SHADOW OF
THE MOON

This magnificent novel tells the story of the Indian
Mutiny of a hundred years ago, one of the most dramatic
events in India's and the British Empire's history. It is
also the story of Alex Randall, far-seeing Assistant Commissioner of Lunjore, and the spirited Winter de
Ballesteros.

Randall is charged with the unwelcome task of fetching Winter from Britain to marry his superior, Conway
Barton, whom he dislikes and despises. This mission
involves him in even greater difficulties than he had bar-
gained for, particularly when, back in India, he is confronted with the arrogant, ruthless Lord Carlyon who
has his own ideas about Winter's future.

Through a colourful array of characters, the author
recaptures the atmosphere of gaiety and irresponsibility
of British life in India just before the Mutiny, with its
lavish dances and shooting parties; for there were few
who detected the ominous signs of trouble or who knew
of the ceaseless agitation, the messages passed from hand
to hand, and the secret meetings at which barbaric rites
were performed.

Amid the rising tension between the two races Randall
gradually but against his will, develops an intense love for
Winter. They are then engulfed by the cataclysm of the
Mutiny, with its orgy of bloodshed and destruction. It is
as fugitives in the jungle that they are brought together,
but this only leads to further hardships and dangers, until
they meet their destinies in the final climax.

The author's personal experience of the country has
enabled her vividly to portray the Indian scene in all its
exotic detail; while she has used her wide knowledge of
Indian history to create a wholly authentic and engross-
ing picture of the events.

SHADOW OF
THE MOON

M. M. KAYE

1724

LONGMANS, GREEN AND CO
LONDON · NEW YORK · TORONTO

LONGMANS, GREEN AND CO LTD
6 & 7 CLIFFORD STREET LONDON W I

BOSTON HOUSE STRAND STREET CAPE TOWN
531 LITTLE COLLINS STREET MELBOURNE

LONGMANS, GREEN AND CO INC
55 FIFTH AVENUE NEW YORK 3

LONGMANS, GREEN AND CO
20 CRANFIELD ROAD TORONTO 16

ORIENT LONGMANS PRIVATE LTD
CALCUTTA BOMBAY MADRAS
DELHI VIJAYAWADA DACCA

First published 1957

PRINTED IN GREAT BRITAIN BY
WESTERN PRINTING SERVICES LTD BRISTOL

To

Sir John William Kaye

who wrote a history of the Indian Mutiny,

Major Edward Kaye

who commanded a battery at the Siege of Delhi,

my grandfather, William Kaye of the Indian Civil Service,

my father, Sir Cecil Kaye,

my brother, Colonel William Kaye,

and to all other men and women of my family

and of so many other British families who

served, lived in and loved India.

And to

The Lovely Land

and all her peoples,

with admiration, affection and gratitude.

. . . and there you can see
Our English sun, convalescent after passing
Through the valley of the shadow of the moon.
CHRISTOPHER FRY (*Venus Observed*)

CONTENTS

PART I—WARE

Page 1

PART II—THE SHADOW BEFORE

Page 29

PART III—KISHAN PRASAD

Page 73

PART IV—CONWAY

Page 195

PART V—MOONRISE

Page 305

PART VI—THE HIRREN MINAR

Page 455

PART VII—THE GULAB MAHAL

Page 569

I

WARE

1

THE chill wind that was driving tattered regiments of cloud across a watery moon brought with it a sudden and vicious spatter of raindrops and a hint of snow. It jerked unexpectedly at the folds of a long military cloak that wrapped the solitary rider on the moor road, and wrenching it back sent it flapping out behind him like the wings of some monstrous bat.

Captain Alex Randall swore into the cold night and reining in his horse gathered the heavy folds about him again, gripping the slack beneath his arm. He rose in his stirrups and peered ahead into the wind-torn darkness, but could see no sign of light or human habitation. The moon, momentarily shaking itself free from the millrace of the clouds, showed nothing but a desolation of moorland, across which the lonely road cut a pale track like the wake of a ship running before the wind.

A fresh gust of rain whipped out of the darkness, and Medusa jerked at her bit and sidled on the rough roadway, impatient to be off. Randall gave the mare her head and rode forward into the driving wind.

It was on Medusa's account that Captain Randall was on the road at this late hour. He had hoped to reach Ware before dark, but just beyond Highelm the mare had cast a shoe. A passing yokel having informed him that the next smithy lay over ten miles ahead, he had had no choice but to turn back and get the damage repaired by a smith in Highelm.

There had been considerable delay before a new shoe could be fitted and Medusa ready for the road again, and the smith, enquiring as to Captain Randall's destination, had advised against a resumption of his journey that day. There was, he affirmed, an excellent coaching inn at Highelm, and the road to Ware lay

3

over a lonely stretch of moor, unpleasant enough by daylight in bad weather, but certainly to be avoided by night, with the sky darkening to storm clouds, a rising wind, and the threat of snow before morning. Only last week, said the smith, a London doctor, hastening to his lordship, had been overtaken by darkness on the moorland road and had perforce to spend the night in his stationary coach owing to the loss of a wheel—his coachman having mistaken the lie of the road in the darkness: 'An' 'e might 'av saved hisself the journey. It's for Thursday we hears. There's bin many goin' past this day.'

The smith, a well-meaning man, had urged Captain Randall to spend the night at the George and resume his journey on the morrow, but Randall was not to be persuaded. His distaste for his errand was sufficiently great for the prospect of further delay to be unpalatable. The sooner he was finished and done with it, and away again, the better. He thanked the smith for his well-meant advice but persisted in his intention of continuing on his way, and night had overtaken him while some eight to ten miles still lay between him and the tall towers and florid battlements of Ware.

The rain that drove under Captain Randall's hat-brim and trickled icily down his neck was turning to snow. Intermittent gusts of gradually thickening flakes streamed out of the darkness, touching his face with a thousand soft, furtive fingers and clotting in the folds of his cloak, and he began to think regretfully of the warm beds and roaring fires of the George Inn, and to regard his chances of reaching Ware that night with a less optimistic eye. His hands, encased in heavy gauntlets, were so frozen that he could barely feel the reins, and his booted feet ached with cold. He flexed his numbed fingers and smiled wryly into the darkness.

How many times during the last ten or eleven years had he longed for the sight of grey skies and the smell and bite of east winds blowing across English soil? How many times, in the merciless, grinding heat of an Indian summer, lying panting under a flapping punkah that merely disturbed but could not cool the molten air, had he yearned in imagination for the ice and frost and snow of an English winter? Well, he had them now, and he should be satisfied. But perhaps the blazing suns of the last twelve years had thinned his blood, for the icy wind that disputed his passage chilled him to the bone and his whole body ached with cold and fatigue.

To distract his thoughts from his physical discomforts he turned them to the counter-irritant of his present mission, and for perhaps the hundredth time, and with a deepening sense of exasperation and distaste, mentally reviewed the events that had led to his riding along this moorland road by night, and in the teeth of a rising gale, towards the great house of Ware.

Almost twelve years ago, in the autumn of 1843, Alex Mallory Randall, having completed his training at the Honorable the East India Company's Military College at Addiscombe and celebrated his eighteenth birthday, had embarked for the shores of India. He had served with distinction in that vast and turbulent land, and it was a day in which young men possessed of ability and ambition could find full scope for their talents and energy in the colourful cauldron of 'John Company's' rapidly expanding Empire.

Alex had fought at Ferozeshah and Sobraon and at Chillianwallah—that disastrous shambles that had cost Lord Gough over two thousand four hundred lives, and had been claimed as a victory by both Sikhs and British. He had been fortunate enough to catch the eye of the irascible Commander-in-Chief himself, and had been rewarded by a brevet to the rank of Lieutenant. As a result, he was removed almost immediately from Regimental duty and set to work in an administrative capacity under the eye of that great administrator, Henry Lawrence. Lawrence's passionate love and understanding of the country and its peoples were untainted by the lust for conquest, and he expected—and got—as gruelling a standard of work from his subordinates as he himself gave to the task before him. Under his tutelage Alex had been in turn surveyor, road builder and magistrate, and had helped to govern and control vast expanses of lawless territory at an age when many a man is licking stamps or running errands. His handling of a swift and ugly crisis on the North West Frontier had led to a second brevet, but he had not been permitted to return to his Regiment, and had once more found himself employed in a capacity that was more political than military.

His immediate superior in his present appointment was one Mr. Conway Barton, Commissioner of Lunjore. Alex Randall had not taken to his chief. There were too many aspects of Mr. Barton's character and habits that failed to commend themselves to him, but the two men had worked together reasonably amicably. Alex avoided his chief's company as far as possible and, as that gentleman was only too willing to transfer the bulk of the work to his junior's shoulders, went his own way to a large extent, unhampered by much interference.

It was on the eve of his departure on a year's furlough that Mr. Barton had thrust an unwelcome commission on him, and looking back on it Alex was surprised to find how clearly he remembered the events of that evening. He had seen that the last of his packing was completed, and in response to an unexpected summons from Mr. Barton had walked over in the hot, harsh moonlight to the Residency. He was conscious of a twinge of anxiety as to what the sudden summons might portend, for he had already made his formal farewell visit, and as far as he knew all official matters had been handed over to his successor in good order. He could think of nothing that had not already received his attention; but supposing some sudden crisis had arisen at the last moment to delay his departure? It did not bear thinking of.

He was to leave the next day for Calcutta, and from there, via the overland route, for England. What would England look like? —feel like?—smell like? Could it really be as cool and green and fragrant as his memory had painted it for him during the last hot and crowded and eventful years? Could two such places as the England of his imaginings and the India of the stifling present really exist in one and the same world?

His footsteps made no sound on the thick dust that blanketed the ground between the avenue of shade trees, and overhead a bone-white moon blazed in a sky that seemed almost iron-grey. The air under the great gateway of the Residency was cooler than that of the hot night outside, and Alex lingered there, grateful for the small relief of that coolness.

Standing in the shadow of the thick archway he was struck by the uncanny stillness of the night, but presently he became aware of a faint sound that came from somewhere deep in the black shadows of a banyan tree that grew to the left of the gateway and just inside the Residency walls.

From an angle of the archway, where the shadow cut across the white, moonlit drive, Alex could see the dark mass of the banyan. There was a stone idol among the roots of the great tree; a crude, obscene figure roughly carved on an upright slab of stone, hideously bedaubed with orange paint, and, on feast days, wreathed with garlands of fading marigold flowers. As his eyes became accustomed to the shadows he could make out figures crouched about the main trunk where the idol stood. One of them was speaking in a voice that was barely a whisper, for only the sibilance of the sound reached his ears. But the whispering voice was quick and urgent, and somehow conveyed an indefinable impression of authority.

Alex's first and instant suspicion was that he had stumbled on a gang of dacoits intent on robbery; but as he watched he abandoned it, for the group among the roots of the banyan tree was becoming more distinct, and one of them, surely, was Akbar Khan the gatekeeper, while another was the oily down-country *khansamah*, cook to the Commissioner. He caught a momentary glimpse of a third profile as it turned against a narrow bar of moonlight that struggled between the hanging fringe of banyan roots, and recognized the Havildar of one of the native infantry regiments stationed in Lunjore.

There were at least a dozen men in the shadow of the great tree, and Alex came to the conclusion that they were for the most part Residency servants. These were largely Mohammedan with a sprinkling of low-caste Hindus; but the Havildar was a Brahmin. What, then, were they all doing, meeting in secret conclave at this hour at the feet of a Hindu idol? And why did they consider it necessary to speak in whispers?

As he listened the speaker ceased, and a low-toned murmur of conversation broke out, and presently a lone figure detached itself from the group among the tree roots and moved out into the moonlight. Alex saw with surprise that it was a sadhu, a Hindu holy man. The tall, spare figure was naked except for an intricately tied loin-cloth, and in the clear moonlight the man's ash-smeared body and long rope-like locks of ash-covered, uncombed hair appeared grey and ghost-like.

The sadhu reached the path before the gateway and without pausing walked directly towards Alex, his naked feet making no sound on the baked earth. The long, carved rosary he wore about his neck swung and clicked in the silence and Alex waited, expecting the man to check at the sight of him. He had a momentary glimpse of a grey, skull-like face blotted with a dark caste mark, in which a pair of glittering eyes showed astonishingly alive; and then, before he had quite realized it, the man had walked swiftly past him and through the dark arch of the gateway.

Alex swung round and ran after him, but the road beyond the gateway was empty, and the sadhu had vanished as completely as though he had indeed been a ghost.

Alex stared unbelievingly at the long expanse of roadway, white in the moonlight, that stretched away to the left and right past the Residency gateway. But the road was lined with shade trees, grey with the dust of breathless days, and the sharp-edged shadows of any one of them might have swallowed up the figure of the sadhu. It was only then that Alex realized that the man had probably not been aware of his presence, for the sadhu had come from the deep shadow of the banyan out into the bright moonlight, while Alex had been standing in the shadow near the mouth of the gateway, his white drill backed by the whitewashed stone. He must have been as nearly invisible in that setting as the sadhu's ash-smeared greyness among the moonlight and shadows of the long cantonment road.

Alex heard a slight sound behind him and turned quickly. Akbar Khan, the gatekeeper, a shadow among the shadows, stood salaaming under the archway.

'Where hast thou been?' demanded Alex harshly in the vernacular, 'and what hast thou and the others to do with a sadhu? What evil is toward?'

'No evil, Huzoor,' said Akbar Khan tranquilly. 'We do but make prayer for rain.'

'What child's talk! Thou art a follower of the Prophet. Imal Din also; and Ustad Ali. Since when have Mussulmans made prayer to the gods of the Hindus, or consorted with their holy men? And what has Havildar Jodah Ram to do with such as Bulaki of the sweeper-*log*?'

'Huzoor,' said Akbar Khan, 'in evil times, when the rains fail, we suffer as one. The monsoon tarries and the crops die. Soon, if the rains delay over-long, there will come a great famine and many will die—Mussulman and Hindu, Sikh and Bengali together. Yonder *fakir* makes petition to his gods for rain. While we Muslims call upon Allah for rain the Hindus of the city call also upon their gods. That is all.'

'*Hmm*,' said Alex. 'In the circumstances it is almost conceivable that you might be speaking the truth. But I don't believe it and I don't like it. And don't leave the gate unattended again, you old reprobate.'

Akbar Khan, to whom these last remarks, spoken in English, were unintelligible, salaamed deeply and drew back against the wall as Alex walked past him and up the long, curving drive towards the big white single-storeyed house among the flame trees.

From a courtyard behind the house a woman's voice could be heard singing a shrill, quavering Indian song to the accompaniment of a *sitar*. It stopped suddenly, as though checked by an order, as Captain Randall mounted the verandah steps, his boots ringing loud on the stone. A white-clad figure rose with a

rustle from the matting and, salaaming low, pattered away to a
lighted doorway screened by a *chik*—a curtain of split cane—that
led into the Commissioner's drawing-room. Alex could see the
crouching figure of a punkah coolie seated cross-legged in the
shadows, his body bowing to the rhythmic tug and release of
the rope, and from inside the room came the familiar flap and
fall of the punkah cloth, a clink of bottles and glasses and the
murmured Urdu of the native servant.

'Wha's that? Wha's that?'

The Commissioner's voice was thick and blurred and Captain
Randall's mouth twisted in a fleeting grimace of impatience and
contempt.

The servant lifted the split-cane curtain and the Commissioner's
bulky figure appeared in the doorway, black against the yellow
lamplight.

'Tha' you, Alex? Come in! Come in! Jus' the man I wanted
t'see. Siddown. Have a drink. Know why I sent f' yer?'

'No, sir. Nothing gone wrong with my furlough, I hope!'

'No, no. Tha's all right. It's about that I wan' t'talk. Wan'
you t'do something fer me. Favour. Long story. It's m' future
wife . . .'

He took a deep pull at the glass in his hand while the sweat
trickled down his pale, puffy features and soaked into the thin
short-sleeved Indian-style garment he wore in lieu of more
formal attire.

Alex sat down and resigned himself to listen. He knew the
Commissioner for a bore and a snob, and both attributes were apt
to colour his conversation to an intolerable degree. He was also
aware—as who was not?—that Mr. Barton was affianced to a
distant cousin; a great-granddaughter of the Earl of Ware.

Conway Barton was proud of his connection with Lord Ware
and lost no opportunity of mentioning the relationship. But in
actual fact the connection was of the slightest. The Lady Emily
Grantham, only daughter of the fifth Earl, had married an
elderly nabob, Sir Ebenezer Barton. This Sir Ebenezer's youngest
brother was Conway Barton's father. Lady Emily's niece,

Sabrina Grantham, had apparently married a Spanish nobleman, and it was to her daughter that Mr. Barton was affianced. The match had been arranged some five or six years previously, during the Commissioner's last furlough in England, and it had been intended, explained Mr. Barton, that there should be a long engagement—no unusual thing in the circumstances—and that the marriage should take place during his next Home leave. But this would not fall due for several years, and meanwhile the Earl of Ware, the lady's relative and guardian, was failing in health and had written to urge the return of Mr. Barton and his immediate marriage to his betrothed. This course, however, was impracticable, and therefore he had decided upon an alternative arrangement. . . .

Captain Randall smothered a yawn and shifted uncomfortably in his chair. He could feel the sweat trickling down between his shoulder blades, and his body itched with prickly heat. The punkah, flapping gently to and fro above their heads, had drifted to a stop as the weary punkah coolie dozed at his post, and Alex wondered tiredly why the Commissioner had found himself unable to go home. For one of his seniority it should have been easy enough to arrange. The districts were always intolerably short of officers, but Conway Barton's reputation did not stand so high as to class him among the irreplaceables. And why should the Commissioner have sent for him, Alex, at this hour, merely in order to discuss his projected marriage?

'The mountain must come to Mahomet!' said Mr. Conway Barton, and laughed heartily at his own wit. 'An' this, m'dear Alex, is where you come in——'

'I, sir?' Alex sat up with a jerk, roused from his bored lethargy into apprehensive attention.

'Yes, you, m'dear fellow. Wouldn't trust anyone else. But yer a gentleman. Can't shay the same of some others. An' though yer a sight too good-lookin' fer a man, or would be if yer'd only grow some hair on y'lip—wasser marrer with yer anyway? it ain't decent at your age, shavin' yer face like a demned nigger!—yer don't go much with women. Never known yer tie up with a petticoat yet. Can't shay the same of some others. 'Tisn't normal, but there it is. Sho when I had to decide, I said "Randall! Just the f'llow. He'll do!" '

The Commissioner stopped as though he had fully explained himself, and lay back in his long cane chair and drank deeply.

'Do what, sir?'

'What? Wha's that? Oh; fetch her of course, m'boy. Bring her out here. Mountain t' Mahomet! Hope she ain't a mountain. Half Spanish y'know. They can run to fat. Mountain t' Mahomet!'

For a few minutes Alex had thought that the Commissioner could not possibly be serious, but he was speedily disabused. The Commissioner was perfectly serious. He had given prolonged thought to the problem, and had spent the greater part of the day in writing letters. They lay on an inlaid ivory and sandalwood table beside him as he spoke. His plans were all made. Captain Randall was to carry letters to the Earl of Ware, to his lordship's great-granddaughter who was Mr. Barton's betrothed, to Mr. Barton's solicitors, Mr. Barton's uncle and Mr. Barton's bankers. He was in addition to explain the whole matter in person to the Earl, and add his entreaties to those of the Commissioner that the Condesa de los Aguilares should set sail for India in the following year under the charge of Captain Alex Randall, and of any suitable chaperon that could be provided, when Captain Randall returned from furlough.

'I leave it to you,' said the Commissioner expansively. 'Very capable f'llow. Always said so. "Randall's the man for this," I said! Once they shee you they'll realize it's safe enough to shend —send 'er out. Gen'leman to protect her. Makesh a difference.'

Alex had argued and protested, but to no purpose. The Commissioner was not a man to be deflected from any course of action which he had once decided to follow, and short of a flat refusal— and the incurring of the Commissioner's enmity thereby—there was nothing he could do about it. To make an enemy of his chief over such a matter seemed absurdly quixotic. After all, he had to return and work with the man. That work must come first, and it could be made difficult, if not impossible, if Mr. Barton's antagonism was aroused against him.

Alex fought a perpetual battle with the daily problem of how to do what appeared to him as obviously right, sensible and just, and at the same time steer clear of a direct collision with some senior official who resented his early promotion and his impatience with bumbling ineptitude. He had learned long ago the necessity of riding his temper and his impatience on a curb, but he still found it the hardest part of his work. He could not afford to quarrel with Mr. Barton, and so it had ended with his accepting the distasteful commission that had been thrust upon him by his superior. But with certain inward reservations.

Alex had considered those reservations often since that hot night at the Lunjore Residency, but had been unable to come to any definite decision. There were two alternatives before him, and both were distasteful. On the one hand he was to make himself responsible for conveying a gently nurtured woman to an unknown land seething with sedition and unrest—to say nothing of the dangers and discomforts of such things as disease, intolerable heat and an almost total lack of sanitation—and eventually hand this fellow-creature into the care of a man whom he knew to be both a drunkard and a libertine. On the other hand, should he warn Lord Ware of these aspects of the affair, he would be betraying the trust of his superior officer, and stand guilty of disloyalty.

It was always possible of course that the Commissioner's betrothed was well aware of the disadvantages of the match. According to Conway Barton the marriage had been arranged some five years previously, and as the earliest that a young lady of rank would be likely to be affianced was seventeen, that would make her at least of age. But possibly she was a good deal older than that, and plain into the bargain, which would account for the aged Earl's anxiety to get her suitably bestowed. If so it was likely that the lady herself was fully prepared to accept the prospect of life in the East, and a drunken husband of loose morals, as an escape from spinsterhood. Women were unpredictable in

such matters. The solution of the problem would have to rest
on the outcome of his visit to Ware, and the character and
understanding of the aged and possibly senile Earl. Nothing of
course could be said to Mr. Barton's betrothed, but if her guardian
was a sensible man Captain Randall had little doubt that the
Commissioner of Lunjore would wait in vain for the arrival of
his bride.

Medusa stumbled and recovered herself, and Captain Randall's
tired brain jerked itself back from the past and into the immediate
and uncomfortable present.

The snow had turned back to sleet, and now it was raining
again. No heavy, tropical, lukewarm downpour this time, but
the icy stinging sleet of the northern latitudes, that lashed at
him as the wind blew in uneven gusts. For the last mile or so
Medusa had been moving at a walk, picking her way uncertainly
in the darkness and confused by the whirling snowflakes. But
now all at once she lengthened her stride and began to trot.

Alex roused himself from his stupor of cold and fatigue and
peered ahead. There were trees nearby. And surely that was a
glimmer of light? They were leaving the moors behind them and
entering a more hospitable country of fields and hedges and
woodland, and Medusa shook her head and snorted as though she
knew that a warm stable and a feed of oats lay not far ahead.

The road dipped downwards, sheltered now by trees, and the
whine of the gale over the moorland changed to the surf-like
croon of wind among branches. A high wall loomed up out of
the darkness; sensed rather than seen, for the wind was cut off
abruptly and the sound of Medusa's hooves rang hollowly on the
roadway. The wall followed the line of the road for a mile or so
and then turned away almost at right angles in front of a vast
stone gateway topped by the heraldic wolves of Ware.

Lights glowed behind the windows of the lodge-keeper's cot-
tage and it seemed that Captain Randall was expected, for the
heavy wrought-iron gates stood open. Beyond them lay a long
avenue of oak trees rising out of a sea of dead bracken, and on

either side stretched the open spaces of a park across which the wind, unhampered now by the high stone wall that had sheltered the road, blew in savage gusts between the tree trunks.

Medusa broke into a gallop, and ten minutes later the park and the avenue ended in a wide sweep of gravel before the towering bulk of a great house, half-castle, half-mansion. A faint gleam of light showed from a high window, but except for that the house was in darkness.

Captain Randall dismounted stiffly, and knotting the sodden reins, looped them about the neck of a dimly seen griffon carved in weather-worn stone, and mounted the wide steps that led up to the front door. He tugged at the iron bell-chain and waited, stamping his feet on the wet stone to restore the circulation to them. After what seemed an unconscionably long wait he heard a sound of slow footsteps, and the great door creaked open. An aged man, bent and wrinkled, his white hair dressed in the manner of an earlier day, peered out at him, and then setting the door a little wider drew back to let him pass.

Captain Randall found himself standing in a vast hall that appeared even vaster in the dim light of the single branch of candles that formed the only illumination in all that wide place of shadows. He looked about him in some surprise. In such a hall one might have expected to see family portraits, weapons or trophies adorning the enormous expanse of wall. But here there was nothing. Nothing but a blackness that seemed to move and sway and shiver as the draught blew in through the half-open door and eddied about the hall.

The candle flames flickered wildly in the rush of cold air, to flare up again as a tall footman in black livery leant his weight against the door, shutting it upon the wild night. Captain Randall stared about him in the grip of an odd sense of unreality. Weariness appeared to be playing tricks with his eyesight. Was it only imagination, or the effects of cold and fatigue that made the shadowy walls about him seem to move and tremble?

The ancient steward who had peered at him through the half-open door tottered across the hall and lifted the branched candlestick, holding it high, and Alex saw with a sense of shock that the walls of the vast hall were hung from ceiling to floor with black curtains that still swayed and shifted uneasily from the wind that had blown in from the night.

The old man tapped on the stone floor with the long steward's wand he held in one shrivelled hand, and two more sombre-liveried flunkeys materialized out of the shadows. 'Your horse shall be attended to, sir, and Thomas will see that you have all you require. You will be one of the family? I do not for the moment recall the name. Forgive me, sir—your lordship—we were not expecting——' The old man's voice quavered to a stop and Alex spoke curtly:

'You mistake me. I am Captain Alex Randall. Lord Ware requested me to wait upon him on this date. I was delayed upon the road, or I should have reached here before dark. You will find my valise strapped to the saddle.'

'His lordship requested you . . .?' The words appeared to carry a note of disbelief, and Alex thrust a hand into the bosom of his coat and drew out a folded sheet of paper that bore a few lines written in a wavering, spidery hand. 'I received this a week ago, and sent a letter in reply, informing Lord Ware that I would do myself the honour of waiting upon him. Was my letter not received?'

'I—we—there have been so many letters,' said the aged steward uncertainly. 'Perhaps it was overlooked. A week ago, you say——'

To Alex's puzzled amazement he saw that tears were standing in the old man's eyes, the feeble tears of old age that brimmed over and trickled down the furrowed, parchment-like face and flashed in the candlelight. And suddenly several things that had meant nothing to him a moment before took on shape and meaning. The smith at Highelm who had said: 'It's for Thursday we hears. There's bin many goin' past this day.' The London doctor who might have saved himself a journey. The open gates at the entrance of the oak avenue; the black liveries of the servants and the funereal hangings that draped the walls of the great hall.

He said suddenly, sharply: 'The Earl———?'
'His lordship died five days ago,' said the old steward.

2

THE morning dawned wet and cold. It had snowed again during the night, and although the snow had once more turned to sleet, patches of it still lay in the hollows of the park and along the margins of the long oak avenue. The wind moaned among the bare branches, and the draughts whined uneasily along the dark corridors of the great house and bellied the funereal hangings that draped the walls.

Captain Alex Randall awoke with a headache and a sense of acute irritation. He had slept little, and that uneasily, for the problem that he had intended to transfer to the Earl of Ware was once more back upon his own shoulders. Lord Ware, thought Alex crossly, had no right to die before settling his ward's affairs. Now what was to be done? It was one thing to explain the true state of affairs to an elderly man of the world; quite another to interview Mr. Conway Barton's betrothed herself. What the devil was he to do now? Simply deliver the letters, discharge his duty as courier, and let the woman go hang? After all, it was no concern of his whom she married or did not marry. Who was he to play Providence? And yet— Here he found himself back once more at the interminable argument.

He breakfasted alone in a small panelled room warmed by a blazing log fire, and an elderly and sedate secretary waited upon him with a message from the Earl. Lord Ware, owing to pressure of work, found himself unable to see Captain Randall until late in the day. He trusted that it would be convenient for Captain Randall to spend another night or so at Ware, as the business he had come upon was not one to be dealt with in haste.

'It is most damnably inconvenient,' said Captain Randall sourly. 'But I suppose there is no help for it.'

Left to his own devices he passed a tedious morning, and the company at luncheon proved unenlivening. They were all, with the sole exception of himself, relatives or connections of the family, who had assembled for the funeral of the late head of their house which was to take place the following day. They were dressed in deep black, and conversed in the hushed undertones deemed suitable in a house of mourning, but bereavement had evidently not impaired their appetites. The meal was rich, indigestible and interminable, and the conversation, of necessity, lacking in sparkle.

Alex spent the greater part of the afternoon moodily watching a stream of black-clad tenants and their families who, despite the inclemency of the weather, were moving slowly up the oak avenue to pass through the guardroom where the late Earl's coffin lay in state. Presently, more for lack of other occupation than from any desire to pay his respects to the unknown dead, he abandoned his post at the window and went down to join the sombre procession.

They moved forward slowly and in silence through a low stone porch in the oldest part of the castle and entered a long passage leading to the guardroom. The air was heavy and cold and the walls were hung with black drapery that billowed continuously in the draught. A short flight of stone steps led down into the guardroom, and at the foot of them stood the catafalque.

Alex drew to one side and stood looking down on a strangely impressive scene. The walls were draped in the same unrelieved black, and the catafalque itself and the floor about it was covered with heavy black cloth and lit by four massive candles in iron sconces. But the rest was colour and glitter and magnificence; a magnificence made even more startling by very contrast with its funereal setting. A defiance and a boast in the face of death.

The ornate hatchment suspended above the coffin-head gleamed with all the colour and gilding and pride of heraldry, and below it crimson velvet drapery covered the heavy oak of the coffin. Placed upon the coffin on a velvet cushion stood the Earl's coronet and the Star and Garter. The diamonds flashed and blazed as the candle-flames wavered in the draught, sending out splinters of brilliant light—violet and green and blue, scarlet and white. The breastplate, surrounded by various orders and badges of honour, was surmounted by the Earl's own arms, and below them, together with the gilt spurs of Knighthood, lay two crossed swords; the dress sword of a Knight of the Garter and one which Alex took to be the sword of some Militia Regiment.

At the foot of the coffin hung a Knight's gold collar, and beneath it were grouped on either side of the bier the Earl's mantle and the velvet and ermine of a Knight of the Garter, the hat of a Colonel of Militia and a military scarf. Servants dressed in black livery stood guard at each side of the coffin, and as the silent procession of mourners passed slowly by the bier and out through the low stone arch at the far side of the room Alex found his lips moving in scraps of remembered poetry: '*The boast of heraldry, the pomp of power, and all that Beauty, all that wealth e'er gave, await alike the inevitable hour. The paths of glory lead but to the grave.*' A sobering reflection. Yet there was no meek acceptance of the latter end here. His aged Lordship was moving to the grave with all the pomp and ceremony that had attended him in life.

The steady stream of mourners thinned gradually to a mere trickle, and beyond the narrow stone embrasures of the guardroom windows the grey daylight took on the purple hue of dusk.

A woman, veiled and in heavy mourning, brushed past Captain Randall and went swiftly down the steps to pause beside the resplendent bier, her clothing outlined with a faint nimbus of gold from the candle-light beyond.

The thick veil that fell from her bonnet's edge almost to her feet permitted no glimpse of her features and did not betray even the colour of her hair. But the vast hooped crinoline, the heavy crape veil and a deeply fringed pelisse, unwieldy as they were, failed to conceal the wearer's youth. They failed, too, to conceal something else. Despite its rigidity there was about the slight figure in its cumbersome mourning a poignant impression of intense and hopeless grief. Alex could not have explained even to himself why this should be so, for the girl stood stiffly; head erect and black-gloved hands pressing back the spreading skirts of her dress. But he was aware of a sudden sense of guilt, as though he were eavesdropping on some private and personal conversation, and turning abruptly he walked quickly away.

Darkness had fallen by the time the secretary appeared to request Captain Randall's presence in his lordship's private apartments, and to lead the way along interminable corridors to a more recently constructed wing. He turned the handle of an ornate white and gold door and ushered Captain Randall into a large high-ceilinged room whose original Regency character had been successfully submerged in a wave of taste generated by the Great Exhibition of 1851. But it was the Countess, and not the Earl, who waited to receive him.

Lady Ware rose with a rustle of heavy silks. Julia, lately Viscountess Glynde and now Countess of Ware, was a tall woman, verging on middle age, with a coldly handsome face and smooth loops of light brown hair already lightly streaked with grey. She held out a thin white hand with a gesture that was almost royal, and Alex Randall bowed over it and straightened up to meet the critical gaze of a pair of slightly prominent blue eyes, cold, pale and calculating. She studied him for a moment in silence and apparently liked what she saw, for her somewhat thin-lipped mouth relaxed in a faint smile.

'My dear Captain Randall,' said the Countess of Ware, 'you must forgive me for being unable to receive you earlier, but under the present sad circumstances—well, I am sure that you will understand how difficult it has been for us. Pray be seated. My husband has asked me to convey to you his regrets that he cannot, after all, find the time to see you today. He hopes that he will be able to do so later.'

The Countess seated herself again, the vast expanse of her black silk mourning billowing about her in impressive folds, and waved Captain Randall to a chair beside her. Captain Randall sat down warily. He had never had much to do with women, and apart from several light and lovely ladies who had provided him with amusement and a substitute for love, had met singularly few of them. This, it may be added, was not from lack of opportunity. Alex Randall was no celibate, but two things obsessed him to the exclusion of all others; India and 'John Company'. The glamour of India—the vast, glittering, cruel, mysterious land teeming with violence and beauty—and the romance of John Company, that prosaic collection of merchant traders from London who had conquered a sub-continent and now maintained their own armies and administered justice and law to sixty million Indians. These were the things that held his heart and his imagination and his loyalty, and he had little time for other matters.

Now, facing the imposing figure of the Countess of Ware, he knew himself to be at a disadvantage. He could have dealt with a man. He disliked having to deal with a woman.

'I must apologize for my inopportune arrival,' he said stiffly. 'I had of course no idea——'

Lady Ware cut him short in her clear, incisive voice:

'My dear Captain Randall, no apology is necessary, I assure you. We are exceedingly grateful to you for all your trouble in being the bearer of these letters. We have heard of you from Mr. Barton of course. He sent other letters through the post, apprising us of your arrival and giving us some indication of the nature of your mission, although naturally he did not write so fully as in the letters he entrusted to your personal care. You must know that we had expected to see you some months earlier.'

'Yes. I am sorry. I had myself expected to arrive a good deal earlier, but I visited the Crimea *en route*, and was delayed. I wrote to Mr. Barton and the late Lord Ware to explain matters.'

'We quite understood. You were wounded, were you not. Did you see much fighting?'

'A certain amount,' said Alex uncommunicatively.

Lady Ware lost interest in the Crimea and returned to Mr. Barton.

'. . . and now that we have had the opportunity of meeting you, and of reading the letters you brought with you,' she concluded, 'the position is of course quite clear.'

She lifted one of the letters under discussion from an ormolu table at her side, and the thin sheets of paper, covered with the familiar, erratic handwriting in heavy black ink, crackled sharply in the stillness, echoing the sound of the burning logs in the wide hearth. One letter was still unopened and the seal intact. 'We have not,' said Lady Ware, 'given Winter her letter as yet. I shall now do so at the earliest opportunity.' The shadow of a frown passed over her face and her narrow mouth drew itself into a tighter line.

'Winter?' Captain Randall's voice was puzzled.

'My cousin. The—Condesa,' explained Lady Ware, pronouncing the title with palpable distaste. 'Naturally she will be allowed to express her views. But I am convinced that she will consent to dear Conway's plan. It is unfortunate that he cannot come home, but in the circumstances I feel that to delay the marriage for a further, and possibly indefinite, period would be unnecessarily harsh. Both on dear Conway and on Winter herself.'

Winter! thought Alex Randall. What an impossible name! Probably the diminutive of some more lengthy Spanish one.

'There are times,' said Lady Ware with the air of one who is prepared to be both broadminded and magnanimous, 'when one must sacrifice one's own wishes in order to forward the happiness of others. I am sure that you will agree with me.'

Captain Randall was far from being in agreement with her. He felt tolerably certain that the dear Conway of five years ago bore little resemblance to the Commissioner of Lunjore as he had last seen him. Five years in the East were apt to leave their mark on most men, and with a man of Conway Barton's character and habits the change was not for the better.

'Have you any knowledge of the East?' enquired Alex abruptly.

Lady Ware looked a little taken aback. 'If you mean, have I ever been there, I have not. Why do you ask?'

'I only wondered if you have any idea as to what life, and to what conditions of life, you are sending your cousin? It is no

country for a young lady who has been brought up in such surroundings as these.'

'Nonsense!' said the Countess crisply. 'Thousands of Englishwomen—many of them well bred—have managed admirably
out there. I myself am acquainted with some of them. Lady
Lawrence, Sir Henry's wife——'

'She is dead,' interrupted Alex curtly. 'Did you not know?'
It seemed to him incredible that anyone who had known Honoria
Lawrence should not know that she was dead.

'Dear me!' said the Countess inadequately. 'I had not heard.
Poor Sir Henry! Of what did she die?'

'India,' said Alex laconically.

The Countess stiffened indignantly. 'I do not understand you,
Captain Randall. You yourself have spent some years in that
country——'

'Twelve,' interjected Captain Randall.

'Then surely you have met many of your fellow-country-
women out there? Are you trying to tell me that none of them
find life supportable? I cannot believe that you are serious.'

'No,' said Alex slowly. 'Many of them would be nowhere else
if given the choice. But as a general rule these fall into two
categories: those who remain, and endure every hardship that
heat and disease and exile can bring, for love of husband or
father. And those whose social status in this country is such that
India gives them a sense of position and importance that they
cannot obtain here. The rest hate it. The latter consideration
will hardly apply to your cousin. Can you be sure of the first one?
I understand that it is five years and more since she last saw Mr.
Barton.'

'That is a matter that must be left to my cousin,' said the
Countess frostily. 'It is no concern of ours. No doubt she will
decide for herself.'

She rose with an impressive rustle of silk, and held out her
hand. Captain Randall stood up and bowed over it.

'I hope,' said the Countess with a return to graciousness, 'that
you will not mind extending your stay for another two days? My

husband hopes to be able to see you tomorrow afternoon. Most of our guests will be leaving after the funeral, and he will then be able to give you his undivided attention.'

Captain Randall murmured his thanks and turned to go, and as he did so he noticed for the first time a large portrait that hung above the clutter of a velvet-draped overmantel. It depicted a young girl in a white crinoline and a blue sash. A pretty creature, barely more than a child, with pale gold ringlets falling on to sloping shoulders, and one small hand holding a single rose. He had observed the original of the portrait at luncheon that day, and looking at the painted likeness he had a sudden and disturbing vision of what a few years of scorching heat, difficult childbirths, cholera, typhus, dysentery, and the society of a dissolute and drunken husband would do to that face. It did not seem made of the stuff of endurance. 'No stamina,' thought Alex with a stab of anger and frustration. It would be unthinkable to have a hand in condemning such a defenceless creature to the life that awaited any wife of Conway Barton, Commissioner of Lunjore!

'My daughter, Sybella,' said the Countess complacently, and Alex drew a quick breath of relief. At least the future of that fragile-looking child need not be on his conscience. He turned and smiled at the Countess. Few women were proof against Alex Randall's smile, and Julia Ware proved no exception. She thawed visibly. 'Such a dear child! You must meet her, Captain Randall. Herr Winterhalter informed me that of all his subjects Sybella was——' The discreet entrance of an elderly lady, evidently a companion, interrupted her. 'What is it, Mrs. Barlow?'

'Lady Augusta: you asked that she——'

'Yes, yes. I shall not be a moment. Good night, Captain Randall. I have so enjoyed our little talk.'

She inclined her head in a slight but gracious nod of dismissal and turned her attention to the elderly companion.

*　　　*　　　*

There was no sign of the young lady of the portrait at dinner that night, and Alex concluded that she must be dining with her parents. He found himself seated between a portly clergyman and a Lady Wycombe who, having demanded an explanation of his presence at Ware, remarked: 'For one can see that you are not one of the Family!'

'How?' enquired Alex, interested.

'The Family favours fair hair. Have you not noticed? Yours is dark. And you are burnt so exceedingly brown. India, I presume?'

Alex introduced himself and explained his presence in the house. He did not go into the details of his errand, merely allowing it to be inferred that he had had business to transact with the late Earl.

'Yes, of course. He was a shareholder, was he not? Of the East India Company I mean. A very interesting country, India, I feel sure. But too hot. You were looking for someone, were you not? Whom did you expect to see here?'

'No one, I assure you,' said Alex with a smile. 'But there was a young lady sitting opposite me at luncheon. I noticed that she is not here tonight.'

'Ah, you must mean Sybella,' said Lady Wycombe. 'She is having a light supper in her room. Do not tell me that you too have fallen a victim to her charms! If so I must hasten to warn you that you stand no chance; no chance at all! When Bella marries it will be to the heir of a great name or a great fortune. Probably both.'

'I have met Lady Ware,' said Alex gravely.

His companion laughed. 'Oh, I was not referring to Julia! Naturally *she* thinks that no one under a Prince of the Blood is good enough for her dazzling daughter, but she could be brought to consent to anything that her child demanded. No, it is Sybella herself who sets the mark high. And she will hit it, of that I have no doubt. That is, if she can rid herself of her cousin. Winter may yet spoil her aim. It is a way she has.'

'Winter. That is a curious name. Does it derive from the Spanish? It sounds a trifle bleak.'

'You have not met her yet?'

B

'No. What is she like?'

Lady Wycombe laughed on rather an odd note.

'No woman can describe her to you without injustice. But I am sorry for Julia—and Sybella. Sybella is a spoilt, selfish chit who will grow up into a spoilt, selfish woman. Nevertheless one could not help feeling for her. Do you see that young man over there? On the far side of that candelabrum; sitting between old Lady Parbury and Camilla Grantham—the girl with the red hair. That is Amberley's heir, and the greatest *parti* in Europe. He is also Sybella's first cousin, though that will not stop them! There is only one thing that may stand in the way of a satisfactory conclusion, but now that Henry is dead I am quite sure that suitable steps will be taken. Yes, they will certainly get rid of Winter!'

Alex said: 'I am sorry to appear so dull-witted, but you forget that I am a stranger here. I have never met any of these people before, and I must confess that I have not the least idea what you are talking about.'

'And why should you, indeed?' said Lady Wycombe.

'Enlighten me!'

'You will find it very tedious stuff. What is it you wish to know?'

'About the Condesa with the chilly name. And Lady Sybella. What was it that she could do nothing about while Henry—the late Earl I collect?—was alive, and why will she get rid of this Winter now that he is dead? You perceive that you have aroused my curiosity.'

'Wait until you know them better, and then you will see for yourself.'

Lady Wycombe had clearly lost interest in the subject. She turned her shoulder upon him, and Captain Randall found himself engaged to listen to a long monologue from his right-hand neighbour, a portly ornament of the church, anent the disgraceful advance of the railroads, which were spreading a pernicious network all over the country to the great detriment of the natural scene and a decline in the use of that noble animal, the horse.

*   *   *

The morning of the funeral was cold and windy. Hurrying ranks of clouds streamed endlessly overhead against a louring background of grey skies that failed to show a glimpse of blue, and patches of discoloured snow still lay about unmelted. But among the roots of the oaks and the beech trees in the park an occasional early primrose showed a pale splash of yellow.

The body of the late Earl had been laid to rest in the ancestral mausoleum attached to the chapel in the grounds of the castle, and, the service over, Captain Randall found himself standing next to his neighbour of the previous evening, Lady Wycombe.

'Let us wait in the porch until the crowd thins,' said Lady Wycombe. 'At least it is out of the wind. It will take some time to get the carriages away, and I do not intend to walk.'

The crowd about the mausoleum was thinning rapidly, for the keen wind did not encourage loitering. Those who had come or were returning on foot had already set off at a brisk pace, and the carriages that waited to one side of the yew-lined avenue were being filled and driven away.

A lone woman was standing apart by the nearest yew tree, using it as a shelter against the wind and evidently waiting, as were Alex and Lady Wycombe, until the major portion of the crowd had left the avenue. Something about her attracted Captain Randall's attention, for despite the heavy veil that obscured her features he had the impression that he knew her, or had seen her before. She stood quite still: so still that he suddenly realized when and where it was that he had seen her. It was the woman who had entered the guardroom yesterday, and had stood in that same rigid attitude beside the old Earl's coffin.

He watched her idly, wondering how it was that such complete immobility could yet manage to convey such a vivid and unmistakable impression of grief. And as he watched, a freakish gust of wind, sweeping about the trunk of the aged yew tree, snatched at the long black veil and whipped it out and above her head, revealing a young, unguarded face.

It was a small face, the colour of warm ivory. Wide at the

brow and pointed at the chin, with enormous dark eyes under delicate black brows that curved like a swallow's wings. The black hair that sprang from a deep widow's peak on her forehead held a blue, burnished gleam that made the mourning hue of bonnet and gown appear dull and rusty by comparison, and though her mouth was too wide and too full to suit the accepted standards of beauty in that age, it was a mouth, all the same, to set a man's pulses beating.

'Who is that?' enquired Captain Randall of his companion. 'The young lady by the tree——'

Lady Wycombe turned. 'That? We were discussing her last night—the Condesa de los Aguilares. That is Winter.'

II

THE SHADOW BEFORE

3

'*WINTER!* Who ever heard of such a name? It is not a name at all. Pray be sensible, my dear Marcos! You *cannot* call the poor mite anything so absurd!'

'She will be called Winter.'

'Then at least let her have some sensible second name! There are so many pretty and unexceptionable names to choose from.'

'No. Only Winter.'

Kindly Mrs. Grantham threw up her hands in a gesture of exasperation. 'My dear boy! Winter de Ballesteros de los Aguilares. Only think how absurd it will sound.'

'Sabrina wished it,' said the distraught young husband stubbornly.

Mrs. Grantham knew when she was defeated. There was no arguing with Marcos in his present frame of mind. If only the christening could be postponed he might yet be brought to see reason. But the baby was a sickly infant whose chances of survival appeared to be so slight that it had been considered expedient to baptize it without delay, and Marcos, who was a Spaniard and a Catholic, had even agreed to allow the ceremony to be performed by an Anglican parson; cholera having struck down the only available priest, and the child's mother having belonged to the Anglican Church. Marcos had been sufficiently distraught to agree to anything, but he had been adamant over the matter of his daughter's baptismal name.

'*Winter!*' repeated Mrs. Grantham dabbing ineffectually at her swollen eyes. 'Poor 'Rena must have been out of her mind!'

But Sabrina—poor, pretty Sabrina—dying in childbirth in the

31

merciless heat of an Indian May, had not been out of her mind.
She had been thinking of Ware . . .

*   *   *

Sabrina had never known her parents. Her father Johnny
Grantham, youngest son of the fifth Earl of Ware, had been
killed at Waterloo, and her mother, Louisa, had died in giving
birth to his only and posthumous child. Sabrina had been brought
up in her paternal grandfather's great house, and she was nine-
teen when her Aunt Emily, who had married an elderly nabob,
asked that her niece be allowed to accompany her on a visit to
India. The Earl might have been expected to veto such a suggestion, but the invitation happened to coincide with the appearance
among the ranks of his granddaughter's suitors of a certain
dashing Captain of Hussars. The Hon. Dennis Allington was
known to be a gambler and a spendthrift, and his reputation—
particularly where women were concerned—was not of the best.
Sabrina, however, had accorded him a greater degree of favour
than she had previously shown to any of her numerous suitors,
and the Earl had become seriously alarmed. Recalling the old
adage that out of sight is out of mind, he had given his consent to
the proposed visit, and three weeks later the Lady Emily Barton
had set sail for Calcutta, accompanied by her niece, Sabrina
Grantham.

Sabrina was enchanted with India. She possessed a gay and
uncritical nature, and everything that she saw there delighted
her. Her Uncle Ebenezer, as a prominent member of the Governor General's Council, often went on stately tours during the cold
season, upon which Lady Emily and Sabrina would accompany
him, and it was in the course of a visit to the court of the King
of Oudh that Sabrina met Juanita de Ballesteros.

Juanita's father, the Conde de los Aguilares, was a wealthy
and eccentric Spanish nobleman who as a young man had
travelled much in the East. Arriving in Oudh almost half a
century earlier he had been greatly attracted to the country and
its people, and in particular to a nephew of the ruling King.

The two young men, Spaniard and Mussulman, had become fast friends. They were curiously alike both in feature and temperament. Perhaps the blood of some dark-eyed daughter of Islam from the days of the Moorish conquest of Spain had been transmitted down the ages to this son of Castile and Aragon.

Ramon de Ballesteros, Conde de los Aguilares, never returned to Spain. Oudh became his home, and the rich, barbaric, colourful kingdom his country. The King of Oudh made him a grant of land on the banks of the Goomti, and there, surrounded by groves of orange and lemon trees and green formal gardens, he built a house; a vast Spanish castello in the heart of India.

The Casa de los Pavos Reales, the House of the Peacocks, merged into the Eastern scene with the same ease and grace as its owner—Spanish architecture, with its cool open courtyards and splashing fountains, its high rooms and secretive balconied windows, being to a large extent the legacy of a conqueror from the East.

In due course the Conde married; not, as might have been predicted, a daughter of the Royal house of Oudh, but the only child of a French *émigré* who had fled with his family from the bloody massacre of the Revolution, and had subsequently taken service in the Army of the East India Company.

Anne Marie de Lazencourt was a gentle dark-eyed creature who could not remember the country of her birth, and the Urdu and court Persian of Oudh were as familiar to her as the Tamil and Telegu of the South, the English tongue, or her own native French. She settled into the colourful polyglot life of her husband's great house on the Goomti and never realized its strangeness. Her friends were the slender, olive-skinned, dark-eyed wives of the Princes and nobles of Oudh, and her fourth child, Juanita, was born in the house of Aziza Begum, wife of her husband's great friend, Mirza Ali Shah.

Only two of Anne Marie's seven children survived their infancy: her son Marcos and her daughter Juanita. The others fell early victims to cholera and typhus, those two deadly plagues of the East. When Marcos was fourteen his father dis-

B*

patched him to Spain in order that his son might complete his education in his native land, and Marcos did not return for nine years. By then he was a slim young grandee with the dark, hawklike handsomeness that is so frequently seen among the great families of Aragon and Castile, and his sister Juanita had married her childhood playmate, Wali Dad, son of Ali Shah and Aziza Begum.

The marriage had aroused considerable opposition from both Christian priests and Mohammedan Maulvies but had in the end received the consent and approval of both families. The world was changing, but the old friendship between the two families had not changed. Handsome young Wali Dad, Aziza's first-born, fell in love with Anne Marie's gentle dark-eyed daughter: his parents had never denied him anything, and why should they deny him this? 'There is no God but God,' said Ali Shah to the Maulvies, 'but is not Hasrat Isa (Jesus Christ) numbered also among the Prophets? and are not Christians also Children of the Book?'

'One of our own line was a Moorish maiden,' said the Conde Ramon. 'Ali Shah is my oldest friend, and Oudh has been the country of my adoption. If the young people desire it, I will not refuse my consent.'

Sabrina Grantham, visiting Oudh with her aunt and uncle in the year 1857, met Juanita de Ballesteros, wife of Wali Dad, at a banquet in the women's quarter of the Chutter Manzil Palace in Lucknow, and they were friends from the first moment of their meeting. Sabrina came to spend more and more time at the Gulab Mahal,* the little pink stucco palace in a quiet corner of the city where Juanita lived, for Sir Ebenezer Barton was making an extended stay in Oudh.

The Honorable the East India Company—'John Company' —was a company of merchants and traders. They had come to India to buy and sell, and Trade and Profits were what they desired. They did not want an Empire. Yet slowly and insidiously, or so it seemed, an Empire was being thrust upon them.

* Gul (rhymes with 'pull') *arb* Ma-*harl.*

In the days of the Great Moguls a British ship's surgeon had successfully treated the badly burned and beloved daughter of the Emperor Shahjahan, and when asked what he wished for in reward had requested permission for the British to trade in Bengal. Those first small trading-posts had flourished and paid rich dividends, but in their very success they had aroused the envy and resentment of other traders from beyond the seas. The French, the Arabs, the Dutch and the Portuguese were also rivals for the golden prizes of Indian trade, and to protect their factories, together with their own lives, the British merchants had been forced to arm themselves and to hire mercenaries. They had in time succeeded in defeating their rivals and in establishing a monopoly of trade, but as their interests grew and expanded, and more and yet more factories and warehouses were built, the need of larger forces for their protection grew also, for the times were troublous and India a medieval medley of small and warring states, riddled with corruption, trickery and intrigue. The Company of Merchants made treaties with many of these petty kings, and on behalf of their allies fought with others, while their arms, of necessity, kept pace with their profits. The Genie of Force had been let out of the bottle and it became impossible to replace it. Instead of reaping a harvest of gold, as they had in the early years, the Directors of the East India Company found themselves pouring out treasure upon what had become no less than a vast private army, and acquiring, in order to protect their trade, a huge and ever-enlarging Empire.

It was Robert Clive, one-time clerk in the service of the Company, who conquered most of India and propounded the revolutionary theory that if a country is taken over from its rightful owners, then it must be governed for the greater benefit of those owners and not merely to the advantage of the conquerors; and the erstwhile merchant adventurers found themselves, to the dismay of many of their members, dealing more and more in territorial administration and less and less in trade. Their armies policed the land, and they appointed Governors and Residents and Political Agents to dispense law and justice to this vast country to which they had come to barter and remained to conquer, and their profits dwindled away.

'No man goes so far as he who knows not where he is going,' said Oliver Cromwell. The men of John Company had not known where they were going, and they had travelled a long and far road from the days of the seventeenth century and the first small trading settlement on the coast of Coromandel. They had defeated Tippu Sultan, ruler of Mysore, and divided and apportioned his territory. They had defeated the Mahrattas and the Gurkhas, and deposed the Peishwa and added his lands to the Presidency of Bombay. Would the ancient Kingdom of Oudh now go the same way, and its rule pass from the hands of its Royal house into those of the Company? Sir Ebenezer Barton, for one, was resolved to do all he could to prevent it. The whole question of India, he considered, was getting out of hand. The greater the Company's territorial power and possessions, the less profit in terms of trade. John Company was not only losing money, it was heavily in debt. It was out of the question that they should take over the sole Government of Oudh.

The warm November weather gave place to the sharp, sparkling mornings, cool nights and brilliant days of December: Juanita's daughter was born, and the old, old lullabies of Spain and France and Hindustan were sung above her cradle. And Sabrina, paying a morning call at the Casa de los Pavos Reales with her Aunt Emily, met Marco de Ballesteros, newly returned from Castile.

It was of course inevitable that they should fall in love. Marcos, dark-haired and romantically handsome, with his gay laugh and the novelty and charm of one newly come from that most charming of countries, Spain, and Sabrina Grantham who had, surprisingly enough, not been in love for over a year, and who was so small and slim and blondly beautiful.

'My niece, Sabrina Grantham——'

'My son Marcos——'

They had stood looking at each other in the cool white hall of the Casa de los Pavos Reales where the orange trees grew in tubs as they do in Spain, and where the sunlight filtering through the lemon trees planted about the house filled the hall with a green, aqueous light.

'*Sabrina!*' thought Marcos, staring at her entranced. '*Sabrina fair—listen where thou art sitting, under the glassy, cool translucent wave.* Yes, she is like a mermaid. A water nymph.'

'He is like a knight of the Round Table,' thought Sabrina. 'Like the picture of Sir Tristram in that book in Grandpapa's library.'

They stood and looked at each other and fell in love.

For Sabrina it was a time of enchantment: a page cut from a fairy story. But Emily was full of anxiety and foreboding. Lady Emily was staunchly and stubbornly British; possessed of all the ingrained insularity of her race. Her two children had both been born, lived their brief days and died in this hostile foreign land, and had been laid to rest in this alien soil. She did not find India beautiful or exciting. She saw it only as the graveyard of her children; an uncivilized and barbaric country with a medieval standard of morality, sanitation and squalor that it was the divinely appointed but distasteful task of men like Ebenezer to govern and control and lead into the path of enlightened Western living.

'We will remove to Delhi immediately,' decided Lady Emily, 'and I think it would be as well if Sabrina returned to England in the spring.'

'But I cannot do that,' said Sabrina, starry-eyed with happiness. 'I am going to marry Marcos.'

'Oh dear!' sighed Emily, 'it is all going to be very difficult. I hope you may not find that you have made a sad mistake. You think now that this country is beautiful and romantic. But how are you going to like living all your days here? Heat, disease, wars, famines——'

'I shall have Marcos,' said Sabrina.

Emily gave it up, and waited with as much resignation as she could muster for the arrival of the mails from England that would

bring her father's answer to the request for his blessing upon the
marriage of his favourite granddaughter to Marcos de Ballesteros.

The New Year dawned over Oudh in a blaze of saffron-yellow
light. A new year that was to see the Coronation of the young
Queen Victoria, the Austrian evacuation of the Papal States,
France declare war on Mexico, the abolition of slavery in India
and the start of the disastrous Afghan war. But the year that
had dawned for Sabrina with so much sunshine and happiness
darkened swiftly. Anne Marie died in the first week of February
and old Conde Ramon, stricken with years and grief, took to his
bed and did not rise from it again, and three days later his body
lay beside that of his wife in the marble mausoleum of the Casa
de los Pavos Reales.

March brought with it a steadily rising temperature, dust
storms, the monotonous, maddening call of the *köil*, whom the
British had nicknamed the 'Brain Fever bird', and the dispensa-
tion that Marcos had written for to Rome. And on a hot evening
towards the end of the month, while a dry wind rattled the dying
leaves of the bamboos and neem trees, and the pariah dogs of the
city bayed a sultry yellow moon rising through the hot dusk, the
letter they had been awaiting for so long arrived from England.

It was short and to the point. On no account whatsoever would
the Earl of Ware consent to the marriage of his granddaughter
to this expatriate Spaniard who had settled in the East. He had
no intention of allowing Sabrina to throw herself away on any
man, however wealthy or well born, who was not only a foreigner
but had made his home in such a barbarous and uncivilized spot.
As for Emily and his son-in-law, to whose care he had entrusted
his granddaughter, the Earl could only think that they had gone
out of their minds to entertain any thought of such a preposterous
marriage. Sabrina would return home instantly. In the event
of her refusing to do so and of persisting in this outrageous folly,
she would be cut out of his will and cut off from all future contact
with him or his family. This was his final word upon the subject.

But Sabrina had no intention of being sent home to England.

She had promised her aunt and uncle that she would wait until her grandfather's views on her marriage were made known, but she had not promised to abide by those views. Now that her grandfather's letter had arrived, offering her the choice of giving up Marcos or being cast off and disinherited, there was no further need for delay. She left a note pinned to her pincushion in the traditional manner, and slipping out of the house, had her horse saddled, and rode away to Marcos.

They were married in the little chapel of the Casa de los Pavos Reales in the presence of two young officers of the 41st Bengal Cavalry, friends of Marcos on their way to rejoin their Regiment after a leave spent shooting in the Terai, and of Juanita, who had been hurriedly summoned from her home in the city.

Sabrina wore a dress of Anne Marie's that she and Juanita had found stored away in a camphor-wood chest in Anne Marie's rooms, for she had brought nothing with her except the clothes she stood up in and the pearls that Marcos's mother had given her on the night of her birthday ball.

Someone had put jasmine and white roses in the chapel, and the cura had lighted candles on the altar. The ring that had been one of Anne Marie's slipped on to Sabrina's finger; a broad gold band set round with small pearls. Anne Marie's fingers had been plumper than Sabrina's and the ring was heavy and a little loose. Sabrina looked down at it—this symbol of her marriage to Marcos that had belonged to Marcos's mother—and as she looked at it she was aware of a strange feeling of timelessness and of the continuity of life. It was as if she realized for the first time that she and Marcos, who were young and gay and with all their life before them, must one day die as her own father and mother and Anne Marie and Don Ramon had died. That life was not long at all, as it appeared when one was young and impatient, but very short and very swift, like the shadows of the clouds racing silently over the unheeding earth; but that this was not a sad thing, because all time was one. She seemed to see it stretching back behind her and away ahead of her. Anne Marie who had

been young once had worn this ring, and now she was dead and
her son's wife wore it—as one day a daughter of Sabrina's would
wear it in her turn. Anne Marie was still here in Marcos and
Juanita as she would be in their children and grandchildren.
All time was one, and Sabrina was suddenly filled with a warm,
shining happiness and an assurance of immortality.

*   *   *

Wali Dad's father, who had been Conde Ramon's friend, died
that spring, and Sir Ebenezer and Lady Emily left for the cool
air of Simla, where Emily's health improved and Sir Ebenezer
attended those endless conferences that were to result in the
disaster of the First Afghan War.

Sabrina remained in her husband's house on the banks of the
Goomti, and the furnace heat of the Indian summer closed
upon Oudh like a steel trap from which there was no escape.
But the high white rooms of the Casa de los Pavos Reales,
with their thick walls and shuttered windows, and the patios with
their fountains and orange trees, had been built for coolness, and
Sabrina did not suffer too greatly from the heat that first summer,
though she grew pale from the enforced inaction of the long
months. She occupied her idle hours with the study of Urdu,
and as a compliment upon her progress in the language Juanita's
mother-in-law, Aziza Begum, sent a woman from the Gulab
Mahal, Zobeida, to be her personal servant. Zobeida was the
daughter of a zenana slave; brown-skinned and sturdily built,
with a quick brain, willing hands and a faithful heart, and
Sabrina grew to love her and rely upon her as though she had
been some trusted nurse from the days of her childhood. A love
that Zobeida reciprocated with the protective devotion of a
mother for her child.

Sabrina might well have been lonely that summer had it not
been for Juanita and the Gulab Mahal, for old Conde Ramon,
who had from time to time acquired land in outlying parts of
Oudh, had left vast estates, so that Marcos perforce spent much
of his time in the saddle. But during the long hot evenings, if

he were away from home, Sabrina would visit her sister-in-law; and as the moon rose they would sit out on the flat roof of the zenana quarter, looking out across the minarets and white roof-tops, the green trees and gilded cupolas of the beautiful, evil, fantastic city of Lucknow, while old Aziza Begum cracked jokes and shook with silent laughter, stuffed her mouth with strange sweetmeats from a silver platter, or told long, long stories of her youth and of kings and princes and nobles of Oudh these many years in their graves.

But while the plains gasped in the grip of the hot weather, in the hills, among the pines and deodars of Simla, the Governor General, encouraged by the irresponsible advice of men whose lust for power and conquest had made them deaf to the dictates of prudence, justice or common sense, had decided to declare war on Afghanistan.

It mattered little to Lord Auckland and his favoured advisers that Dost Mohamed, the Amir of Afghanistan, was the chosen ruler of a people who infinitely preferred him to that elderly weakling, Shah Suja—the ex-ruler whom they had driven from his kingdom many years before. The Governor General's advisers distrusted a man of the Amir's ability, who had proved that he could both think and act for himself. They considered it a vital matter of policy that Afghanistan should be an ally of Britain, and suspecting that Dost Mohamed might intrigue with Russia, decided to force the rejected Shah Suja back on his unwilling people in the belief that gratitude and self-interest would bind him to the British. With this end in view they con-cluded a treaty that amounted to nothing less than an offensive alliance with the dying Ranjit Singh, 'Lion of the Punjab' and ruler of the Sikhs, and in November, with the onset of the cold weather, the grandiloquently named 'Army of the Indus' assembled at Ferozepore before marching on Afghanistan.

Sabrina was pregnant by then, and after the new year Juanita did not come so often to visit her, for the birth of her own second child was imminent and she preferred to remain within the se-clusion of her house. But when Marcos was absent Sabrina still spent much of her time at the Gulab Mahal, talking and laughing with Juanita and Aziza Begum and playing with her niece, Juanita's black-eyed, dimpled first-born. She was there on a golden morning in early February when Juanita's pains began, and would have stayed with her but that Aziza Begum and Juanita herself would not permit it.

'Send her away, my mother,' whispered Juanita urgently, the sweat already pearling on her brow. 'The English are not as we. They tell their maidens nothing of these things, and because it will go hard with her when her time comes, it were better she were not now made afraid.'

'*Arré!* and who should know better than I?' nodded the Begum. 'Her time will indeed be hard. She is not made for the bearing of children. *Hai Mai!* I will send her away, do not fear. Rest now, my daughter, and in a little while my son's son lies in thy arms.'

Aziza Begum stuffed her mouth with pan leaves and waddled out to summon the carriage and reassure the anxious Sabrina: 'Do not fear. It is but a time that comes to all women, and what woman amongst us all would forgo it had she the choice? Not one, my bird!—not one. For is not this the end for which we were born? All will be well here. I, who have borne many children, tell you so.'

To Sabrina the obese old woman who was Juanita's mother-in-law had always seemed a grotesque figure; but now, suddenly, she saw her with new eyes: saw the kindness and the shrewd wisdom in the bright eyes that peered out of that fat, wrinkled mask; the firmness and character that lay in those small dark hands; and, all at once, the vanished beauty and charm that had once been possessed by this stout and shapeless old woman who had been Anne Marie's lifelong friend.

Moved by a sudden impulse Sabrina put out her hand and groping for those small beringed fingers, clung to them tightly. The Begum embraced her. It was surprising how comforting that plump sandalwood-scented shoulder was to lay one's head against. 'Haste now, little daughter, and return to thy husband's house, and I will send word when my son's son is born.' The old woman patted Sabrina's shoulder and whisked away a sudden tear with the corner of her veil.

Juanita's son was born before moonrise. A lusty, dark-haired creature with his mother's fair skin and his father's black eyes. 'He is born in an auspicious hour,' said the Begum. '*Arré, arré,* do not cry, thumbling! Thou shalt be a great king and have seven sons!'

Far to the north, as April drew to a close, Shah Suja with the British Envoy, Macnaghten, riding behind him, entered Kandahar. And in the last week of that month Marcos left for the South.

Anne Marie's father, on his retirement from the service of the East India Company's army, had acquired land on the Malabar coast and settled down to the life of a planter. His estate had prospered and he died a wealthy man. Anne Marie had been his sole heiress and the property had passed on her death to her children, Marcos and Juanita. But news had been received of the overseer's death from snakebite, and also of disaffection among the coolies employed on the estate. Marcos, and Juanita's husband Wali Dad, discussing the matter, decided that their best plan would be to sell the Malabar estates and reinvest the money in Oudh, as the property was too far away to be administered except at second hand and at long range; an arrangement which the present news had proved to be unsatisfactory.

Marcos and his brother-in-law rode south in the last week of April, promising to return by the end of May.

'It will not be for long, *querida*,' said Marcos, comforting Sabrina. 'I shall be back before May is out, I promise you.'

But Sabrina would not be comforted. 'Why must you go? Why cannot Wali Dad go alone? Marcos, you cannot leave me now! I could not bear it. I am afraid!'

'*Que pasa?* Afraid of what, my heart?'

'I do not know! I only know that I cannot bear to let you go. Let Wali Dad go!'

'We must both go, *querida*,' said Marcos, his arms about her. 'If only one were to go, it would have to be I. Wali Dad comes to help me. If he went alone the local officials and administrators might cause him trouble; he is not of the South, but of Oudh. And once we have disposed of the estates we need never be worried by business in the South again. Does that not please you? I shall never again have the need to go more than a night's journey away from you.'

'She must come to me,' said Juanita. 'I know that she does not wish to leave 'Pavos Reales, and that it is cooler there. But it is not right that she should be alone just now. Loneliness is not good for her at such a time. Send her to me, Marcos.'

So Sabrina moved from the Casa de los Pavos Reales to the pink stucco palace in Lucknow city, and watched Marcos and Wali Dad ride away under the flaming glory of the gold-mohur trees in Juanita's garden with eyes that were misted with tears.

Marcos, turning in his saddle for a last look as he rode under the arch of the gateway, saw her standing among the hard, fretted shadows of the garden; an incongruous little figure with her white skin and soft blonde curls in that flamboyant oriental setting; and did not know that he was seeing her for the last time.

With Marcos's departure it was as if the shining world of beauty and contentment in which Sabrina had walked had shattered like some fragile and iridescent soap bubble at the touch of a rough hand. She missed him with an intensity that grew rather than diminished as the days wore on. She missed the cool stately rooms of 'Pavos Reales and the quiet of the vast park-like grounds that surrounded it.

Gulab Mahal—the 'Rose Palace'—was full of noise, and the rooms with their walls painted and carved or inlaid with vari-coloured marbles, semi-precious stones or shining pieces of mother-of-pearl, and their windows screened with stone tracery, were stiflingly hot. Below the innumerable carved balconies lay paved courtyards and gardens thick with mango and orange and gold-mohur trees, while beyond and all about the high wall that hemmed them in pressed the teeming city with its crowded bazaars and gilded mosques, green gardens and fantastic palaces.

The noise of the city beat about the pink walls of the Rose Palace night and day, filling the small, hot, stifling rooms with sound, as the unguents and essences used by Aziza Begum and the zenana women filled them with the heavy scent of sandalwood and attar of roses, and the cooking-pots of the kitchen courtyards filled them with the smell of boiling *ghee*, curry and asafoetida.

Even the nights brought only a diminution of the noise: never silence. Tom-toms beat in the crowded mazes of the city, mingling their beat with the piping of flutes and the tinkle of *sitars*, the barking of pariah dogs, the crying of children, the clatter of armed horsemen riding through the narrow streets, or the drunken shouts of revellers returning from some debauch at the King's palace.

With the passing of each slow day the heat became greater. During the hours of daylight the walls and the roofs of the houses and the stone paving of the courtyards would steadily absorb the fierce rays of the sun, so that when night fell it seemed as though every stone and brick in the city gave off the stored heat in waves, as from the open door of a furnace. Sabrina found it possible to sleep a little during the day, for a hot dry wind frequently blew during the day-time, and then the doors and windows would be opened and hung with curious thick matted curtains made of woven roots, which were kept soaked with water. The hot winds blowing through the damp roots cooled the rooms and filled them with a not unpleasant aromatic odour. But often the wind did not blow; and always it died at sunset.

Sabrina's thin body felt hot and dry and shrivelled with heat, and she began to long for the cool pine-scented air of the hills as a man parched with thirst longs for a draught of cold water, and to regret that she had not gone to the hills with Emily in March as Marcos had wished her to do. But she would never again go to the hills with Emily. Marcos had been absent just over three weeks and May was halfway over when a brief letter arrived from Sir Ebenezer Barton. Emily was dead. She had contracted malarial fever, wrote Sir Ebenezer, and had died two days later. Her distant relative, Mrs. Grantham, had been with her. Sir Ebenezer's handwriting, normally so clear and firm, wavered like that of an old man far gone in years.

There had been no news of Marcos or Wali Dad beyond a brief note dispatched from the village where they had spent the first night of their journey. The lack of news did not worry Juanita or the Begum, who knew only too well the state of the roads and the difficulties of sending word through the Dâk from out-of-the-way stations. But it worried Sabrina, and during the long hot hours of the sleepless nights her imagination would conjure up pictures of horror and calamity, and she would remember the overseer who had died of snakebite. Marcos too might be bitten by a snake—attacked by a tiger—murdered by the wandering devotees of Thugee—fall a victim to fever or cholera or the plague, or die terribly of hydrophobia. The India that had once seemed to her so glamorous and beautiful a country began to wear a different aspect. She knew now that underneath that glamour and beauty there lurked undreamed-of depths of cruelty and terror, just as the graceful minarets and gilded domes of the palaces rose above narrow, filthy streets and the squalid hovels of the poor.

On the far side of the high wall that bounded the garden of the Gulab Mahal, and immediately fronting Sabrina's window, stood a mosque. It was an unpretentious little mosque built of whitewashed brick and plaster, its bulb-like dome crowned by an iron horned moon that is the symbol of Islam. The sun rose directly behind it, and with every dawn, while the air was still faintly cool from the long hours of darkness, Sabrina would see it framed by the curve of the open window and silhouetted darkly against the saffron sky. And when, too soon, the sun rose, it would cast the curved shadow of that horned moon across the floor of her room.

The shadow would creep slowly across the matting as the sun rose into a brassy sky, and sometimes at night Sabrina would awake to find it lying black in the moonlight. It came to symbolize for her all the fear and loneliness of those long days, and that growing sense of being alone in an alien country and surrounded by people of an alien race. It was a threat and a warning. A

token of the inescapable and grinding heat of the coming day.
Heat that sapped the strength from Sabrina's body and the power
of connected thought from her brain.

She had not visited the Casa de los Pavos Reales since Marcos
had left, but one breathless evening, after a day in which no wind
had blown and the heavy curtains of wet *kus-kus* roots had served
only to make the hot rooms of the Gulab Mahal more stifling,
she was seized by a sudden desire to see it again and to walk
through the gardens and along the river terrace. May was at best
a burning month in the plains, but now a heat-wave held all
Oudh in its grip, and the mercury mounted steadily. But out at
'Pavos Reales it would be cooler. The trees and the open spaces
and the terrace by the river would not hold this sweltering,
remorseless heat as the city did.

Juanita offered to accompany her, but Sabrina preferred to go
alone, and attended only by Zobeida she was driven through the
narrow, burning streets where the heat appeared to be imprisoned
between the houses as water between the banks of a river, and
out to the open country where the Casa de los Pavos Reales lay
surrounded by acres of parkland and groves of trees.

The dim, shuttered rooms were close and stuffy and the patio
fountains were silent, but after the noise and heat and colour of
the Gulab Mahal it seemed to Sabrina incredibly cool and peaceful. She wandered through the quiet, darkening rooms, touching the heavy Spanish furniture and the fragile French ornaments
with a caressing hand, as though they were friends whom she
was greeting—or bidding farewell.

There were still a few late roses by the river terrace, and fallen
petals lay among the parched grasses and made small splashes of
colour on the hot stone paving. The river was low and barred
with the faint silver ripples of shoal water, and white long-
legged egrets picked their way along the warm shallows, ghost-
like in the dusk. A peacock called harshly from among the
bamboo thickets, its cry waking the echo from the curved wall
at the far end of the terrace. Pea-oor! ... *Pea-oor!* Pea-oor! ...
Pea-oor! Sabrina had always loved to hear the peacocks cry at

dusk and dawn at the Casa de los Pavos Reales, but tonight it seemed to her that the harsh call held a strange aching note of sadness, and she was seized by a sudden and uncontrollable spasm of fear. A fear of India. Of the savage alien lands that lay all about her, stretching away for thousands of miles and yet hemming her in. Of the dark, secretive, sideways-looking eyes; the tortuous unreadable minds behind those bland expressionless faces. The incredible cruelties that were practised within the King's Palaces, of which the zenana women whispered. The stories that Aziza Begum would tell by starlight, sitting on the flat rooftop overlooking the crowded city. Stories of battle and intrigue and murder. Of queens and dancing girls and zenana favourites burnt alive on the funeral pyres of their lords. Tales of the savage sack of great cities. . . .

India had not changed greatly because a handful of London merchants had brought much of her territory under subjection. She had been conquered before, many times, since the days when *Sikander Dulkarn* (Alexander the Great) had fought his battles on her soil and built his roads and tanks and left behind his nameless Viceroys. Greeks, Huns, Arabs, Mongols, Tartars, Pathans, Persians—India had seen them come and had watched the fires of their power blaze bright and die away again leaving nothing but ashes; and had gone on her way.

Some of all this was in Sabrina's mind as she stood on the river terrace of the Casa de los Pavos Reales while a vast yellow moon rose through the hot, dusty twilight. Daylight does not linger in the East as it does in cooler lands, and the Eastern twilight is barely a breath drawn between day and night. One moment the river ran gold in the last reflected glow of the sunset, and the next the moon had laid a shining pathway across its dark surface and Sabrina's shadow lay black on the moonlit terrace. A jackal howled from somewhere far out across the darkening plain, and although nightfall had brought little or no alleviation of the oppressive heat, Sabrina shivered as though with a sudden chill, and drawing the light scarf of Indian gauze closer about her, she turned away.

The heat of the city met her like a blast from a furnace, but the streets and bazaars were uncannily quiet. It was too hot for speech or movement and men had dragged their string cots into the roadways and lay in the hard moonlight, sprawled and silent like the victims of some medieval pestilence.

There was a riderless horse standing just within the gateway of the Gulab Mahal. A tired horse, lathered with sweat, its head drooping and the white dust of the roads thick on its heaving flanks. It stood among the dappled shadows of the flame trees, but Sabrina knew it. She knew all the 'Pavos Reales horses, and this was Suliman, who had been ridden by one of the servants who had accompanied Marcos to the South.

Her heart leapt with a sudden wild joy and she stood up, swaying to the movement of the carriage as it jolted over the uneven paving of the courtyard.

But it was not Marcos. A messenger only, bearing letters, said the servant who opened the carriage door. Sabrina brushed aside Zobeida's hand and sprang to the ground. A letter from Marcos at last! Perhaps to say that he would be back in a few days. Only a few more days to wait! She ran down a short passage and up the two steep flights of narrow ill-lighted stairs that led to Juanita's rooms, laughing as she ran.

Juanita's room seemed to blaze with light after the dimly lit stairways, and it was full of people. Aziza Begum was there and two of her daughters, and Wali Dad's younger brother Faiz Ullah, and several serving women. Juanita herself was holding a letter in her hand and her face was white and frightened.

Sabrina stopped on the threshold and stood quite still. Her mouth was still curved with laughter and for a moment it stayed that way as if Juanita's face had been Medusa's head and had turned her to stone. Then her lips closed stiffly and she said: '*Marcos!*'

Juanita ran to her, putting her arms about her and holding her close.

'Do not look like that, *querida*! He will not die. Many recover. Do not look so!'

Sabrina put her aside, pulling herself free of the clinging arms, and spoke across the small, hot, crowded room to Aziza Begum: 'What is it? Tell me.'

'It is the cholera, my daughter. One of thy husband's servants brought a letter from my son. He thought it best that we should know, so that——' The Begum checked herself and then said: 'But thy husband is a young man and strong. He will recover, never fear. There is no need for thee to be over-anxious, lit⁺le heart. In a few days he will be well again. Many recover from the cholera who are not so young or so strong as he.'

But Sabrina did not hear her. She had heard only the one word —Cholera! The swift, dreaded plague of the East. Marcos had cholera. Even now he might be dying—dead! She must go to him. She must go at once. . . .

The heat of the small room pressed upon her with an almost tangible weight, but it seemed to her that her brain was suddenly very clear and cold. The only clear thing in this queer hot room full of oddly hazy faces and bright spinning colours. The only cold thing in this furnace-like city. She looked at the faces around her, trying to focus them. Dark anxious faces. Dark anxious eyes. Juanita's blanched cheeks. They were kind. She knew that. But they would try to stop her. They would prevent her going to Marcos. But Suliman was tethered by the gate. If she could only reach him she could ride away to Marcos and they could not catch her.

She backed away from them very slowly. Juanita took a swift step towards her, her hand outstretched, and the roomful of faces seemed to surge up and forwards. Sabrina whirled round and ran towards the stairs. The steep dark stairway yawned below her feet and she heard footsteps running behind her and glanced over her shoulder. And then she was falling—falling into a hot spinning darkness that reached up and engulfed her.

Sabrina's daughter was born as the sun rose, after a night of agonizing labour, and Juanita, watching the white lips move, bent closer to catch the whispered words.

'Don't . . . let . . . it . . . touch——'

'No, no,' comforted Juanita, not knowing of what she spoke.

'The shadow——' persisted Sabrina. She was too exhausted
to turn her head, but her eyes turned, and Juanita following their
gaze saw them rest on the curious curved shadow of the crescent
moon that the early morning sun threw across the wall, and
she rose quickly and drew close the heavy wooden shutters
that should have been closed an hour earlier to conserve what
little coolth the night had brought into the room.

Sabrina lay motionless on the low Indian bedstead and her
mind wandered back to Ware in wintertime; to keen biting winds
and a white expanse of snow against which the yew trees and the
leafless woods cut sharp black silhouettes; to icicles fringing the
leaden gutters at the roof's edge, and to frost patterns on a
window-pane; to grey skies and softly falling snow. In imagination she touched the snow and felt its crisp coldness. Plunged her
arms in it and held handfuls of it to her burning cheeks. If
only she could lie quite, quite still—if she did not move or
breathe—perhaps she could will it to be true . . .

At sundown Zobeida opened the shutters and sprinkled water
on the stone balcony outside the window, and Sabrina, waking,
heard the water hiss upon the hot stone. The sky beyond the
window was already green and a star hung low over the rooftops.
But the air was no cooler and she gasped for breath. As the room
darkened Juanita lit a small oil-lamp. The shadows made a mist
under the curved ceiling so that it was difficult to tell how high
it was, and the moulded reliefs of trees and birds and flowers
which decorated the walls appeared to move in an unfelt breeze.
Aziza Begum, seeing that she was awake, brought her the child.

The tiny creature moved and uttered a thin cry, and the weak
sound penetrated through the mists that were clouding Sabrina's
brain. She turned her head, forcing open her heavy eyelids, and
looked at the child who lay beside her. It was so small that it
seemed more like a doll than a living infant, and it was not red
like most new-born babies, but milk white, with curling dark
hair like black silk. Looking at her Sabrina remembered a fairy

story that someone—was it Aunt Emily?—had told her one
winter's day at Ware. A story about a Queen who had sat at
her window on a snowy day and wished for a daughter with a
skin as white as snow and hair as black as ebony.

'What shall you call her?' asked Juanita. 'She is half a day
old, and should have a name.'

'Winter,' whispered Sabrina.

'*Winter?* But that is not a name, *querida*. She must have a
beautiful name.'

'It is a beautiful name. . . .' Juanita did not realize how
beautiful! She had never seen the snow or the dark December
woods of Ware. She only knew the harsh flaming colours of this
sun-scorched land, and the heat was not an intolerable burden to
her as it was to Sabrina, pressing her out of life.

A sudden sharp fear—a purely maternal fear—took possession
of Sabrina. If Marcos were to die—if she herself were to die—
what would become of the child? Emily will take care of her!
But Emily was dead. Juanita? No—*No!* thought Sabrina,
agonized. Not this life for my baby!

Grandpapa! He would take care of her child. He loved her.
Those angry letters meant nothing. It was only Grandpapa in a
rage. Sabrina was aware of a quivering sense of urgency. Of time
running out like sand between her fingers. She must send a letter
to Ware, at once, before it was too late. She set her teeth, and sum-
moning up all her will-power, dragged herself up on to the pillow.

'What is it, *cherie?* Lie still,' begged Juanita.

'I must write a letter,' whispered Sabrina. 'A letter to Ware.
I must write at once.'

'Tomorrow, *querida*—tomorrow——'

'No,' said Sabrina desperately, struggling feebly against the
restraining hands. 'Now. At once.'

'Then I will write it for you,' said Juanita soothingly. 'You
shall tell me what to say. See, I will sit beside you and write.'

So Juanita wrote at Sabrina's dictation, setting down the
words that came so slowly and with such difficulty in that soft
gasping whisper. She wrote in French, for although she spoke

English well and fluently she could not write it with ease. And looking at Sabrina's face, and the faces of Aziza Begum and Zobeida, she was afraid, and the tears that she would not let Sabrina see fell and blotted the written words.

'Look after her,' begged Sabrina of her grandfather. 'If anything happens to me or to Marcos—if we are not here to care for her—I leave her to you. Dearest Grandpapa, look after her for me. I do not know how to write a will, but this letter is my will. If Marcos dies I leave everything to my daughter, and I leave my daughter to you.'

When she had finished, the Begum and Zobeida lifted her, and with Juanita steadying her hand she signed her name to it. Juanita folded the paper and addressed it and put it away, and Sabrina smiled at her. It was as if a great weight had been lifted from her. She turned her head on the hot pillow and looked out at the moonlight beyond the open window, and as she looked it seemed to her that the white dome of the mosque and the moon-washed walls and black shadows of the orange trees were snow-covered fields and dark, leafless woods, and she began to talk in a clear light voice.

It was winter and the snow was falling, and Sabrina wept because she had been locked into the hot schoolroom and could only see through the barred windows the white park where she had been forbidden to play. She could see it so clearly: the snowy levels dotted with leafless trees, sloping up to the barrier of the dark woods that ringed the park. She struggled to reach it, but hands held her back. And then all at once the hands fell away and the door was open. She ran out of the room and along the familiar passages and down the wide staircase. The wind blew about her, smelling of the winter woods, and now she had reached the snow and it was cold and shining and wonderful, and she was not hot any more but cold, cold, cold.

Zobeida and the Begum fetched padded quilts and tucked them about her shivering figure as the fever mounted, but Sabrina did not feel them, and towards morning she died.

The sky beyond the balcony paled with the dawn, and presently the sun rose, filling the quiet, airless room with harsh light and throwing a curved shadow across the wall from the mosque outside the gardens of the Gulab Mahal.

Juanita, remembering how Sabrina had feared that shadow, rose from her knees, and crossing softly to the window, closed the heavy shutters against the burning day.

*   *   *

Marcos did not die of the cholera. He was, as Aziza Begum had said, both young and strong. He returned home; but by that time Sabrina had been two weeks in her grave, and to stay here in the Casa de los Pavos Reales where he had spent his brief year of happiness was suddenly intolerable to him. Through Sir Ebenezer Barton's influence he obtained a commission in the Company's army: there was always work for the Army, and Marcos yearned for change and hard work, and, if possible, hard fighting. He placed his daughter in the care of his sister Juanita, and having installed a reliable caretaker and overseer at the Casa de los Pavos Reales, put his affairs in order and rode north to join the Army of the Indus, reaching Kabul by way of the Khyber Pass with the advance guard of a motley army under the leadership of Shah Suja's son.

In the pink stucco palace in Lucknow city Sabrina's daughter grew and thrived. Zobeida had taken on the duties of nurse, and a strong and healthy hill woman, Hamida, whose latest infant had been stillborn, had been engaged as wet nurse. Her nickname among the household was *Chota Moti*—small pearl— because of her whiteness and because her given name had no meaning for them and its syllables were harsh to their ears.

The child would lie in the room that had been Sabrina's, her eyes on the colourful walls where formalized trees and flowers in the Persian style were moulded in high relief in *chunam*, a polished cement that had the appearance of coloured marble, and as soon as she could crawl she would spend hours running her small hands over the flower designs, tracing their stylized curves with a tiny finger.

Every animal and every bird in those colourful friezes had had its own name, and there had been one that was her especial favourite—the first within reach of her small, clutching hands. A stylized parrot with a wise expression who held one claw upraised as though he were commanding attention. He was called Firishta, after a celebrated Muslim historian who had lived in the days of Akbar and Jehangir, and the Begum would pretend that it was Firishta who told many of the tales of dead Moguls and heroes that the children loved to hear, prefacing them with 'Firishta says——' so that always, to Sabrina's daughter, Firishta was alive and could speak. When she was older, and the days were hot, she would stand by the pink plaster wall, pressing her small cheek against Firishta's cool, smooth greenness, and talk to him as though he were a friend and a playmate.

She had many playmates in the Gulab Mahal, chief among them Juanita's two children, Khalig Dad and the little Anne Marie who was a year and a half her senior and had been named after Juanita's mother. Anne Marie the Second, despite her name, had not inherited her looks from her mother's side of the family. She was all Wali Dad. Golden skin and eyes like sloes, a mouth like a curled rose petal and hair as black as jet. 'She is her father again—and as I also, when I was but a child,' said the Begum complacently. 'My son had great beauty, as also had I, his mother, when I was in the bloom of my youth. *Hai mai!* but that was long since, and I grow old. It is good to see my children's children growing up about me. As for thee, Little Pearl, thou also art a grandchild of my heart, and were it not inauspicious I would tell thee that, when thou art grown, thou wilt be a very moon of beauty!'

But while life in the Rose Palace went its peaceful way, the storm-clouds gathered over far-off Afghanistan.

Dost Mohamed had fought a victorious battle and had followed it up by voluntarily surrendering himself to Sir William Macnaghten, the British Envoy. He had been sent under strong escort to India where he was received with the honours of war and granted a substantial pension, and the Directors of the East India

Company, convinced that now the ex-Amir was in their hands his country would be less unsettled, and disliking the prospect of continuing to lavish a million sterling a year on bribing the allegiance of the Afghan people, decided upon retrenchment. Sir William was forced to economize in the only possible way— the cutting off or curtailing of the subsidies that alone had kept the tribes quiet—and as a result of this policy in the space of a few months the entire country was hostile, and urgent warnings of the ill-feeling among the tribes came in from every outpost.

Early in November the storm broke. Alexander Burnes and his brother were hacked to pieces by a screaming mob, and soon all Afghanistan was aflame. The distant outposts were attacked and their defenders massacred. General Sale was besieged in Jalalabad and Colonel Palmer in Ghazi. Food became short, there was no hope of relief, and the senile and incompetent Elphinstone was totally incapable of the prompt and daring action that alone might have saved the doomed Army. Akbar Khan, son of the Dost, murdered Sir William Macnaghten, and General Elphinstone remained supine and took no action to avenge the Envoy's death. Instead, a treaty was made with the chiefs by which the British forces were to be allowed to leave the country under a guarantee of safe conduct, Akbar Khan promising to send a strong Afghan escort to see them safely through the passes.

The retreat began early in the new year, and more than four thousand fighting men, with twelve thousand camp followers including many women and children, marched wearily out of the cantonments towards the snow and the bitter cold of the barren hills that lay between them and the fortress of Jalalabad where General Sale still held his besiegers at bay.

But once among the steep defiles of the passes Akbar Khan's escort deserted them, leaving them to the vengeance of the hostile tribes. Hundreds died of exposure in the intense cold, and those who dropped by the way and did not die met a less merciful death from mutilation at the hands of the tribesmen. At some time during that long martyrdom Akbar Khan, with an eye to the future, offered his protection to those few Englishwomen who were still alive, together with their husbands and General Elphinstone. They had no option but to accept, and they turned back with him. The remainder fought their way forward against the snowdrifts and the murderous tribes, and on the thirteenth day of January a sentry on the ramparts of Jalalabad saw a solitary rider, emaciated, ragged, bloodstained, drooping with exhaustion on a starved and exhausted horse. It was Dr. Brydon—the sole survivor of the sixteen thousand souls who had set out from Kabul on that tragic retreat.

Somewhere back in those terrible passes, among the butchered thousands who had paid the price of Lord Auckland's folly, Marcos de Ballesteros had died as Sabrina had imagined herself in her last hours—face downwards in the cold and glittering snow. And his corpse, and those other thousands of mutilated corpses that rotted in the passes, were the seeds from which sprang the rank growth of rebellion that was in time to deluge all India in blood. For the power and the prestige of the Company had been humbled to the dust. Their troops had been defeated in battle and herded and butchered like sheep, and their bones lay bleaching in the sun and wind to bear witness that the mighty John Company was mortal. All along the Border and through the length and breadth of India the news spread swiftly, and many men sharpened their swords in secret—and waited.

In the little pink palace in Lucknow Juanita wept for her brother, clutching his orphaned daughter in her arms until the child too wept aloud in bewilderment and alarm.

When her first grief had spent itself she wrote to the Earl of Ware enclosing Sabrina's letter and another packet: papers relating to the de Ballesteros estates, together with the will that Marcos had left with her instructing her to send them to Lord Ware should anything happen to him. She wrote in March, but summer had gone and the leaves were falling by the time that the packet reached Ware.

The Earl was eighty, but he did not look his age. He read Juanita's letter telling of her brother's death in the Afghan passes, and the will that Marcos had made in favour of his only child

C

in which he had concurred, in the tortuous legal phrases required by the law, with his wife's desire that the child should become the ward of her grandfather. He untied the strings of a small brocaded bag that still smelt faintly of sandalwood, his lip curling with distaste. The letter within it was sealed with a large circle of wax and impressed with curving Persian characters, and he broke it with a silver fruit knife, flicking the broken pieces away as though they were unclean.

The letter was written in French and the ink was blotted in places as though the writer had been crying and her tears had fallen upon the paper. The Earl read it once slowly, and then again. And suddenly there were tears on his own cheeks. He sat there oblivious of them. Oblivious, too, of the startled and embarrassed glances of his family and the servants waiting at the table.

*   *   *

It was not until the autumn of 1844 that Sabrina's daughter, Winter de Ballesteros, Condesa de los Aguilares, arrived at Ware, for mails were slow and travel slower, and the loss at sea of the Earl's first letters, followed by the death from typhus of a lady who had agreed to bring the child home, had delayed matters considerably. She was six and a half years old, and with her, to the mingled curiosity and consternation of the Viscountess and the servants' hall, came a dark-skinned attendant—Zobeida.

Save for one notable exception the small Condesa made an unfavourable first impression. She was a tiny creature, small-boned and, according to Lady Julia, sickly-looking. The white skin that had reminded the dying Sabrina of snow at Ware had ripened with time and the suns of the East to a warm ivory that her newly found relatives described as 'yellow'. Her enormous eyes, the dark, velvet brown of pansies and over-large for her small face, and the rippling blue-black hair that already fell below the child's waist, were pronounced 'foreign', and they resented her sonorous Spanish title.

She was a silent child who spoke English haltingly and with a pronounced accent. The complete change of scene and environment, the contrast between the warm, colourful, casual life of the Gulab Mahal and the cold, gloomy rooms, Victorian discipline and stately routine of Ware, coupled with the bitter pangs of homesickness for the loving friends and the only home she had as yet known, reduced her to a state of dumb misery. Had she wept and displayed her fear and loneliness it might have aroused compassion and understanding even in the breast of so unimaginative a person as Lady Julia. But the child possessed a dignity and reserve beyond her years, and she would not weep and cling to these foreign strangers. Her silent, dry-eyed misery was taken for sullenness and her slow speech for stupidity, for her relatives were not as yet aware that the child spoke four languages, of which English, owing to the fact that it had been taught her by a woman of Franco-Spanish ancestry, was the least fluent.

To Julia the fact that Sabrina's daughter was a plain, sallow and silent child proved a relief, for the Viscountess possessed a jealous nature, and her small daughter Sybella was the apple of her eye. She did not relish the appearance of a rival, and from what she remembered of Sabrina, Sabrina's daughter might well prove to be a formidable one. The subsequent arrival of such a notably unattractive child therefore relieved her of some anxiety. But her relief was of short duration, for the single exception to the disparaging view that her noble relatives had taken of Sabrina's daughter was provided by the Earl himself.

Between the old man and the small silent child there sprang up a strong bond of sympathy and understanding. He alone came to realize what the child must be suffering in heartache and homesickness, and young as she was she sensed the loneliness and need for affection that lay behind the old man's forbidding exterior and irascible manner.

Julia saw her worst fears realized. It seemed to her nothing less than a deliberate affront that her own beautiful child should fail to hold first place in Ware's affections owing to the presence of this silent, pallid, Anglo-Spanish brat. She could not forgive Sabrina's child for stealing what she considered to be her daughter's birthright, and her resentment made itself felt in numerous small ways.

The child herself did not know what she had done to merit the Viscountess's dislike. She was merely aware of it and did her best to keep out of Julia's way. But the next few years of her life were not entirely unhappy, though except from her great-grandfather and Zobeida she received little attention and no affection. Which was understandable, for only when she was in the company of the two people who loved her did she display any qualities worthy of either.

She was a lonely child, driven in upon herself by the circumstances of this new life; her only companions the silent Indian woman and the old man crippled by years and gout. It was therefore not surprising that her memory painted India as a place of wonder and beauty where the sun always shone and where people did not live in vast, chilly rooms fully of ugly dark furniture, but in gardens full of strange and beautiful flowers and tame birds. 'One day,' Aziza Begum had said, taking tender farewell of the weeping child, 'you will come back to the Gulab Mahal, and we shall all be happy again!' Zobeida too longed for her homeland, and kept it alive in Winter's memory, repeating that promise and retelling the tales that Aziza Begum had been wont to tell of an evening seated on the flat rooftop of the zenana quarters and looking out across the beautiful, garish city of Lucknow.

At first Juanita had written two or three times a year, sending news of all at the Gulab Mahal and messages to Zobeida, who could not read. But one year the letters ceased, and there was no one to tell them that the cholera had swept like a forest fire through the packed mazes of Lucknow and had claimed ten victims from the pink stucco palace; among them Juanita, her husband Wali Dad, and old Aziza Begum. Inevitably the past became shadowy and unreal to Winter, for as the years went by Zobeida came to talk less and less of her own country, and Winter's days were fully occupied with lessons in the schoolroom. India retreated into a golden haze and she began to forget many things, until in time only that impression of rose-pink walls, sunshine, flowers and brightly coloured birds—and happiness— remained. As lovely and as far out of reach and as unobtainable as the moon.

*   *   *

Winter was eleven years old when her distant cousin, Conway Barton, accompanied her great-Uncle Ebenezer on a visit to Ware. Sir Ebenezer was getting old and his contacts with India, together with his interest in it, had shrunk with the years. But his influence had been sufficient to assist the advancement of his nephew in that country, and it was largely owing to him that the younger man had obtained a well-paid administrative post in a newly annexed district.

Conway Barton was at that time in his thirty-seventh year, and still a personable enough figure of a man. Already moving towards stoutness he was of sufficient height to make it appear that he was powerfully built rather than overweight, and his blond hair and blue eyes appeared lighter in colour than they actually were, owing to the sun-tanned skin of one newly arrived from the East. He was an ambitious man, not too scrupulous where his ambitions were concerned, with an easy address and an excellent opinion of his own capabilities.

The Earl of Ware had always considered himself to be a good judge of character, but he was old and tired and in this instance his judgment was at fault. His eyesight too had dimmed, and so he failed to mark the signs of weakness and dissipation that were already written clear on Conway Barton's face. He took a great fancy to his son-in-law's nephew, entrusted him with much of Winter's affairs and, when Sir Ebenezer left, pressed the younger man to extend his stay.

It was at some time during this visit that the idea occurred to Conway Barton, who was already familiar with Winter's story and now heard for the first time the full tale of her possessions and estates, that this sallow and unprepossessing child would one day make a most eligible wife for some ambitious man. From this reflection it was but a short step to substituting Conway Barton for this anonymous future husband. The more he thought about it the better it appeared. He was only thirty-six. He could afford to wait for six years—or ten if need be. But only if he were assured of the outcome.

Mr. Barton reviewed the problem carefully. At the moment few people were likely to take much interest in the Anglo-Spanish orphan, but a time would surely come when a succession of titled fortune-hunters would present themselves at Ware, and when that day came Mr. Conway Barton would have little to offer in competition with other and more eligible applicants for the hand of such an heiress. Therefore it would be as well to consolidate his position in advance. It had not taken Mr. Barton long to gain a fair knowledge of Winter's position at Ware, and he made the best possible use of it.

Except for her great-grandfather and Zobeida, no one at Ware had ever troubled to single Winter out for attention or kindness. But this tall yellow-haired man was kind to her, noticed her, talked to her, flattered her. She thought him wonderful. The Earl was pleased that his favourite should show such partiality for a man who had taken his fancy, and put it down to an unconscious endorsement of the soundness of his own judgment. 'Children and dogs,' said the old Earl, producing the platitude as though he himself had originated it, 'they always know! Can't fool a dog. Can't fool a child!'

Conway Barton left Ware with a pressing invitation to return, and it was on his last visit, when less than two weeks of his furlough remained, that he spoke of Winter to the Earl. He had given the matter considerable thought, and chose his words with care. He had, he told the Earl, become greatly attached to the child and would now be returning to India for a further period of some eight to ten years. Before there was any likelihood of his returning, Winter would be a young woman. He suggested, delicately, that the Earl's expectation of life could not be great and should anything—er—unforeseen occur, Winter would be left to the care of Lady Julia, with whom the child did not appear to be entirely in sympathy. He realized of course that no such thing as a formal engagement could be entered into with a girl in the schoolroom, but he would like to feel that when he returned from the East he might, with the permission and approval of Lord Ware, approach her as a possible suitor for her hand. Conway Barton had a great deal more to say on the subject—all of it well phrased and calculated to make the best possible impression—and the aged Earl was much moved.

Lord Ware had always known that Julia disliked Sabrina's daughter, and he placed no reliance upon her being either kind or considerate towards the child once he himself were dead. He had worried sometimes, when waking from the light sleep of old age, about Winter's future. When he was no longer here, could he trust Julia to care for her? He very much doubted it. But now here was a way out of all his difficulties. This admirable young man, who was so sensible and steady and whom Winter herself was so fond of, was surely a right and proper person to care for his little ward. He could not expect to live much longer. Winter's future must be safeguarded now.

Winter was summoned to her great-grandfather's room, the situation explained to her, and her future decided. It seemed to her the most delightful thing in the world. To the eleven-year-old child her great-grandfather's age was terrifying, for if he should die she and 'Beda would be alone and friendless. But now dear Mr. Barton, who was so kind—almost as kind as great-grandfather himself—would take care of them. They would not be left alone at Ware. He would come for them and take them away; back to that golden enchanted land whose memories he had reawakened for her. He was a yellow-haired knight, St. George himself, come to stand between her and the cold-eyed and cold-hearted dragon that was Cousin Julia.

Later during the week the Earl's solicitors called at Ware and drew up various legal documents with which Winter, a minor, had no concern, her great-grandfather signing on her behalf. And on the day he left Ware Conway had presented her with a ring. It was a small thing, made to fit a slim finger, yet still too large for Winter's childish hand. An unpretentious little trinket, for Mr. Barton knew that Lady Julia would take strong exception to any more ostentatious piece of jewellery. It consisted of a small pearl set in a plain gold band. 'You cannot wear it on the right finger yet,' said Conway Barton, slipping it on to the third finger of Winter's small right hand, 'but it is only a token. One day, when you are grown up, I shall put another one there. The brightest diamond I can find for you in India. You must grow up quickly, and you must not forget me while you are doing it.'

Conway Barton patted her head encouragingly and rode away, looking smug and well satisfied with himself. He had always known that he would do well, but what luck—what incredible luck!—that Fate should have thrown this chance of acquiring a vast fortune in his way and given him the brains to profit by it!

Mr. Barton broke into a snatch of song. He had every reason to feel pleased with himself.

The years that followed his departure from Ware dragged by very slowly for Winter and, as they passed, her memory of him became more and more romanticized and unreal. He became to her a tall and broad-shouldered bulwark against unhappiness: handsome, kind, endowed with all the virtues. One day he would come riding up the long oak avenue with the sun glittering on his blond head, and would carry her and 'Beda far away over the seas to the lovely land of her birth, where, like the princess of a fairy story, she would live happily ever after.

She was fourteen when Zobeida died.

The damp cold and fogs and frosts of the English winters had always been a torment to Zobeida, and of late years her once-sturdy frame had seem to shrink and shrivel until she was barely more than skin and bone. She had contracted a chill that turned to pneumonia, and had died within three days, babbling in her native tongue words that only Winter understood.

After Zobeida's death Winter turned more and more to her make-believe world of the future. The years might be passing slowly, but at least they were passing: only a few more of them, and Conway would come home and marry her. She would write long letters to him, telling him of her small doings and asking news of him and his work, but Mr. Barton's replies were infrequent and disappointing, and inclined to contain complaints against his superiors. Conway Barton's superiors were, it appeared, an envious lot who were jealous of his outstanding talents and did their best to keep him from preferment, and Winter would burn with indignation against these stubborn and meanminded officials who could oppose so good and kind a man.

Mr. Barton was still occupying the post of Commissioner of Lunjore, a district bordering on Oudh, which he had originally obtained largely owing to the influence and reputation of his Uncle Ebenezer. He had expected to be promoted before now to some more prominent position, and did not hesitate to accuse several senior political officers and various members of Council of envy, malice and all uncharitableness in that he had not. It was a day in which influence in high places formed an excellent substitute for talent, but Sir Ebenezer neither could nor would do anything more for him, and Conway Barton possessed a love of two things that have never yet failed to ruin those devotees who have worshipped them to excess: Drink and Women.

For a time his strength of body and natural health stood him in good stead, but eventually indulgence and dissipation began to take their toll, aided as they were by climate and the conditions of life in the East.

His work deteriorated with his figure, but the fact that he was Sir Ebenezer's nephew saved him from much interference, and Fortune was kind to him in that it sent him as an assistant Alex Randall, one of those younger men, protegés and pupils of Sir Henry Lawrence: soldiers who had perforce become administrators—some of them the best administrators the world has ever seen. Randall was content to do the work and let his chief take the credit; an arrangement that suited Mr. Barton admirably.

It was from this comfortable state of affairs that he was abruptly aroused by the arrival of a letter from the Earl of Ware.

Winter would be seventeen in the following spring, wrote the Earl in a wavering senile hand, and although he had not intended

c*

that she should marry for some years to come, he felt himself to be failing fast. The doctors held out small hopes of his surviving for another year, and he wished Conway to return as soon as possible so that he might have the happiness of seeing his dear child safely married before he died.

So the day had come! Fortune lay at last within Mr. Barton's grasp, and all that he needed to do was to send in his resignation or, to hasten matters, demand sick leave on the score of ill-health—and indeed he did not feel at all the thing these days—and as soon as it could be arranged, which would probably not be before the cold season, he would take ship for England. The Commissioner heaved himself out of his chair and rolled across the living-room towards his office. And as he neared the door he saw a face . . .

It was a fat face, sallow and puffy, with pendulous jowls and heavy dark pouches under pale, protuberant eyes; the hair above it thin and straggling, as was the long ragged moustache, much stained with nicotine. His own face, looking back at him from a glass-fronted cabinet that a trick of the light had turned into a looking-glass.

Mr. Barton stopped dead, staring at that reflected face with a sort of horror. It was rarely that he saw himself in a looking-glass—the idle luxurious life of the East having made it virtually unnecessary for him to do so, for he was shaved, bathed and dressed, his hair combed and his nails cut by soft-footed, deft-handed servants. And on those few occasions when he did look at himself in a glass he saw only the reflection of what he expected to see there. The Conway Barton of a dozen, or even four years ago: a little older perhaps—that was not to be wondered at—but still, not too bad. Not too bad. But now he had been taken off guard, and because he had not expected to see his own reflection he had thought for a moment that it was some stranger that he saw, and had not immediately realized that what he was looking at was his own face.

He stood where he was, swaying a little and breathing heavily, staring at the glass-fronted cabinet. After a full five minutes he walked unsteadily into his bedroom, and unhooking the looking-glass that hung on the wall above his dressing table, carried it over to the window and stared down into it.

Thoughts were churning round in his head. Some of them familiar ones. 'If I give up drink and all this rich, greasy food, and take cold baths and walk and ride every day, I could get fit again by the cold weather. I could do it.' But he knew he could not. He knew that he no longer possessed the will-power. He knew too, as he stared down at his reflection in the glass, that if he were to present himself as he now was to his betrothed and her guardian they would almost certainly show him the door. He was seeing himself for the first time as others saw him; as the seventeen-year-old Winter would see him, and even the senile, half-blind Earl of Ware.

What a fool he had been! What an unutterable fool to take chances when such a dazzling future was at stake! If he were to return to England he might lose it all. And yet if he did not go—Conway Barton flung the looking-glass from him in a spasm of futile rage and it smashed against the wall and strewed the carpet with a score of glinting fragments that winked up at him, reflecting a score of gross, middle-aged men with fat white faces and bulbous red-rimmed eyes.

He could not go to England! To go would mean to lose the fortune that he had come to look upon as already his own. And yet he could not ignore the Earl's summons. Then all at once a solution presented itself and he laughed aloud. A cackling, half-hysterical laugh of relief. Of course!—if the mountain cannot come to Mahomet, Mahomet must come to the mountain! He laughed again, and uproariously, at the pleasantry.

The girl must come out and marry him here! He would write to Ware. He would think of some plausible excuse. Once let her arrive in Lunjore, alone and without friends, and the marriage could be hurried through before she had time for thought. It would be easy. She was young—she would be barely seventeen —and to return alone to Ware, unmarried, when she had left it with her bridal clothes and her trousseau, *en route* to her wedding, would be unthinkable. He would write at once. Letters to Ware and to his solicitors. Alex Randall should take them. And, better still, Captain Randall should escort the bride back to Lunjore, for although some respectable female returning to the East must be found to act as chaperon, a male escort to protect her would establish confidence. And who better than his trusted personal assistant?

Mr. Commissioner Barton repaired to his office, and having stimulated himself to the effort by a large glass of brandy, wrote steadily. A terse letter to his solicitors: a more lengthy and explanatory one to Lord Ware: another, requesting her assistance and relying on her good offices, to Lady Julia, and finally an affectionate and affecting letter to Winter herself, hinting at ill-health incurred through zeal towards duty, and the patriotic necessity of remaining at his post in anxious and troublous times when it would be inadvisable for the guiding hand to be summarily removed from the helm.

Mr. Barton regarded this last epistle with considerable satisfaction. It conveyed just the right note of pathos and manly devotion to duty, and should serve to remind his betrothed that womanly duty as well as inclination should send her flying to his side.

It was late by the time the letters were finished and sealed, and the Commissioner summoned an attendant who squatted native-fashion just outside the door and bade him send a messenger to Captain Randall's bungalow requesting that officer's immediate presence. After which, well pleased with his handling of a difficult situation, he called for more brandy and drank deeply, congratulating himself upon the fact that although his outward appearance might have suffered some temporary change for the worse during the past five years there was still, thank Heaven! nothing wrong with his brain.

*   *   *

In the year that had followed Zobeida's death Winter had grown paler and thinner and more silent than ever. Her skin appeared to be stretched too tightly over the fine bones of her skull, making her mouth seem even wider and her eyes far too large for her small sallow face. But even the deepest sorrows outwear their first bitterness, and although the cruel void left by Zobeida's death remained unfilled, the natural health and resilience of youth eventually reasserted itself and a change came over her. Almost overnight, or so it seemed, Sabrina's daughter grew from a plain child into a young woman of strange and disturbing beauty.

It was a beauty that many—and these were all women—could not appreciate or understand, for England was in the throes of a sentimental age. It was an era when the ideal of feminine beauty consisted of a smoothly oval face of a stereotyped pink and whiteness, a small rosebud mouth, limpid eyes—preferably blue— and long sleek curls *à la* Stuart caressing the cheeks and dressed so as to accentuate the oval of the face, or at least to give that effect to those unlucky enough not to possess the fashionable features.

Sybella was the very embodiment of the Victorian ideal of Beauty, but Winter possessed none of these attributes. Her wide forehead and small pointed chin gave her face a heart-shaped appearance, and her mouth was considered far too large. It was therefore not altogether surprising that to the majority of feminine beholders she should appear entirely unremarkable, if not actually plain.

But it was quite otherwise with their men. By the time Winter had reached her sixteenth birthday men's heads began to turn when she passed by, and men's eyes to follow her whenever she entered a room. The scrawny, angular child had grown into a slender girl whose slim seductive shape even the overblown hoops of the newly fashionable crinolines could not entirely disguise. Her thin little face had filled out, setting her features in proportion at last, and the wide mouth was seen to be curved with beauty and of a rich and lovely redness. The sallow skin had warmed to ivory, and the sweet curve of her young breasts owed nothing to the ruffles and padding so often resorted to by Victorian maidens. Winter's expressive dark eyes tilted slightly upwards at the outer corners, which women pronounced un-

becoming and men found irresistible. But even the sternest of
feminine critics were obliged to allow that her long slender neck
and the thick sweep of her silky black lashes were both exceptional beauties. The girl appeared to have acquired too the
graceful carriage that is possessed by so many Spanish women.
Perhaps, like her colouring, it was a legacy from Marcos, and
possibly she had always possessed it, only no one had troubled to
notice it until now.

It was not until the summer of 1855, when Winter was sixteen, that Julia awoke to the fact that the ugly Anglo-Spanish
duckling had turned into a swan. Julia had given a young
people's party for Sybella. A summer dance. It was not to be
termed a ball, for Sybella would not make her official début until
the following spring. But it was a ball in all but name, and Ware
was filled with young ladies of title and eligible gentlemen—
young and not so young—of quality and wealth. Julia had every
reason to feel proud of her child, but Winter had had an astonishing success and the Viscountess was both angry and bewildered.
She could not understand why the girl received so much attention
from men whom she had confidently expected to have eyes for no
one but Sybella. It was not that Winter had outshone her cousin.
She could not do that. Sybella had attracted the lion's share of
attention, but Julia was not slow to note how the older and more
eligible men turned to look again and yet again at Sabrina's
daughter.

Lord Carlyon, handsome, wealthy, bored—thirty-five and still
a bachelor—had enquired of Sybella who the beautiful creature
in white might be. Sybella had not recognized her cousin by this
description, and Lord Carlyon had been more specific.

'You mean *Winter*?' demanded Sybella, astounded.

'Winter?'

'My cousin Winter. Such a peculiar name, is it not?'

'*Winter!*' Sybella had heard him repeat the word almost with
awe. 'But how perfect!'

'What *do* you mean?' Sybella's fluting voice had a sudden
sharp edge to it.

'I mean that it suits so admirably. She is like snow and black shadows: cool and mysterious and yet——' He laughed on an odd note. 'So this is the plain cousin from the East! I have heard of her. The ugly duckling in person. Pray introduce me, Lady Sybella.'

Arthur Carlyon was no impressionable youth but a coldly handsome rake with a considerable experience of women. Matchmaking mammas, attracted by his fortune and undeterred by his reputation, had cast hopeful eyes in his direction for well over a dozen seasons past, but Carlyon had remained languidly aloof and more interested in mistresses than marriage. He had attended Lady Julia's ball expecting to be bored, but with a mild feeling of curiosity as to the appearance of the Lady Sybella, whom report had rumoured to be outstandingly beautiful. He had been bored. Considering Sybella with an indolent and experienced eye he had summed her up as spoilt and insipid. Blondes, though fashionable, were not in his line. He considered that they lacked fire. In the role of eligible bachelor he had had occasion to meet most of the other young ladies who were present, and had found nothing to interest him. He was considering an early retreat from the festivities when his eye had alighted on Winter de Ballesteros.

Carlyon's confident approach and suavely experienced manner had, however, made no impression on Sybella's young cousin. Winter had not been in the least sensible of the honour implied by his interest, and Carlyon, who had imagined that such a youthful creature would be easy game, had found himself being put in his place and dismissed with a cool grace that would have done credit to an experienced London hostess. He was unwise enough to treat her dismissal of him as a piece of girlish coquetry, and Winter had been driven to administer a snub that left no room for doubt as to her opinion of him. It was an entirely new and salutary experience to Lord Carlyon, and an unpleasant one.

But he had by no means been the only one to comment on Winter's unusual style of looks, and Sybella was astounded and outraged, and Lady Julia coldly angry. There was only one thing

to be done. Conway Barton must come home and marry the girl
as soon as possible. She would be seventeen in the spring and
quite old enough to be married.

'I have already written,' said the old Earl.

In the early autumn a reply arrived from India. Mr. Barton
had received Lord Ware's communication and was deeply
grieved to hear of his failing health. He could only hope that
Lord Ware was by now fully recovered. Naturally it was the
dearest wish of his heart to marry the Earl's ward, but various
unforeseen difficulties had arisen which necessitated his remaining at his post for the present. However, he had a suggestion to
make that he hoped might meet with the Earl's approval. He
had written more fully on the matter and was sending that letter
by the hand of a trusted subordinate, Captain Alex Randall, who
should reach England sometime in the autumn. Owing to the
unreliability of the mails he had thought it better to make
Captain Randall his courier, despite the fact that this would cause
some delay. In addition to which the Captain was in his confidence and empowered by him to discuss the matter with Lord
Ware.

But Captain Randall, as it happened, was considerably delayed.
He had met with friends at Gibraltar, and instead of continuing
on his way had turned back with them and gone instead to the
Crimea, where he had managed, entirely illegally, to get himself
attached to General Windham's Staff, had fought at the taking
of Sebastopol and been wounded in the bloody battle for the
Redan. He had not reached England until late in February, and
it was not until the second week of March that he arrived at
Ware.

III

KISHAN PRASAD

4

THE majority of the guests who had stayed at Ware for the funeral left the same afternoon, and those few who remained kept to their rooms. Towards dusk on that cold and windy day the sixth Earl sent a footman to find Captain Randall, and once again Alex was led through the corridors and galleries of the west wing. But this time he was not taken to Lady Julia's drawing-room, but ushered instead into a small panelled room where a fire crackled in the hearth and the new Earl sat warming himself at the blaze.

Huntly, Lord Ware, was a stout and undistinguished man who disguised his lack of character behind an impassive and somewhat pompous manner. He greeted Captain Randall graciously enough, regretted his inability to see him earlier and hoped that he had not been put to too much trouble in coming to Ware. He spoke at some length on the subject of Mr. Barton and his young cousin's approaching marriage, and concluded by saying that he understood that the Captain was returning to the East in June, and that he would make arrangements for the Condesa to travel on the same packet.

Alex's hard grey eyes ran over him in a comprehensive glance and summed him up dispassionately as a nonentity. The last of the Wares! The old man whose funeral he had attended that morning must have had more hot blood in him than this, if all accounts were true!

'I have heard of you, Captain Randall,' said Huntly graciously. 'I understand that you obtained a brevet for conspicuous gallantry at Chillianwallah, and a similar promotion only a few years later. Quite a remarkable achievement.'

A faint tinge of red deepened the dark sun-tan of Alex's face and he said expressionlessly: 'There are many opportunities for such advancement in India, sir. It was kind in Mr. Barton to speak well of me.'

'Oh, it was not Barton. A gentleman I met at the Granchesters, who was lately home from the Punjab. We have always as a family been greatly interested in India, on account of our connection with the East India Company. I regret that I have had no opportunity for discussion with you on a subject of such interest, but my time is lamentably occupied. You will be leaving in the morning? I hope I may see you again before you go.'

It was evidently a dismissal, but Alex disregarded it. He had been unable to speak plainly to the Countess, but no such scruples need weigh with him now. This fat, pallid man with his air of consequence had presumably inherited the guardianship of the little Condesa and must therefore be apprised of the truth. But there was a faint chance that he might be dissuaded from sending the girl to India without being informed of the facts about Mr. Conway Barton. It was at least worth trying, and Alex tried it:

'Might I suggest, sir, that it would be advisable to postpone the Condesa's departure for—for a few years? Until the country is in a less unsettled condition. You cannot, I think, fully appreciate the present state of unrest that prevails in India. I am aware that I hold what is perhaps a minority view, but it is one that is also held by such men as Sir Henry Lawrence and General Jacob. There have been disturbing signs of late, and Sir Henry and many others have warned of the possibility of grave troubles arising out of the policy of annexation of sovereign States, in particular if it is pressed over the matter of Oudh. India, and the Bengal Army, is far from being in the condition of tranquillity that some would have us suppose, and I would urge on you most strongly, sir, that this is no time to send any woman to that country—let alone a young girl.'

Huntly raised his eyebrows and observed coldly that Captain Randall was mistaken in supposing that he had no knowledge of the situation prevailing in India. He had had occasion to attend, only the previous August, the banquet given at the London

Tavern by the East India Company in honour of Lord Canning, the Governor General designate, where he had been assured, through the medium of public speeches and private discussion, that our Indian dependency had never before been so peaceful or so prosperous. He ventured to think that the speakers on that occasion had at least as much knowledge of the conditions pertaining in that country as had Captain Randall.

Alex said: 'If I cannot speak with their authority, sir, I can at least speak from experience, for I have of necessity come into far closer contact with the natives of the country than many senior officials, whose very seniority debars them from a too-intimate approach. Lord Dalhousie's policy of Annexation and Lapse, although it has added immeasurably to our territories, has aroused the bitterest enmity among those nobles whom we have dispossessed. They, or their agents, are engaging in active intrigue against us, and their numbers increase yearly. It is known that Lord Dalhousie and the Directors in Leadenhall Street favour the annexation of Oudh, but if Oudh too passes into the Company's possession the present unrest will become gravely aggravated.'

'I think that you exaggerate,' said Huntly, bored. 'Several of the Directors are well known to me, and my cousin Grantham has informed me that a gratifying number of sons and relatives of the princely houses have even gone so far as to enlist in the ranks of the Bengal Army.'

'That is true,' said Alex grimly. 'But what your cousin Grantham and others like him fail to see is that many of these men have a particular reason for accepting such employment. It gives them unparalleled opportunities for spreading sedition and disaffection in a quarter where it can do us the most harm: among the sepoys—the Indian soldiers. A large-scale revolt on the part of the Bengal Army would be a difficult thing to deal with, and it may yet come to that.'

'I should be sorry to think that you are serious, Captain Randall,' said Huntly frigidly. 'Such faint-hearted and alarmist views are hardly what I should have expected rom one of your reputation. I can only suppose that overwork and the rigours of the climate have affected your spirits.'

Alex smiled. It was an unpleasant smile, but his voice remained level, though the faint drawl in it was suddenly more pronounced:

'Possibly, sir. But not my wits. There is such a thing as overplaying one's hand. The arbitrary acquisition of Oudh will mean, once again, a province almost the size of England awash with disbanded soldiery and embittered nobles to whom annexation will have meant the loss of power and privilege and, in many cases, of even the bare means of existence. In addition to which, Oudh—although its people are largely Hindu—is one of the last remaining Mohammedan states. Its annexation will not only antagonize all Mohammedans, but give rise to the fear that we intend to swallow the rest of India, and that no state is safe from us. We have not at present sufficient British troops at our disposal with which to garrison newly acquired territory, so that it would have to be done, if at all, by native regiments who are bound, in the nature of things, to resent such an annexation.'

Huntly said pompously: 'All these aspects of the situation must have occurred to those in authority. And you forget, I think, that the bulk of the population cannot but look upon us as their deliverers from the long reign of oppression, torture and extortion inflicted upon them by their native rulers. We are not only giving them better government, but bestowing upon them the blessings of progress and civilization, for which they are bound to be grateful.'

'That is a view only too commonly held by our race,' said Alex dryly. 'It is a comforting one with which to justify conquest, but, unhappily, entirely untrue. The blessings of Western civilization are seldom appreciated by Eastern races; especially when rammed down their gullets with a musket. I would assure you, sir, that I am no alarmist. And neither has my nerve failed me. We shall hold India. But all that I have heard and seen and felt during the past few years has served to convince me that we are moving blindly towards disaster. I am entirely sure of that. No less sure than I am that we shall survive it. But this is no time to cumber ourselves with women, or to send out a young girl who knows nothing of the East.'

Huntly drew himself to his full height and looked haughtily down his somewhat fleshy nose. 'My dear Captain Randall,' he observed in chilling tones, 'had there been any risk attached to sending my cousin to India you may be assured that Mr. Barton would never have suggested such a thing. As your superior officer his knowledge as to the true state of affairs is bound to exceed yours. In the circumstances I cannot but feel that you are needlessly alarmed.'

Alex said ruefully: 'I am afraid that I shall have to speak plainly, sir. I am well aware that in doing so I am open to a charge of disloyalty to my superior officer, but the occasion appears to me serious enough to warrant plain speaking. What I have to say is naturally in confidence, but as the Condesa's relative and guardian it is a thing that you should know.' And he spoke clearly and dispassionately on the subject of Mr. Barton. . . .

Lord Ware's prominent eyes bulged palely in the firelight and he remarked a little nervously that of course he had no idea . . . What Captain Randall had divulged was most disturbing . . . Surely he exaggerated? He could not bring himself to believe . . .

Captain Randall cut him short: 'I must ask you to believe, sir, that what I have told you of the Commissioner is less than the truth. I could not reconcile it with my conscience to escort your young cousin to India without first acquainting you with these unpleasant facts. Now that I have done so I have no further obligation in the matter, as it will now be for you to decide whether she goes or not. Your servant, sir.' He bowed curtly and withdrew.

Once again, as on the evening of his arrival, Captain Randall dined alone, but at the conclusion of the meal the secretary, Mr. Harrowby, made his appearance with a message from Lady Ware. The Countess, said Mr. Harrowby, wished to see Captain Randall at his earliest convenience, in order to make him known to Miss Winter—er—that is, the Condesa. Captain Randall heaved a resigned sigh, and pausing only to possess himself of a small package that had been entrusted to him for personal delivery into the hands of the Commissioner's betrothed, followed Mr. Harrowby to Lady Ware's apartments.

'Captain Randall, your ladyship,' murmured Mr. Harrowby, ushering him in and closing the door softly behind him. The Countess turned with a rustle of silk: 'So good of you to come, Captain Randall. I trust you have been well looked after? You will forgive us, I know, for dining *en famille* on this sad occasion. You have met my husband, have you not? This is my daughter, Sybella. And this is dear Conway's future wife—Winter de Ballesteros. Winter, this is Captain Randall——'

Alex bowed briefly. Lord Ware did not meet his gaze, but Lady Ware returned it with a coldly smiling blandness that told its own story. 'So her husband has told her,' thought Alex, 'and she means to ignore it. She will tell that child nothing, and neither will she do anything to prevent the marriage. That Wycombe woman was right!' He became aware that Sybella was smiling at him and was abruptly recalled to a sense of his social obligations. He murmured a few words of conventional greeting and looked beyond her into the wide, wary eyes of the Commissioner's betrothed. He looked long and deliberately, studying that young and guarded face; noting the wariness and schooled immobility with cool interest.

A faint flush of colour rose into the pale cheeks, and Alex put his hand into his pocket and drew out a small sealed packet that the Commissioner had given him. He said briefly and without preamble: 'Mr. Barton requested me to give this into your hand.'

The girl's fingers closed about it, holding it tightly, and colour and life flamed up into her face so that she was suddenly beautiful. She made a small swift gesture with the clenched hand as though she would have hidden it among her billowing skirts, but Lady Ware spoke with calm authority:

'You may open it, my dear. It will be your betrothal gift.'

Winter looked down at the small packet in her hand. She knew without opening it what it contained. She had never forgotten anything that Conway had said to her, and had he not said that he would one day give her a diamond—'the brightest diamond I can find for you in India'—to wear on her finger instead of the little gold and pearl ring that she had worn for so long on a ribbon about her neck? He had sent for her, and he had sent the diamond. All her dreams were coming true at last. She did not want to open Conway's gift in the presence of Cousin Julia and this stranger who studied her with such cool and speculative interest. This was not something for critical and unsympathetic eyes to appraise. It was something intensely personal to herself.

'We are waiting,' said Cousin Julia.

The lovely colour faded from Winter's cheeks and she broke the seal with cold, unsteady fingers.

The firelight gleamed on an enormous carved emerald in a curiously wrought setting of Indian gold, and Alex, recognizing it, was unprepared for the sudden shock of anger and disgust that the sight of it gave him. He had seen that stone before, many times. Three years ago it had adorned the hand of a member of a princely house, by name Rao Kishan Prasad.* Alex knew a good deal about Kishan Prasad, for the man had aroused his interest. There had been odd whispers about him, and the subsequent appearance of that ring in the possession of the Commissioner of Lunjore had caused Alex to wonder more than once just what piece of bribery the fabulous stone had represented. It had been flaunted thereafter by the Indian woman, a dancing girl from the city, who was the latest occupant of the *Bibigarh* attached to the Lunjore Residency, and she had worn it as she gyrated for the amusement of the guests at one of the Commissioner's more questionable parties which Alex had reluctantly attended. Alex had also seen Kishan Prasad comparatively recently and in unexpected surroundings, and he scowled down at the great carved jewel with incredulous distaste.

Sybella gave an audible gasp of envy and admiration and even Lady Julia's cold eyes widened in involuntary astonishment, but to Winter it was as though a small chill wind had momentarily

* Pra-*shād*.

breathed upon the shining warmth that Conway's letter had lit
in her breast. He had forgotten! The next second she had taken
herself to task. Why should he take literally a sentence spoken
to a child? He had meant only that he would one day send her
a jewel of beauty and price to wear on her finger in place of the
modest trinket he had given her at parting. And he had remembered, and sent it.

She slipped the barbaric thing on to the third finger of her
left hand where it hung as loosely as that other ring had done
five years before, and thought as she did so that soon Conway
would put a wedding ring on that same finger, and after that she
would be safe and protected and loved, and free from loneliness
for ever and ever. She smiled down at it; a little secret smile; and
looked up to meet the anger and disgust in Captain Randall's eyes.

For a moment the intensity of that cold disgust startled her.
This man for some unknown reason was hostile to her. No.
Not to her—to Conway! Yet that was surely impossible, for
Conway himself had sent this man, his trusted subordinate, to be
his emissary and escort his future wife to India, and if Conway
trusted him he could not be an enemy. She must have mistaken
that expression: and indeed it was there no longer. The face that
looked back at her was blankly impersonal; the grey eyes remote
and expressionless.

The brief moment of silence was broken by Lady Ware, who
thanked Captain Randall for his good offices and assured him
that the young Condesa and a suitable chaperon would be only
too happy to avail themselves of his escort and protection on the
journey.

'You will forgive me I know if I say goodbye to you now,' said
Lady Ware, dismissing him. 'I fear I am not an early riser, and
you will, I feel sure, be anxious to be on your way. You sail
on the *Sirius*, I believe? I shall of course inform you by letter
of the arrangements I have made for dear Winter.'

It was plain that he was to be given no opportunity for private
conversation with the Condesa herself. The entire affair had
filled Alex with boredom and irritation and, finally, disgust; but

he had never had any intention of exerting himself in the matter beyond informing the Condesa's guardian of certain aspects of the Commissioner's character and mode of living of which he believed her relatives to be ignorant. He had discharged this office and his conscience was clear. But now, unaccountably, he found himself angry.

This was no poised and mature woman who was to be tied in matrimony to the obese roué who was Commissioner of Lunjore. This was a girl. A child. And for reasons that the gossiping Lady Wycombe had made abundantly clear, her august relatives, far from pausing before consigning her to the fate that must inevitably overtake any wife of Conway Barton, had every intention of hurrying her towards it without uttering one word of warning.

All the impropriety of bluntly informing her himself of the true state of affairs occurred most forcibly to Captain Randall. The robust outspokenness of the Regency had given place to an age of extreme and mealy-mouthed prudery, in which young girls were sedulously guarded from the facts of life and were expected to have no inkling of the coarser aspects of masculine amusements. Twelve years in the East had, however, robbed Alex Randall of any particular respect for the polite conventions, and he was suddenly and stubbornly resolved that the Commissioner's betrothed should not walk blindly upon her fate if he could prevent it. Once back in his room he found letter paper, a quill pen and a standish, and having written a brief note, folded the paper, sealed it and tugged at the bell-pull.

It was answered by a maidservant in a neat print dress; young and presumably romantic, noted Alex, relieved that some more elderly and conservative retainer had not answered his summons. The note and a gold coin changed hands, and the girl, her eyes round with pleasurable interest, assured him in a conspiratorial whisper that Miss Winter would receive his communication without fail. Alex yawned largely, scowled at his reflection in the vast oval looking-glass that adorned one wall of the room, and retired to bed.

The morning dawned cold and grey, and a white layer of mist lay over the park and pressed against the wet window-panes.

In the great hall a covey of servants were busied with removing the funereal trappings from the walls under the eye of the aged major-domo, and on the wide sweep before the main door Medusa sidled and snorted in charge of a groom. Captain Randall swung himself thankfully into the saddle. In some obscure fashion Medusa typified action as opposed to intrigue, and he was grateful to see the last of Ware.

The mist lay thicker under the over-arching boughs of the oak trees that lined the long avenue, and the trees themselves appeared pale and ghostly. For a mile or more Alex gave the mare her head, exhilarated by the speed, the rush of the cold misty air and the swift, hollow drum-beat of Medusa's flying hooves, but presently his ear caught what at first seemed an echo of that sound, and he slowed Medusa's pace to a trot and then to a walk. There was another rider in the long oak avenue, and Alex, listening, made a wry grimace in which distaste and relief were oddly mingled, and reined to a stop. Medusa's ears pricked and she whinnied softly as a moment later a horse and rider materialized out of the mist and drew level with them.

There were raindrops like a spangle of moonstones on Winter's dark hair, and the cold air and exercise had whipped a glow of colour into her pale cheeks. Those enormous dark eyes—the eyes of her father Marcos de Ballesteros, who in turn had inherited them from some long-forgotten Moorish ancestress—were wide and young and wary; and looking at her Alex was conscious once again of that unexpected flood of anger and exasperation. It must have shown briefly in his face, for some of the colour faded from her cheeks and her voice was breathless and a little uncertain:

'You—you have a message for me, Captain Randall?—from Conway—Mr. Barton?'

Alex shook his head.

'But . . . you wrote——'

'You must forgive me for the subterfuge,' said Alex curtly, 'but I wished to see you privately. I have something to say to you that your relatives would apparently prefer to remain unsaid. I took this method of ensuring that you would see me.'

He saw the slender figure stiffen and draw itself erect, and the dark eyes became guarded. 'What is it you wish to tell me?'

Alex studied her for a moment, frowning. 'How old are you?' he enquired abruptly.

The unexpectedness of the question appeared to take her by surprise, and she answered in unconscious obedience to the authority in his voice. 'Sixteen. But I shall soon——'

'*Sixteen!*' said Alex, exasperated. 'It's not decent! Have you any conception as to what you are going to? Of the life you will be expected to lead? Of the country in which you will live?'

Winter looked at him in surprise. 'Why—you are kind!' she said. Her voice held a note of wonder, and Alex realized with a sudden stirring of pity that kindness had been a rare thing in this young creature's life. She leant forward with a little confiding gesture and said: 'You think that I am going to a foreign land and that I might be unhappy there. But you are wrong. I am going home. Did you not know that my father was a Spaniard who lived and was born in Oudh, and that I was born there too? India is more my home than this will ever be. I spoke their tongue before I spoke my own. I can speak it still. Shall I show you?' She turned from English and spoke in liquid Urdu: 'How should I fear when I do but return to mine own people and to my father's house?'

Alex heard the familiar tongue with a renewal of his previous anger, and seeing it she said breathlessly, watching his face: 'What is it? Is Conway ill? Is that what you meant to tell me? Is he——'

'No.' Alex's voice was hard and expressionless. 'He is not ill. Not in the way that you mean. But I imagine that he has changed considerably since you last saw him.'

'Of course he has changed!' said Winter quickly. 'I have changed too. I was only a child then, and now I have grown up. He has had years more of hard work and sickness and heavy responsibility. I know all that. He has written to me of his difficulties. He will look older, but it will not matter.'

'You do not understand,' said Alex curtly. 'I felt it my duty

to explain something of the true state of affairs to your cousin
Lord Ware, but he apparently did not think fit to inform you of
the facts, or indeed to take any action to prevent your marriage.'

'To *prevent?*' Winter stared at him, white and rigid.

'Yes. To prevent it. I cannot say what Mr. Barton may have
been five or six years ago. But I know what he is now, and I can
do no more than to urge you, in your own interests, to abandon
your journey to India and postpone your wedding until such
time as he can return to this country, so that you may have the
opportunity of judging for yourself.'

Winter's eyes were suddenly bright with anger and her voice
shook: '*You* say this? You—his trusted subordinate!' She saw
the sudden flush on Alex's brown cheek and her voice sharpened
to scorn. 'So I *was* right! You are one of them! One of his
enemies who scheme against him behind his back because you
are envious of him! And you dare to speak against him to me—
to *me!*' Her chin lifted haughtily. 'Well, have you nothing
else to say?'

'Yes,' said Alex, unmoved. 'I cannot expect you to accept
the word of a stranger—even a "trusted subordinate"—who
speaks against his chief. I can only repeat that you would be
well advised to wait here with your relatives until Mr. Barton
can come home and claim you. You will then have the evidence
of your own eyes.'

'That is not enough,' said Winter steadily. 'I must ask you
to be plain, sir. You cannot make veiled accusations and not
qualify them. Or do you prefer imputation to plain speaking?'

'No,' said Alex slowly, 'but I do not wish to offend your ears
with matters that cannot be within your comprehension. However, if you will have it, your betrothed is no fit husband for any
young or decently bred woman, and——'

He saw the small face turn as white as the mist around it and
her gloved fingers clench on the riding-whip they held, and knew
a fraction of a second before she raised her hand what she would
do. But for some reason that he could not have explained he
made no attempt to avoid the blow. The lash of the whip cut

savagely across his face and he felt a thin trickle of blood run
warmly down his chin from a corner of his mouth, and suddenly
and unexpectedly he laughed.

'The Ware women,' said Captain Randall, 'would at least
appear to be ruthless. I see I have misjudged you. You may
well be a match for him after all.'

The bright colour flamed up into the girl's face once more,
and she brought the whip down again, but this time on her
horse, who sprang forward and galloped away down the long
avenue to disappear into the mist.

Captain Randall lifted his hand to brush the blood from his
chin and laughed again. So much for the popular conception of
gently bred young ladies as frail and tender plants given to
swooning and the vapours! He wondered if he had seen the last
of Winter de Ballesteros. It seemed likely. He could not believe
that after what had just occurred she would avail herself of his
escort to India. She would now take a passage on some other ship
and dispense with his services, and she would undoubtedly warn
her betrothed against him. In that event the Commissioner
could be counted upon to effect his removal from Lunjore. He
had, in fact, bungled the whole affair; branded himself as disloyal
to his chief, incurred the enmity of the young Condesa and her
influential relations, and probably brought about his own dismissal—and all for nothing! The weal that the Condesa's whip
had raised across his face throbbed painfully. 'My just deserts,'
said Captain Randall philosophically, and gave Medusa her head.

Firm in the belief that he would not now receive any further
communication from Ware, and having, if the truth be known,
succeeded in dismissing the whole matter from his mind, he was
surprised and more than a little annoyed by the arrival, some
three months later, of a letter from the Countess. A passage had
been procured, wrote Lady Ware, for her young cousin on board
the steamship *Sirius* sailing from London on the twenty-first of
June. Mr. Barton was to meet his betrothed in Calcutta, and the
marriage would take place on the day following her arrival
at that port. She would be travelling in the company of a

Mrs. Abuthnot, who with her two daughters was proceeding to India in order to rejoin her husband who commanded a regiment of Bengal Infantry at Delhi. The ladies would be pleased to avail themselves of Captain Randall's protection and assistance on the voyage. The Countess trusted that Captain Randall was in good health, and was confident that under his escort her young relative could come to no harm.

Captain Randall scowled at the single sheet of paper with its thinly elegant handwriting and florid seal, and crumpling it in his hand tossed it impatiently into the waste-paper basket, mentally consigning all women—with the possible exception of a certain charming and accommodating *première danseuse*—to the same receptacle.

He had had other things to think about than the doings of the Granthams. On the thirtieth of March the news had spread slowly that the Great Powers of Europe, together with Turkey and Sardinia, were at last at peace after one of the most futile and wasteful of wars. It was Sunday, and in order not to interrupt the evening services the salute of a hundred and one guns was fired at ten o'clock that night. Alex had gone out into the cold starry night and listened to the crash of the guns in St. James's Park, the blare of military bands playing the National Anthem, and the answering salvoes from the Tower of London; and had thought of the dead who rotted on the heights of Sebastopol—and of the smiling face of Kishan Prasad taking gloating note of the ragged and demoralized British Army as they fell back after their failure to capture the Redan. He did not know why such men as Kishan Prasad had ever been permitted to visit the Crimea. But they had done so, and Alex was sure that no good would come of it.

Earlier in March he had seen a brief notice in the Press, sandwiched casually in between the arrival of the Far Eastern mails and a paragraph relating to Lord Canning's arrival in India, which had stated baldly: '*Oudh is to be annexed, with General Outram as Chief Commissioner.*' There had been a longer one a week later. '*An army of 16,000 men is now collected at Cawnpore,*

*and in a few days will be pouring towards Lucknow. No resistance
is expected, but Lord Dalhousie never leaves opportunities to the
disaffected by any mistimed affectation of security. The King will
be dismissed with a pension of a lac of rupees a month.'*

The Marquis of Dalhousie, Governor General in India, had
every reason to feel pleased with his achievements. He had
added the Punjab and lower Burma to the British Empire, the
Koh-i-noor diamond to the British crown, secured the western
frontiers of India and brought to the country the blessings of
civilization in the form of the railway and the telegraph. He
had been succeeded in office by Lord Canning, who before he
sailed had reminded the complacent Court of Directors of the East
India Company that 'in the sky of India, serene as it is, a small
cloud may arise, at first no bigger than a man's hand, but which
growing larger and larger may at last threaten to burst and over-
whelm us with ruin'.

But that cloud, thought Alex uneasily, listening to the guns
that celebrated the Peace Treaty and broke the sabbath silence
of the cold March night, had already arisen. He and many like
him had been aware of it for some considerable time—a small,
ominous stain on the clear blue sky of the East India Company.
Only two years previously Sir Henry Lawrence had written to
Lord Stanley: '*You ask me how long Oudh and Hyderabad are
to last? It is the fashion to cry out for their annexation . . . and
bad as we are I believe that we are better than any native ruler of
the present age; but that does not justify us in picking their pockets.
The Oudh treaty permits us to take over the management of their
country, if necessary. We can protect and help the peasants without putting their rents in our pockets. . . . I am however in a
terrible minority. The Army, Civil Service, Press and Governor
General are all against me. I still say—look at our treaties. We
have no right to make one day and break the next.*' But Oudh
had been annexed, and Alex Randall, walking through the
crowded, gas-lit streets where the people had gathered to cheer
a peace treaty and the end of the long and costly Crimean War,
thought of the words of Henry Lawrence and of a knot of

D

servants and sepoys who had whispered together in the shadow
of the banyan tree by the gate at Lunjore; and was afraid.

As March gave way to April and spring warmed to summer the
problems and policies of the land that he loved continued to
obsess him, and he became impatient to return, for Lunjore
touched the very borders of the newly annexed province, and
there would be work to do: work that Mr. Commissioner Barton
was entirely incapable of performing. Mr. Barton's district, which
took its name from its capital city, was largely inhabited by petty
chiefs who had been involved in a rebellion some twelve years previously. The rebellion had been put down and the district
brought under the control of the Company's government, whose
policy it was to discourage large landowners. It was a policy that
had the full approval of Mr. Conway Barton, and Alex Randall
had done what he could to mitigate the hardships and injustices
that the purblind pursuance of it had so often involved. With
these and other things on his mind he had had no time to think
about the problem of the Commissioner's bride, and when reminded of it his only feeling was one of impatience as he con-
signed Lady Ware's letter to the waste-paper basket.

He himself had been equally dismissed from Winter's mind.
Conway's promised bride entertained no doubts or forebodings as
to the future. The long waiting was over. She had grown up at
last and Conway had sent for her. She was to see India again—
the enchanted country—and leave behind her the cold walls of
Ware and the cold eyes of Sybella and Cousin Julia. Ware held
nothing for her now that the only two people she had loved were
dead. The old Earl lay in a marble vault below the mausoleum,
while Zobeida, denied burial in consecrated ground by a bigoted
clergyman, lay in a quiet corner of the park with only the wind
in the alien yews to sing her lament.

Julia herself had taken the unprecedented step of travelling to
London in order to see her young relative safely bestowed into
the care of Mrs. Abuthnot. She had stayed only one night,
putting up at the Pulteney Hotel, and had left the following
morning to visit friends in Surrey. But she had stayed long

enough to see the cab containing Sabrina's daughter drive away in the rain towards the docks and the steam-packet *Sirius* that was to take her to India.

5

MRS. ABUTHNOT was kind, stout and talkative. She had been barely Winter's age when she had married her George and first set sail for the East, and she was not yet forty. But the long years spent in India, the birth of seven children and the death in infancy of five of them, had left their mark on her, and she might well have been ten or even twenty years older.

Lottie and Sophia Abuthnot, in contrast to their stout and voluble mamma, were slim and shy and silent and, it was to be presumed, took after their papa, for they in no way resembled their mother, being small and fair where Mrs. Abuthnot was an ample, though greying brunette.

Sophie, the younger by two years, shared a cabin with her mother, while the eighteen-year-old Lottie was to share an adjoining one with Winter. The cabins were small and cramped and sparsely furnished, and the first few days of the voyage had been anything but pleasant.

The early summer had been wet and cold, and the rain that had been falling as they drove to the docks had later given place to blustering gusts of wind that drove the dark banks of cloud before them and whipped the water of the Thames Estuary to a white froth of broken wave-tops. Lottie, Sophie and Mrs. Abuthnot had retired to their berths while the ship was still in sight of Sheerness, but Winter had returned to the deck to watch the coast of England fade into the wet greyness of that June evening.

Seagulls screamed and wheeled above the churning wake, and the acres of straining canvas overhead roared and sang to the rush of the wind, while spray drove over the bows in a fine,

stinging veil of mist. It had been raining, thought Winter, on
that long-ago day when she and Zobeida, cold, wet and shuddering with sea-sickness, had landed at Southampton. She had not
been seven years old; and now she was seventeen and sailing away
again—sailing away to be married and to live happily ever after....

The ship rolled and pitched and a sharp hiss of spray stung
Winter's cheek. She began to feel distinctly uneasy, but she
could not face the prospect of descending once more to the
cramped cabin where Lottie Abuthnot, prone upon her berth,
had already succumbed to the pangs of sea-sickness. The fresh
air, despite the drenching spray, was preferable to the narrow,
reeking cabin, and setting her small jaw she turned instead to
pacing to and fro.

The deserted deck heaved up and sank away again beneath
her feet, and presently she began to regret her decision not to
go below. She should have retired to her cabin while she still
had the strength to do so, for now, quite suddenly, it was
impossible to move. Impossible to do anything but cling to the
wet rail, oblivious of the driving spray and the fact that the wind
had whipped her cloak from her grasp and was billowing it out
in imitation of the straining sails above her, or that her bonnet
had fallen off and was now only attached to her by its ribbons.

Her head appeared to have swollen and to be full of whirling
sparks, and she leant on the rail; wet, chilled, and racked with
nausea. She did not hear the footsteps behind her, and she would
not have cared if she had. She was beyond caring. She only
knew that arms were around her, holding her, and that she need
no longer cling to the rail.

Someone lifted her as easily as though she had been a small
child, and a man's voice with a hint of a laugh in it said: 'I suppose this is included in the duties of a courier?' And then she
was being carried down into heaving darkness to her cabin.

She was aware of the cabin door being thrown open, and above
the creaking pandemonium of the labouring ship she could hear
the alternate moans and retching of Lottie Abuthnot. Winter
turned her head feebly away from the sound and buried her face

against the shoulder of the man who carried her. She heard him say, 'Good God!' in tones of half-humorous resignation, and then he had closed the door on Lottie's woe and turned abruptly away.

A moment or two later he laid her down and Winter opened her eyes and found herself looking up into Captain Randall's face. He appeared to be amused, and she closed them again, and pressing a hand over her mouth managed with an enormous effort to say in muffled tones: 'Please go away. I—I fear I am about to be very unwell.'

'I've seen worse things,' remarked Captain Randall philosophically, reaching for a basin. And presently it ceased to matter to Winter whether he went or stayed.

It had been morning when she had awakened. A cold wet morning in which rain fell steadily and the ship creaked and shuddered and groaned as it thrust its way through the steep choppy seas, driven onward by a shrill wind.

The small cabin rose and fell alarmingly before Winter's eyes and she shuddered and closed them again quickly. Presently, struck by a sudden thought, she opened them once more. This was not the cabin that she was to share with Lottie Abuthnot. She was in a strange cabin. Captain Randall's of course! He had brought her there yesterday evening because Lottie had been so ill. He must have slept elsewhere; probably in the saloon. She could only be surprised that he had bothered to remove!

Winter lay still, remembering the details of yesterday's deplorable collapse with horrified dismay. How could she have behaved so? Instead of insisting on decent privacy she had done nothing to prevent Captain Randall from remaining in the cabin and rendering aid, but, if she remembered rightly, had actually welcomed his assistance! She had a distinct recollection of him holding her head over a basin when she no longer retained the strength to perform that necessary office for herself. He had laid her back on the pillows and washed her face in cold water, removed her spray-sodden cloak and bonnet and forced brandy down her throat with a matter-of-fact competence and a total lack of embarrassment that surprised her.

Winter did not realize that the life of a political officer in the India of that day called for a greater degree of proficiency in dealing with the unexpected than was required of the average man. Alex Randall had in his time been called upon to perform a variety of actions in excess of his official duties, which had included amputating the leg of a man who had been mauled by a wounded tiger, hanging a murderer, housing and feeding thirty-seven small children ranging in age from one month to approximately eight years in a year of plague and famine, acting as midwife to a woman in childbirth and dragging another one screaming from the pyre that consumed her husband's corpse and on which she had intended, following the custom of her people and in defiance of the Company's new law, to immolate herself.

In the circumstances it was hardly surprising that he had behaved as though dealing with a young woman in the throes of sea-sickness was nothing so unusual. Winter could only be surprised that he had not also thought fit to remove her dress. She moved cautiously, aware that her head was aching badly, and discovered that he had in fact done so. The voluminous folds of her grey *batiste* travelling dress and the whalebone hoops of her crinoline were flung over a chair-back, and the blankets that had been drawn up over her concealed only petticoats and pantalettes. Further investigation revealed the horrifying fact that Captain Randall had unlaced her stays.

The indignity of this discovery impelled her to sit upright, but it proved an unwise move. The cabin swam unpleasantly before her eyes and she was forced to lean her aching head against the polished boards that formed the wall of the berth.

Someone rapped on the panels of the door and after a momentary pause it opened to disclose Captain Randall himself, looking, thought Winter resentfully, almost offensively well. He encountered her hostile gaze, and smiled.

It was a disconcertingly pleasant smile, and the fact that even through a haze of acute physical misery and social embarrassment she could recognize it as such, increased rather than diminished her hostility.

'I've brought you some food,' said Captain Randall. 'May I come in?'

'It's your cabin,' said Winter bitterly. 'I cannot prevent you from coming in, but at least you might have sufficient consideration to avoid any mention of food!'

Alex laughed, and entering the cabin closed the door behind him and set down a small tray. 'You'll feel a great deal better when you have had something to eat,' he assured her. 'It's only hot soup and biscuits.'

Winter glanced at it and shuddered. The small cabin dipped and rose, tilted, sank and steadied again in an endless, sickening rhythm, and the soup in the thick china mug slopped over the rim on to the tray. 'Go away!' said Winter in a gasping whisper. 'Take it away and go away!'

Alex sat down on the edge of the berth beside her. 'If you intend to go on being sea-sick, you will find it is far better to have something to be sick with,' he remarked prosaically. And then, she did not quite know how it happened, he was holding her against his shoulder and feeding her with soup and dry biscuits as if she had been a sick child—and with much the same manner that Nurse Sedley or Mrs. Flecker the housekeeper might have employed in similar circumstances.

The soup was hot and sustaining, and unlikely though it had seemed, she managed to swallow a fair proportion of the biscuits he had brought, and felt considerably better for having done so. Captain Randall's shoulder was strangely comforting to lean an aching head against, and she tried to remind herself that this man was an enemy; a traitor to Conway. That she had once cut him across the face with her riding-whip—and deservedly! But it did not seem to matter any longer. She was conscious only of an unfamiliar and inexplicable feeling of being safe: a feeling she had been a stranger to ever since the day when a small, weeping and bewildered child had been torn from the comforting arms of Juanita and Aziza Begum and the safe, familiar walls of the Gulab Mahal. She did not know why the presence and the touch of this man who was Conway's enemy—and therefore, surely, hers?—should give her this warm feeling of safety, and she was too physically exhausted to puzzle it out. It was enough to feel relaxed and protected. The uneasy motion of the ship seemed to be lessening, or perhaps it was true that the food had benefited her. She felt infinitely better, but strangely disinclined to move.

Alex put down the empty cup and said: 'It is just as well that your chaperon and every other woman on board is prostrated with sea-sickness, or I am afraid that I should have damaged your reputation beyond repair. As it is, the ladies have no attention to spare for anything but their own sufferings, so for the moment I think you can safely stay here.'

'I cannot do that,' said Winter drowsily. 'I must go back to my own cabin.'

'I wouldn't advise it,' said Alex. 'Your cabin companion is showing no signs of recovery as yet, and ten minutes in there will undo any good that a night's sleep and a meal have done you.'

'How do you know?' enquired Winter, interested. 'Have you been looking after them too?'

'I have,' admitted Alex with the ghost of a laugh. 'I must admit that had I realized earlier that the duties of escort would include those of sick-nurse, I might have declined the office. The stewards are doing their best, but they are only possessed of one pair of hands apiece, and as your chaperon and her daughters are technically in my charge, I felt obliged to offer assistance. I have no doubt that when she is feeling better Mrs. Abuthnot will find it hard to forgive me for it, but at present she is tolerably grateful.'

'If you unlaced her stays for her,' remarked Winter, 'I should not think she would ever forgive you!'

She had spoken without thinking; a thing that she had schooled herself not to do for a third of her short life, and the moment the words were out she would have given anything to recall them. She jerked herself away from Captain Randall's supporting arm, her hand to her mouth and a hot wave of colour dyeing her throat and her pale cheeks. How could she have said such a thing! Underclothes were considered an unmentionable subject, and she had spoken of them to a man!—and to a strange man at that. A man who had had the incredible effrontery to act as lady's-maid to her. Cousin Julia would have swooned with horror. Captain Randall, however, remained unmoved. The enormity of her observation appeared to have escaped him and he replied to it in all seriousness:

'It wasn't necessary. She seemed to have managed it herself.'

His attitude, had Winter but known it, was entirely genuine, for owing to the nature of his work he had escaped to a large extent the corroding prudery of Victorian England that muffled and enshrouded almost every aspect of domestic life in layers of shibboleth and taboo. It did not strike him as outrageous that he should have taken it upon himself to remove this child's drenched outer garments and unwieldy crinoline, and as it happened the mechanics of the corset were no mystery to him. It seemed to him a ridiculous and torturous garment, but possibly no more ridiculous than the close-fitting, high-stocked coat with its elaborate frogging and heavy epaulettes that he himself wore when in uniform despite a temperature that frequently reached well over a hundred in the shade.

The sight of Winter's scarlet cheeks and wide, horrified eyes brought home to Alex for the first time the fact that his proceedings might be considered shockingly unorthodox. A muscle twitched at the corner of his mouth and he said gravely: 'May I give you a piece of advice, Condesa? Common-sense will nearly always stand you in better stead than a slavish adherence to the conventions! If I had left you to spend the night in wet and uncomfortable clothing it might have saved you some temporary embarrassment, but it would have done no good at all to your health. And in the country to which you are going, health is an important thing. You cannot afford to be ill in India.'

The shamed colour faded from Winter's cheeks, and the horror in her eyes was replaced by interest. That common-sense was

D*

preferable to convention was a point of view so diametrically
opposed to the teachings of Cousin Julia that for a moment it
seemed almost to smack of heresy. Yet on consideration it was
so obviously right that Winter was conscious of a sudden sense of
release from bondage; as though some mental form of tight
lacing had suddenly been unloosed.

She had never had a very high opinion of her Cousin Julia,
but it had not occurred to her to question her authority and the
rightness of her views in matters of behaviour and etiquette.
But Cousin Julia, she knew, would not only have looked upon
Captain Randall's eminently sensible proceedings as entirely
scandalous, but have regarded Winter, as the recipient of them,
as next-door to a fallen woman. Cousin Julia's inflexible code
would visualize no alternative for Captain Randall but to abandon
Winter to be sick in decent seclusion, and that such a course of
action might well have resulted in a severe chill, or even pneumonia, would have carried no weight at all when placed in the
balance against the strict preservation of the social conventions.

Winter considered the matter and came to the conclusion that
Captain Randall's point of view was infinitely more practical.
A dimple broke the smooth curve of her grave young cheek and
she smiled.

It was the first time that Alex had seen her smile, but he did
not answer it. He sat quite still, looking down at her and no
longer seeing her as a forlorn child, but as a young woman. The
small heart-shaped face was unusually pale, and the shadows
under the great dark eyes made them appear even larger. The
crumpled whiteness of petticoat and corset cover served to turn
her bare arms and shoulders to a warm shade of ivory, and the
loosened hair that tumbled about her in rippling profusion
glinted with blue lights in the cold greyness of the small cabin.

Alex had a sudden and disturbing vision of the moist, unsteady
hands of the Commissioner of Lunjore twining themselves in
that soft darkness and sliding over those smooth ivory shoulders,
and the lines of his face hardened and set. He stood up abruptly,
and retrieving the tray said brusquely: 'The Captain appears to

think that we shall run out of this bad weather by sunset. You had better stay where you are for today at least. I have this cabin to myself as far as Madeira.'

'But—what about you?' asked Winter hesitantly.

'I can manage,' said Captain Randall briefly.

The cabin door closed behind him and Winter did not see him again for some considerable time. It was a steward who knocked at her door with a tray of food at midday, and towards the late afternoon she felt sufficiently recovered to resume her discarded dress and find her way to her own cabin. It proved to be a mistaken move. In the peace and privacy of Captain Randall's cabin she had succeeded in throwing off the worst effects produced by the boisterous seas, but ten minutes in the company of Lottie Abuthnot sufficed to bring on a renewal of nausea. The cabin reeked of sickness and resounded with Lottie's lamentations, and Winter took to her berth where she remained for the next few days.

The Captain's optimistic assertion as to the weather proved incorrect, but a Mrs. Martha Holly, who had recovered her sealegs after a temporary set-back of twenty-four hours, had come to the rescue of the Abuthnot party.

Mrs. Holly was stout, brisk and motherly, and had once been a nursemaid. She had borne and lost several children in India, but sorrow and adversity did not appear to have damped her invincible spirits, and after a year spent in England, to which she had returned in the capacity of nurse to the invalid wife and two small sons of a Colonel of Native Foot, she was returning to rejoin her husband.

'Not that I can stand the place, miss,' she confided. 'The 'eat kills me, and I don't 'old with foreigners—bein' British. But 'Olly's bin a good 'usband to me and 'e's lost without me. Those blacks 'ave no idea 'ow to darn a man's socks and iron 'is nightshirt right. Like as not they'd use starch—I'd put nothin' beyond 'em! Yes, I've been sixteen years in India. It's a long time. I suppose it 'as its points, but give me Islington any day. Now, Miss Lottie, just you swallow down that soup while I go and see to your poor ma. If you don't keep nothing down you'll keep on bringing nothing up, an' that's uncomfortable as well I knows. I made meself eat ship's biscuit, and in less than no time I was up and about again.'

Her energetic ministrations had the desired effect, and when four days later the *Sirius* finally ran out of bad weather and into sunshine and blue seas, even Mrs. Abuthnot was able to appear on deck.

Their fellow-passengers included several other ladies, in addition to officers of all ranks—the majority of them returning to India from leave—and at least two persons who were well known to Captain Randall: a Colonel Moulson, who commanded one of the regiments of Bengal Infantry stationed at Lunjore and was a bosom friend of Mr. Barton's, and a slim, pleasant-mannered Indian who spoke excellent English and was accompanied by several dark-skinned servants. That same Kishan Prasad whom Alex had last seen outside Sebastopol.

Kishan Prasad and his retinue had attracted Winter's immediate attention. The sight of the brown-skinned faces and the sound of the swift familiar speech revived memories of her childhood and of Zobeida's dear dark face, and reminded her not of a foreign land, but of home.

Kishan Prasad had spoken to her one evening. She had been standing under the awning on the poop deck watching the sun sink into the Atlantic while Cape Finisterre showed like a violet shadow on the horizon behind her. The evening breeze had tugged unexpectedly at the light shawl that she wore and had tangled its long silk fringe about a stanchion, and Kishan Prasad, who had been passing, had come to her assistance. She had thanked him prettily, and he had been about to turn away when his gaze had fallen upon her left hand. She had been wearing Conway's ring; the great carved emerald in the curious setting that Alex Randall had brought with him from Lunjore, and Kishan Prasad had checked at the sight of it. The pupils of his eyes had narrowed like a cat's in the light, and he said in his soft voice whose faintly sing-song intonation alone betrayed the fact that it was not an Englishman who spoke: 'That is a very unusual ring you are wearing. May I be permitted to ask where it came from? It looks as though it were a jewel from my own country—from Rohilkhand.'

'Perhaps it is,' said Winter, holding it out for him to see. 'It was sent to me by the man I am going out to marry. Mr. Conway Barton.'

'Ah!—Mr. Barton. That is very interesting. He is the Commissioner of Lunjore, is he not?'

'Yes. Do you know him?'

'I have some slight acquaintance with Mr. Barton. I own land in Lunjore district.'

Kishan Prasad was an agreeable man and an entertaining conversationalist and was soon on good terms with the majority of his fellow-passengers. Even Mrs. Gardener-Smith, who did not consider that it was at all the thing for an Indian gentleman to converse freely with young ladies of European birth, pronounced him to be a very pleasant-mannered man. 'Who is he?' she enquired of the Captain.

'No one of any special importance, ma'am. He is merely a wealthy Indian who has been visiting Europe. Doing a Grand Tour of the Continent, I imagine.'

'One wonders what he made of it,' remarked Mrs. Abuthnot. 'The contrast between our great cities and the squalor of the East must cause such visitors the greatest amazement! Lottie, dear, pray move under the awning. The sun is so strong, and freckles are *so* unbecoming!'

'Yes, Mamma,' murmured Lottie dutifully, her eyes under their soft lashes busy with a party of gay young officers who were lounging on the rail at the far side of the deck. Freckles might be considered unbecoming in a young lady, thought Lottie, but on a man they could be strangely endearing.

Lieutenant Edward English was a large young man who possessed a generous supply of freckles, red hair and charm. He also possessed a pair of deeply blue and openly admiring eyes, and Lottie's fairness and fragility had made an instant impression upon his susceptible heart. He had lost no time in making her acquaintance, but Mrs. Abuthnot had no intention of allowing any young man to fix his interest with her daughter at such an early stage of the voyage, and she had contrived to keep Mr. English at a safe distance.

Mrs. Abuthnot had every intention of marrying her sweet Lottie to the first really suitable *parti* who offered for her: marriage being in her opinion a woman's sole purpose in life. But was Edward English suitable? She would have to find out. Meanwhile there was plenty of time—and plenty of other men on board.

There were also, of course, several other young ladies. Notably Miss Delia Gardener-Smith. Miss Gardener-Smith possessed sufficient pretensions to beauty to cause some slight anxiety in the breast of any mother of marriageable maidens, being tall, blue-eyed and inclined to plumpness, and possessing a spectacular wealth of chestnut curls.

Mrs. Gardener-Smith, who was also bound for Lunjore, was distantly related to a peer and had an inflated opinion of her own consequence; but on hearing that Mrs. Abuthnot was acting as chaperon to a young lady of title, a cousin of the Earl of Ware and the affianced wife of the Commissioner of Lunjore, she had hastened to make her acquaintance. She pronounced Lottie to be a sweet girl and Sophie a charming child, but she had not known what to make of the young Condesa de los Aguilares.

Mrs. Gardener-Smith, like Julia before her, could see little to admire in the girl's unusual beauty. 'Her father was a Spaniard, you say? It is a pity that she should be so sallow—and have such very black hair. And those eyes! I fear such colouring will be misunderstood in the East. It is almost Oriental, is it not? She looks to be very reserved.'

'I think she is shy,' said kindly Mrs. Abuthnot. 'The poor little thing is an orphan, you know. But she is a dear child, and does not push herself forward at all. In my opinion Mr. Barton is a singularly fortunate man!'

There were others who were of the same opinion, but they

were exclusively male. Winter's unusual style of beauty might
not appeal to Mrs. Gardener-Smith, but it was very much to the
taste of the male passengers on board the steamship *Sirius*, and
in particular to Colonel Moulson.

Colonel Moulson was a bachelor and a lover of women, and he
fancied himself as a connoisseur of female charms. He had been
something of a rake in his youth, and had managed in later years
to purchase what he could no longer obtain on his own merits—
a fact that his vanity would not allow him to admit. Lottie and
Sophie, who were too shy and inexperienced to know how to
avoid his amorously avuncular advances, were frankly terrified
of him, but Winter's cool dark eyes had a way of looking through
him that he found more than a little disconcerting. As the
affianced wife of one of his greatest friends, he felt, he informed
her, a special responsibility towards her.

Winter could only be surprised that such an unlikable man
should be a friend of Conway's, but she concluded that Conway
must of necessity, and in the course of his official duties, remain
on friendly terms with many people whom he would not choose
as friends in a private capacity. For Conway's sake she tried to
be as polite as possible to Colonel Fredrick Moulson, and it was
an easy enough matter to avoid being left alone in his company,
there being a great many other men on board who were only
too ready to make themselves agreeable to the young Condesa.

There was, indeed, only one gentleman who appeared to be
wholly uninterested in her. Captain Randall had not addressed
more than a dozen words to her since her emergence from her
cabin, and during the succeeding days, while the *Sirius* sailed
southward through blue seas and the passengers spent the greater
part of the day in sociable converse in the shade of the awnings,
although he made himself pleasant to Mrs. Abuthnot and won
golden opinions from that warm-hearted lady, he never made one
of the group that surrounded Mr. Barton's betrothed, and Winter
came to the conclusion that he was deliberately avoiding her.

The discovery filled her with a vague feeling of resentment,
and she was forced to remind herself yet again that this man had

spoken against Conway, and that had he not kept his distance she herself would have been compelled to avoid his society. The fact that he had come to her rescue during the early stages of the voyage, and had treated her with a casual familiarity that could only have been socially excusable had she been his sister, should not be allowed to weigh in the balance against his disloyalty. Captain Randall had obviously realized this, and therefore kept out of her way; which was understandable. What was not understandable was why she should resent his doing so. She found herself covertly watching Captain Randall and comparing him, to his disadvantage, with Conway.

Alex Randall was slim and deeply tanned and undeniably good-looking. His rather hard grey eyes were fringed with thick black lashes as long as Winter's own, and although he was not much above medium height while the Conway of Winter's memories was exceptionally tall, his slimness and grace of carriage conveyed an impression of more inches than he possessed. But Conway—blue-eyed and blondly handsome—was of a size to make Alex Randall appear insignificant by contrast, and his luxuriant corn-gold moustache enhanced his masculine beauty and compared most favourably with Captain Randall's unfashionably clean-shaven countenance. Conway was also great-hearted and the soul of chivalry, and he would have scorned to speak against a man behind his back as Captain Randall had done.

Nevertheless that irrational feeling of resentment remained. He might at least speak to her! After all, had he not been deputed to look to her comfort and safety?

She had encountered him one evening in the dark passage-way that led to the cabins, and he had stood aside to let her pass. Winter drew back her hooped skirts, for the passage was narrow, and was about to pass him when she changed her mind and stopped. Her crinoline, released, brushed the walls of the passage on either side and effectually prevented Captain Randall from moving.

She said hesitantly: 'I—I never thanked you for—for your help. It was most kind in you, and—and I would not wish you to think me ungrateful.'

Alex bowed but he did not speak. A sudden colour tinged Winter's pale cheeks and she said abruptly, her voice unexpectedly breathless: 'I am sorry about—striking you with my whip. It was unforgivable of me.'

'But entirely understandable,' said Alex gravely.

She waited, expecting him to apologize for the words he had said that day: confident, now that she had given him the opening, that he would retract them, or at least admit that he should not have spoken as he had; but he remained silent.

The colour deepened in Winter's cheeks and her small chin lifted haughtily. She gathered up her wide skirts, and as she did so the ship heeled to a sudden fresh breath of the evening breeze that blew off Africa, and threw her against him. For a brief moment his arms held her, and once again she was conscious of that warm sense of safety that she had experienced before on the first morning of the voyage. She lifted her head from his shoulder and saw that his eyes held a glint of something that was uncommonly like anger. Then he had set her on her feet again and walked quickly away.

After that Winter made no further attempt to speak to him. She acknowledged his occasional brief civilities with even briefer replies, and found no difficulty in ignoring him.

6

THE long, hot, monotonous days passed slowly enough for Winter, but to Lottie Abuthnot and Edward English they were all too brief.

The voyage had been less than half over when Lieutenant English had approached Mrs. Abuthnot to ask her permission, in the absence of Lottie's father, to pay his addresses to her daughter. He had been so earnest and engaging that Mrs.

Abuthnot's heart had quite melted, and she had ended by assuring him that although the last word must of course lie with Lottie's father, if Lottie reciprocated his feelings she herself would not stand in the way of her daughter's ultimate happiness.

And indeed, thought Mrs. Abuthnot complacently, although Lottie might have made a more dazzling match, Edward English was of good family and appeared to possess both prospects and adequate means. It might do very well!

The heat became more intense, but the weather remained fine until a storm in the Indian Ocean drove the ladies to seek refuge in their cabins again, while many of the gentlemen lay about the decks and groaned in various stages of sea-sickness. Winter had acquired a certain degree of immunity, but she owned to some queasiness, and prudence dictated that she should keep to her cabin and risk no repetition of the humiliating collapse of the first days of the voyage.

The storm blew itself out after twenty-four hours of tossing discomfort, and on the last evening before they sailed into fine weather they passed the waterlogged wreck of a dismasted ship, its decks swept by the sullen seas.

Captain Ross of the *Sirius* had manœuvred his ship as close as he dared, and had launched a mail-boat, in charge of the first officer, with a boarding party. They returned wet and exhausted with the news that the vessel had apparently been a troopship bound for China, but that there was no one on board and few papers or particulars to be found on her. It was to be presumed that all on board had taken to the boats, for all the boats were gone. The bulkheads of her captain's cabin had been carried away, the port anchor and the cathead had gone, and from the appearance of the tattered sails and broken spars it was obvious that a sudden squall of hurricane force had carried all away at once. It was unlikely that the men on board would have lived to reach any shore, but there was nothing that could be done about it now, and the *Sirius* went on her way in the swiftly gathering twilight.

Winter, who had crept up on to the windy, spray-swept deck, watched the abandoned wreck fade into the stormy dusk; a forlorn sight with jib and staysail hanging in shreds from her bowsprit and jibboom, her masts shattered and her broken spars trailing over the side into the surging seas that washed her deserted decks.

A cold shiver ran down Winter's spine as she looked. In spite of the wild weather the fact that she was actually in the Indian Ocean, and that India itself lay ahead of her at last, had filled her with a sense of glowing happiness. But the sight of that battered and broken ship, drifting and sinking in the lonely wastes of the sea, dimmed the glow and brought with it a chill breath of apprehension and foreboding.

She heard a sigh beside her that was not the wind, and turned quickly. It was Kishan Prasad who stood near her, his eyes fixed on the fast-vanishing wreck. But for once his bland, inscrutable face had dropped its guard, and it was as though a mask had been stripped from it, leaving it naked and exposed. He did not appear to be aware of Winter, and he did not move or speak. But quite suddenly, and as though he had shouted it aloud, she knew his thoughts with a complete and horrified certainty.

He was thinking, with a fierce, gloating pleasure, of the men who had been on that ship. Seeing them in his mind's eye swept away by the savage seas; sinking down into the hungry fathoms, dragged under by the weight of their sodden uniforms; choking and drowning, their struggling bodies torn and ripped by sharks and barracudas. He sighed again. The same long-drawn sigh of hatred and satisfaction, and Winter shrank away, and backing from him, turned and ran headlong, stumbling down the steep stairs and tripping on her full skirts.

Alex Randall was coming down the passage towards her, and he caught her arm and steadied her: 'What's the matter? Feeling ill again?'

'No,' said Winter on a gasp. She had forgotten that she had meant to avoid all conversation with Captain Randall beyond social necessity, and she clung to his arm, her eyes wide with shock. 'It was Kishan Prasad——'

She saw Alex's face change and his mouth tighten, and said

breathlessly: 'He was looking at that ship. And he was glad! He hated them and he wanted them to drown! He was glad that they had been drowned—I could see that he was!'

Alex said: 'It isn't so surprising. They were soldiers—British troops. If he could have drowned them singly with his own hands he would probably have done so.'

'Why? Do they—do they hate us?'

Alex said impatiently: 'Did you suppose that they loved us? The benefits of Western civilization are not necessarily looked upon as an unmixed blessing when imposed by a foreign conqueror.'

'Who is he? Why is he here? You know him, don't you?'

'Yes. I know him.' Alex leant against the wall and stared thoughtfully into space. He said slowly: 'He is a member of one of the great families of Rohilkhand. An exceedingly clever man, and an embittered one—always a dangerous combination. He went to one of the better Indian colleges and took top honours in all English subjects. He studied engineering for the Company's service, and passed out as the senior student of his year with higher marks than any European there. But because he was not a European he was only nominated to the rank of jemadar, where he was actually subordinate to a European sergeant—a man who was his inferior in every possible way, and who was at the same time arrogant, insolent and stupid, and who lost no chance to insult him. Kishan Prasad is a proud man and a descendant of princes. He found the position intolerable and resigned from the Company's service. We lost a good man when we allowed that to happen—and gained a dangerous enemy. He went on a tour of Europe a year ago: a strange thing for a man of his caste to have done. I saw him last in the Crimea, where he saw us fail in the assault on the Redan at Sebastopol, and met Russian agents. And now he is returning to his own country. . . . We should never have allowed any Indian to see the British Army in the Crimea. Or, having seen it, to return and tell of what he had seen . . . to return alive . . .'

Alex's voice had dropped until it was almost inaudible; as though he was speaking to himself rather than to Winter, and there was that in his face that made her shrink away from him. She said with a catch in her voice: 'You mean—you mean you should have *killed* him?'

Alex laughed shortly. 'Perhaps. But assassination is unfortunately alien to the British temperament. We consider it socially indefensible—which must on occasions be a matter for regret!'

He looked down at Winter's small white face and glimpsed something of the shock that had been dealt her. This girl had probably never thought of India as a conquered country. She had imagined herself to be coming home, and the realization that many of the inhabitants of that land could hate all those of British blood with a savage and implacable hatred was like a blow in the face to a trusting child. He wanted to say: 'Don't look like that! It isn't safe to be so vulnerable—to expect too much of anything or anyone!'

He said instead, with a kind of exasperated anger: 'I warned your cousin Ware that this was no time to send any young woman out to India, but he would not listen. None of them will!' And turning from her abruptly he went on down the passage and up on to the wet deck.

But it was only two days later that Kishan Prasad fell overboard, and it was Alex who went after him.

Alex had not known that it was Kishan Prasad who had fallen. Perhaps if he had done so it might have altered the course of a great many lives.

The day had been hot and still and all that remained of the storm was a long, heaving, barely perceptible swell that swung the cabin doors idly to and fro and made the line of the horizon lift slowly and fall again as slowly in a leisurely rhythm. The sea was blue with the intense midnight blue of the Indian Ocean, and so clear that floating squadrons of jelly-fish far below the surface appeared as though embedded like bubbles in blue glass. The sun blazed down from a cloudless sky and even under the shade of the awnings the deck planks were uncomfortably hot to the touch.

It was after four o'clock and the decks were comparatively deserted while the passengers changed for dinner. Lottie had come up early, intending to meet her Edward, and she had looked up and seen Kishan Prasad standing on the paddle-box gazing out to sea. Even as she looked the ship rolled suddenly in the trough of an unexpectedly deep swell and she saw Kishan Prasad, taken off guard, slip and fall and slide under the rail. The next moment he had vanished, and Lottie shrieked and ran.

Two of the lascars, together with a ship's officer and Colonel Moulson, had also seen him fall, and they ran along the deck shouting, Colonel Moulson, with what he considered to be admirable presence of mind, picked up two deck-chairs and heaved them overboard into the creaming wake, where they were joined almost immediately by a hen-coop thrown after them by one of the lascars.

'*Man overboard!*' bellowed Colonel Moulson and the ship's officer.

Alex, who had been lying asleep face downwards in a patch of shade with his head buried in his arms, woke at Lottie's shriek and came to his feet. She stumbled towards him, her face chalk-white, screaming and pointing, and he turned and raced aft along the deck and caught a brief glimpse of a despairing hand that reached up from the foaming wake.

'It's all right, Randall,' snapped Colonel Moulson. 'Only one of those blacks. He'll be drowned by now—they can't swim.'

A sudden flash of pure rage hit Alex with the force of a blow; he kicked off his shoes, and in the next second he had vaulted over the rail and dropped feet first, and the rush of the sea closed over his head.

The water was unexpectedly cold and the churning wake sucked him down and down until the sea felt like a ton weight upon his shoulders. Just when it felt as though his lungs must burst, the weight lifted. and he was being shot to the surface like a cork and there was air again. He gulped deep draughts of it and struck out strongly, aided by the swirl of the wake. After the sweating heat of the *Sirius* the cold rush of the foaming water was incredibly exhilarating and he shook his wet hair out of his eyes and laughed.

It was, he presumed, one of Kishan Prasad's servants who had fallen overboard, for had it been a member of the crew Moulson would have said 'a lascar'. 'Of all the goddamned, bloody, idiotic things to do!' thought Alex anathematizing his own conduct. 'What the hell is the life of one heathen lackey worth that I have to make a quixotic exhibition of myself trying to fish the man out! Why does common-sense betray one in a crisis?'

He saw a dark struggling shape ahead of him and the next moment it had disappeared. Alex filled his lungs with air and dived. The man struggled feebly, and for a minute that seemed like an endless hour they sank down together through the blue water. And then Alex had got a grip on him and had kicked strongly and they were rising once more into light and air.

Even then he did not realize who it was that he held. He caught the half-drowned man under the arms and swam towards the heavy wooden hen-coop that was lifting to the swell not twenty yards away. After several fruitless efforts he managed to heave his limp burden face downwards across the stoutly built coop and hold him there while he trod water.

The swell that had been barely perceptible from the decks of the *Sirius* was a very different thing when viewed from the level of the sea itself, and in the trough of it the sea appeared to be empty and the *Sirius* had vanished. The next swell swung them slowly upwards, and far away—miles away it seemed—the ship showed small against the blue. It would take a long time for them to heave-to and circle back, thought Alex. They would lower a boat as soon as possible but it would be a long wait. The distant ship vanished as the burdened hen-coop slid once more into the glassy trough of the swell, and the Indian coughed, retched, lifted his head and moved feebly.

'Lie still, fool!' said Alex in the vernacular, and the man obeyed, but presently he turned his head and Alex saw for the first time who it was whom he had rescued.

The two men stared at each other for a long moment and Alex

was conscious of a queer twisting wrench at the pit of his stomach: a helpless, futile, sick anger against fate and himself and the fatuous, foolish instinct of his class and his kind and his creed that had driven him to leap unthinkingly to the rescue of a drowning man, and by so doing had betrayed him.

Alex had been convinced for a long time that Kishan Prasad was deeply involved in treasonable activities, and had reported as much to Mr. Barton. The Commissioner had demanded concrete proof, which Alex had been unable to supply. Had he been able to do so, and thereby bring Kishan Prasad legally to the gallows, he would have done so. But owing to the blindness of those who did not wish to see, he knew that he might never obtain such proof as would satisfy them. And now Providence had stepped in and done its best to put an end to Kishan Prasad, and he, fool that he was, had risked his neck to save the man whom he regarded as among the most dangerous enemies to British supremacy in India.

If he had only waited! If he had asked questions before he had jumped. It had been Moulson's remark that had done it. Moulson had said: 'It's only one of those blacks——' and Alex had instantly lost his temper. With the result that he had fallen into a booby-trap, for it was Kishan Prasad whom he had saved.

The salt sea water was bitter in Alex's mouth and he looked into Kishan Prasad's grey face and laughed. Kishan Prasad's lips drew back from his teeth in an exhausted grin that was a grimace of complete comprehension. He said in a hoarse voice between difficult breaths: 'Whom did you think you had saved—*Sahib*?' —the appellation was nearer an insult than a term of respect— 'One of your own kind? The General Sahib, belike?'

'No,' said Alex, treading water. 'I had thought it was one of your *naukar-log* (servants).'

He saw the flare of astonishment and disbelief in the dark eyes. 'My *servant*?'

'Yes,' said Alex shortly. 'Had I known it was you——'

'You would have let me drown,' finished Kishan Prasad fighting for each breath.

'Yes,' said Alex bluntly. 'Do not talk. You will tire yourself and the boat will not reach us for some time yet.'

Kishan Prasad was silent for a long while. The slow swell lifted them up lazily so that at intervals they could see the distant ship and the small speck that was a boat rowing towards them. Then it would slide them down into a long blue-black hollow and the ship would vanish and there were only two men and a wooden hen-coop alone in all those endless leagues of ocean.

Kishan Prasad looked down into the glassy water and thought of the unimaginable depths that lay beneath him: the cold fathoms that stretched downwards and ever downwards to the slimy darkness of the sea floor; and his fingers tightened convulsively on the rough wood that supported him.

He spoke at long last, and softly, in a voice that despite himself he could not keep quite steady: 'You say that had you known it was I who had fallen, you would have left me to my death. But it would seem that death is here now for one of us. Look there——!'

Alex turned his head and his diaphragm seemed to contract and turn to ice.

In the glassy swell beyond them lay a long, silvery-brown body, the triangular dorsal fin just clear of the water. Shark! . . .

The sea was darkening below them, and the low sun burned along the water, turning the surface of the swell to gold and outlining the creature with fire. It did not move, but hung motionless like a fly embedded in amber.

Alex seemed to have lost all power of movement. He held on to the edge of the hen-coop with one hand and stared back at that small cold eye. It had seen them and was watching them, idly curious.

Kishan Prasad said in a hoarse whisper: 'This wooden thing will not bear two upon its surface, and my life is forfeit to thee.' He had forgotten to speak in English. He began to slide softly from the coop and Alex said furiously: 'Don't be a fool! Get back on to that! You can't swim!'

At the first movement the shark had flicked away and now they

saw its fin cut the water on the far side of them. The swell
swung them up once more and they could see the boat, the low
sun flashing along the oar blades. But it was still a long way off.

Alex remembered having heard that sharks disliked noise
and he beat the water with his cupped hand. The fin sheered
away, circled and came back. Kishan Prasad was in the water
holding on with only one hand, and Alex said again: 'Get back,
you fool!' He grasped him about the waist and heaved, and
releasing him, caught his legs and thrust him on to the top of the
hen-coop where he remained on all fours gripping the edge. It
was a perilous and inadequate raft, and now that it bore Kishan
Prasad's full weight it lay barely an inch or two out of the water.
But at least it held his body clear of the surface.

The fin cut slowly through the water, cruising gently along
the flank of a long glassy slope parallel to them, and Alex suffered
a spasm of cold, crippling panic. 'Oh God, if only I had a knife!'
he said in a whisper, unaware that he had spoken aloud.

'Here,' gasped Kishan Prasad. He fumbled among his wet
clothes and drawing out a knife with a slim wicked eight-inch
blade, thrust it into Alex's hand. It was an inadequate enough
weapon to pit against the fourteen-foot monster who circled
warily about them, but the feel of it in his hand gave Alex a
sudden surge of hope. It was something. He had read of pearl
divers off the coast of Ceylon who fought off sharks with a knife.

He beat the water again and shouted and the creature shot
away, hovered and returned. It seemed to hang in the water
above him and he realized suddenly that if it came at him while
he held to the hen-coop the rush of its great body would overturn
that makeshift raft and dislodge Kishan Prasad. He had forgotten
that this was an enemy whose death he would have welcomed,
and whom a few short minutes ago he had been passionately
regretting that he had not left to die. The man on the raft was
a fellow human and as such they were leagued together against
this finny cold-blooded killer from the deeps beneath them.

He released his hold and swam away at a tangent, his eyes on
that cruising dorsal fin. The swell lifted it up and once again

the creature seemed to hang in the water above him. It came at him quite slowly, and as it came it turned. Alex avoided it with a superhuman effort, kicking backwards with all his strength and twisting again to face it. He heard a hoarse shout of warning from Kishan Prasad and the thought flashed through his mind that the boat had come.

'Just in time!' thought Alex grimly. And then he saw a flicker of movement to his left. Another fin! There was a second shark—a third. They circled him as though merely curious, and he felt the heave of the water under him as the first shark returned to the attack, and somehow he avoided it. Now they would all rush in. He would not wait for them to come at him, and be torn to pieces without a fight. His fingers tightened hard on the haft of the knife and he swam towards the nearest shark.

It was apparently an unexpected movement, for the creature sheered off at lightning speed, and he turned quickly and saw in the slow swell that bore down upon him the swift shape of another coming in. For the flash of a second he saw too, with uncanny vividness, the tiny striped bodies of the pilot fish which raced before and beside it; and then he had dived to meet it and as it rolled to bring the wicked jaws into play he struck with all his strength.

The knife sliced through a foot of the creature's side and was wrenched from his grasp, and there was a cloud of blood in the water. For a moment the other sharks lay motionless, and then suddenly the sea boiled into foam as they rushed in upon their wounded companion, fighting, snapping and tearing like hounds upon a fox. The dark water was red with blood and Alex turned and swam desperately away. He was still swimming when someone grabbed his shoulders and shouted above his head, and then hands were pulling at him and he was dragged over a gun-wale to tumble gasping and helpless among the feet of the boat's crew.

'That was a near thing!' said the first mate, beating him on the back. 'Touch and go! Here—get down, Mr. Prasad! Holy

Moses! Look at the brutes! They'll have us over. Hit with oars, *sumjao*!' The boat rocked dangerously as a ten-foot blue shark, attracted by the taint of blood, rubbed along the keel, and the sea seemed alive with triangular fins and lithe rolling bodies. And then they were rowing back to the ship into the eye of the setting sun over a sea that was no longer blue, but black below them and bright gold beyond.

Alex sat up dizzily and grinned at Kishan Prasad, and Kishan Prasad laughed and lifted his hand in a brief gesture of salute. For a moment they were no longer enemies but men who had seen no escape from death and yet by some miracle had escaped it, and were whole and alive. They drank the fiery grog proffered by the first mate and grinned weakly at each other and looked with dazed thankfulness at the clear sky above them while the lascars chattered and tugged at their oars, and the *Sirius*, its deck-rails lined with excited cheering passengers, grew larger and nearer and at last loomed solid and safe above them.

Alex was aware, as though through a thick fog, of noise and shouting voices and people who shook his hand and thumped his shoulders. He felt absurdly sleepy and rather as if he were very drunk. It was an effort to keep his head erect and his eyes from closing, and he yawned largely in the faces of the congratulatory passengers, and pushing his way through them, stumbled down to his cabin and collapsed on to his berth, where the ship's doctor, following him, found him so deeply asleep that he did not even wake when his wet clothes were removed and a blanket thrown over him.

He woke early the following morning, feeling refreshed and fitter than he had for many days. The long swim and the violent exertion of the previous evening, followed by almost twelve hours of uninterrupted sleep, had apparently proved more beneficial than the hot idle days and sweltering sleepless nights. His cabin companions had evidently slept on deck, and Alex lay looking about the small cramped space and the low ceiling above his head with a strange new appreciation of mundane things and the miraculous fact of being alive. He rolled out of his bunk and pulling on a pair of trousers went up on deck to breathe the dawn air.

The sun had not yet risen but the sky was already bright and the decks glittered with the night dew and the salt water with which a busy group of lascars were washing down the planks. The sea lay colourless in the dawn light except near the ship where it appeared coldly black and clear as glass. The whorls of foam and bubbles sank down into the blackness, still visible a fathom and more below the surface and turning from white to silver to grey until they vanished into nothingness. The deck-hatches were strewn with the bodies of those who preferred a cool night under the stars to the close heat of the cabins, and only the lascars were as yet awake.

Alex went aft and leant against the rail, idly watching the long white track of the wake. He heard footsteps behind him and turned to see Kishan Prasad. The two men looked at each other for a moment or two in silence and with the cool, narrowed, calculating look of adversaries who measure swords.

Kishan Prasad said slowly: 'I wish to thank you——'

'You have nothing to thank me for,' interrupted Alex curtly.

'You mean because had you known that it was I you would not have saved me? Is that indeed the truth? If you had known —and knowing that I could not swim, must drown—you would not have gone after me?'

Alex returned his look with eyes that were hard and level. 'No. I would not have lifted a hand to save you.'

Kishan Prasad bowed gravely as though he had received an answer that he both expected and understood. He said: 'It is for that reason that I come to thank you. Not for what you did for me, but for what you would have done for one of my servants. There are very few who would have risked their lives for—a black man and the servant of a black man.'

'You overrate me,' said Alex brusquely. 'There was no risk. I am a strong swimmer.'

'And the sharks?' said Kishan Prasad gently.

'You force me to admit,' said Alex with a grin, 'that I had

clean forgotten that there might be sharks. If I had remembered it, I give you my word that I should not have jumped! So you see, you owe me nothing.'

'Nevertheless,' said Kishan Prasad, smiling, 'willingly or unwillingly, you gave me back the life that the Gods would have taken from me. In the past I have intrigued against your race——' He saw the sudden flare in Alex's eyes and laughed, lifting a protesting hand. 'Oh no! That is not evidence. I tell you nothing that you did not already know. And here there is no one to overhear. We two speak under the thorn tree. Your Commissioner will not move against me. That I know.'

'And I also,' said Alex bitterly. 'Are you by any chance telling me that you have suffered a change of heart because I risked my neck to pull you out of the sea?'

Kishan Prasad smiled and shook his head. 'Alas, no. I have suffered no change of heart. In the name of my country and my people and my Gods I will do all in my power to pull down your Company's Raj.'

'And I,' said Alex, 'will do all in my power to get you hanged or transported—for the sake of my countrymen who govern your country.'

'It is good,' said Kishan Prasad gravely. 'We understand one another, and we are not children.'

He turned a small ring that he wore on his right hand and pulling it off held it out to Alex. It was a trumpery thing of little value, fashioned out of twisted silver in a curious design set with three small red stones that might have been flawed rubies. An odd ornament for the hand of such a man as Kishan Prasad. He said: 'Will you wear this for me? As a token of my gratitude? It is worth less than ten rupees, but it is a talisman that may one day save you from much evil. If ever the day comes, as I pray it will, that the Company's Raj falls and its charter for robbery and confiscation is destroyed, look on that ring and remember Kishan Prasad. For in that day—who knows—it may repay a part of my debt.'

Alex looked at the outstretched hand with a frown and made

no attempt to disguise his hesitation. Then he reached out and taking the ring slid it on to the little finger of his right hand. He said slowly: 'I did not remember that there might be sharks when I went over that rail yesterday, but you would have had me take your place on that damned hen-coop when you saw them come. I will wear this because it is the gift of a brave man.'

Kishan Prasad put his hands together, the finger-tips touching, bowed gravely above them and turned and walked away.

7

'WE shall be in Calcutta tomorrow,' thought Winter. 'Only one more day—and then I shall see Conway!'

It did not seem possible that the long waiting that had begun six years ago at Ware could be over at last, and that in only two days' time she would no longer be 'Miss Winter' or the Condesa de los Aguilares, but Mrs. Conway Barton, driving away from the church with her handsome husband to live happily ever afterwards like a princess in a fairy-tale.

The *Sirius* was anchored off the Sandheads awaiting the first light and the turn of the tide when, with the pilot on board, she would begin the slow journey up the Hooghly to Calcutta. Winter turned restlessly in her narrow berth and wondered if Conway would meet her at the mouth of the river or at Diamond Harbour. He might take a launch down the river and board the ship on her way up. Mrs. Abuthnot seemed to think it possible . . .

The sky beyond the open porthole was already turning to grey, and a cock in the galley began to crow. Soon the sun would turn the silt-stained sea to gold, the boatswain's whistle would shrill and there would be a patter of feet on deck and the rattle of the anchor chain. The last day!

Winter had completed her packing on the previous afternoon, except for the last few necessities, for she could not bear to waste a moment of that enchanted day. Every foot of the way was wonderful and exciting to the girl who had passed that way as a child almost a dozen weary years ago, held in the arms of Zobeida who had wept as she looked her last on her homeland. The tangled thickets of bamboo, the thatch-roofed huts surrounded by groves of tamarind, jackfruit and custard apple, the low brown land, the temples and the wide, mud-coloured Hooghly with its treacherous shifting shoals and unpredictable currents. Every approaching craft, every carriage seen upon either bank, might be one that contained Conway. A horseman riding behind a far belt of trees or a figure carried in a rough palanquin might be he . . .

Alex Randall, seeing her run to lean over the deck-rail as a river launch approached the ship, felt again the same half-angry, half-exasperated desire to tell her that she must not look like that: that she should not let such glowing expectation show on her face, for before the day was out she would have seen for herself what the years had done to Mr. Commissioner Barton, and she would never wear that look again. Alex, watching that young and vulnerable face, thought entirely dispassionately that it would be a pleasure to choke the life out of Mr. Barton.

The sky was ablaze with sunset by the time the *Sirius* reached the Calcutta anchorage, and boat after boat shot out from the shore bringing relatives and friends of those on board or coming to fetch the passengers away. Mrs. Abuthnot, who had informed Lottie only the day before that any public display of affection was not only intolerable but indelicate, abandoned all reserve and cast herself into the arms of a tubby little gentleman with a cherubic face, silver-white hair and mild blue eyes, who proved to be Colonel Abuthnot, and the reunited family retired to shed happy tears in the privacy of their cabin.

Winter stood apart from the turmoil of welcome and departure, her eyes anxiously scanning every boat: but none contained a familiar face. She had seen Kishan Prasad leave, loaded with scented garlands of flowers and tinsel that had been brought by the friends who had welcomed him; and had watched a boat with two rowers bring an Indian wearing an odd sandy-coloured uniform out to the ship, and seen Alex Randall go quickly to meet him.

The man had saluted stiffly as he reached the deck and then his brown face had creased into a grin of pure pleasure. Winter saw Alex's hand go out and grip the man's shoulder, holding it hard, and saw that he was smiling the same smile. For a moment the two men had looked at each other without words, as brothers might look who meet again after a long separation, with affection and relief in each other's safety. Then Alex's hand had dropped and they had both laughed and turned away together, talking rapidly.

The crowded decks emptied and Winter watched anxiously as boat after boat drew away laden with passengers for the shore. At last someone touched her on the arm and she turned quickly. But it was only Alex Randall. There was a look on his face that was dangerously near pity and it stiffened Winter's small shoulders and brought her chin up with a jerk. She looked very young, thought Alex, and despite the haughtiness of that lifted chin, very frightened and wary. He said bluntly: 'He has not been able to come. My orderly has brought letters from Lunjore.'

Winter took the proffered packet with a hand that was not quite steady, and her fingers closed on it so tightly that the stiff paper crackled. She could feel tears prickling behind her eyelids, and she forced them back. If she let Alex Randall see tears in her eyes she would never forgive herself. Or him. She said: 'Thank you,' in a small cold voice, and Alex turned away abruptly and left her.

Winter caught at the rail to steady herself. She found that she was trembling, and the tears that she would not let Alex see stood in her eyes so that she saw the river and the trees and the houses on the bank through a swimming mist. The disappointment was almost too bitter to be borne. Today was to have been the end of a long journey, but the journey had not ended after all. She looked down at the letter she held clenched in her hand, and after a moment broke the seal.

E

Pressure of work, wrote Conway, had made it impossible after all for him to meet her in Calcutta. She must know how great a disappointment this was to him. As great, he knew, as it would be to her. But duty must come first, and he was persuaded that she would not have him neglect his duty even for her. He had written to Randall asking him to make all arrangements for her journey north, and as he had heard that the Abuthnots, who had so kindly escorted her out, were proceeding to Delhi, she had better remain under their protection and travel as far as Delhi with them. It was a little out of the way, but as he himself would have occasion to go there in the near future and would be staying with the Commissioner, Mr. Simon Fraser, it would suit very well. They could be married in Delhi and spend their honeymoon in that historic city, visiting the various places of interest with which the ancient Mogul capital abounded. It would mean a delay of a few more weeks, but what were a few more weeks when they had the rest of their lives before them? He hoped that she had had a pleasant voyage and remained, as ever, her affectionate, devoted husband-to-be . . .

The writing was straggling and uneven and the lines ran crookedly across the page. He must have been very tired when he wrote it, thought Winter with loving compassion. Tired and disappointed. It made her own disappointment seem a selfish emotion. It was noble of Conway—and so like him!—to put duty before personal happiness. Dear, dear Conway!

She crushed his letter between her hands, pressing it to her breast and fighting a desire to put her head down on the top bar of the deck-rail and cry. But she must not cry here in the open deck, and there was no privacy anywhere on the ship that day. To let her bitter disappointment be seen might be taken by others to imply a criticism of Conway, and that would be unforgivable in her. She turned away from the rail and walked steadily down to her cabin with her head high, her face calm and composed and her eyes very dry and bright.

Mrs. Abuthnot was motherly and sympathetic. Dear Alex had already informed her of the state of affairs and had handed

her a most *charming* letter from Mr. Barton. So disappointing!
But then life in India was sadly full of such disappointments.
One had to learn to bear them. Officers in the service of the
Company were not their own masters. India, said Mrs. Abuthnot
profoundly, was not England. Naturally dear Winter would
remain in her care. It would be delightful to have her!—
although she feared that it would mean some delay, as Colonel
Abuthnot had official business to transact in Calcutta and
Barrackpore which might keep them here for a little time. He
had arranged for them to stay with a friend—Mr. Shadwell, a
Calcutta merchant. The Shadwells, she knew, would be only
too pleased to welcome Winter as an additional guest, for Mr.
Shadwell had known her Uncle Ebenezer well. And what could
be more delightful than to travel to Delhi in company? Dear
Lottie was overjoyed at the prospect!

The Shadwells' house proved to be a palatial two-storeyed
mansion on Garden Reach surrounded by lawns and gardens,
and to Winter's relief she was given a room to herself.

She shut the door behind her and leant tiredly against it,
released at last from the necessity of keeping her features composed and her lips smiling. She could cry now that there was
no one to see, and let tears relieve some of the strain and the pain
of disappointment that the day had brought her.

But she did not cry. She looked about the huge, high-
ceilinged room with its whitewashed walls and long french
windows opening on to a deep verandah. A room that was as
utterly unlike an English bedroom as the vast, slow-moving
Hooghly was unlike an English stream. The tight band that had
seemed to be tied about her heart relaxed, and the fever of
excitement and the leaden weight of disappointed hope both
faded.

She walked slowly across the room and out on to the verandah,
her wide skirts rustling softly on the matting. Below her a long
lawn sloped down between thick groves of trees to where the
river ran gold in the brief twilight. The sky was a wash of clear

pale green in which the first stars were already ghostly points of light, and the evening air was full of sounds: half-forgotten and yet wholly familiar sounds. Conches blaring in a temple; a distant throb of tom-toms; peacocks calling and a jackal-pack wailing; the barking of pariah dogs and all the many noises of an Indian city. The air smelt of sun-baked dust and cow-dung fires; of wood-smoke and marigolds and jasmine and the rank scent of the river, and in the gathering dusk a myriad fireflies spangled the bamboo brakes with glinting pin-points of light, while overhead a dark flight of fruit bats flapped silently across the garden.

Winter leaned on the broad verandah rail and drew a long, long breath of happiness. It did not matter any longer that Conway had been unable to come to Calcutta to meet her, or that tomorrow would not after all be her wedding day. She could wait. She had come home.

*   *   *

Winter was awakened in the diamond-bright morning by a scream from Lottie, whose room gave on to the same verandah, and a moment later Lottie herself, clad in a pink cotton peignoir over a cambric nightgown and with her soft fair curls in tangled disarray, appeared in Winter's bedroom.

A man, an Indian! had walked into her room, she announced in trembling tones. 'A *man*, Winter! He did not even knock! He just walked in! I thought I should have swooned with fright!'

'What did he want?' enquired Winter.

'Oh, he did not want anything. He brought me tea and fruit. He just put them on a table beside my bed and went out again. Don't laugh, Winter! It is most unkind of you! I was never so frightened in my life!'

'That was only the bearer,' said Winter, continuing to laugh. 'He brought me some too. You will have to get used to it, Lottie, darling. I do not think servants in India ever knock.'

'I shall *never* get used to it!' declared Lottie, shuddering.

'Oh yes, you will. I prophesy that within a year you will find yourself quite unable to support life or run the simplest *ménage* without the assistance of at least a dozen servants, with another ten for Edward. Mrs. Shadwell informed me last night that they run a very modest establishment here—a mere thirty-five servants!'

But the mention of Edward had instantly diverted Lottie. She blushed pinkly and said with a small gasp: 'Oh, Winter, Edward is to call on Papa today! Mamma has told him all, and Papa has been so kind. And only think!—he knows Edward's uncle! They were at school together. He would not commit himself, but—but he did not look at all displeased. And he said that it was hard for a father to find his daughter again after so many years, only to lose her before he had time to know her. That does not sound as though he meant to refuse his consent, does it?'

'No, of course it does not! What possible objection could he have? Edward is most eligible. And so handsome!' added Winter with a twinkle.

'He is handsome, is he not?' sighed Lottie, accepting the tribute as a simple statement of fact. And indeed to her adoring eyes Edward's blunt-nosed, blue-eyed, freckled face and flaming red hair embodied all that was admirable in masculine good looks, although barely two months ago her mental vision of the ideal male would have been found to resemble the late Lord Byron; a gentleman who had borne no recognizable likeness to Lieutenant Edward English.

'You are so lucky, Winter,' sighed Lottie. 'I do not think that it is fair. You are a whole year younger than I am, and yet you are going to be married in a few weeks' time, whereas I shall have to wait for at least half a year, and probably a great deal longer. Mamma says that an engagement of only six months would be considered scandalously short, but Edward hopes to be able to persuade Papa to allow it, so that we may be married in the spring. Do you think he will agree? It is delightful, of course, to be with Papa again, but—Oh, I know that it sounds most undutiful in me—but he is not *Edward*!'

But as it happened Lottie had not to wait for as long as that.
Incredible as it seemed, Lottie was to be married within a few
weeks of their arrival in Delhi.

It was Edward who had not only advanced such an unheard-of
suggestion, but had actually succeeded in carrying the day
against the scandalized opposition of Mrs. Abuthnot.

There was an unauthenticated rumour in Calcutta of tension
brewing between Great Britain and China, and Edward had
received information—unofficial but believed to be reliable—
that his Regiment, who were Queen's and not Company's troops,
might be sent to augment Admiral Seymour's forces in China
early in the New Year. In the light of this information he
desired to get married as soon as possible in case such a calamity
occurred. As he pointed out, he had already known Lottie for
over two months, during which time he had seen her daily, and
this surely constituted a long acquaintance, for had they been in
England he might well have seen her at the most once or twice
a week, even if they had been betrothed. There was little point,
he argued, in being separated from Lottie for the next few
months, only to be married on the eve of his departure and when
faced with the prospect of indefinite separation. Let them at least
enjoy a short spell of happiness, and then if the worst occurred
and he was indeed ordered to China in the following year, they
could face it with more fortitude as husband and wife. While
should he be killed, added Edward bluntly, his wife would be
amply provided for, as all he possessed would revert to her.

From this last and strictly worldly point of view Edward's
arguments carried considerable weight, and when reinforced by
the appeals of sentiment and emotion they had carried the day,
for Lottie, upon hearing of the possibility of her Edward being
sent to China, had instantly swooned away, and only the promise
of an early wedding had prevented her—upon her being revived
with the aid of burnt feathers and hartshorn—from repeating
this affecting gesture.

Mrs. Abuthnot, alarmed by her daugher's pallor and despair,
had withdrawn all opposition, and the entire party had repaired

to the drawing-room where Mr. Shadwell, despite the unsuitability of the hour, had called for champagne so that all might drink to the health and happiness of the betrothed pair.

It was at this point that a servant announced Captain Randall, who was greeted affectionately by Mrs. Abuthnot, introduced to the Shadwells, and once again thanked by Colonel Abuthnot for his assistance on the journey. Informed of the betrothal and wedding plans of Lottie and Edward he congratulated them in a somewhat preoccupied voice, and announced that he had only called in order to make his adieu. He regretted that he could not accompany them to Delhi, but he could not delay his return to Lunjore any longer.

Winter had spoken a few stiffly formal words of thanks when he had said goodbye to her, to which Alex—his eyes on a massive clock at the far side of the room—had replied briefly that he was happy to have been of any assistance to her. He was quite obviously in a hurry and impatient to be off, and having swallowed half a glass of champagne with absent-minded haste had shaken hands with the assembled company and left. The rattle of his carriage wheels died away on the long drive, and Winter was astounded and disturbed to find that the sound brought her a sudden feeling of being alone and unprotected. Which was of course absurd, for was not Colonel Abuthnot here to take his place and see that she came to no harm?

But as the slow days dragged by she was surprised how much she missed him. Not the man himself, but the feeling he had given her that as long as he was there she was safe. She had not stopped to analyse it, and she would not do so now. But the fact that he had gone, and that it would never again be any part of his duty to see to her comfort and safety, did not bring her any feeling of relief, but rather a vague sensation of insecurity and loss. Which must, she decided, be because he had been a link with Conway.

*   *   *

Edward English had left for Meerut on the day following his momentous interview with Colonel Abuthnot, and Lottie had found what comfort she could in planning her wedding, which was to take place late in October. But their stay in Calcutta was by no means spent in idleness, for the kindly Shadwells arranged numerous entertainments for their guests, and cards of invitation for balls and Assemblies, including a State Ball at Government House, arrived at the house on Garden Reach in an apparently never-ending stream. Mrs. Gardener-Smith and Delia were also in Calcutta, for Colonel Gardener-Smith having obtained three months' leave they had decided to remain there for a week or two in order to rest and recuperate after the long voyage, and they had driven over several times to visit the Abuthnot ladies and accompany them on shopping expeditions to Calcutta city.

Calcutta, as the capital and headquarters of the Governor General and the Council, and seat of the Supreme Government, had a reputation to keep up in the way of gaiety, and the State Ball had been a revelation to Lottie and Sophie, who had never attended such a function before. Even Winter, accustomed to the almost unrelieved black and white attire of the men who had danced at Ware and in the London ballrooms, had imagined for one dazzled instant that the Governor General was giving a fancy-dress ball.

Men in the gorgeous dress uniforms of regiments whose names were rarely heard outside India, regiments of Cavalry, of Irregular Horse, of Bengal Infantry and Artillery—men wearing the pale blue and gold of the Light Cavalry, the canary yellow of Skinner's Horse, the green of the Rifle companies and the scarlet of Infantry regiments—vied with the shimmering silks and frothing tarlatans of feminine ball-gowns in richness of colour and glitter of gold lace, and outnumbered the women by six to one.

Moving among them in more sober attire, crows among a flock of peacocks, were the rich Calcutta merchants—men such as Mr. Shadwell—or, distinguished by ribbons and orders, the members of the Governor General's Council and high officers of the East India Company. Indian guests, many of them ablaze with jewels and wearing brightly coloured brocades and muslins, their dark

faces often no darker than the sunburned skins above the high
tight collars of dress uniforms, mingled with the company but
did not dance, and Mrs. Abuthnot, covertly regarding them and
uneasily conscious of the décolleté bodices above many a crinoline,
confided in a whisper to Delia's mamma that it was an odd cir-
cumstance that toilettes which had seemed unexceptionable in
England should appear almost daring when worn in the East.
'I suppose it is because there are so many Indian guests present
tonight,' she concluded unhappily.

Mrs. Gardener-Smith bristled slightly and observed that for
her part she considered the present fashions *quite* charming, and
that several people had complimented her upon Delia's appearance. Lady Canning indeed had been more than kind. *Such* a
pleasant creature!—although to be sure it was a pity that she
had elected to wear crimson, as it made her appear sadly pale.
It was probable that she found the climate trying, this being her
first visit to the East. As for the Governor General, though Mrs.
Gardener-Smith had not yet spoken to him, she considered that
he too did not look to be in the best of health.

Lord Canning's health, as it happened, was excellent; but he
was having a troublesome time. The new Governor General, a
remarkably handsome man in his early forties with a noble brow
and a somewhat womanish mouth, had taken over the reins from
the dynamic Dalhousie less than eight months previously, and
had early discovered that his predecessor's confident prediction
that all was well with India was unfounded. Dalhousie had
enlarged the bounds of Empire to a previously unthinkable
degree, but there had been no corresponding enlargement
of the number of Company's men needed to control and
administer it. The Bengal Army had been stripped of officers,
who had been sent on special service to administer newly
acquired districts, to act as judges, to build roads and bridges and
pacify revolting populations; and efficiency in the regiments
suffered in consequence—an aspect to which the new Governor
was not blind, but which he found himself unable to rectify.

The annexation of Oudh had been one of the last acts of Lord

E*

Dalhousie's reign, but the settling of the province had fallen to Lord Canning, and his appointment of a Mr. Coverley Jackson as Chief Commissioner of this newest of the Company's possessions had not proved a happy one. Mr. Jackson appeared to be more interested in conducting a lively paper war with his subordinates, Gubbins and Ommaney, than in the affairs of Oudh. Mr. Gubbins, equally irascible, entered with enthusiasm into the combat, and the hapless province—the main recruiting ground for the Company's Sepoy Army—was left to limp along in chaos while its chief British administrators expended a large part of their time and energy in mutual recrimination, and in formulating charges and counter-charges which were forwarded almost daily to Calcutta.

To add to Lord Canning's worries the war clouds were massing over Persia, and he knew that if war were to be declared he would be required to send troops from India which could be ill spared. There was also the problem of Wajid Ali, the deposed King of Oudh, who had settled in Calcutta, bringing with him a large following of relatives and retainers who lived a life of idleness and occupied themselves with intrigue and the formulation of endless complaints against the behaviour of the British officers in Lucknow who, they alleged, were inflicting disgraceful sufferings and indignities upon the dispossessed nobles of the State, plundering their possessions, turning their women into the streets, and using their palaces to house horses and dogs.

The Marquess of Dalhousie, sailing away from India towards an early death, imagined that he had left behind him, in effect, peaceful agricultural acres reclaimed from the savage forests of medievalism and barbarity. But the dragon's teeth that had been sown in them were springing up under the feet of his successor, and Lord Canning watched his carefree guests dancing the waltz in the ballroom of Government House with an abstracted eye and a mind that was on other matters.

8

COLONEL ABUTHNOT, who was no dancer, left his wife to gossip among the older women and to keep a watchful eye upon Lottie, Sophie and Winter, and removed himself to the more congenial company of several like-minded gentlemen who were smoking a quiet cigar in an anteroom some distance from the ballroom. His appearance was hailed by a portly civilian whose high stock seemed to be in danger of choking him:

'Hullo, Abuthnot!—you're the very man I wanted to see! Fallon here has been talkin' a lot of twaddle about disaffection among some of the regiments around Delhi way. That's your part of the world, ain't it? I tell him he's too credulous by half. The Army's as sound as a bell!'

'Well—there have been rumours, of course,' admitted Colonel Abuthnot cautiously. 'But I have certainly had no trouble with my own men. 'Evening, General. 'Evening, Fallon.'

'Pah! *Rumours!*' snorted the stout civilian scornfully. 'There are always rumours. Wouldn't be India without 'em! But it's only the alarmists who go quackin' about, takin' them seriously.'

Colonel Fallon's bronzed countenance took on a distinct tinge of purple. 'I resent that aspersion, sir! I am no alarmist. But neither am I a Government ostrich burying my head in the sands of complacency! I tell you that there are dangerous ideas stirring among the sepoys. Ideas that we have fostered ourselves —or done nothing to prevent. Grievances that we have given insufficient attention to!'

'Such as what, sir?' demanded the first speaker, bristling. 'The sepoy is better fed, better treated and better paid than ever before!'

'Ah, that's the trouble,' cut in an elderly man with fierce white mustachios, who wore the uniform of a famous Bengal Infantry regiment. 'They used to be as tough as hickory sticks in my young days; but now we pamper 'em. Yes, by God! we pamper and pet 'em as though we were running a demned girls' school instead of an army. The whole thing's going soft!'

'Not soft,' snapped Colonel Fallon. 'Rotten! Rotten from top to bottom. Why, half the younger officers don't even know their men! and the best of them are for ever being removed from regimental duty on special appointment to civil posts—or the staff. Then there's all this damned Brahminism. We should have done something to limit it.'

A tall handsome man with cold blue eyes and a marked air of fashion added a languid voice to the discussion:

'Brahminism? Pray enlighten an ignorant globe-trotter, Colonel Fallon. I was not aware that there were political parties in this country.'

'It is not a political party, Lord Carlyon; it is an aspect of Hinduism. The Brahmins—the "twice born"—are the priestly caste of the Hindus and as such are held in great reverence by all other castes, who dare not offend them for fear of the fearful penalties that would follow not only in this world but the next. It is no uncommon thing to see an Indian officer of a lower caste grovelling to a mere sepoy who happens to be a Brahmin. It rots discipline, and we should have put a stop to it long ago—clapped a limit on to the number we recruited, and kept the whole Army on a lower caste level! It is the Brahmins who are at the back of all this present trouble.'

'What trouble, sir?' enquired Lord Carlyon in a bored voice. 'I understood Mr. Halliwell here to say that reports of trouble were entirely without foundation.'

'So they are!' snorted Mr. Halliwell. 'No foundation! Lot of chicken-hearted flapdoodle!'

'Henry Lawrence ain't exactly my notion of a chicken-heart,' murmured a thin man with a brown, nutcracker face who wore the blue and silver of a Punjab Cavalry regiment.

Mr. Halliwell swung round on the speaker, his face above the high stock becoming dangerously empurpled. 'I have every respect for Sir Henry's capabilities as an administrator,' he said angrily, 'but the man's a demned nigger-lover! He was against the Oudh annexation. Made a devil of a nuisance of himself, and Dal' had to put him in his place pretty sharply.'

'Sir Henry was not the only one whom his lordship put in his place,' said the thin man dryly. ' 'Seem to remember him doin' the same to Napier in 'fifty—and for much the same reason.'

'Two of a kind!' retorted Mr. Halliwell. 'Alarmists, both of 'em! Sir Charles would have it that the Bengal Army was on the verge of mutiny and the Empire in danger. Quite fantastic!—and he was proved wrong.'

'If you mean that the danger was temporarily averted owing to the prompt action taken by Sir Charles, yes,' said Colonel Fallon with a snap. 'But I think that you have forgotten, sir, that the disaffection Sir Charles Napier feared might lead to mutiny arose out of disappointment over pay and allowances, which he attempted to remedy himself.'

'And wrongly! And wrongly!' blared Mr. Halliwell. 'It is not the province of the Army to meddle in such matters! It rests upon the decision of the civil Government, who——'

'Who do not know the mind of the sepoy!' countered Colonel Fallon angrily. 'Are we never to learn by our mistakes?'

He was interrupted by a large blond gentleman whose countenance was adorned by a magnificent set of Dundreary whiskers and whose manner suggested—correctly—the House of Commons. Mr. Joseph Leger-Green, who had lost his seat in the last election, was but newly arrived in Calcutta. He intended to make a short stay in the Orient with the object of writing a book on the subject of 'Our Eastern Empire', and had already compiled an impressive collection of notes. He turned now on Colonel Fallon and fixed him with a glittering eye:

'May I ask what mistakes you refer to, Colonel? I confess to being at sea.'

'I am sorry, sir,' apologized Colonel Fallon. 'This must be an exceedingly tedious discussion for you. Let us abandon it.'

'On the contrary, Colonel. I am intensely interested. I intend,' said Mr. Leger-Green impressively, 'to study the whole question of our foreign possessions during my tour. What question of pay and allowances do you refer to?'

The Colonel took another deep draught from the glass in his

hand and regarded his interlocutor critically. Like most of his
kind he had little use for visiting writers and politicos who arrived
in Calcutta for a brief stay in the cold weather and returned to
pose as experts on all Eastern questions, but the subject under
discussion was one on which he felt strongly. He said:

'The sepoys, sir, were granted special allowances for service
outside British-held territory. We have used them to conquer
vast new provinces which, once annexed, we have pronounced
British, and thereafter, with shortsighted parsimony, cancelled
the "foreign" allowance of all sepoys serving there. The sepoys
resent annexation at the best of times, but when it is followed by
loss of allowances that resentment is gravely aggravated. They
resented it in Sind and later in the Punjab, and finally resorted
to mutiny. The mutinies were put down. But concessions were
made; and because they were made as the result of mutiny
the sepoy gained the impression that they were made from fear,
and that has given him a sense of power. And now there is this
final folly of Oudh——'

'Sir——!' began Mr. Halliwell hotly, but was unable to
continue, for once again the smooth tones of Mr. Leger-Green
intervened.

'I am greatly interested in this question of Oudh,' said Mr.
Leger-Green. 'Pray, why do you consider it a folly? Taking
the humanitarian view——'

'I was speaking from a purely military one,' said Colonel
Fallon impatiently. 'We recruit the bulk of our sepoys from
Oudh, and they had certain privileges in that state as servants of
the Company. But now that every citizen of Oudh is equally
under Company's law, those privileges have gone, and there is
no special advantage any longer in being in the service of the
Bengal Army.'

Colonel Abuthnot, who had so far taken no part in the discussion, coughed gently and remarked in a diffident voice: 'I think
you possibly exaggerate the effects of the recent annexation. I
myself feel that it is this matter of foreign service and the
General Services Enlistment Act that has given rise to any

uneasiness that may prevail in some regiments. It will pass, of course. But they are bound to regard it with some suspicion to begin with.'

Mr. Leger-Green turned on the speaker and produced a small notebook in which he jotted down a hurried line of script. 'The General Services Enlistment Act, did you say? And what is that?'

'Service overseas, sir. The Bengal sepoy enlisted on the understanding that he should not be required to cross the sea.'

'Caste again,' interpolated Colonel Fallon. 'The men believe that crossing the sea will deprive them of their caste, and they would have to pay heavily to the priests on their return, to be cleansed of the defilement. But the Governor General, with the approval of Mr. Halliwell here and his friends in the Council, recently issued a General Order to the effect that no recruit would in future be accepted who would not undertake to go wherever his services might be required. And that means Burma, sir!— or Persia—or China! Is it not understandable that a caste-ridden, bigoted and superstitious people are willing to believe any agitator who whispers that the British plan to destroy their caste?'

'Rubbish, sir!' exploded Mr. Halliwell. 'You exaggerate grossly, Colonel!'

'I do not think so, sir! I think I may claim to have met and conversed with more of the people of this country than you gentlemen in Calcutta! Mohammedans and Hindus alike have regarded the advent of railways and telegraphs with the gravest suspicion, and when we permit the Missionary Societies to publish a manifesto to the effect that our trains and steamships, by facilitating the material union of all races of men, are to be the instruments for bringing about their spiritual union under one Faith—ours!—is it to be wondered at that the wildest rumours are given credence?'

'Am I to take it, Colonel Fallon,' said Mr. Halliwell contemptuously, 'that you consider your own regiment to be a hotbed of sedition and unrest?'

A dark spot of colour burned beneath the brick-red of Colonel Fallon's sunburnt cheeks and his hand made a small instinctive gesture towards his dress sword, and fell again. He said hotly: 'No, sir! I thank God that my own men are loyal! But I am not blind to the attacks that are being made upon both their loyalty and their credulity by agitators and troublemakers. Neither am I blind to the fact that we have done our best to give the sepoys an overweening sense of their own importance, while at the same time reducing their respect for authority. The Commanding Officer of the Regiment should be the final arbiter of their fate, but he may now neither reward nor punish them according to their deserts. I and my fellow colonels are reduced to impotence by red-tape and our decisions are overruled by Headquarters. The only advancement an Indian may obtain is by seniority. Merit is apparently of no importance, and——'

A tall man with a thin grey beard and wearing the insignia of a Brigadier General said coldly: 'You forget yourself, Colonel.'

Colonel Fallon turned quickly and the flush faded from his cheeks as he became aware that he had permitted his temper to lead him into openly expressed criticism of military policy, but his indignation was supported by the wine he had drunk and he was in any event no coward. He returned the Brigadier's cold gaze with composure and said hardily:

'Perhaps, sir. But I do not forget that our native troops number two hundred and thirty-three thousand men, while the European soldiery totals barely more than forty-five thousand of all arms! Those are sobering figures, sir.'

'*I* do not find it so,' declared Mr. Halliwell. 'It is well known that one Britisher is a match for fifty Asiatics any day. Are you not agreed, gentlemen?'

There was a chorus of assent and Colonel Fallon said sharply: 'That, if I may say so, is a remark that could only be made by a civilian and a politician! I will bid you good evening, sir.' He bowed stiffly and walked angrily away.

'Disgraceful!' puffed Mr. Halliwell indignantly. 'Man's a menace! a rumour-monger! Taken to nerves and the vapours like some mewling female. He ain't fit to command troops if he's started listening to that sort of flapdoodle!'

'Two hundred and thirty-three thousand . . .!' It was the ex-Member for Chillbury and Howersford who spoke, and his mellifluous voice had a startled note in it. 'And how many British did he say? Forty-five thousand odd? It is indeed a sobering thought! You are quite sure that there is no danger to be apprehended? I had intended to pay a brief visit to Delhi and the interior, but——'

'I can assure you, sir,' said Mr. Halliwell, 'that there is no need for any anxiety. The country is pacified from end to end and basks, if I may say so, in the beneficial sunshine of our benevolent rule. As for the Bengal Army, it is loyal to the core—I am sure that all you gentlemen will agree with me.'

'Undoubtedly,' concurred the grey-bearded Brigadier. 'The finest army in the world! Naturally, when one reflects that they have served us for a century, there are bound to have been a few unpleasant incidents from time to time. But those mean nothing. Mere ripples. The vast mass of the country and the army are well content. In fact I can safely say they have never been more so. Those who prate of disaffection are cranks and alarmists, but fortunately they are few in number. If you intend to visit Delhi, sir, Colonel Abuthnot here can tell you more about it than I can. His regiment is stationed there, and I am quite sure that he does not consider them to be on the verge of revolt!'

'Hardly, sir,' said Colonel Abuthnot with a smile, 'or I should not be taking my wife and daughters to Delhi.'

'Indeed? That is most reassuring.' The ex-Member of Parliament appeared relieved. 'I cannot suppose that you would contemplate putting your wife and daughters in any danger, and if the ladies can proceed in safety there can be no cause for anxiety. I had intended to venture into Oudh, should time permit, in order that I might be able to gain first-hand information on this newest addition to our territorial possessions. I have been given a letter of introduction to a Mr. Coverley Jackson——'

'What is that about Coverley Jackson?' enquired a new voice, and the group turned as one to see their host advancing upon them. 'Are you contemplating a visit to Lucknow, Mr. Leger-Green?'

'Only if time permits, your Excellency. I have an introduction to Mr. Coverley Jackson from a mutual friend.'

'Ah, yes,' said Lord Canning. 'Competent fellow, Jackson—if only he were not so quarrelsome.'

'You're looking fagged, Charles,' remarked Lord Carlyon. 'India don't appear to agree with you. Too many social functions and too much heat.'

'And too much work,' said the Governor General with a smile. 'You should try it, Arthur. It would at least have the charm of novelty.'

'That is too bad of you, Charles,' protested his lordship indolently. 'I work like a demned nigger.'

'You surprise me. At what, may I ask?'

'Keeping boredom at bay. And here I am flogging round the globe in proof of it!'

'Stay here awhile and try some real work instead,' advised Lord Canning. 'We can even use someone as ornamentally useless as yourself.'

'Then you must be devilish hard up for hands, Charles!'

'We are; or we shall be if this Persian business blows up into anything. The annexation of Oudh has stretched our resources to the limit. But this is no time for such dull talk. You gentlemen are neglecting your duty. You should be dancing.'

'We leave that to our juniors, your Excellency,' said Mr. Halliwell. 'Every lady is at least three deep in would-be partners already, and such old fogeys as ourselves would receive short shrift from them.'

'Speak for yourself, Halliwell,' said the Brigadier, straightening his befrogged tunic. 'I intend to dance the lancers with my wife —if I can persuade her from the whist table.'

'Bravo, General!' approved Lord Canning. 'I trust that the rest of you intend to follow such an intrepid lead. A word with you, Arthur——'

The Governor General took Lord Carlyon's arm and moved away in the direction of the ballroom.

'What's on your Excellency's mind?' enquired Carlyon, his

lazy-lidded eyes unexpectedly observant. 'You were not by any chance serious just now?'

'When I suggested that I could use your services? Certainly.'

'My dear Charles! In what capacity? To dance with the ladies who attend your crushes? It is the most that I am capable of—and then only providing they are pretty. I cannot dance with a plain woman. I lose all sense of rhythm and am instantly abroad.'

'You underrate yourself, Arthur. I know you to be a superlative horseman and a first-class shot.'

The younger man stopped suddenly and turned to regard his host narrowly. He said slowly: 'What exactly do you mean by that? Do you too think as that Colonel in there—that there is going to be trouble?'

'What Colonel? Was someone prophesying trouble?'

'Fallon, I believe the name was. Elderly little man with a face the colour of a brick wall. Tell me, Charles, is it one of the rules of the Indian Army that a man must be at least a grandfather before he is considered fit for command? Damme if I've ever seen such a gaggle of grey-beards! Your colonels are all tottering on the brink of gout and the grave, while your generals would appear to have both feet already in it. And they told me that this was a young man's country!'

'So it is—for those who make the most of their opportunities.'

'Not if they stay in the Army, I collect! I am no military strategist, but isn't it time that the Company overhauled its policy of promoting by seniority? I gather that no one can become a senior officer in the Bengal Army until he is senile and consequently useless. No wonder some of the less moribund go around croaking of impending disaster!'

'Was Fallon croaking of impending disaster?'

'Like a raven!' said Carlyon lightly. 'But he appeared to be in the minority. What are your own views? Do you too anticipate the deluge?'

'No, of course not! Nothing wrong with the country. Some people enjoy croaking of doom. The effects of this prophecy, I suppose. It is quite astonishing how superstitious even the most level-headed can become.'

'What prophecy?' enquired Carlyon, interested.

'Oh, it's an old tale now. It cropped up after Plassey. The Company's Raj—rule—was to last for a hundred years after the battle that established it. And Plassey was fought in 1757.'

'So the hundred years are up next year,' commented Carlyon. 'Very interesting. But surely you cannot take this seriously?'

'Naturally not! I wish you will not be ridiculous, Arthur!'

'Then what is worrying you?'

'Nothing! Nothing! It is just that—well, I would like you to extend your visit, if that is possible. Will you do that?'

'Why?'

The Governor General looked down upon the crowded ball-room and spoke in an undertone that was barely audible above the chatter of voices and the gay music of the fiddles: 'It would be of use to me if you were to decide to go on an extended tour of this country—in an entirely private capacity, of course; as a casual sightseer only—and give me your impressions. I find that too many people tell the Governor General only what they think will please the Governor General. It is this question of Oudh. The ex-King and his swarm of hangers-on are here in Calcutta, and they deafen me with their complaints as to the behaviour of our people in Lucknow. I have sent the strongest representations to Coverley Jackson, the Commissioner, but his replies have been evasive.'

'Sack him,' recommended Carlyon, bored.

'I can hardly do so without hurting his feelings,' said Lord Canning unhappily. 'The charges are quite possibly without foundation, and they are certain, at worst, to be grossly exaggerated. But they are doing our reputation a great deal of harm and providing fuel for the malcontents. If only I could have effected the Commissioner's removal without the necessity of direct dismissal . . . I had hoped——'

He paused, frowning, and Carlyon threw him a glance of friendly contempt. He was aware of Canning's tendency to avoid harsh measures, and of the conscientiousness that would not allow him to give an arbitrary decision on any matter that he had not thoroughly and personally sifted to the bottom. Carlyon, less patient, had little sympathy with such an attitude, and no intention of prolonging his stay in the East. He intended to reach England by the New Year, and the prospect of proceeding to Lucknow in order to test the accuracy of charges brought against the British administration of the newly acquired province by its deposed King did not appeal to him. His languid gaze rested without interest on the dancers, and he allowed his attention to wander.

'You could not of course proceed direct from here,' said Lord Canning, 'but were you to go first to Delhi and return via Lucknow, it would give the appearance of a sightseeing tour, and——'

He became aware that Carlyon had ceased to lounge and was gripping the balustrade with both hands and watching someone in the ballroom below with every appearance of lively interest.

'By Jove!' said Lord Carlyon under his breath, 'it *is* the ugly duckling!' He turned to his host with an unwonted gleam of animation in his bored eyes. 'Forgive me, Charles. I see an acquaintance of mine below. Perhaps we may continue this conversation at some other time.' He turned to descend a flower-decked staircase and was lost to view.

Lord Canning sighed a little tiredly and retreated to his study to wrestle with the contents of a dispatch box, leaving his wife to do the honours. He had emerged in the grey dawn, when lamps and candles were burning low and carriages drawing away laden with yawning men, sleepy dowagers and excited, laughing girls, to find Carlyon escorting a stout matron in a crimson opera mantle across the hall and into a closed carriage. The lady's face was unfamiliar and she did not look to be at all in Carlyon's style —both her dress and her *coiffure*, even to the Governor General's disinterested eye, being far from the first rank of fashion. Lord Carlyon however handed her into the carriage with a display of affability that was most unusual in him; bowed over her hand, expressed his intention of calling upon her at the earliest opportunity, and stood back to allow a tubby gentleman in the uniform of a Colonel of Native Infantry, presumably the lady's husband, to enter the carriage. There were half a dozen young officers grouped upon the steps, and they dispersed as the carriage drove off.

Lord Carlyon turned and made his way slowly back across the hall between the crowd of gorgeously uniformed servants, and stopped at the unexpected sight of his host.

'Ah, Charles—I imagined that you had very sensibly decided to retire to bed.'

'Who was that?' enquired Canning without much curiosity.

'No one of interest. A Mrs. Abuthnot.' Lord Carlyon glanced down at the wilting flower in his buttonhole, removed it and dropped it on to the polished marble floor. 'By the way, Charles,' he said softly, 'you will be interested to hear that I have decided to take your advice. I intend to extend my stay in India. I shall visit Delhi, and I may even return by way of Oudh.'

9

'CAN we take our own road from here?' asked Niaz* Mohamed.

Alex turned away from the window of the sparsely furnished dâk bungalow room and dropped the split-cane curtain back into place.

'Is there need?'

'Great need,' said Niaz, busy with the straps of a dusty valise. 'It was not advisable to speak while there were many to overhear, but now——'

'Here also there are ears,' said Alex with a jerk of his head towards the verandah outside, where the shadow of a loitering servant lay long upon the sun-warmed stone.

* Nee-*ahz.*

Alex and his orderly had left Calcutta by train. The new railway, one of Lord Dalhousie's most admired strides towards the Westernization of his Eastern Empire, now reached as far as Raniganj—a distance of over a hundred and forty miles north of Calcutta. But from that point the remainder of the journey must be accomplished by road.

Alex and Niaz had left the train, hot and dusty and coated with grit and cinders, and having slept the night at Raniganj in company with Colonel Moulson and a varied assortment of troops and travellers moving north, had proceeded for several days' journey towards Benares by dâk *ghari*—a four-wheeled, cab-like vehicle drawn by two horses. The roads, as a result of the monsoon, were unspeakably bad; the half-starved ponies made poor time, and Alex's travelling companion, a morose Major on his way to rejoin his regiment at Benares, did little or nothing towards improving the discomforts of the journey.

On the fourth day the *ghari* overturned down the side of an embankment. Its passengers, including the coachman, escaped unhurt, and owing to the fact that the shafts and traces had snapped as though they had been made of so much matchwood and string, the two starveling and evil-tempered horses had not only been unharmed but had bolted across the plain.

The driver had wasted an unconscionable time in rending his garments and calling down a variety of picturesque curses upon the heads of the absent horses, and had eventually, urged forcibly by Niaz, started off in half-hearted pursuit. The Major had high-handedly commandeered the *ekka*—a two-wheeled vehicle in which the servants travelled—and leaving its lawful occupants to follow on foot had ordered the driver to proceed to the nearest dâk bungalow, which was happily only a matter of two miles ahead, with himself, his bearer and Alex on board. Niaz had elected to remain with the baggage and had arrived at the bungalow some two and a half hours later, having transferred himself and his master's luggage to a passing bullock cart.

There were several other dâk *gharis* at the bungalow, where their passengers were partaking of such refreshment as the *khansamah* could provide, and the morose Major lost no time in arranging for one of them to take him up. Fresh horses were brought from the stables, the passengers embarked once more, and after a prolonged and invigorating struggle the reluctant steeds started off at a headlong gallop and the *gharis* disappeared in a cloud of dust. Alex and Niaz were alone in the dâk bungalow and quiet descended upon the scene.

It would be some little time before a new conveyance could be procured, said Niaz, and as the sun was already low in the sky they would have to spend the night here. He would prepare a room, and he suggested that it might be possible to procure two horses locally for very little cost, so that they might dispense with the services of a dâk *ghari*.

'When there is work to do it is better to travel alone,' said Niaz, his dark face blandly expressionless. 'I have a friend in the village who I think will find horses for us.'

Alex had nodded and turned to enter the room at the far end of the verandah in which his bedding and valise had been placed. He had had few opportunities for private conversation with Niaz since he had landed, for the hotel in Calcutta had been overcrowded and he had been compelled to share his bedroom with another officer.

Niaz was a Punjabi Mussulman whose home was north of Karnal. Born in the same year as Alex Randall, he came of a family of well-to-do landowners of some consequence whose daughters would seem to have married far from the family acres, for he appeared to possess blood relations in half the provinces of India. He had served in Alex's regiment and fought at his side at Moodkee and later at Ferozeshah. Alex's horse had been hamstrung at Moodkee by a wounded Sikh in the charge that silenced the guns of the Khalsa, and Niaz had risen in his stirrups and by some miracle of horsemanship had gripped Alex and dragged him clear as the horse fell. A moment later he had slipped to the ground and Alex was in his saddle with Niaz holding the stirrup leather and fighting beside him in the swaying, maddened mêlée, yelling joyfully as he had yelled in the charge: '*Shabash, bhayan! Dauro! Dauro!* (Well done, brothers! Ride! Ride!).'

Four days later, at Ferozeshah, Alex had repaid the debt when Niaz had fallen with a bullet through his chest, and Alex, his own horse killed, bestrode the wounded man and fought above him in the storming of the Sikh entrenchments. Since then Niaz had attached himself to Alex as orderly and body servant, and when Alex had been removed on special duty he had managed, through the judicious use of influence in the right quarters, to gain permission for Niaz to accompany him. Niaz had been granted extended leave during the past year, and Alex had left certain specific and unofficial instructions that he had no doubt at all that Niaz would have carried out.

The shadow of a loitering servant that the evening sun had laid across the dusty verandah did not move, and Alex said reflectively: 'Bring my gun. There will be quail and partridge in the open country beyond, and I am stiff from jolting in that dâk *ghari.*'

Niaz grinned appreciatively, and went out to inform the *khansamah* that the sahib wished to shoot and would return to an evening meal which had better be of the first quality or he, Niaz, would have something to say on the subject.

Alex strolled down the shallow stone steps of the verandah and walked slowly away through a mango tope that lay to the left of the bungalow. The low sun thrust shafts of dusty gold between the tree trunks, and a troop of monkeys chattered and quarrelled among the thick leaves. Facing the bungalow the jungle through which the road had run swept almost to the compound wall, but behind it and to the left lay comparatively open country; a few fields where crops of maize and sugar-cane had been planted, grazing-grounds, a glimmer of water that indicated a distant jheel and the probable presence of waterfowl, and the level plains stretching away to the far horizon.

The ground in the mango tope was hard and dry and splashed with the droppings of green pigeons, and a warm shaft of sunlight probing the shadows illuminated a slab of stone crudely carved with the lingam, the emblem of fertility, that stood propped against the bole of a tree. The obscene thing was daubed with red paint and there were offerings heaped upon the ground before it. Humble offerings: a handful of parched grain, a bunch of marigold flowers, a string of red jungle beads and the remains of a *chupatti*—the flat cake of unleavened bread that is the staple food of half India. Two small striped squirrels were tugging at the *chupatti*, and a group of seven-sisters—those drab grey-brown birds who hop and twitter in small gangs like a covey of nervous spinsters—were disposing of the grain.

Alex paused and regarded the crude emblem with some interest. There was nothing at all unusual in the sight, for India was littered with such things. It was the offerings that surprised him. The flowers were unfaded and the grain and the cake of unleavened bread must have been placed here comparatively recently, for the birds and the squirrels would make short work of them. Yet it was unusual for villagers to bring offerings to a shrine at such an hour.

There was a light step behind him and Alex turned to see Niaz who carried a shot-gun and a bag of cartridges. Niaz glanced at the red-daubed emblem of Mahadeo and said cheerfully: 'Misbegotten unbelievers!' He spat on the ground and jerked a thumb over his shoulder in the direction of the bungalow: 'The drivers of two of the dâk *gharis*, and he who drove the *ekka*, brought the offerings. There was, I think, a message also, but it has gone. See, there in the dust——'

The hard dry ground of the mango tope did not hold the print of footmarks well, but the day was windless, and dust, twigs and fallen leaves betrayed a well-worn track from the bungalow to the shrine, while beyond it the print of unshod feet showed where a single man had approached from the direction of the grazing grounds and the open plain, and returned again.

Niaz moved slowly out of the shadows of the tope, his eyes on the ground. Presently he said: 'Here he turns aside and returns to the village. It is an old trick to thrust a message into a *chupatti* and bake it so that it is well hid. But the driver of that *ekka* was a Mussulman and no Hindu.'

Alex nodded without speaking and turned to look out across the plain, his eyes screwed up against the low sunlight. A black partridge called again, and he held out his hand for the gun. He was an excellent shot, and Niaz was carrying half a dozen limp, feathered forms by the time they reached the edge of the jheel— a shallow stretch of water fringed with straggling rushes, stray clumps of elephant grass and a few scanty palms that stood up against the bright evening sky like worn broomsticks.

Alex sat down on a tussock of dry grass at the end of a narrow arm of stony ground that reached out into the jheel, and pulling a packet of papers and pouch of tobacco out of his pocket, rolled two cigarettes—a habit he had acquired in the Crimea— and tossed one over to Niaz who squatted beside him.

Niaz struck a sulphur match on the sole of his shoe, and having lit the cigarettes blew the flame out carefully and flicked the spent match into the placid water. 'There are no ears here,' he remarked approvingly, 'and none can approach by the water. We need watch to landward only.' He drew the tobacco smoke deep into his lungs and expelled it slowly through his nostrils. The evening was warm and very still. So still that they could hear the leap of a little fish a dozen yards away, a quack of water-birds far out on the jheel and the rustle of a small snake that slid through the grass stems.

Alex had learned patience with much else from the East, and he sat relaxed and silent; watching the shadows lengthen and the smoke from his cigarette rise unwaveringly into the quiet air. He knew that Niaz would speak when he wished to, and not before. Meanwhile it was pleasant to sit here and smell the familiar scents of an Indian evening while the sky behind the ragged palm-trees blazed with the spectacular glories of a sunset unimaginable to those who live only in Western countries.

At last Niaz said reflectively: 'I did as thou asked. I took my leave and went on horseback, as befits one of the *risala* (cavalry), to visit those of my relatives in Oudh and Rohilkhand and Jhansi; and from them I heard much. And when that was done I went on foot, and no longer as Niaz Mohamed Khan of

the Company's *Risala*, but as Rahim, a man of no consequence.
From Ludhiana of the Sikhs to the north of my own *ilaqa*, to
Benares of the Unbelievers, and further south to Burdwan went
I, listening to much talk in the twilight and hearing many things
in the bazaars and by the way.'

He was silent for a moment or two, drawing deeply at his cigarette, while the sunset painted his face with a wash of vivid light so
that it seemed to glow like polished bronze, and presently he said:

'Thou wert right, my brother. There is devil's work toward;
and this time it is not a plague that will break out in one spot
only and may thereby be kept from others. This runs north and
south, and the infection is carried by many and to all men. Even
by such as the drivers of these dâk *gharis*!'

'There is always talk,' said Alex laconically, his eyes on a high-
flying wedge of Garganey teal that cut a thin dark pattern against
the evening sky.

'That I know, for when has it ever been otherwise? But this
time it is more than talk.' Niaz cupped his lean brown hands
about the stub of his cigarette and drew on it, his gaze on the
quiet water. 'It has long been a custom of Hind,' he said
slowly, 'for a man who has no heir to adopt one who shall
succeed him; for the son, say the unbelievers, delivers his father
from the hell called *Pat*. If there be no son to perform the
funeral rites, they believe that there can be no resurrection
to eternal bliss. Therefore their priests and lawgivers have permitted the adoption of sons where the male line has failed.
Comes the order of the Company saying that where there is no
male heir of the blood the lands and titles of a prince shall not
pass to any adoptive son, but pass instead into the possession of the
Company, and that man's line shall die out and cease. Thus many
states, by right of lapse, have been swallowed up into the maw of
the Company and their ancient names have become as dust.
Satarah . . . Nagpur . . . Jhansi . . . Sambhalpur . . . Their greatness has departed.'

Alex said softly: 'These be Hindus, O follower of the Prophet!'

'That is so. But now there is Oudh also. And therefore Hindu and Mussulman, unbelievers and the Elect of God, plot together in fear and hatred, and the word goes up and down the land.'

'And what is that word?'

'That the *feringhis* (foreigners) are few and their councils are divided, and that the men of the north, the Russ-*log*, have made a great slaughter of their armies so that there are none left to come to the aid of those in Hind. It runs from *pulton* (regiment) to *pulton*—from *risala* to *risala*. Men on pilgrimage to the shrines of Kashi and Haramukh; merchants, maulvies, sadhus; Mussulman, Brahmin, Sikh and Jain; the woman who draws water at the well and the man who drives a plough—all or any of them may be a carrier of the word. They spill the powder, and when the train is laid it will need but a spark to ignite it.'

Alex flicked his cigarette end into the water where it went out with a little hiss, startling a paddy bird which undisturbed by the rise and fall of Niaz's low voice had pricked through the shallows a yard beyond them. The rose and saffron of the sunset had faded, leaving the sky awash with clear green light in which a single star blazed and glittered in lonely splendour.

Alex rolled another cigarette and said: 'Has that spark been found?'

'Not yet. Those who plot seek for one. It wants only that to set the land alight. But it must be something that touches Mussulman and Hindu alike, for if one rise without the other, the Company, few and weak as they have become, may still triumph. So they search diligently, and wait.'

'Yes,' said Alex reflectively, handing over another cigarette, 'but a thing that will make Mussulman, Hindu and Sikh sink their differences and unite against us will not be easy to find.'

'Doubtless the Company will of their charity supply it!' said Niaz ironically. 'Are thy people blind or mad, or both, that they cannot see what is toward?'

'Neither,' said Alex. 'It is a national conceit. They—we—can only see ourselves as benefactors whom such as thou'—he grinned maliciously at Niaz—'must perforce regard only with admiration and gratitude.'

'And do they never learn?' enquired Niaz scornfully.

'No. We *Angrezis* (British) are as God made us. The mould is set. All this that you have told me, word for word and letter for letter, happened once before some two score years and more ago, in the Kingdom that was Haidar Ali's.'

'I have heard that tale,' grunted Niaz. 'But this time if the fire be lit it will not be so easy to stamp it out, for it will not be in the south only, as it was in that day, but north and west and east also; and many will die in that burning. *I* tell you this! I who have hearkened this past year to the talk in the lines and in the bazaars; in the cities and the *serais* and at the wayside halts!'

Alex shifted restlessly. The swift tropic twilight was almost gone and he could no longer see Niaz's face clearly. He said abruptly: 'All this is talk. Have you proof?'

'*Proof!*' said Niaz, and laughed shortly. 'Spoken like a sahib —*Sahib!*'—he gave that title the same scornful emphasis that Kishan Prasad had once done. 'Have I ever lied to thee that thou shouldst demand proof of what I tell thee as though I were some *vakil* (lawyer) of the court?'

'*Gulam* (slave),' said Alex gently, 'were it not that thou art as my brother in all but blood, I would throw thee into the jheel for that word!'

Niaz flung up a hand in mock appeal: '*Marf karo* (have mercy) —Sahib!'

Alex caught the upflung hand about the wrist and bent it backward, and for a moment the two men wrestled silently, hand against hand.

'Is it to be the jheel, then?' enquired Alex.

'Nay, it is enough! *Marf karo—bhai* (brother).'

'That is better,' said Alex, releasing him.

Niaz rubbed his wrist and grinned. 'At least thy sojourn in *Belait* has not softened thee! But what is that gaud thou art wearing? A love token belike?'

'That——?' Alex looked down at the twisted silver ring with its three small red stones, and shook his head. 'It was given me by a man whom I would have given much to see dead.'

He told the tale and heard Niaz draw a short hissing breath between his teeth at the mention of that name. 'Kishan Prasad!' said Niaz. 'I have heard of that man. And if all that I have heard is true, it had been better that thou hadst cut off thy right hand rather than have given him his life.'

'These things are written,' said Alex philosophically.

'*Beshak!* (assuredly),' said Niaz grimly. 'Nevertheless I think that that bauble will serve its turn. It may yet help thee to this proof that thou hast demanded.'

'It is not for myself that I require proof,' said Alex composedly. 'All that thou hast told me I knew without the telling. But those in authority are hard to convince. The *Burra Lāt Sahib* who has lately gone to his own land has told them that all is well—the land never more peaceful and the people filled with content.'

'More fool he!' grunted Niaz.

'Wherefore,' continued Alex, ignoring the interruption, 'those in high places are unwilling to lend an ear to warnings.'

'As they were in the days before the massacre of Vellore!' interjected Niaz scornfully.

'Yes. As in the days before Vellore. There is a saying among our people that those whom the gods would destroy they first make mad.'

'A true saying indeed,' said Niaz. 'But thou shalt have thy proof, though small good will it give thee!'

'Ah!' said Alex, his eyes suddenly bright. 'I thought that there was something more. Tell me swiftly and let us have no more of this talk that runs in circles.'

Niaz laughed. ' "We are as God made us," ' he quoted. ' "The mould is set." It is only the English who rush straight upon the heart of the matter looking neither to the right hand nor to the left. Yes, there is indeed something more. I would not have troubled thee on account of bazaar rumours.'

He glanced uneasily over his shoulder as though to make sure that there could be no third person near them, and despite the fact that nothing larger than a jackal could possibly have approached unseen to within fifty yards of them he lowered his voice until it was barely audible.

'I have learned,' whispered Niaz, 'that there is to be a meeting of certain men in a place near Khanwai that lies to the north of Bithaur within the borders of Oudh. It is dangerous knowledge and known only to a few. Perhaps a hundred in all Hind: no more.'

'And how didst *thou* come by it?' enquired Alex softly.

Niaz threw his hands out palm upwards in a brief, indescribable gesture. 'A woman. How else? Her husband is old and moreover he drinks wine. The Prophet forbade the drinking of wine, and rightly, for by indulgence in this are tongues loosened and many plans brought to ruin. When a woman has discovered a matter that should be hid she will tell it for idleness or mischief or'—Niaz grinned—'for love's sake.'

'But is it true talk that she has told thee?'

'It is true. That I would swear on my life. I do not know what it is that they who meet will speak of or do, but this I know—that it bodes no good. And I have had the thought that it would be well if we two learned what is afoot. It is set for a night but twelve days hence, when there is a fair at Khanwai. I have been to spy out the land. The place of meeting is a ruin; no more than a handful of stones and a broken wall which the jungle has swallowed. A foolish spot for such talk, but these men are assuredly bitten with madness. There is but one path to it, for the jungle grows thick behind it, and that path leads through a deep nullah where was once a gateway that has fallen. Only one man at a time can pass through, and each as they pass must say a word. That word I have.'

Once again Niaz paused to peer into the gathering dusk, and in the silence they heard from somewhere far out across the darkening plains a jackal howling at the evening star. Niaz's gaze returned to Alex and even the green dusk could not disguise the glitter of his eyes and the flash of his teeth.

'You old devil!' said Alex in English—the same glitter in his own eyes. 'Niaz, thou wilt surely end thy days in a hangman's noose! Was the overturning of that dâk *ghari* thy work?'

Niaz waved a deprecatory hand. 'I judged it to be necessary,' he said airily. 'Also the driver was an un-friend of mine. I owed him somewhat in the matter of repayment for certain insolence that he had spoken. He was an eater of opium and he dozed upon the box. A twitch of the reins, and the thing was done.'

'And if my neck had been broken, O son of Eblis?'

'There was no fear of that. A few scratches and a bruise or two at most. No more. It was necessary that we should separate ourselves from those others who travelled by the road. Do we go to Khanwai?'

'Assuredly!' said Alex, and laughed. It was a laugh that men hear sometimes in the heat of battle or as the order is given for a cavalry charge, and that no woman would recognize. Niaz recognized it and his own laugh answered and echoed it.

A rush of wings swept the darkening sky above them and Alex snatched up his gun and fired. There were two splashes within a yard of each other some twenty feet away, and the placid surface of the jheel broke into ripples that spread out across the water in ever-widening circles to slap against the rushes. Niaz came to his feet in one lithe movement and waded out to retrieve the fallen birds as Alex snapped open the smoking breech and ejected the spent cartridges.

'That is a new toy,' said Niaz returning. 'I have not seen one that is loaded thus before.' He examined the mechanism of the pin-fire breech-loading gun with interest, peering at it in the dim light, and then snapping it shut he shouldered it and picked up the dead birds: 'Come; it is time we returned.'

10

TEN days later an itinerant toy-seller, his pack laden with crudely painted plaster trifles, trudged down the dusty road that led from Cawnpore into Oudh. He had no assistant, but he was of a

F

cheerful and gregarious disposition and always ready to enter into conversation with fellow travellers upon the road and at the wayside halts. At one of these he had attached himself to a party of jugglers who were proceeding to the fair at Khanwai, a small village on the borders of Oudh not far from Bithaur.

His ready wit and the quick-fire patter with which he accompanied the sale of his gimcrack toys appealed to the leader of the troupe, and after some haggling it was agreed that the man, Jatu by name, should act as barker to the jugglers in the intervals of pursuing his own trade. In return for which the troupe would provide him with food and, if profits allowed, a small percentage of the takings; an arrangement that appeared highly satisfactory to all.

From the opposite direction, that of Fathigarh, a slim, wiry Pathan, sitting astride a bony and bad-tempered down-country stallion and trailed by two sorry-looking hacks on a lead rein, was also riding towards the fair at Khanwai. His dress and speech, and the hard, light-coloured eyes in the brown face, proclaimed him as a son of the border tribe of the Yusafzai, and he too was of a cheerful disposition, for he sang the songs of the Border—the more questionable ones—as he rode, and was always ready to fall into talk with any he met upon the way.

His cousin Assad Ali, he explained to any who were interested, had brought a string of horses down from the north hoping to sell them for greater profit in the Punjab and Rohilkhand. He had done well with his string but he had died of the cholera at a village on the outskirts of Delhi, and his horseboys, fearing the disease, had run away taking with them the greater part of the profits, so that now he, Sher Dil, with only three unsaleable hacks picked up at Karnal, had taken the road alone, hoping to dispose of them farther south. He had heard talk of a fair at Khanwai and intended to try his luck there. He carried a long Pathan knife in his broad waist-belt and an antiquated but serviceable *jezail* slung over his shoulder, and he took for preference the centre of the road. Alex had always been a believer in the old saying that it is darkest under the lamp.

The town of Khanwai was little more than a village, and distinguished only by an annual fair which was held in honour of a treaty between two warring clans who centuries ago had endeavoured to exterminate each other for reasons long lost sight of in the mists of time. The fairground was surrounded by the booths of sweetmeat-sellers, toy-makers and hucksters, and there was plenty to entertain the idle: jugglers, acrobats, fire-eaters, a sad and ragged performing bear, snake-charmers, and fortune-tellers. And as night fell a troupe of firework-makers brightened the sky with a display of their wares and frightened the timorous with the crash of exploding rockets. But as the fireworks flared, dyeing the awed faces of the spectators red, green and amber by turns, it might have been noted, had any been interested in such a thing, that sundry men were drifting away from the fairground by ones and twos and making their way through the fields beyond the village to the uncultivated land and the dark barrier of jungle that backed on to the grazing grounds.

Sher Dil of the Yusafzai, following the same path, caught his garments on an unseen branch of thorn tree and swore softly and fluently in Pushtoo as he freed himself, and a shadow that followed noiselessly on his heels lengthened its stride and spoke in a whisper: '*Hai!* thou from the north——' Alex checked and his hand went to the knife in his belt '——what dost thou here? Thou art a Pathan, and no man of Hind.'

'I come that I may carry the word to those who wait beyond the Border,' replied Alex in whispered Urdu. 'And thou?'

'I likewise; but to Bengal go I. To Berhampore by Murshidabad. Of what *pulton* art thou?'

'Of none. But my cousin's brother is a Duffardar in the Guides,' said Alex mendaciously. 'He too is like-minded with us. And thy regiment?'

'The 19th Bengal Infantry.' He was a sepoy on leave; a lance-naik and a man of some influence in his regiment. He hurried on ahead and was lost in the shadows.

The flare of the fireworks from the fairground lit the path with intermittent flashes of light, and in these brief glimpses Alex could see that there were men ahead and behind him, hurrying forward down the narrow track that wound between thickets of thorn, bamboos, *dhâk* trees and elephant grass, but keeping a safe distance from each other. Niaz had studied the ground with the eye of a general, and a map that he had drawn in the dust of the roadside, though crude, had been remarkably accurate, so that even by night and on strange ground Alex could guess the lie of the land and knew what to expect.

The path—it was little more than a goat-track—wandered with apparent aimlessness between tall clumps of grass and finally descended a sandy slope into a dry nullah. To the right the nullah ran straight on into the darkness, but to the left it narrowed and appeared to be blocked by a fall of rock. The sepoy could not have been half a dozen yards ahead, but he had vanished, and Alex, turning unhesitatingly to the left, was once again grateful for the care with which Niaz had reconnoitred the ground. There was a space between two huge slabs of fallen rock that would have been invisible to one who was not aware of it, for the rocks overlapped each other and were overgrown with creepers and the roots of a tree, and only a close inspection by full daylight would have discovered the gap. It was barely wide enough to allow one at a time to enter it, and behind it—Niaz had told him—lay a narrow, walled tunnel; for this had once been the outer gateway of a fortress whose walls ran back to left and right, hidden and overgrown by the trees and creeper of the jungle. Alex heard feet slither on the path behind him as another conspirator entered the nullah, and he set his teeth and walked between the rocks.

He had taken no more than four steps in the blackness when his outstretched hands touched the shaft of a spear that barred his way. It dropped instantly and after a moment's pause he moved forward again and heard it lift once more behind him, and heard, too, a man's quick breathing. 'Making sure we go through one at a time,' thought Alex grimly. He could see no glimmer of light and his hands brushed against rough stonework. Niaz had said that the tunnel of the ruined gateway was no more than eight fair paces in length; that meant that there was something or someone blocking the far end of it. And then he saw a glimpse of greyness and something touched his chest—an iron-bound *lathi* such as night-watchmen carry—and a voice almost in his ear whispered: 'Give the word.'

' "*A goat for Kali.*" '

'Pass, brother.' The *lathi* dropped and Alex moved on into the open air.

The sides of the nullah were steeper and narrower here than on the far side of the concealed entrance, and the jungle arched above it and excluded the moonlight so that the place was almost as dark as the tunnel behind it. Then the darkness thinned and torchlight glowed through the undergrowth ahead, and presently the track ran out into a clearing before the ruins of a long-forgotten fort or palace.

The starlight and a half-moon, the flaming torches and the occasional flare of a rocket illuminated roofless walls and fallen pillars half-hidden by weeds and creepers. A giant peepul tree split the stones of what had once been a hall of audience, and in the uncertain light it was difficult to tell which were fallen pillars and which the roots of the great tree. India is full of such ruins; relics of cities and dynasties that have passed away and been forgotten; the haunt of snakes, foxes and monkeys and the lair of the wild boar.

It seemed to Alex an odd spot to choose for a meeting of malcontents, except that there was little doubt that the place had a certain eerie atmosphere about it, and though it lay less than half a mile from Khanwai and the beaten track, its presence would never have been suspected by the casual passer-by. He could see now that the clearing was not a natural one, but the remains of what had once been a large stone-paved courtyard open to the sky. Thorn bushes and the tough jungle grass had thrust their way between the sandstone blocks, but the jungle had been unable to obliterate them, and stood back from it, walling it about with impenetrable vegetation.

The open space was crowded with shadowy figures and sibilant with whispering voices, and Alex stood still, the lance-naik of the

19th breathing heavily beside him. At the far side of the square before the ruined entrance to a roofless hall stood two men holding torches—flaring country-made things of dried grass, branches and pitch. They stood as though waiting, and the orange light flickered weirdly on the rolling eyeballs of the shifting, whispering crowd and threw grotesque shadows on the wall of the watching jungle.

Presently there was a stir among the men at Alex's back and the crowd drew aside, Alex with them, as half a dozen men muffled in dark cloaks entered the clearing by way of the nullah. It seemed that they had been expected, for the crowd made a lane for them, parting to left and right, and they passed quickly through and came to a stop before the torch-bearers. They stood for a few moments talking in undertones with a small group of men who had apparently been waiting for them, while the crowd ceased its whispering to listen.

Alex was too far away to hear what was said, and it is doubtful if any but a handful heard them, for at that point the fireworks on the distant fairground let off a very fusillade of rockets. 'This is too easy,' thought Alex, waiting for them to mount the ruined steps behind them from which he imagined that they would harangue the crowd. 'There must be a catch in it somewhere.' A line from a nursery-rhyme drifted through his brain: '*Will you walk into my parlour? said the spider to the fly.*' It had been easy enough to walk in—would it be as easy to walk out again?

The group of men by the torch-bearers turned, but they did not mount the steps behind them as Alex had half-expected. They walked between the torches and simply disappeared as though the ground itself had opened and swallowed them up.

From where Alex stood the illusion was so complete that he heard the men about him gasp and shrink back, and saw the sepoy put up a hand to clutch at some hidden amulet he wore concealed under his shirt. Then the crowd began to move forward slowly and Alex realized suddenly that the torch-bearers stood either side of a shaft that descended into the ground, and as he drew nearer he saw that the two men with the torches scrutinized the faces

of all who went past them. A hand touched him in the press and
he turned to see Jatu, the seller of toys.

'They will never let me pass. Try the ring!' The words were
barely a breath against his ear and then the man had melted
into the darkness and was gone.

*   *   *

Alex moved forward, a step at a time. He was conscious of a
cold tingling sensation between his shoulder-blades and was
aware that his mouth was dry. For a fleeting moment he wondered
what would happen if the ring meant nothing to the guardians
of the shaft. Would they let him stand to one side and wait as
others were waiting, or would they——? The light of the torches
flared full in his face and his nerves tightened and leapt, but the
hand he held out was entirely steady.

The three small stones in Kishan Prasad's ring gleamed redly
in the torchlight, and the ring appeared a small and insignificant
thing; but the men who held the torches evidently recognized it.
One of them, bending forward to stare at it, muttered something
that Alex did not catch, and salaamed low, and Alex walked
between them and down a steep narrow flight of steps, aware that
the palms of his hands were wet and that there were drops of cold
sweat on his forehead.

The entrance to the shaft had been concealed by a huge flag-
stone that had been drawn up with ropes, and it must have taken
at least two men, and probably more, to move it. The walls of
the shaft were smooth and dry and the worn steps so steep and
narrow that only one man at a time could possibly have descended
them. They went down farther into the ground than Alex
would have believed possible, and once again he had the sensation
of walking into a trap. A bat flew up past him, its leathery wings
brushing his cheek—proof at least that there was some other
entrance—and then he had reached the foot of the steps at last
and was standing in a vaulted chamber, the roof of which was
supported by crude stone pillars.

It was impossible to gauge the full extent of the underground room, for the walls beyond the pillars were lost in darkness and the only illumination was supplied by a single brazier supported on an iron tripod that stood at the far end of the vault, in which an uneasy flame burned flickeringly. The stone floor and the pillars were slimy to the touch, and not dry as were the walls of the stair shaft, and in the faint light of the brazier Alex could see tree roots that had thrust down between the curved slabs of the vaulted ceiling. That accounted for the bats and the fact that the air was breathable. Perhaps this underground room had once held the hoarded treasures of a king, or been used for some dark priestly purpose. Possibly the latter, for there appeared to be carvings on the wall behind the brazier.

There seemed to be about thirty or forty men squatting on the stone floor between the pillars, but it was difficult to tell in that uncertain light whether there were more of them whom Alex could not see. He edged his way towards a pillar and squatted down by it, Indian fashion, keeping his back to the stone. He could hear hard breathing all about him and smell the rank smell of unwashed human bodies, and as his eyes became accustomed to the dimness he saw that many of those present were sadhus— holy men of all sects and persuasions—wild-eyed and ash-smeared, naked or wearing the ill-cured skins of animals, their long hair matted and hideous. Bairagis, Sannyasis, Bikshus, Paryrajakas; Aghorins whose custom it is to steal and eat the flesh of corpses; devil worshippers, mendicants and mystics.

Alex shuddered and felt his skin crawl, and was grateful for the feel of the dank stone at his back. But it was not the presence of the Hindu ascetics that made him afraid. It was the unbelievable, impossible fact that there were others in that ill-lit underground vault. Not only Sikhs, but Mussulmans also; followers of the Prophet to whom all Hindus were dogs of unbelievers, crouching side by side with the worshippers of Shiva the destroyer, of Vishnu and Brahma and Ganesh of the Elephant head, of many-armed Mother Kali the drinker of blood, and of a hundred other gods and godlings. It was true, then. Mussulman and Hindu were prepared to unite against the men of John

Company—against the white-faced foreign conquerors whose dominion had lasted for a hundred years. Nothing but a common cause and a common hatred could have brought about this weird gathering.

A man stood up at the far end of the chamber, towering above the crouching figures that filled the aisle between the stone pillars. His back was to the fitful flame of the brazier and Alex could not see his face, but the voice and dress told him much.

The man was a Mussulman and probably from Oudh. A tall man with a silver tongue. He spoke quietly and with a curious suggestion of a chant; the voice of a priest or a story-teller; and the tale he told was the story of a conquered people—oppressed, cheated, robbed and exploited by the men from the West, from the land beyond the Black Water. He spoke of kings and princes who had died fighting the Company, or been defrauded of their rights. Of great names and great houses that had become as the blown sands of the deserts of Bikaner. Of cherished laws and customs and religious freedoms that had been curtailed or put aside. Of sheltered zenana women, queens and princesses in their own right, sent to beg their bread in the streets.

His voice rose and sank and the men before him swayed and groaned in unison as though they were so many puppets pulled upon a single string. Even Alex, listening—Alex who knew just how much of that tale was truth and how much fable, exaggeration or falsehood—found himself stirred to anger or intolerably moved by that wild, bitter, sorrowful saga. He forgot that he was an Englishman and a servant of the Company, and swayed and groaned with the swaying, groaning mob.

He did not know for how long the man spoke—it might have been for an hour, or two hours, or three. The flame in the brazier flickered and danced and the shadow of the speaker leapt and shrank and leapt again across that motley mob of listening men with an effect as hypnotic as the remarkable voice. The man ended with an impassioned plea for unity: 'They of the Company be few! A handful only, scattered up and down the land. We of Hind have risen against them many times, but the risings have

F*

always failed. They have failed because we of this land were divided one against the other. But it is well known that ten men with one heart are equal to a hundred men with different hearts; and it needs only this—that we hold together with one heart—and we are rid of them for ever. Let us put aside our differences and strike as one!'

He flung up his arms with a wild gesture and the crowd gasped and shrank back, for a green fire seemed to run up his arms and leap for a moment from his spread fingers. But the spell had snapped for Alex. He had seen that trick performed by an illusionist at a London theatre, and sanity returned to him: and with it an icy sense of danger. If this man could sway others as he had swayed this bigoted, caste-ridden, creed-divided assembly tonight, he was more dangerous to the Company than anything that had as yet risen against them.

Another man was speaking. A Hindu this time. His theme was the same, but his shrill, impassioned oratory lacked the almost hypnotic appeal of the previous speaker, and Alex allowed his attention to wander, and concentrated instead on trying to memorize as many as possible of the audience and to file their features away for future use. It was no easy task in that wavering light, but there were several faces that he thought he would recognize again.

The talk went on and on and Alex shifted restlessly. During his first years in India, when he and Niaz would take leave together and go off shooting, he had taught himself to squat native-fashion on his heels. It had amused him to study and copy the habits and customs and speech of many kinds of men—a game which Niaz, who was a natural mimic, had entered into with enthusiasm—but his grey eyes had made it impossible for him to pass as any but a hill-man or a northerner, and so he had selected his present role and worked hard to perfect himself in it. He had used it upon several occasions, in company with Niaz, to gain sorely needed information, but he had spent the last year and more in Europe, and his muscles had grown unused to the treatment they were receiving. They ached abominably and he wondered how much longer this performance was going to last, and if he had not already heard sufficient for his purpose.

Yet another man was speaking. A sadhu this time. His message was less general and more specific. Spread the word! Carry it into every town and every village. Tell every man to be ready; to procure arms and secrete them; to steal them if necessary! To sharpen his sword, his axe or his knife and to tip his *lathi* with iron. The coming year was the Year of the Prophecy in which the Hundred Years of Subjection would be accomplished. Man, woman and child, the oppressor would be slain, so that not one would remain to carry the tale to the West.

'Carry the word! Carry the word!' The hoarse hysterical voice rang and echoed uncannily under the vaulted stone. 'See! now we prepare a sign as in the old days, so that all men may know!'

A shaven priest arose and threw something on the brazier and the flame flared up with a sudden intolerable brightness that for a brief moment threw the avid faces into harsh relief. It died again and in the near darkness that followed a second priest began a chant that was taken up by other voices.

The light flickered up again, though dimly, and the two priests moved about it, coming and going. The crowd craned their necks to see, and Alex would have given much to stand upright and look over the heads and backs that obscured his view, but he did not dare to draw attention to himself by doing so. He could catch only glimpses between the silhouetted heads. Something was being poured on to a platter; it appeared to be *ata*—the coarse-ground flour of the villages. A man squatting near the brazier began to beat on a small drum; softly at first, so that it was barely more than a rhythmic accompaniment to the chant, but growing slowly louder and more insistent. Gradually the chant changed its note and became a frenzied incantation, and Alex recognized it as a hymn to Kali.

'*Kali! Kali! Oh dreadful-toothed goddess! Devour, cut, destroy all the malignant—cut with an axe! Bind, bind, seize! Drink blood! Secure, secure! Salutation to Kali!*'

The ranks of half-seen men began to jerk and sway and once more one of the two priests flung something on the brazier. But this time the brief flare of the flame was followed by a dense smoke that whirled upward and filled the darkness with a choking smell akin to incense: a heady, stupefying smell that drugged and yet exhilarated. The other priest who had moved back into the shadows returned dragging something that struggled feebly and gave a small bleating cry. A sacrifice, of course, thought Alex. '*A white goat for Kali.*' They would cut the creature's throat with suitable ritual.

He saw the light glint on the long blade of a knife, and the men nearest the priests and the brazier drew back and caught their breath in a harsh and simultaneous gasp that was clearly audible above the thudding beat of the drum. A shudder swept back through the crowd as a wave sweeps in from the open sea, so that even those who could not see felt the surge of that savage emotion, and Alex was seized with a sudden sick horror, inexplicable and paralysing. A horror that crisped his hair and dried his mouth and brought the cold sweat out on his forehead.

He would have moved then if he could, but he could not. His muscles would not obey him, for he was helplessly afraid with a fear that he had never known before. A primitive, primeval fear; not of death, but of Evil. . . . He could hear the harsh panting breath of the men about him, and it seemed to him as though they breathed as a pack of wolves might breathe; avidly, tongues lolling, circling about a wounded buck.

The smoke from the brazier faded and the flame leapt clear, and as it did so a man near it sprang to his feet with a hoarse cry. It was, thought Alex, the tall man who had first spoken, and for a moment his face showed clear in the leaping light: a harsh, hawk-nosed face whose deep-set eyes were white-ringed with horror. He called out something that Alex did not hear, for the drum beat louder and the chant rose to a frenzy. Someone in the crowd pulled the man back, and the knife flashed and fell. There was a bubbling, agonized cry, shrill and high and almost instantly drowned in the concerted groaning howl of the crowd.

But it had not been an animal's cry, and Alex stumbled to his feet and stood pressed against the slimy stone of the pillar, and saw what it was that had cried out.

It was not the body of a white goat that lay on the slab of stained and reeking stone below the flickering brazier, but the naked body of a child. A white child. Alex caught a momentary glimpse of yellow hair and a small mouth that gaped from that last shriek of terror, above the gaping scarlet gash of the severed throat. It was a boy of no more than three or four years of age, his small body startlingly white against the dark stone and the bright blood.

A blind, killing rage laid hold of Alex, blotting out reason and any thought of caution. His hand fumbled in the breast of the flowing Pathan shirt and closed upon the warm metal of the pistol he carried hidden there. At that range he could not miss the priest who stood above the child's body. He would kill him and his fellow priest who held the bowl, and three others. And after that there was still his knife. . . .

He jerked out the pistol and levelled it, and as he did so the man immediately in front of him rose, momentarily blocking his view, and turned to grope his way into the blackness beyond the line of pillars. But that moment had been enough. Sanity returned to Alex and the red fog of rage cleared from his brain. There were more important things at stake than avenging the slaughter of a child. The lives and safety of other children and of countless men and women might hang upon his ability to leave that underground den alive. It would do no good to anyone were he to die too, even though he were to take a dozen of that evil company with him to the grave. The thing was too big. It would go forward and spread, and there would be one less voice to cry a warning. Niaz too would not live to tell that tale, for he too would fight.

Alex slid the pistol back into hiding and wiped the sweat out of his eyes. The horrible ritual of the sacrifice had drawn all eyes and there had been no one watching him. He sank down again on to his heels and found that he was shivering violently. The man who had stolen away into the darkness had left him a clearer field of vision, and once more someone threw a substance on the brazier which hissed and flared and burnt with a bright flame, throwing the faces nearest to it into strong relief. One face in particular caught Alex's attention. A dark gloating face contorted with hate and excitement; the eyes wide and glittering and avid. Red stones—rubies from their colour—adorned his ears and flashed upon his quivering hands. 'I shall know that man again, at least,' thought Alex.

There was some ritual being performed that he could see but not understand, and then he realized that the fresh blood was being mixed with the flour on the platter. He caught the familiar movements of kneading that he had seen a thousand times before in the lines and beside camp-fires and in the bazaars. They were making a *chupatti*; the daily bread of India. To the droning accompaniment of strange incantations and the ceaseless, maddening thud of the drum the cake was kneaded, shaped, flattened and baked on a metal platter laid across the glowing brazier. And all the while, to the sound of that chanting, the rows of watching men swayed and bowed and grovelled in a state of half-hypnotic frenzy.

At last the platter was lifted off the fire and the priests of Kali broke up the cake that smoked upon it, mumbling and grunting invocations to gods and devils—invocations as old and as evil as those chanted in the temples of Moloch. The man with the ruby earrings was handed a square of silk by someone behind him, and laying it across his hands he received the broken pieces of the *chupatti* from the priests.

'Let the token be sent forth!' howled the tallest of the priests, tossing his arms above his head. 'Let it go up and down the land. From the north to the south, from the east to the west! And wheresoever it passes, there shall men's hearts be turned to hatred of the oppressors. For this is the pestilence—this is the evil—this is the blood of the British!' His eyeballs rolled in his head and there was froth on his lips. 'Hear me, Kali! Hear me, O drinker of blood! From the north to the south! From the east to the west!'

He fell to the ground and writhed upon the stone floor as the second priest flung oil into the brazier and a crackling flame leapt upwards to the roof, blazed furiously for a moment and died. The drum crashed and was still. The chanting ceased on a long wailing note and the vault was plunged into darkness and silence—a darkness in which only the red coals of the brazier gleamed like a single malignant eye.

A cold voice spoke softly into that silence: 'This that ye have witnessed shall be binding upon all; for were it known, there is not one here whom the *feringhis* would not hang at a rope's end for this night's work. In the eyes of the Company's Government all who have seen it would be held guilty of the blood that has been shed. It were well to remember this, lest any be tempted to speak unwisely.' The voice ceased, and presently man after man rose noiselessly and groped their way to the stair shaft to pass up it and out into the clean night air.

Once there they did not linger, but seemed anxious to avoid each other's company, emerging from the shaft like ants debouching from a hole in the ground, to hurry furtively away into the darkness.

The torch-bearers had gone and the stone-paved square with its surrounding wall of jungle was shadowy under the starlight and the waning moon. Alex made his way down the black length of the nullah, guided by a spark of light that proved to be a single *chirag*—a tiny earthenware saucer filled with oil in which a wisp of cotton did duty as a wick—which had been left on a ledge by the narrow cleft of the gateway. He saw the spark vanish briefly as the man ahead of him passed in front of it and entered the tunnel, and then he himself had reached it.

11

THREE minutes later Alex was climbing the goat-track on the far side of the nullah and presently he was among the high grass at the edge of the plain.

A hand touched his arm as he passed under the black shadow of a thorn tree, and a voice whispered: 'It is I, brother!'

'Back!' said Alex softly. He caught Niaz by the wrist and dragged him swiftly back into the high grass beside the path, crouching down beside him. A moment later another man climbed the slope out of the nullah and passed along the path at a jog-trot. It was a sadhu, his ash-smeared body grey in the moonlight. 'Down,' whispered Alex to Niaz, who would have moved. 'Keep down!' They flattened themselves against the dry warm ground in the shelter of the dusty, sharp-edged grass and lay still as man after man hurried silently along the narrow goat-track towards the distant village, each man keeping his distance from the next and each one glancing furtively from left to right and quickly over his shoulder: sadhus, sepoys, merchants, townsmen and zemindars; followers of the Prophet or wearers of the sacred thread; disciples of Baba Nanak, and worshippers of Kali.

'Divide and rule,' thought Alex watching them as they passed, their feet almost noiseless on the dusty goat-track and their breathing loud in the warm silence of the late September night. As long as these people were divided by their castes and their creeds into antagonistic factions they would always be at the mercy of a conqueror, but if they once combined they could stand against any from sheer weight of numbers. 'But they will never combine,' thought Alex. 'Never. Half of them hate each other more than they hate us. This will not last. . . .'

Niaz jerked at his sleeve and whispered: 'Why do we wait? It is not good to linger here. Let us go.'

'Hush,' said Alex softly. 'There is a debt to pay. When these have gone we go back. There are some few who will remain. The priests will leave last, for there is work to do. They cannot leave the dead unburied.'

'Has there been killing, then?'

'Yes. Quiet—here is another——'

Two men this time. One tall and turbaned, his hawk nose clear-cut against the starlight; the other stout and muffled in a

shawl that was wound about his shoulders and over his head as
though to guard against the night air. The tall man did not walk
furtively as the others had done. He strode past, brushing
against the grasses, careless of noise, and although he spoke in an
undertone his words were clearly audible.

'Dogs and devil-worshippers!' said the tall man furiously.
'Must they stoop to such filth to ensure that none shall betray
them for gain? Now are all our heads forfeit for this night's
work!'

'Hush!—oh, hush!' begged the stout man, pausing to peer
anxiously over his shoulder. 'Surely thine is forfeit already,
Maulvi Sahib, for the words thou hast spoken against the
Angrezis.'

'They will not hang me for a word,' said the tall man scornfully, 'for with the purblind vanity of their race they do not fear
such talk. But let them but hear of this killing and they will
hunt us down like mad jackals—each one of us! Dogs and devil
worshippers——!' The sound of their voices faded as they
disappeared into the darkness.

'That is Ahmed Ullah, a Talukdar of Faizabad,' whispered
Niaz. 'He is one who goes up and down the land speaking against
the Company's Raj. They call him the Maulvi of Faizabad.'

At last the steady procession of shadowy figures ceased and for
a full ten minutes no one passed along the narrow path. Alex
stood up with infinite caution and remained for a further minute
or two listening intently. The moon hung low in the sky like
a pallid wedge of sweet lime above the dark tangle of cane brake
and *kikar* trees, and the night was silent and nothing moved.

'It is foolishness to go back into the tiger's lair having once
escaped,' said Niaz. 'Forgo thy revenge and come away. There
is more in this than one life.'

'It was a child,' said Alex. 'An *Angrezi* child.'

'Ah!' said Niaz. 'Let us go back, then.'

There was no other way of reaching the ruined fort except by
the way they had taken before, and they crept down the steep
sandy slope that led back into the nullah, their nerves tensing to

each rattle of a dislodged pebble or slither of dry earth crumbling beneath their feet. The bed of the nullah was by now in complete darkness, but Niaz possessed eyes like a cat and though Alex was not his equal in this he could see well enough not to be unduly troubled by it.

The huge stone-paved courtyard lay bathed in starlight in which the clumps of coarse grass, thorn and stunted saplings that had thrust up here and there between the paving stones took on the appearance of crouching men, but nothing stirred except a breath of night wind in the grasses. The two men stole forward silently, moving from one clump of shadow to the next, and reached the shelter of the peepul tree that straddled the entrance to the roofless hall.

The block of stone that closed the shaft still leant upright against the lowest step of the ruined stair that rose behind it, and from the shaft itself came a dim glow of light and the sound of a man's voice, faintly familiar and speaking in tones of cold rage:

'—so all are endangered!'

'Nay, all are now bound one to another!' replied another voice, a shrill, hysterical voice. 'None dare now betray us, for all are guilty of the blood—as thou thyself hast said! They will keep silence for their lives' sake. And was not this thing thine own scheme? A ruse—an excellent ruse!—for the unsettling of men's minds? The making of this first one with spells and priests and incantations and the calling up of spirits, so that the tale of its beginning might hasten the work? For such things a sacrifice is necessary—yes, necessary!'

'A goat!' snapped the first voice. 'Had I known that aught else were planned——'

'Yea, a goat!' interrupted the second speaker. '*A white goat for Kali!* It was thyself who chose that password! But now'— the voice rose shrilly—'now is the spell doubly sure! Of what use to Mother Kali is the blood of one starveling *bukri* when we may offer her the blood of a thousand—nay, a hundred thousand! *feringhis*? In this sacrifice we have given a sign and a promise of that which is to come! A child of the Abominable Ones—the eaters of cattle, the defilers of caste!—a male child. May it be the first of many! Would that their throats were as one throat, men, women and children together, that I might slit them with one stroke!' The voice rose until it was a scream of rage.

'That would I too,' said the first speaker. 'But to slaughter a defenceless babe in this fashion is an abomination before Gods and men!'

'Thou wouldst spare the young of the serpent? Pho! That is indeed folly! One such, if allowed to live, will one day sire many! They must be destroyed; leaf and branch, root and seed! Not one must be spared. Not one—*not one!*'

Alex heard the man stamp his feet furiously upon the ground so that the vault echoed. There was a brief silence and then the first speaker said shortly: 'Well, it is done now and it cannot be undone. But though this may do well enough for the villages it will not serve for the sepoys. For them it must be something that strikes deeper and that touches every man. They are already as tinder, but there is as yet no spark. No matter; we will find it.'

Alex felt a touch on his arm and Niaz whispered in his ear: 'Let us let down the stone. I do not think they will lift it from below. They will be trapped like rats and die slowly.'

Alex's eyes gleamed in the starlight and he rose to his feet, and then checked and shook his head. 'No. They could, I think, find a way out. There are bats in that place, and where a bat can enter men might burrow a way out. We will wait. They must come up one by one.'

A moment later a head appeared above the hole in the paving. Niaz's muscles tensed involuntarily but Alex's fingers clamped down upon his arm and checked him as four men, one after another, emerged from the shaft, the light from the vault below glimmering redly on the rubies that one of them wore in his ears. The men conferred together in whispers and he of the earrings said querulously: 'It is late, and I have far to go before morning. The two down there can close the stair. Let us go.' It was the same voice that Alex had heard screaming shrilly of death.

One of the men turned and called down the shaft: 'We go now. Close the stone when all is finished.' The faint light from below brightened for a brief moment as though more fuel had been thrown on the brazier, and for an instant the speaker's face showed clear against the surrounding darkness. It was Kishan Prasad. The next moment the group by the stair shaft had turned away and vanished as quietly as they had come, and the night was silent again.

The two who crouched in the shadow of the peepul tree did not move for a full five minutes after the last faint rustle had died away, and then Alex rose and crept forward, and after a moment Niaz followed him. They crouched down on either side of the tilted slab of stone and waited, listening to the faint sounds from below while the shrunken moon sank below the horizon and the sky darkened. A jackal howled mournfully from the plain beyond the jungle and a little breeze awoke and rustled through the surrounding scrub, whispering through the leaves of the peepul tree and filling the silent night with a hundred small stealthy sounds.

At last the light below was extinguished and presently feet groped on the stairs and a man's head lifted out of the black well of the stair shaft. Alex waited until his shoulders were clear of the shaft and then he reached out and took him round the throat. The man uttered one choking gasp and then he was struggling frantically, his hands clawing the air. His bare feet beat a tattoo against the steep stone steps, and Alex lifted him clear with one savage heave as though he had been of no more weight than a sack of vegetables.

'What is it? Hast thou fallen?' said a voice from the darkness below, and a second head appeared above the pavement. Niaz's lean fingers closed about the fat throat and he jerked the man up and backwards across the rim of the shaft and brought his head down upon the stone with a sharp sound like the cracking of an egg. It was enough.

'This one at least will cut no more throats,' said Niaz. 'Is thine sped?'

'Yes,' said Alex breathlessly, and let the limp thing drop in a huddled heap at his feet. His hands were wet and sticky with the blood that had burst from the man's mouth and nostrils, and he stooped, panting, and wiped them on the priestly robes.

'What now?' asked Niaz.

'Throw them back. If any raise the stone to seek for them, they shall find them waiting.'

They tumbled the bodies back into the shaft and lowered the stone above it. They could not see how the thing had been raised or on what principle the two dead priests could have lowered it into place, and they had no time to discover the trick of it. They put their shoulders to it and discovered that it took the last ounce of their combined strength to send it crashing into place. The noise of its fall broke the silence of the night as though it had been the crash of a cannon, and awoke a hundred echoes from the ruined walls.

'Quick,' gasped Niaz. 'If there be any within earshot they may return.'

They ran together across the wide, ruined courtyard and plunged into the blackness of the nullah, and ten minutes later they had reached the edge of the grazing grounds and the grove of trees where Alex had tethered the horses.

'Where now?' whispered Niaz, mounting a fidgeting horse with an ease that consorted ill with the character of Jatu the toy-seller.

'Lunjore. I go by way of Pari.'

'It were better to take a road south of Gunga,' said Niaz. 'It is not safe to ride the roads of Oudh after this night's work.'

'No roads are safe now,' said Alex grimly.

'True. Let us go swiftly, for in another hour it will be dawn. I would that I had my own mare between my knees in place of this bag of bones!'

By first light they were no more than a dozen miles from Khanwai, for the roads were rough and now that the moon had set the darkness made it necessary for them to keep the horses to a walk. As the dawn broke and the morning mists turned from silver-grey to rose and saffron and the long low veils of smoke from the cow-dung fires of the villages stretched out across the plain, Niaz fell behind and Alex rode on alone through open country where peacocks screamed from the standing crops and the dew diamonds on every blade and twig glittered in the first rays of the rising sun.

It was barely more than a hundred miles from Khanwai to Lunjore; less, as the crow flies. He should be able to reach there some time during the night, but the horse would need rest. Alex had always been able to sleep in the saddle when necessary, but for the sake of the animal he rode he would be compelled to halt for some part of the day. The thought of any halt oppressed him, for his instinct was to keep going with all possible speed. He could not rid himself of the thought that at any hour the word might go out to look for Sher Dil of the Yusafzai who had stood in the full glare of the torchlight and shown Kishan Prasad's ring.

Alex looked down at the ring now, and dropping the reins he wrenched the thing off in a sudden spasm of loathing, and flung it away into the rank grass by the roadside.

It had been Kishan Prasad whose voice Alex had heard in the vault protesting against the murder, and it had undoubtedly been the priests and the unknown man with the ruby earrings who had been responsible for that foulness. But Kishan Prasad, whether he had condoned it or not, had convened that unholy coven, and as the instigator of it he could be held to account for all that had happened there, and summarily hanged for his part in the night's work. Alex wondered yet again why he had not let the man drown. He had had the chance, and some absurd, inexplicable quixotic streak born of background and upbringing had forced him into saving his life. And yet only a few hours ago he had killed another man, and the dried blood of that killing was still on his hands, spotting his clothing and dark under his finger-nails. But a hundred such men were less dangerous than one Kishan Prasad. Was rage then, and not justice or reason, the incentive for killing?

Alex scowled down at his stained hands. There must not be a

rising! It must be prevented at all costs; for if such a thing were
to occur, and the blood-lust that he had witnessed last night were
to be let loose, the British, who would do little now for the sake
of reason, would do much under the spur of blind rage, and the
retribution that would follow an armed rising would be both
harsh and horrible, engulfing innocent and guilty alike. His own
behaviour was proof enough of that, for he, who had not been
able to leave Kishan Prasad to die, had killed a man for rage and
revenge—because he had seen that man murder a child. Yet if
the fear and hatred that men such as Kishan Prasad were coaxing
into flame were to flare out into rebellion, a thousand children
would die worse deaths. 'It must not happen,' thought Alex
desperately. 'If it does it will leave a legacy of hatred and suspicion that will go on into the future until one day——' The
mare shied at a snake that had been sunning itself in the dust,
and the action brought his thoughts back from the problems of
the future to those of the immediate present.

Shortly after midday, having watered his horse and tethered
it some hundred yards within the borders of the surrounding
jungle, he lay down and slept, and an hour later Niaz, jogging
along in the hot dust with a party of armed men—the erstwhile
retainers of an Oudh noble whose estates now lay under threat of
confiscation by the Company's Government and whose acquaintance he had made on the road—noted that the print of a misshapen horseshoe no longer appeared upon the dusty surface of
the road. Niaz nodded to himself, realizing that Alex must have
turned aside to rest his horse. That meant night riding, and it
was safer to ride by night.

12

THE low sun was shining gold between the grass stems and the
bamboo canes when Alex awoke, and a jungle cock was calling
from a crane brake above a nearby stream. Alex rummaged

among the folds of his garments and produced the remains of a *chupatti*, which he ate hungrily. The stream would provide water to quench his thirst and he need not stop again for food or rest until he reached Lunjore. As he ate he thought of the ritual making of the *chupatti* that he had witnessed last night, and of stories that he had heard of food prepared with special incantations, in time of plague, being taken out and left beside the roadside in the belief that any passer-by who picked it up would carry away the infection from the house or village. Was that the meaning of the making of the *chupatti*? The symbolic ridding of the community—of Oudh—of the misfortunes that had befallen it?

A flock of green parrots fluttered up from the edge of the stream and screeched indignantly away between the trees as Alex emerged from the jungle and bent to scoop the water up in his cupped hands, and a line of egrets passed overhead, chalk-white against the blue sky, making for the distant river. Alex dried his hands against the full Pathan trousers, and mounting, rode out of the jungle and into the warm evening light.

He made considerably better time over the next twenty miles or so, for the horse appeared to have benefited from its rest. The sun plunged below the horizon and a sharp sweet smell of wood smoke stole across the plain, and presently a little chill wind arose, a precursor of the cold weather and a promise of cool nights. Alex wrapped a length of cotton cloth about his throat and shoulders, and as the swift dusk swallowed up jungle and plain and the ghost of the wedge-shaped moon gathered strength in the darkening sky, he settled himself down to ride hard, using all the skill he possessed to coax the best speed from his shoddy mount.

It was late and the road was white in the moonlight as he neared the little town of Pari. He had covered over eighty miles since he had left Khanwai before dawn that day, and only a matter of some six or seven more separated him from the river that formed the border between Oudh and Lunjore. Once across the river an hour's ride would bring him to the cantonments, for Lunjore city lay barely ten miles from the border.

The road that had run for the past few miles in the shadow of overarching trees ran out into the clear moonlight and crossed an open plain dotted with tussocks of tall grass and the sparse shadows of thorn trees, on the far side of which a few warm pinpricks of light marked the outskirts of Pari. The plain lay milky in the moonlight and patterned by the misshapen shadows of the grass clumps and an outcrop of rock that loomed tall and sharp-edged against the night sky. Something moved in the black shadow of the rock and Alex reined in hard as Niaz moved out into the moonlight.

Niaz did not speak, but catching the mare's bridle he turned her off the road. He was breathing quickly and the flanks of his own weary beast were white with foam and heaving as though it had been ridden to exhaustion.

'Thou canst not go forward,' said Niaz, speaking in a whisper as though even in that wide plain he feared to be overheard. 'The word has gone out against thee. There were men in Pari asking if any had seen a Pathan horse-dealer—one Sher Dil, a man of the Yusafzai. Some matter of a stolen horse—or so they said. They will look for thee to enter the town. We can ride on for half a *koss* and then turn away from the road and make a circle through the fields. It is on the far side that we shall find it more difficult, for there is only one place where the river may be crossed—by the Bridge of Boats into Lunjore—and that will be watched!'

'We will deal with that when we have the town behind us,' said Alex. 'Can that beast bear thee farther?'

'Needs must,' said Niaz, and laughed.

Fifteen minutes later they turned off the road on to the open plain and went at a foot-pace, the horses picking their way wearily between rocks and tussocks of grass, and presently they were skirting the cultivated land to the south of Pari. Two pariah dogs barked at them as they crossed a shallow irrigation ditch where Niaz's horse stumbled and all but threw him, and a watchman, perched in a ramshackle *machan* in a mulberry tree to scare the deer and wild pig from the crops, shouted hoarsely and discharged an ancient fowling-piece. The pellets rattled through the leaves

and something like a red-hot knife sliced into Alex's arm and he
felt the warm blood pour down it and wet the fingers of his left
hand. Then water glimmered in the moonlight, and they
found themselves on a narrow track bordering the marshy margin
of a jheel that stretched away and to the left.

The frenzied barking of the pariah dogs died away behind them
and the track curved north again under the shadow of a steep
bank topped by a towering hedge of cactus, and presently came
to what appeared to be a dead end, for the bank and the cactus
hedge bent sharply at a right angle, barring their path and continuing in an unbroken line towards the glimmering stretches
of the jheel.

Niaz drew rein in the shadows and slid to the ground. 'There
is a lane ahead,' he whispered. 'Thou canst not see, for it
runs——' He stopped suddenly. 'Art thou hit?'

'It is only a flesh wound,' said Alex, and dismounted awk-
wardly.

Niaz rolled back the sodden sleeve. A raw-edged fragment of
the scrap-iron with which the watchman's gun had been loaded
had ploughed through the fleshy part of the arm midway between
shoulder and elbow, making an ugly jagged tear that bled freely.
Niaz ripped two strips of cloth from his turban and making a
pad of the first bound the wound skilfully. 'And the lane?' said
Alex.

'It runs back to the right; there by the turn of the bank. It was
not watched when I came by this way, but it may be that there
are watchers now. Wait here while I go forward to see.'

He vanished silently into the shadows and Alex waited, listening to the many night noises and coldly calculating the chances
of survival. A breath of wind rattled a dead and dried cactus leaf,
jackal packs bayed the moon, and from the edges of the
jheel frogs croaked a noisy and monotonous chorus while an
occasional clucking proclaimed the presence of water-birds feeding
farther out from the shore.

Niaz returned as noiselessly as he had gone, his shod feet making
no sound on the soft carpet of the dust. 'The path is shut——'

his voice was barely a breath of sound. 'They have run a cart across the far end and there are two men there. Perhaps three.'

Alex said: 'And the jheel?'

'It would take us until morning to cross it, if we were not drowned among the weeds. Moreover, we could not swim the horses.'

'That may be no loss! There will be a watch kept for a mounted man and the horses may well be recognized. But it is true that——' He was silent for a moment or two, his eyes ranging along the banks and the cactus hedges above them. But the banks were steep and the cactus hedges impenetrable to anything larger than a mongoose. He thrust the reins at Niaz and said: 'Wait while I see.'

He walked soft-footed in the shadow of the bank and found, as Niaz had said, that the bank that apparently took a sharp-angled turn to the left was not the same bank as that which they had followed, but another that cut across it. The two banks turned back towards the town and ran parallel for about thirty yards, forming a narrow steep-sided lane. A country cart had been backed into the mouth of the lane at the far end and Alex could hear a murmur of voices and see a gleam of firelight. He crept forward to within a dozen feet of the cart and observed with satisfaction that it carried a bale of fodder slung beneath it between the clumsy wheels, and that a blanket hung down between the shafts and provided a rough screen for a small fire of dung-cakes that smouldered on the ground in front of the cart and warmed the feet of the watchers. Two men squatted beside it and were apparently playing cards by its glow, and a third man leant against a wheel and appeared to be asleep. There was just room for a man to pass between the cart and the left-hand bank, but not for a horse. Alex wriggled backward with infinite caution and presently rejoined Niaz.

'It is easy.'

He outlined a plan in a few terse sentences and Niaz nodded: 'We will try it. If it come to the worst they are only three to our two.'

'We cannot allow one to run away, or the alarm is given. Give me five minutes.' He turned and crept back the way he had come.

The lane was inches deep in dust and even the long-thorned fragments of dead cactus with which it was strewn only pressed deeper into the dust under Alex's feet, and the faint snap of their breaking was drowned by the purr and bubble of a hookah and the slap of falling cards. A dozen yards short of the cart he flattened himself against the ground once more and began to crawl forward inch by inch, the end of his turban wrapped about his nose and mouth as a protection against the choking dust. Then he had reached the cart and was under it, shielded from view by the bale of fodder and the hanging blanket, with his head barely a foot from the legs of the man who leant against the off-side wheel. Less than a yard away the two card-players muttered, cursed, coughed and drew by turns at the bubbling hookah.

The dust and the acrid smoke of the dung fire penetrated even through the folds of turban cloth and tickled Alex's nostrils maddeningly, and the wound in his arm throbbed painfully. A procession of ants crawled across his legs and a myriad night-flying insects that had been attracted by the dim glow of the fire fluttered and crept about his face. The slow minutes seemed like hours and he began to wonder if some mishap had befallen Niaz. And then at last he heard the sound he had been waiting for. A voice—a raucous and untuneful voice that sang an obscene ballad enumerating in detail the charms of a certain Delhi courtesan. The song, interrupted by hiccoughs, came nearer, and the card-players broke off their game and turned to listen, while the dozing sentinel roused himself and unslinging the musket he carried, held it at the ready.

'It is only some drunkard from the town,' growled one of the card-players. '*Ola!* Who comes? Thou canst not pass! The road is closed. Go back, O servant of Baihron!'

'Go back?' hiccoughed the newcomer. 'Wherefore? And since when has this path been closed to honest men?'

'It is an order of the new Government,' said the man with the musket.

'What *zulum*! (oppression). First it is a wandering pig of a Pathan whose horse thrusts me into the jheel so that I am be-mired with mud, and now the road is closed against me and——'

The man with the musket gripped Niaz and dragged him into the light of the fire. 'What is that? What Pathan!'

'He is back on the road there—may his horses fall into the jheel and drown! He desired to know where he might obtain a fresh mount, his own being spent, but what do I know of horse-dealing? A song is better—let us sing together, thus—"Oh, Moon of Beauty"——'

'It is the very one!' said the man with the musket. 'Hush, fool! Does he come this way?'

'Who?'

'The Pathan, O owl!'

'How should I know? He sits by the path while his horses graze. Must I indeed go back? What if he should beat me? Pathans be men of evil temper and this one is angry.'

'Let us go,' said one of the card-players, his hand on the handle of a serviceable-looking knife. 'There is a price on his head. Stay by the cart, Dunnoo, and let none pass. And thou, O son of a noseless mother! remain thou here until we return, and if it be that thou hast not spoken truth concerning the Pathan thou shalt suffer a sore beating!'

'Why should I not speak truth?' demanded Niaz, tripping over his feet and sitting down heavily in the dust. 'It is as I have said. He sits by the jheel and curses his gods. If I may go no farther I will sleep here. One place is as good as another.'

He yawned largely; a yawn that broke off into a hiccough as two of the men turned and disappeared down the lane. Presently the remaining sentinel turned back to squat by the fire. There was the sound of a dull blow, a coughing grunt and a thud, and Alex crawled out from under the cart and beat the dust off his clothes.

The man who had been addressed as Dunnoo lay face downwards by the smouldering fire, and Niaz was composedly replacing a long-hafted knife in its sheath and concealing both in the folds of his clothing.

'I said there was to be no more killing!' said Alex angrily.

'He is not dead,' said Niaz, rolling the man over with his foot. 'I used the hilt only, and these *pūrbeah* pigs have thick heads. It may be that he has a crack in the skull. No more. Do we go now? It will be a long journey on foot.'

'All the more reason to go on horseback,' said Alex. 'Even a spent horse may travel swifter than a man. We will wait. Those two will be back soon, and I think that they will bring us the horses.'

He stooped above the unconscious man and began swiftly to strip off his outer clothing, donning them himself while Niaz scientifically bound and gagged the man and rolled him out of sight under the cart.

Ten minutes later the two men returned, leading, as Alex had surmised, the horses that they had found grazing by the jheel.

'We could not find him. But there were two horses and we brought them away. He cannot get far on foot,' said the man with the gun, edging his way between the wheel and the steep bank of the lane. He crumpled and fell as Alex's fist took him under the jaw, and a choked cry from the rear of the cart showed that Niaz had risen from beneath it and struck down a second victim.

'Pah! It is easy,' said Niaz with scorn, ducking under the wheels and reappearing. 'We must pull this thing clear, else the horses cannot pass.'

They dragged the cart forward, and having led the horses out of the lane tied up the two groaning men—the first had still not moved—and bundled them into the cart. 'It would be better to kill them,' said Niaz judicially, 'then they can tell no tales.'

'There has been enough killing. They will not be found until morning and we shall be across the river by then.'

'Mayhap!' grunted Niaz pessimistically. 'But there is the bridge to be crossed.'

The brief period of rest appeared to have put new life into the

jaded horses and they made good time along the moon-splashed
road towards the river, but Alex's arm had begun to stiffen and
from the pain that it gave him he realized that the jagged scrap
of metal that had caused the wound must still be embedded in it.
He would have to get it out soon or it would fester.

An hour's riding brought them the smell of the river, and they
led the horses off the road and tethering them in the jungle went
forward on foot to reconnoitre. The unmade road became rougher
and more sandy and the air cooled perceptibly and smelt of wet
sand and stagnant shallows. There was a square mud toll-house
where the road ended, and behind it, screened by plantains and
bamboo, lay a meagre huddle of huts that housed the family of
the toll-keeper and the bridge guard. Pedestrians were not
required to pay a toll, which was only levied on carts and wheeled
vehicles whose approach was audible from a considerable distance,
and the toll-house was in darkness. Alex and Niaz kept to the shelter of the trees on the far side of the road, and gave it a wide berth.

The near bank was low and fringed with casuarina scrub, and
the white sands and wandering shallows stretched far out into the
moonlight. But beyond the sands and the shallows the river ran
deep and wide, bounded on the far side by a steep bank and a
solid wall of jungle. A raised stone causeway ran from the Oudh
bank to the edge of the deep water where a bridge of boats
spanned the main arm of the river. There was no sign of life
on or near it, and it lay open and innocent in the waning moonlight, creaking to the sluggish pull of the slow-moving current.

'They are on the other side,' muttered Niaz.

Alex nodded, frowning. He knew the far bank of the river
well. Even if they could swim the horses across there was no
point for several miles, either up- or down-stream, where they
could get them ashore, for the current ran strongly on the far
side and had worn away the bank until it overhung the river.
The only possible landing-place was the cutting where the bridge
of boats ended and the road ran up a long, gentle slope to where
a brick-built toll-house and half a dozen mud huts huddled on the
fringe of the jungle. They would have to leave the horses.

'We must swim,' said Alex slowly.

Niaz did not speak but he pointed silently, and Alex looking
along his raised arm as a man sights along the barrels of a gun
saw a long grey object at the water's edge; something that might
have been a log washed down by the river, and which lay at the
exact angle that such a log would have grounded. Mugger. The
blunt-nosed, man-eating crocodile of the Indian rivers.

'If I die, I will die on land,' said Niaz, 'and not in the belly
of such as that! Besides, I am no swimmer, and it will go hard
with thee to swim against the current with a wounded arm. It
may be that we can win back to the Khanwai road. They will
not look to see us there, and we have the horses. Let us go back.'

'And be hunted through Oudh? No. We must go forward—
or die.'

'Then I think we die tonight!' said Niaz grimly.

Alex digested this statement in silence. He had had barely
three hours' sleep in the last two days and his head was aching.
His wounded arm was absurdly painful and it throbbed to a steady
burning beat of pain that seemed to find an odd rumbling echo
in the night. An echo which slowly drowned the throb of his
blood, until he realized suddenly what it was. There were carts
approaching down the road towards the bridge. A long line of
creaking, bullock-drawn country carts of the kind that might be
met with on any Indian road at any time of the night; their
drivers asleep while the patient beasts plodded slowly onward
hour after hour in the darkness.

Alex touched Niaz on the arm and jerked his head in the direction of the distant sound. He said: 'Turn the horses loose. We
shall not need them again. I do not think that we shall die
tonight, for these will take us across.'

They left the weary horses to graze in the jungle and ran back
along the road towards the carts, keeping to the shadows. There
were nine carts rumbling and creaking down the moonlit road,
moving as slowly as crawling beetles; the torpid bullocks lumbering through the dust in a ruminative trance, noses almost to the
ground and horns swaying, while their drivers crouched upon the

cartpoles, miraculously preserving their balance, and slept. A
flickering oil lantern swung from the leading cart and the moonlight showed that four of the carts were piled high with sugar-
cane while five carried sacks of *bhoosa*. Alex and Niaz slipped
across the road between the carts, and Niaz, walking behind one of
them, dragged out several of the light, bulging sacks and flung
them away while Alex watched the man on the cart immediately
behind for fear that he should wake.

'In!' whispered Niaz, and Alex swung up on to the cart and
wriggled into the cave that Niaz had made among the sacks. The
plodding bullocks did not slow their crawling pace by a step at
the additional weight, and Niaz thrust two sacks on top of Alex
and dropped back to burrow his way into the heart of a pile of
sugar-cane with the celerity of a grass-snake.

Left alone in the dusty sweet-smelling darkness Alex shifted
the sack beneath him and worked his way down and farther
forward into the pile until he lay in the centre of the stifling
load. The carts rocked and squeaked and rumbled forward on the
rutted dusty road, and presently, as the wheels met the dry sand
near the river bank and a sleepy voice called from the toll-hut,
they jolted to a stop. The carters, jerked abruptly into wakeful-
ness, entered into surly argument with the yawning toll-keeper,
and after some delay the carts started forward once more, and
with shoutings, tail twistings and belabourings, jolted down the
sandy slope on to the causeway. One by one they rolled out on to
the bridge which swayed and groaned beneath the rumbling
wheels, and one by one, as the bullocks grunted and strained
under the hail of blows and shrill yells of encouragement, they
breasted the slope on the far side and were on the road again.

Alex did not catch the shouted orders that checked the carts,
for the creaking and rumbling had deafened him and the close-
packed sacks muffled all other sounds, but the wheels ground to a
halt and there were men all about the carts and hoarse angry
voices.

'What is this? Yet another toll?' called one of the carters.
'A Pathan? Nay, we have seen no Pathans. . . . Look then and

G

see! . . . Horses? Horses? These be no horse-drawn *gharis*!
Bullocks only. We carry fodder and such stuff to Barowli village,
and to Lunjore.'

There was another burst of angry shouting and a man's voice
said: 'Any fool would have known that the bridge would be
watched once the word had gone out, and this man we seek is
no fool. He will have doubled back to the Ganges. *Ohé!* thou
upon the cart there; didst thou see no horses upon the road?'

'Have I not said that I saw no horses? And no Pathans either!
It may be that I slept a little on the way, but if thou thinkest
that we carry horses and Pathans in our carts thou art welcome
to search for them. Perchance thou wilt find more than horses—
elephants belike, and men of Turkistan! Search then!—we
cannot wait through the night.' A torch flared as men passed
along the carts prodding and peering, but the task of unloading
and reloading each cart was clearly impossible.

'Thrust with thy spear!' growled a voice.

'And who is to pay me for my sacks?' shrilled the carter
furiously.

A voice farther down the line said angrily that there was no
spear made that could be stabbed down through sugar-cane,
adding: 'Do we play at tent-pegging, then?'—the speaker's spear
had evidently stuck fast in a piece of cane. The wrangling voices
passed down the line and presently someone climbed upon the
sacks that concealed Alex, crushing them down stiflingly upon
him, and something jabbed down, ripping through sacking and
bhoosa. It missed Alex by a millimetre, but it caught the edge of
the bandage that Niaz had tied about his arm and ripped it away.
The blood had clotted and dried, but the wrench tore open the
wound again and he could feel the fresh blood well out once more.
But either the spear had been pulled back in the fractional second
before the blood flowed again or the *bhoosa* and the sacking had
cleaned any traces from the metal, for the man jumped down
upon the road again and passed on to the next cart.

Alex pressed his wounded arm against a yielding sack and tried
to get his right hand across to cover it, for if blood should drip

upon the white dust of the road it would be seen when the carts
moved on again. He managed to clench his fingers over it but
the warm sticky tide seeped between them. And then, after what
seemed an eternity, the carts jerked forward again. It was
over—and they were through. The dusty airless darkness closed
in upon him, and he was still asleep when Niaz pulled him out
from among the blood-stained sacks in the yellow dawn.

*   *   *

Three hours later, bathed, shaved and fed; clothed once more
in his own clothes and with his wound probed, cleaned and bound
and his arm in a sling, Alex presented himself at the Residency.

The Commissioner was engaged with a visitor and sent out
word asking Captain Randall to wait. He would not, he said, be
above half an hour.

Alex sat down in a verandah chair and stretched his legs out
before him. He could hear a murmur of voices from the large
living-room on the far side of the Commissioner's office, and supposed that Mr. Barton's visitor must have called in a social
rather than an official capacity. After a time the gorgeously
uniformed *chuprassi* who squatted farther down the verandah
by one of the outer doors of the living-room, sprang to his feet
and held aside the split-cane curtain that hung in front of it,
and Alex could hear the Commissioner's voice raised in affable
farewell. A man, an Indian, came out past the salaaming *chuprassi* and turned and walked down the length of the verandah.
It was Kishan Prasad.

Alex did not move and not a muscle in his face quivered; nor
was there any alteration in his lounging pose to betray the shock
and the incredulous surprise that the sight of Kishan Prasad had
given him. Kishan Prasad, walking softly, came to a stop in
front of him and bowed. Alex did not return the greeting. He
looked up at Kishan Prasad under his black brows with eyes
that were as cold and hard and passionless as grey granite, and
smiled.

Kishan Prasad drew back involuntarily and for a fractional

moment some of his assurance seemed to drop from him. Then
he recovered himself and his voice was smoothly urbane:

'Ah, Captain Randall! This is an unexpected pleasure. The
Commissioner was telling me that he did not expect you back
until next week when your replacement, Mr. Parbury, is due to
leave. I am sorry to see that you have suffered an injury to your
arm. Nothing serious, I hope?'

'No, nothing serious,' said Alex from behind that cold smile.
'It was kind of you to come here. It will save me the trouble of
sending an escort to bring you in.'

'To bring me where?' enquired Kishan Prasad affecting polite
surprise.

'To the jail—and the gallows.'

'My dear Captain Randall! I must admit that I do not understand you. Is it some English joke?'

'You understand me perfectly,' said Alex softly. 'Murder has
always been a capital offence.'

'Murder?'

'What else? "*This thing that ye have witnessed shall be
binding upon all, for were it known there is not one who would
not hang at a rope's end for this night's work,*" ' quoted Alex
in the vernacular. He saw Kishan Prasad's pupils widen,
and said: 'Yes, you were right. I am the man whom your cut-
throats are hunting through Oudh. You should be more careful
whom you admit to your meetings.'

'I do not understand——' repeated Kishan Prasad woodenly.

Alex said: 'But I do. I had heard many tales, but until two
nights ago I had no proof. Now I have it. And your life and the
life of every man who was there is twice forfeit—for sedition and
for murder.'

Kishan Prasad released his breath in an audible sigh and after
a moment he said very softly: 'That killing was by no will of
mine. I do not war on babes, and had I known what was planned
I should have prevented it. I am no ignorant worshipper of
devils to dabble in such foulness. As for the rest, I have told
you before that I desire to pull down your Company's Raj, and

to that end I will use any and every means that lie to my hand. But you cannot hang me, for this proof that you have is no proof. It is only your word, and it will not be believed. No'—he held up a hand to check the words that Alex would have spoken—'hear me out. I do not know how you knew of that meeting or how you came by the password, but I know that had I not in a foolish moment given you a certain token you would not have seen—what you saw. But having used that token to gain admittance, there was a penalty. It was told to me that a certain Pathan had entered, having shown it. I could not believe—yet it was possible. The word went out against that Pathan; but in case he were not stopped certain other things were done. If you send men now to Khanwai there will be nothing found in proof of your tale. As for me, a hundred witnesses can prove that I was elsewhere, and not at Khanwai two nights ago.'

Alex said grimly: 'I think you will find, Rao Sahib, that my word will be taken against a hundred thousand of your witnesses.'

'Even when one of those witnesses is the Commissioner of Lunjore?' enquired Kishan Prasad softly.

Alex's face stiffened and there were suddenly two white patches at the corners of his mouth. He came to his feet with a swiftness that made Kishan Prasad flinch as if in expectation of a blow, and said in a harsh whisper: 'That I will not believe!'

'But you will find that it is so. He does not know that he lies,' said Kishan Prasad. 'You see, there was a—a little party that night at the house of a mutual friend, and the Commissioner perhaps indulged too freely in perfumed brandy. He does not remember very much of what occurred and he is convinced that I also was present. He was good enough to admire a trinket that I had brought back from France; an ingenious toy that he was pleased to accept. He has even mentioned it to Colonel Moulson, who is with him now. So you see——'

Kishan Prasad sketched a deprecatory gesture with one slim brown hand, and Alex saw: saw with a complete and bitter understanding. Kishan Prasad had made full use of both Mr. Barton's drunkenness and his vanity. It must have been so easy

—so fatally easy. A prearranged party at the house of one of the more disreputable noblemen; drink and dancing girls, champagne laced with brandy and probably opium. A man—any man with a superficial resemblance to Kishan Prasad—and his name repeated until it was impressed upon a fuddled brain. Alex knew his chief only too well. If the Commissioner had admitted seeing Kishan Prasad at such an affair he would never go back on such a statement, because to do so would be to admit instead that he had been drunk enough to be deceived, and at the house of a prominent Indian.

'They will say that you must have been mistaken,' said Kishan Prasad softly. 'As for this meeting you will tell them of, they will say it was a mere gathering of malcontents. Talk—but no more than talk. Shall I tell you why they will not believe? Because they do not wish to! The colonels who command the sepoy regiments here suspect that their regiments are rank with sedition. Their Indian officers are insolent in many small ways. But for shame's sake they will not admit it and each cries louder than the other that all is well. You see, I speak frankly to you. What need is there for pretence between us, who know what we know?'

He looked at Alex's rigid face and he lowered his voice until it was barely a whisper: 'You know that you cannot win this fight. The Company is only a handful of men and its power is an illusion. I have seen the slaughter at Sebastopol and I know that your Queen has no more regiments to send. Do not fight us. Join us! It will not be the first time that men from the West have risen to greatness in the armies of Hind. There have been many —Avitable, George Thomas, Ventura, Potter, Gardiner——'

Alex laughed and the laugh brought a sudden flush into Kishan Prasad's olive cheeks. His hand dropped and he stepped back. Then: 'I am sorry,' he said gravely. 'That was a foolish thing to say.'

'Very,' agreed Alex.

Kishan Prasad smiled. 'I am sorry too that our blood makes us enemies. Perhaps in your next life it may be that you will be born a Hindu.'

'Perhaps,' said Alex, 'when I have hanged you in this one.'
'That too may come about,' said Kishan Prasad. 'But the time is not yet.'

He saluted Alex with grave courtesy and turning from him walked down the shallow flight of steps into the bright sunlight of the garden and was driven away in an open carriage, his servants running beside it.

But the hours that followed, and the days that followed those hours, bore out all that he had said. Mr. Barton listened with entire incredulity to Alex's story. Alex had made a mistake—a very natural one. All niggers looked as like as two peas when in a crowd. The suggestion that he himself might have been mistaken drove him to blustering and apoplectic indignation. Such an assertion was absurd and insulting! Why, the Rao Sahib had actually shown him a toy that he had bought in Paris—a musical-box ornamented with a naked dancer who contorted her waxen limbs in time to a tinny little tune. There it was, standing on the table to prove his words! Kishan Prasad had begged his acceptance of the trifle and had called only that morning in order to bring the duplicate key—a very sensible idea; these fiddling things were so easily lost.

Alex had brought him remorselessly back to the subject under discussion, and Mr. Barton had been horrified and disbelieving. It was obvious, he said, that Alex had happened upon some queer religious rite; it never did to pry into such things—leave 'em to wallow was his motto. At such ceremonies the blacks were bound to get above themselves and talk a lot of inflammatory nonsense. It meant nothing. As for Alex's assertion that an English child had been murdered in cold blood, he could only suggest that Alex had been carried away by the—er—the unusual circumstances; the atmosphere, the fumes from the brazier he had spoken of, or the effects of fatigue. He would not like to suggest that Alex had been drinking; although some of these country-brewed spirits were far from mild. Of course it had been a young goat that he had seen killed! A very common form of sacrifice. And if Alex took his advice he would refrain in future from play-acting in native dress and mixing himself up in such affairs. It did not consort well with the dignity of a Company's officer, and might lead to a deal of trouble. That wounded arm should be a lesson to him!

And now that that matter was settled, Mr. Barton would like to know what news Alex had brought of the Condesa. He hoped that she was well. No beauty, what?—but looks were not everything. A good child, though plain. He had thought it better to allow her to proceed to Delhi in the care of Mrs. Abuthnot as he himself would be going there shortly on official business, and it would therefore save him a tedious journey to Calcutta. Two birds with one stone!

Alex had dismissed the Condesa in a single brief sentence and returned grimly to the question of Kishan Prasad and the meeting of seditionists at Khanwai. He had argued, expounded and pleaded, but Mr. Barton remained obdurate: there was nothing he could do. It was all an unfortunate business and had best be forgotten. No sense in stirring up a hornets' nest.

The same opinion was expressed by Colonels Moulson and Packer, commanding two of the three regiments of Native Infantry stationed at Lunjore, and Major Beckwith, in temporary command of the third in the absence of Colonel Gardener-Smith.

Colonel Moulson, who had taken particular pains to be offensive, had brought all his influence to bear to prevent the Commissioner from taking any official notice of the report, and had done his best to discredit the whole story, while Colonel Packer, an earnest Christian, appeared content to leave the entire matter in the hands of the Almighty, assisted by prayer. Major Beckwith, uncertain of himself and convinced of the indestructible loyalty of every sepoy in his regiment, listened to Colonel Moulson's scathing and outspoken criticisms of jumped-up and over-promoted pets of the Civil Service, and took refuge in the fact that in Colonel Gardener-Smith's absence he could do nothing.

Alex asked for a week's extension of leave on account of his wounded arm, and rode to Agra to see Mr. John Colvin, Lieutenant

Governor of the North-west Provinces. But the mission had proved abortive.

The Lieutenant Governor was that same Mr. Colvin who twenty years ago, as Lord Auckland's Private Secretary, had been one of the primary instigators of the disastrous folly of the Afghan War. He had never been able to forget it, or ever again trust entirely to his own judgment. Mr. Colvin did not believe that disaffection was rife in the country and still less that the army was affected. There had been rumours, of course—but then there were always rumours. He could not take it upon himself to order the arrest of men like Kishan Prasad—influential men whom there was no reason to suspect of being anything but loyal —especially when, as Captain Randall had admitted, the Commissioner of Lunjore was prepared to swear that the man had been nowhere near the scene of this—um—gathering at Khanwai. He too thought that Captain Randall must have been mistaken, and that he was surely exaggerating the dangers of the situation. He too suggested that it was hardly suitable for an officer of the Company to take such investigations upon himself. There were paid spies among the native population who were entirely trustworthy, and better qualified for the work on account of their dark skins. He would of course pass on the information Captain Randall had given him to the proper authorities, but in the meantime . . .

Alex had set his teeth and listened with a gathering sense of frustration and bitterness. This was what it must feel like to be a lunatic confined in a cell, beating your head against the padded walls and convinced that it was you, and not your keepers, who were sane. Perhaps he had indeed been mad to imagine that anyone would listen to him when men like General John Jacob were written down as alarmists. He had thought that if he could produce proof he must be believed, but it seemed that the evidence of his eyes was not proof and, as Kishan Prasad had so truly said, the great majority did not wish to believe: they found it more comfortable to close their eyes and look the other way in the hope that if they ignored its existence the danger would pass.

G*

To take any form of preventive action, they reasoned, would be to advertise a lamentable want of confidence and possibly precipitate thereby the very dangers whose existence they refused to admit.

The most that Alex could gain was permission to take six *sowars* and three British officers to see if any concrete evidence could be brought back of the murder that he professed to have witnessed. There had been a report of the disappearance of a child a week earlier, admitted Mr. Colvin reluctantly. The three-year-old son of a private in a British regiment stationed in Cawnpore; and it was always possible, though hardly credible . . .

Alex had ridden back to Khanwai with six troopers and three sceptical but enthusiastic officers. They had found exactly nothing. The stair shaft leading to the underground chamber was open to the sky and choked with fallen debris that had the appearance of being there for some considerable time. There had been a heavy and recent fall of earth and stonework from the spot where the roots of the peepul tree had forced their way downwards, and the vault appeared to be in too dangerous a state to encourage a thorough search.

Ten paces within the jungle behind the ruined fort they uncovered a grave, but it contained only the rotting carcase of a white goat.

IV

CONWAY

13

IT was over six weeks since the Abuthnots had left Calcutta on the long journey northward to Delhi. A journey on which they had been accompanied, somewhat unexpectedly, by Lord Carlyon and the Gardener-Smiths.

Lord Carlyon, having taken a fancy to visit the old Mogul capital of Delhi, had requested permission to avail himself of the pleasure of their company on what he must otherwise find to be a singularly tedious journey. Such a pleasantly worded request had been impossible to refuse, and it had been a source of some annoyance to Mrs. Abuthnot that the Gardener-Smiths, having made a last-minute change in their plans to allow for a few weeks' visit to Delhi, had also attached themselves to the party.

Mrs. Gardener-Smith had announced that the heat and humidity of Calcutta were not to be borne, but Mrs. Abuthnot, without wishing to be uncharitable, could not rid herself of the suspicion that Mrs. Gardener-Smith's dislike of the Calcutta climate had only manifested itself when she had heard that Lord Carlyon would be travelling to Delhi with the Abuthnot party. She could also not entirely bring herself to believe that it was the pleasure of their united company that had prompted Lord Carlyon to make his flattering request. He was of course well aware that both Lottie and dear Winter were affianced and shortly to be married, but could it possibly be that he was attracted to her Sophie? Sophie, though a mere child, was such a sweet thing! *Could* it be Sophie?

Mrs. Abuthnot indulged in a few maternal daydreams, and her lack of enthusiasm over the addition of the Gardener-Smiths to the party was understandable. Delia, thought Mrs. Abuthnot with a sigh, was so *very* striking!

The majority of travellers were apt to find journeys in India uncomfortable, fatiguing and insufferably tedious, but to Winter there had been interest and enchantment in every mile of the way: in the sun-baked silence of the dusty roads and the cheerful tumult of the *paraos*; in the little villages with their small bazaars, creaking well-wheels, tanks and temples. In the scream of peacocks in the dusk and the cry of wild geese and sarus cranes at dawn. How could anyone travel through such a country and find it, as Lord Auckland's sister, Emily Eden, had found it, 'a shrivelled cinder of a country', and 'quite hideous'? How was it possible that the self-same thing should hold such enchantment and beauty for one pair of eyes and yet appear only ugly, daunting and repellent in another's?

But there was one aspect of the journey to Delhi which she had not found pleasant—the presence of Lord Carlyon. Winter had not been favourably impressed by Carlyon on the occasion of their first meeting at Sybella's Summer Ball at Ware, and although his manner towards her since their meeting in Calcutta had been outwardly unexceptionable, his languid gaze had a way of resting on her with a look of insolently comprehensive appraisal, as though she had been a slave girl on the block or a blood horse whose purchase he contemplated.

Carlyon had never previously been in the least interested in single young ladies. They were, in his opinion, too raw, too uninstructed and too dangerous, and he had never yet distinguished one of them with his attentions. But Winter de Ballesteros had not been in any way like the general run of demurely blushing débutantes. Her unusual looks had attracted him sufficiently for him to pay her some attention, and he had been considerably taken aback by her reception of the compliment. To be put in his place and given a sharp set-down by one so young and inexperienced had, by its very novelty, both piqued and intrigued him.

Carlyon was the product of an age in which wealthy members of the aristocracy considered themselves to be above the laws that governed the behaviour of the lower and middle classes, and he had always considered the '*Droit de Seigneur*' an admirable institution and regretted that it could no longer be enforced. It would do no harm—and should prove quite delightful—to give this delicious young creature an advance course of instruction in some of the pleasanter aspects of matrimony, and she would enjoy the subsequent embraces of her Indian Service nonentity all the more for having been introduced to the delights of passion by an expert. A girl with such a mouth and so sweetly seductive a figure would not, he was convinced, prove anything but an apt pupil in the art of love, and a journey of several weeks had seemed to offer endless opportunities for sentimental dalliance by the way.

But however carefully he manœuvred he found it impossible to speak to the little de Ballesteros alone. She kept close to Lottie or Sophie and could not be drawn into private talk with him, and Carlyon, who had started the journey in a spirit of pleasurable and entirely confident anticipation, began to lose his temper. Had he *really* wasted his charm and his conversation on ingratiating himself with this set of middle-class bores, not to mention delaying his departure from India and embarking on a long and uncomfortable journey, made the more uncomfortable by the fact that his hitherto faithful valet had flatly refused to accompany him, and all to no purpose? He could not believe it! But as day succeeded day and the travellers drew nearer to Delhi he found himself no nearer to obtaining his objective. Winter remained as cool as her name and tantalizingly out of reach, and Lord Carlyon, angry, frustrated and piqued, had ended by doing what he had always pronounced to be the very height of folly. He fell in love.

Carlyon had played with that emotion for so long that he did not at first recognize it. Love had been an amusement and the gratifying of a strongly developed sexual appetite, but it had never once touched either his heart or his emotions, so that he had come to believe that he at least was immune from this particular form of madness. The discovery that he—Arthur Veryan St. Maur Carlyon—had actually fallen in love with a chit of seventeen astounded and angered him. Nevertheless, he was in love; and being so found himself incapable of avoiding any one of the agonies and ecstasies inherent in that condition, or of behaving in a rational manner. The *finesse* that had led him scatheless through a score of affairs deserted him, and he behaved like a boor and knew it—and could not prevent it. Mrs. Abuthnot took fright and Mrs. Gardener-Smith took offence; the older men, with more understanding than their wives would have given them credit for, regarded him with sympathetic concern, while Delia sulked and pouted and Winter remained warily withdrawn. The days that had been a delight ended by becoming a torment of embarrassment and strain, and Carlyon was the only member of the party who was not inexpressibly relieved by the sight of the rose-red walls of Delhi.

The Abuthnots' bungalow was situated in the Cantonments on the stony ridge some four miles outside the walled city, and Carlyon had had no difficulty in obtaining an invitation to stay with them, although before the journey was over Mrs. Abuthnot would have given much to get out of it. What a relief it would be to see Mr. Barton, who must have arrived by now and would be staying until the wedding at Ludlow Castle with Mr. Simon Fraser, the Commissioner of Delhi. He would be sure to present himself at their bungalow on the very first evening. She did hope that he would allow dear Winter sufficient time to bathe and change her dress before making his appearance. The child would wish to look her best for such a momentous meeting. Six years——! Mrs. Abuthnot sighed sentimentally and remarked encouragingly that another half-hour would see them at the end of their journey.

There were no fewer than seven letters awaiting Lottie at the bungalow: fat, sealed packets, each as large, as Sophie remarked teasingly, as one of Mrs. Heyman's novels, and all of them from Edward English. But there was neither letter nor message for the Condesa de los Aguilares.

Of course there would be none, thought Winter, comforting herself. There was no longer any need for letters when Conway himself would be at Ludlow Castle only a mile or so from the Cantonments. In an hour—perhaps less—she would see him. She must hurry and change into her prettiest dress. Her hair was dull from the dust of the roads and there was dust too on her long lashes and at the corners of her nose and mouth. She must wash and change quickly—quickly!

An hour later she took a last anxious look at herself in the looking-glass, wished yet again that she possessed Lottie's blue eyes and yellow curls, and crossing the hall went into the drawing-room from where she could watch the gate and see Conway arrive. The servants were already laying dinner so it must be nearly five o'clock. Surely he would come soon! She heard someone enter the room behind her and close the door, and turned, expecting to see Mrs. Abuthnot.

'Who are you waiting for?' asked Carlyon. 'The tardy lover?'

Winter stood quite still. Her dark eyes widened a little and a pulse beat at the base of her throat, for it needed only one look to see that Carlyon had been drinking. He was far from drunk, but his flushed face and over-bright eyes and the slight slurring of his drawling voice were sufficient indication that he was not entirely sober.

She said in a cool, steady voice: 'I am expecting Mr. Barton. I will wait in the garden, I think. It is quite pleasantly cool out there now that the sun is so low.' She pressed back the wide flounces of her crinoline and walked quietly towards the door.

Carlyon waited until she was almost level with him and then moved with unexpected swiftness, blocking her way. 'I think not. I haven't had a chance like this before. You've avoided me, haven't you? You've done it very cleverly. Why won't you let me speak to you?'

Winter steadied her voice with an effort, doing her best to keep it light and level: 'But I do. You have often spoken to me.'

'But never alone. Do you know that I have never once been alone with you—even for a moment? Why do you behave like this? Do you do it to pique me, Winter? No!—don't go! I won't let you.'

She had tried to pass him and he had moved again, keeping between her and the door. Winter said a little breathlessly: 'Lord Carlyon, please let me pass. I—I think I hear Mrs. Abuthnot in the hall——'

'No, you don't. And my name is Arthur. Do I have to tell you that? Do I have to tell you that you are the loveliest and most seductive creature that I have ever known. That I——'

'Lord Carlyon, please——'

'Arthur! And I love you. Isn't that absurd?'

'Lord Carlyon, you must not speak to me like this,' said Winter desperately. 'You know that I am to be married shortly, and——'

'And to some clod of a Commissioner? What nonsense! What ridiculous, damned nonsense! You know it's nonsense, don't you? Don't you, my beautiful swan?—my snow maiden. Shall I melt that snow and teach you to be as warm as summer instead of as cold as your name? Shall I? Shall I?'

Above his soft, slurred voice Winter could hear horses' hooves on the drive. *Conway!* She tried again to pass Lord Carlyon, and he reached out and caught her wrist. The touch of those hot fingers sent a sudden shock of revulsion through her, but she knew that she must not struggle. It would be fatal to struggle. In a moment the door would open and they would come looking for her. She could hear voices on the verandah. She must not let Conway find her struggling degradingly in the arms of another man! What would he think! He might even think she had encouraged Lord Carlyon. She must keep calm.

She said quite steadily: 'If you do not let me go I shall call out.'

Carlyon laughed. 'No, you won't! It would make a vulgar scandal, and this is no moment for a vulgar scandal if this is your chosen clod arriving. So as time is short——'

Before she realized what he meant to do, or had time to cry out, he had jerked her to him and caught her close, pinning her arms to her sides in a grip that was agonizingly painful, and kissing her with a bruising violence that deprived her of breath. She struggled wildly and soundlessly, anger and disgust swamp-

ing out thought as the greedy mouth moved to her throat, kissing
its cool whiteness with a savage intensity and travelling downwards to the warm hollows of neck and shoulder.

She tried to cry out but the only sound she could make was a
choking gasp for air. And then the door into the hall opened, and
at the sound of it the arms that had held her dropped and she
leapt back, one hand to her bruised throat and the other clutching
desperately at a chair-back. But it was not Conway who stood
there. It was, astonishingly, Captain Randall.

'*Alex!*' She was not in the least aware that she had called
him by his Christian name, and the word was barely more than
a gasping breath.

Carlyon turned. He was entirely self-possessed and it did not
seem possible that this was the same man who only a moment
ago had been gripping her in a paroxysm of greedy physical
desire. 'Ah,' said Lord Carlyon blandly, 'Mr. Barton, I presume?'

Alex's hard grey eyes took in Lord Carlyon from head to foot
in one coldly speculative glance, and he raised his brows: 'No,
sir. Am I to take it that you were expecting him?' He looked
past Carlyon at Winter and bowed slightly: 'Your servant,
Condesa.'

A sudden flush burnt in Carlyon's cheeks and his lips tightened.
He drew himself up to his full height and said in his coldest drawl:
'You have mistaken the room, sir. You may find Colonel
Abuthnot in his office, I think.' He nodded a brief dismissal, but
for once that quelling manner which had hitherto invariably
succeeded in putting the pretentious in their place entirely failed
in its effect.

'Very likely,' said Alex, strolling forward into the room. 'But
I did not come to see Colonel Abuthnot. I am charged with a
message to the Condesa de los Aguilares.'

'Then pray deliver it, sir, and go,' snapped Lord Carlyon.
'You interrupt us.'

'So I observe,' said Alex, his gaze dwelling lazily on the red
blotches that disfigured Winter's white neck and shoulders. 'The
message, however, is of a somewhat personal nature, and when

I tell you that it is from this lady's future husband I am sure
that you will permit me to deliver it in private. I shall not keep
you above a moment.'

He walked over to the door, and holding it open smiled at Lord
Carlyon. Alex's acquaintances would have recognized that smile.
Carlyon did not. The fury died out of his face and contempt took
its place. He looked at Winter and said: 'For a moment then,
my dear,' and walked past her into the hall. Alex closed the door
upon him and Winter sat down very suddenly on the ottoman,
feeling ridiculously weak at the knees and seized with an absurd
desire to cry.

'Who was that?' enquired Alex without interest.

Winter looked away from him and said in a difficult voice:
'Lord Carlyon. He—accompanied us from Calcutta and is staying
here. But you must not think—I would not want you to——'

She broke off and bit her lip. There was, after all, no reason
why she should justify herself to Captain Randall, and he could
not possibly suppose that she had been a consenting party to the
scene that his entrance had interrupted. But how much had
he actually witnessed? Carlyon had released her so swiftly, and
she had not cried out. Alex must know that if she had cried out
he would have heard her. Did he imagine——?

She looked up quickly, the hot colour in her cheeks, and said:
'I know that it must look most singular to you, but——' And
then she saw for the first time that Alex carried his left arm in a
sling, and forgetting what she had been about to say, said instead:
'You are hurt! What has happened?'

'A shooting accident,' said Alex indifferently.

'An accident?' A sudden recollection of stories of risings and
the murder of men in outlying districts drove the blood from her
face, and she stood up quickly: 'Conway! Has there been trouble
in Lunjore? Is that what you have come to tell me? Is anything
the matter with him? Is he ill?'

'Not as far as I know,' said Alex in a completely expressionless
voice.

'Then why are you here?'

'The Commissioner found himself unable to come to Delhi after all. He asked me to explain the matter to you and to arrange if possible for you to travel to Lunjore with the Gardener-Smiths, who will be going there shortly.'

'But——' Winter put out a small hand and clutched at a chair-back as though for support—'but they are not going for nearly three weeks!'

'I know. I am sorry. But there appears to be no one else going there at present, and you cannot travel alone.'

'Why can't I go with you?'

'The Commissioner does not consider it would be suitable,' said Alex dryly. 'Besides, I do not go myself for at least two weeks. I have some business here that the Commissioner wishes cleared up.'

Winter sat down slowly, the apple-green flounces that had been intended to please Conway foaming about her. She looked very small and forlorn, and as once before on the deck of the *Sirius* at Calcutta, Alex found himself reflecting that strangling was probably too good for Mr. Barton. Yet was this slender young thing quite as unsophisticated as she appeared? It would be interesting to know just what was behind the scene that he had interrupted. Young ladies—particularly young ladies who were engaged to be married—did not normally indulge in *tête-à-têtes* with unwelcome admirers, and if she had not wished to be alone with Carlyon she had only to call out. The bungalow appeared to be swarming with servants, not to mention four Abuthnots.

Lord Carlyon, decided Alex dispassionately, appeared to be a strikingly handsome man of a type who might be expected to exercise a considerable appeal to women of all ages; and if he had travelled from Calcutta to Delhi with the Abuthnots it would not be surprising if he had succeeded in making an impression upon the Commissioner's betrothed. If he had indeed done so Alex could not feel sorry for it, for he was of the opinion that almost anyone would be preferable to Mr. Barton as a husband for the Condesa. He wished that he did not feel so responsible for the girl. It was an absurd feeling and it irritated him, for there was no reason for it. What happened to her was no concern of his, and she was, when he came to consider the matter, an extremely fortunate young woman and one whom many might envy.

Alex looked down at the bent head and the small hands that were clasped together so tightly among the absurd apple-green ruffles, and frowned; aware of a disturbing tug at his heart, and thinking again that India was really no place for such women, and that if there ever should be a rising on a serious scale they were going to be a devilish responsibility.

Winter, looking up at this point in his reflections, caught that frown, and it brought back her courage and a sudden spark of anger. She rose, straight-backed, and said in a cool, composed voice: 'It has been most kind in you to trouble yourself on my behalf. I hope you will not think me ungrateful. Did Mr. Barton not send a letter?'

'There was no time. The alteration in plan came at the last moment and I myself left at less than half an hour's notice,' said Alex curtly. He considered it unnecessary to explain that the Commissioner had been in no condition to stand upright, let alone write a legible line, when he had last seen him.

If the truth were known, Mr. Barton, faced with the journey to Delhi, had once more been attacked by his old fears—the same fears that had kept him from sailing to England to claim his bride. Supposing—just supposing—that she should not like what she saw of him? Might she not, supported by the Abuthnots, even go so far as to break off her engagement? Better perhaps to bring her to Lunjore where she would be in the society of strangers (he did not count Colonel Moulson or the Gardener-Smiths), for once there she would have no chance of changing her mind. He would see to that!

Mr. Barton decided to play safe and cancel any idea of going to Delhi. He had celebrated this decision by getting exceedingly drunk, and was barely able, on the morning on which he had originally intended to set out, to do more than mumble a few directions to Captain Randall, the gist of which had been that Alex must see to that Delhi business—he would find the documents relative to it among the office files—and make his excuses to Winter. She had better come to Lunjore with the Gardener-Smiths. He was damned if he could go chasin' to Delhi to get married. She must come here. Mountain t' Mahomet! Alex must arrange it. He would write when he felt more the thing; and where in the name of damnation that black brute of a contractor had procured the last consignment of brandy from he could not imagine——

A description of this scene would, Alex considered, only lead to further misunderstanding, and if the Commissioner's betrothed had indeed found herself growing attached to Lord Carlyon the problem would probably solve itself without any further interference on his part. He could only hope so; for if the girl did not marry either Carlyon or Barton he could see himself being landed with the unwelcome task of finding a suitable chaperon to escort her back to Ware.

14

LOTTIE was to be married at St. James's Church in Delhi on the twenty-sixth of the month, and preparation for the wedding kept the ladies of the household in a constant ferment over silks and muslins and the mysteries of feminine underwear. There were also expeditions, picnics, parties and balls, and Carlyon received a flattering amount of attention from the garrison, and was even asked to call upon the ragged old ghost who lived surrounded by a tatterdemalion court in the Palace within the Red Fort of Delhi —Bahadur Shah, descendant of the House of Timur and last of the Moguls. But Winter remained as elusive as ever and Carlyon's exasperation mounted daily.

His temper was not improved by the frequent addition of Captain Randall to the party, and he found that his first and instant dislike of the man increased with every sight of him. But the contempt he had first felt for him had vanished, and try as he would he had been unable to recapture it. There was a look in Captain Randall's coolly observant eyes, and something in his bland manner, that disconcerted and frequently infuriated Lord Carlyon; but it was difficult to pick a quarrel with a wounded man, and in addition to carrying his arm in a sling Captain Randall was not an easy man to quarrel with. He appeared to be entirely uninterested in Lord Carlyon and his proceedings. Nor did he seem particularly interested in the social gaieties of the Delhi season, and Carlyon was frequently puzzled to know why he troubled to accept invitations to affairs that he so obviously found uninteresting.

Alex was finding it hard to explain this to himself. The business that was occupying him in Delhi consisted mainly of the collecting, correlating and checking of evidence in a contested case of accession of territory by lapse, and the bulk of the documentary evidence was being dealt with by the clerks of Mr. Fraser and Sir Theophilus Metcalfe. He found himself with a fair amount of time on his hands, and the Abuthnots were pressing with their invitations; but he had previously experienced no difficulty in refusing equally pressing invitations, and he was not entirely sure why he did not refuse these.

Was it only on account of that irksome feeling of responsibility that he could not rid himself of? Because he was aware, without quite knowing why, that Winter was frightened and unhappy? She certainly gave no outward signs of being either, but there was a difference in her that had not escaped him. She had lost that look of expectation, and was once again the withdrawn, wary child of the early spring; but he sensed that in some way— perhaps because she looked upon him as a link between herself and Conway Barton?—his presence reassured her.

In this he was partly right. Winter had understood and for-given Conway's failure to meet her at Calcutta, for Captain Randall had not been in Lunjore then and possibly there was no one competent to be left in charge of affairs. But if Alex was able to take over the work that was to have brought Conway to Delhi, then surely he could have been left in Lunjore for a matter of a week or ten days in order to allow Conway to come here?

She knew that it was disloyal of her even to think such a thing. Conway must be right, and of course duty must come before personal happiness: he had never failed to impress that upon her in his infrequent letters. But she could not help feeling that just this once he might have arranged things so that he could have left his desk for a few days to come for her. If he had been in ill-health she could have understood it better, but Captain Randall had denied that he was ill, and in a letter that had arrived a few days later Conway had mentioned only pressure of work. He was, he explained, anxious to clear up the more pressing business of the district so as to enable him to take a really adequate spell of leave for their honeymoon. The letter was a more affectionate one than Conway usually wrote and it had dispelled much of her unhappiness. But despite it she was still conscious of a return of that frightening feeling of loneliness and insecurity that had been so familiar a part of her childhood, and which had so nearly vanished with the arrival of the letters that Captain Randall had brought to Ware.

Winter suspected that Captain Randall was inclined to regard her as a somewhat tiresome responsibility, but she could not help feeling grateful for his continued presence in Delhi, if only because it protected her from Lord Carlyon's more than unwelcome attentions. When Alex was there she could forget about Carlyon and relax from the strain of being perpetually upon her guard.

That she was bent upon avoiding him and was not merely being coy was gradually borne in upon Carlyon, and he began to realize that vanity and self-assurance had led him into making a grave tactical error. Far from awakening Winter to the delights of dalliance he had only disgusted and frightened her, and if he were not careful he would lose her to the nonentity after all. But he could not make his apologies and set himself right with her in the presence of others, and it seemed as though he were never to see her alone.

His opportunity came at a ball when he stood up with her for a waltz that she had been unable, in the interests of politeness, to refuse him, and he made the most of it. He attributed his unforgivable conduct on the day of their arrival to brandy and laudanum drops which, he explained, he had taken as a precaution against a suspected bout of fever. He abased himself and begged for forgiveness, employing all his considerable charm and facility of address. Having received it, he proceeded with confidence to make her a proposal of marriage.

He was fully aware, said Carlyon, of the impropriety of addressing such a proposal to an engaged lady, but he must beg her to make allowances for a man deeply in love. The fact that she had not seen her betrothed since she was a child had given him grounds for hoping that she might bring herself at least to postpone the wedding, in order to allow him time in which to make her change her mind. Carlyon had expressed himself with fervour and humility, and had received in return an unqualified refusal that contained nothing which he could conceivably take as encouragement to persist in his suit. The music had ceased, and Winter had not granted him a second dance.

She had been touched by the humility of Lord Carlyon's apology, and disagreeably surprised by his subsequent proposal. But having left him in no doubt as to her feelings she had expected him to leave the Abuthnots' house and Delhi more or less immediately, for if, as he had assured her, she was his sole reason for being there, there could be no further point in his remaining.

But Carlyon had not removed. Instead he had written her a carefully worded letter, delivered to her by his bearer, in which he had assured her that he had not intended to distress her, promised never to mention the subject again or enact her any more tragedies, and hoped that he might be honoured at least by her friendship, though he must be denied that nearer relationship he had so ardently desired. If he could at any time be of any service to her, his life was at her disposal. He remained—etc.

Winter could not help feeling that she had misjudged Lord

Carlyon, and she had smiled at him shyly when they next met. She was, however, entirely ignorant of the feelings that had prompted the writing of that letter, and had she had any inkling of them she would have been considerably alarmed. For Carlyon had written that letter with no other motive than the hope that by doing so he might prevent the little Ballesteros from pressing for his removal from Delhi. He had every intention of removing shortly, but he had made up his mind to take her with him.

Having much to his own amazement decided that he actually wished to marry the girl, it had never occurred to him that she would not be willing to jilt the nonentity once she discovered his intentions to be honourable. He had never proposed marriage to any woman before, and possessed sufficient vanity and bland self-assurance to consider that to do so would be to bestow a very considerable honour. To have his offer incontinently refused was something he had never considered to be remotely possible. She could not mean it!

Carlyon had passed from stunned incredulity to dangerous rage. His languid manner had always disguised a hot and uncertain temper, and now suddenly he lost control of himself. He wanted the girl. Wanted her more than he had ever thought it possible to want anything; and by God he would have her!

His plan was quite a simple one. Make his peace with Winter, and having made a few necessary arrangements, carry her off and compromise her so that she would be glad to marry him. The clod might cause a little trouble at first, but Carlyon could always use his influence to procure him some advancement, and as he had not seen his prospective bride for six years there could be no question of love on either side. The man was obviously only interested in her fortune, and Carlyon was sufficiently wealthy to apply a generous gold-plaster to any wounds he might receive.

*　　　　*　　　　*

Now that Winter would be staying for Lottie's wedding it had been decided that she as well as Sophie must be a bridesmaid. They were to wear pale blue muslin profusely decorated with satin bows and quilling, and diminutive bonnets of blue straw trimmed with roses. The wedding-dress was pronounced to fit admirably, and Mrs. Abuthnot, watching her elder daughter try on her bridal array before the looking-glass, shed motherly tears and announced that she did not know how she should support the loss of her dearest, sweetest Lottie!

'You will have me, Mamma,' comforted Sophie.

Mrs. Abuthnot embraced her and said tearfully that it would not be long before Sophie too would be wearing a wedding-gown.

'I do not think I shall ever marry,' said Sophie with a small unhappy sigh. 'I shall stay single and be a comfort to you and Papa.'

'Nonsense, dear!' said Mrs. Abuthnot bracingly. 'Lottie, my love, I really think that we shall have to change your hair-style a little. I am not sure that it would not look better dressed a little more forward, to suit a wreath.'

Sophie reached up to rearrange the veil on Lottie's golden head, wondering as she did so if she herself would ever wear bridal array. Would Captain Randall ever look at her as Edward looked at Lottie, or as Lord Carlyon—Sophie was not unobservant —looked at Winter? Sophie doubted it. Captain Randall treated her more as though she were a pleasant child still in the school-room, or, worse, as though she were his younger sister. Sophie fancied that she would have been happier if he had ignored her or treated her to the disinterested civility he extended to older women.

'But I will grow older,' thought Sophie hopefully. 'Perhaps it will be different next year. . . .'

There was a sound of stir and bustle in the hall and the next moment the door opened to admit Mrs. Gardener-Smith who swept in, accompanied by Delia, exclaiming that she was sure that dear Mrs. Abuthnot would forgive this unceremonious entry but that the butler had told her that the ladies were trying on clothes for the *shadi* (wedding) and as she would not dream of dragging any of them away from such an absorbing occupation, she had come to add herself to the admiring audience.

It soon became obvious, however, that Mrs. Gardener-Smith was not in the least interested in Lottie's trousseau and had called in expectation of seeing Lord Carlyon. There was to be a ball at Metcalfe House, the residence of Sir Theophilus Metcalfe, Chief Magistrate of Delhi, and Mrs. Gardener-Smith hoped that Lord Carlyon might, if reminded of her presence, think to engage Delia for a waltz or the cotillion.

But Carlyon was not in. He had ridden over to the Artillery Lines to see some carriage horses that an officer wished to sell, and would not be back for at least an hour, explained Mrs. Abuthnot. Mrs. Gardener-Smith signified her willingness to partake of refreshments and wait, and the two ladies fell to discussing the arrangements for the wedding and the various social engagements of the coming week.

A moonlight picnic on the walls of Delhi had been arranged by the livelier spirits among the younger officers, and neither lady was entirely sure that they approved of such a festivity. Naturally no young lady would be attending it unchaperoned, and both Mrs. Abuthnot and Mrs. Gardener-Smith would be there to keep a maternal eye upon their daughters. But all the same they were not sure that such an entertainment was not a little *fast*.

'Although, of course,' said Mrs. Abuthnot hopefully, 'when the moon is at the full it really is almost as bright as day, and I hear that it is to be quite a large party. We are to start an hour before sunset so as to be able to observe the moon rise. It should be a very pretty sight.'

'Does Lord Carlyon intend to go?' enquired Mrs. Gardener-Smith.

'Yes, indeed! We are all to go. Except Colonel Abuthnot of course. He says that such things are not at all in his line. But with Carlyon and dear Alex to accompany us we shall not want for male escorts, and shall do very nicely.'

Carlyon returned before the visitors left, and in reply to Mrs. Gardener-Smith's questions said that he had purchased a carriage and pair with the object of travelling in his own conveyance

instead of by dâk *ghari* when he left Delhi. He was at present
engaged in the purchase of spare horses for the carriage, for
although he himself preferred to ride, on a long journey a
carriage was sometimes necessary.

Mrs. Gardener-Smith was desolated to hear that Lord Carlyon
intended to deprive them of his society, and hoped that he would
perhaps find the time to visit Lunjore. She was sure that Colonel
Gardener-Smith would be able to show him some tiger-shooting
in the jungles there. She then turned the conversation to the
ball at Metcalfe House and tomorrow's moonlight picnic, where
it remained until they were interrupted by the return of Colonel
Abuthnot, and the two ladies took their leave.

There were clouds to the north-east of Delhi on the following evening; a threatening bar of greyness that lay along the far
horizon and caused Mrs. Abuthnot some anxiety, though Alex
assured her that their presence merely indicated rain somewhere in the foothills. He had added that if it had been raining
up north he might well find himself being held up on his way
back to Lunjore, but that the picnic party stood in no danger of a
wetting that night.

Carlyon, Winter and Alex had ridden to the picnic, while
Mrs. Abuthnot and her daughters had driven in the carriage.
The ride had been a pleasant one, though a trifle dusty, for Carlyon had behaved in an exemplary manner. He could be excellent
company when he chose, and this evening he had exerted himself
to please, so that by the time they arrived at the Kashmir Gate
Winter was feeling quite in charity with him.

They rode in under the massive arch of the gate, and dismount-
ing before the Main Guard, left their horses to the care of the
attendant syces and walked up the sloping stone ramp to the
battlements, where earlier guests had already assembled.

Alex had not accompanied them there. He had stopped to
speak to a Jemadar of the guard and had been hailed by a man on
horseback who was approaching the gate from the direction of
St. James's church.

'Alex, by God!' The man had spurred forward and leaning

down from the saddle had smitten Captain Randall between the shoulder-blades. 'When did you get back? I haven't had so much as a word from you in half a year, you ingrate!'

Alex had turned swiftly and gripped the proffered hand. 'William! What the devil are you doing here? They told me you were in Dagshai.'

'So I am—officially.'

Alex said: 'Get down off that horse and join us. Condesa, may I introduce Lieutenant Hodson. William, the Condesa de los Aguilares and Lord Carlyon.'

Lieutenant Hodson had reached down a hand to Winter and said: 'Will you forgive me if I do not dismount? I have been suffering from a dislocated ankle and can do little more than hobble when on the ground.'

He was a slim wiry man, as slim as Alex, though a little taller and looked to be a few years older; but where Alex was dark-haired and deeply sunburned, this man was of almost Nordic fairness. The Indian suns, that had apparently had no power to tan his intensely white skin, had bleached his blond hair and long cavalry moustache to a yellow so pale as to be almost white, and only his eyes were dark. They were remarkable eyes, of so deep a blue as to appear black at first sight, and large enough to have graced a girl, but as hard and fierce and glittering as a hawk's.

He shook hands with Winter, favoured Carlyon with a direct look that appeared to sum him up, analyse him, and dismiss him in one brief second, said: 'Your servant, sir,' and turned back to Alex with an enquiry as to his injured arm.

Winter and Lord Carlyon continued on their way and joined the remainder of the party on the ramparts, and Alex said: 'William, your manners are as abominable as ever!'

'Nonsense! You cannot expect me to waste time uttering social inanities when I have not seen you for close on two years. Get back on to that spavined animal you have there and ride with me. I can't talk to you here.'

Alex swung himself back into the saddle and the two men rode out through the gate and turned right-handed along the far side of the deep ditch that formed a wide, dry moat between the walls of Delhi and the open country and jungle-like greenery of the Kudsia Bagh.

'Who was the Spanish beauty?' demanded Hodson, 'and what are you doing in such company?'

'Acting as duenna,' said Alex with a grin. 'The Spanish beauty has come out to marry my respected chief, and I have had the thankless task of seeing to her safety during the journey. I escorted her out from England.'

'*What!*' Hodson threw back his head and shouted with laughter. 'Now I have seen everything!'

'It has its humorous side,' admitted Alex with a somewhat rueful smile. 'But then I admit I had not visualized, when I joined the Bengal Army, finding myself called upon to act in almost every civil capacity from magistrate to midwife. Being employed to bring out brides for senior officials should be no surprise, and not much worse than being saddled with the care of a stray orphan, which I seem to remember you suffering from on one occasion.'

'My God, yes! Shall I ever forget it! The tasks we are called upon to do in this country would raise the hairs on the head of any Horse Guards officer. Who was the lordling? Do not tell me that you have been press-ganged into bear-leading the globe-trotting nobility in addition to nursemaiding your unspeakable chief's betrothed?'

'Not yet. Though I daresay I shall come to it!—all is grist to the mill in this service. Lord Carlyon is merely visiting in Delhi.'

'Dangerous look in his eye,' commented Hodson. 'Had a horse like that once. Thoroughbred with the lines of an archangel, and as full of vice as Beelzebub. I shot him. Which reminds me, you didn't tell me what you've been doing to your arm. Riding accident? Or did someone put a bullet through you?'

'The latter,' said Alex, drawing rein among the scrub and the grasses that fringed the banks of the Jumna river. 'It's a long story, but I propose to inflict it on you. The sling, however, is merely a façade. It could have been discarded some days ago, but I find it useful.'

He smiled, and Hodson, who unlike Lord Carlyon had reason to know that particular smile, said accusingly: 'What devilry are you up to, Alex?'

Alex laughed. 'No devilry, I assure you, Will. But it does not happen to suit me just now to involve myself in a brawl with his noble lordship. And while I carry one arm in a sling he can hardly be as offensive as he would wish. One cannot insult a man who appears incapable of repaying the insult with a blow.'

The hard blue eyes regarded him with a speculative interest not untinged with surprise. 'What's plaguing you, Alex? Afraid of a scandal?'

'Good God, no! It is only that I, like you, distrust the type. He does not care to be crossed and is, I think, egotistical enough to go to almost any lengths to avenge an injury. He has influential friends, and at the present moment I have no particular desire to have complaints laid against me in Calcutta—or anywhere else for that matter—and possibly find some uninstructed Johnny Raw replacing me while I am sent to kick my heels in a useless backwater.'

'As I have been,' said Hodson grimly. 'You heard, did you not, that I had been removed from command of the Guides and that there had been a court of enquiry on my actions?—yes, of course you did! You wrote. They proved nothing of their case, but the findings exonerating me have been filed in some government pigeon-hole, there to gather dust while I kick my heels in Dagshai. I tell you, Alex, it is damnably hard to begin again as an infantry subaltern after more than eleven years' hard work. I shall not stand it much longer.'

Alex said: 'Come on down out of that saddle if you can hobble as far as those trees. I have more to say to you than can be comfortably said sitting this fidgeting animal.'

He offered a hand, and having tethered the horses the two men moved off between the tussocks of grass and seated themselves on the river bank, looking out across the Jumna that lay all pearl-pink and glinting in the evening light. Up-stream stretched the curves of the river, the wide white sands and wider plain with the

H

white roof of Metcalfe House showing above the thick green of trees while behind them, a mile or so distant, ran the low line of the Ridge, while to their right the walls of Delhi glowed rose-red in the dusty glamour of the setting sun.

Alex looked over his shoulder at the thicket some ten paces behind them, and Hodson, interpreting the look, said: 'There are peafowl in that cane-brake. I saw them move as we passed. If anyone comes that way they will warn us.'

Alex grinned appreciatively. 'You are a great man, William.'

'Not yet. But I will be. God willing, I will be!' Hodson put up an impatient hand, and pulling off the peaked pith helmet that he wore, tossed it away and ran his fingers through his yellow hair. 'What is this long story I was to hear?'

Alex settled his back against a tree-trunk and retold the tale of Khanwai, and Hodson listened without interruption, and when he had finished remarked: 'Very interesting. At least it's something to know for certain that Kishan Prasad is one of the inner ring! I've met the man. A clever devil, and likeable.'

'And damnably dangerous,' said Alex tersely.

'Oh, yes. As a king cobra—or a krait! And a bosom friend of your delightful Commissioner Barton's, I gather.'

'That, too.' Alex's voice was edged with bitterness, and Hodson reached out a hand and gripping his uninjured arm gave it a little shake.

'I know how it is. God—don't I know! Sometimes I've lain awake at night feeling like—like Krishna urging Arjuna on to slaying his kin and justifying the deed! If only we could sweep out some of these obese fools, what an empire this would be!'

He threw out a hand in a gesture that seemed to embrace the vast plain and the quiet river, the ancient city of Delhi and all of India, and there was a sudden glow in his eyes. Then his hand dropped again and he said bitterly:

'There are so many men whom one could follow blind. Lawrence, Nicholson, Edwardes—oh, and a dozen other first-rate fellows. But not even a hundred good men can undo the harm that one Barton can create—or one hide-bound octogenarian, for that matter! I am not sure which is worse; the frankly venal—of whom there are mercifully few—or the aged, osseous ineptitudes which this fatuous seniority system forces on us by the score. I tell you, Alex, one of the brigadiers I served under in the affair of 'forty-nine could not even see his regiment! I had to lead his horse by the bridle until the animal's nose was on their bayonets, and even then he had to ask me which way the men were facing! The Company's policy of promotion by seniority may be a boon to poor men, but it is a godsend to fools, for it enables them to rise equally with men ten times their worth; and for the purposes of discipline in peace and effective action in war there never was a worse system! One day we are going to pay heavily for it.'

'Probably sooner than we think,' said Alex grimly. 'By the way, Will, you have not told me yet what you are doing here. Have you taken French leave?'

'More or less. I came because I heard a rumour that a certain elusive and assiduous subject of the Czar was expected in Delhi, and I thought it worth while to make a few enquiries.'

'Gregori Sparkov?'

'The same. A persevering gentleman, you will allow.'

'And at the same old game, I suppose. Helping to sow the wind in the pious hope that we shall reap the subsequent whirlwind.'

'What else? Farid Khan sent me word that he was expected, but he did not say how he had come by the information, so I came down because I thought I might be able to get more out of him. But something or someone has scared him badly, and he isn't giving anything away. I wonder . . .' He relapsed into silence, staring meditatively at the distant walls of Delhi until his shadow, that the setting sun had thrown long and blue on the white sands of the Jumna, lay black behind him in the full blaze of the risen moon.

A jackal scuttled out across the silvered sands to feed on the rotting remains of a half-burnt corpse that had stranded in shoal water, and a peacock called harshly from among the cane-brakes

of the Kudsia Bagh. The tethered horses stamped uneasily and
Alex's mare whinnied softly.

'That will be Niaz,' said Alex, glancing over his shoulder.
He stood up and reaching down his right hand helped Hodson
to his feet. 'I shall have to go back and do my social duty. Join
us, Will.'

'Not a chance. I must be in Dagshai tomorrow.'

'*Tomorrow!* Are you mad? William, you cannot do it! Not
with a bad ankle. Why must you always ride hell-for-leather?'

'Prefer it. And it may come in useful one day. Besides you
know I can sleep in the saddle. As for the ankle I've got it
strapped into splints for the occasion. That's why I'm so lame.
Damnably painful, but entirely serviceable.'

He limped over to his horse and called out: 'Holla, Niaz
Mohamed. Is it thou?'

Niaz rode forward into the moonlight and slipping from his
horse gave the salute that is only given to elders of high rank.

'*Salaam Aleikum.* Is it well with thee, Hodson Bahadur?'

'Nay. Ill. My star is sinking.'

'That I have heard,' said Niaz gravely. 'No matter. It will
rise again.'

He held the stirrup for Hodson to mount and Alex said: 'Have
they sent thee to look for me?'

'Nay; I followed, for there was a sadhu who also came this
way. A Shakta of the Left Hand. He came very quietly, keeping
among the trees, and I came after to see what he would do. But
hearing my horse move among the dried grass he turned back
and went away to the northward. I waited to see that he did not
return.'

'Some more of your friends, Alex?' enquired Hodson over his
shoulder, as his horse picked its way across the rough ground to
the narrow footpath at the edge of the counterscarp.

Alex shrugged his shoulders. 'India is full of sadhus. Do you
really ride for Dagshai tonight, William?'

'I am afraid so.'

'Then I shall not be seeing you for some time. I'm for Lunjore

on Monday. The business here is cleared up a good three or four
days earlier than was expected, but Fraser has asked me to remain
on over the week-end. I should get back, but I have accepted, for
he is having a guest who I shall be interested to meet. Dundu
Pant. The Peishwa's heir. Met him?'

'Once. Another krait. What is he doing here?'

'Oh, purely a private visit, I gather. Unofficial. He stays in
Delhi for only two days. I admit I have always had a certain
amount of sympathy for the man. There is no getting away from
it that the Hindu law has allowed the right of adoption for
centuries, and we cannot sweep it out of court merely because it
is not a custom of the West. Sir John Malcolm had pledged the
Government to bestow that pension, and had this man been the
true son of the old Peishwa he would have fallen heir to it. I
cannot help feeling that it was a niggardly gesture to refuse it to
him on the ground that he was adopted, when in the eyes of
every Hindu he is the legal heir.'

'Trouble with you, Alex,' Hodson threw over his shoulder, 'is
that you will see both sides of a question. It makes life too
complicated.'

Alex made a wry grimace. 'I am aware of it. I wish I had
your singleness of purpose. What is your star, William?'

'Leadership!' said Hodson promptly. 'I would like to be able
to make men follow me blind—as I would follow a man like
John Nicholson. To damnation if necessary.'

'They will,' said Alex with a smile. 'Niaz does not hold my
stirrup, nor call me Bahadur!'

Hodson laughed. 'Do you know, I believe they will. That is
if I can prevent myself being hamstrung by a lot of incompetent
old women in trousers! But I'll get my chance one day, and then,
by God, I'll show 'em!'

He reined in his horse as they reached the Main Guard and
held out his hand. 'God bless you, Alex.'

Their hands met in a brief hard grip, and then he had touched
his spur to his horse's flank and galloped back under the dark
arch of the Kashmir Gate while Niaz, who had dismounted, stood

stiffly to the salute. Alex heard his horse's hooves drum hollowly
on the bridge over the moat and then he had gone.

'What does Hodson Bahadur do here?' enquired Niaz in an
undertone, holding the horse for Alex to dismount.

'He sees a friend in the city.'

'Does he so!' said Niaz thoughtfully. 'Dost thou remember
how in the year following the taking of the Punjab an astrologer
in Amritsa cast his horoscope, and foretold that in seven years his
star would arise and burn bright among much blood? Those
years be all but sped, and it may be that he smells that blood!'

He took the reins and led the horses away into the shadows,
while Alex walked up the ramp to the battlements and into a
babble of voices and laughter and the clink of glasses and silver.

15

'MY dear Alex, we had quite given you up! Where have you
been?' Mrs. Abuthnot edged her chair back a little and pulled
aside her ample skirts as Alex came over and subsided on to the
carpet at her feet.

'I am sorry. I met a friend whom I had not seen for over two
years and who leaves Delhi tonight.'

He accepted a plate of cold food and ate it abstractedly, his
mind still on his conversation with William, but presently he
became aware that someone had addressed him by name, and
he roused himself and turned to find that it was Winter who sat
on the opposite side of him.

Winter had kept close to Mrs. Abuthnot since her arrival, for
try as she would she could not bring herself to share in the
universal high spirits. She had done her best to appear interested
and entertained, but the iron band that had seemed to fasten
itself about her heart when she had learned that Conway would
not be coming to Delhi had only drawn tighter among the prevailing merriment. A shy young Lieutenant of Bengal Artillery,

George Willoughby, had been seated on her left, and Mrs. Abuthnot's voluminous skirts had effectively protected her right until Alex had materialized out of the moonlight and sat down at Mrs. Abuthnot's feet.

With his arrival some of her fear and tension and doubt faded. There was something about Alex that was instantly reassuring, and Winter fought down a sudden and childish desire to clutch at his sleeve and hold it tightly. She doubted if he would have noticed had she done so, for he appeared to be singularly distrait and as if his own thoughts were of sufficient interest to make him oblivious of the babble of talk about him. She answered Lieutenant Willoughby's shy attempts at conversation so much at random that he could only feel relieved when at length she turned to Alex and said: 'Who was that man whom you introduced to me, Captain Randall? Is he stationed in Delhi?'

Alex turned towards her with something like a frown and then his face cleared and he said: 'Oh, it's you. I'm sorry. I was not attending. What did you say?'

Winter repeated the question and Alex said: 'William Hodson. No, he was only here for the day. His regiment is at present in the Simla hills. I rather think that he has taken French leave.'

'You mean left without permission? Are officers allowed to do that?'

'No! But William is a law unto himself—which has caused him a great deal of trouble in the past and will probably cause him more in the future! But if ever we get into another war in this country I would rather have William at my back than a whole army corps. Not that he'd be at one's back. He'd be twenty paces ahead!'

Winter said: 'You are fond of him, aren't you?'

'Yes,' said Alex briefly.

'Tell me about him.'

Somewhat to his surprise Alex found himself complying with the request and telling her something of William—that dynamic, unpredictable person whose physical endurance matched his enthusiasm and impatience.

'The trouble with William,' concluded Alex, 'is that he says what he thinks, and people don't like that. And what he does is usually proved right, and they like that even less! He has been sent to kick his heels doing a subaltern's job in Dagshai—and this at a time when we need his kind of man more than we have ever needed them before! My only consolation is that if there ever is any serious trouble no one will be able to hold him!'

Alex had forgotten that he was talking to the promised wife of Mr. Commissioner Barton who had caused him a great deal of inconvenience and irritation. He had been speaking as though it were to someone with whom he was entirely at ease, and he looked down at her now, realizing suddenly that he had been talking uninterruptedly through three courses, and as though the two of them had been alone: which indeed they might have been, for Mrs. Abuthnot and a Mrs. De Tessier had kept up an animated discussion above their heads, and Lieutenant Willoughby had been engaged in conversation by Miss Jennings, daughter of the Chaplain of Delhi.

Alex looked away again and caught a smouldering glance that momentarily held his own. So Carlyon, at least, had noticed that he had been monopolizing the little Ballesteros for the last twenty minutes or so! Observing that look Alex was reminded vividly of Hodson's comment of an hour ago. 'Dangerous look in his eye,' William had said, and he had been right. Alex looked thoughtfully back at Winter and then reached out and removed the empty plate that she held in her hands.

He said: 'I seem to have been talking a deal too much. What a subject for a moonlight picnic! William should feel honoured. Have I bored you?'

'No.'

A swift and appreciative smile lit Alex's eyes. He found the brief monosyllable, shorn of the polite protestations with which a more socially experienced young lady would have adorned it, curiously touching. Alex, himself a man who did not trouble to say 'Yes' or 'No' unless he meant it, appreciated not only its obvious sincerity but the fact that the speaker was as yet sufficiently unversed in social small-talk to say exactly what she meant and no more.

He bent to remove a large moth that appeared to be in danger of drowning in a bowl of fruit salad, and said: 'Why were you interested in him?'

But this time the answer took him completely by surprise, for Winter said simply: 'Because he was a friend of yours.'

Alex looked up, startled. 'You see,' said Winter slowly, and as though she were explaining something to herself as much as to Alex, 'I do not really know very much about you, but one gets to know a little more about people when you know something of their friends.'

'And do you know more about me now?' enquired Alex with an odd note in his voice.

'I think so.' She looked away from him and traced a small aimless pattern with one finger on the close pile of the Persian rug before her. 'Alex——' Once again she was unaware of having used his Christian name.

'Yes?'

'Why could not Conway come to Delhi? Was there any—any other reason?'

Alex did not answer and Winter said: 'Other than his work, I mean?'

Damnation! thought Alex, taken off-guard and completely at a loss. How did one answer a question like that and at a time like this? And what was the good of answering it? He had told her once and been slashed across the face for his pains. Was that because he had been a stranger? Now that she knew him better would she take it from him and believe it? or—— 'I cannot throw it into her face in the middle of this bloody picnic-party,' thought Alex. 'I *cannot*. It will have to wait——'

'Was there?' persisted Winter.

'No,' said Alex shortly. 'That is—no. I——'

He was interrupted by Mrs. Abuthnot who leant forward and tapped him upon the shoulder with her fan. 'Alex, dear boy, you are sitting on my flounce and I wish to move. Thank you——' She rose and shook out her skirts as Alex came swiftly to his feet. 'The servants are to clear away and then we are to

H*

have some singing, I believe. I see that Lieutenant Larrabie has brought a guitar and Miss Clifford has her mandolin. Winter, my love, Mrs. De Tessier tells me that we are to remove for a while so that the gentlemen may finish their wine. Come, dear. Come, Lottie.'

There was a ruffle and a rustle of silks and muslins as the crinolines ceased to be flattened circles and their owners drifted away in the moonlight like a flight of enormous bubbles blown along by a light breeze.

By the time they returned the debris of the picnic had been cleared away. Only the carpets and cushions remained, and an officer possessed of impressive whiskers and a luxuriant moustache was playing a sentimental ballad on a guitar. The majority of the guests did not immediately reseat themselves in a compact group, but scattered along the ramparts talking, laughing and admiring the moonlight and the view. Winter could see no sign of Alex and wondered if he had gone home, but Sophie informed her that he had walked along the wall towards the Water Bastion.

Why had Alex looked so disconcerted when she had asked him about Conway? He had looked—guilty . . .

'Winter, my love,' said Mrs. Abuthnot bearing down upon her accompanied by an unknown gentleman, 'here is someone whom I am sure you must be pleased to meet. Only fancy! Mr. Carroll here passed through Lunjore less than a week ago and stayed the night with Colonel Moulson—you remember Colonel Moulson, do you not, dear?—and they both dined with Mr. Barton. So he can give you the latest news of him. Mr. Carroll, this is the lady who is shortly to marry Mr. Barton. The Condesa de los Aguilares.'

Mr. Carroll, a large man with a red face that even the white moonlight could not pale, stared at Winter and muttered that he was honoured to meet her. He took her hand doubtfully and bowed over it, and in reply to her eager questions said that he had indeed seen the Commissioner at the previous week-end. He was often in Lunjore and had had the pleasure of his acquaintance for some years. Mr. Barton had in fact been kind enough to urge him to stay on and keep him company, there being little to occupy him at present. But though the Commissioner of Lunjore might find time hanging heavily on his hands, he himself had had too many calls upon his time to allow him to——

Mr. Carroll became aware of the amazement and shock reflected on the faces of the Abuthnot ladies and the young Condesa, and stopped, disconcerted and alarmed.

'But that is absurd!' said Mrs. Abuthnot sharply. 'Perhaps you did not know that we expected Mr. Barton in Delhi, but pressure of work did not permit him to leave Lunjore. You must be mistaken.'

'Oh—er—yes,' said Mr. Carroll unhappily. 'I must have misunderstood. Yes, of course. I——'

Winter broke in upon his flounderings. 'Mr. Carroll, please tell me. Why could not my—the Commissioner—come to Delhi? Is he—is he not well?'

Mr. Carroll, embarrassed and distressed, caught at the excuse with the fervour of a drowning man snatching at a passing straw, and overplayed his hand.

'Yes! Yes, I am afraid that is it. He—er—did not wish to distress you. Naturally wished to spare you anxiety. Most awkward, being taken ill at a time like this—felt it very keenly.'

'But—but why did he not tell me?' said Winter, her hands gripped tightly together.

Mr. Carroll gulped, groped wildly for a suitable answer and was visited by inspiration: 'Would not mention it of course, for fear that you would consider it your duty to proceed immediately to his side. Sickroom no place for a delicately nurtured lady. Fever you know—er——' Mr. Carroll had a momentary vision of the corpulent, bloated face of the Commissioner of Lunjore, and improvised glibly: 'a swelling fever. No, no, nothing serious, I assure you. Merely—er—disfiguring. Not catching. But no man of sensibility would wish to meet his betrothed looking so.'

'Oh, the poor, dear man!' exclaimed Mrs. Abuthnot, touched. 'How *well* I understand! How could he wish to allow you to see him in such a sad state? And of *course* he would not permit you

to endure the discomforts of a sickroom! Perhaps that is also
why he could not come to Calcutta? I expect he hoped to be well
enough to proceed to Delhi instead, and suffered a relapse!'

Winter said in an eager, breathless voice: 'Is that so, Mr.
Carroll? How long has he been ill?'

Mr. Carroll looked unhappily at the small, tense face. He had
roistered with Mr. Barton on more than one occasion and considered him a bad man with a bottle or with women. But he
could not tell this white-faced young woman the truth. A lie
was better, and he'd drop a line to Con Barton in the morning,
giving him the tip.

'Er—not above six weeks,' said Mr. Carroll. 'Or it may be a
little more. Slow business. He hopes to be recovered shortly. On
the mend now. You will not let him know that I have told upon
him? He—he did not wish you to suffer any anxiety on his account.'

'No,' said Winter unsteadily. 'No, I will not tell him. But I
am so *very* glad to know—to know that he is better. Thank you,
Mr. Carroll. I am truly grateful to you.'

She gave him her hand and Mr. Carroll bowed over it and
removed himself hurriedly, mopping his brow with a large
bandana handkerchief and breathing hard.

'The poor, dear man!' said Mrs. Abuthnot, presumably referring again to the absent Mr. Barton. 'How truly noble of him
to wish to spare you anxiety. And how very *human* to wish not
to be seen by you except when looking his best! Gentlemen would
like us to think that it is only we who are vain of our looks, but
we know better! Ah, I see that we are to have some music.
Let us join the others. I believe Miss Clifford to be an exceptional
performer on the mandolin. Such a treat! Come, Sophie, dear.
Why, Winter—where are you going, my love?'

Winter did not answer her and it is doubtful if she even heard
the question. She caught up the short train of her riding-habit,
and turning from them went quickly away down the long stretch
of the moonlit ramparts towards the Water Bastion.

There were few people strolling now upon the broad ramparts,
for most of them had returned to join the party and seat them-

selves on the carpets and cushions preparatory to being entertained by the talented Miss Clifford and the romantic Lieutenant Larrabie, and the few who passed Winter were returning from the far end of the wall. There was still, however, a lone gentleman who remained seated in an embrasure of the battlements overlooking the river, the end of his cigar making a small warm pin-point of light in the blue and black and silver of the night.

Alex had no wish for company. He was feeling angry and irritable and irrationally guilty. He had hoped that he need do no more in the way of warning off Mr. Barton's betrothed, for once she reached Lunjore and saw the man, the whole affair—apart from arranging for her return to England—would be over. And, what was more to the point, the breaking of the engagement would have nothing whatever to do with him, Alex Randall, and therefore it would not lead to the Commissioner having him removed from Lunjore and sent to eat his heart out—as William was doing—in some useless and junior appointment. But Winter had asked him a direct question and it must be answered. He had answered it with a lie because she had taken him off-guard and it had been impossible to answer it truthfully in those surroundings. She had asked it because she was frightened and unsure. He knew that. Had she also asked it because now that she had come to know him better and to regard him with less hostility, she had remembered what he had told her in the avenue at Ware, and begun to wonder if, after all, it could be true?

He would have to tell her, and this time she would believe him and go back to Calcutta and to England instead of to Lunjore. And that meant that the Commissioner would ask questions and—— 'Oh, damn all women!' thought Alex savagely. 'What has come over me?' Surely this was no time to allow one small, white, frightened face to come between him and the work there was to do. And yet——

Various couples passed him, chattering and laughing, but he kept his shoulder turned to them and no one broke in upon his thoughts, and presently they drifted back towards the Main Guard again and he was alone with the moonlight, the glittering river that wound between the wide ghostly sandbanks below the walls, and a white egret that had alighted softly on the battlements some half a dozen yards to his right.

Someone at the far end of the wall was singing 'Where are the flowers we gathered at morning?' to the accompaniment of a mandolin: a plaintive ballad that he had last heard in England. He heard a sound of quick light footsteps and the rustle of a woman's dress, and the egret rose with a flap of silver wings and flew off into the night as the footsteps came to a stop beside him. Alex tossed the end of his cigar over the battlements, turned, and rose to his feet.

Winter's small face appeared drained of all colour in the white moonlight, and she breathed unevenly as though she had been running. The close-fitting pearl-grey habit she wore in place of a crinoline moulded the lovely lines of her figure and lent her an illusion of maturity and height, but she could not control the childish trembling of her lips or keep the hurt and anger from her eyes, and Alex, looking at her in the full moonlight with his own face in shadow, felt an odd pain at his heart and a hurt and anger that matched her own.

She said in a quick breathless voice that she tried to keep steady: 'You knew what was the matter with Conway, didn't you? You knew all the time! You could have told me, even if he did not want me to know. I had a right to know! And all these weeks I've thought—I've thought——'

Her voice broke and Alex said curtly: 'I did try to tell you once, but you would not listen.'

'You never told me! I asked you, on the day that you came to tell me that he could not come, if there was anything the matter with him, and you said there was not. And I asked you again tonight——'

'I'm sorry,' repeated Alex, relief and pity submerging that inexplicable anger. It did not occur to him to wonder how she could have come by the knowledge. It was enough that she knew the truth at last without any further attempt on his part to force her to it. But, unaccountably, the fact that she had trusted him to tell her the truth hurt him unbearably.

Winter said: 'You knew the reason why he did not come to meet me in Calcutta. You had a letter from him too. He must have told you in that.'

Alex's brows twitched together in a sudden frown. 'Told me what?'

'Oh, I know that he did not want me to know! Mr. Carroll told me so. He thought it would distress me, and—and he wished to spare me anxiety. And I know he cannot have wanted me to see him looking——' Her voice stopped on a sudden gasp of horror and her eyes widened: 'Why—why! he may even have thought that I might turn from him if his illness had affected his appearance! He should have known I should not! But he has not seen me for so long. *You* knew, though! You must have known that I was not like that. If you had told me——'

Alex cut harshly across the sentence: 'We seem to be at cross-purposes. I find I have not the remotest idea what you are talking about. What is it that Mr. Carroll has told you?'

'He told me the truth! That Conway has been ill.'

'*Ill?*'

Winter's small chin came up with a jerk. 'I hope you do not mean to deny having had any knowledge of it?'

'I most certainly do!' said Alex, 'although I suppose it is just possible to describe his condition by such a term. But it is not the one I would have used myself. Perhaps you will be good enough to tell me just exactly what Mr. Carroll had to say?'

Winter told him; her voice quick with indignation and reproach. 'I—I suppose you meant it for the best,' she finished. 'But you should have known that I would prefer to be told the truth. I did not think it of you. I thought that you——'

She stopped and bit her lip, and Alex said curtly: 'You are right. I should have told you the truth. Will you hear it now?'

'I know it now.'

'Oh no, you do not. No——' His hand shot out and grasped her wrist as she made a move to leave him. 'This time you are not going until I have said what I have to say.'

Winter tugged furiously at her imprisoned wrist, but Alex's

lean fingers were hard and unyielding, and realizing that she could not free herself without an undignified struggle, she let her arm go slack and stood still:

'Very well. I will listen.'

He released her and she snatched her hand away and stood rubbing it, her breath coming unevenly. There was doubt, and something else in her face—a dawning apprehension.

Alex said: 'Mr. Barton is not ill. Not in the accepted sense of the word.'

'What—what do you mean?' The words were barely a whisper.

'I mean,' said Alex with brutal clarity, 'that Mr. Barton suffers from over-indulgence in drink, drugs and women.'

Winter caught her breath in a harsh gasp and turned swiftly, but again Alex was too quick for her. He caught her by the arm and jerked her round to face him.

'I'm sorry, but you are going to hear me out. I told you once before that Barton was not a fit person for you to have anything to do with, let alone marry. I meant it. A libertine and a drunkard is hardly a suitable husband for such a woman as yourself—or for any woman, for that matter. He would not come to England to marry you because he must have been well aware that, should he do so, one look at what he had become would have been enough to ensure that the engagement was broken. I do not know why he did not meet you in Calcutta. Probably for the same reason. I do know, however, that the after-effects of a debauch, if nothing else, prevented him from leaving for Delhi. He was incapable of standing upright when I left him.'

He let her go, but Winter did not move. She stood quite still, her eyes wide and frightened, and once again Alex was conscious of that bewildering pain in his heart. He said harshly: 'Well, now that you know the truth, I can only suggest that you return to Calcutta and sail for England as soon as there is a passage available.'

She did not answer him, and the moment seemed to stretch out interminably. A mongoose ran along the parapet, keeping to the shadows, and checked by the sight of the two motionless humans, fluffed out its tail and whisked away with a little chattering cry of rage. But neither of them moved or spoke, and in the moonlit silence the words of a tender, plaintive melody that drifted down the long length of the ramparts, sung by a dozen voices and blurred and sweetened by distance, filled the night with a strange, nostalgic magic—

> *Believe me, if all those endearing young charms,*
> *Which I gaze on so fondly today,*
> *Were to fade by tomorrow, and fleet in my arms . . .*

Winter saw Alex's set mouth soften and twitch, and she spoke in a whisper: 'No! Oh, no . . . I don't believe it. Alex——'

She stretched out a small groping hand in a gesture that begged for reassurance, and as it touched him something as vivid and as elemental as a flicker of lightning seemed to shiver between them. The next instant his arm was about her and he was holding her hard and close. For a brief moment she resisted him violently, her body taut with shock. And then his mouth came down on hers, and all at once the rigidity and resistance left her and the ground was no longer solid under her feet. . . .

Thou wouldst still be adored as this moment thou art . . .

Her skin smelt faintly of lavender and her body was soft and sweet and fragrant in his embrace; as soft and sweet and fragrant as her lips and her closed eyelids and her shining hair.

Alex's mouth was not hot and greedy as Carlyon's had been. His lips were cool and firm and his slow-moving kisses were a warm, drugging wonder that deprived her of all power of thought or movement and narrowed the night and the moonlight, the wide world and the wider sky, down to nothing more than the close circle of his arm. She felt him free his left arm from the sling, and then his fingers were on the nape of her neck, pressing upwards slowly and caressingly through the thick soft waves of hair; fondling the curve of her head and holding it as closely and possessively as his right arm held her body. His mouth moved from hers at last, and his cheek was cool and harsh against her smooth warm one:

'*Darling* . . . *darling* . . .' His voice was no more than a
breathed caress, but at the sound of it the passionate spell broke
and dissolved before the cold inrush of reality. Winter tore
herself free and backed away from him, shaking with rage and
shame and the shock of a sudden revelation:

'So *that's* why you hate him——!'

Her voice was low and breathless and edged with scorn:
'You're jealous of Conway, and so you made it all up! You
haven't even enough honour and—and decency to prevent you
making love to his future wife! *You!*—you and Carlyon! Mr.
Carroll *did* tell me the truth. Why should he lie to me? Conway
is ill—and because you are jealous of him you do your best to
blacken him to me so that you can make love to me behind his
back! I hope—I hope I never have to see you again!'

Her voice broke on a sob, and then she had whirled about and
had run from him, and he heard the sound of her flying feet die
out along the wall and lose itself in the sound of the distant
singing.

Alex made no attempt to follow her. He stood where she had
left him, staring into nothingness. Presently he lifted an uncertain hand and rubbed it dazedly across his forehead, and sitting
down slowly in the embrasure, felt mechanically in his pockets
for tobacco and matches. He rolled a cigarette with careful concentration and struck a match against the worn stonework. It lit
with a hiss and crackle of sulphur, and the vivid flare of the small
yellow flame momentarily dimmed the brightness of the moonlight.

> . . . *the heart that has truly lov'd never forgets,*
> *But as truly loves on to the close;*
> *As the sun-flower turns on her god when he sets*
> *The same look which she turn'd when he rose.*

The singing ceased and the night was silent once more. Alex
appeared to have forgotten about the match, for it burnt out
between his fingers. He dropped it with a quick grimace of
pain, and removing the cigarette from his mouth, flicked it away
into the shadows.

'*Hell!*' said Alex, aloud and softly, addressing the moonlight, the ancient city of Delhi and all India.

16

CARLYON'S plans were at last reaching some sort of shape, and in pursuance of the policy of lulling Winter's fears he had studiously avoided her and had devoted himself instead to entertaining Delia Gardener-Smith.

He had seated himself as far away from Winter as possible, but this had not prevented him from observing that Randall had held her in conversation for the greater part of the meal, or that they appeared to be on remarkably easy terms with one another. He had tried not to watch them, but he could not keep himself from doing so, and the unusual animation on Randall's face and the interest on Winter's had infuriated and alarmed him. Thank heaven Randall would shortly be leaving Delhi, and that he himself would before long be shaking the dust of this deadly place off his shoes. Only a few more days—he could not stand it much longer.

Carlyon looked across the laden cloth at Winter, trying to observe her dispassionately and decide what it was about her that had become such a fever in his blood. He had known many beautiful women; women far lovelier than this slender young creature whose wide-set eyes were full of a sweet unsureness that gave the lie to that full-lipped, passionate mouth.

Perhaps it was that—the youth and unsureness and the unawakened passion—that attracted him? To a palate jaded by experience, inexperience alone had a charm that was strangely and sharply new. He had been a fool. He, with all his knowledge of women, had handled this unsophisticated girl as though she had been some opera dancer to be seduced for the price of a trinket. Did she know that she was disturbing and desirable? . . . What had Randall been saying to her? He had met Alex's reflective gaze and for a long moment he had stared at him, his throat tight with rage; and later that evening, when the singing had begun, he had not failed to mark that neither Winter nor Randall was present, and judging from the direction of Sophie's anxious gaze he had little doubt as to where they were.

He had endured it as long as he could, but as the minutes slipped by and they did not return his jealous rage had increased until it had suddenly become past bearing, and he had risen and walked quickly away in the direction of the Water Bastion. Halfway down the stretch of wall the shadow of a huge neem tree lay across his path, and as he reached it he heard a sound of running footsteps, and someone ran into him and would have fallen but for his arms.

'"Oh, it's you——' Winter's voice was breathless and sobbing, and she had forgotten that she disliked this man. She had forgotten everything but the fact that Alex had betrayed her—lied to her—shamed her. 'Take me home! Please take me home. I cannot stay here!'

Carlyon drew her out of the shadows and into the bright moonlight, and looking down at the small distorted face saw that it was wet with tears. He said furiously: 'What has he done to you? My dear—don't! I'll go back and break his damned neck for you!'

'No—no, please don't.' Winter's fingers clung to his arm. 'I want to go back to the bungalow. Please take me back!'

'Of course.' He took her hand and drew it through his arm and turned back towards the group near the Kashmir Gate, but they had not taken more than a dozen steps when he stopped. 'We shall have to pass through all those people. There is no other way down. You will not like them to see you like this. May I——?'

He proffered a clean handkerchief and Winter accepted it gratefully. Presently she said in a more rational voice: 'You are very kind!'

'No, I am not!' There was an unexpected bitterness and sincerity in his voice, and Winter looked up, startled. Carlyon recovered himself swiftly: 'I told you, did I not, that if I could serve you in any way it would give me great happiness to do so. I meant it, you know.'

'I—I know.'

Did she know? Had she been wrong about Lord Carlyon? She had been wrong about Alex. If she could be wrong about Alex——

Quite suddenly she found herself telling him everything. Conway's illness. Captain Randall's perfidy. Her own fears and doubts when Conway had failed to come to Delhi: 'I could not understand it! I thought that he could surely have left the work to Alex—Captain Randall—just for a few days. Just to fetch me! But now that I know, I must go to him at once. I cannot wait another week in Delhi! I could help nurse him—I would not mind a sickroom. He might have another relapse and I not there. If he is ill he needs me. Will you—would you help me to go to him?'

Carlyon looked down into the wide, appealing eyes and saw that she was shivering violently. He knew nothing of this man that the little Condesa was to marry, but what he had seen of Captain Randall led him to suppose that Captain Randall's revelations concerning his chief were probably correct. Randall did not give him the impression of a man given to that particular form of lying. On the other hand Randall appeared to have made —or attempted to make—advances to his superior officer's future wife, and Carlyon found himself torn between an entirely primitive rage that he should have dared to touch her, and satisfaction that by doing so he had played his, Carlyon's, game for him by presenting him with an opportunity that appeared to be little less than a gift from the gods.

He said: 'I will take you to Lunjore myself. You cannot go unescorted.'

Winter drew a quick breath, her hands clasping and unclasping against her grey habit. 'Would you? Would you really?'

'Of course. It is a piece of the greatest good luck that I purchased that carriage. You and your serving woman can travel in it and I will ride. There is only one thing——' He paused, frowning, and Winter said anxiously: 'What is it?'

'Well, I do not know,' Carlyon spoke doubtfully, 'but I think perhaps it would be as well if you did not mention this matter to the Abuthnots.' He saw that he had startled her and said quickly: 'I am sure that they would sympathize with your intentions, but they would be obliged to prevent you from going until you could do so under the charge of Mrs. Gardener-Smith. They would not consider it at all suitable for you to travel either alone or in my care, and I do not imagine that Mrs. Gardener-Smith could be prevailed upon to put forward the date of her departure.'

'No,' said Winter slowly. 'No, she would not. And you are right about the Abuthnots. But I will not wait. I will not! I— I am my own mistress. No one can stop me.'

'They will try,' said Carlyon dryly.

'Yes, I suppose so.' Her eyes were suddenly dry and bright and she straightened her slim shoulders and lifted her chin, stilling the trembling of her body with a visible effort of will. 'When can we leave? Tomorrow?'

'I could arrange it.'

'You are very kind. I will speak to Mrs. Abuthnot tonight and tell her that I wish to leave immediately for Lunjore. I must do that. If she will assist me then I will not have to trouble you. But if she will not, then—then I think it would be better if we left as early as possible.'

Carlyon said gravely: 'You are quite right, of course. Perhaps she may assist you.'

He had no qualms on that score, for he was quite certain that the Abuthnots would do no such thing. He offered his arm to Winter and said: 'Shall we go now? Do you ride home, or shall you go in the carriage? I will tell Mrs. Abuthnot that you have a headache. I do not think, you know, that you should leave without her. It would be remarked.'

Winter had returned in the carriage, and Mrs. Abuthnot, who had been alarmed by the girl's looks, had hurried her into bed and prescribed hot milk and chlorodyne drops. Her solicitude provided the opportunity Winter had needed to beg her permission and approval for an immediate departure to Lunjore, but

Mrs. Abuthnot, although deeply sympathetic, would not hear of it. Such a plan was out of the question!

'After waiting for so long, dear, you can surely wait another eight days. Only think of poor Mr. Barton's chagrin if you were to see him after all these years when he is not in looks!' To Winter's passionate assertion that Conway's looks could not make a particle of difference to her feelings for him, Mrs. Abuthnot had replied that it was not dear Winter's feelings that were in question, but poor Mr. Barton's. Winter had argued and pleaded and Mrs. Abuthnot had wept sympathetic tears, kissed her fondly but remained adamant.

'You will see that Colonel Abuthnot will agree with me. And Alex too.' She had turned out the light and left the room, and Winter had lain awake in the darkness and made her own decision. She would not wait another eight days—or even one day! She would leave at once. Alex would be leaving Delhi on Monday and if she left tomorrow she would be in Lunjore by then: married to Conway and safe from him. She did not know why she had to be safe from Alex, or stop to realize that a part of the driving impulse to get to Lunjore and to Conway arose from a panic desire to escape from him.

Conway would have to get rid of Alex. He must arrange for him to be sent to some other appointment, and until that happened she at least need not see him again. As for Carlyon, she had forgotten both her dislike and distrust of the man and thought of him as no more than a means to an end. He was no longer a person with a character and passions of his own, but something of no more, or not so much, importance as the carriage and horses that would take her to Conway.

She groped for matches, and having found and lit a candle, slipped out of bed and wrote a brief note to Carlyon. The ayah should deliver it first thing in the morning. She wrote a second and longer one to Mrs. Abuthnot, sealed it with a wafer, addressed it and put it away. Her trunks would have to be sent after her. To be packing trunks would not do at all. She lit a second candle, and making a selection of garments and other necessities, packed a small valise and a capacious carpet-bag. Carlyon would have to devise some means of smuggling them into the carriage. Struck by another thought she scribbled a hurried and loving note to Lottie. Lottie at least would understand!

That done she blew out the candles, and fell at last into an uneasy sleep.

Mrs. Abuthnot had evidently given the question of Winter's proceeding immediately to Lunjore no further thought, for she did not refer to it on the following morning, and having enquired affectionately as to whether Winter had quite recovered from her headache, was full of plans for pre-wedding festivities in the forth-coming week. A seemingly endless list of engagements which tripped off her tongue was only interrupted by Carlyon's enquir-ing of Winter if she would care to drive out with him that morning to try the new carriage.

Mrs. Abuthnot was not at all sure that it was quite the thing for dear Winter to be seen driving *à deux* with Lord Carlyon, but consoled herself with the reflection that she was, after all, engaged to be married. Besides the child really did look remark-ably pale, and a drive, even in the heat of the morning, would doubtless be of benefit to her. As they drove away, she was sur-prised to see that Carlyon did not intend to sit in the carriage with his guest, but to ride beside it. The hood of the carriage had been raised against the morning sun and Mrs. Abuthnot did not leave the shade of the verandah. Winter kissed her with unusual affection and Mrs. Abuthnot, unsuspicious by nature, was touched.

The carriage rolled out of the drive under the shadows of the pepper trees, and ten minutes later, happening to look out of her bedroom window, Mrs. Abuthnot saw Carlyon's down-country bearer and two of his syces riding out of the side gate that led from the stables, taking with them the two spare carriage horses. She supposed that they must have had their orders, but it seemed to her an odd time of day to exercise horses, and she could only imagine that it was Carlyon's ignorance of the country that had led him to order them out in the hottest part of the day. For a moment an odd twinge of uneasiness disturbed her, but Lottie

demanding advice on the set of a pagoda sleeve turned her
thoughts into more congenial channels.

Twelve o'clock brought no sign of the carriage, and by one
o'clock Mrs. Abuthnot was seriously disturbed. Neither Winter
nor Carlyon, she was persuaded, would be so thoughtlessly incon-
siderate as to hold up luncheon to this extent. There could be
only one explanation. The carriage must have broken down, or
—horrifying thought!—the horses had bolted with it!

Mrs. Abuthnot was immediately seized with the conviction
that Winter was at that moment lying in some nullah with a
broken neck. 'Oh no, Mamma!' cried Lottie turning alarmingly
pale. 'You cannot think——! You cannot really believe——
But Lord Carlyon would have sent back word had there been an
accident! One of the syces would have ridden back.'

Investigation, however, proved that the procession that Mrs.
Abuthnot had witnessed leaving the stables that morning had
also not returned. 'Mamma,' said Sophie thoughtfully, 'you do
not suppose that they can have eloped?'

Mrs. Abuthnot uttered a small shriek. 'Sophie! How can you
suggest such a thing!'

'I am sorry, Mamma; but you will own it is a little strange that
all Lord Carlyon's servants and his horses have left, and none of
them returned. And anyone could see that he admires Winter.'

'Dear Winter would never——' began Mrs. Abuthnot, and
stopped. She had suddenly recalled the kiss that Winter had
given her before setting out that morning. The kiss that had
seemed so unusually demonstrative for that undemonstrative
child. She had imagined at the time that it was intended in part
as an apology for her outbreak on the previous night when she
had pleaded to be allowed to leave immediately for Lunjore.

Lunjore——! Mrs. Abuthnot fell back in her chair with a
groan that brought Lottie and Sophie running to her side. 'Oh
no!' gasped Mrs. Abuthnot, pressing her plump hands to her
ample bosom. 'Oh no! She *could* not do such a thing! She
would at *least* have left a letter!'

Lottie flew for the hartshorn while Sophie, more practical,

departed in the direction of Winter's bedroom. She returned a few minutes later with the two letters that she had found propped up on the chimney-piece where they could not fail to catch the eye of the first-comer.

Colonel Abuthnot, summoned from the lines by an entirely unintelligible missive from his wife, gave it as his opinion that Carlyon had behaved shockingly, and that come to think of it he had never quite trusted the fellow. Something a sight too smooth and cynical about him. But he had not thought it of the little Condesa. Probably foreign ways; he had heard that they were surprisingly lax on the Continent.

To his wife's plea that he would set off immediately in pursuit of the runaways he had replied with an unqualified refusal. He was far too busy a man to go tearing about the country in pursuit of a young chit who was old enough to know better.

'It's no good, Milly, my dear. I will not do it! The girl is going to her future husband. Very understandable. I cannot conceive what possessed Carlyon to agree to such a mad scheme, but if she was set upon going he may have considered that her protection on the journey was of paramount importance. Though he must also have realized that his presence was enough to ruin her reputation! I can only hope that the Commissioner of Lunjore will take a lenient view of it. As for suggesting that I should go in pursuit of them, the idea is preposterous. If anyone is to go in pursuit it had better be Captain Randall. The girl is betrothed to *his* superior officer, not mine. And he is a deal younger than I am; he might even overtake 'em. I should not!'

'*Alex!*' exclaimed Mrs. Abuthnot frantically. '*Why* did I not think of that!'

She hurried away to dash off a brief note requesting Alex's immediate presence, and having underlined 'immediate' with three black lines that tore the paper, added a postscript, also underlined, stressing the urgency of the matter. This missive had been dispatched post-haste to Ludlow Castle, the residence of Alex's host, Mr. Fraser, with instructions to the bearer of it that it must be delivered into the Captain Sahib's own hand.

But Alex had been out, and the bearer of the letter, whose instructions had not included scouring Delhi for the Captain Sahib, had settled down to sleep away the afternoon in a convenient patch of shade in the compound until such time as the sahib should return.

Alex had arrived back barely half an hour before sunset in no very good humour, and had not been pleased to receive Mrs. Abuthnot's agitated summons. He had no idea what Mrs. Abuthnot's note portended, but imagined that Winter had poured out to her something of the scene last night, and that she wished to hear from himself if he had really made such accusations against the Commissioner, and were they true.

Alex supposed that he would now have to convince the Abuthnots that he had, if anything, understated the case, and then perhaps they would be able to prevent Winter from proceeding to Lunjore at the end of the month. The possibility that she might leave at once, and with Carlyon, had never occurred to him, and he was entirely unprepared for the announcement with which the tearful Mrs. Abuthnot greeted him.

She saw the colour leave his face and a white line show about his mouth. He said: 'What time did they leave?'

'Quite early,' sobbed Mrs. Abuthnot, dabbing her eyes with a handkerchief. 'Ten o'clock, I think.'

'Good God, ma'am!' said Alex violently, 'could you not have sent for me before?'

'But we did not realize what had occurred until Sophie found this letter——' She held it out to Alex, who having read it with eyes that were almost black with anger, crushed it into a ball and thrust it into his pocket. 'And then you were out,' explained Mrs. Abuthnot, 'and the stupid man never thought to enquire after you. And George——Colonel Abuthnot—positively declines to go after them!'

'Quite out of the question!' confirmed Colonel Abuthnot, who had caught the end of the sentence. He entered the room by the verandah door, and having nodded gloomily at Alex said: 'What do you propose to do about it, my boy?'

'Bring her back,' said Alex tersely.

'Too late for that now. She'll have been out all night with that fellow Carlyon before you can catch up with her. And I can't see that it will do any good for you to go along too. Two men ain't any better than one when it comes to playing propriety. Worse, if you ask me. Not sure I'd trust Carlyon very far. He had an eye to that girl. Wanted her himself. Any fool could see that. Probably ruined her by now.'

He caught Alex's eye and took an involuntary step backwards, saying hastily: 'No, no! I don't expect he'd do such a thing. But as far as her reputation is concerned——'

Alex cut him short. 'May I take it that you would be willing to allow her to remain here when I bring her back, Mrs. Abuthnot?'

'Of course I should! I know only too well that the dear child means no harm. It was only that she was upset by the news of Mr. Barton's illness and wished to go to his side without loss of time. One can understand that so well. The *best* of motives! But she may not wish to come back.'

'Her wishes,' said Alex through shut teeth, 'have nothing whatever to do with the matter. I shall hope to be back at a tolerably early hour tomorrow, and if this matter has not been mentioned outside the house I see no reason why it should become known.'

'You need have no fears in that score, my boy,' said Colonel Abuthnot firmly. 'We ain't likely to blab about such an affair. Though if it were not for that fellow Carlyon fancying himself in love with the girl, I'd advise you to let well alone and let her press on for Lunjore. I daresay Barton may be persuaded to take a lenient view of the matter once he has her safe, and if you don't try fetching her back it's he who'll have the handling of her.'

Alex, who had turned to leave the room, stopped with his hand on the door-knob and looked back. 'It is precisely on that account,' he said savagely, 'that I intend to bring her back. Lord Carlyon can go to the devil!'

The door slammed behind him, and Colonel Abuthnot, who

had been giving the matter thought, said reflectively: 'Damme if I don't believe he's fallen in love with the girl himself! Now look what you've done, Milly!'

'Done? What have I done? I've sent him after her. Someone had to go. And of course he is not in love with her!'

'You're a fool, Milly,' said Colonel Abuthnot affectionately. 'Always were. Why else should he be in such a taking? He ain't the type to lose his temper for nothing. Now there'll be the devil to pay!'

'What *can* you mean, George?'

'Mean? I mean that if I'm right about him, and he overtakes those two before they reach Lunjore, he'll murder that fellow Carlyon. And if he doesn't, he'll probably murder Barton!'

Mrs. Abuthnot, who had borne enough, took refuge in a strong attack of the vapours.

*   *   *

Alex's mood was so nearly murderous that Colonel Abuthnot's prediction might have come unpleasantly near the mark had it not been for one factor that he had not taken into his calculations. The ford at Jathghat.

He had stopped at Ludlow Castle barely long enough to inform his host that he would be unavoidably absent, and to collect Niaz, a third horse and his revolver. He had proffered no explanation for his actions and had left, riding at a breakneck speed that had taken them far on the road by the time the moon was high. He knew that the carriage could not travel at any great speed owing to the poorness of the roads, and he imagined that it would halt at some dâk bungalow for the night, so that he calculated, with luck, on being able to come up with it well before midnight.

He had no very clear idea what he intended to do when he did overtake it. Carlyon was bound to be difficult and he apparently had at least half a dozen servants with him. Niaz, however, could be trusted to deal with the latter, and as for Carlyon, it would give Alex the greatest pleasure to deal with his languid lordship himself. He had not given much thought to Carlyon—

beyond considering him a more suitable husband for Winter de
Ballesteros than the Commissioner of Lunjore—and the murderous rage that had taken possession of him at the news of their
flight had been almost entirely on account of Mr. Barton.

If Winter had gone to Lunjore in the care of the Gardener-
Smiths they could not have refused to shelter her and assist her
to return to Delhi or Calcutta when she discovered, as she must
almost immediately do, the impossibility of marrying Mr.
Barton. But if she were to arrive in Lunjore alone, with no one
to turn to, there was no knowing what might happen. In all
probability Mr. Barton would see to it that any return was made
impossible, and Alex had turned sick at the thought.

Even Colonel Abuthnot's reference to Carlyon's wanting the
girl himself had done little more at the time than add to his fury;
but now he remembered it again, and a cold fear took the place
of that fury as he remembered also the scene he had interrupted
on the evening of Winter's arrival in Delhi, and the look he had
seen in Carlyon's eyes only last night. 'If he has harmed
her——' thought Alex savagely. 'If he has harmed her——' He
set his teeth and bent far forward in the saddle, riding as though
he rode in a race, and with a recklessness that startled Niaz.

But he had forgotten the ford at Jathghat and the unseasonable
clouds that Mrs. Abuthnot had commented upon on the previous
evening.

There had been rain in the foothills and on the plains beyond
Moradabad and Rampur, and now, twenty-four hours and more
later, the river had risen and was still rising. It had been dangerously high, though still fordable, when Winter and Carlyon
had reached it some four hours earlier. But what had then been
a ford of no more than fifty yards in length was now a brown,
turgid torrent measuring a quarter of a mile from bank to bank,
and swirling sullenly past in the moonlight with an ominous
chuckling gurgle that spoke of whirlpools and hidden currents.

Alex had been riding at a hand-gallop and paying little attention to the road, and he reined in hard at Niaz's shout of warning,
and dismounted to stare at the ugly stretch of water in blank

dismay. He knew that road only too well, and knew too that when the river ran high there was nothing to do but wait for it to fall again, for the nearest alternative route meant a detour of fifty miles, and over such country as to make it, on a normal occasion, a matter of less delay to wait for the flood-water to pass. But this was no normal occasion.

Alex swung himself back into the saddle, his face harsh and haggard in the bright moonlight, and turned north on the long detour to the nearest bridge.

Half an hour later a python slithered across the narrow and little-used track almost under the hooves of his tired horse. Shalini shied wildly and the low branch of a *kikar* tree slammed against Alex's wounded arm. He hit the ground with the point of his shoulder, and in the fractional second before his head struck against the rocks by the roadside, heard his collar-bone snap as he went down into darkness.

17

WINTER lay back in a corner of the carriage and closed her eyes. The setting sun shone in with a golden glare under the heavy leather hood above her, and the surface of the road was unbelievably bad. The carriage wheels jolted into ruts and out again, and every jolt threw her body sideways or jerked it back against the squabs until her head began to ache dully.

She told herself again that she was going to Conway and that in four days' time—less, if the roads improved—she would be with him at last: no more waiting; no more doubts or fears or loneliness. But the spell had begun to lose some of its first potent charm.

Perhaps it had first failed a little at the ford. The horses had jibbed at the swirling brown water and the coachman had looked frightened and had protested that it would be better to turn back or to wait until the water fell. For one inexplicable moment Winter had experienced a feeling of overwhelming relief. They would have to go back! The next second shame at such cowardice had stiffened her resolution and she had feverishly seconded Carlyon's decision to cross.

The sight of the rising river had given Carlyon an exceedingly unpleasant shock, for the prospect of having to return to Delhi was not one that he cared to contemplate. Such an absurd anti-climax did not bear thinking of. The frightened faces of the coachman and the servants had infuriated him, but threats and bribery had prevailed, and they had made the crossing.

They had rested a while on the far bank and had watched the river rise steadily, inch by inch. 'No more will pass that way for some days,' remarked a villager who had crossed with them, and Winter had looked back at the swirling water and thought, 'Now there is no going back. Now, whatever happens, we must go on.' The thought had been oddly frightening. She did not want to go back. Of course she did not want to go back! But now even if she had wanted to do so, the road was barred behind her and the flooded river lay between her and Alex. *Alex*—her mind shrank violently away from the thought of Alex as though it had touched something that could not be faced. She would not even think of Alex.

The road on the far side of the river had been almost worse than the one they had travelled on since leaving Delhi, but Carlyon had handed the reins of his horse to one of the syces and joined Winter in the carriage. She had had little speech with him since they had started out, for it had been impossible to carry on a conversation with anyone riding beside the carriage. Carlyon had seen to it that the horses kept up a creditable speed, and his behaviour during the brief halts had been courteous and considerate. But now that the river had been crossed and lay impassable behind them, his manner had undergone a noticeable change. Or was it only weariness that made her imagine that it had?

Ever since the scene in the Abuthnots' bungalow that Alex

Randall's arrival had interrupted, Carlyon had appeared to avoid looking directly at her, and she had not again encountered that slow appraising gaze that had so often disturbed her on the journey from Calcutta. Now, however, as though the need for restraint were gone, she found that she could not look up without finding his eyes upon her.

He did not talk much and Winter, finding the silence obscurely alarming, did her best to keep up some show of conversation. As the sun sank behind the trees and the carriage began to fill with shadow she asked that the hood might be lowered so that they could get the benefit of the cooler air. With open sky above her and the accompanying servants in full view, she fancied that the uncomfortable tension would be largely relieved, but Carlyon, although he had stopped the carriage and complied with her request, had laughed and said: 'Why? Are you afraid of what I might do?'

There had been no possible answer to that, and Winter had forced herself to meet his gaze calmly and with a faint touch of disdain that had aroused his admiration. Despite her youth and inexperience this was no vapourish miss who would fall into a swoon and capitulate to a show of masculine force. She would be a wife worth having. His gaze rested upon her with possessive appreciation, and it crossed his mind that he must remember to see that none of the horses was left unattended and within her reach. The providential flood that had closed the ford behind them had solved one problem, for he had felt tolerably certain that Randall at least would not take the news of their departure with equanimity; but now there was no longer any need to look over his shoulder or listen for the sound of hoofbeats on the road behind them. There was apparently a dâk bungalow some few miles farther on which they should reach before darkness fell, and where they could pass the night. And tomorrow they would resume their journey, not to Lunjore, but to Oudh; and from there, by way of Cawnpore and Benares, to Calcutta.

Winter would be unlikely to discover for several days that their destination was not Lunjore, and Carlyon intended to use those

I

days to eradicate the unfortunate impression that he had made in Delhi. He had no doubt at all that given time and the opportunity he could eventually make her love him, for too many women had done so in the past for him to harbour any fears on that score. But should he fail to win her heart by the time that she discovered their changed destination, he could then make plain to her an aspect of the affair that had as yet not dawned upon her unsophisticated mind—that Mr. Barton would hardly wish to ally himself to any woman who was known to have travelled under the sole protection of Lord Carlyon, and that marriage with anyone other than himself was now quite out of the question.

The dâk bungalow when they reached it shortly before moonrise was, to Carlyon's annoyance, already sheltering what looked to be a large party. It had not occurred to him that they might have company, but his Calcutta bearer, who spoke sufficient English to make himself understood by his master, informed him that it was only an Indian lady and her servants who had broken her journey for a few hours at the bungalow and would be leaving shortly, and that meanwhile there were rooms in plenty for himself and the Miss-sahib.

They had eaten a tolerable meal in the main room of the bungalow, while the moon rose over the plain and someone—the *khansamah* said it was the Mohammedan lady in the room at the far end of the verandah—played a tinkling tune on a stringed instrument.

It was a haunting thread of sound, oddly familiar, and Winter found herself listening to it with a feeling that she had heard that particular plaintive tune before. She was very tired, and anxious to get to her own room and be free of Carlyon's disturbing gaze and the necessity to appear calm and composed, and the meal seemed interminable. She had excused herself as soon as it was over, and stepping out on to the verandah had seen a *ruth*, a closed, double-domed cart, to which a pair of trotting bullocks were being harnessed.

'It is the Begum Sahiba,' said one of the bungalow servants in reply to Winter's question. 'She stopped only on account of a broken wheel, which has now been repaired. She stays the night at a village farther on the road. She is from Oudh and returns to her home.'

Winter walked slowly to the door of her room, her wide skirts rustling on the dusty stone of the verandah. 'I am from Oudh,' she thought, 'and I too am returning home.' The thought gave her fresh courage and she turned and gave her hand to Carlyon, thanking him once more for his help and bidding him good night.

He took her hand: but he did not release it . . .

Carlyon had imagined that he could keep his passions under control. There had indeed been a time when he had contemplated rape, but that was before he had fallen so helplessly and unwillingly in love. He did not intend to force his future wife. He had meant to treat her instead with all the tenderness and consideration that such a situation permitted; but now, suddenly and without warning, the touch of her slim fingers snapped his resolution as though it had been no more than a thread of yarn, and forced him to folly.

He held her hand in a hard grasp with fingers that were feverishly hot and unsteady, and lifting it to his lips, he kissed it.

It was not a light gesture of gallantry, but a kiss as greedily passionate as those which he had forced on her once before, and which the shock of Mr. Carroll's revelations and Alex's perfidy, coupled with her frantic desire to escape to Conway, had driven into the background of her mind. She tried to drag her hand away but he held it hard, kissing it again and again; moving his hot, hungry mouth against its cool softness. And when he lifted his head at last and looked at her in the moonlight, his cold eyes were cold no longer, but as hot and avid as his mouth had been.

He stared at her for a long moment, breathing hard and unevenly, a dark flush on his cheeks and his eyes bright with a feverish excitement that was as inexplicable to Winter as it was terrifying, and her body shrank and turned cold with a primitive fear and a misty comprehension that the passion she had aroused in him was beyond her control—and his. Then he had released her hand at last, and she turned and stumbled across the threshold and into the safety of her room.

She closed the door behind her and leant her weight against it as though she feared that he would follow her, and presently she fumbled for the bolt and shot it home. The flame of the single oil-lamp swept the huge, balloon-like shadow of her crinoline across the coarse matting and the bare whitewashed walls as she walked unsteadily across the room and sat down on the low bed, her legs feeling suddenly too weak to support her, and disjointed thoughts whirling in her brain as helplessly and as frantica ly as the moths that battered their wings against the smoky glass of the lamp.

She should have known—she must have known!—that it was madness to accept Lord Carlyon's offer to escort her to Lunjore! What had possessed her to set off with him, alone and unchaperoned? How could she possibly have allowed herself to forget—or at least excuse—his behaviour on the day of her arrival in Delhi? How could she have been so foolish as to imagine that she could use him to further her own ends? She should have known that Lord Carlyon would be no woman's tool. Now, suddenly, she began to doubt if he had ever had any intention of taking her to Lunjore. And even if he did so, what would Conway think of this escapade? Would Conway think (as Cousin Julia would undoubtedly have thought!) that she was lost to all sense of shame, and had deprived herself of every shred of reputation? Would it harm his position as Commissioner of Lunjore to marry a wife who had behaved in such an improper manner? Why had she never thought of that before?

There was only one thing that she could do now, and that was to remove instantly from the dâk bungalow. For reasons that were still obscure to her she was aware that no woman's reputation was entirely ruined unless she had slept a night, unchaperoned, under the same roof as a man. Therefore, as she had as yet only spent the greater part of a day travelling in Lord Carlyon' company, she might still retrieve herself in Conway's eyes, and her own, by leaving immediately.

But how was she to leave? And where was she to go? The road back to Delhi was closed by the swollen ford, and she could not—she *would* not—ask Lord Carlyon to allow her to proceed to Lunjore alone. Supposing he were to refuse? Supposing he——

A sound of wrangling voices and laughter from the compound outside cut across her disjointed thoughts, and her attention was caught by a jingle of bells as one of the bullocks tossed its head. The other travellers who were to leave tonight! Of course! She would beg help from the lady from Oudh. Surely another woman would not refuse to help her? And Lunjore lay only a mile or so off the road that led into Oudh——

Winter stood up resolutely, and, remembering the size of the Indian lady's conveyance, she pulled up the spreading yards of chintz-flowered balzarine that had seemed suitable for a short drive in a carriage, and unfastened her crinoline. The hooped underskirt fell to the ground with a rustle and a click and she stepped out of it and ran to fetch the carpet-bag.

The door hinges squeaked protestingly as she eased it open, but the verandah was deserted. A flare of torches and oil-lamps and a chattering group of retainers surrounded the tinselled *ruth*, and a square of orange light from the window of the end room showed that the Indian lady had not yet left. Winter gathered up her trailing skirts in one hand and the carpet-bag in the other and ran lightly down the moonlit verandah.

The door was not locked and she could hear women talking on the other side of it. She pushed it open and went in.

There were three women in the room. A young and strikingly beautiful woman wearing the silk tunic and full trousers of a Mohammedan lady of family, and two older women who were obviously servants, the younger of whom uttered a small scream of alarm at the sudden appearance of a stranger.

Winter put a finger to her lips in a gesture that implored silence, and spoke in a soft, breathless voice, explaining what little she could of her predicament and begging that they would take her with them. The Indian girl—she could not have been

very many years older than Winter—listened in wide-eyed
astonishment, and when she had finished clapped her hands like
a child and said: 'But it is wonderful!' She turned to the elderly
serving maid: 'Is it not wonderful to hear a *feringhi* speak as
one of us? Who art thou? What is thy name?'

'Winter. Winter de Ballesteros. If the Begum Sahiba would
be so kind as——'

'*What?* What is that you say?' said the girl sharply. She
snatched up the oil-lamp that stood on the floor and held it so
that the light fell full on Winter's face.

Winter blinked at the sudden blaze, and the girl stared in
silence, moving the lamp so that it lit first one side of Winter's
face and then the other, lifting it so that the light poured down
upon the black waves of hair.

'It is!' said the girl. '*Allah Kerimast!* It is so. Little sister,
do you not know me?'

'I—I do not think——' began Winter breathlessly.

'Ameera!—dost thou not remember Ameera? Hast thou
indeed forgotten the Gulab Mahal and my mother Juanita
Begum, and the tales that *nani* told us on the roof-top?'

The older serving woman, a stout grey-haired old lady, threw
up her arms with a little wailing cry: '*Aie! Aie!* It is the *Chota
Moti*! It is Zobeida's baba whom I nursed as a babe!'

Winter's eyes widened until they were dark pools in her white
face, and she looked from the elderly woman to the girl who had
called herself Ameera.

'*Anne Marie!*' All at once there were tears in Winter's eyes,
and her voice was a shaken whisper. 'It is Anne Marie!'

And then quite suddenly they were in each other's arms,
laughing and crying and pulling away to look at each other and
clinging together again.

The soft silk, the smell of sandalwood and attar of roses; the
liquid Eastern vowels. The touch and the scent and the sound
of home!

A sudden tumult from the compound outside brought Winter
back from the past to the recollection of her present predicament.

and she pulled away, listening, her face once more strained and anxious:

'Anne Marie, you will take me with you? I *cannot* stay here!'

'But of course, little sister!' said Ameera, who was Juanita's daughter and granddaughter of Anne Marie de Selincourt who had also been Condesa de los Aguilares. 'We go now. Those are my servants out there. They make ready to leave.'

'Then let us go quickly,' urged Winter. 'I—I do not wish Lord Carlyon to know that I am leaving tonight.'

'As thou wilt,' said Ameera, 'and on the road thou shalt tell me of this *feringhi* from whom thou wouldst escape. Is it thy husband?'

'No. It is someone who—— I cannot explain now!'

Ameera laughed. 'No matter, Little Pearl—dost thou remember thy pet name in the zenana?—thou shalt tell me later. See! we will put Hamida's *bourqa* upon thee, thus!' She snatched up a voluminous white cotton garment that lay on the floor and dropped it over Winter's head. It was a long, full, tent-like cloak that shrouded her from head to foot, leaving only an inset of coarse net over the upper part of the face through which the wearer could see but not be seen. 'There!' said Ameera triumphantly. 'That is more seemly. Hamida must cover her face with her *chuddar* if she fears that men will attack her for the sake of her beauty!'

The older waiting-woman, who had been the infant Winter's wet nurse, mopped the tears from her wrinkled face and chuckled like a parrot, and Ameera donned her own *bourqa* and said: 'Come now, we are ready.'

'No—wait!' said Winter suddenly. 'I must leave a message. If I do not, he will think me lost and rouse the country looking for me, or go to the police. He could not just leave me and go back. Hast thou paper and ink?'

'Paper and ink? No. But Atiya here shall fetch some from the *khansamah*. Quick, Atiya—run!'

Ameera gave the girl a push, and she scuttled away, looking like a Halloween ghost, to return breathing hard a few minutes later and bearing a soft sheet of native paper, a bowl of black and gritty ink and a quill pen. Winter threw back the folds of the *bourqa* and wrote swiftly, Ameera holding the lamp. She thanked Lord Carlyon for his kind assistance, but she had met with a relative, a cousin, and so need put him to no further trouble on her behalf. He need be in no anxiety about her as she would be quite safe, and was continuing her journey immediately.

She held the paper above the lamp to dry the ink, and folding it, begged Atiya to take it to her room and leave it there, where it would be found in the morning. The girl had slipped out again, and Winter had waited in a fever of impatience and dread until she had returned, giggling reassuringly and carrying the small valise. 'No need to leave thy gear,' said Atiya.

They hurried down the verandah steps and out into the night, and a moment later they were in the dark, close-curtained *ruth*. There was a startled ejaculation from one of the entourage, and a fierce request to be silent from Hamida. The man who had exclaimed at the sight of four women where he had expected three enquired anxiously if all were well. 'All is well, Fateh Ali,' called Ameera. 'Drive on. It is late.'

The driver of the *ruth* shouted, the bullocks grunted and the *ruth* jolted forward and precipitated Winter into Ameera's lap, where the pent-up strains and anxieties and emotions of the last twenty-four hours found relief in a gale of laughter. She clung to Ameera and laughed, and Ameera and the two serving women laughed with her so that the driver and the four elderly mounted retainers who accompanied the *ruth* stared at each other in bewilderment and ended by chuckling in sympathy with that joyous sound.

'And now,' said Ameera, drawing breath and dabbing her eyes with the edge of her veil, 'tell me all! How dost thou come to be here? Art thou not yet wed? and who is this *feringhi* from whom we escape?'

She received no answer. Winter's head was still against her shoulder, but she had fallen asleep.

.   .   .   .   .

Carlyon did not discover that Winter had left the dâk bungalow until breakfast-time on the following day, and then he had shouted for his horse and ridden after her at breakneck speed along the dusty Lunjore road.

He had overtaken a curtained *ruth* accompanied by a motley escort of mounted retainers, but had galloped past it without a second glance, and it was only after several hours of hard riding that he had been forced to realize that Winter had escaped him, and had turned back, rage contending with fear for her safety. Whom had she gone with? How could she have left without his knowledge? A *relative*? How could she have met a relative? Had she planned it all, and known that there would be someone here to meet her? The Indian woman in the end room did not so much as cross his mind, for Carlyon had never heard of Juanita de Ballesteros, who had married Wali Dad, son of her father's great friend, Mirza Ali Shah of Oudh.

The frightened servants could give him no information, and he cursed his inability to understand this barbarous language and the incapacity of his Calcutta bearer as an interpreter. He had headed for the ford on the chance that Winter's letter had been a blind and that she had, after all, turned back to Delhi. But a raging torrent ran where the ford had been and Carlyon had returned to the dâk bungalow, white with fury and convinced at last that Winter had tricked him. He had spent two appalling days of enforced idleness at the bungalow, alternating between the extremes of rage and boredom, and on the morning of the third day, having heard that the river had fallen, he had returned to Delhi.

*   *   *

Winter awoke to find sunlight lying across her in a fretted pattern thrown by a carved wooden shutter. She was still wearing the crushed and crumpled morning dress of balzarine that she had put on in her bedroom at the Abuthnots' bungalow in Delhi Cantonments—how long ago? It seemed an age; another existence.

I*

She pushed away the thin cotton *chuddar* that covered her and stretched her arms above her head. She was lying on a charpoy, a low string bed with carved and painted legs, in a small bare room whose walls were painted a gay pink while the floor was covered with rush matting. Except for the charpoy and the matting the room was devoid of furniture, and once again Winter had a sudden mental vision of her room at Ware with its clutter of cumbersome furniture, gloomy wall-paper, dark heavily-framed engravings and thick fringed and tasselled draperies. The contrast made her laugh aloud, and there was a rustle of silk and a scent of sandalwood, and Ameera was there, smiling down at her.

'We did not like to wake thee,' said Ameera, 'but the sun is high and if we do not wish to lose a day's journey we must be on our way.'

Winter sprang up and immediately tripped on the voluminous folds of her crumpled dress and would have fallen if Ameera had not caught her.

'*Tenga cuidado!*' exclaimed Ameera, unexpectedly relapsing into Spanish. 'Why do you wear a garment in which it is impossible to walk?'

'My hoops,' explained Winter, looking ruefully at her trailing skirts and suddenly collapsing into laughter. 'I took them off, and I suppose they are still on the floor of that dâk bungalow.' Forgetting more pressing matters she described to the fascinated Ameera the working of a crinoline. 'They hold the skirts out—so.'

'Like a tent!' exclaimed Ameera, delighted. 'But it is ridiculous, is it not so? How does one sit down? Or walk through a door?'

Winter demonstrated and Ameera went off into peals of laughter.

'But have you never seen one?' asked Winter curiously. 'Are there no European women in Oudh?'

Ameera's laughing face sobered. 'Yes,' she said slowly, 'there are European women, but I do not meet them.'

'But your mother?'

'My mother is dead,' said Ameera. 'Did you not know?'

'No. I am sorry. She used to write, and then she wrote no more, and—and that is all I ever knew.'

'She died in the year of the cholera, when more than five hundred died in one day in Lucknow,' said Ameera. '*Ai de me!* you will find few who remember you at the Gulab Mahal.'

'Yet you still speak Spanish,' said Winter.

'As you see. But badly now. We kept it as a child's language amongst us. I do not often speak it in these days, for my husband —my husband does not care for *feringhis* and their ways.'

'Your husband? You are married, then!'

'But of course!' said Ameera in surprise. ' I have been married these five years. Have you no husband as yet?'

Winter laughed. 'You are taking me to my wedding!'

Ameera clapped her hands in a childlike gesture of delight. 'Is it really so? Then there is all the more need for haste. You shall tell me the whole; but first you must eat, and then we will find you some clothes. You cannot travel in comfort in such garments as you wear now.'

She ran to the door and called a variety of orders down the steep little stair, and presently Winter was being bathed and fed, and dressed in a replica of Ameera's own graceful costume by a horde of chattering, inquisitive, laughing women.

'Zobeida has cared for this well,' said Hamida approvingly, combing out the heavy silken waves of hair that reached almost to Winter's knee. 'It is softer and finer and even longer than Ameera Begum's! Is Zobeida no longer alive that she is not with thee now?'

Winter shook her head and Hamida sighed. '*Hai Mai!* We all grow old. Stand still, child, while I braid it. We shall need no black sheep's wool to lengthen this!'

Her gnarled brown fingers braided the rippling silken cloak into two long thick plaits, and fastened them with coloured thread. 'There! it is finished. Now thou art no longer of *Belait* (England) but of Hind.'

' And is not that dress more comfortable than thy tent of wires and fish-bones?' demanded Ameera. 'Thus do I remember thee when we played together in the women's quarters of the Gulab Mahal.'

Dressed alike in full trousers, loose tunics and veils of fine *shabnam* from Dacca, with their blue-black hair braided to the knee, the relationship between the two women was suddenly apparent. But the face of Juanita's daughter was not broad at the brow and pointed at the chin like Winter's; Ameera's face was a smooth, laughing oval, and though she was the elder by less than two years, early marriage and her Eastern blood had ripened her to an opulent maturity that would have made her seem the younger girl's senior by as much as ten years, had it not been for the laughter that danced perpetually in her dark eyes and lurked in the dimples at the corners of her small curving mouth.

Winter, whom life at Ware had starved of laughter, looked into Ameera's merry eyes and experienced a sudden relief of tension. An uprush of gaiety and high spirits and an irrational desire to run out into the sunlight and shout and play foolish games. To laugh for the sheer joy of laughing—and to make up for all the laughter that had been lost during the lonely years at Ware.

'A *bourqa* for the bride!' called Ameera. 'My little cousin goes to her wedding, and we cannot let other men's eyes peer at her by the way!'

And at that they had all laughed together with a noise like a flock of starlings, and swept out to the door of the women's quarters to see the guests off on their journey.

That journey was perhaps the happiest time that Winter de Ballesteros, going to her wedding, had known since the long-ago days of the Gulab Mahal. Here was a friend and a companion of her own age, and here once more was all the warmth and wonder of the old happy memories coming alive again. The very scent and sound of the days that she had kept alive with Zobeida's help and a desperate and tenacious effort of will, because it had so often seemed all that she had to cling to. She told Ameera all that had happened to her, and heard in return all the news of the Gulab Mahal.

There were, as Hamida had said, few left in the Rose Palace who would remember the Little Pearl, for the cholera had taken a heavy toll. Dasim, son of old Ali Shah's brother, was now an elderly gentleman whose wife, a soured and shrewish woman from Faizabad—Ameera pulled her laughing face into an expression of mock malice—was the senior lady of the household, though Dasim had acquired two junior wives and now possessed the three permitted by the Prophet. Ameera's brother, the baby who had been born in the same year as Winter—Kalig Dad who was to have been 'a great king and have seven sons'—had died too of the cholera, as had the little sister who had been born in the fateful January that had seen the retreat from Kabul and the disastrous end of the first Afghan War.

Ameera had married her second cousin, Walayat Shah; a petty nobleman who had occupied one of the numerous hereditary and lucrative sinecures at the dissolute court of the King of Oudh. The annexation had dispossessed him of employment and livelihood and he and his family lived now at the Gulab Mahal. The loss of power, privilege and revenue had enraged Walayat Shah against the *feringhis*. Men, explained Ameera regretfully, were apt to get hot and angry. They had less patience than women, and although she herself considered that the action of the Company had been high-handed and unnecessary—for were there not others of the royal line to replace Wajid Ali if he had offended? —she was happy to be back in the Gulab Mahal and had no wish to kill and burn. She had heard no good of Wajid Ali while he had reigned, and she had her children's safety to think of, and for their sake would be content to live quietly in the Gulab Mahal under any government that could be trusted to keep order.

'Your children!' exclaimed Winter, instantly diverted from politics to the personal. 'Have you children? How lovely! How many?'

'I have two sons,' said Ameera proudly. One was four years old and the other three, and they had been left in the care of her husband's mother while she had been away on a visit to attend the wedding of a near relative. She would have taken the children with her, but that her husband's mother had forbidden it for fear that they might fall ill or meet with some accident on the journey, and Ameera could not wait to get back to them.

'Three weeks! I have not seen them for three weeks—and it has been like three years. If it were not that I cannot spare even another hour from them, I would remain for thy *shadi*, Little Pearl. When thou art married and have sons of thine own thou wilt know how it is with me.'

Ameera's road lay through Lunjore and across the bridge of boats, but when some five days later they neared the outskirts of the city she would not come to the Residency, but stopped the *ruth* and sent one of her servants to fetch a hired carriage. 'I have thought,' said Ameera lovingly, 'that it were better if thou didst not arrive at thy bridegroom's house with a cousin who is not of thy own race. I have heard that there are those among the Sahib-*log* who do not look kindly on such things. But we will meet again. Surely, surely we will meet again! And now, as thou hast no woman of thine own to attend thee, Hamida here will go with thee. Nay, nay, we arranged it all last night whilst thou wert asleep! It is not seemly for thee to go to thy husband with no woman to attend thee. If he has procured another for thee, then she can return.'

The two young women embraced, and Hamida collected her own and Winter's belongings and followed her out into the road. A moment later the gaily decorated *ruth* with its mounted escort had rumbled away down the long, tree-shaded road. A slim hand waved briefly from between the embroidered curtains, and Ameera was gone.

Winter, no longer in native dress but wearing a light-coloured riding-habit, stood by the side of the road, looking after the dust cloud that hid the *ruth* and blinking back tears from her eyes, until Hamida, scandalized by the staring crowd of country folk who had paused to gape at the sight of a strange memsahib, hurried her into the hired carriage, and they were driven away through the hot sunlight towards the cantonments and the Residency.

18

THE Residency was a rambling house that had once been part of the palace of a local princeling. A former John Company official had altered it to a great extent, retaining all the larger reception rooms, to which he had added considerably. The house stood in extensive grounds on the edge of the jungle, which was separated from it by a deep nullah that formed a natural moat on three sides. On the fourth side a fort-like rampart, honeycombed with small rooms once occupied by an army of retainers, had been pulled down and replaced by a high wall of whitewashed brick, and only the massive gateway now remained to mark the fact that this had once been a royal residence.

The carriage drew up under a stone porch festooned with flowering creeper, and a startled *chuprassi* gaped at the girl in the close-fitting riding-habit who descended from it. The Residency servants had been aware for many months of their master's approaching marriage, but they had not expected the bride for another two weeks, and several of them gathered to stare and exchange agitated whispers.

Yes, agreed Durga Charan the head *chuprassi* cautiously, straightening his turban with an agitated hand, the Commissioner Sahib was at home. But he could see no one. He was indisposed—far too sick to receive visitors!

'I know,' said Winter. 'That is why I have come. I will see the sahib at once. Show me to his room.'

The head *chuprassi*, already bewildered by this young white woman who showed such an unexpected command of his own language, made an ineffectual attempt to stop her, but Winter swept past him and into the wide hall.

Conway's bedroom was darkened by curtains drawn across the windows, and it smelt unpleasantly. There was a woman in it. A plump native woman dressed in brightly coloured spangled muslin, who crouched on the floor beside the bed and waved a palm-leaf fan. The woman looked up, startled by Winter's

entrance, and rose with a clash of anklets and jewellery. She
was fat and past her first youth, but in a bold, florid manner,
not unbeautiful. She had been chewing *pan*, and the smell of
it, added to the musk with which she was scented, almost overpowered the stench of sickness and brandy. She seemed an
unsuitable sickroom attendant, and she stared at Winter in
indignation and hostility, her *kohl*-blackened eyes enormous in
her plump dark face.

'The sahib is not well!' said the woman in a shrill, angry voice.
'He can see no one. No one!'

'He will see me,' said Winter, and walked past her to the bed.

The heap on the bed moaned, grunted and stirred and said in
a thick voice: 'Wha's that? Wha's that? Shurrup, can't yer!
Filthy din——'

It turned over on its back and groaned aloud, and Winter
looked down at a bloated, unrecognizable face. Was this—*could*
this be Conway? She had expected to find a worn, haggard,
perhaps even grey-haired man, wasted by fever, and this fat
bloated face, yellow in the dim light of the curtained room, was
entirely and unexpectedly shocking. A reek of stale spirits and
foul breath made her draw back sharply. They had been dosing
him with brandy! Surely that could not be a good thing for fever?

And then suddenly she remembered what Mr. Carroll had
said. 'A swelling fever.' Of course! That was why Conway
looked so bulky and bloated. No wonder he had not wished her
to see him like this! No wonder, not knowing her well enough
to trust in her devotion to him, he had feared the effect it might
have upon her. Pity and love choked her and her eyes filled with
compassionate tears. She leant over him and laid a cool hand on
his forehead.

Conway grunted and opened his eyes with an effort. He stared
up at her for a long time, trying to focus her and completely at a
loss. Must have been drunker than he had thought last night—
or was it the opium? God, what a head he had! Tongue like a
roll of dusty matting. He'd seen things before, but they had
been strange spotted things that had crawled or hopped. Not

women. Not young and beautiful women. Couldn't be the brandy. Must be the opium. The creature was speaking. He wished that she would stop speaking and go away. He liked women, but not after a thick night. At the moment noise—any noise—hurt his head abominably . . .

'. . . Winter! Conway, it's Winter. Conway, dear, don't you know me? Why did you not tell me you were ill? I have come to look after you. You will be well soon, dearest. Conway, it's I—Winter. Dearest, I am here——'

At long last, through the thick, sick, agonizing torment that filled his head and stomach, the sense of the words penetrated. . . . *Winter!* It wasn't the opium or the brandy. This was the fortune that he was going to marry. The ugly, skinny, dark-eyed creature from Ware. She was here! How she had got here he did not know. Surely he could not have collapsed from the effects of a debauch and been unconscious for weeks? Hardly. What did it matter anyway? The girl was here. Must get rid of her. He was going to be sick again any minute, and that would finish it. Must get rid of her——

He was sick. Exceedingly sick. But in the more lucid interval that followed he discovered with amazement that she was holding his head and bathing his forehead with cold water; whispering endearments and telling him that he would soon be well. Fatima, standing by in stunned fury, began to protest, and Conway turned his head slowly—he could not turn his eyes—and spoke a single virulent word of dismissal.

The small, cool hands pressed his head back upon the pillow and he lay still with closed eyes, trying to think; dimly aware of disaster and the need for action. Presently he opened his eyes a little, peering at her under puffy, half-closed lids, and said thickly: 'Didn't expect you. Good of you t'come. Call Ismail, there's a good girl. M'bearer.'

The portly bearer, who had been hovering outside the door with a whispering and curious crowd of servants, hurried to his master's side, and after a brief and muttered colloquy turned to Winter and salaamed deeply. If the Miss-sahib would follow him he would show her to her room, and refreshments would be brought. The Huzoor wished Ismail to attend upon him.

'Go with him,' said Conway, forcing the words with an effort. 'Yr' can come back later.'

When the door had closed upon her he crawled out of bed and dragged himself to the bathroom. The water in the earthenware *gurra* was cold from the cool night, and he took a tin dipper and sloshed it over his head and shoulders, shuddering at the shock of the chilly cataract on his hot, sweating body and coldly sweating head. Ismail, returning, applied a variety of well-tried remedies, and the Commissioner groaned and staggered back to his bedroom to subside heavily into a chair, dazed, half-stupid and racked with recurrent waves of nausea and futile rage.

Damn the girl! What had possessed her to come gallivanting off on her own? It was unheard of! It would ruin all. He would not have had this happen for the world. He had intended to arrange for the wedding to take place within an hour or two of her arrival, so as to allow her no time to change her mind. And now she had arrived unexpectedly, and alone, and had found him suffering from the after-effects of a debauch in a house stinking of spirits and the sandalwood and essences of the five nautch girls from the city who, with Fatima, had entertained his guests at a bachelor party he had given on the previous night. What had possessed her to descend upon him like this? Or had she heard rumours, and wished to catch him out unawares?

'The Miss-sahib, hearing that the Huzoor was suffering from illness, hurried from Delhi in her haste to care for him,' said Ismail, laying out clean linen.

Illness! She had said something to that effect, so she had. Why, of course! An innocent creature like that could have had no experience of drunkenness. She had imagined him to be suffering from some illness!

The way opened before him with such surprising simplicity that he would have laughed aloud if such a physical effort had not been too painful. She was here alone and unattended. There was no one she knew in Lunjore and she could not stay the night

in his house unless she were married to him. It was all going to
be quite easy after all. He would send for the padre and explain
why, in order to protect the young bride's reputation, the wedding
must be performed immediately, and until the knot was tied
he must keep up the fiction that he had been suffering from
fever. It could not be better!

Revived and invigorated by the prospect he stumbled back to
bed and ordered Ismail to send a message instantly to the padre-
sahib requesting his immediate presence, and another to Colonel
Moulson to say that he wished to see him. 'And send in the
barber to me, and get this room cleaned up, and open all the
windows and clear the air a bit—no, don't draw the curtains, you
black bastard! Oh—and keep the Miss-sahib out of here, d'you
hear? Tell her I'm asleep—in me bath—anything! But keep
her out. Now *hut jao*—and *jaldi*!'

The padre, a thin young man suffering from weak eyes and
incipient malaria, listened with an attempt at concentration to
the explanation of the young Condesa's unexpected arrival and
unprotected state, and agreed, shivering with ague, that immediate marriage seemed the best solution to the difficulty, and
that as the bridegroom was unfortunately in poor health the
ceremony could be performed in the house. He would make the
necessary arrangements, but the Commissioner must procure
two witnesses.

Three hours later, in the cool, dim drawing-room, Sabrina's
daughter stood before a makeshift altar between burning candles
and was married to the nephew of Emily and Ebenezer.

She had brought her wedding-dress with her, but she did not
wear it, for she had no hoops to support its spreading folds, and
she had no desire to explain at this juncture why she should be
without a crinoline. She wore instead the pale grey riding-habit
in which she had arrived, and carried a bunch of the white
jasmine that grew by the porch. Hamida had tucked jasmine
blossoms into her black hair, and dropping the filmy bridal veil
over her head had frowned, saying that white veils were more
suited to widows than to brides.

Hamida was uneasy. She had no knowledge of the ways of white men, but the Commissioner's servants appeared to hold him in scant respect behind his back, and half an hour in the house had left her under no delusions as to what type of woman it was who occupied the *bibigarh*—the small detached set of rooms that lay behind the main building and screened from it by a discreet hedge of poinsettia and a cluster of pepper trees.

But if Hamida had qualms, Winter had none. Her only anxiety was on the score of Conway's health, and she had been alarmed at hearing of his intention to leave his bed for the ceremony. Surely a man who had been ill for so long should not be allowed to rise and be kept standing even for a short time? Supposing he should suffer a relapse? Conway had, however, assured her that her arrival had worked such wonders on his spirits that he felt himself to be a new man, and as he was already on the mend such a small exertion on so happy an occasion could do him no harm.

That had been in the course of a brief interview in the darkened bedroom where the curtains had remained drawn against the strong sunlight. The Reverend Eustace Chillingham, who had also been present, had been surprised to learn that the Commissioner had been so ill, as he had previously heard nothing of such a thing; but he was feeling too ill himself to pay much attention to the matter.

Winter had not seen Conway again until Colonel Moulson had appeared to lead her to the drawing-room. The sight of Colonel Moulson, whom she had never liked, was a shock to her. She had forgotten that he would be in Lunjore, and although she knew him to be acquainted with Conway, she had not expected him to be on such intimate terms with her betrothed as to warrant his being asked to give away the bride. She would rather have had anyone but Colonel Moulson to give her away, but Conway must know that she had met him, and it was out of delicacy and consideration for her that he had asked the Colonel to give her away rather than some stranger.

Winter looked at Colonel Moulson, her pale cheeks pink, her eyes very bright and young and a little frightened; not seeing him at all, but seeing instead the old, familiar picture of Conway, golden-haired, blue-eyed, wearing bright armour and standing between her and Cousin Julia and unhappiness.

That picture did not fade when she looked through the mist of her veil at the gross elderly man with the pale protuberant eyes, the greying hair and slack, twitching mouth, who stood or knelt beside her, and whose damp fleshy fingers were so unsteady that it was only with difficulty that he managed to put the ring upon her finger.

There was nothing about this bulky stranger that was familiar; but he was Conway, and he had been ill. So ill, and so disfigured by illness, that he had not wanted her to see him. That was proof enough of his affection for her, and of his kindness. The change that she saw in him was only physical, and now that she was here to nurse him and take care of him, to help him and to love him, he would recover soon enough and become strong and well again. She looked down at the ring that was too loose for her finger, as the first ring that he had given her had been, and her eyes were suddenly full of happy tears.

The Reverend Eustace had left immediately after the ceremony, but to Winter's distress Conway had refused to return to his bed.

'Bed? Nonsense! Nonsense! Never felt better in me life! Told you I was on the mend! Don't get married every day of the week. I've sent out to tell some of m' friends, and they'll soon be over. They'll want to see the bride. You're the Commissioner's Lady now, m'dear. You'll have to learn to do the honours. Have some champagne! Capital stuff for putting life into yer! You'll find we keep a good cellar. Hey there, Rassul, bring another bottle!'

He toasted Winter and looked her over with considerable approval. Between pain and nausea, and his fear that her unexpected arrival might result in his losing the fortune that she represented, he had been able to spare little attention for her personal appearance. Now, however, secure and in triumph, he took stock of his bride and decided that fate had indeed been kind to him.

Who could have believed that the plain, skinny, owl-eyed child whom he had last seen six years ago would have turned out so well? She was not precisely in his style—there were enough dark-haired women in India, and when it came to Europeans he preferred 'em blonde and buxom—but she was well enough. Those eyes were magnificent, and if he knew anything of women that mouth promised a very pleasant wedding night. As for her figure, if her riding-habit did not lie, it left little to be desired.

'Fred told me you had turned out quite a beauty,' said the Commissioner, 'and by Gad he was right! A fortune and a beauty too! I'm a lucky man.' He put an arm about Winter's slim waist and squeezed it, and the champagne slopped over and splashed down his waistcoat.

Winter said anxiously: 'Conway, please sit down! I am sure that you cannot be strong enough to stand. Colonel Moulson, please persuade him to return to his bed.'

'Persuade him to go to bed?' exclaimed Colonel Moulson, who had been lacing his champagne with brandy and had already downed three glasses in rapid succession. 'You shouldn't have any difficulty about gettin' him there! If I were in his place the difficulty would be in holdin' me back from it—the lucky dog!'

Winter had not fully understood the allusion, but the coarseness of the laugh which accompanied it had made her colour hotly and draw back from him in shocked distaste, her slim body stiffening with disgust. But Conway had only laughed and said: 'Time and to spare for that, Fred—time and to spare!' And then carriages and men on horseback had begun to arrive, and the room had filled with noisy strangers.

There had not been many of them—perhaps a dozen in all— and only two of them had been women; but to Winter there had appeared to be twice or three times that number. The noise, the loud laughter, the congratulations, the curious appraising stares and the bold approval of the men bewildered and disconcerted her, and the women were neither of them of the kind whom she would ever have felt drawn towards. They made her feel young and stiff and gauche, and they appeared to know Conway very

well, for they addressed him—and every other man in the room
—by his Christian name, so that Winter had some difficulty in
deciding which were their husbands.

Mrs. Wilkinson was small, plump and pretty, and made no
secret of the fact that she used rouge. She jangled a great many
bracelets, smelt strongly of violet essence and had rolling blue
eyes and a high-pitched laugh.

Mrs. Cottar was tall and thin, red-haired, green-eyed and ugly.
She was dressed with extreme smartness, though in a somewhat
outré style, and she appeared to be a general favourite with the
men. Her remarks were invariably greeted with a burst of
laughter and applause, but as they were mostly delivered *sotto
voce* Winter heard few of them, and those she did hear conveyed
nothing to her; she could not understand why they should so
amuse the gentlemen who hung on Mrs. Cottar's words, applaud-
ing her and addressing her as 'Lou'.

Winter herself stood silent; a small, rigid smile on her face
and her anxious eyes fixed on Conway. Once, when a particularly
uproarious burst of laughter had greeted one of Mrs. Cottar's
more audible sallies, he had observed that his bride had failed to
join in the general mirth, and had urged her in rousing tones not
to be such a little innocent.

'She ain't likely to remain one long; not in your company,
Con!' observed Colonel Moulson with a hiccough.

'Damn you, Fred!' protested the bridegroom; adding jovially:
'Not that I wouldn't say you were right!'

'Not like you to take to milk and water after years of champagne and country-brewed brandy, eh, what?' said Colonel
Moulson. 'Shouldn't have said it would suit you at all!'

'But then I do not suppose that he will be putting down his
cellar,' said Mrs. Cottar softly.

There was another burst of laughter in which the Commissioner joined uproariously, and Mrs. Cottar looked from the
bridegroom's face to the bride's, and frowned.

Lucy Cottar possessed a caustic and malicious wit, and little
kindness towards her own sex; an attitude which the majority of

them reciprocated with active dislike, for despite her lack of beauty many men found her attractive as well as entertaining, and Mrs. Cottar enjoyed playing with fire and had no conscience in the matter of other women's husbands. But something in Winter's bewildered eyes gave her a momentary twinge of compunction.

'Con,' said Mrs. Cottar in an undertone, 'you shouldn't have done it. It isn't decent.'

'What ain't decent?' demanded Mr. Barton.

'You aren't! What possessed that child's family to send her out to you? Why, it's no better than rape! Didn't they know you?'

'I took dam' good care that they didn't!' said Mr. Barton, and shouted with laughter. He was feeling light-headed with triumph. All over—all the waiting! All the work. He'd married the fortune. He was a rich man. A rich man and a dam' clever one! He'd planned it all, and it had all come about just as he had planned it. Not a hitch. Clever!

Mrs. Cottar, still under the influence of that unexpected feeling of compunction, left him and addressed herself to his wife:

'You must find it a little bewildering at first—meeting so many people whom you do not know and who all know your husband so well. But you will soon get to know us just as well as he does. Though you must not expect much gaiety in Lunjore! We do our best, but if you have been led to expect a gay life from what you will have seen of Calcutta and Delhi, I am afraid you may be sadly disappointed in Lunjore.'

'Oh, but I never expected it to be gay,' Winter hastened to assure her, 'and I know that Conway—Mr. Barton—will be far too hard-worked, once he is well again, to have much time for entertainments.'

'Has he been ill?' enquired Mrs. Cottar in some surprise. 'I did not know. But then I have not seen him for above a week. You must know that that is most unusual, for we all meet a great deal. Your husband has been used to give a small party as a regular thing each Tuesday night for his special cronies, and

you do not know how welcome they have been during the hot
weather. To sit at home all day in the heat is bad enough, but to
be compelled to sit there every night as well would be insup-
portable! And this is such a cool house. But I had a migraine
last week and could not attend, although Josh went—the selfish
creature.'

She saw that Winter was looking at her with a stunned bewilderment and said in explanation: 'Josh—Joshua—is my husband. The large dark one by the door——' She pointed with
her fan.

Winter said slowly and as if she found it difficult to articulate:
'But—but Conway—Mr. Barton, has been ill, you know. Since
—since late August.'

'Ill? Feathers! Did he tell you that? He was joking. Perhaps
he meant you to believe that he was sick for love!'

'But Mr. Carroll told me——'

'Carroll? Do you mean Jack Carroll? So you know him? Oh,
that would be just his way of saying that Con gave one of his
bachelor parties when Jack was last here, and they were all in a
melancholy way the next morning. I know Josh was! I told him
that the next time he came home from one of Con's bachelor
dinners he could sleep it off in the verandah. I am afraid that the
men will sadly miss those parties now that Con is married, but I
hope that you do not mean to discontinue our Tuesday sociables?
We gamble, you know. Not very heavy stakes, but enough to
make it exciting. Do you play cards?'

'No,' said Winter. 'No, I—I have never . . .'

'We must teach you. And you need not be afraid that Con
will be too overworked to enter into our few entertainments.
Why, he is the idlest of creatures! And so we all tell him. He
lets Alex Randall do all the work while he takes all the credit.
Quite shocking—is it not, Con?'

'No idea what you're talkin' about, Lou, my witch. But I am
ready to be shocked,' said Mr. Barton, coming to anchor beside
them. 'What is it? A new scandal?'

'On the contrary. An old one. It is you I was referring to.

I was telling your wife that you allow Alex Randall to do all the work while you take all the credit.'

'What's shockin' about that?' demanded Mr. Barton. 'Randall likes work. Meat and drink to the man! Peculiar taste. Shockin' fool I'd be if I wore myself out doing what someone else will do for me! *I've* better use f' my time, m' dear. But Alex is a cold fish.'

'Oh, no, he is not,' said Mrs. Cottar with a twisted smile. 'You're out there, Con!'

'Ha! I am, am I? Trust you to know! Speakin' from personal experience, Lou?'

'No, alas!'

'Which means that you tried your lures on him, eh?'

'But of course! Any woman of spirit would have done the same. But he does not mix business with pleasure, and Lunjore is business. Such a pity!'

'Not for me!' said the Commissioner, holding out his glass to be refilled by an obsequious *khitmadgar*. 'He deals with the business while I take care of the pleasure. Very satisfact'ry arrangement, Lou, my love!' He drank deeply and looked down at his wife's white, rigid face. 'Mustn't forget I'm a married man now. Have to watch m'self! Not so much straying from the straight and narrow, eh, Lou?—eh, m' dear?' He pinched his wife's chin and slopped a quantity of brandy down her dress in the process.

The rest of the evening was a nightmare to Winter. A dreadful, feverish dream of babble and noise and the clink of glasses, in which she did not hear one word of what was said. She sat on a sofa with her back straight and her head high and a small social smile frozen on her face. She answered when she was spoken to, but her voice did not seem to belong to her any more.

The sun sank and the room filled with shadows. Lamps and candles were lit and the *chiks* rolled up to let in the cool night air, but still the noise went on and still no one left. Hours later—or so it seemed—a meal was served in the big dining-room, and Winter sat beside her bridegroom at the head of the table, white-faced and dry-eyed, smiling with stiff lips and trying to force herself to eat the food that was placed before her. Toasts were drunk and speeches were made, and still she sat there as if she were held in a strange trance in which her body had turned into some inanimate jointed thing and her mind had ceased to function.

It was midnight before the guests departed, and they would not have gone then but for Major Mottisham, the second witness at the marriage ceremony, who, suddenly recollecting that this was a wedding-party and not a carouse, had made a short and garbled speech full of distressingly broad allusions, and herded the wedding guests into the hall.

Winter stood on the porch steps beside her husband with her hands hanging at her sides and her face still wearing that frozen smile, while carriage wheels rolled away and horses' hooves scattered the gravel. They had gone at last, and the house was quiet.

The garden was full of moonlight, and in the drawing-room the servants were stacking glasses and removing cigar-stubs, turning out lamps and blowing out candles. 'Well, we may not have had a full-dress weddin',' said Conway, 'but we cer'nly had a capital celebration! Don't get married every day of yer life, s'just as well to enjoy it. Eat, drink and ge' married! That's it, ain't it, m'dear?'

He appeared to expect some reply, and Winter said in a stiff, expressionless voice: 'I am very tired. I think, if you do not mind, that I will go to bed.'

'Tha's right. You go to bed. I won't keep y' waiting!' He laughed uproariously and Winter turned away and walked slowly and unsteadily to her room, as though it were she and not Conway who was drunk.

Hamida was waiting for her, and the sight of the girl's white face and dazed eyes filled her with clucking alarm. But Winter paid no attention to her words and did not even hear them. She allowed herself to be undressed and bathed and put to bed as though she were not even a child but a large doll. Her world—the dream world that she had built up for years and planned for and longed and lived for—was in ruins about her, but she could not even think.

At least it was quiet at last. The noise and the babble, the meaningless talk, the incomprehensible jests, the shouts of laughter and the clink of glasses had stopped, and she was alone; for now even Hamida was gone. Now perhaps she could think again —could cry, to ease the terrible pain in her heart. And then the door opened and Conway was there.

Winter sat up swiftly, pulling the sheets up about her, wondering dully why he was here and what he wished to say to her so late at night. She had not taken in the sense of his last remark to her, and in the dazed nightmare of that terrible wedding-party she had forgotten that people who were married shared the same bed. She watched stupidly while he came towards her, weaving a little in his walk, and put his candle down upon the bedside table and began to remove his dressing-gown. And then, quite suddenly, the numbness left her and gave place to sheer panic and horror.

This man—this gross, repulsive, drunken stranger—was going to get into the same bed with her! To lie down beside her— perhaps touch her—kiss her! She dragged the sheets up to her chin and her eyes widened until they were enormous in her small face.

'Go away! Please go away at once!' Her voice was hoarse with fear and loathing. 'You cannot sleep here tonight—not tonight. Go away!'

Conway gave a drunken chuckle of approval. 'Coy, are you, my shy little virgin? Tha's as it should be! But yer a wife now.' He looked down at her and his red-rimmed eyes lit with a look that she had seen before. A look that had been in Carlyon's eyes.

'By gad, yer a beauty, after all!' The thick voice held a note of awe. 'It would a' been worth marryin' any ugly wench with that fortune, but to get a beauty into the bargain——!'

He reached out an unsteady hand and lifted a long tress of the black, unbound hair, and Winter struck at his hand in fury and terror.

'Don't touch me! Don't dare to touch me!'

Conway lunged towards her across the bed and she flung aside
the sheets and leapt out, in the grip of the same frantic shuddering panic that she had experienced when Carlyon had looked at
her by the door of her room at the dâk bungalow beyond the ford.
But her husband's clutching hands were on her hair and they
gripped it and jerked it brutally, so that she fell back and was
caught. And this time there was no escape.

19

ALEX was both strong and healthy, and Niaz had sufficient knowledge of such matters as concussion and broken collar-bones to
deal more than adequately with the situation. Having assured
himself that the injury was not serious he had eased off Alex's
coat and set the collar-bone, binding it securely with his pugaree,
and having retrieved Shalini had ridden back to a small village
they had recently passed, where he had procured a ramshackle
palanquin and bearers to carry it. An hour later Alex had been
installed in the hut of the village head-man and under the care
of a wrinkled crone well versed in the use of healing herbs.

He had not recovered consciousness until a little before dawn
on the following day, and all through that day, while Niaz held
him down so that he should do no further injury to his arm and
shoulder, he had talked; sometimes in English, sometimes in
Urdu or in Pushtoo, muttering and raving; exhorting a gang of
labourers who built a road through wild and trackless territory;
shouting in a cavalry charge; whispering to a Havildar, eight years
dead, as they crawled forward under cover of darkness to attack a
fort; discussing philosophy with a Mullah in the foothills beyond
Hoti Mardan; arguing with the Commissioner of Lunjore—
expounding policies, pressing for action, explaining patiently the
need for reforms—or muttering of Khanwai and white goats, of

sharks and sacrifices and the stupidity of fools who would neither see nor hear, look nor listen. But towards sunset he became quieter and lay still at last, talking to Winter, his hoarse, exhausted voice barely a whisper.

Twenty-four hours later Alex woke to drugged sanity and a splitting headache. He could remember nothing of the past few weeks; his last coherent recollection being of a dâk *ghari* overturning on the journey up from Calcutta. He supposed that he must have suffered some injury in the accident and wondered what had happened to his fellow-passenger, the morose Major.

Niaz, discovering this gap in his memory, made no move to repair it, for instinct told him that once Alex remembered what it was that he had set out for, he would start off again long before it was safe for him to do so. But Alex was drowsy and stupid and in pain, and he drank the beldame's drugs obediently and slept; woke to a smell of dung-fires and sun-baked earth, the aromatic scents of masala and cardamoms and all the familiar sounds and smells of an Indian village, grinned at Niaz and swallowed the infusion of herbs and hot milk that he was offered, and slept again.

It was not until the morning of the sixth day that, awaking to the first brilliant rays of the sun and the squeaking of a well wheel, he remembered Delhi and all that had happened there. It had taken him some time to realize how many days had elapsed since he had ridden in pursuit of Winter and Carlyon, and when he had done so he had propped himself on his unwounded arm and cursed Niaz with a savage, concentrated fury for having let him lie there; for having given him drugs and for not having put him on his horse and taken him on to Lunjore or back to Delhi.

'Had I done so, it had gone ill with thee,' said Niaz, unmoved. 'Saddle the horses. We go now.'

'To Delhi?'

'To Lunjore.'

Niaz shook his head. 'If we go today thou wilt be able to ride two *koss*. Perchance three, but no more. Wait here yet another day and I will ride to Delhi for Latif and our gear. I sent word to Fraser Sahib in Delhi, and also to Barton Sahib, that thou hadst met with an accident and would be delayed. There is no need for thee to ride to Delhi and back. I will go; and tomorrow, if I return in time, we will go on to Lunjore.'

'We will go today, and within the hour,' said Alex.

Niaz observed him with a thoughtful eye and said in a non-committal voice: 'I sent a man to get news at the ford. The river fell three days back, and the Lord Sahib returned with the carriage and horses and his *naukar-log*. They go to Delhi.'

Alex looked at him for a long moment, then he said: 'Was the Lady Sahib with him?'

'No. But the man spoke with one of the syces, and it was said that she had met with friends upon the road and had gone forward with them to Lunjore.'

Alex lay back slowly on the string bed and stared up at the smoke-blackened ceiling above his head. He was silent for so long that at last Niaz cleared his throat and said carefully: 'Do we ride today?'

'No.' Alex closed his eyes and spoke without looking at him. 'I will wait here. Fetch the gear from Delhi.' He turned over on his right side with his face to the wall and did not speak again.

Niaz did not return for two days, and those days had given Alex plenty of time for thought. His shoulder still pained him and his head still ached, but the dizzy stupidity had gone. He would drink no more of the old woman's drugs and his brain was clear. There had been a moment when he had been tempted to return to Delhi and demand an account of his behaviour from Lord Carlyon, but five minutes' reflection had convinced him of the uselessness of such a proceeding. He had no shadow of right to take Carlyon to task, and Colonel Abuthnot could be counted upon to say all that was necessary upon that head. As for Winter, if she had indeed met with friends upon the road she would have reached Lunjore days ago, and there was nothing more that he could do about that either. She would have learned by now what sort of man Conway Barton was, and would probably be staying with these friends until she could arrange to return to England.

Whether he wished her to return there was another matter, and one which he was not in the least desirous of facing. He had kept free of entanglements with women of his own class and kind, largely because of a conviction that work and women in such a country and climate, and under the conditions that prevailed in India, did not mix. One or the other of them were bound to suffer. Those wives who endured the heat and hazards of hot weather in the plains in order to be with their husbands grew old before their time, and yet to go to the hills meant months of separation. Children were less a blessing than a continual and terrible anxiety: Hodson had lost his only and beloved child the previous year, and India was strewn with the graves of children.

Winter . . . If he should see her again, would he try to stop her from returning to England, or would he let her go? He did not know. Barely more than a week ago he would have been thankful to see her go. But that had been before he had kissed her. He had kissed other women, lightly or passionately, and had forgotten them. But he could still feel that warm, rounded slenderness in his arms and the way in which, for a long moment, she had seemed to melt against him and become so much a part of him that her every nerve and pulse and breath and heart-beat had been as though it were his own.

Behind his closed eyelids Alex saw the small heart-shaped face, and the dark eyes that were so unsure; one moment so brimful of hope and happiness and the next so still and so wary—and sometimes so frightened. She had learnt to school her face. To wear a dignity and calm and composure beyond her years. To hold her chin high and her slim figure erect, and to hide loneliness and hope and hurt. Perhaps in time she would learn to force her eyes to do these things too, unless happiness and security saved her from that sad necessity. But he, Alex, was the last person who could offer her either. . . .

In the evening, when the cooking-fires were lit, the headman and some of the village elders, finding that he was sufficiently recovered to sit up and eat the first solid meal he had eaten in days, came to squat by the door, smoke their hookahs and converse.

Their talk was a talk that Alex understood and had listened to on many occasions—the all-important problems of village life. Crops and harvesting, the drying of a well, the damage done by deer and wild pig, the failure of certain crops owing to a poor monsoon, a dispute over a marriage dowry—the half of which had not been paid—and a vexed question of grazing rights. This was the India that he knew and loved, and which, as far as any European may understand the mind of India, he understood.

India to Alex was the land. The cultivator and the herdsman and the hundreds of thousands of small, humble village communities whose way of life had not changed in the slow centuries since Alexander of Macedon and his warriors had poured through the passes to conquer the unknown land that had been old when Greece was young. The villagers were more tolerant and charitable than the city dwellers, for ploughing, sowing, reaping and irrigation would not wait while men sat in circles and listened to windy and grandiloquent phrase-makers who promised overnight Utopias provided that this or that class or sect, creed or colour were first destroyed or routed. They toiled hard and they were a kindly people, and Alex listened to them now and felt more relaxed and at peace than he had for many days.

He had accomplished the remainder of his journey by easier stages than he would normally have done, for he found the long hours in the saddle more tiring than he would admit; and Winter had been married almost a week by the time he reached Lunjore.

His lamp-lit bungalow was pleasantly cool after the heat of the dusty roads, and Alam Din, who combined the offices of butler and bearer, had prepared a meal, for Niaz had sent forward word of their arrival. Alex had ridden less than thirty miles that day, but he was intolerably tired and impatient with himself for being so. He had intended to go straight to bed and merely send word of his arrival to the Commissioner, reporting to him on the following morning, but Mr. Barton had sent over to say that he wished to see him that same evening.

Alam Din, handing dishes, had mentioned the Commissioner's marriage—it being a matter of considerable interest in Lunjore

K

—and had expressed approval that there should at last be a memsahib at the Residency, but Alex had answered at random and had not taken in a word of what had been said. Alam Din was inclined to be talkative and Alex's mind was on other things. He walked over to the Residency in the starlight and was ushered into the Commissioner's drawing-room.

The big room was brightly lit and empty, and there was something unusual about it. It was no longer the untidy and somewhat raffish apartment with which he was familiar. The furniture had been rearranged and the place was clean, and there were no fewer than three vases of flowers. Alex was frowning abstractedly at an arrangement of orange lilies and yellow jasmine when a door at the far end of the room opened and he looked up and saw Winter.

He should have been prepared for it, but he was not. He had been so sure that, young as she was, she possessed too much character and courage to allow herself to be forced by circumstances into this marriage once she had seen again the man to whom she was betrothed, and had realized, as she must immediately do, what he had become. It had indeed occurred to him that she might still be in Lunjore, but he considered it more likely that the friends she had met with on the road—possibly friends she had met at Ware or at Sir Ebenezer's?—had already helped her to return to the Abuthnots or to Calcutta, and he could only be grateful for it. That she could have married that sodden debauchee was—must be—impossible. He was neither prepared for the sight of her nor for what it did to him.

Winter had not known of Alex's return. Conway had not thought to mention it, and she had imagined that she need never see him again. Knowing her husband to be sitting over the wine with two of his friends, she had slipped into the drawing-room by the side door to fetch a pair of embroidery scissors that she had left there earlier in the evening. She had opened the door and seen Alex. . . .

They stood quite still and looked at each other; their faces white and drawn with shock, and their eyes wide and fixed and unbelieving. There was a clock in the room; a massive affair of marble and gilt. The pendulum swung to and fro counting the ticking seconds into the silence, and the sound of them seemed to grow louder and louder in the stillness. Alex put out a hand with the groping gesture of a blind man and caught the back of a chair and held it, and Winter saw his knuckles shine white, and saw too that there were bright beads of sweat on his forehead.

Her own fingers tightened about the door-knob, gripping it desperately as she fought with a tide of shame and despair that equalled the shame and desperation of her wedding night. Alex had told her the truth about Conway and she had not believed him. He had done what he could to prevent her from falling into this horrible quicksand into which her own foolishness had led her, and it was unbearable that she should have to face him now.

Alex said harshly: 'Did you marry him?'

'Yes.' The word was barely a breath.

'Why?'

Winter did not answer him, but she moved her head in a slight, helpless gesture that was less a refusal to answer than hopelessness.

Something in that small despairing movement hurt Alex with savage pain that was as entirely physical as the touch of a hot iron. 'Was it because you had no one else to go to? You could have——' He stopped abruptly, aware of the futility of questions or answers. What did the whys and wherefores matter now? The thing was done. His hand tightened for another instant on the chair-back and then fell to his side. His head was aching abominably and it was suddenly an effort to stand erect. He said in a curiously formal voice that somehow gave the impression that he was a little drunk:

'I suppose I must offer my congratulations. Will you make my excuses to your husband? He sent for me, but I have had a somewhat tiring day and I feel sure he will forgive me if I postpone the interview until the morning. Good night.'

He turned on his heel, and Winter heard him stumble as he went down the porch steps, and then the sound of his footsteps

died away into the silence until there was only the clock ticking
again, louder and louder, and presently a muffled bellow of
laughter from the direction of the dining-room where her husband and his friends were finishing the port.

Alex had gone. She had let him go, though she could have
stopped him. Even now, if she ran after him, he might help her.
He could not dissolve her marriage. That was irrevocable. But
he would not refuse to help her. He would do something—she
did not know what—but something. Yet how could she possibly
appeal to him after what had occurred at Delhi?—after the
insults she had flung at him? She could only hope that she need
not see him again. And there was no one else she could appeal to.

She could not run to Ameera or return to Delhi, for she had
no money and no means of getting any. Conway had taken
charge of her jewel box and any valuables she possessed, saying
that such things were better under lock and key. Even Hamida
had gone. . . .

The morning after her wedding Winter had awakened from
the deep sleep of utter mental and physical exhaustion to the full
and despairing realization of what she had done. There had been
a heavy arm lying across her, its inert weight hurting her breasts,
and beside her, his mouth open, her bridegroom snored in sodden
slumber. He had groaned and rolled his head on the pillow when
she had moved, but he had not wakened, and Winter had crept
shuddering from under that arm, dizzy, bruised, sick with loathing and despair, and stumbling into the dressing-room had bolted
the door behind her.

Hamida had been there waiting for her, and Winter had clung
to her; shivering, dry-eyed and desperate. Hamida had crooned
over her and petted her, but it was obvious that she considered
such things to be a normal part of life. She herself, said Hamida,
had been many years younger than Winter when she had been
wed, and her husband had been a lusty man—a bear!—so that
Hamida too had screamed in terror on her wedding night and
had wept and shivered for many days afterwards. But in time
she had come to love her husband and to welcome his embraces,

and she had borne him five sons of whom four still lived, so that her grandsons were many. Husbands, said Hamida, were often rough and brutal in the marriage bed, but wives must bear such things and learn to please their lords, lest their lords turned to light women. Winter's hysterical assertion that she intended to leave Lunjore immediately was received with scandalized horror. Such a thing was impossible—unthinkable! Wives did not behave thus. They had their duties and their responsibilities, and to run away because they found a bridegroom not entirely to their taste was unheard of! She was married now, and that could not be undone. She had not even been forced into the marriage. It had been of her own choosing, and she could not now run away from it.

Winter had listened numbly to Hamida's voice holding forth on the duties of wives, but only one thing that Hamida had said made sense to her—she was married now, and that could not be undone. Hamida was right. But within a week Hamida had gone.

It was the plump painted woman whom Winter had found sitting beside Conway's bed on the morning of her arrival who was responsible: Fatima Bai; the woman who lived in the *bibigarh* behind the scarlet poinsettias and the feathery screen of pepper trees, with her sister and her own serving women. Fatima Bai had recognized an enemy in Hamida and had taken steps to remove her. Conway had told his wife that she must dismiss the woman she had brought with her, as he had already made arrangements for an ayah, and an outsider would only cause trouble among the other servants.

Winter had refused flatly to part with Hamida, and Conway, to his wrath, had found that he could do nothing to alter her decision. He had lost his temper and had said things that had stripped the last rags of her illusions from her. She had not given way, but the next day Hamida had been taken ill, and had whispered to Winter that her food had been poisoned. 'Do not fear, child. I ate only a little, and tomorrow I shall be well again. But after this I must buy all my own food and cook it apart, letting no one near, so that they cannot try again.' But Winter would not hear of it. She would not risk Hamida's life, and she sent her away, sending gifts and messages by her to Ameera. And with Hamida went her only link with the outside world.

Conway had mentioned casually that Captain Randall had met with some accident that would delay his return, and that it was cursed careless of him; but Winter had not believed it. She had been sure that after the incident on Delhi wall Alex would prefer not to return to Lunjore, and was probably arranging to get himself transferred to some other post. She had no knowledge of officialdom and it seemed to her an obvious course of action. Alex had no illusions about his chief. He had spoken of him in unmeasured terms, and he had kissed his chief's betrothed and had been accused by her of jealousy and lying. He would not wish to return to Lunjore, and she would at least be spared the humiliation of facing him.

There remained Mrs. Gardener-Smith, who had called upon her from mixed motives on the afternoon following their arrival. Perhaps Mrs. Gardener-Smith would help her?—lend her money so that she could return to England and to Ware. To Ware! She had never believed that she could ever desire to return there. But anything—*anything*—was better than life in this horrible house, with this coarse, brutal stranger who was her husband and who had told her furiously to her face that he had only married her for her money.

But Mrs. Gardener-Smith's views on young wives and their duties towards husbands—especially husbands as senior as the Commissioner of Lunjore—proved to be much the same as Hamida's. She had not only been unsympathetic, she had been scandalized. Of course all men drank! and on occasions drank too much and behaved accordingly. But ladies did not mention such things. They looked the other way. As for the suggestion that she, Mrs. Gardener-Smith, should assist Winter to leave her husband, she would have nothing whatever to do with such a preposterous proposal! Such a course could only involve her in unpleasantness with the Commissioner, and on those grounds alone she would not think of it. But even if Winter *should* be

mad enough to run away she would not get far, for the law would
be on Mr. Barton's side and could force her to return to him.
Mrs. Gardener-Smith had pronounced herself shocked that dear
Winter should be so lacking in restraint, and so lost to all sense
of responsibility towards her husband and to society, as even to
think of such a thing! She must remember that she was no
longer a heedless girl but a married woman, and marriage
entailed responsibilities. . . .

Winter had driven away down the dusty, shadow-barred roads
of the cantonment with her last hope gone. Mrs. Gardener-
Smith had been right, as Hamida had been right. She had
married Conway and she could not run away; because there was
nowhere to run to, and because however far she ran it would
not be far enough. The law would send her back to her lawful
husband. She had indeed made her bed and now she must lie
on it.

Returning wearily to the big white house that was now her
home she had not thought it was possible to experience more
humiliation or more despair. Until on the evening of that same
day she had opened the door into the drawing-room and had seen
Alex Randall, and known that she was wrong.

In the slow days and weeks that followed she had seen him
only rarely, and never to speak to. For he had not left Lunjore,
and Winter, who had once—how long ago it seemed!—meant to
influence Conway to send him away, had grown to be almost glad
of it. The fact that he was there, even if she did not speak to
him or see him, was curiously comforting; the one strong link
in a rotted and rusty chain. If ever life and living became more
than she could endure, there was Alex—he at least would not
refuse to help her. He knew Conway.

Alex spent a large part of his time in the outlying areas of
the district, and when he was not on tour he avoided entering
the living-rooms of the Residency. But he was often in the
Commissioner's office, and Winter would hear the murmur of his
level voice that always seemed to her, when he was addressing
her husband, to hold something of the deliberate restraint of an

adult explaining a problem patiently and tactfully to a backward and fractious child. She was obscurely aware that Alex rode his temper on a tight rein, and often wondered why he should trouble to do so, for the truth of Mrs. Cottar's flippant remark that Captain Randall did the work while Mr. Commissioner Barton took the credit was soon patently obvious.

Conway did little work and was content to leave the greater part of his duties in Alex's hands. He signed papers that Alex laid before him, and agreed to decisions that Alex had made, imagining, from the way in which they were presented to him, that the decisions were his own. He had not, after all, sent in his resignation, for rumour had it that the Governor General was contemplating an extensive tour, which would include Lunjore, in the following year, and the Commissioner scented a possible knighthood. The prospect of being able to retire not only as a rich man but as 'Sir Conway' appealed strongly to his vanity, and he decided to postpone his resignation for a year, and also to make that year as pleasant as possible. He ceased to take even a casual interest in the affairs of Lunjore, and Alex's work was greatly simplified thereby, though it meant that he spent more time in Lunjore itself and less out in the district.

Secure now in the possession of large wealth, the Commissioner entertained lavishly, and the Residency was always full of guests. He was proud of his wife's looks and poise, and it pleased him that her dresses and jewels and her youthful dignity made an impression on his guests. But he had early tired of her as a woman. She had never again screamed and wept and fought him, but the passive, rigid disgust with which she had endured his subsequent embraces had soon robbed them of all pleasure, and he had returned to the coarser and more co-operative Fatima for his entertainment.

20

CONWAY did not allow the fact that he was now married to alter his way of life to any great extent, and his more raffish friends were frequent visitors at the Residency. Mrs. Cottar, acidly witty, and Mrs. Wilkinson, plump, pouting and feline, were often to be seen there, with or without their husbands, and the Tuesday parties of which Mrs. Cottar had spoken were not discontinued. Winter played hostess at any of the Commissioner's parties that might be considered official entertaining, but she had refused to preside at the long sessions of gambling and drinking that constituted these particular entertainments, and on Tuesdays she would retire early to bed with the plea of a headache.

Conway had attempted to take her to task on this score, and to insist on her remaining, on the grounds that her early retirement was an insult to his guests. But here he had found, as he had found over the question of Hamida, that his young wife was not to be browbeaten. She would perform the duties of the Commissioner's wife to the best of her ability, but these duties did not include lending her countenance to such questionable and noisy entertainments as the Tuesday parties.

She made no friends among the British community in Lunjore, and she did not like the Residency servants, but she was given no opportunity to dismiss them. The capacity for gaiety and warmth and happiness that had shown itself, although shyly, on the long voyage from England, and the laughter that Ameera had released, had been cut off like flowers in a black frost, and Lunjore society found young Mrs. Barton a cold little thing.

Mrs. Gardener-Smith did indeed claim that her daughter Delia was Mrs. Barton's greatest friend, and Delia was often to be met with at the Residency, though if the truth were known she came there more on Colonel Moulson's account than Winter's. Winter had been surprised and disconcerted to find that Delia was becoming one of the 'Tuesday crowd' at the Residency, for she had not thought that Mrs. Gardener-Smith would permit it,

K*

and she was sure that Colonel Gardener-Smith—a silent, elderly, earnest man, wrapped up in his beloved regiment—would not wish his daughter to attend such affairs. But Delia's papa had other things to think of.

Colonel Gardener-Smith had recently succeeded in putting into practice a long-cherished scheme for improving the lot of the sepoys' families: the opening of a school and a medical centre run on European lines. But the scheme was proving a grave disappointment, for he had now discovered that his philanthropic venture was regarded by his sepoys as a subtle method of destroying their caste, and he had no hesitation in laying the blame for this attitude at the door of Lionel Packer, the commanding officer of the 105th Bengal Native Infantry, stationed at Lunjore.

Colonel Packer, a bigoted Christian, placed his duty towards his God above that of his duty as an army officer. An admirable attitude with which no one could quarrel, save on the score that as his interpretation of these duties conflicted it would have been wiser for him to resign his command.

Colonel Packer's duty towards God impelled him to make every effort to spread the Gospel to the heathen, and he was at present engaged in an earnest attempt to convert his entire regiment to Christianity. A project which Colonel Gardener-Smith, together with almost every other thinking British officer and every sepoy in Lunjore, regarded with hostility and dismay, while Captain Randall, in the name of the Commissioner of Lunjore, had sent a strongly worded protest to the Commander-in-Chief, General Anson, suggesting that Colonel Packer should be either restrained from 'spreading the Word' or instantly removed from his command.

Colonel Gardener-Smith refused to see that the suspicion with which his own schemes towards bettering the lot of his sepoys was regarded was anything more than a reflection of the alarm and dismay that Colonel Packer's assaults upon the religion of his men had produced among the ranks of the native regiments, and he did not abandon hope of popularizing both school and medical centre. He had too much on his mind to pay overmuch attention to the social activities of his wife and daughter, and Delia continued to frequent the Residency and attend the Tuesday parties.

Winter had made at least one friend in Lunjore; Zeb-un-Nissa, the nine-year-old granddaughter of Akbar Khan, the gatekeeper. Nissa was a frail little creature whose enormous dark eyes had a curiously blind look as though they looked through people and not at them. She was reported to be subject to fits and to have second-sight, and the servants were afraid of her.

She was a solitary child who spent much of her time among the roots of the big banyan tree near the Residency gate, watching the birds and squirrels, who appeared to have no fear of her and would feed from her hand and take grain from between her lips. Winter had noticed a flock of green parrots fluttering about the roots of the tree early one morning, and had gone out to see what had attracted them. She had stayed to talk to Nissa, and the two had become fast friends.

Winter became less actively unhappy as the weeks passed, and a dull resignation took the place of the raw wound in her heart. There was still India, and that alone, in the ruin of her dreams, had not betrayed her.

She would ride out every evening, and in the early morning before the sun rose; galloping across the plain and along the banks of the distant river, or riding through the dew-wet crops where the peafowl screamed at the dawn and skeins of wild geese honked overhead on their way to the jheels of Hazrat-Bagh and Pari. The glory of the sunrise over the limitless plains and the wide, winding river; the quiet beauty of the evenings when the sun sank with incredible swiftness, dyeing the river and the long silver sandbanks, the city and the plain and every tree and cane-brake to a warm, glowing apricot; the swift, opal twilight, and night unfolding like a peacock's tail, green and blue and violet, flecked with the last gold of day and spangled with stars—these were things that comforted Winter and held for her a never-failing enchantment, daily renewed.

The wide land and the wide river and the enormous sky were

beautiful to her. The vastness soothed her. The sense of space—
of the plains stretching away and away to the deserts of Bikaner
and the blue waters of Cape Comorin, to the jungles and valleys
of Nepal; wrinkling up into the foothills, to rise in range after
range to the white barrier of the Himalayas where the remote
passes led into the unknown land of Tibet, into Persia and the
Pamirs and the great plains and lakes and ranges of Central
Asia—the Kara-Koram, the Hindu Kush, Tien Shan and Turkes-
tan; Balkash and Baskal; the white wastes of Siberia and the
yellow leagues of China. Here there was none of the sense of
being shut in and enclosed behind high walls that she had sometimes experienced at Ware. The mile-wide rivers and the enormous mountain ranges seemed less of a barrier than the neat
English hedges and the trout stream that had separated the
paddocks from the park.

There was a fatalism too about the East that appealed to her,
and the filth and squalor and cruelty that everywhere underlay
the beauty did not in any way lessen her love for the land. The
city was ugly and foetid and full of sights that were unbelievably
horrible to Western eyes, and Winter's eyes did not miss them.
But she loved the city too. The heaped colours of fruits and
vegetables and grain in the bazaar. The rich smell of mustard
oil and masala, of musk and spices and ghee. The shops of the
potter and the silversmith. The stalls that sold glass bangles as
fine and light as silk and as fragile as a dried leaf, in glittering,
sparkling, burning colours—red and blue and gold and grass
green. The silk-shops with their gay bales piled high in the
shadows. The drifting, jostling crowds and the great, lazy
Brahmini bulls, sacred to Shiva, who shouldered through the
narrow streets taking toll of the baskets of the vegetable-sellers.

White women were seldom to be seen in the city, and on the
rare occasions on which they went there they went in carriages
and escorted by white men. But Winter would go with only
Yusaf the syce, and at first the crowds would collect to giggle and
stare and follow her, peering and whispering. But she went so
often that they became used to her, and to the fact that she spoke

their language with an idiomatic fluency that they had rarely met with in others of the sahib-*log*. She came to have many friends and acquaintances in the city. Unexpected friends and strange acquaintances who would have horrified and disgusted her husband had he known of it. But Conway took little interest in his wife's doings, and he did not know or care where she went.

Alex knew, and though it had at first disturbed him that Winter should go so freely and so far afield about the countryside and the city, he had come to the conclusion that her greatest safety might one day lie in such friendships, and he had withdrawn the unobtrusive watch he had set on her.

He seldom saw her, and then only at a distance when he rode abroad, and might never have spoken to her again—or indeed to anyone else!—had it not been for an unexpected drop in temperature on a night early in the new year.

The cold had awakened Winter who slept alone in the wide bed, for Conway had moved back into his own room once more, and seldom visited her. Rain had fallen during the day, but towards sundown the sky had cleared and now the moon rode high and shone into the windows of her room. Winter sat up and reached for the quilt that normally lay folded at the foot of her bed, but it was not there and she remembered that she had taken it into the dressing-room earlier that evening.

She slipped out of bed, shivering, and pulling a light Cashmere shawl about her shoulders, crossed the room and pushed open the door of the dressing-room. She had left the quilt on the couch by the bathroom door, and her hand was upon it when she became aware that somewhere quite close to her a voice was speaking in a whisper.

The sibilant sound held something of the faint, hollow clarity of an echo and seemed to come from the bathroom, the door into which had been left open. Winter stood clutching the quilt, shivering and a little frightened, until quite suddenly she realized that the voice was speaking in Urdu, and that the ghostly echoing quality was accounted for by the wide stone sluice pipe that carried off the bath water, for she had heard that sound once before and been startled by it.

Someone was squatting on the far side of the blank bathroom wall, safely out of sight and hearing of anyone within the house, but unaware of the fact that the exit of the sluice was acting as a speaking-tube, so that it seemed as though a soft, echoing voice whispered under the curved roof of the bathroom. Winter heard the bubbling sound of a hookah, and supposed that it must be Dunde Khan, the night-watchman, whiling away the long hours with a wakeful friend from the servants' quarters. She had a sudden childish impulse—the first young or gay impulse she had experienced in three months—to creep into the bathroom and wail down the sluice pipe. The windowless wall would be in black shadow, and such a sound, coming out of nothingness, would startle old Dunde Khan considerably. She dismissed it reluctantly, visualizing the household aroused by a piercing yell of panic, and was turning away when the soft, disembodied voice whispered again in the silence:

'He will be riding Chytuc or Shalini, for the Eagle has cast a shoe. And either will show up far against the crops——'

Winter stood still, her attention suddenly arrested. Those were Captain Randall's horses. Was it Alex Randall whom the men in the darkness by the blind wall were speaking of? She waited, listening intently, and then a second voice spoke, less distinct this time, but still audible:

'But what of Niaz Mohamed? It is seldom that Randall Sahib rides without him, and——'

'That has been arranged. By now I think he will be suffering from a little sickness. Only a little—it would be unwise to arouse suspicions—but enough to keep him to his bed tomorrow. And the syce has a poisoned hand. I think the sahib will ride alone.'

Yet another voice spoke, but this time the speaker must have been farther away, for Winter could not catch the whispered words. She found that she was shivering again, but not with cold, and she crept forward into the darkness, feeling for each step, with a hand outstretched before her. The window shutters were closed and there was no gleam of light in the dead blackness of the bathroom. The matting whispered under her bare feet, and then her foot touched the raised rim that surrounded the space where the bath stood and from where the sluice led out. She crouched down so that her head was nearer the level of the pipe, and started as a voice appeared to speak almost in her ear:

'And what if he does not ride by way of Chunwar?'

'He will. There is a report that the canal bank has been breached by Mohamed Afzal for his fields, and sitting by the office door I heard him tell the Commissioner Sahib that he would go on the morrow, when he rides at dawn, to see if the report be true. And as all know, to ride to Chunwar he must cross the nullah near the *dhâk* trees. There is no other way for a horseman. It will be thought an accident.'

'But—but if I should fail——' the voice had a shiver in it, either from cold or fear.

'Thou wilt not fail. A child could not! And there will be Mehan Lall also. And afterwards there will be witnesses to tell that the sahib's horse took fright, which all will believe, for did not he fall from his horse not three months agone, and lie sick with a cracked head? When a man has been dragged by a foot that is caught in the stirrup of a bolting horse it is difficult to tell which injury caused his death. I have seen one such in my time!'

Another voice growled: 'Why not a gun or a knife, and be done! There are two score times a day when a man might bring him down with either!'

'And be caught! No. Besides, we want no open killing. If he be killed openly it might be that word would go out that Lunjore is a place of trouble, and then, who knows, an *Angrezi* regiment might be sent here, and that we do not want. He must not be killed unless it be made to look an accident. That is the order that has been given.'

There was a pause in which the hookah bubbled again, and a faint scent of tobacco smoke drifted into the cold blackness of the bathroom. Winter heard a man clear his throat and spit, and then the voice with the shiver in it said: 'Why is this necessary? It is but one sahib, and there are many.'

'There be many fools to one wise man,' grunted the first speaker. 'Up by Peshawar way they say that there are many sahibs—but only one Nikel Seyn! It is the same everywhere and with all men. If those who see where others are blind be removed from the path, the matter is thereby made easier.'

'But—but this is a good man——' another voice, farther away and almost inaudible. 'He knows our ways, and though at times he is hot and very angry, he is just. He righted the matter of the crop tax, and Balu Ram has said——'

'*Fool!*'—the epithet echoed hollowly in the cold room—'it is not those who spit upon us and treat us as dogs and slaves who are of danger to us, for they do but light a fire for their own burning. It is men such as Randall Sahib, who speak our tongues as one of us, and who have many friends amongst us and are seen to do justice to all men, who are a stumbling-block in the path; for many of our people will listen to their words and many more follow them to the death, taking up arms even against those of their own blood. It is these who must first be slain!'

There was a murmur of agreement and again the purr and bubble of the hookah. Winter's teeth began to chatter with cold, but she clenched them tight and continued to crouch in the darkness, straining her ears to listen. But something had evidently startled the group outside, for she heard sounds of hurried movements and an unintelligible mutter, and after that for a long time there was silence, and she did not know whether the men had gone or were still crouching against the wall. Then there was a sound of footsteps, an asthmatic cough and the rattling of a chain from beyond the shuttered window at her back, and she realized that it was old Dunde Khan the night-watchman, making his rounds, whom the men by the wall must have heard approaching.

She waited for perhaps a quarter of an hour longer, huddled in her shawl and numb with cold, but she heard no more voices, though the night was so silent that she could hear the sound of her own breathing and the rustle of a mouse which scuttled across the matting in the darkness behind her. At last she stood up stiffly and crept back to bed, closing the dressing-room door softly behind her. She had forgotten about the quilt and she did not go to sleep, but dragged the blankets up about her and sat with her chin on her knees, shivering and thinking and waiting for the dawn.

Chunwar . . . That was a village to the south of the city. She had ridden out that way before, though she did not often ride in that direction, for the first mile or so was crop-land threaded by water-courses, and to walk a fresh and restless horse along the narrow paths between the crops or along the crumbling edge of irrigation channels was tedious. Beyond that there lay several miles of open dusty plain dotted with *kikar* and *dhâk* trees; rough, stony ground, full of unexpected potholes and dry nullahs.

The nullah that the man had spoken of cut diagonally across the plain a mile or so short of the village, which lay behind a thick belt of trees. It was more a wide, steep-sided ravine, and riding to Chunwar from the direction of the cantonments there was only one practicable place where it might be crossed; where the narrow, rutted cart-track ran. The ravine was full of trees and scrub and high grass, and someone—or perhaps several men—would be waiting there for Captain Randall to pass. It would be easy enough to unhorse a man in such a place, for they would see him coming from a long way off across the plain, and be ready. A rope or a wire laid across the steep path and suddenly jerked taut. A man dropping from an overhanging bough on to the shoulders of a horseman passing beneath. There would be a dozen ways. And when they had dragged him off and stunned him, his foot would be jammed into the stirrup and his horse lashed forward to drag him at a gallop across the sharp stony plain.

Winter had a sudden vision of Alex Randall's brown, clean-cut face torn and battered into a shapeless mass of blood and dirt, and she shuddered as she stared into the darkness. The hours

crawled past and the moonlight left the window and then the
verandah beyond, and the room was dark and very cold. The
cold began to make her drowsy, but she dared not sleep for fear
that she should awake too late and not be in time to stop Alex
from riding to his death.

At long last a hint of grey crept into the blackness, and a cock
crowed from somewhere behind the servants' quarters at the far
side of the compound. Winter lit a candle and began to dress
herself hurriedly; her fingers clumsy from cold and weariness and
a sudden fear that perhaps after all she might be too late. The
thought terrified her and she ran through the quiet house and
shook awake the sheeted, corpse-like figure of one of the house
servants who slept in the hall at night, and told him to tell her
syce that she wished her horse brought round immediately.

Fifteen minutes later she was cantering down the long drive
in the grey, aqueous light of the early morning. She had never
been to Captain Randall's bungalow, though she had passed it
almost daily. There was a light burning in one of the rooms and
a syce was walking a restive horse up and down in front of the
verandah. So he had not yet left! Winter restrained her mount
with difficulty, for Furiante was feeling fresh and above himself
and did not relish being kept to a gentle canter; but Winter had
no intention of going too far ahead. She reined him in and made
him walk sedately down a narrow lane under a feathery canopy
of tamarisk boughs while she listened for the sound of Chytuc's
hooves behind her.

She did not know the identity of the men who had whispered
against the wall last night, and she had heard only one name—
an unfamiliar one. But the men would not have been there if
some of them at least had not been connected with the Residency.
One, or all of them, must be in the Commissioner's employ.
Winter could not believe that her syce Yusaf had been one of
them, but she had been too frightened by what she had heard to
take any chances, and she would have left him behind except
that she had never ridden out without him before, and to do so
now might cause comment. She must avoid any appearance of

deliberately turning Alex back from Chunwar, and make it look as though she had met him by chance.

The lane came out upon an open stretch of ground beyond which lay a mango tope and a deep belt of crop-lands. To the right lay the city and the river, while half a mile to the left lay the *maidan* and the rifle-range. Winter drew rein a little beyond the mouth of the lane, as though undecided which way to turn. She heard Yusaf's horse, Shiraz, fidgeting behind her, and then the sound that she had been waiting for, and turned; swinging Furiante so that Alex had no choice but to stop. He pulled up, and Winter saw that he was alone. So they had been right in that at least!

She said on a note of surprise, and for the benefit of Yusaf: 'Captain Randall! How fortunate that I should have met you. I have been wishing to see you. May I ride with you?'

It was the first time that she had met or spoken to him since the night of his arrival in Lunjore almost three months previously, but if Alex was in any way surprised at being thus accosted he gave no sign of it. He bowed slightly and said in his most expressionless voice: 'Certainly, Mrs. Barton, if you wish. But I am riding to Chunwar this morning and I am afraid that you would not find it very amusing. The going is rather rough.'

'Then perhaps you will ride with me to the *maidan* instead,' said Winter, turning her horse's head. 'You can ride to Chunwar some other morning.'

'I am sorry to sound disobliging,' began Alex, 'but——'

Winter looked over her shoulder at him with raised brows, letting the reins lie loose, and under cover of her long habit used her spur on Furiante. Furiante needed no second invitation. He had been sidling and snorting and seething with impatience for the past quarter of an hour, and he responded to the spur with all the outraged velocity of an exploding rocket.

Winter screamed once for Captain Randall's benefit, and thereafter concentrated on remaining in the saddle without making the smallest attempt to arrest Furiante's headlong flight. She was not, if the truth be known, in the least sure that she could do so if she wished, for Furiante had the bit between his teeth and was galloping as though he were pursued by seven devils.

Mercifully the ground was level, and once they were through the trees the vast stretch of the *maidan* lay ahead. The path through the trees was a narrow one and branches whipped at Winter's skirt; her hat fell off and her hair streamed out behind her like a black silk flag, and then they were racing across the open *maidan*. She could hear Chytuc's hooves behind her and Alex's voice shouting 'Left!—pull left!' and remembered then the wide ditch that bounded the far side of the ground. She pulled on the near-side rein with all her strength, but she could not turn the maddened horse. And then Alex was gaining on her and she saw Chytuc's black head and laid-back ears draw level with her, and Alex had caught her bridle and turned Furiante— still galloping at full stretch but tiring at last—away from the ditch and towards the open country. Two minutes later he had brought them to a stop.

Winter bowed over Furiante's neck in sudden weakness and felt Alex's hard fingers grip her shoulder and heard him say: 'Are you all right?'

She lifted her head and looked at him—and saw the sudden comprehension in his face as he met that look. His hand dropped and he said incredulously: 'Did you do that on purpose?'

Winter straightened up and drew a deep breath to steady herself: 'I—I had to. I'm sorry. But I had to talk to you. I had to! Tell Yusaf to keep behind.'

Alex looked at her for a long moment. His eyes were black with anger and his mouth had closed in a hard unpleasant line. He threw a curt word of command over his shoulder and touched Chytuc with his heel, and the two horses moved forward at a sober pace, Yusaf falling back out of earshot and following at a discreet distance.

Alex said abruptly: 'You had better do something about your hair. Give me the reins.'

He leant across and took them from her, and watched her as she attempted to gather up and re-roll the shining mass into some semblance of order. The anger went out of his face and he smiled a little crookedly:

'You might almost be one of the Spartans "combing their long hair for death" in the passes of Thermopylae. Don't look so tragic! What is it?'

Winter said: 'I—I am sorry about—about that, but I had to stop you from going to Chunwar.' Her voice was all at once small and unsteady and she glanced at him and saw that his brows had drawn together and his eyes held a look that was hard to read. She said abruptly: 'Why did you ride alone today? Doesn't your orderly usually ride with you?'

'He is ill,' said Alex briefly. 'Why do you ask?'

Winter drew a little gasping breath. 'Because—because that means it is true. I didn't imagine it all.'

Alex looked at her, frowning. 'What is true? What is all this?'

'They were going to kill you,' said Winter. 'In the ravine on the road to Chunwar. I heard them talking last night, and I had to stop you. But—but I did not want them to know that I knew, so when you would not come with me I had to do something to make you. That is why I made Furiante bolt, and pretended that I was being run away with, so that you——'

Alex said: 'Wait a minute. Do you mind saying that all over again, and slowly? I must be singularly slow-witted this morning.'

Quite suddenly there was a hint of a laugh in his voice, and Winter stiffened and the colour rushed up into her face. 'You don't believe me! You think that I am—— But it is true! They said that Niaz Mohamed would be given something to make him ill, and that your syce had a poisoned hand and so you would be riding alone, and——' She checked and said: 'I—I am sorry. I do not seem to be telling it very well.'

'Begin at the beginning,' advised Alex. 'Who are "they"?'

'I don't know. I only heard voices——' She told him the story of those voices that had whispered in the shadow of the blank wall where the bathroom sluice ran out, and of how it was that she had come to hear them, and Alex listened without interruption. When she had finished he was silent for a moment or two, and then he asked if she had recognized any of the voices. Winter shook her head. 'No. They were speaking very quietly, and the echo made it sound strange.'

'No names?'

'Only one. A man named Mehan Lall would be in the ravine to—to help. There is no one of that name among the servants.'

'But there is among my acquaintances,' said Alex grimly.

He snapped his fingers at the level of his shoulder without turning his head. It was a brief and almost inaudible gesture, but Yusaf, twenty yards behind, saw it and spurred forward. 'Huzoor?'

'Hast thou a gun?'

Yusaf thrust a hand into the bosom of his coat and produced a small five-chambered Colt pistol; a surprising item of equipment for a syce. Alex held out his hand for it and slid it into his own pocket, and said: 'I may have need of two. Take the memsahib home by way of the cantonments, and keep a still tongue in thy head.'

He noticed Winter's startled face and smiled: a smile that did not quite reach his eyes. 'It's all right. Yusaf is one of my own men. I did not think that you should ride so far afield without a trustworthy escort. The times are not as settled as some people suppose.'

He made as though to turn Chytuc, and Winter snatched at his rein.

'No! Alex, no!' Her voice was sharp with panic.

Alex looked down at her white frightened face and the harsh lines of his own face softened. He dropped his hand over hers for a brief moment and gripped it hard and reassuringly.

'I shall be all right. I promise you. Forewarned is forearmed, you know.'

But Winter's fingers still clung to the bridle. 'What are you going to do?' she demanded breathlessly.

Alex grinned unexpectedly. 'To tell the truth, I am not sure.

But I do not like being gunned for, and I intend to discourage it. There is a deal of difference between falling into an ambush and walking into one with your eyes open.'

Winter said: 'I'm coming with you—and Yusaf can come too, and——'

Alex shook his head. 'Oh, no, you're not. That would spoil everything. They are expecting me to come alone, and if they see anyone with me they will abandon the idea and wait for another opportunity. And I might not be warned next time.'

'Alex——'

Alex wrenched her hand from the bridle and said suddenly and savagely: 'For God's sake don't look at me like that!' He saw her flinch as though he had struck her, and said with harsh impatience: 'I'm sorry. I am very grateful to you for warning me. Now get on—go on back to the house.'

He wheeled Chytuc, and was gone, galloping back across the open ground towards the distant belt of trees, and Winter turned her horse's head and sat watching him grow smaller and smaller across the colourless plain until at last the trees swallowed him up.

The sky that had been pearl grey when she had ridden out under the arch of the Residency gate was growing bright now with the sunrise, and only the morning star still shimmered faintly in the wash of saffron light that flooded upwards from the east. It was less than an hour since she had left the Residency, but it seemed as though hours had passed—or years. As though she were not even the same person who had ridden out under that gate.

Why had she not known before that she loved Alex Randall? Why was it only now, when he was riding away from her to what might be his death, that she should realize how much he meant to her? She had loved him for so long, and been too obsessed with her childish, foolish, pasteboard and tinsel image of Conway to recognize it. When he had kissed her at Delhi she had been shamed and startled by her own instinctive response, because it had seemed a betrayal of Conway and she had hated herself for it. And hated Alex who had trapped her into it. It was only now, facing the possibility of his death, that all the mixed and unmanageable emotions had suddenly sorted themselves out and left only the one fact—that she loved Alex. But whether he lived or died, it was too late, because she had married Conway Barton.

Yusaf cleared his throat in a gently deprecatory hint that his orders had been to see that she returned to the Residency, and Winter straightened her slim shoulders and lifted her small chin in the familiar gesture of her childhood when she had braced herself to meet reproof or hurt or humiliation and to endure it in silence, and turning Furiante she rode back through the brightening dawn to her husband's house.

But she did not enter it. She dismounted within the gate, and dismissing Yusaf and the horses, went across to the great banyan tree to sit silent among the roots and watch Akbar Khan's little granddaughter share her morning meal with the birds. The sight of the small, still figure with its slow unhurried movements, surrounded by a host of friendly birds and squirrels, was always a soothing one to Winter, and the creatures had become sufficiently used to her frequent presence to pay little attention to her. But today they appeared wilder than usual, and would barely come to Zeb-un-Nissa's soft, wordless call.

'It is because they know that thou art afraid,' said Zeb-un-Nissa. She turned her enormous, unfocused eyes on Winter and smiled her sweet vague smile: 'There is no need to fear. He will come to no harm.'

The words were spoken with entire conviction, and though she could only have been referring to a bird or a squirrel, Winter was suddenly and strangely reassured. The terror and the tension ebbed away from her, and a bold blue-jay, its plumage glinting like a handful of jewels in the morning sunlight, swooped down to take a fragment of bread from Nissa's small palm.

V

MOONRISE

21

THE sun was still below the horizon when Alex left the green crop-lands behind him, and gave Chytuc his head across the wide stretch of the open plain where his hooves clicked against the bleached bones of cattle and his black body as yet cast no shadow.

A rough cart-track idled across the plain towards the ravine and Chunwar, but the heavy dew and the rain of the previous day had laid the dust, and the prints of Chytuc's hooves lay clear on a surface that showed that no cart and only two men on foot had passed within the last few hours.

Alex noted the fact, but without optimism. There was no reason to suppose that reinforcements had not entered the ravine from the opposite side, and he could only hope that there were not more than three, or at the most four, men lying in wait for him. Experience had taught him that out of four there is generally one who will run away, and out of three one who gets in the way of his allies. The conversation that Winter had repeated to him made it seem likely that there would be only two men, but it was not safe to count on that.

Mehan Lall . . . Yes, he remembered Mehan Lall, and he had a fairly clear idea as to why the man had been selected to carry out this particular form of assassination. Mehan Lall possessed an unusual accomplishment, and Alex had once seen him use it to bring down a galloping leopard that had broken cover during a partridge shoot. The creature had bounded across an open stretch of ground, and Mehan Lall had swung and released a weighted silken rope with unbelievable swiftness and accuracy. The rope, swung by its weights, had whipped about the leopard's fore-paws and brought it to a rolling, snarling stop. It was said of Mehan Lall that he could bring down anything from a galloping horse to a long-legged heron with his weighted rope, and Alex did not doubt it.

He slowed Chytuc to a canter as the clump of *dhâk* trees loomed larger and the tops of the scrub and trees and cane that choked the ravine showed as a dark line above the level of the plain. As he neared it he reined in to a walk: there was no necessity to risk Chytuc breaking a leg, though he doubted if anything would be tried in the way of tripping the horse. That Chytuc should be capable of dragging his dead body for a reasonable distance appeared to be an essential part of the scheme.

Alex had ridden through the ravine comparatively frequently, and he tried now to visualize it and put himself in the place of two men who wished to ambush a third and kill him, preferably by a blow on the head. There was a tree that grew on the bed of the ravine and spread its branches above the track. A man lying along one of those branches might strike down at the head of a horseman riding beneath. But would the leaves be thick enough to hide such a man? He could not remember, but of one thing he was sure; on the downward slope it would be easier to see into the branches, for they would for a moment be on a level with the eye. Therefore there would be nobody in that tree. It would be as he breasted the slope on the opposite side.

Alex drew out the slim skinning-knife that he carried under the saddle flap. It was an item of equipment that was useful on long rides in rough country, and had in its day been put to a multitude of uses. Niaz kept the blade sharpened to a razor-like edge and Alex ran his thumb lightly along it and grinned appreciatively to see the blood start at its touch. He held the knife with the blade uppermost against his sleeve and touched Chytuc with his heel, and they passed by the *dhâk* trees and down over the rim of the ravine.

Chytuc's hooves slipped a little on the slope and Alex spoke softly. He was riding loosely, sitting relaxed in the saddle, and there was nothing about him to betray the fact that every nerve and faculty was tense and alert. He heard the faint rustle to one

side of the track, and the whistle of the weighted rope; and because he had been waiting for it he pulled back on the rein and
brought up his left hand in the same movement.

The rope whipped about him like a live thing with a life of
its own, but instead of pinning his arms to his sides, his arm was
raised to meet it. The knife blade shored upwards and Chytuc,
reined in savagely on the slope, had backed instead of plunging
forward.

Almost simultaneously a man rose from the high grass by the
track and clawed at Alex's boot, but Alex had dropped the reins
after that one savage jerk and there was a pistol in his right hand.
The explosion and the howl of pain sent Chytuc rearing wildly
on the narrow track, and the slashing blow of an iron-tipped
lathi from the opposite side missed its mark and caught the
horse's flank, raising a vicious weal. Alex dropped the knife and
fired again, as with a squeal of rage Chytuc reared up with flaying
hooves. The next moment horse and rider had burst out of the
ravine and on to the level plain with the speed and violence of a
thunderbolt.

Alex made no attempt to check the infuriated horse but let him
have his head until his pain and panic had subsided. They rode
into Chunwar by way of the canal bank, and Alex noted that the
report that it had been illegally breached was correct, but that
it was another cultivator, and not Mohamed Afzal, whose fields
had reaped the benefit. He called upon the Kotwal—the village
headman—and having dealt with the matter of the breached
canal, rode back to the ravine accompanied by the Kotwal and
some of the more responsible villagers.

A man who gave his name as Sobha Chand was discovered
hiding in the thickets a quarter of a mile above the track. It had
not been difficult to trace him, for he had a bullet through the
shoulder and was suffering from severe loss of blood. He appeared to imagine that he was either dead or dying. Mehan Lall
had not gone so far. A smashed knee is a painful thing, and he
crouched in the tall grass by the path and groaned. There had
been a third man, but he had fled.

Alex had seen the two wounded men loaded into a bullock-cart, their wounds roughly bandaged, and had ridden slowly back to the cantonments in the wake of the cart, where having handed the groaning pair of would-be assassins over to the care of the police, he had returned to his bungalow for breakfast. He hoped that the morning's work might act as a deterrent to others interested in his removal, for the average native of the country, though for the most part careless of death, possessed a disproportionate fear of being painfully wounded.

Having breakfasted he walked over to the Commissioner's office and paid particular attention, without appearing to do so, to the demeanour of every servant whom he met. No face expressed any surprise at his appearance, but he noted with interest that although Durga Charan, the head *chuprassi*, could control both his face and his bland, unwinking eyes, he could not prevent his hands from quivering. Alex dropped his gaze to those unsteady hands and allowed it to linger on them thoughtfully.

'Durga Charan,' said Alex softly, 'I think that I have heard some talk of *taklif* (trouble) in thy village. It may be that thou shouldst take leave and see that all is well with thy house—while thy health permits.' He had passed on, and the man had said nothing, but an hour later he had asked the Commissioner for leave to go to his home.

Winter had heard Alex's footsteps and his quiet voice, and she had gone to her bedroom and locked the door behind her and wept for the first time since her wedding night: weeping for relief and thankfulness as she never wept for the loss of her illusions.

It had been a Tuesday, and that evening the 'Tuesday crowd' were to dine as usual at the Residency. Winter had been too tired and too worn out by the anxieties of the previous night and the varied emotions of the day to be able to stand up to a scene with Conway, and she had agreed to dine with them on the understanding that she could retire immediately afterwards. Provided she sat at his table, said Conway, he had not the smallest objection to her feigning a headache and retiring at the conclusion of the meal. In fact he would appreciate it, by God he would! She cast a damned damper on such parties, and they would do very well without her!

He looked at her with scowling irritation, wondering how he could ever have imagined, even for so short a time, that she had grown into a beauty? He had not paid much attention to her of late, and it suddenly struck him that she had lost a lot of weight and was looking remarkably sallow. A pity. He disliked skinny women. And her eyes were too big. He had thought them amazingly fine when she had first arrived in Lunjore. The most speaking eyes he had ever seen in a woman's head. Lashes like —like black butterflies, dammit! mused the Commissioner, surprised at himself for such an unusually poetical flight of fancy. But now there was a blankness about them and they seemed to look round him or through him, but never at him, and there were blue shadows beneath them like bruises.

He said a little uneasily: 'You are not looking at all the thing, my dear. Are you not feeling well? Lunjore is not held to be a good station for women. The climate is not all it could be. Perhaps it might be a good thing if you were to go away on a short visit, to set you up before the hot weather. The Abuthnots would I feel sure be pleased to see you. Or we might consider a visit to Lucknow. You will like to see your father's house—our house. What do you say to that?'

He saw the bright, transient colour flood up into his wife's pale face and her eyes lose their blankness and become brilliant again, and thought with baffled amazement: 'Why, dammit, she *is* a beauty——!'

Winter said with a tremor in her voice: 'Could I really go to Lucknow? I have wanted to so much! Could I really?'

The Commissioner was gratified by her response to his careless suggestion. He patted her shoulder with condescending affection and said well, well, they would see about it. It might not be a bad idea at all. The Casa de Ballesteros—he believed that it had once been called something fanciful to do with peacocks—was really a very fine house. He had stayed there once or twice when inspecting the property on behalf of her guardian.

Pleased with that momentary flicker of beauty and his own magnanimity, he had put an arm about her waist, and pulling her against him had planted a wetly alcoholic kiss upon her cheek. It had been intended for her lips, but Winter had turned her head away, though she had done nothing else to avoid his embrace but had stood quite still, enduring it with her eyes closed; wishing with a sudden passionate intensity that it was Alex who held her. She heard footsteps in the hall and Imam Bux's murmured 'Huzoor', and realizing that in the next moment a visitor would be ushered into the drawing-room, attempted to free herself: 'Conway—please. Someone is coming in——'

'Let 'em!' mumbled Conway thickly. He had started his drinking early so as to be in good spirits for the arrival of his guests, and had found, as always, that the feel of a woman's body in his arms—even that of so slim and unyielding a one as his wife's—was remarkably pleasant.

Winter's arms had been hanging stiffly at her sides, but now she put up her hands and caught at his coat sleeves in an endeavour to thrust him away, so that for a moment it appeared as though she were returning her husband's embrace. She heard the door open and found herself looking into Alex Randall's expressionless face.

It was a sudden and nightmare repetition of the day at Delhi when he had walked in and found her in Carlyon's arms. A nightmare with a cruel twist to it, because then she had been so afraid that it would be Conway who would find her in that degrading position; but it had been Alex. And now it was Conway who held her, and again it was Alex. But it was Alex whom she loved.

Conway released her and turned. 'Hullo, Alex, m'boy. Walked right in on the turtle doves, dammit! Have a drink. Make yerself at home. Nothin' urgent, is it? because I ain't got the time to look at it now. Here's Mrs. Barton already dressed, and I still to have a bath and change.'

He shouted for drinks to be brought, took one himself and moved to the door. 'Don't go. M' wife'll look after yer. Why

don't yer stay t' dinner? Good party on tonight. Capital crowd!
We shall all be as jolly as grigs. Time you got yourself out of a
rut. Shall expect you.'

'I am afraid, sir——' began Alex, and stopped. He looked at
Winter's small rigid face, and after a perceptible pause said quite
deliberately and as though he had intended to finish the sentence
that way—'that I have been neglecting my social duties of late.
I should be glad to.'

'Good! good!' approved the Commissioner heartily. 'Look
after him, m'dear.'

He removed himself, and Winter said stiffly: 'I am sorry that
Mr. Barton should be unable to give you his attention, but we
are expecting guests within the hour. I hope that your business
with him will keep?'

Alex strolled across the room and came to a stop before her.
He was feeling angrier than he had ever felt in his life. An
entirely illogical anger, for surely he should be glad that she was
not after all as unhappy in her marriage as he had supposed?
Because of that anger his slight suggestion of a drawl was suddenly more marked.

He put his glass down on the chimney-piece and said: 'I did
not come here to see Mr. Barton. I came to pay my debts.'

'Your debts?'

'Let us say, my thanks. I am afraid that I cannot have
appeared particularly grateful to you this morning. But I am.
I think I owe you my life, and the least I can do is to thank you
properly for the gift.' He looked down at her and smiled, not
entirely pleasantly, and added: 'I believe that I had intended to
say something to the effect that it is now of course wholly at your
disposal, but such statements are apt to sound better in a theatre,
do you not think? So I will confine myself to saying "thank you".
I am indeed grateful.'

He reached out, and before she had realized what he meant to
do he had taken her hand and bent above it formally, lifting it so
that it barely touched his tight mouth.

Winter snatched it away and took a quick step backwards:

L

afraid of his proximity and what it did to her, and bewildered by the derisive note in his voice. She said a little breathlessly: 'You have nothing to thank me for, Captain Randall. I did nothing that anyone else would not have done in the same circumstances.'

Making a determined effort to steady her voice and appear calm and composed, she moved to a chair and sat down, her wide skirts spreading crisply about her, and said: 'You have not told me what occurred this morning. Was there no one in the ravine, then?'

'No, they were there,' said Alex. He gave her an edited and colourless version of the happenings in the ravine, and passed on to other topics, mentioning that he had recently received a letter from Mrs. Abuthnot, and enquiring if Winter had had any news of Lottie.

Winter had, in fact, received a long and rapturous letter from Lottie by the last dâk, but as it had been largely concerned with the many perfections of Edward and the sweetly pretty furnishings that Lottie had contrived for her drawing-room, there was little in it that could be expected to interest Captain Randall; while its only really important item of news—that Lottie had begun to cherish hopes of a child who would be born in mid-summer—could not be imparted, for such things were unmentionable before gentlemen.

Captain Randall, however, did not stay long. He finished his drink and excused himself, saying that if he were to dine at the Residency that night he would have to change into more formal wear.

Winter rose with a rustle of yellow *gros de chine*. She had not looked directly at him during the past ten minutes or so, but she looked at him now. 'Why did you change your mind about dining here tonight, when you had meant to refuse?' she demanded abruptly. 'I know that you do not like parties, and if you only wished for an opportunity to thank me, you have done that, and need not dine here if you do not wish to. I will make your excuses to Mr. Barton.'

'What makes you think I do not wish to?'

'Well—you have never accepted any previous invitation to dine.'

Alex lifted one faintly ironic eyebrow. 'Have I not? You must put it down to pressure of work. I daresay I offered some such excuse. But you are quite wrong. I like parties. It is only their after-effects that I have sometimes found tiresome. And I seem to have attended several this season.'

'But none in this house.'

'That was churlish of me,' said Alex gravely. 'But it will be remedied tonight.' He bowed and went away, leaving her question unanswered.

He had returned some thirty minutes later, and Winter had had the doubtful felicity of observing that he appeared entirely at his ease among the inner circle of the Commissioner's friends. Mrs. Cottar addressed him familiarly by his Christian name and devoted a large part of her attention to him, and her conversation had seemed to afford him considerable amusement. He had also made himself unusually pleasant to Delia Gardener-Smith, while at the same time blandly refusing to be drawn into any argument with Colonel Moulson, who continued to regard him with a hostile eye.

At the conclusion of the meal the guests had repaired to the drawing-room, where the furniture had been moved to allow space for a long table covered with a baize cloth on which cards and dice were laid out. There were usually several Indian guests on these occasions: rich landowners and noblemen, or their sons, who gambled heavily and were on that account on easy terms with the Commissioner and his more raffish friends. Those who were Hindus, and whose caste raised difficulties in the matter of eating, would arrive after dinner, and tonight they were joined by Kishan Prasad, whom Winter had not seen since the day of her arrival at Calcutta.

She had been about to excuse herself on the plea of a headache, but two things had made her change her mind—the arrival of Kishan Prasad and something that had been in Alex's face when he had seen him. Alex had been standing at the far end of the room among a noisy group which had gathered about Mrs.

Cottar, and Winter had been covertly watching him. She had seen his gaze rest briefly upon Kishan Prasad, and had been suddenly sure that he had known Kishan Prasad would be present that evening, and it was for that reason that he had accepted her husband's invitation to dine. Perhaps he had even arrived at that particular moment in the hope of obtaining such an invitation, and for reasons of his own had made it appear as though he had at first intended to refuse? His expression had not altered noticeably at the sight of Kishan Prasad, but it seemed to Winter as though there was a glint of satisfaction in his eyes, as though he had bet on the turn of a card and won. Then he had turned his back and engaged Mrs. Cottar in conversation as Winter moved forward to greet the new arrival.

Kishan Prasad bowed formally in the Indian fashion and expressed his pleasure at meeting her again. She had never been able to rid herself of a slight feeling of revulsion towards him ever since the day that she had surprised that look of gloating hate upon his face as he had watched a waterlogged wreck sinking in the wild dusk. But he was of a very different kidney to those of his fellow-countrymen who frequented the Commissioner's less reputable parties, and she could not imagine him tipsy, obsequious or insolent, or permitting himself to be cheated at cards—treatment that she uneasily suspected was not unknown when the Tuesday parties had lasted well into Wednesday morning.

Card play had not yet begun, and Kishan Prasad, having greeted Colonel Moulson and one or two other acquaintances, drew up a chair beside the sofa on which Winter had seated herself, and addressed her in his own tongue. She was well aware of his proficiency in English, and appreciated the compliment. Kishan Prasad did not talk the trivialities of the station. His conversation was dryly entertaining and rich with the imagery of the East, and Winter found herself conversing with him with more interest and ease than she had as yet experienced since her arrival in Lunjore, and could only be sorry when they were joined by Colonel Moulson and Delia Gardener-Smith and he reverted to English.

He enquired politely where Mrs. Barton intended to spend the summer months, and on hearing that she would not be removing to the hills, advised her earnestly to do so. She would, he assured her, find Lunjore unpleasantly hot from mid-April until the monsoon broke, as it had a bad reputation in the matter of high temperatures during May and June. He himself had visited Simla on more than one occasion, and he dilated upon its charms. She must persuade the Commissioner to permit her to sample the delights of the cool airs and the pines.

Delia had been pleased to be arch. She had informed Kishan Prasad that no loving wife would ever voluntarily allow herself to be separated from her husband, and that were *she* married she knew that for her part she could never bear to leave her husband's side even for a week. No mountain airs could compensate for such deprivation! She had allowed her gaze to rest innocently upon Colonel Moulson, who had twirled his moustache and expressed approval of such womanly sentiments.

Kishan Prasad remarked dryly that Miss Gardener-Smith had yet to experience a hot weather in the plains, and turned the conversation to the forthcoming duck shoot at Hazrat Bagh, a jheel which lay some fifteen miles to the west of the cantonments. Hazrat Bagh—the 'Grove of a Thousand Trees'—had once been the site of a hunting park of some forgotten king, but nothing remained of it but the lonely stretches of water and the intersecting bunds on which the 'thousand trees'—*kikar* and an occasional peepul tree—stood among high grass and reeds and provided excellent cover for sportsmen. There were no villages near the jheel, and the waterfowl came there in their thousands.

The shoot was being arranged by some of the local talukdars, and food and beaters on an elaborate scale were being provided for the guests, who were to include most of the British officers stationed in Lunjore. Those ladies who had been invited to attend as spectators would watch the *battue* from the tree-lined bunds or from an artificial 'hide' to one side of the jheel, and several hundred sepoys were to be lent for the occasion to keep the birds from settling on outlying jheels and inaccessible stretches of water. A road was in process of construction so that the ladies would be able to drive there in their carriages, for the jheel lay far from any made road and was at present difficult to reach even on horseback, owing to the roughness of the going.

'I hope that we are to have the pleasure of seeing you there, Mrs. Barton?' said Kishan Prasad. 'I am to be one of the hosts, you know.'

'No, I did not know,' confessed Winter. 'But I shall certainly be there. I have never been out on a big shoot yet.'

'You must let me arrange a tiger shoot later on,' said Kishan Prasad. 'One may shoot duck in Europe, but a tiger shoot is something that you will see only in the East.'

'For my part, I could not endure to attend such a thing!' declared Delia with a shudder. 'I am sure I cannot conceive how *any* lady could do so!'

'Why?' enquired Kishan Prasad. 'Would it distress you to see so beautiful a creature shot? But tigers are vermin, you know. They prey upon the herds of the villagers, and in their old age they often take to killing men, while the duck you will see shot do no harm.'

'Oh, but I did not mean that!' said Delia opening her eyes at him. 'I meant the danger, of course. There can be no danger in a duck shoot, but a tiger shoot cannot help but be dangerous.'

'That is why it is exciting,' said Kishan Prasad with a smile. 'No sport is worthy of the name that does not include an element of risk.'

'Is that a creed, or merely an opinion?' enquired a pleasant voice behind them. 'Good evening, Rao Sahib. When did you arrive in Lunjore?'

They had none of them observed Alex approach, and Winter saw Kishan Prasad's slight involuntary start at the sound of that voice, but he turned a bland countenance and his voice was as pleasant as Alex's own:

'A creed, of course, Captain Randall. I seldom advance opinions. I arrived at midday.'

'In good time for the obsequies, in fact,' said Alex with a grin. 'I am sorry to have had to disappoint you.'

'Yes?' Kishan Prasad's slim brows rose and he looked puzzled though polite, as though he imagined Alex to have attempted some Western joke, the point of which had escaped him.

Winter looked sharply from one face to the other, for Alex's apparently pointless remark was entirely clear to her, though she could not conceive why he had made it. To suggest that Kishan Prasad could have had any hand in an attempt upon his life was absurd, for the man owed his own life to him and was not likely to forget it. Yet she did not think that Alex was in the habit of making pointless remarks.

Had Kishan Prasad known that there was to have been an attempt to kill Alex? No, of course that was impossible! . . . Or was it? She could not be sure, and because she was not, she was all at once afraid.

Alex laughed, but did not explain himself. He said instead: 'I hope you mean to invite me to your tiger shoot. When is it to be?'

'I have not thought,' said Kishan Prasad gravely. 'It was not a plan, merely a suggestion.' He met Alex's gaze blandly, holding it for a long moment, and then said gently: 'Some time in the hot weather, shall we say? They are always easier to deal with in the hot months, for instead of ranging at large they are forced to keep near water, and are less active.'

'That is not a thing that I should care to count on,' said Alex, regarding him under drooping eyelids.

Kishan Prasad shrugged his shoulders: 'But of course not. Did I not say that there is always an element of risk? It is for that reason that one should take particular precautions when ladies are of the party. But there can be few ladies who would care to go on such a shoot during the hot weather, and I do not imagine that Mrs. Barton will be with us then. I feel sure that she will have removed to some hill station to escape the worst of the heat. I have just been warning the ladies that Lunjore can be a veritable furnace in the months before the monsoon breaks, but coming from Europe they have as yet little idea of how fierce our Indian hot weathers can be.'

'I shall do my best to impress it upon them,' said Alex.

'I am sure you will, Captain Randall,' said Kishan Prasad with a smile, 'though I fear your warnings are doomed to be disregarded. You will find that those ladies who have not yet experienced a hot weather will be sure that you are grossly exaggerating the discomforts, while those who have will have forgotten just how bad they can be. So you see I am really quite safe in playing traitor to the climate of my native land.'

Delia said brightly: 'Maudie Chilton, who has been four seasons in Lunjore, says that it is best not to think of such things while it is cool, as once it becomes hot there is nothing to be done about it, and when it is over one can forget all about it until the next time.'

Winter could see nothing amusing in the remark, but both Alex and Kishan Prasad laughed, and their laughs contained a disturbing and identical note of grimness. It was almost, thought Winter uneasily, as though their casual conversation had possessed two separate and distinct meanings, and that each knew exactly what the other had implied. She looked at the two men, and for a fleeting moment it seemed to her that there was a strange likeness between them. A likeness that had nothing to do with colouring or feature, but that went deeper than externals.

Kishan Prasad rose at the approach of Mrs. Cottar and presently walked away with Alex, amicably discussing the forthcoming duck shoot, and Winter decided that she was letting her imagination run away with her. But she had not, after all, left the party early that night. She had stayed for the first time; watching Alex and watching Kishan Prasad, and telling herself that there was nothing there—nothing! That Kishan Prasad had not blandly presented Alex with some obscure piece of information or warning, or Alex recognized it as such.

The Commissioner had as usual drunk too much, and had eventually abandoned cards in favour of lolling upon a sofa at the far end of the room with his arm about Mrs. Wilkinson's waist— Major Wilkinson being at present in no state to resent such a proceeding, having succumbed early to the effects of the Commissioner's port.

Winter looked at her husband's coarse, flushed face with its pale, protuberant eyes and drooping brandy-sodden moustache, and watched him fondle Chrissie Wilkinson's plump bare shoulder while he whispered something in her ear that sent her off into peals of laughter. She knew that she should not remain and lend her countenance to such proceedings, and that she need not even trouble to make any excuses for her removal, for few if any of the guests would notice that she had gone. But she did not go. She sat stiffly upright, the yellow silk flounces of her wide skirt spreading out from below her slim waist like the petals of an overblown rose, and the same small frozen smile on her face that she had worn during the nightmare hours that had followed her wedding.

She could not leave, because Alex was there and all at once it had become enough to be in the same room with him: to be able to watch his face and to hear his voice and his laugh. To realize, having visualized him dead, that he was alive and safe and real; and to feel the ache of loving him tug at her heart. Tomorrow, or the next day or the next, he might meet with another carefully planned accident, or die of cholera or typhus or black-water fever or any one of the deadly diseases that ravaged India. Life was cheap in such a country, and a face seen laughing across a luncheon-table one day might well lie slack-mouthed in death less than twenty-four hours later, and be hidden under six feet of earth before another sun had set.

Death was an all-too-familiar visitant, and as Maudie Chilton had said of the hot weather, it was better not to think of such things. But there were also other and less disastrous things that could remove Alex from her orbit just as effectually. He might be transferred to some other district, or returned to regimental duty. He might fall in love and marry some pretty creature like Sophie Abuthnot who, with infinitely more sense than Winter, had wasted no time over falling in love with him. Or someone like Delia— No, surely not Delia! He had never been more than polite to Delia. But he was being more than polite to her now. Winter watched him unobtrusively across the width of the

L*

room, and suspected him of being a little drunk. His eyes were very bright and his thick dark hair was ruffled, and he appeared to be in excellent spirits and to have no objection to entertaining Miss Gardener-Smith—or, for that matter, Mrs. Josh Cottar. Josh Cottar, that coarse rich vulgarian who had made a fortune out of beer and army contracts, was discussing a business deal in a far corner of the room with one of the Commissioner's Indian guests, but Colonel Moulson, seated at Delia's left, was showing every sign of losing his temper.

Kishan Prasad had left at midnight, but his departure had not been the signal for any of the other guests to leave. The Tuesday parties seldom ended before three and sometimes four o'clock in the morning, but shortly before one o'clock the Commissioner, who had passed successively through the convivial, the amorous, the quarrelsome and the maudlin stages of intoxication, finally arrived at the unconscious; and as though he had been waiting for that, Alex put down his unfinished drink, flung his cards face upwards on the table, and rose.

'Where are you going, Alex?' demanded Mrs. Cottar.

'Bed,' said Alex briefly. 'And so are the rest of you.'

Unbelievably, he had managed to get rid of them. Winter did not know how he had done it, but within a quarter of an hour the last carriage had rolled away down the drive and only Alex remained. He had looked thoughtfully at the Commissioner's snoring bulk and then at Winter and said: 'Do you need any help?'

Winter had not been entirely certain as to what he had meant by that question, but she had chosen to put the obvious interpretation upon it and had said a little stiffly: 'You need not trouble. Ismail will help him to bed.'

Alex shrugged his shoulders very slightly and had been turning to go when she had stopped him.

'Captain Randall——'

Alex turned back. 'Mrs. Barton?'

Winter said: 'Did you know that the Rao Sahib would be coming to the house tonight?'

'I had heard that he might be.'

'Is that why you were here tonight?'

Alex regarded her with raised brows. 'My dear Mrs. Barton, I was here tonight because your husband invited me.'

'But you would have refused if you had not thought that the Rao Sahib might be coming.'

Alex shrugged again. 'Perhaps.'

'Why did you want to see him?'

Alex's lazy glance dwelt reflectively on her for a moment or two and then he said: 'Because I happen to be interested in him. There is a reason for everything that Kishan Prasad does, and it is always the same reason. He is a man with only one idea.'

'What idea?'

'My dear girl,' said Alex with sudden impatience, 'you know as well as I do! You once saw his face in the raw when we passed the wreck of that transport. He has only one aim in life. To throw off the rule of the Company. And to achieve it he would, if it were necessary, be prepared to cut the throat of every white man in this country with his own hands—with one possible exception.'

'You mean—yourself? But you thought that he had told those men to kill you. You told him so! That is what you meant, didn't you?'

Alex shook his head. 'No. He will not deliberately take my life, or plot to take it, because I once made the grave mistake of saving his. But if someone else should do it, that would be quite a different matter.'

Winter sat down again a little abruptly. She said, looking up at him: 'What were you talking about? It sounded just like ordinary talk, but it wasn't, was it?'

Alex subsided on to the sofa opposite her and drove his hands into his pockets. He said slowly: 'Not exactly. I think that he intended to do you a service—or me—and that he is sufficiently sure of himself to be able to afford to do so. Perhaps he is right.'

Winter said: 'I don't understand,' and Alex looked at her under lowered lashes.

'That may be just as well. Are you going to the hills this summer?'

'No. I do not think that I shall mind the heat so much. Why are you changing the subject?'

'I'm not. I think you should go, and I shall do all that I can to see that you do. Are you so particularly anxious to stay?' His gaze wandered to the sofa on the far side of the room where her husband lay and snored.

'Yes,' said Winter, watching the turn of his head against the lamplight. Had that been what Kishan Prasad meant? Had he been hinting that there might be trouble in Lunjore in the coming months? But if that were so, how could she go to the hills, knowing that Alex would still be in Lunjore?

She said almost inaudibly: 'There are times when—when one would so much rather not be sent away.'

Alex misinterpreted the hesitant words. He turned sharply, his mouth suddenly white. 'Are you going to have a child?' he enquired bluntly.

Winter did not move, but he saw her face set in a dreadful silent stare and felt the shudder that went through her body as clearly as though she had been touching him instead of separated from him by a full two paces.

It would be absurd to say that Winter had never contemplated such an eventuality, for she had often imagined herself as the mother of Conway's children. But that had been before her marriage. It had, incredibly enough, never once occurred to her since; perhaps because, subconsciously, she could not believe that anything could be conceived as a result of happenings that inspired only fear and repulsion. Alex's abrupt question had faced her with something that filled her with sick horror; as though she had been a sleep-walker waking to find herself balanced on the lip of a yawning gulf. The colour drained out of her face, leaving it pinched and sallow. That could not happen to her—it could not! Children should be born of love——

Alex said: 'Are you?' The harshness of his own voice surprised him.

Winter steadied her white lips with an effort, too shaken to resent the question. 'No.'

Alex stood up abruptly and crossing to the table that was still littered with cards and dice, picked up his unfinished drink. The brandy burned his throat and he drank it as though he were parched with thirst, and refilling the glass at a side-table by the door, came back with it in his hand and stood looking down at her: 'I'm sorry. Perhaps I should not have asked you that.'

Winter did not raise her eyes farther than the glass in his hand, and noting the direction of her gaze he smiled a little wryly: 'No, I am afraid I don't get drunk. It does not happen to be one of my failings, so I cannot excuse myself on that score. I thought that was what you meant, and it seemed to make it even more necessary that you should remove from Lunjore for the hot weather.'

Winter did not look at him. She said: 'I only meant that I will not run away.'

'From what?'

'From—from anything.'

'No,' said Alex thoughtfully, 'I don't believe you will.'

He sat down again, stretching his legs out before him and leaning his head against the back of the sofa, and the silence lengthened and drew out and filled slowly with small sounds; the Commissioner's stertorous breathing, the ticking of the clock, the chirrup of a gecko lizard and the monotonous flutterings of a large moth that had found its way in from the night and was battering its wings against the glass of the large oil-lamp, throwing whirling, wavering shadows across the walls and the high white ceiling.

Winter sat motionless, her body still rigid from shock. She did not look at Alex's face where it lay thrown back against the gold-coloured brocade of the high-backed sofa. She looked at the hand that held his glass: brown, thin, long-fingered and nervous; a hand possessed of unexpected strength and equally unexpected gentleness; and she seemed to see beside it the damp, fleshy, unsteady fingers of the man she had married. She knew then that she could not bear children to Conway. To do so would be the ultimate indecency. She would go to Lucknow as Conway had suggested. Not to the house that had been her father's, but to the one that had been her only home. To the Gulab Mahal. To Ameera, who might understand, and even if she did not, would be loving. If she could only get back to the Gulab Mahal she might be able to see things clearer; to stand back and get them into some sort of perspective. She could not do that while Alex was here and her need for him was so great; while Conway was here and her shuddering aversion for him filled her with such sick despair. She would go home. . . .

She saw Alex's body relax, slackening perceptibly until the glass that he held tilted a little as his fingers loosened about it, holding it only lightly. He was still silent, but his silence was as devoid of tension as his body, and the familiar sense of safety and reassurance that his presence could bring to her gradually smoothed out the turmoil in Winter's mind. The strained rigidity left her and she leant back tiredly against the furry plush upholstery of the tall chair-back, feeling the strain and tension of the last twenty-four hours seep slowly away from her.

The drawing-room smelt stalely of cigar smoke and spirits, of fading roses and the heavy violet scent affected by Mrs. Wilkinson, and the furniture still stood pushed out of the way of the card-table and against the walls. The room looked as cluttered and untidy and forlorn as any room when a party is over and the guests are gone, but despite its unattractive aspect it was all at once curiously peaceful. Alex had always been able to give her this feeling of security, and looking at his abstracted face Winter thought how strange it was that this should still be so. Surely now that she had discovered that she loved him she should feel embarrassed or shy or ashamed in his presence? She was a married woman, and it was shockingly improper of her to allow herself to fall in love with another man. She should by rights be overcome with shame. But then she had not allowed herself to fall in love with Alex. She had only discovered the fact when it was far too late to do anything about it. She had not even had sense enough to realize it when he had kissed her. She wondered, now, why he had done so? Had it only been a sudden impulse, born of the romantic beauty of the warm moonlight and the strains of a sentimental song? Or had he after all loved her a little? She knew that he had felt responsible for her, and that the feeling of responsibility had irked him. She knew too that it had not died with her marriage. Sitting relaxed and silent she watched his quiet face and wondered what he was thinking of.

Alex was not thinking of Winter. He seldom had time to think of her, or allowed himself to do so. There were too many other things to think about. Too much that needed to be done, and always too little time in which to do it. . . .

So Kishan Prasad was to be one of the hosts at the duck shoot—Kishan Prasad who never did anything without a reason. What then was behind this shoot at Hazrat Bagh? Could there be an ulterior motive behind such an arrangement? or was its aim merely to lull the senior officers and officials into a deeper sense of security and belief in the goodwill of the local talukdars than they already possessed? It would of course mean that for the best part of a day the station would be practically denuded of British officers, as the majority of them were attending the shoot. Had anything been planned to take place in their absence? The armoury—the magazine——?

No, that was absurd. Kishan Prasad had said the hot weather, and he would not have troubled to say that if it had not been true. The real hot weather did not officially start until the end of April or the first week of May. Or had he been playing a double game? That would be like him. And yet—— No, he had meant it. He could afford to hand Alex that piece of information, carelessly secure in the knowledge that no one else would believe it.

Sepoys—— They had asked for sepoys to help put up the birds. Why, when there were so many villagers and coolies that they could call upon? Was there anything in that? *This may do well enough for the villages, but it will not serve for the sepoys. For them it must be something that strikes deeper and touches every man. They are already as tinder, but there is as yet no spark. No matter, we will find it.* Had Kishan Prasad found the spark he had spoken of? What had made him sure enough of himself to give that warning?—for it had been a warning . . .

'I must see Packer and Moulson and Gardener-Smith in the morning,' thought Alex, 'though they will none of them believe a word of it. Surely they must know that their sepoys are being got at? What the devil *is* behind this duck shoot? I'll swear there is something. . . . Maynard says the police are firm: I wonder. Oh God, why won't they send us out more British officers—call off the civil from mucking about with the army, and throw out some of these decrepit senior officers! Look at the way we leave magazines and arsenals unguarded. If there is a rising in Lunjore, who is going to hold the magazine if they are all involved in it? Thank God we've only got a small one! But there's the arsenal at Suthragunj: guns, arms, powder enough to blow up half India, and only one Queen's regiment against three of Native Infantry and one of Native Cavalry if ever it came to⸻ Oh, what's the good of thinking of it! It's none of my business. . . .' His thoughts left the wider issues and drifted into-the familiar pattern of planning for the welfare of his own district.

The clock on the chimney-piece struck two, and Alex removed his abstracted gaze from the ceiling and turned his head to look at Winter. He said slowly: 'I didn't mean to keep you up so late. I'm sorry. . . . Riding this morning?'

'Yes.'

'Where?'

'Anywhere. To Parry's mound?'

'All right. Six o'clock, then.'

They smiled at each other, their faces dim and peaceful, and Alex finished his drink and stood up. Winter rose with a rustle of silk and walked beside him into the hall where a sleepy servant squatted nodding by the dining-room door.

Alex said curtly: 'Send the Sahib's bearer to him,' and the man scrambled to his feet and scurried away into the darkness as Alex turned to Winter and held out his hand:

'Good night. Or good morning! And I suppose I should also
say "Thank you for a very pleasant evening."'

'Was it pleasant?'

Alex considered the question, still holding the hand she had
put into his. He had a habit of considering a question before he
answered it, rather than returning a conventionally empty reply.
He said thoughtfully: 'Instructive, at all events. And I suppose
tolerably amusing.'

He seemed about to say something else, but he changed his
mind and was silent for a moment or two, looking down at
Winter and not quite smiling, the line of his mouth unexpectedly
tender. Then he lifted the hand he held, and turning it palm
upwards, kissed it lightly and deliberately, and folding her fingers
upon the kiss, released it.

There had been nothing in the least passionate in the gesture:
it might have been either a wordless apology or a comforting
caress given to a child. Then he had turned and gone out into
the night, and Winter had heard him speak to a servant in the
porch, and had waited, standing in the silent hall, until the sound
of his footsteps died away in the darkness.

22

LESS than four hours later Alex had been waiting for her on the
Residency road, and they had ridden out through the quiet
cantonments and across the rifle-range to the open country
beyond, Niaz and Yusaf riding behind them.

The rifle-range was hard and level and the horses were fresh,
so they did not talk much. But beyond the range the ground
became broken, and they slowed to a walk, threading their way
between rough tussocks of grass, *kikar* trees and thorn bushes,
feathery clumps of pampas and outcrops of rock, to draw rein on
the crest of a lonely knoll that was crowned by a banyan tree
and the weather-worn slab of an ancient grave whose inscription

was still faintly legible: *Here lyes the body of Ezra Parry of the Honorable Company of Merchants of London trading to the East Indies, the son of Thos: Parry and Susanna, who departed this lyfe the eleventh of October 1666.*

The sun rose as they reached it, and they sat looking out across the country beyond, while every blade and spear of grass flashed and glittered with dewdrops, and the morning mists lifted in veil after veil so that the land seemed to unroll itself, stretching back and back into limitless distance.

Doves cooed among the branches of the banyan tree, and a flight of wild duck whistled overhead, making for the jheel that lay ten miles and more to the northward. Winter turned to watch them as they dwindled into specks against the pale blue of the morning, and saw that there were other lines in the sky, long and wavering or forming neat dark arrow-heads; duck and teal and geese flying in from a night spent on the river or among the ploughed lands.

'That is Hazrat Bagh out there, isn't it? Are they making a road?' She pointed with her riding-crop to a thin brown line that wandered away across the plain, and Alex, following the direction of her gaze, said: 'Yes. That is a temporary track so that the ladies from Lunjore can all drive out in comfort to watch the duck shoot. No expense is being spared to impress upon your husband and the garrison how friendly and co-operative our local landowners are, and I should dearly like to know——'

He did not finish the sentence and Winter said curiously: 'What would you like to know?'

Alex did not answer. Winter had discovered that he seldom answered a question unless he wished to do so; he merely ignored it. He turned away, screwing up his eyes against the dazzle of the newly risen sun, and said: 'Listen to those partridges calling! I must bring a gun out here one evening.'

Winter was silent for a moment or two, listening to the clangour of the partridges and thinking of other things, and presently she said: 'You had one yesterday, didn't you? A pistol, I mean. Do you always carry one?'

'No. Only recently.'

'Have you got one now?'

Alex nodded, his eyes on a covey of partridges that whirred up from among the low thorn scrub and skimmed away across the tops of the sun-gilt grass where Niaz sat his fidgeting horse at the foot of the knoll.

Winter said abruptly: 'Will you give it to me?'

Alex turned sharply. 'What?'

'Will you give me a pistol?'

'What for?'

'I should feel—safer,' said Winter lightly, affecting an interest in a pair of weaver birds who were fluttering anxiously about their dangling nest in a thorn tree below.

Alex surveyed her with narrowed eyes and said dryly: 'Thinking of shooting anyone?'

'No,' said Winter soberly. 'Not even myself.'

The Eagle snorted and backed as though he had felt a sudden jerk on the bridle, and there was a momentary silence while Alex brought him under control. When he had done so he enquired shortly if she had ever used firearms before.

Winter shook her head. 'No. But I do not suppose it is very difficult, is it?'

'Try.' Alex dismounted and pulling the Eagle's reins over his head whistled to Niaz and turned to help Winter from the saddle. The sunlight glinted on the barrel of the small Tranter revolver as he explained its mechanism.

'Is it loaded?' enquired Winter.

'My dear girl,' said Alex impatiently, 'do you really imagine that I should carry one that wasn't? Here—take it. No, don't aim as low as that. Fire it in the air.'

The report sent Furiante dancing and snorting indignantly, and startled a peacock and his five demure brown wives who had been roosting unseen on the far side of a clump of pampas grass, sending them squawking away.

'Well done,' said Alex approvingly. 'You didn't jump; but you must allow for the recoil.'

'Show me how,' said Winter, handing it back to him.

There was a bright blue jay's feather caught among the thorns of a *kikar* tree less than a dozen yards away, and Alex jerked up his hand and fired. The feather vanished and Niaz, behind them, gave a grunt of approval.

Winter said: 'Is that really the way to do it? Not taking aim?'

'No,' admitted Alex with a grin. 'That was just showing off. I apologize. I'll do it slowly for you this time. Stand behind my shoulder and look along the barrel.'

He levelled the revolver and fired. 'Think you can do better now?'

'Yes, I think so.'

Winter took the weapon less gingerly, selected a mark and pulled the trigger. Her slim wrist jerked to the kick of the discharge and the bullet went high of the mark. Alex made her fire the remaining rounds and then remarked: 'Not bad. You can keep it.'

'Thank you,' said Winter gravely. She held it out to him and said: 'Will you reload it for me, please?'

Alex shook his head. 'No. Not until I've taught you how to use it. For the present it is safer unloaded. And probably just as effective a deterrent.'

He saw the hot colour rise in a wave from her throat to the roots of her hair and had a sudden, startled suspicion why she had wanted a pistol. Winter thrust the weapon into the pocket of her riding-habit and turned away to where Yusaf held the indignant Furiante, and Alex, following her, helped her to the saddle and stood holding her stirrup-leather and looking up at her under frowning brows. Winter did not return his look. The bright colour was fading from her face and her expression gave nothing away, and after a moment he dropped his hand without speaking.

They cantered back in single file between the high tufts of grass, the rocks and the flat-topped thorn trees, and when they reached the rifle-range broke into a gallop and did not draw rein until they came to the outskirts of the cantonments. Alex had stopped before the gate of the Residency, for his own bungalow lay barely a hundred yards beyond it, and said briefly: 'Bring that pistol with you tomorrow and I'll teach you how to use it. It may come in useful.'

He had asked no further questions as to why she had wanted a pistol, and he did not know that three days after he had given it to her she had used it, unloaded but with, as he had predicted, a satisfactorily deterrent effect, against his superior officer.

Conway rarely visited his wife's room, but he had done so on the night following the Tuesday party and had found it locked against him. He had created a scene, which availed him nothing. The next night, finding it still locked, he had decided to teach his wife a lesson, and on the following evening he had walked in upon her as she was dressing for dinner. He had been tolerably sober and therefore more dangerous, and had bellowed at Johara, who was sulkily assisting with his wife's toilet, to get out and stay out.

'Now, my dear wife,' said Conway unpleasantly, his pale eyes red-rimmed with rage and brandy, 'you will find that there are other times of day when I can demand your obedience. You can take that dress off again. You won't need it.'

Winter had remained unruffled. She had opened a drawer of her dressing-table and turned towards him with the Tranter revolver in her hand. She had been perfectly polite and quite definite. He had not married her for love, but for money, and he had got what he wanted and must be content with that. She would fulfil her duties as his wife in every way but this, but if he ever attempted to force his attentions upon her again she would shoot him.

'Not to kill you, Conway. I shall stop short of murder. But just to hurt you painfully enough to ensure that such a thing does not occur again. I hope you realize that I mean it?'

If she had screamed or raged Conway might not have believed it. Because she did neither, but faced him with white-lipped calm, he had blustered and shouted and called her unprintable names, but had backed out of her room and had not attempted to enter it again. The revolver had served its purpose, but Winter continued to take instruction in how to fire it. Partly because it amused her, but largely because it gave her an excuse to see Alex.

Alex had taught her with a grim, unsmiling efficiency, making her load and fire, reload and fire again until her wrist ached. 'You never know when it may come in useful,' was all he would say.

Once he had brought a rifle with him on the morning ride, and had told her to fire it. It was, he said, one of the new issue; the Enfield rifle that was to replace the old-fashioned infantry musket—the famous 'Brown Bess' that had long outlived its usefulness.

He had made her lie down to fire it, holding the heavy weapon as though she had been on the range, and had lain beside her on the dew-wet ground explaining the method and mechanism, and exhorting her not to hold it as though it were made of glass. The recoil had bruised her cheek and shoulder badly, and the bullet had gone far wide of the towering ant-hill, over two hundred yards distant, at which she had been aiming. Alex had refused to let her fire it again. He had fired it himself, and Niaz, seeing the distant explosion of dust, sucked in his breath and said '*Wah!*' in an awed voice.

Both Niaz and Yusaf had regarded the rifle with considerable interest. 'Is it true that these things will fire a ball many times the distance of the old ones?' enquired Niaz. 'How is it done?'

'It has grooved bores,' said Alex.

'They will be difficult to load; especially when they are fouled,' commented Niaz, squinting down the barrel.

Alex shook his head. 'No, for the cartridge papers are greased.' He took one out of the pocket of his riding-coat and biting off the end, rammed it down the barrel to demonstrate, and fired again.

'May I try?' enquired Niaz.

Alex handed over the gun and another cartridge and Niaz bit off the end and spat it out upon the ground. 'Pah!' he said with a grimace. 'With what is that greased?' He lay down, cuddling the butt against his cheek, sighted carefully and fired. A fluff of dust showed that the bullet had chipped the ant-hill, and Niaz laughed.

'*Hai!* This is indeed a good weapon! Now all that we require is a war so that we may try it on an enemy!'

'May a man buy such a gun for his own use?' enquired Yusaf, his eyes sparkling. 'Beyond the Border such a thing would be worth many times its weight in silver.' Yusaf was by birth a Pathan, and blood feuds added much to the excitements and hazards of life in his own territory.

Alex did not answer. He was staring down at the small scrap of greased paper that Niaz had spat out upon the ground, and there was an odd, still look on his face. He drew another cartridge from his pocket and stood looking at it, turning it over in his hand and rubbing the ball of his thumb slowly across the greased paper wrapping until Winter said: 'What is it?'

'Hmm?' He turned towards her, but his eyes were blank and unfocused and they looked past her as though she was not there.

Yusaf said: 'Huzoor, may I too try the gun?'

Alex's eyes narrowed suddenly. The abstraction left them and his hand clenched hard over the cartridge that he held. 'Assuredly.' He turned slowly and held out the cartridge, and Winter, watching him as she always watched him when he was not looking at her, was all at once aware that behind that casual gesture his nerves were tense and alert as if he were waiting for something to happen; for some expected—or unexpected?—action. She was so sure of it that she turned quickly to look at Yusaf, half-expecting to see him recoil from Alex's outstretched hand; but he took the cartridge without hesitation, and biting off the end of it as Alex and Niaz had done, rammed it home.

Yusaf did not lie down to fire in the manner of a sepoy. He handled the musket as a tribesman, and the ball struck the top of the ant-hill and disintegrated it. '*Shabash!*' applauded Niaz.

Alex handed him a second cartridge without ever taking that quiet, intent gaze from him, and a curious spark leapt to life in his eyes as Yusaf, having bitten off the top of the second cartridge, rubbed his mouth swiftly with the back of his hand.

Yusaf fired again, and missed. 'That is bad shooting,' said Niaz. 'Thou shouldst come and fire on the range. The second shot should be better than the first.'

'In my country,' said Yusaf, 'it is the first shot that counts. If a man fail with his first, he may not live to fire a second. Come over the Border on thy next leave, Niaz Mohamed, and we will show thee!' He handed the gun to Niaz and once more drew the back of his hand across his mouth.

Alex saw the gesture, and he turned away and stood looking out across the plain with his hands in his pockets, and after a moment or two Winter heard him say something under his breath that sounded like '——and furnish the pretence'.

'What is it?' she asked, as she asked five minutes earlier, troubled by something in his manner that she could not understand.

Alex looked round at her with a faint frown as though he had forgotten that she was there. 'What is what?'

'You said something about furnishing a pretence.'

'Did I? I must have been thinking aloud.'

'What about?' enquired Winter, unaccountably disturbed.

Alex gave a short laugh. 'I was thinking of some lines of Dryden's. "When churls rebel against their native prince, I arm their hands and furnish the pretence, and housing in the lion's hateful sign, bought senates and deserting troops are mine." It seemed remarkably appropriate.'

He turned on his heel, and although it was still early they rode no farther that day, but returned to the cantonments—Alex riding with a speed and recklessness that he had never shown before when he had been out with Winter, and as though he had once again forgotten that she was there.

An hour later he had been ushered into Colonel Gardener-Smith's office, where he had been forced to wait for some considerable time.

'Good morning, Captain Randall,' said the Colonel making a belated appearance and eyeing Alex with some uneasiness, 'sorry to have kept you waiting. Awkward time of the day for me—'

He wondered what Randall had come about this time, and hoped that it was no more alarmist nonsense about an armed rising planned for the coming hot weather. Efficient young man, very: Colonel Gardener-Smith had a profound respect for Captain Randall's knowledge and ability; but all these outstanding young men who were pets of the political—'Lawrence's Young Men'— had bees in their bonnets. Randall's was the fear of mutiny; not a localized affair, but something on a far larger scale that would involve the whole of the Bengal Army and not merely one, or at the most two, regiments.

Such an idea was of course complete nonsense! Not that Colonel Gardener-Smith imagined that India had seen the last of mutinies and rebellions. That was perhaps too much to hope for. Now and again one was likely to hear of some dissatisfied and mismanaged regiment causing trouble. But as for the entire army, absurd! It would need something more than local grievances to do that—a common denominator that would set off a panic among all sepoys everywhere. But misuses and abuses of authority were always localized affairs, and would not disturb the army as a whole. His own regiment, for instance, was loyal to the core, and he had recently written a letter to the *Calcutta Times* expressing his indignation on the subject of those men who had so little respect for the known character and fidelity of the British-led sepoy as to attempt to blacken him in the public prints by suggesting that he was ready to turn against his masters. No such thing! The Colonel was almost tempted to agree with Colonel Moulson (a man whom he could not bring himself to like) that men who expressed such views must be considered to be losing their nerve and should resign from the service of the Company.

Not that Randall appeared to be deficient in either physical or moral courage, but that last interview, at which both Colonel Packer of the 105th N.I. and Colonel Moulson of the 2nd Regiment of Lunjore Irregulars had both been present, had been distinctly trying. One could not help thinking that Captain Randall was, at the very least, guilty of exaggeration. And at the worst must be suffering from overstrain or sunstroke. He had put his case with a convincing lack of heat, and had kept his temper remarkably well in the face of what the Colonel could not help thinking was unnecessarily insulting behaviour on the part of Moulson; but all the same——

Colonel Gardener-Smith frowned and said with more hostility than he had intended: 'Well, what is it now?'

Alex had been standing by the window when he entered, looking out over the sunbaked parade-ground and turning something over and over in his hand. He replied briefly to the Colonel's greeting, and walking over to the table tossed the object down upon it and said without preamble: 'That is one of the cartridges for the new Enfield, sir. Can you tell me what they are greased with?'

The Colonel stared, considerably taken aback both by the question and the tone in which it was uttered. He picked the thing up, examined it and dropped it, and marked his displeasure by seating himself behind his desk and keeping Alex standing. Randall might occupy a reasonably senior civilian post in Lunjore, but in the presence of a Commanding Officer he was a mere brevet captain and must remember to conduct himself as such.

He said coldly: 'I have no idea. And I hardly think that the composition of cartridge-grease lies within your province.'

Alex said: 'Perhaps not, sir, but it must be within yours. Those cartridge-papers have to be bitten, and if there is any doubt as to the composition of the grease it is a thing that will affect the caste of every sepoy in the army. A grievance that will unite men of every regiment. A common denominator.'

The mention of a term that had so recently passed through his own mind checked the Colonel's rising anger, and he cast a startled glance at the innocent-seeming object that Alex had thrown down on his desk. He looked at it for a minute or two in silence and then looked up again at Alex's expressionless face and thought fleetingly that Randall appeared to have aged a lot recently. He said slowly: 'You mean, if it were animal fat——?'

'If it should contain any lard or animal fat,' said Alex harshly, 'no sepoy should be asked to touch it, let alone bite it. The pig is an unclean animal to a Mussulman and the cow a sacred animal to the Hindu, while the fat of any dead creature is an abomination to both. But no one knows that better than you, sir.'

Colonel Gardener-Smith's worried gaze returned to the cartridge and he frowned at it, pulling at his lip. He said uneasily, but without conviction: 'That is a point that cannot have escaped the attention of the responsible authorities.'

'Why not? The method and manufacture of these things was worked out in England, not India, and the men responsible for it are not likely to possess any special knowledge of the caste system that prevails here.'

'I do not believe . . .' began the Colonel unhappily; and then once more a sense of irritation and frustration came over him. Of *course* there was always the danger of trouble breaking out in a conquered country! And he too had lately been aware of a changing atmosphere and a lack of that sympathy and close co-operation between officers and men that had obtained in earlier and more troublous days. But it was the New Order, that was all. New methods. A new outlook. The lack of large-scale wars and operations to keep the troops occupied, and an inevitable slackening of discipline. Not what it had been in his young days. But *his* men were all right. They were his own men and he could handle them. They would follow him anywhere: hadn't he proved that? He wished Randall would leave well alone and stop this continual harrying . . . bees in the bonnet. *Buzz-buzz-buzz* . . .

He banged the table suddenly with his clenched fist and said violently: 'What do you expect me to do about it, anyway? It's none of my business—or yours! I'm not Master-General of the Ordnance! These things will be issued to every regiment in India shortly.'

'I know,' said Alex tiredly. He reached out a hand and picked up the cartridge, and his face was suddenly bleak: 'But at least it can do no harm to ask for the official analysis of this stuff, and in the meantime it might be possible to manufacture our own wrapping papers here in Lunjore, so that the men can see for themselves what is used.'

'That would be impossible,' said Colonel Gardener-Smith shortly.

'Nothing is impossible now,' said Alex slowly. 'Not even a mutiny of the Bengal Army.'

Colonel Gardener-Smith stood up abruptly and pushed his chair back with unnecessary violence. 'That is a point upon which we are unlikely to agree! If that is all you wished to see me about, I must ask you to excuse me, as I have a great many calls upon my time. I will bear in mind what you have said, and write at once to enquire into the composition of the lubrication which is being used. But you may be quite confident—as I am—that your fears will be proved groundless.'

'Thank you, sir,' said Alex in a colourless voice, and went out into the bright blaze of the mid-morning sunlight.

*   *   *

He rode less with Winter after that and he did not again take out the Enfield rifle.

Winter missed those early-morning rides in his company, and did not know that the reason for their curtailment was the fact that it is difficult to arrive home in the early hours of the morning and still wake in time to ride before sunrise.

Alex spent a great many of his nights in unexpected places; listening, watching, and occasionally—very occasionally—asking questions. It was an easier matter by night to pass unnoticed in the crowded bazaars and alleyways of the city, and he had sources of information there whose usefulness would have been severely curtailed had they been observed coming to his house. It was better that he should meet them outside the cantonments and in some other guise, and he had managed in this way to acquire a considerable quantity of curious information.

Niaz too spent much of his time similarly occupied, but he did not frequent the city. Niaz had friends among the sepoys and was often to be found visiting the lines. Much of his information tallied with Alex's, and none of it was in any way reassuring.

'It is said,' reported Niaz, chewing a grass stem while Alex lying full length in a small patch of dusty casuarina scrub sighted carefully along the barrel of a heavy Westley Richards rifle, 'that it is the purpose of the Government to make all men Christians. This the Jemadar of Colonel Gardener-Smith Sahibs *pulton* himself told me. But they say that as the *feringhis* are few, to force their faith upon all in Hind would be difficult; therefore they will accomplish it by fraud.'

'With what purpose?' asked Alex, screwing up his eyes against the low sunlight that glowed on the river.

'So that they may use the sepoys to conquer all the world for them. When the sepoys go on ships, and to far countries, they become sick, and do not fight so well; but it is not so with the Sahib-*log*, and this, it is said, is because of the food that the Sahibs eat. Therefore if the army were all of one caste— Christians—they too would eat the same food and be as strong, and as slaves of the Sahib-*log* would fight their battles in a hundred countries. There is even now a tale that to this end the Company have ground up the bones of pigs and cattle and mixed that dust with the flour and with the grain, so that all who eat of it will thereby lose their caste. And being casteless will have to become Christians, and—hast thou heard this then?'

Alex nodded. 'I have heard. Do they in the lines believe it?'

'Many believe. What do they say in the city?'

'They have refused the last consignment of Government flour,' said Alex. 'It lies still unloaded in the carts. I have sent for grain from Deesa, so that they may grind it for themselves. Are there no elder men among the *pultons* who can see that these are lies made to frighten the foolish into ruin?'

'They are like sheep,' said Niaz scornfully. 'The leading one tumbles down and all the rest fall over him! And surely the days of the Company are numbered when those who command the *pultons* no longer know the minds of their men. *Ah——!*' His voice dropped from an undertone to a whisper, 'that *manji* (boatman) spoke truth. He said that it came daily at this hour——'

A ripple broke the gleaming surface of the river and glittered in a dazzling shiver of light, and presently, inch by inch, an iron-grey shape drifted in towards the flat white sandbank and grounded as gently as a floating log.

'It is a long shot,' murmured Niaz, 'and into the eye of the sun. We should have gone lower.'

Alex said nothing. He waited patiently, as he had waited for the best part of the last two hours, until the creature drew its ten feet of ugly armour plating out of the water and turned slowly and clumsily, lying full length at an angle to the stream.

The crashing detonation of the shot echoed along the quiet river and sent a score of basking mud-turtles flipping back into the water while a flock of paddy-birds flapped off the far shallows. The big mugger jerked once and was still. Alex fired a second time and rose to his feet, beating the sand off his clothes as Niaz ran forward.

The bullets had ploughed into the beast's neck, severing the spinal cord, and it had moved no more than a foot.

'Do we keep the skin?' enquired Niaz, pacing the length from jaws to tail on the wet sand.

'No. That creature has taken the lives of over twenty men to my knowledge, and I have no wish to be reminded of it. Leave it to the kites. They will make short work of it.' Alex turned on his heel and walked back across the hot white sand with the evening sun stretching his shadow long and blue before him.

The mugger had taken a heavy toll of the city and the village five miles above it for many years, and only the day before it had taken Mothi, the eight-year-old son of Alex's grass-cutter. Mothi had been a friend of Alex's, and Alex had taken an afternoon off to lie up for the killer. But as he walked back across the sand he wondered why he had done so. To kill a dumb beast for revenge was surely a pointless action, for the creature had killed by instinct and for food, and its death would not bring back the child or any of the countless other humans whom it had fattened upon. The mugger too had a right to live, and who was to say that its victims had not been born and appointed to their end?

'We interfere too much,' thought Alex tiredly. 'Am I God that I should arbitrate?' He looked out across the flat lands and the quiet river, dusty gold in the low sunlight, and thought wryly: 'I am thinking like a Hindu!'

A slow-moving shadow sailed across the white sands and a raw-necked vulture flapped clumsily to rest a yard or two beyond the red and grey shape at the water's edge, and waddled cautiously towards it.

'That too was appointed,' said Niaz quietly, 'for none may die before their allotted time.'

Alex turned his head and looked at him reflectively, wondering how it was that this man should be able to follow his thoughts when there were so few of his own kind who could do so. His own kind, as represented by the garrison and officials of Lunjore, were as far out of touch with him at the present time as though they had been occupying separate worlds and speaking different languages. He had been unable to do more than scratch the surface of their determined blindness and complacency, and they were inclined to take anything he said as a reflection upon their own efficiency.

There had been that matter of the Government issue of flour. He had brought up at a general conference earlier that day the question of the refusal of the bazaars to accept or handle it, but the Commissioner had merely observed that if they didn't like it they could go without. The majority view appeared to be that the whole thing was a storm in a tea-cup which would blow over if ignored, and Colonel Moulson had remarked unpleasantly that he did not know what the garrison was coming to when members of it allowed themselves to be panicked by every petty rumour in the bazaars.

Alex had glanced down at his hands in the shadow of the table and had been surprised to see that they were comparatively steady when he had felt physically sick with rage and exasperation. The windy, unconstructive debate had dawdled to an indecisive close, and he had flung out into the sunlight in a fury and had taken his own measures to deal with the situation without consulting the Commissioner or anyone else. And two hours later, still possessed by that fury, he had gone out after the mugger.

The long crawl across the hot open sands to the dusty and inadequate shelter of a thin outcrop of grass and casuarina that provided the only possible cover within rifle shot, and the enforced stillness of the lengthy wait that followed, had done a great deal towards calming him. And looking down at the dead creature he had tasted a brief satisfaction in the knowledge that he had avenged the death of a friendly brown imp of whom he had been fond. But the satisfaction had been only momentary, and Niaz, watching him, had by some alchemy of friendship followed his thought and replied to it.

But the thought recurred as they walked back in the evening light along the river bank and across the dun-coloured plain towards the green belt of trees that hid the cantonments. 'I have taken the life of that creature for the sake of Mothi, who will not care, and to work off my rage, which will return. And yet I could not kill Kishan Prasad, or even leave him to drown, although that might have saved the lives of many more men, women and children than the mugger would have taken in all his life. Why? Because I believe that Kishan Prasad has a soul, and that the beast has not? But if that were so, I have taken all that the mugger had, while Kishan Prasad would still have a soul. But then so had that priest at Khanwai whose life I took. And so has that girl who would have burned herself with her husband on his funeral pyre if I had not heard in time and prevented it. But is she any happier for being forced to keep her life? If she had committed *suttee* she would have gone with her man, and her name would have been honoured in the villages: her very ashes would have been sacred. Now she will never re-marry, but live out her life as a childless drudge, despised and neglected. We interfere too much. We take too much upon ourselves. By what right?—by what right?'

'And why in the name of the four hundred and ninety-nine

thousand angels,' thought Alex impatiently, as he had thought so often before, 'can I not rid myself of this habit of seeing both sides of a thing instead of only my own? Which is my own? . . .'

He had been dining out that evening, the occasion being a Guest Night of the 105th N.I., and had been half-inclined to send his excuses until it had occurred to him that his absence would undoubtedly be regarded as a fit of the sulks, and as it behoved him to try to keep on terms with the senior officers he had donned the tight, high-collared mess dress of his Regiment, with its elaborate frogging and jingling spurs, and driven over to the barracks which lay two miles distant on the far side of the cantonments.

The Guest Night had been late and noisy, and it was long after midnight before he had been able to leave. The sleepy syce deposited him in the porch of his bungalow and drove the trap round to the stable, and Alex walked stiffly up the verandah steps, tugging at the fastening of the braided collar and throwing it open with a sense of relief.

There was a light burning in his room, and the *chowkidar*, his *chuddar* drawn over his head, lay sleeping soundly on a string cot in the porch and did not stir as Alex passed him.

Alex's spurs jingled in the silence and two shadows rose to their feet from the far side of the soft square of orange light that the oil-lamp in his bedroom threw across the matting of the verandah. One of them moved forward and lifted the *chik* that hung over the doorway to allow him to pass in.

'Who have you there?' asked Alex in an undertone.

'It is the Kotwal of Jalodri,' said Niaz. 'He would have gone away, saying that he would come again in the morning, but I constrained him to stay, for he has news that concerns thee somewhat.'

'Send him in,' said Alex.

The man slipped in under the lifted *chik* and stood blinking nervously in the yellow lamp-light. Alex greeted him gravely and offered an apology for his having been kept so late. 'What is the trouble with thee, Chuman Lal?'

M

'I do not know,' whispered the Kotwal, and his eyes rolled and started like those of a frightened horse. 'It is a thing I do not understand, and therefore I brought one to thee, and by night. But they told me thou hadst gone out to eat with the *pulton*, and I would have gone back to my house, but thy servant constrained me to wait. He—he said that this was a matter of which thou hadst knowledge. If that be true, and there be some evil charm in this, it may be that thou canst draw it out.'

The man looked back quickly over his shoulder, but there was only Niaz behind him, and thrusting a trembling hand into the folds of his garments he drew out a *chupatti*.

Alex's expression did not alter, but it was a moment or two before he spoke:

'What evil is there in that?'

'I do not know,' whispered the Kotwal, shuddering. 'It was brought to me last night by a runner from Chumri, which is four *koss* to the north. He brought with him five of these things, together with a fragment of goat's flesh, and told me that I must prepare five more, breaking one of these which he had brought and mixing a little with the new five. These I must dispatch by a runner to the next village, sending also a portion of goat's flesh, to be given into the hand of the watchman of that village, saying to him that he must do likewise and send in turn to the next village. And with it must also be said certain words that the runner from Jalodri had spoken to me: "From the North to the South, and from the East to the West." Then did I know that it was a charm.'

Alex stretched out his hand and took the small flat cake of coarse-ground flour, and stood looking down at it with the smile that he had taught himself to wear when his face was being watched by tense or frightened men for a clue to his thoughts. Niaz, who knew that faint, abstracted smile, grinned in recognition of it, and the Kotwal, looking anxiously from one to other, visibly relaxed.

'Here it comes,' thought Alex. 'The fiery cross. This is the fruit of that devildom at Khanwai. "*It will do well enough for the villages, but it will not serve for the sepoys . . .*"'

He handed the *chupatti* back to the Kotwal and said: 'And what hast thou done?'

'I did as it was told me,' said the Kotwal. 'Five I prepared and had sent by runner. Those that I received, saving only this one, I wrapped in a cloth and buried deep. Huzoor, what is the meaning of this thing? I am a poor man and ignorant, and I fear that it may bring misfortune upon my house and my fields.'

'There is nothing to fear,' said Alex quietly. 'It is only, as thou knowest, that last year the rains failed and many of the crops failed also. That thing in thy hand is the food of all, and if it be a charm it is one that is sent for good; in propitiation, so that this year the rains will not fail and the crops of every village through which the *chupattis* pass may be abundant.'

'Ah!' said the Kotwal gratefully. 'That is good talk. I will tell the village, for they feared greatly, wondering what evil this might portend. I will strew these things about the fields, and then surely my crops will prosper. And the goat's flesh? What is the meaning of that? Tara Chand, whose fields lie by mine, said that it foretold the fall of the Company's Government, for is it not said that——' The Kotwal stopped abruptly and coughed a small dry cough of embarrassment.

'——that he who kills an Englishman sacrifices a goat to Kali,' finished Alex grimly. 'So I also have heard. But the goat's flesh that was sent thee is but a sign that the flocks and herds shall increase, for in a good year there is grass and water for many. Tell them this in the villages, that they may know that it is a sign for good.'

The Kotwal salaamed deeply, and stowing the crumbling *chupatti* with reverent care among the folds of the blanket he wore wound about him, he backed out of the room, and they heard his feet patter away on the matting of the verandah.

'So it comes at last,' said Niaz softly, echoing Alex's own thought. 'That was quick thinking. Will he believe?'

'Let us hope so. It is the Government who will not!'

'All Governments,' said Niaz cheerfully, 'are as blind as the monkey of Mataram who did not wish to see.' And he squatted down to help Alex remove his boots and to regale him with the gossip of the lines.

Alex wrote a report on the mysterious distribution of the *chupattis* the following morning and sent it across in triplicate to the Commissioner, who was pleased to be facetious on the subject that evening.

'Damned if I ain't beginning to think Fred Moulson is right about you, Alex. Megrims and the vapours! Yes, yes, yes—I know y' had a wild tale last year about some hocus-pocus at Khanwai. But as I told yer then, it's a mistake to go pokin' about in that side of native life. Probably no connection with this at all! Far more likely that this is only some local big-wig propitiating the gods by a distribution of cakes; it ain't unusual— you should know that! And if you think I'm going to forward such a farrago of nonsense to the Governor, y' *must* be mad! Fiery cross, indeed! Tell you what, y' should relax. Yer gettin' a sight too fidgety. Get a woman instead!—do you all the good in the world! Comin' on this shoot tomorrow? Good, good. Day in the open will blow some of these cobwebs away.'

Alex, who spent the larger part of his day in the open dealing less with paper-work than with people, and who had recently spent half his nights there as well, forbore to comment. He refused the offer of a drink, and walked back to his bungalow wondering if he had ever really imagined for a moment that the Commissioner would take any other attitude. He supposed not, and he felt slightly ashamed of that report in triplicate, realizing that he had only put it in writing so that he could justify himself later from the files. But of what use to him, or to anyone else, would such justification be? 'I told you so' was a cheap form of satisfaction at the best of times, and he despised himself for having given way to it. He would have to go more often to the villages and talk with the head-men and the elders, and see what he could do towards allaying any panic that the distribution of the *chupattis* might have caused.

Did the things carry any specific message? or were they merely a means of creating an atmosphere of suspicion and alarm, and thus providing a fruitful breeding-ground for deeper and more savage hates and fears? Five . . . Did that mean anything? He was familiar with the Indian custom of sending a message by means of a handful of oddments—flowers, leaves, fruits, bangles; things that each carried its own meaning in the language of signs and were in common use as messages between lovers. In that language any object appearing in duplicate stood for a number indicating time, unless it were accompanied by a pinch of saffron or incense, in which case it stood for place. Five *chupattis*. The fifth month? That would be May, and Kishan Prasad had said 'in the hot weather'.

An open carriage passed him bearing a Captain and Mrs. Hossack, their four children and an ayah. Mrs. Hossack was a pleasant woman with a somewhat anxious manner, and the four children, the youngest of whom, wrapped in innumerable shawls, lay in the arms of the ayah, were pale-cheeked, leggy little creatures whose pallid fragility was a cause of endless anxiety to their mamma. The two older children, recognizing Alex, waved enthusiastically as they passed, and Mrs. Hossack smiled and bowed.

'Thank God I'm not married!' thought Alex with sudden vehemence. 'At least I have not got that fear to face!' And thought instantly: 'I must get him to send her to the hills. She will have to go if he orders her. After all, he is her husband.'

But he was not thinking of Mrs. Hossack.

23

THE duck shoot at Hazrat Bagh was timed to begin soon after eight o'clock in the morning, to allow the guns and the guests to assemble, and breakfast to be eaten on a prepared ground half a mile from the jheel.

Previously it had always taken several hours of riding over

difficult country to reach the jheel, and no carriage or cart could have attempted the trip. But the temporary road that the hosts had caused to be constructed for the convenience of their guests proved remarkably good, and the carriages that had started from Lunjore as dawn was breaking had reached the rendezvous in ample time for breakfast.

To Winter's surprise many of the guests proved to be strangers to her, and she found on enquiry that they were officers and officials from Suthragunj, a large cantonment town beyond the borders of Lunjore.

As the crow flies Suthragunj lay less than thirty miles from the Lunjore Cantonments, but the main road ran far to the southward for more than double that distance before a branch road to Suthragunj added yet another fifteen miles to the score. There were various small footpaths and side-tracks that wandered between the villages, but as none were capable of taking a carriage, the British residents of Suthragunj and Lunjore seldom met. Now, however, two of the hosts having acquaintances among the Suthragunj garrison, the *kutcha* road had been extended beyond the jheel so that they too might attend, and at least a dozen members of the garrison were present.

The jheel was not in the least as Winter had pictured it. She had imagined a mile-long lake fringed with reeds, but the narrow bunds divided the shallow water into numerous squares and triangles, few of which were more than two hundred yards across. *Kikar* trees and high grass grew thickly along the bunds, which were fringed with reeds and red water-weeds, and the guns with their loaders and beaters took up positions along them at intervals of fifty to a hundred yards apart.

Winter had seated herself on the hard ground with her back to a tree trunk a few yards from where her husband had taken up his stand, and she took off her wide-brimmed hat and let the faint breeze ruffle her hair. There was a continuous coming and going among the thousands of waterfowl who blackened the open water, and the noise of quacking and quarrelling birds and the ruffle of wings made a soothing and monotonous music. The

bright morning sunlight chequered the banks with patterns of
light and shade, and the sky no longer appeared to weigh down
upon the wide earth as it seemed sometimes to do in the heat of
the day, but to curve high and cool and cloudless; as full of peace
and serenity as the placid water that reflected it.

A green-bronze feather drifted down through the warm air and
came to rest in Winter's lap, and looking at it she thought of all
the far places to which the birds would soon go, and all the
strange, wild forests and lakes and tundras that they would see.
They would go to Central Asia and Outer Mongolia and Siberia;
but they would come back again to Hazrat Bagh—flight upon
flight of mallard and teal, widgeon, pintail and pink-feet, white-
fronted geese and the long-legged storks who built their nests
and reared their foolish, flapping babies in the isolated *kikar*
trees that grew out in the open water. And in the summer there
would still be the doves and the hoopoes, the black-and-white king-
fishers, the green pigeons and the blue jays, and a hundred other
birds and beasts who lived their placid lives beside the jheel. . . .

A little striped squirrel which had crept within a yard of
Winter's foot whisked away with an indignant chirr, and turning to see what had alarmed it, she saw the loader hand her husband a gun, and was seized with a sudden, desperate desire to
cry out to him, begging him not to fire.

The first shot broke the drowsy, murmurous peace of the
morning with a shattering impact. It was followed by a crashing
fusillade and a sound that Winter had never heard before—the
slow, rushing roar of a hundred thousand birds rising off the
water—and the day was no longer peaceful, but full of noise and
violence.

The quiet air was ripped by wings and deafening explosions
that crashed and echoed and crashed again as the panic-stricken
birds whirled towards the bunds, banked and rose, wheeled and
broke, to sweep up over the tree-tops and rise higher and higher
in dark, lacy patterns against the high blue sky. And then the
birds began to fall; plummeting into the water to float inertly or
flutter wounded into the temporary shelter of the reeds.

Winter stood up, backed against the rough bark of the tree, and pressed her hands over her ears to keep out the noise of the shots and the shouting; staring in shuddering horror at the falling birds and their helpless dying flurries as they strove to dive and could not do so, or thrashed upon the water with broken wings, striving to evade the men who waded in to retrieve them, but whose caste forbade them to put a dying creature out of its misery. She shut her eyes, trying to shut out the sight; but she could not shut out the sounds. And then something crashed through the thin branches and struck against her, and she opened her eyes to see a huge goose struggling on the ground at her feet. It dragged itself away, one wing trailing and its beak wide as though it gasped from fear or for air.

'Good shot, that!' commented Conway lumbering up. 'Better wring its neck, or it'll get away. Surprising how tough these birds are——'

He stooped, but Winter was before him. She caught the great bird in her arms, her face white with all the accumulated pain and horror and panic of the last months, and backed away from him, her mouth open in a soundless scream.

'Here, give it to me,' said Conway. 'Can't kill it yourself. You'll find it takes a deal of doing.'

'Don't touch it!' The words were almost a scream. 'It's only hurt. It isn't going to die! You shan't kill it!'

Conway stared, his pale eyes bulging with anger. 'Don't be a fool! Put it down at once, d'you hear me!'

He lurched towards her and Winter evaded him with a frantic leap, and turning, fled down the bund clutching the wounded bird to her breast, its warm neck across her shoulder and one huge helpless wing almost brushing the ground as she ran.

The bund bent at a right angle less than fifty yards from where her husband had taken up his position, and high grass closed in about it, reaching up to the lower branches of the thorn-trees. Winter ran blindly, in the grip of a breathless, reasonless, gasping panic, and she did not see Alex until she had run into him.

Alex had been given a less exposed position just beyond the

turn of the bund, but he had not been shooting well that morning. He had been thinking of other things. Seeing at last and
very clearly the reason for this elaborate shooting-party, and
wondering why it had not occurred to him before, when it was
so simple and so entirely obvious. Was it this climate? Did the
hot suns that sapped one's strength also slow down one's thinking?
Well, it was too late now. He should have stopped it before.
How? Barton would never have let him. But perhaps—who
knew—it would cut both ways. So simple, and yet he had not
seen it!

'*Mark!*' yelled an unseen man—Captain Garrowby of the
93rd—from fifty yards farther down the tree-shaded bund. A
lone goose swished overhead and Alex fired and saw the bird fall
wounded somewhere along the further arm of the bund. Niaz
gave a grunt of disapproval and Alex threw the gun across to him
and said: 'Damn the birds!' He turned away and walked towards
the turn of the bund, feeling in his pockets for a cigarette, and
Winter brushed through the grass and stumbled against him.

Alex caught her by the shoulders and held them in a hard
grasp, staring down into the wide, panic-stricken eyes. For a
moment she had tried to wrench herself free, and then she had
seen who it was who held her.

'*Alex!*—Alex, don't let him kill it! Don't let him——' She
thrust the warm heavy body at him, and as she did so the soft,
feathered neck slid down from her shoulder and hung limp.

'It's dead, dear,' said Alex quietly, and took it from her.

'No! no! it can't be dead. It was only wounded.' Her dress
was splotched and spattered with bright scarlet drops, and a wide
patch of blood stained the breast of the grey habit as though it
were she who had been shot, and not the bird; and at the sight
of it a savage wave of fear lashed at Alex as though something
had struck him over the heart.

He let the bird slip to the grass, and Winter caught at his arm
as though she would have snatched it from him. And then quite
suddenly she dropped her head against him and wept.

Alex stood very still, holding her: feeling the shuddering of

M*

the slim warm body under his hands. Her hair smelt faintly of lavender as it had on the walls of Delhi, and he held her quite gently because he wanted so much to hold her hard against him —because he wanted so much to thrust her away from him. The sound of that helpless broken sobbing tore at his heart, and his face above her bent head was twisted with pain and scored with harsh lines that had not been there before. 'Oh God,' thought Alex, 'not this! Not now. I can't stand it!' The sun was hot on his shoulders and the warm silence was drowsy with the hum of bees among the *kikar* blossoms and sweet with the scent of lavender, and the crackle of shots seemed to come from very far off as though he were hearing them from the other end of a long tunnel. At last the choking, shuddering sobs quietened and ceased, and he put her gently away from him.

She made no attempt to turn away, but stood facing him, her long lashes sticking wetly together and her face streaked with tears, searching in the pocket of her habit for a handkerchief. It was a flimsy enough affair, and stained too with the blood that had run down the great wing. Alex produced his own and handed it over. His nostrils were pinched and there was a white shade about his mouth, but he spoke quite pleasantly. 'Try this one,' he advised. 'It's larger and a good deal cleaner.'

He watched her with a wrenching tenderness as she dried her eyes and blew her small nose with a complete lack of self-consciousness, and wondered how many women would have been sufficiently oblivious of their own looks as to face his direct gaze instead of turning away to repair the ravages of tear stains and dishevelled hair.

Winter folded his handkerchief into a careful square and drew a deep breath. 'I'm sorry,' she said, her voice under control once more. 'I don't know why I should have behaved so stupidly.'

She considered the matter gravely, looking down at the dead bird that lay beside them on the grass, its strong wings and soft breast dabbled with bright blood, and said slowly: 'I think it was because it was such a lovely day, and when the shooting began that seemed to make it worse—because it had been so beautiful before, and so peaceful. I couldn't bear it being spoilt. And then the goose came down on top of me, and it was hurt. Conway wounded it—he wanted to kill it, and . . .'

'I wounded it,' said Alex.

'You?' She looked up at him, startled, frowning a little.

'Yes. I saw it fall and I was coming to get it.'

'Oh.' She was silent for a moment or two and Alex, watching her, said gently: 'Does that make a difference?'

Her gaze came back to him and she said thoughtfully: 'Yes. But I don't know why it should.'

'Better?—or worse?'

She did not answer him and Alex lifted a hand that was not entirely steady and brushed his fingers lightly across her forehead: 'Don't frown, dear. It can't matter as much as all that. Give me that handkerchief.'

She held it out to him and he took it and pushed through the grass and reeds to the water's edge, and returning with it wet and dripping, washed the worst of the stains from her habit, remarking that it would dry very quickly in the sun. 'And now come and try a shot at the duck yourself. You've never tried to fire a sporting-gun.'

Winter shuddered and jerked back, her face blank with hurt, and Alex met the look squarely. 'You think that's callous and brutal of me, don't you?—after what has just happened. But it's sense, you know. Like getting back into the saddle after you have been badly thrown, when you're learning to ride. Didn't they ever make you do that? And you'll find that hitting a moving target isn't as easy as you think. It takes a lot of skill, and that makes a difference too.'

Winter said, shuddering: 'I don't want to kill anything—*anything!* And if I did hit a bird I might only wound it, and not kill it outright. Like—like that goose.'

Alex said with deliberate harshness: 'What do you suppose happens to any wild creature when it gets old? Nine times out of ten it dies a slow and very painful death. And it's the same with most of the animals in this country. I passed a buffalo yesterday that had fallen into a nullah and broken two of its legs. The crows had already picked out its eyes and the pariah dogs were tearing at it. It was near the village track and twenty people an hour passed it, but though it was still alive not one of them thought of killing it.'

Winter swallowed convulsively. 'Did you kill it?'

'I did. And got lectured by the local Brahmin for doing so: a friend of mine, but bigoted. Shooting duck isn't really slaughter, whatever you may think. For one thing it's food, and none of it will be wasted. And it takes skill. You may not like the idea of trying it yourself, but it will take the bad taste out of your mouth to see it in a different light. An antidote to sentimentality.'

His voice was suddenly mocking and devoid of pity or sympathy, and its hardness had a tonic effect upon Winter. She had needed that hardness. She came reluctantly, but she came. Alex handed her a gun and gave a few brief directions.

'You won't find it the same as firing at a stationary object. Swing with your mark and allow for its speed. Those are pintail coming in from your left. Now——!' Winter fired, and the three birds that had been flying towards her jinked and rose and were gone. 'Not far enough ahead. Try again.'

He made her fire again and again, and after the first three or four attempts the panic and sick distaste that had begun to rise again to her throat died down, and she thought only of the science and theory of the shot, concentrating tensely on the flashing marks, so that when, fifteen minutes later, Alex took the gun from her and demonstrated, bringing down two birds within a yard of each other, interest had replaced horror.

'Well?' enquired Alex, looking down at her where she sat among the freckled shadows. 'Feeling better about it now?'

Winter nodded. 'Yes. But I still don't want to shoot anything myself.'

'There's no reason why you should. But a sense of proportion is a useful thing to cultivate.' He laid the gun away and sat down on the warm grass beside her. 'I've suffered from the same kind of mental indigestion myself. I killed something the other day—not for food nor even for the sport of trying out my skill on a difficult target, but for revenge and because I was in a damnably bad temper. I wasn't sorry for it, but it seemed point-less, and for some reason or other I lost a lot of sleep over it—at least ten minutes!'

'A man?' asked Winter with a catch in her voice.

Alex gave a short laugh. 'No. That is where the inconsistency comes in. I killed a man not so long ago for precisely the same reasons; but it did not seem in the least pointless, and neither did I lose any sleep over it. Don't let yourself get hurt by some-thing like this——' he jerked his chin in the general direction of the jheel. 'Put it in its proper place. I dislike these large-scale *battues* myself. I prefer to do my shooting on my own, or with one or two people at most, instead of indulging in this type of mass slaughter.'

'Then why did you come?—if you knew what it would be like?'

'Curiosity. I wanted to see if I could find out why Kishan Prasad and his friends had arranged this elaborate shoot.'

'And have you found out?'

'Yes.'

Alex did not add anything to the affirmative, but looked out across the stretch of sunlit water that lay beyond a narrow belt of grass and reeds fringing the bund, his eyes narrowed against the sun glare. There were fewer birds moving now, for many had risen far out of range and were making for the quieter reaches of the river or the jheels within the borders of Oudh, and those that remained were too wild to offer a reasonable mark. The firing had died down to no more than an occasional shot, and a warm sleepy silence returned to the morning, broken only by the soft monotonous cooing of the imperturbable doves.

Winter pulled a grass stem and bit it thoughtfully, watching Alex's brown profile against the sharp criss-cross lines of sunlight that fell between the branches of the *kikar* trees and the tall spears of dry grass. His silence contained no quality of withdrawal, and presently she said: 'Why do you think that they gave this duck shoot?'

'Hmm?' said Alex absently.

Winter repeated the question.

'It isn't a duck shoot,' said Alex, his eyes still on the glittering expanse of water. 'That was merely a means to an end—and also, possibly, a rehearsal.'

'A rehearsal? I don't understand. What are they rehearsing for?'

'They aren't. We are very kindly doing it for them.'

He stretched out at full length and turned, facing her: 'It was quite simple really. Lunjore lies across one of the main roadways into Oudh, and that road crosses an iron bridge ten miles to the south. If there was a rising in the Punjab, or Delhi way, we could hold that bridge; or if the worst came to the worst, blow it up and not only isolate ourselves from rebel troops, but prevent them from using this route into Oudh, which is at the moment a hot-bed of disaffection. There is an arsenal at Suthragunj. A very large one which is, in my opinion, inadequately protected against the possibility of a large-scale rising. Some of our local talukdars have not missed that point, and under cover of a lavish and well-organized entertainment for the garrisons and officials of both districts they have constructed a very adequate road that avoids the bridge and brings Suthragunj within roughly twenty miles of us. We have very kindly tested it for them, both from the point of surface and timing, by driving a variety of carriages along it, while the officers from Suthragunj have done the same from the opposite direction. And where a carriage can go, guns and ammunition-wagons can follow.'

Alex rolled over on his back with his hands linked beneath his head and watched an industrious procession of red ants hurrying along the underside of a branch above him, and presently Winter said a little uncertainly: 'Are you—do you really think that there is going to be trouble?'

She had half-expected that he would not reply, for Alex when he chose to answer a question did not lie, and she knew that the majority of men, when faced with such a query from a woman, would resort to denial or some soothing generality; but Alex said bluntly: 'Not trouble. A rising. Yes, I do. I've thought so for about five years. We've been asking for it. Napier warned us that there would be one sooner or later if certain reforms were not instituted, but no one paid any attention to him. We cherish a theory that to listen to warnings, or act upon them, is a sign of panic and shows loss of confidence, and we would rather lose our lives any day than be accused of either. It is an exasperating trait. The kind that curls in on itself and ends by eating its own tail, because precautions that are not taken in time of peace cannot be taken when a crisis is imminent, for the simple reason that to take them then creates panic and loss of confidence at a time when one can afford to do neither.'

'What will happen?' asked Winter.

Alex was silent for a moment or two, and when he spoke his voice held a savage bitterness that startled her:

'We shall see the ruin, in one day or in twenty days, of what might have been the finest army in the world. We shall build it up again, but it will never be quite the same. We shall turn half the army against its fellows, and play off Sikh against Mussulman and Mussulman against Hindu and Gurkhas against both. There will be atrocities on both sides—all sides. The East drops straight into barbarism when it is frightened or enraged, and we shall follow its example and call it revenge—as I myself have done! There will be murders and massacres, for these people have no conception of the ultimate strength that we can bring out of Europe against them, and they imagine that they can stamp us out—' Once again Alex was talking more to himself than to Winter—talking angrily and despairingly:

'Even men like Kishan Prasad have no idea what they are challenging. Kishan Prasad watched the shambles at Sebastopol when the Russians threw us back and we failed to take the Redan. He saw the mess and the muddle and the raging incompetence, and missed the fact that, despite it, sheer physical courage and guts and endurance triumphed over it. He and men like him do not realize that even if they murder every white man, woman and child in the whole of India, England, and not

John Company, will go on sending out troops until she has smashed all opposition. And the reprisals that will follow will leave a legacy of hatred that will be handed down to future generations, from father to son and from mother to daughter. We shall forget—but they will not!'

A breath of breeze whispered across the jheel, ruffling the water and rustling through the reeds and the harsh grasses, and bringing a sharp reek of black powder to mingle with the faint scent of the yellow, mimosa-like blossoms of the *kikar* trees and the dusty incense of the dried grass. There was another burst of firing from away to the left and the voice of Captain Garrowby arose once more upon the quiet air: '*Mark!*'

A dozen teal, bunched together, swished overhead almost brushing the tree-tops with their wings, and Alex came reluctantly to his feet. 'Energetic beggar——' He appeared to refer to Captain Garrowby. 'Perhaps I had better do something towards upholding the honour of the visiting team.' He glanced down at Winter and said: 'Your habit seems to have dried. Hadn't you better be getting back?'

Winter ignored the remark. 'Is that why you wanted me to go to the hills?—and taught me to shoot?' she enquired, leaping womanlike from the general to the personal.

'Yes,' said Alex briefly and without qualifying the statement.

Winter stood up and shook out the grey folds of her skirt. She said quite lightly, 'I will think about it,' and was turning away when she remembered the goose. She hesitated for a moment and then said a little diffidently: 'The—that goose. Conway thought that he had shot it. Can I take it back? Then perhaps he will not be so——'

She stopped, flushing painfully, and bit her lip; suddenly ashamed of her desire to placate her husband in this unworthy manner. But Conway would be angry enough as it was, and she could not bear another scene just now.

Alex was watching a flight of mallard who were approaching from the open water, too high to allow them to pass within range. He said: 'Of course,' without turning his head.

He did not look round as she went away, but he heard the tall grass rustle behind her, and he stood quite still, listening until he could hear it no longer; his face drawn and bleak in the harsh sunlight.

'Why,' demanded Alex, asking the despairing question that has been asked so often of heaven, 'does this have to happen to me?'

An hour and a half later a horn blew, conjuring odd echoes from the water and the wandering, intersecting lines of the bunds. Beaters and shikarris collected the dead birds, and the guns walked back to the tents where refreshments awaited them. During the afternoon they had walked up partridge and sand grouse over the open country to the west of the jheel, leaving the duck to settle again, and Alex had walked alone with Kishan Prasad to the top of a low stony ridge that overlooked the distant jheel, and spoken bluntly and to the point, telling him what he had told Winter earlier that day—that British regiments would be sent out to take over the country if the Company fell.

'If the Company fall, it is enough,' said Kishan Prasad. 'If I can but live to see that, I will die content.'

'We shall still hold India,' said Alex. 'If it takes a year— five years, ten, twenty!—we shall go on fighting you, if only for the sake of one thing—the women. If there is a rising there will be women of ours, and children too—many of them—who will be murdered by your friends without mercy. Who should know that better than you, who were at Khanwai? You will not be able to prevent it, and it is the one thing that my countrymen will not forgive. All else perhaps, but not that. Their deaths will arouse a hatred and a rage that will seek only revenge and not rest until it is obtained. And that revenge will fall on the heads of the innocent as well as the guilty, because men are blinded by such rage. I have seen troops run amuck, and it is not pleasant. In the last it will be your own people who will suffer most, and they will suffer to no purpose, for you will not be rid of us. We shall send out more and more British regiments.'

'You will find it too costly,' said Kishan Prasad. 'Your Queen and your Queen's Ministers will say, "Let be. It is not worth it."'

'Never. You do not understand. We are a rising power, and with every day we become richer and more powerful. When we have had our day the time may come when we will stomach an affront, and turn from a fight. But not now. Not yet.'

'Then I will wait for that day,' said Kishan Prasad softly. 'And if I am dead, then my son will be ready—or if it be not him, then his son's son—or the son of that son! Would you yourself not do likewise?'

Alex did not answer and Kishan Prasad repeated the question in Urdu, using the familiar title: 'Tell me, Sahib, wouldst thou not do likewise, wert thou of my blood and this thine own land?'

Alex stared at him, his eyes hot with a helpless anger that was as much against himself as Kishan Prasad, and he said violently and as though the words were wrenched from him: '*Yes*—God damn you!' and turning on his heel he walked blindly away without once looking back to where Kishan Prasad followed more slowly behind him.

24

THE carriages and the ladies had left Hazrat Bagh early so as to get home before dark, but the guns had remained to shoot once more on the jheel, and had ridden back three hours later by the light of a half-moon to attend a large party given by the Commissioner to round off the day's festivities.

The gathering at the Residency had consisted of the larger part of those who had been at Hazrat Bagh, and had included the members of a self-styled Italian Opera Company who had sung excerpts from a number of light operas and followed them by a selection of popular songs.

Alex, who had attended the party, had arrived in a singularly unpleasant frame of mind, and for perhaps for the first time in his life had deliberately set himself to drink too much. The Commissioner's port, wine and brandy were of the best obtainable, but they had little effect upon Alex beyond increasing his ill temper, which the sight of Mr. Barton openly making amorous advances to Signorina Aurora Resina, the auburn-haired ornament of the Opera Company, did nothing to mitigate.

It had been verging on midnight when a not unpleasing baritone voice embarked upon a familiar ballad:

> *Believe me, if all those endearing young charms,*
> *Which I gaze on so fondly today,*
> *Were to change by tomorrow, and fleet in my arms . . .*

The music and a memory hit at Alex with an unexpected, wrenching pain, and some control in him seemed to snap, as though a wire drawn taut had parted. He put down his glass, walked across the room and calmly removed Signorina Aurora from the Commissioner's orbit. He had some experience of such women, and he had drunk enough to make him reckless for once of arousing the Commissioner's animosity. It suddenly did not seem to matter any longer if he did so or not. And there was Winter, who should not be made to endure the insult of her husband's behaviour towards this ogling actress. But he did not want to think of Winter. . . .

Alex could be charming enough when he chose, and he chose now. He had blandly ignored the glowering indignation of his chief, the hostility of Colonel Moulson and the momentary shock he had seen on Winter's face, and had taken the lady away— ostensibly to view the garden by moonlight. They had not returned, though the majority of the guests, despite a long and tiring day spent in the open, had stayed until well after two o'clock. The Commissioner had been crudely outspoken on the subject of Captain Randall's behaviour when the guests had departed, and had ended by observing that Lou Cottar had been right about the man, by God!—he was a dark horse, and they were always the worst with women: trust a woman like Lou to know! Lou had said that Randall was no cold fish, and he'd

certainly taken home a hot enough piece to keep him warm
tonight! It was only he, Conway Barton, who had a curst cold
fish on his hands.

The Commissioner had returned to the deserted drawing-room
to drink more brandy, and Winter had gone to her room and had
sat for a long time on the edge of her bed, staring before her and
thinking of Alex: Alex with his hard, nervous fingers caressing
another woman's hair; Alex's slow kisses on another woman's
mouth, and his dark head lying pillowed on that opulent powdered breast or buried in the suspicious brightness of those auburn
curls.

She had cried only that morning for a dead bird. No, surely
not for a dead bird?—for the wanton destruction of something
beautiful. Was it for the beautiful day, or the strong, beautiful
bird? or for her illusions and all that had happened to them? She
did not know. But she could not cry now because Alex could be
like Carlyon and Colonel Moulson, and—and Conway.

'I must go away,' thought Winter, as she had thought on that
day when she had first discovered that she loved Alex. 'I will
go home to the Gulab Mahal. If only I can get back there I shall
be safe again—safe from everything.' And she thought, as she
had thought so often, of the rose-pink walls and brilliant flowers;
of the brightly coloured birds which had been so tame that
they had allowed her to touch them, and of old Aziza Begum's
comfortable sandalwood-scented lap where she had sat in the
warm, star-twinkled dusk to listen to tales of Gods and Heroes.

'I will go back,' thought Winter staring dry-eyed into the
shadows of her room. 'If only I can get back I can start again . . .'

She had fallen asleep at last, fully clothed, and she had not
ridden that day, either in the morning or the evening, because
she had been afraid of seeing Alex.

She had not seen him again for some considerable time. Alex
had taken care of that. The night he had spent in the arms of
la Resina had resolved nothing and solved no problems. It had
not even made him forget, as he held her, the feel of Winter's
slim body in his arms. In the cold grey light of the early morning

the auburn-haired Aurora had looked blowsy and coarse—the lip rouge with which she had deepened the red of her pouting mouth smeared and ugly, and the black from her lashes smudging her cheeks. She smelt faintly of perspiration and rice powder and overpoweringly of patchouli, and Alex had looked at her with impatience and pity and a twinge of disgust, and thought of Winter sobbing jerkily against his shoulder for the death of a wild bird. And had found that his anger had not evaporated with the morning but was still a hard hot stone in his breast. The complexity of his emotions exasperated him, and he had woken the woman and driven her back in the dawn light to the dâk bungalow where the troupe were lodging.

He had attended no more parties at the Residency, and he had not ridden again with Winter. His bungalow had not seen him for days at a time, for he spent more and more of his time in the outlying villages of the district, picking up what information he could between and in the course of his official duties, and doing what lay in his power to allay the uneasiness that he could see and sense in and behind every cautiously worded greeting or enquiry.

The villagers would bring him rumours—tales such as the story of the bone-dust that was reported to have been mixed with the Government flour—and he would deny them, explaining and exhorting, and his listeners would agree. Yes, yes, he was right. The Huzoor was right. It was only a tale, and untrue. A tale spread by evil men to alarm the simple . . . But he knew that they did not eat the flour and that it lay rotting in the Government-stamped sacks in warehouses and carts.

He could not reach them. Their processes of thought were not of the West. They accepted an order if it were backed by force, but that did not mean that it was of itself acceptable. They respected Alex, and many of them liked him; but he was a *feringhi*—a foreigner. Impassable gulfs gaped between them, and they looked at each other helplessly across them, seeing the same things by entirely different lights and weighing them by different standards so that they appeared as dissimilar as rocks and rivers. Is there a meeting-point? thought Alex. Is there any real neutral ground? But there was Niaz, who was as much his friend as William. How did one explain his strong kinship for this man of his own age who would turn from his own race to serve one of alien blood?

He had asked Niaz that question one evening when they were lying up in a patch of high grass waiting for a slow-moving herd of blackbuck to pass within range—Alex was in camp and they were shooting for the pot—and Niaz had replied lightly: 'I have eaten the Company's salt.'

'That is no answer. Many have done that, but the bread that is eaten is soon forgotten.'

Niaz shrugged. 'We are brothers, thou and I. Who can say why? Were I a dog of a Hindu I would say that perchance in some other life we were indeed kin, for I have met none other among thy race whose mind I knew—or cared to know. Yet I know thine.'

'And if it come to bloodshed, as it may come, wouldst thou stay with me against thine own kin?'

'*Beshak!*' the answer was prompt and leisurely. 'I owe thee my life—and thine is forfeit to me. That alone were a rope that is hard to cut. Quiet, now!—they move this way . . .'

It was Niaz who had brought him a copy of a pamphlet that was being circulated in the city calling on all Mohammedans to prepare for a *Jehad*—a Holy War. 'This thing is in the hands of all Mussulmans,' said Niaz, 'and in the mosques also they preach a *Jehad*. I have heard too that it has been promised that Ghazi-ud-din Bahadur Shah, the King of Delhi, shall be restored to his own, so that once more the Mogul will rule in Hind.'

'And what say the Hindus who hear such talk?' asked Alex.

'They do not speak against it. And that is a strange thing, for they would not wish to see us rule them as once we did. Yet they say that they will accept the Mogul because he is of Hind, and no foreigner. Sikandar Dulkhan (Alexander the Great)'—Niaz looked at Alex with a half-smile—'I will fight at thy side and take thy orders when the bloodshed begins—and *I* do not say "if it begin"!—but I too would like to see a Mussulman rule once more in Delhi; Sunni though he be, while we of my family be Shiahs!'

Alex said: 'Art thou so sure then that it will come to an uprising?'

'As sure as thou art! And were it not for thee I myself might well cry *Deen! Deen!* for the Faith.'

Alex shivered involuntarily. He had heard that fanatical war-cry in his time, and seen the green flags wave and the hot-eyed hordes of the Faithful sweep yelling up to and on to and over the guns, and he had not forgotten. He said now: 'Who is behind this thing that comes? Is it the Hindu or the Mussulman? Or is it the work of foreigners—Russians and Persians?'

Niaz laughed and made a gesture of negation with his hand. 'There are many Russian spies; and Persian too. They, the Russ-*log*, plot with both, as is their custom—but always against thy people! And in despite of the police and the spies of the Company they still go about the land, even to the walls of Delhi, bringing money and arms and many promises, and their sayings and promises are printed openly in the Hindu press. But their words are of little account: they help to boil the pot, that is all. Nay! this that will come is the Rising of the Moon,' said Niaz with oriental imagery. 'We who were once great in the land have lost almost all that we had of power; and Revolt may serve us where Peace will not. This will be a *Jehad*—and I think it comes close. Dost thou remember the day preceding the earth-quake at Hoti Mardan?'

Alex nodded. He knew only too well what Niaz meant, for he too was aware of an ominous feeling of expectant stillness. But it was a stillness that was not to last long, and the first warning mutter came from far-away Bengal.

The thing that Alex had visualized in the moment following Niaz's casual comment on the greased cartridge-paper—the fire that unthinking officialdom had put into the hands of Kishan Prasad and his like—had caught the fuel that officialdom had itself prepared. And the fuel was dry and ready.

On that same January morning that had seen the garrison of

Lunjore ride gaily out to shoot duck at Hazrat Bagh, a man of low caste, a lascar who worked in the ammunition factory at Dum Dum near Calcutta, had stopped a high-caste sepoy during the heat of the day and begged a drink from his *lotah*—the brass water-pot carried by every caste Hindu and religiously preserved from defilement. The sepoy had stared less in anger than astonishment at the outrageous request. 'How can that be, fool? I am a Brahmin, and my caste forbids it.'

'Caste? What is caste?' grinned the lascar. 'The cartridges that we prepare here are defiled with the fat of hogs and cattle, and soon ye will be as one—casteless together—when the new guns are given out to the *pultons* and ye bite the cartridges daily.'

'What is that?' said the sepoy thickly. 'Tell again!'

The lascar had done so, with embellishments, and the sepoy had not waited to hear to the end, but had run to his comrades in the lines. Here was proof at last of the duplicity of the *feringhis*! The hated policies of Annexation and Lapse, the suppression of *suttee*, the seizure of land, the deposing of kings and the curtailment of pay and power and privilege were as nothing to this; for this struck at the deepest beliefs of men, in that it destroyed their souls.

Hindu and Mohammedan together recoiled in horror from sacrilege and defilement. Panic spread through the lines, and from there, with the incredible swiftness that fear lends to evil tidings, it swept out across India, its progress sped and fanned by those who had been ready and waiting for such an opportunity, and who made the best use of this brand that had been given into their hands.

A hundred men—a hundred thousand—picked up the fearful whisper and passed it on: 'It is an order from *Belait*! from the Queen and her Council, that by means of the cartridges all sepoys, both Mussulman and Hindu, be defiled—as all men in the towns and cities are defiled by the eating of bone-dust in their flour—so that being made casteless they shall do the will of the Sahib-*log* as slaves for ever! We are betrayed by the *feringhis* who have stolen our country and now wish to steal our souls!'

It was then that the nocturnal fires started. The thatch of an officer's bungalow would catch fire, set alight, more often than not, by a blazing arrow shot by some unseen hand. The telegraph station of the big cantonment of Barrackpore burned to the ground, and night after night, despite guards and sentries, flames would glow bright in the darkness, spreading up northward from Calcutta and Barrackpore.

There were midnight meetings of men with muffled faces who kept to the shadows of walls and where no guards challenged them. There were letters—for the sepoy had learned to use the post in the days before the privilege of free postage to the army had been abolished. Letters that went out by every dâk, calling upon the soldiery to resist the attempts to defile them. The news that the 19th Regiment of Native Infantry at Berhampur, a hundred miles to the north of Calcutta, had broken out into mutiny spread upwards through India and fanned the panic.

But that mutiny which had flared up so suddenly died out, and without violence. An enquiry into the question of the greased cartridges was instituted and proceeded upon its ponderous way, and officers who had begun to eye the men under their command with an anxiety they would not own to, relaxed again.

The rumours died down, and the Commissioner of Lunjore, who had consistently pooh-poohed the possibility of any serious trouble arising, remarked complacently that he had always known it was a mere tempest in a tea-pot, and there was too much panic about among fellows who ought to know better. Why, he had even heard some preposterous story of a manifesto being circulated to all Mohammedans calling for a *Jehad*! All nonsense, of course! There hadn't been any such thing circulated in *his* district.

'About eight hundred of them, I think, sir,' said Alex expressionlessly.

'*What's that?*' The Commissioner's voice had cracked with angry amazement. 'You're telling me we've had 'em in Lunjore? Then why the devil wasn't I told!'

'You were, sir. I sent in a full report—in triplicate. It will be somewhere in the files.'

'Oh,' said the Commissioner, disconcerted. He glowered angrily for a moment or two and then observed sulkily that he hadn't the time to read every damned, panicky paper that came into the office.

Relieved by the passing of the temporary uneasiness caused by the cartridge scare and the abortive mutiny of the 19th N.I., he had at long last turned his attention to the question of leave, and a visit to the Casa de Ballesteros in Lucknow.

25

THERE was nothing in Winter's first sight of the beautiful, barbaric city of Lucknow that awoke even an echo of memory, and her father's house was as unfamiliar to her as the city had been. But the golden ghost of Sabrina would have found little changed, for the years had been kind to the House of the Peacocks. The groves of lemon and orange and pomegranate still scented the twilight, and the fountains still made a splashing, tinkling music in the patios. The peacocks cried at dusk and dawn, and often Winter would find a glittering gold-powdered tail-feather on the grass or the stone flags of the river terrace. The servants would collect the fallen feathers, tying them together and using the gorgeous things to dust the carved furniture and the dark, magnificent portraits that her grandfather, Don Ramon, had brought from Spain.

But although she had returned at last to Lucknow she did not find there the haven and the homecoming for which she had longed, for the city seethed with bitterness and rage and rumours, and the Gulab Mahal was closed to her.

Ameera's husband, Walayat Shah, had at no time felt any friendship towards the British, but he had admired force—when it was successful—and as long as the British won battles and crowned their mercenary armies with glory he had been prepared to view them with toleration and a certain degree of respect. Now, however, they had deprived him at one stroke of all rights and privileges and put an end to his means of livelihood, so that almost overnight, from holding a position of some power and authority, he had become little more than a pauper; forced even to prove his right before a British official to land that his family had held for generations, and which was now his only source of income. And the proving of such rights, in a land where the sword had always carried more weight than the pen, was no easy matter when written evidence of possession was almost non-existent.

Walayat Shah's toleration of the *feringhis* changed to a corroding and vindictive hatred. And with that hatred had arisen, like a phoenix from the fire, the memory of the past glories of his race. He had rarely thought of the history of his people while the Muslim Kingdom of Oudh still stood, but now that Oudh, almost the last Mohammedan state in India, had fallen, he and many like him turned to look back on that glorious past when the horned moon of Islam had blazed above India from Peshawar to the Deccan, and the Great Moguls had ruled all Hind. The fire of that great Empire had sunk now to a feeble flicker, as though it had been no more than the light of a thousand *chirags*—the small oil-lamps lit for such festivals as Dewali—that together blaze like a golden bonfire, but which die out one by one as the oil burns low or the night winds blow. Only a few of the lamps that had once made that bright glare now remained, for the hot winds of the warlike Marathas, of the Rajputs, of Guru Nanak, founder of the Sikhs, had extinguished them one by one. And now a greater wind had arisen: the cold wind of John Company, blowing in from beyond the Black Water and breathing on the last dying flicker of the Empire of the Moguls.

The British had conquered the conquerors: Maratha, Rajput and Sikh; and now if the British themselves were to fall, chaos would follow. Out of that chaos might not the moon of Islam rise once more, and the followers of the Prophet rule the land as they had ruled it in the great days of Akbar—of Jehangir—of Shahjehan—of Aurungzebe, '*Holder of the World*'?

Walayat Shah, brooding on present calamity and past glory, listened to the words of those who preached a *Jehad*, and dreamed the Mohammedan dream. For now a *Jehad* meant far more than the spreading of the Faith and the slaying of Unbelievers. It meant revenge: and perhaps, once more, an Empire.

'He is changed even toward me, his wife,' said Ameera sadly. 'And therefore I cannot ask thee to enter the Gulab Mahal. Some day, surely; when all this has passed. But for the present it were wiser to keep away.'

Winter had come back at last to Lucknow, but not to that charmed and peaceful starting-point whence she had hoped to draw strength and find a purpose in the pattern of her life. She had seemed within reach of it at last, but she might not stretch out her hand and touch it. The door was barred against her.

Sir Henry Lawrence, perhaps the best-loved man in India, had arrived in Lucknow late in March to take over the administration of Oudh from Mr. Coverley Jackson. He was aged by grief and disappointment, and in failing health, but at Canning's request he had once again abandoned the hope of sorely needed Home leave and had hurried to the help of Oudh. '. . . *man can die but once,*' wrote Lawrence to his friend and pupil Herbert Edwardes, '*and if I die in Oudh—after saving some poor fellow's health or skin or* izzat (*honour*)—*I shall have no reason for discontent . . . But the price I pay is high for I had set my heart on going Home . . .*'

No one knew better than the man who had settled the conquered Punjab and won the respect and affection of the defeated Sikhs what unavoidable tragedies resulted from such a change of Government, or how best to soften and mitigate the hardships and heartaches and hopelessness that inevitably followed in its wake. The news of his appointment sent a sigh of relief through half India. If anyone could tame the sulky, suspicious, wild-eyed stallion that was Oudh, it was Henry Lawrence.

He was a tall man, thin to emaciation, and his grey hair and straggling beard were already turning white. His haggard, hollow-cheeked face was scored with the lines of weariness and anxiety and the unending strain of sorrow for Honoria, who had died three years before. But the grey deep-set eyes were quiet and far-seeing, and they could still glow with the same fire and fervour and enthusiasm with which he had faced his task as a young man newly come to India.

The Lucknow Residency was always full of guests these days, for the newly appointed Chief Commissioner kept open house for the nobles, landowners and gentry of the district, as one method of inspiring confidence and getting in touch with the opinions prevailing in Oudh. His jurisdiction did not extend beyond the borders of his own province, but as Lunjore touched upon those borders he had been anxious to meet Mr. Barton, of whom he had heard little good. Mr. Barton had not impressed him favourably, but Winter had struck up a friendship with Mrs. Daly, who had been temporarily acting as hostess and housekeeper for Sir Henry, and Mrs. Daly had asked if she might invite Mrs. Barton to spend a few nights at the Residency: a scheme to which Conway had raised no objection, it having occurred to him that his wife's absence would provide an excellent opportunity for him to arrange a few entertainments of his own at the Casa de Ballesteros.

The Residency was a large, three-storeyed building whose deep verandahs and pillared porticoes looked out over the beautiful city and the winding river. It stood on high ground, among green lawns and gardens full of roses and flowering trees that held at bay an area of crowding, crowded buildings that surrounded and pressed about it, and which housed a numberless horde of unemployed musicians, entertainers, and other humble hangers-on of the vanished court of Wajid Ali Shah, last King of Oudh.

'Sir Henry does what he can for them,' Mrs. Daly told Winter, 'but I do not think it can be easy. He cannot give them *all*

employment. But he is always so ready to listen to anyone who
asks for help, and to give any aid he can. I think a great deal of
it comes from his own pocket. I do not believe that there can be
a kinder or more charitable man to be met with anywhere!'

Winter had been happier as Sir Henry's guest than she had
been for months past. The relief of being free of Conway's
society was itself immeasurable, and she had been charmed by
the atmosphere that prevailed at the Residency, and the casual-
ness and complete lack of ceremony shown by its host. But her
peace of mind did not survive the arrival of an unexpected visitor
who walked in on a breakfast-party on the last day of her stay.
The house-party had been animatedly discussing the rival merits
of Buddha and Confucius as religious teachers, when a caller had
been announced, and Captain Daly had looked up and jumped to
his feet:

'Alex—by all that's wonderful!'

Winter had been peeling an orange and her hands were suddenly still. As still as her heart. Alex's voice spoke behind her:

'Hullo, Harry; I hadn't heard you were here. I hope you may
forgive me for walking in on you like this, Sir Henry. I arrived
an hour or so ago, but Mr. Barton cannot see me until later, so I
thought——'

'You know that you need no apology for walking in on me at
any hour, Alex,' said Sir Henry, and smiled.

Winter laid the orange down very carefully on her plate and
turned slowly, but Alex was not looking at her. He was not even
aware that she was present. He was looking at his old chief, and
Winter was seized by a helpless, foolish pang of pure jealousy.
A resentment, as keen as it was ridiculous, because neither she
nor any woman would ever be able to bring that look to Alex's
face—or to any man's face.

Sir Henry pushed away his plate and stood up to grip Alex's
hand, and Captain Daly beckoned to a *khitmadgar* to bring
another chair.

'Had any breakfast?' enquired Sir Henry.

'At about five o'clock this morning, sir.'

'Then you can do with another one now. *Hazri lao Sahib kiwasti*, Ahmed Ali. What are you doing in Lucknow, Alex?'

'The Commissioner sent for me, sir.'

Alex's voice was entirely expressionless, but Sir Henry regarded him with a twinkling eye in which there was a good deal of comprehension. 'Called up to explain yourself, eh? What high-handed action have you been taking this time without consulting the higher authorities?'

Alex laughed. 'Something like that. You are too acute, sir.'

'And entirely mannerless, for I have not yet made you known to my guests. But then you know all of them except Dr. Ogilvie, I think. Mrs. Barton is staying with us for a few days to keep Mrs. Daly company.'

Alex looked round with a sudden startled frown in his eyes. 'I'm sorry, Mrs. Barton; I did not see you were here. Hullo, Mrs. Daly. It's good to see you again. How do you do, sir—no, I do not think we have met.'

'How long will you be staying?' enquired Sir Henry.

'Not above a day, I imagine, sir. It depends on the Commissioner, but I hope to start back before dawn tomorrow.'

'Only one night? That is not long. You'll stay here, of course.'

'I would like to, sir, if you are sure——'

'Oh, Mrs. Daly will arrange it. You need not worry. She is in charge just now. I cannot think what I am to do when she leaves me, but her husband is selfishly removing her on the thirteenth. Daly is off to command the Guides.'

Alex turned quickly: 'Is that true? Congratulations, Harry, I had not heard. You always were a lucky devil. Pleased?'

'Who wouldn't be! But I could wish it had come at any other time. It is hard to leave Lucknow just as Sir Henry arrives.'

Sir Henry smiled. 'My dear Harry, don't think that I do not appreciate the compliment, but as I told you before, you could not dream of refusing the finest appointment open to a soldier.'

Alex said: 'You couldn't try pulling a few strings, sir, so that he can stay on here and I can go instead?'

Sir Henry looked at him reflectively. 'I might try, though it would not have a particle of effect. But would you really go if it did?'

Alex returned the look, and his mouth twisted in a wry smile. 'No, sir.' There was an odd note of bitterness in his voice and Sir Henry nodded understandingly: 'I did not think so. Not at this time.' He pushed back his chair and stood up. 'Well, if you will all excuse me, I must go. I'll see you later, Alex. When you have had your wigging!'

The conversation became general after his departure, but though Alex had borne a part in it he had appeared distrait, and Winter found that he did not even glance in her direction. Looking at him across the wide table she was filled with despair. Nothing had changed. She might just as well have never come to Lucknow—have never left Lunjore. She had found no solution to her problems or her unhappiness or her love for Alex. Perhaps there was no solution. And no answer except fortitude.

Alex had left at the conclusion of the meal, and she did not see him again until he entered the crowded drawing-room just before dinner that night. She thought that he looked tired and cross, and she would have given much to have been able to go to him and run her fingers over his forehead to smooth away the frown lines as he had once done to her at Hazrat Bagh. She wondered what he had done that had annoyed Conway sufficiently to send for him to Lucknow at a time like this, and what the interview had been like. She had not seen her husband since her arrival at the Residency, and she found the relief it occasioned her more than a little frightening. Was it really going to be possible to spend the rest of her life in the company of a man whose absence brought her such infinite and blessed relief? Could marriage really be regarded as a sacred and binding sacrament under such conditions?

There had been a large dinner-party that night, and from his seat at the head of the long table Sir Henry's bright, tired gaze had wandered from one to another of his guests and rested on Alex Randall with approval and affection. These were the proper men to govern the country. Men who would keep the peace by mixing freely with the people and doing prompt justice in their shirt-sleeves, and who did not consider *jagirdars* and pensioners as nuisances and enemies. Once, nearly nine years ago, Alex had said hotly in the course of an argument: 'No, I don't believe in a divine right to govern! But I do believe that now we've got this country it is up to us to govern it to the very best of our ability!' He was probably still of the same mind, mused Sir Henry, and he possessed the right kind of ability. He must find an opportunity to talk with Alex during the course of the evening . . .

But it was not until the last carriage had driven away shortly after eleven o'clock, and the house-party had dispersed to their own rooms, that he found himself alone with Captain Randall in the cool darkness of the high verandah.

'Well, Alex?' enquired Sir Henry after an appreciable interval of silence.

Alex turned from his contemplation of the moonlit garden beyond the tall verandah pillars. 'Far from it, sir. Will you forgive me if I omit the reasons for my visit here? I do not feel capable at present of discussing them in a rational manner.'

'In fact,' said Sir Henry softly, 'if anyone were now to offer you command of the Guides you would return a different answer to the one you gave me this morning!'

Alex gave a short laugh. 'If anyone were to offer me any post whatsoever that would enable me to return to regimental duty, I should accept it!'

'Oh, no, you would not,' said Sir Henry placidly. 'If you think that, you know less about yourself than I do. I have been wanting to see you for some weeks past. I would have written, except that there has been so much to do. Colvin gave me news of you when I stayed with him in Agra on my way here. It seems you saw him in October.'

'I did,' said Alex grimly. 'I had a story to tell him which he was not prepared to believe.'

'So I gathered,' said Sir Henry settling himself comfortably in a long verandah chair. 'Perhaps you will find me less hard to convince. Sit down and tell me about it.'

N

'Thank you, sir, but I think I'll stand. I have had a long spell in the saddle, and there is another ahead of me in the morning.'

'Can you not stay over tomorrow? We have the Nana of Bithor in Lucknow on a visit, and I shall be seeing him tomorrow. I have my suspicions of the Nana Sahib, and I should be interested to hear what you make of him. Have you ever met him?'

'No, sir. I missed meeting him once in Delhi, owing to—to unexpected circumstances. And I am afraid that I shall have to miss him again. I cannot delay.'

'I am sorry for it. Tell me this story that you told Colvin. I imagine that your version differs somewhat from his.'

Alex propped his shoulders against the nearest pillar and told again the story he had told in the previous autumn to Mr. Colvin, Lieutenant-Governor of the North-West Provinces, together with much that had happened thereafter.

'I think that it is the army that we have to fear, sir,' he said in conclusion.

'A mutiny,' said Sir Henry quietly. The words were a confirmation rather than a query.

'Yes, sir. Not a spontaneous outbreak, but a planned one set to take place simultaneously in every cantonment in India on a given date. A few months ago I would not have believed such a thing possible, because to achieve it there would have to have been some exceedingly strong grievance that was common to both Mussulmans and Hindus—strong enough to unite them against us. We have, however, very thoughtfully provided that common bond in the greased cartridges. That was all that was needed.'

Sir Henry was silent for a moment or two, stroking his beard, and presently he said gently: 'Any evidence, Alex?'

Alex flung the contents of his glass with a violent gesture over the roses below the verandah rail, and said bitterly: 'None that is acceptable to the Commissioner or those purblind, pig-headed —I beg your pardon, sir!'

Sir Henry laughed and getting up from his chair put out a thin hand, gripping the younger man's shoulder in a hard grasp.

'Hipped, Alex?'

'Damnably,' admitted Alex, meeting his look.

'I know. It's like banging one's head against a stone wall. What's the evidence?'

Alex told him; repeating the words that Kishan Prasad had spoken in the drawing-room of the Residency at Lunjore.

'In the hot weather . . .' said Sir Henry thoughtfully. He had returned to his chair while Alex talked and now he leant back in it, fingering his lip. 'Why are you so sure that he was presenting you with the truth in this oblique manner?'

'I saved his life once,' said Alex shortly. 'It was possibly the greatest mistake I ever made, but he feels some sense of obligation towards me. And I also think he has a liking for Winter—Mrs. Barton. Or else——'

Alex checked; wondering, as he had done once before, if it might not be that Kishan Prasad suspected Alex of liking Mrs. Barton, and for that reason had warned him to send her to safety? He did not complete the sentence but said instead: 'There is another thing that seems to suggest he was speaking the truth. That road, if I am right about it, will have to be used before the monsoon breaks, for it will be useless afterwards. And that limits it to this side of mid-June. Something will happen before then.'

Sir Henry nodded and leaned forward in his chair, his clasped hands on his knees and his head silvered by the moonlight. He said slowly: 'I am in agreement with you. In fact, so much so that I will tell you something that few people are aware of. I have already begun to prepare the Residency to withstand a siege.'

'Then you think——'

'I hope!' interrupted Sir Henry. 'And I will go on hoping until the last possible moment! But I am also doing what I can to prepare, in case that hope fails me. Perhaps it will not. I have a deal of faith in the Punjab. Nicholson and Edwardes are there, and my brother John. They will hold the Punjab quiet. I believe Nicholson could do it single-handed, and if there were only three of him instead of one I should have no fears for India!

But I cannot feel any optimism on the score of the North-Western Provinces, and should Oudh revolt it will go hard with us all. Given time I believe I may be able to hold it quiet even if the rest of India rises: but it is *time* we need—time most of all: and that is a thing that God and the Government may not grant me. The sands are running out, Alex.'

He looked up and smiled his tired, charming smile: 'I am taking a dreary view of the future tonight, am I not? But though I can feel the wind and hear the thunder I do not despair of averting the storm. And if it comes—it comes! and I shall look to you to hold the western road for me, so that if you should be right, and the regiments at Suthragunj mutiny and seize the arsenal, they will not reach Oudh by Kishan Prasad's road!'

'I will do my best, sir. You know that.'

'Even if you were offered command of the Guides tomorrow?'

Alex threw up his hand in the gesture of a swordsman acknowledging a hit, and laughed, but this time without bitterness. 'You could offer me no greater inducement, sir, but I will content myself with trying to hold the western road for you.'

'Let us hope that it will not come to that,' said Sir Henry soberly.

They talked of other things for a space, until at last Sir Henry rose and held out his hand: 'If you are making an early start I shall not be seeing you again before you go. Good luck to you, Alex. God bless you, and——' He hesitated for a moment and then said thoughtfully, and as though the word was not a light one, 'Goodbye.'

His thin hand gripped Alex's for a brief moment and then he turned and walked away, and Alex had a last glimpse of his tall figure outlined against the lighted square of the open doorway as he passed through it and was gone.

'I shall not see him again,' thought Alex with sudden conviction; and was startled by the unbidden thought. Why should he think such a thing? Was it only because he was tired and overworked that he had imagined something indefinably final in that last word of farewell? He found that he was staring at the lighted doorway as though he could drag back that tall spare figure by an effort of will, and that there was an uncomfortable constriction in his throat.

The last months had been full of anxiety and strain and infuriating frustration for Alex, and his recent interview with Mr. Barton had driven him dangerously near to breaking-point. To be dragged from his district at a time like this, to explain a wholly justified action taken against a wealthy and dissolute nobleman who had only escaped his just deserts in the past on account of bribes paid to the Commissioner, was beyond bearing. Yet he had set his teeth and borne it, and as a result had arrived at the Residency that evening in no very amiable frame of mind. He had, for the moment, quite genuinely meant what he said when he had told Sir Henry Lawrence that he would accept any post that would allow him to return to regimental duty, and he had been seriously considering sending Mr. Barton his resignation. But ten minutes of Lawrence's society had been enough to restore him to a sense of proportion and sanity.

'Of course I shall see him again!' thought Alex. 'He is not an old man. He is barely fifty . . .' But in spite of the windless warmth of the night he shivered as though he were cold, and could not rid himself of a sense of foreboding.

It was late, and in a few hours' time he would have to start for Lunjore again. He knew that he should get what sleep he could, but he had seldom felt less like sleeping. The house was hot and it was too warm even in the shadows of the verandah, but the garden looked cool and inviting. Alex walked the length of the verandah and went down a shallow flight of steps and out into the quiet moonlight.

Although it was almost mid-April the night air was clear and mild, for the hot weather was unusually late that year and it might well have been early March, so green and pleasant were the grass and the flowering trees. Alex strolled across the wide lawns, his footsteps inaudible on the grass that the gardeners had watered at sunset, and came by chance to a group of flame trees whose shadows lay velvet-black in the moonlight.

There was someone standing at the far edge of that belt of soft darkness, her wide, pale skirts luminous in the shadows, and despite the fact that her outline was barely distinguishable and that she had her back to him, he knew that it was Winter. He stopped, and would have turned back except that something in the pose of the dimly seen figure arrested his attention. She was watching something, and there was a suggestion of alertness in the tilt of her head that even the deep shadows could not disguise. Curiosity overcame discretion and he went forward and came to stand beside her.

She heard the quiet footsteps and turned her head, but she made no movement of surprise or alarm and seemed as instantly aware of his identity as he had been of hers. She might almost have been waiting for him, though for once she had not even been thinking of him. But it seemed entirely natural to her that he should be there. The warm, moonlit stillness of the garden was another world which had nothing in common with the turmoil and tensions and restlessness that were a part of the daylight hours. She accepted his presence as a matter of course, and turned back to her contemplation of the stretch of gardens beyond the trees, as though her interest in what lay there had absorbed her attention to the exclusion of all else.

Standing beside her Alex could see the pale outline of her profile against the massed darkness of the leaves, and smell the clean, cool scent of lavender that he had come to associate with her. As his eyes became accustomed to the shadows he could make out the curving line of the long lashes, the faint, puzzled crease between her brows, and a stray tendril of black hair that curled childishly above her ear.

Winter did not appear to be aware of his gaze and presently she enquired in a whisper: 'What are they doing?'

Alex looked away from her, and for the first time became aware of what it was that had caught her interest. There were things moving across the open ground between the sharp-edged shadows of buildings that lay within the precincts of the Residency: things that moved in complete silence, keeping for the most part to the shadows and flitting noiselessly across the moonlit spaces like a frieze of trolls; bowed, hunchbacked and grotesque, silhouetted briefly against the silver-washed grass or the wall of a house; lost again in shadow and emerging only to be swallowed up by the ground.

It took him a moment or two to realize that they were men carrying heavy loads, shouldering sacks or bent under weighted boxes, and stowing them away in the underground cellars that lay beneath some of the Residency buildings. He said lightly enough: 'They are only men laying in supplies for the summer. Grain and——'

'And ammunition,' finished Winter. 'Why? And why are they doing it by night? They were doing it last night too. And the night before. They cannot need so many supplies unless—unless they think this place will be besieged. Is it that?'

Alex did not answer the question. He said instead: 'Why have you come out here to watch them every night?'

'I haven't. I mean, I did not come out to watch them. I only came out to walk in the garden.'

'At this time of night? It's very late.'

'I could not sleep, and this gave me something else to think about,' said Winter simply. 'Is there really going to be a rising? Ameera says——'

She stopped and after a moment Alex said: 'What does Ameera say? And who is Ameera?'

Winter turned to look at him in surprise. It seemed incredible to her that Alex should not know about Ameera. Until she remembered that she had barely seen him, and then only at a distance, for almost three months after her marriage, and that he did not even know the story of how she had come to Lunjore. She told him something of it now, and of Juanita and Aziza Begum and the Gulab Mahal; standing among the scented shadows of a garden that overlooked the teeming city of Lucknow and the house in which she had been born.

It had been April when Marcos de Ballesteros had ridden out through the gateway of the Gulab Mahal, and had turned in the saddle to see Sabrina standing among the hard fretted shadows of the gold-mohur trees, and had not known that he was seeing her for the last time. Eighteen years ago. And now it was April again, and Sabrina's daughter told that tale as it had been told to her by Zobeida. . . .

'We never knew what had become of them—Aziza Begum and my Aunt Juanita and the others——' said Winter in conclusion. 'The letters stopped. That was all. I did not even know if Ameera was alive; or anyone I had known.'

She was silent for a time and then she said slowly: 'I think Ameera is afraid. Her husband does not like the British, and I think—I think he does not trust her because of her western blood. She will not let me go to the Gulab Mahal, and I have only seen her twice. She says it is not easy for her to see me, and I do not think her husband knows that she has done so. Perhaps he would punish her if he did. You don't think he would, do you? Jehan Khan told me that Nila Ram cut off his wife's hands because she disobeyed him——' Her voice had a sudden tremor of fear in it and she put out a hand and caught at Alex's sleeve: 'Alex, you don't think he would do anything like that, do you?'

Alex looked down at the small hand on his arm and found himself unable to resist the impulse to cover it with his own. His touch appeared to startle her, for he felt the slim fingers stiffen and become quite still under the light clasp of his own. They withdrew gently and without haste, but her unconscious acceptance of his presence was gone and the ease between them was broken.

Alex said in a matter-of-fact voice: 'No, I don't. I expect you would find that Nila Ram's wife was conducting a clandestine affair. To visit a first cousin, even if that cousin is a European, is hardly a major offence. Does she seem to think there is any danger of an armed rising?'

Winter shook her head. 'She said that the city was full of strange rumours, but she would not say what they were. Only —only she said that I must go to the hills, and not stay in Lunjore.'

Alex said dryly: 'I seem to remember saying that myself.'

'I know you did. But there are twenty or thirty other women in Lunjore, and——' She broke off abruptly, wishing that she had not spoken. The inference was so obvious, and what did she expect Alex to say? That she was the only one whose safety he cared about? She drew back from him involuntarily, feeling the hot colour flood up and burn in her cheeks, and grateful for the darkness that would conceal it. But Alex's voice was clipped and cool:

'I am aware of it. And had I the authority to do so, I would have every one of you sent to the nearest hill station where there are British troops while there is still time. Not for your safety, but for ours.'

'For yours?' said Winter uncertainly. 'I don't understand——'

'Don't you? I should have thought it was obvious,' said Alex brutally. 'Because men are sentimental over women they will throw away military advantages, and hesitate and weigh the chances of failure when attack is their best or only hope, and lose their opportunity because they "have to think of the women and children". Men who would not otherwise dream of surrendering will make terms with an enemy in return for the safety of a handful of women. If a man is killed, it is an accident of war; but if a woman or a child is killed it is a barbarous murder and a hundred lives—or a thousand—are sacrificed to avenge it. It is only a man like John Nicholson who has the courage to write, and mean it, that the safety of "women and children in some crises is such a very minor consideration that it ceases to be a consideration at all". If only more men thought like that you could all stay in Lunjore and be damned to you!'

There was exasperation and bitterness in his voice, as though some prophetic vision of the future had risen before him in all its tragic futility. And then a dry leaf crunched behind them and he turned quickly to see George Lawrence standing in the moonlight beyond the rim of the tree shadows.

'Who is it?' George Lawrence spoke softly but sharply, and as Alex moved out into the moonlight he said with undisguised

N*

relief: 'Oh, it's you, Alex. I thought——' He checked at the sight of Winter. 'Mrs. Barton!'

His eyebrows twitched together in a sudden frown and Winter said: 'I'm sorry, Mr. Lawrence. Did we startle you? I came down to walk in the garden because I couldn't sleep, and Captain Randall found me here.'

The Chief Commissioner's nephew cleared his throat in nervous embarrassment and shot a quick look at Alex that needed no interpretation.

Alex grinned a little maliciously and said: 'No such luck,' as though in answer to a spoken question.

The moonlight did not disguise the dark colour that showed briefly in George Lawrence's face. He said sharply: 'I did not suppose——' and checked again, and then said abruptly and as though Winter were not there: 'How much has she seen?'

'Quite enough,' said Alex laconically. 'But she won't talk.'

George Lawrence turned to look at Winter and she answered an unspoken question as Alex had done: 'I promise. I didn't mean to spy on you, and I won't speak of it to anyone. Word of honour!' She smiled at him and his set face relaxed in an answering smile.

'Thank you. It is not a thing that my uncle would wish to become generally known. It is only a precautionary measure, you understand, but if it were to be talked about it might give rise to panic at a time when it is essential to give the appearance of calm. But I beg that you will not allow it to disturb you, Mrs. Barton. There have been a great many rumours abroad, but I feel sure that this cloud will blow over as others have done. It will pass, if it has not passed already.'

He turned to Alex and said a little stiffly: 'I thought that you were intending to make a five-o'clock start, Alex? It is near two o'clock already. Had you not better be getting some sleep? I will see Mrs. Barton to her room.'

Alex regarded him with a good deal of sardonic comprehension in his gaze. So George considered that he had been gravely imperilling young Mrs. Barton's reputation by being found talking

to her in the garden at two o'clock in the morning, did he? He
wondered what impression would be gained by anyone who might
happen to see Mr. Lawrence escorting Mrs. Barton to her bedroom at that hour. George would not have thought of that!
He said gravely: 'I feel sure I could leave her in no better hands.
Good night, Mrs. Barton. Goodbye, George. I hear you return
to Sikora soon? Good luck to you.'

'Thank you,' said George Lawrence soberly. 'I may need it.'

Alex lifted his hand in a brief gesture of farewell, and turning
on his heel walked away across the moonlit lawn and was
swallowed up by the foreshortened shadow of the Residency
tower.

26

It will pass . . . It has passed . . .

In cantonments and offices, in Residencies and bungalows, in
Government Houses and Council Chambers and in the house of
the Governor General himself, wherever the British met to talk
the soothing phrase that George Lawrence had used was repeated
again and again. The brief flare-up at Berhampur in February
and the uglier and more recent outbreak at Barrackpore had died
down without giving rise to any further incidents, and men who
had been smelling the wind uneasily relaxed again, and concurred with the popular and comfortable conviction that the peak
of the general unrest had passed, and that any serious danger (if
there had indeed been any, which the majority were inclined to
doubt) was now over.

Lottie wrote from Delhi. Edward had been transferred there
on special duty, but they were not living in the cantonments, as
they had been lent a delightful house in the city, not far from
the Kashmir Gate. Sophie was in Cawnpore visiting friends and
would not be returning until the end of May, but Mamma and
Papa sent their love . . .

The letter disturbed Winter, for she had thought that Lottie at least would be safe. Meerut housed the strongest European garrison in the North-Western Provinces, and where there were well over a thousand British soldiers there could be no danger. Sophie too could come to no harm in Cawnpore, where General Sir Hugh Wheeler and his staff had their headquarters. But Delhi . . . There were no British regiments in Delhi.

In Lucknow the Chief Commissioner gave an evening party. Shamianas had been erected on the Residency lawns, the trees were hung with coloured lanterns, and the band of one of the regiments stationed in cantonments provided music for the delectation of several hundred guests, who included almost all the British residents and a large proportion of the nobility and gentry of Oudh.

Perhaps the most spectacular guest, and certainly one who aroused the most interest, was Dundu Pant, the Nana of Bithor, who had attended the party accompanied by an impressively large retinue. The Nana was a man who cherished a grievance against the British—the Government having refused to recognize him as the legal heir or allow him the pension granted to the Peishwa, Baje Rao, who having no son had adopted him in accordance to Hindu Law. But he did not appear to have allowed his grievances to sour him, and was most friendly and affable towards the British guests, with several of whom he seemed to be on excellent terms. He was a fat man, strangely dark-skinned for a Maratha, and very splendidly dressed, and he wore a pair of large diamond earrings that flashed and glittered in the light of the coloured-paper lanterns. Alex, had he been present, would not have recognized the earrings—the ones he had seen had been rubies—but he would have had no difficulty at all in recognizing the wearer.

Conway too had given a party. A farewell party on his last night in Lucknow. It had been a riotous affair lasting well into the small hours of the morning, and he had had to be carried to the carriage in which he and his wife were to make the journey to Lunjore. He had expressly forbidden Winter to ride, saying that he had no desire to have her down with heat-stroke on the journey—nothing could be more inconvenient! But the sight of her husband's brandy-sodden and inanimate bulk being disposed in the carriage proved too much for her, and she had had Furiante saddled.

She had ridden away from the Casa de los Pavos Reales with no regrets, for the gracious, peaceful house held no happiness and no memories for her. It was the Gulab Mahal that held those, and the Gulab Mahal was closed to her. It was still a *fata Morgana* —a glimmering mirage. The moon out of reach.

There had been no word from Ameera—not even a line in farewell—until in a narrow street near the outskirts of the city, where they had been momentarily halted by the passing of a marriage procession, someone had touched Winter's foot. It was no casual touch, but a quick, urgent pressure of frantic fingers that thrust something into the top of her short kid boot, and she had looked down, startled, to see a woman in a soiled and shabby *bourqa*. For a brief instant the eyes behind the square of coarse mesh stared into hers, wide with warning, and then the woman had turned and vanished into the jostling, shifting crowd.

Was it Ameera? or Hamida? It had been impossible to tell. But all at once, riding on through the noisy, crowded streets in the burning sunlight, Winter had been afraid. The small folded square of paper that had been thrust into the top of her short riding-boot pressed into her flesh, but she did not touch it until they stopped at the first rest-house on the dusty Lunjore road. She had removed it then, in the privacy of the shuttered room that had been put at her disposal. It was a brief enough message, and written, save for one word, in *shikast*: 'Dear—*They have set the auspicious day. Therefore go swiftly to the sea and take ship for* Belait, *for tho' no harm will befall thee before the last day of the new month, after that there will be no safety anywhere. Least of all where there be regiments.*'

There was no signature, but Winter did not need one. Only Ameera would have prefaced the broken script with that single Spanish endearment.

It was evening, and the last day of April, when the Commissioner and his wife drove once more through the massive gateway of the Lunjore Residency, and barely an hour later they were dining with the same raffish company that had celebrated the Commissioner's wedding.

They were all there, with the exception of Mr. Josh Cottar who had departed to Calcutta on a business trip: Lou Cottar, Cissie and Edgar Wilkinson, Colonel Moulson, Major Mottisham and half a dozen others. 'Wrote ahead and invited 'em,' said Conway. 'Nothin' like havin' a celebration to welcome us home, eh?'

'I assure you the place has been like a morgue or a Quakers' Meeting while you have been away!' said Lou Cottar. 'I have had such a fit of the bore that I have yawned two more lines into my face, and heaven knows that it has enough already. I get asked to so few amusing parties when you are away, Con, for the majority of your female parishioners do not consider me quite respectable. Odd, is it not? Or else they do not trust their husbands! Though I cannot think why they should not, when their husbands are almost without exception dull enough to send one into a decline!'

'Who are the exceptions, Lou?' enquired the Commissioner with a chuckle. 'Am I one?'

Mrs. Cottar raised her brows at him: 'Not any longer. But you do at least provide the only tolerably amusing parties in Lunjore.'

'It wasn't only my parties you found amusing once,' said the Commissioner, reaching out to stroke her arm. 'Eh, Lou?'

'Ah, but that was at least five years ago. Or was it more? You were a heavy, handsome brute in those days, and I believe I actually lost almost two nights' sleep over you once!'

'Shall I see if I can make you lose two more?'

'You couldn't do it. You're gross, Con. You're fat and bald and you drink a deal too much, and if it wasn't for your parties I'd be tempted to drop you. But you're a habit with me and I'm too idle to break it.'

The Commissioner glowered at her. 'You've got the most poisonous tongue of any woman I know, Lou. By God, I don't know why I put up with you!'

'Because I'm a habit with you, and you've never been able to break yourself of bad habits,' said Mrs. Cottar. She laughed her low, throaty laugh, and crossing to the piano, threw up the lid and began to sing a music-hall song to her own accompaniment for the amusement of the company:

> *Hamlet loved a maid,*
> *Calumny had passed her.*
> *She never had played tricks,*
> *'Cause nobody had ask'd her!*

'Nothing has changed,' thought Winter. 'It is just the same; it is as though I had never been away to Lucknow. . . .'

But that was not true. She herself had changed. The noisy, raffish party and the sight of her husband with his arm about Cissie Wilkinson's waist no longer had any power to hurt or disgust her, for now she too could feel the wind and hear the thunder.

If Ameera was right, all these people here might die within a few months—perhaps in less. The last day of May, Ameera had said—'*and after that there will be no safety anywhere*'. It was the first of May tomorrow. In English villages they would be going to bed early so as to be up with the dawn to pick flowers with which May Queens would be crowned and garlanded on countless village greens. May Day! Thirty days more. *Was* Ameera right?—or was George Lawrence? *It will pass . . . it will pass . . . It has passed.* Had it?

Winter did not ride the following morning. The horses needed rest, and she slept late, but when she had breakfasted she wrote to Alex. It was a short letter and the first she had ever written to him. She gave it to a servant to deliver to him, but the man said that Randall Sahib was in camp among the outlying villages. 'Then someone must take it to him,' said Winter. 'Send Yusaf to me.' The man looked slantingly at her under

lowered lids and went away to summon the syce, but the look
had frightened Winter.

Quite suddenly, in that brief moment, the full meaning of what
a major insurrection in this country would entail came home to
her. She had never really visualized it in its entirety before.
She had, indeed, imagined Ameera being killed or maimed as a
punishment for having warned her, and she had visualized Lottie
and kind Mrs. Abuthnot and hero-worshipping Sophie being cut
down by a howling mob. But these had been isolated pictures,
and behind them had been a whispering voice that said: '*We
hear many of these rumours . . . it will pass.*' But now, standing
in the big, cool drawing-room of her husband's house, she thought
for the first time of exactly what such a rising would mean. Of
the handful of white people who held this vast country, and the
dark, teeming millions who surrounded them and who lived
cheek by jowl with them, watching their every movement and
listening to their every word—and waiting. There was little
privacy to be had in a land where a dozen servants were always
within call, and where a punkah coolie, a *chuprassi*, or a *darzi*
sitting cross-legged before a pile of sewing was as natural a part
of every verandah as the matting on the floor.

She tore up the letter that she had written to Alex and burnt
the pieces, and wrote another. It was not that she did not trust
Yusaf, who was Alex's own servant, but she preferred to take no
chances.

Yusaf had ridden with the letter, and Alex had read it late
that evening by the light of a flaring oil-lamp. There had been
only two lines, but he had read them and re-read them and then
folded the paper carefully and put it into the inner pocket of his
coat, and said: 'Tell the memsahib that I return tomorrow or the
next day.'

Yusaf saluted and slipped back into the darkness, and Alex
returned to his tent and blew out the light that was attracting
too many creeping and flying things to their doom.

Niaz had put up the camp-bed in the open, and lying on it
later that night Alex stared up through the mosquito net at the

blaze of stars, and saw a comet cross the heavens from east to west, not with the rush of a falling star, but slowly, dragging a long train of glowing light that appeared red rather than white or golden, and taking a full ten minutes to traverse the spangled ceiling of the sky. From a dozen yards to his left he heard Niaz move, and looking in his direction saw the silhouette of his lifted head and knew that he had seen it, too.

'They will say that too is a sign—or an omen,' thought Alex, 'and I am not sure that one can blame them for it.'

A red star, smearing a trail of blood from the east to the west. Were there such things as signs and wonders in the sky? A star had once brought Wise Men out of the East to search for that Sword that had come into the world so many centuries ago and had not yet been sheathed. That the heavens foretold the future was perhaps the oldest superstition in the world, and men had watched the skies for ten thousand years and more, believing that their fate could be read there. In the hot weather many men slept out in the open, in roadways and on rooftops and at the doors of their huts. How many would have seen the red comet, and how many—or how few?—would not regard it as a sign from heaven? An evil sign: not because of its colour, for red is worn in the East for rejoicing, but because the times and men's thoughts were evil.

A hundred yards away a pariah dog thrust its gaunt nose at the sky and howled long and very mournfully, and the howl was taken up and repeated again and again in a barking, wailing chorus by all the dogs of the nearby village, as though they bayed the moon. Beyond the tank and the mango tope where Alex's camp was pitched, a light pricked the darkness; and another and another; and presently a conch brayed in the temple and a tom-tom beat. 'They have seen it,' thought Alex. 'This is how legends are born.'

He heard Niaz mutter something in an undertone. It appeared to be uncomplimentary to the villagers. The red-tailed comet sank behind the mango trees, its reflection lingering for a moment longer in the dark waters of the tank, and as the glow faded from the sky the dogs stopped howling as though at an order. But the conch brayed and the tom-toms beat for hour after hour, and Alex heard them in his sleep, mingling with his uneasy dreams.

He did not start for Lunjore until early next afternoon, and leaving the servants to break camp and follow, he and Niaz rode hard through the heat of the day and into the dusty sunset and the brief green dusk. As the sun sank below the horizon they had stopped to eat, for the Mohammedan fast of Ramadan had begun with the new moon, and while it lasted Niaz and all other followers of the Prophet might not eat or drink between sunrise and sunset. Alex too kept the fast when he was away from the cantonments and out among the villages, for he had found it to be good training, and there were times when he needed to keep it. It was dark by the time they reached the bungalow, and Alex took a hot bath to remove the dust and sweat of the long ride, and having changed into the white mess-jacket that was almost a uniform of the hot weather, he walked across in the starlight to the Residency.

The big house was ablaze with lights and there was a trap and a high dog-cart standing on the wide drive. 'Moulson again,' thought Alex, 'and Gidney and Mottisham, I suppose.' He nodded to the *chowkidar* and went up the verandah steps. A servant lifted the *chik* before the hall door and murmured that the Huzoors were playing cards in the small *ghol-kumra* (drawing-room) and the memsahib was in the big drawing-room.

Winter was sitting on a sofa in the centre of the room with the slow-moving punkah stirring the air above her. She had a book in her hands, but it was obvious that she had heard his voice in the hall. There was a suggestion of rigidity about her slight figure and she was smiling. It was a pleasant smile; the smile an actress might have employed to indicate pleasurable surprise. But she was not, as a rule, reflected Alex, walking leisurely towards her, much given to smiling, and it occurred to him to wonder if that smile was for his benefit or for Rassul, who had shown him in. Some instinct for danger made him return it, and as he took the hand that she held out to him he knew that he had been right, for her fingers were cold and not quite steady and they tightened warningly upon his for a moment before they were withdrawn.

Winter said gaily and on the same note of pleased surprise that was in her smile: 'How kind of you to come so promptly! I hope it was not inconvenient? I was entrusted with a message from a friend of yours whom I met in Lucknow.' Her gaze went past him and she spoke to the servant who lingered by the door: 'Bring drinks for the sahib, Rassul.'

'*Hukum*,' murmured Rassul, and the door closed softly behind him.

Winter said: 'Do sit down, Captain Randall. Have you ridden far today? I am afraid my husband is busy just now. A card-party, you know. How much English do these people understand? I did not expect to see you until tomorrow.' She laughed as though she had made some joke.

Alex's eyes narrowed slightly but he replied without the least hesitation: 'There was nothing much to keep me, and camping is hot work in this weather. A good deal more than most people think.'

He saw Winter's quick breath of relief, and smiled. Had she really been afraid that he would misunderstand her and demand explanations? She threw an anxious glance at the two doors that opened on to the verandah. *Chiks* hung before both to keep the room from filling with bats and night-flying insects, but there were, he knew, at least three servants in the verandah. He shook his head very slightly, and the door behind him swung open silently and Rassul was back with a laden tray.

Winter said: 'Yes, I thought it might be so. Mr.—Brown wished to know if there was any good shooting to be had in Lunjore at this time of the year. He has a few weeks' leave soon and was considering coming here. I told him that I could not possibly say, but that you would write. He sent you this——'

She handed him Ameera's note and Alex read it with a half-smile, folded it, and slipped it into his pocket as Rassul poured out a drink and withdrew. Winter talked trivialities for five minutes or so, and then rose with a rustle of starched muslin flounces and suggested that they walk on the roof, as she found the close heat of the drawing-room oppressive. The flat stone levels of the roof were still warm from the burning day, but the night air was unexpectedly cool, and here at least there was no ubiquitous servant loitering within earshot.

Alex listened to the tale of Ameera's message, and he did not say any of the soothing and reassuring things that George Lawrence had said. He said nothing at all for a long time, and when at last he spoke it was only to say: 'If you will excuse me, I think I should let the Commissioner know that I have returned. Did you enjoy your stay in Lucknow?'

He talked of other matters as they left the roof, and having said good night to her he went off to the small drawing-room where he was greeted ungraciously by the Commissioner and stayed to watch a hand of whist. There were no omens in the skies that night, and the pariah dogs were silent; but the city was not. The city was awake and restless, and tom-toms throbbed and conches blared as they had in the little village beyond the tank and the mango tope. 'It is Ramadan,' said Niaz; but he said it uneasily, looking over his shoulder.

'It is *dewanee*—the madness,' said Alex.

He did not sleep well that night, but lay awake hour after hour staring into the darkness and thinking of those few scrawled lines of broken script that Winter had given him in the Residency drawing-room . . .

So he had been right! A day and a date. He was sure that it must be so. Men like Kishan Prasad and the Maulvie of Faizabad would not content themselves with stirring up general discontent. That was an easy enough thing to do. But though sporadic outbreaks of mutiny and violence would embarrass the authorities, they could be dealt with and stamped out without much difficulty. It was a general mutiny of the Bengal army, coupled with a popular rising, that was to be feared, and such a thing called for a day and a date . . .

The last day of May—and it was already the third. Three days gone. Twenty-seven left. Twenty-seven days in which to turn aside the wind that was rising steadily and blowing hot and fitfully through every cantonment in India. How did one stop a wind that had been whistled up by the blindness and obstinacy and egotism of men who imagined that it was a simple matter, and one worthy of all praise, to pry the East loose from its centuries-old laws and customs and force it into a Western mould?

'I can do nothing about the regiments,' thought Alex, 'but some of the talukdars will stand behind me—or at least stay quiet. And so I think will the villages. The city is the trouble. There are always *badmashes* (scoundrels) by the score in the kennels of any city, and the scum of the bazaars and the back alleys will rise at a word simply for the chance of murder and loot . . . Will the police stand if the army breaks? I must see Maynard again . . . Perhaps I can get Barton to demand plenary military powers in Lunjore that would give him the right to order the sepoys to be disarmed if their colonels refuse to take action. I could always get him drunk enough to sign anything, and do the job myself. How does one prove to a set of courageous, pig-headed, devoted die-hards that their beloved men are listening nightly to treason? To suggest as much to a man like Gardener-Smith is almost on a par with telling him that his wife is unfaithful to him. Worse if anything, as it deprives him of the satisfaction of knocking me down.'

Alex went over to see the Commissioner on the following morning, and gave him the substance of Ameera's warning; without, however, disclosing the fact that the message had been received by his wife.

'Nonsense!' said the Commissioner. '*Auspicious day*?—don't believe a word of it! Probably refers to a wedding. You shouldn't listen to bazaar gossip!'

'As you like, sir,' said Alex in his most expressionless voice.

'Why do I do it?' he thought, walking back to his bungalow. 'Why in hell's name do I do it? It's a waste of time and it only puts his back up. Yet I cannot keep him in the dark. I can't have him saying when the mine goes off, "Why did you never tell me?" Justifying myself in advance again!—as if it mattered. Oh well, I suppose I may as well do the thing thoroughly, and be damned to it!'

He spent another exhausting and abortive morning on his feet — he was not offered a chair—placing his views yet again before the three commanding officers of the regiments stationed in Lunjore, but with no better results than before. Leaving them, he rode down to the police lines to discuss the possibility of disaffection in that quarter with Major Maynard, who commanded the Military Police.

Major Maynard alone confessed to uneasiness, though not on account of his police, whom he believed to be staunch. 'It's old Packer,' he said. 'Unless something can be done to stop him preaching the Word to his men, we shall find ourselves in the basket! Can nothing be done to gag the old fool?'

'I've tried,' said Alex tiredly. 'I got him an official wigging, which he holds against me—I gather I am one of those "by whom the offence cometh"! But that was the best I could do.'

'It doesn't appear to have damped his proselytizing ardour,' commented Major Maynard. 'Perhaps he yearns for a martyr's crown.'

'I daresay he does—and at this rate he'll get it! But I have no desire to qualify for one myself. He told me that he was merely "rendering unto Caesar the things that are Caesar's and to God the things that are God's," and as, in temporal matters, he obeyed the orders of his superior officers in the army, so in spiritual matters, as a soldier of Christ, he obeyed the orders of the Lord, which instructed him to save the heathen from damnation. He has a great deal of support in Lunjore.'

'Among the sepoys?'

'Good God, no! Among the ladies. They look upon him as a saintly man and a shining example to the less devout—such as Moulson!'

'Moulson's too much of a martinet,' said Major Maynard gloomily. 'Seems to be no happy medium! There's old Gardener pottering around with his watering-can, cherishin' his fellows as though they were tender plants, and Packer looking upon his as erring sheep to be gathered into the fold, while Moulson goes to the other extreme and slings his sepoys into irons if they so much as blink on parade! He'll go too far one day, but there's no denying that his lot are the best disciplined of the bunch. I'd say there was a lot less chance of them cracking than of Packer's strayed lambs.'

'Or your own?' enquired Alex.

'Oh, they're all right,' said Major Maynard easily. 'But I'll bear in mind what you say and keep a sharp eye on 'em. Personally I'm inclined to think that the worst is past. I hear they hung that Jack who touched off the Barrackpore business— Mangal Pandy? And the Jemadar as well. That ought to stop the rot.'

'I envy you your optimism,' said Alex dryly, and rode back slowly through the blinding sunlight and the hot shadows of the wide cantonment road.

27

THE telegraph did not as yet operate in Lunjore, and so it was not until two days later that the news trickled over the border from Oudh that on Sunday, May 3rd, the 7th Regiment of Oudh Irregulars had refused to accept their cartridges, and had mutinied. Sir Henry Lawrence had apparently acted with great promptness and succeeded in disarming the regiment, a good many of whom had absconded, and fifty of the ringleaders had been seized.

'It is too soon,' said Alex, reading that laconic dispatch. He crumpled up the slip of paper and flung it from him in sudden rage, and rode out in the heat of the day to visit one of the influential landowners in his district.

It was that night that Niaz woke him at one o'clock in the morning.

Alex slept out in the open in the hot weather, and had, in other years, slept in the garden. But this year his bed had been carried up nightly to the flat roof of his bungalow, and Alam Din slept across the stair that led up to it. Alex was a light sleeper at the best of times, and the whispers woke him. There was a quality of urgency about them that sent him out of bed and across the roof within less than ten seconds of his waking.

'*Kaun hai?* (Who is it?)'

'Come down, Huzoor,' whispered Alam Din. 'It is Niaz, and I think he is sorely hurt.'

Alex ran down the stairs and his bare foot slid on something wet. He knew the feel of that sticky wetness of old, and he caught the dark figure that sagged against the bottom of the stair, and said sharply to Alam Din: 'Take his feet!'

'No,' gasped Niaz with an attempt at a laugh. 'I can walk. Give me thy shoulder, brother.'

Alex thrust Alam Din ahead of him: 'Light a lamp in my room—quickly! Where art thou hurt?'

'In the back, to the left. But it has missed its mark. Do not fear.'

Alex pulled Niaz's right arm about his shoulder and half-carried him to the bedroom, where he could see the flicker of a light as Alam Din lit the oil-lamp and drew the curtains. He could feel the warm wetness that soaked Niaz's clothing, and in spite of the heat of the May night he found that his hands were cold with rage. The wound was unpleasant enough, but it had, as Niaz had said, missed its mark, for it had been deflected by the shoulder-blade and Niaz was suffering more from loss of blood than from anything else. He had walked a mile or more after he had been knifed.

'It was in the lines,' said Niaz. 'I had——'

'Quiet,' said Alex curtly. 'Tell me later. We will bind thee first.' He cut away the blood-soaked clothing, and with Alam Din's assistance washed and bound up the wound and sent him off to brew strong tea.

'I can go no more to the lines,' said Niaz ruefully. 'It is finished. For long they have not trusted me, and I too have carried a knife, for fear of this thing. And then to be caught off guard like a fledgling! Pah!' He grimaced with pain and drank the hot, sweet liquid thirstily.

'Who was it?'

'I do not know. I went to talk with those whom I thought to be friends of mine in the lines of the 93rd, and to listen. But tonight they would not talk, and they looked at me out of their eyes, sideways, and there was a constraint upon them. There was a *bairagi* in the lines—a sadhu. I saw him standing in the shadows of a hut. He stayed silent and did not move as I passed, and I made as though I had not seen him. When I came away I looked to see if he was still there, but he had gone, and I put my hand upon my knife and walked as a cat walks in an alley full of dogs.'

Niaz grinned to hide another spasm of pain and drank again, his teeth chattering on the rim of the mug. 'There is a lamp by the peepul tree at the turn of the lines, by the bunnia's shop,' he said between mouthfuls, 'and there was a gun lying in the dust. A revolver such as the Sahibs carry. A child's trick that should not have deceived a babe, yet I stooped for it. I heard the step but I could not avoid the blow. Had I not heard it, that knife would have struck true.'

Alex said: 'Was there nothing to tell who it was?'

'I did not see. I fell, and turned as I fell, but he had gone like a shadow, and I did not wait. But I think it was the sadhu.'

'Why?'

Niaz wrinkled his nose expressively and Alex nodded. He too knew the characteristic smell of the ash-smeared, unwashed ascetics of India.

Niaz had a touch of fever the next day, but the ugly wound had bled itself clean, and he suffered remarkably few ill effects from it. The weather continued unusually mild, and all over India women who had intended to leave for the hills delayed and put off the day of departure while the nights remained cool, and the Commissioner of Lunjore informed his wife that he could not arrange for her to leave for the hills before the twenty-second of the month. It seemed that Mrs. Gardener-Smith and Delia, Mrs. Hossack and her four children, and a Captain and Mrs. Batterslea and their young family were all leaving on that date, and therefore it would be more convenient if she were to travel with them, as Captain Batterslea's presence would save him from having to arrange for an escort for her.

Winter acquiesced without interest. She still rode every morning before sunrise and again in the cool of the evening, but she saw nothing of Alex for several days and heard nothing of him until Colonel Moulson remarked in her hearing one evening that he understood that Captain Randall had taken shooting-leave.

'So much for all this hot air he has been talking,' said Colonel Moulson with scorn. 'Shows how much he believes in it if he can chuck his responsibilities and go off after jungle-cock! Tried to set us all by the ears, and when he found he couldn't panic us, goes off and sulks in the *terai*. I wonder you let him go. I'm damned if I'd have done so! What that cub needs is five years of regimental soldiering under a C.O. who'd knock the conceit out of him. Wish I had him under my command!'

'You have got your knife into him, haven't you, Fred?' said Mrs. Cottar pleasantly. 'Now I wonder why? Con used to feel quite kindly towards him until the Aurora Borealis preferred him to his Excellency the Commissioner—didn't you, Con? But ever since then he's gone sour on him too—just like you. How vain you men are!'

The Commissioner cast her a glance of dislike and said sourly: 'I don't know why I put up with you, Lou! As for you, Fred, to hear you talk anyone 'ud think I'd given the man a month's leave instead of three days!'

'You can give him three years for all I care,' said Colonel Moulson. 'Place is a sight better off without him. Your deal——'

Alex resented the lost days considerably more than Colonel Moulson, but there were certain preparations that he thought it necessary to make, and they could not be made in a night. Niaz, he considered, could hardly have selected a worse moment to be laid up with a knife wound, but time was too short to wait until he had recovered. Niaz himself had angrily asserted that he had taken no harm, and had begged to go with him, but Alex had been adamant. He would need Niaz later on. Returning three days later, after dark, he had enquired after the wound. 'It is healed,' said Niaz impatiently. 'How much longer do I stay here?'

'For another week, I think,' said Alex. He smiled a little grimly at Niaz's face of disgust and said softly: 'It is in my mind that thou wert so sorely wounded that I must ride abroad with a syce for some days yet, so that all will know that thou art still a sick man and unable to go about.'

'Aah!' said Niaz, and smiled. 'What now?'

Alex explained. '. . . and if thou and one other go, on foot and by night, and while it is known that thou art sick, I think that the thing may be done.'

'So do I also,' said Niaz. 'Give out that I am like to die. That should please those dogs in the lines! Who goes with me? Yusaf?'

Alex considered the matter, frowning, and after a moment or two said curtly: 'It will have to be.'

He found Winter sitting under the punkah of the small drawing-room on the following morning, writing a letter to Lottie. It was Sunday, and she had just returned from church. Her formal dress of grey, white-spotted *mousseline de chine* looked fresh and cool, and her discarded bonnet lay on the sofa. She looked up in surprise when he entered and he saw her cheeks flush with sudden colour. She seemed to be aware of it herself, for she stood up rather quickly and turned so that her back was to the light.

'I came to ask if I might borrow Yusaf for a few days,' said Alex, dispensing with formalities. 'Niaz is sick and there is a certain amount of work I need done that I think he could do for me. It will only be for a few days. Can you spare him?'

'Yes, of course. But——'

'Thank you. It will mean that you will have to take one of the Commissioner's syces with you when you ride. Don't go too far afield, and stay away from the city. I'll send him back as soon as I can.'

He turned to leave and Winter said: 'I heard that you had taken shooting-leave. When did you get back?'

'Last night,' said Alex uncommunicatively, and left.

The door closed behind him and Winter regarded it with a smouldering eye. 'There are times,' she said aloud and deliberately, 'when I am almost glad that I once hit you!'

She returned to her desk and the sheet of letter-paper that so far bore only the address, and picking up her pen, dipped it in the standish. But she did not write. She sat nibbling the end of it thoughtfully while the minutes ticked by and the ink dried on the nib.

The punkah creaked and flapped gently and monotonously overhead and a pair of gecko lizards on the wall behind the desk chirruped a small, shrill counterpoint. In the garden outside a *köil*, whom the British had nicknamed 'the brain-fever bird', was singing its maddening hot-weather song on a long, rising scale. *Brain fever . . . brain fever . . . brain fever!* sang the *köil*, finishing at the top of the scale and starting all over again at the bottom, as tirelessly monotonous as the creaking of the punkah. It was hot today: hotter than it had been for many days, and in every room the doors and windows had been closed before sunrise to keep in the cooler air of the night and exclude the burning heat of May. 'There will be no more cool nights now until the *bursat* (the rains),' Imam Bux had said that morning.

'I was a fool not to have sent in m' papers before,' grumbled the Commissioner, mopping at the sweat that trickled down his thick neck. 'I don't believe that dam' man Canning is coming on tour this year, after all. Pretty fool I shall look if he don't— stewing through another hot weather for nothing! Should have gone a month ago. No—take that damned coffee away and give me a cold drink! Hair of the dog!'

He mixed champagne and brandy and started the day with a 'Raja's peg'.

*　　　　*　　　　*

Alex walked back to his bungalow, oblivious alike to the harsh glare of the sunlight and the song of the *köil*. 'We have only one chance,' thought Alex, 'and that is that their ringleaders will not be able to hold 'em until a given day. They're too worked up. Something will set them off. Someone like Moulson will put his foot in it somewhere and provoke a premature explosion that will sound the alarm. But if it does go off on time, and in every cantonment in India, they can write our obituaries now.'

In far-away Calcutta a senior Member of the Supreme Council finished reading Sir Henry Lawrence's telegraphed report on the mutinous behaviour of the Oudh Irregulars, and picked up his pen. '*The sooner this epidemic of mutiny is put a stop to, the better*,' wrote the Member of the Supreme Council. '*Mild measures won't do. A severe example is wanted . . . I am convinced that timely severity will be leniency in the long run . . .*'

In a large bungalow in the cantonment of Meerut, forty miles to the north-east of Delhi, Colonel Carmichael Smyth, the commanding officer of the 3rd Light Cavalry, sat at breakfast. The Colonel was a man whose views were identical with those expressed by the senior Member of Council, and hurrying back from leave to set an example, he had ordered that fifteen picked men from each troop were to parade on the following morning to learn to use the new cartridges. 'I'm not standing any dam' silly nonsense from *my* sepoys!' said Colonel Smyth. The ninety men were duly paraded—and eighty-five of them had refused to handle the caste-breaking cartridges. They were immediately tried by court martial and sentenced to ten years' imprisonment, and a parade of all troops had been ordered by the aged divisional commander, Major-General Hewitt, to watch the sentence put into execution. For hour after hour, in the broiling sun of the Meerut parade-ground, the regiments had stood in stony-faced

silence to watch eighty-five picked men of a picked Regiment
stripped of their uniforms and fettered one by one with the iron
fetters that they would drag with them through ten weary years
of captivity, and when at long last the ordeal was over, the terrible
clanking file of men had marched away in the bright, merciless
sunlight, calling to their comrades: 'Is this justice? Because we
will not lose our caste so that none of our own will speak with us
or eat with us, must we suffer this fate? Is there no justice?
Help us, brothers! Help us!'

'Entirely just!' snapped Colonel Smyth, helping himself to
scrambled eggs. 'Harsh? Nonsense! These mutinous fools need
a sharp lesson. This will serve to stop the rot.'

'Wait, brothers! Wait—wait. Have patience! Remember the
auspicious day. It is too soon!' urged the agents of Ahmed Ullah
the Maulvie of Faizabad; of Dundu Pant the Nana of Bithor;
of Kishan Prasad . . .

'Art thou of the Risala?' shrilled a harpy in the Street of the
Harlots in Meerut city to a group of prospective clients as night
fell. 'The 3rd Risala, sayest thou? Then thou canst not enter
here! Out—out! we do not lie with cowards! Where are thy
comrades who eat dirt and walk in chains? *They* were men!
But thou——! Chicken-hearts!—children!—cowards all! *Pah!*'
She spat in derision, and a chorus of jeering painted faces applauded her from a dozen latticed windows and balconies, screaming like peacocks: 'Out! Out!—we lie with no cowards! If ye
indeed be men, and not the boneless babes we take ye for, release
thy brothers from bondage!'

Their taunts and their jeers pursued the men of the 3rd
Cavalry through the hot, crowded, snarling bazaars of Meerut
city, driving them from rage to a murderous frenzy.

Winter dipped her pen once more into the standish and added
a date below the address that she had already written at the top
of the blank sheet of paper. *Sunday, May 10th 1857—Dear
Lottie . . .*

28

THE night was hot and very still. So still that every small sound of all the small sounds that go to make up silence separated itself from its fellows, and emphasized that stillness. The cheep of a muskrat; the dry scrape of a scorpion crawling up the wall; the flitter of a bat's wings in the dark verandah; the drone of the mosquitoes and, from very far away, the echo of a jackal-pack howling on the plains beyond the river.

Winter lay and listened to those sounds, and could not sleep. Once she thought that she heard whispering voices, and remembering the night that she had listened in the bathroom, she slipped noiselessly out of bed and tiptoed to the bathroom door. But there were no voices. Only the dry whisper of dead and dying neem leaves that drifted down through the hot, windless air and came to rest on the parched stone of the roof or the dry, brittle grass.

'There are no tom-toms in the city tonight,' thought Winter, listening by her open window. 'And no conches. This is the first night for almost ten nights that I have not heard them. Perhaps it is the heat. It has not been really hot until now——'

Somewhere in the dark recesses of the house a clock struck one. Three more hours before she could dress and go out to ride by the river. Would it be cooler by the river? It was so hot here, and so airless. The noise of the flapping punkah had irritated her, and she had sent the punkah coolie away, saying that she could sleep better without it. But when he had gone she wished that she could call him back, for the sweltering, breathless stillness that had closed down upon the room with the cessation of the slow sway of the punkah had been worse than the nerve-racking monotony of that creak and flap.

'I will go up to the roof,' she thought, turning restlessly away from the window. 'It will be cooler up there,' and she groped for her slippers in the darkness and put them on, shaking them mechanically before doing so for fear they harboured centipedes

or scorpions, and slipped her arms into the wide sleeves of the
muslin wrap that lay at the foot of her bed. There was a dim
light burning in the hall, and a slow regular snuffle and snore
came from a corpse-like figure who lay rolled in a thin cotton
chuddar near the front door. Winter walked softly past it, and
lifting the *chik* went down the verandah and up the steep flight
of stone steps to the first level of the flat-topped roof.

It was cooler here certainly, but the brickwork and the stone
were still warm to the touch, and the wall supporting the second
and higher-level roof gave off waves of stored heat. She made a
half-circuit of the lower level and came to where six stone steps
led up to the larger area that covered the high main rooms of the
Residency.

A shadow moved on the stonework and she looked up, startled,
to see a small white figure standing above her by the narrow
parapet that surrounded the upper roof. It was Zeb-un-Nissa.

Winter called up to her in a whisper, but the child did not
answer or make any movement to show that she had heard.
She was staring out across the lawns and gardens and the distant
bulk of the Residency gateway towards the south-west, and her
face and body looked curiously rigid, as though she were straining
to catch some far-away and almost inaudible sound.

'I believe she's sleep-walking!' thought Winter, suddenly
anxious. She waited for a moment or two, looking up at the
child's tense face, and then went up the steps very softly so as
not to frighten her, for she had heard that it was harmful to
waken a sleep-walker too suddenly. Zeb-un-Nissa did not move.
Her eyes were wide and fixed, and standing beside her Winter
could see that her small face was drawn with fear. She laid a
gentle hand on the child's thin arm and spoke softly: 'Nissa——'

Zeb-un-Nissa did not start or turn, but she moved her head a
little and looked at Winter as though she were perfectly aware of
her; her eyes full of horror. 'Hark!' she said in a hoarse whisper.
'Dost thou not hear them?' She began to shiver, and Winter put
an arm about the frail little shoulders and drew the child against
her: 'What is it *piyari* (darling)? What is there to hear?'

The child pulled herself free and turned again to the parapet, clutching at the stone with small claw-like hands, and listening to some sound that Winter could not hear.

'It is the mem-*log*—the memsahibs! They are screaming! Canst thou not hear them scream? Surely thou canst hear them —there be children also . . . Listen!—*listen!* They are killing the mem-*log*. Thou canst hear the sword cuts—and the flames. There! that was a child!—hark to its mother shriek! *Ai! Ai!*——' She wailed aloud and put her hands over her ears, cowering down below the parapet and weeping. 'I cannot bear to hear them scream!—they are killing the mem-*log*—they are killing the mem-*log*!'

Winter dropped to her knees and gathered the small, wailing figure into her arms. 'Nissa—Nissa! There is no one screaming. It is all quiet. Listen—there is no sound. It is only a dream, *piyari*. Only a bad dream. There is no killing——'

She had heard no sound behind her, but a shadow fell across them, black in the moonlight, and she turned swiftly, her heart in her mouth, to see Akbar Khan the gatekeeper salaaming deferentially behind her. His face was dark against the moon and the night sky, but Winter could see the gleam of his teeth and the glitter of his eyes, and though her first momentary panic had died at sight of him, an odd flicker of fear went through her, making her pull the child closer.

'Her mother missed the unworthy one from her bed,' said Akbar Khan softly. 'She has been sick with a fever these few days past and she must have left her bed while her mother slept. I am sorry that the child should have troubled the lady-sahib.'

'She has not troubled me,' said Winter. 'Let her be. She can sleep in my room for what is left of the night.'

'Nay, nay!' said Akbar Khan, shocked. 'The lady-sahib is the fount of all goodness, but it would not be seemly! And her mother is anxious, and sent me in search of her.'

Winter felt the frail body in her arms stiffen and writhe and become rigid, and then quite slowly it relaxed. Nissa sighed and her head nestled down against the shoulder that supported it,

o

and looking down at the small face and feeling the shallow even breathing, Winter realized that she had fallen asleep.

Akbar Khan reached down and took the child from her. 'It was a fit,' he said placidly. 'She has always been a sickly child, and I fear that the time of her release is near. Her mother will grieve; but what is written is written.' He cradled the thin body of his grandchild comfortably in his arms and said: 'Her mother will be very honoured that the gracious lady-sahib troubled herself with the child. Shall I call a servant to light the lady-sahib back to her room?'

'No,' said Winter curtly. 'I will remain here. Tell Zeb-un-Nissa's mother that I will come tomorrow to see how the child fares.'

'The lady-sahib is my father and my mother,' murmured Akbar Khan politely, and went away, his bare feet making no sound on the warm stone.

Winter watched him go and she shivered in the hot night air; a shiver that was not caused by cold, but by uneasiness and foreboding. Akbar Khan had always been courteous and placid, and his greeting to her whenever she passed through the gateway contained no trace of the veiled insolence that she had sometimes detected in the manner of Conway's other servants. But tonight there had been something in his manner that frightened her. No—not in his manner; there had been nothing wrong in that. In what, then? In the fact that he himself had for some reason been afraid? In the glitter of the eyes in that shadowed, bearded face as they had stared down at the wailing, muttering figure of his little granddaughter? No! she was being foolishly imaginative! Yet he had told a lie when he had said that Nissa had been sick for some days. That at least was not true, for she had seen the child daily at dawn.

What did Nissa think that she had heard? It was a dream, of course. She had been dreaming. And yet she had not behaved as Winter imagined that a sleep-walker would do. She had appeared to be aware of Winter, and awake; caught up in horror, but awake. The servants said that Akbar Khan's little granddaughter had second-sight, and they were afraid of her. And there had been that day when she had said—or seemed to say —that Alex would come to no harm; and he had come to no harm. But she could not have known that he was in any danger! It had been a coincidence. 'They are killing the mem-*log*, surely thou canst hear them scream?' Surely, in this waiting stillness, the sound of a scream would carry from the cantonments beyond the trees? But there was no scream—no sound. Only silence.

Almost against her will Winter went to lean on the parapet as Nissa had done, and strained her ears to listen. But nothing broke that silence. Not even a jackal's wail or the fall of a dead leaf. 'She was dreaming!' said Winter aloud and firmly. But she shivered again, and drawing her thin beruffled wrap tighter about her, she left the roof and returned to the hot, dark, silent rooms and her hot, tumbled bed.

*   *   *

Alex heard her running along the verandah of his bungalow at eleven o'clock on the following morning, and knew who it was even before the startled *chuprassi* lifted the *chik* and she was standing before him, tense and white-faced, her hands clutching at the edge of his desk.

There were five other men in the office, but she appeared to be oblivious of them. Alex stood up swiftly and dismissed them with a brief word, and they melted out into the sunlight. Winter did not see them go. She said in a hard, breathless voice that she fought to control: 'Alex, do something! They've killed her! I know they've killed her! Conway won't do anything. He says it's all nonsense. It's her grandfather—it's Akbar Khan. He did it. I know he did it! Alex, you can't let him do that and— and——'

Alex came round the desk and caught her by the shoulders and propelled her forcibly out of the office and into the living-room. He pushed her down into a chair, splashed a generous quantity of brandy into a glass and held it to her mouth while

she drank it. Winter gasped and choked, but it took some of the
shivering rigidity from her.

'Now tell me.'

'It's Nissa,' said Winter, tears standing in her eyes. 'She—
she had a nightmare last night. At least I think it was a nightmare. Akbar Khan said it was a fit——' She described the happening on the roof: 'Then he took her away, and I went to see
her this morning and—and they said she was dead. They didn't
want me to see her, but I made them. Her mother was crying,
and she tried to tell me something but they pulled her away and
said she was hysterical. I—I have never seen anyone dead before.
Only great-grandfather, and he—— But I don't believe—I
think they smothered her——' Her voice broke suddenly on a
shudder of horror.

Alex said quietly: 'You can't know that.'

'No. They said she had had another fit, and—— I don't
believe it! He heard what she said—Akbar Khan—and he was
afraid. I know he was afraid! I knew it last night.'

Alex said: 'I'll see what I can do.'

He walked back with her in the full glare of the blazing morning and saw her go into the house, and an hour later he sent over
a brief message asking if she would ride with him that evening.

Winter heard the wailing in the servants' quarters for half
that hot afternoon, and later a small wooden box was carried out
by a side door in the wall to the Mohammedan burial ground
outside the city; but she did not see it go.

'There is nothing we can do,' said Alex. 'The child appears
to have been subject to epileptic fits, and Dr. O'Dwyer, whom I
asked to look at the body, says that it is quite possible that she
died as a result of one of them—with general debility and the
heat as contributory causes. He was not prepared to take any further action on it. He said—and rightly—that there was enough
tension in the place already without giving rise to any more
alarm and excitement. I'm sorry, but that is all there is to it.'

Winter said in a small, hard voice: 'And what do you think
yourself?'

'What I think has nothing whatever to do with it,' said Alex at his curtest.

'Then you won't do anything?'

'There is nothing I can do, beyond what I have already done. The child was buried at four o'clock. *Ab khutam hogai* (now it is finished).' He turned his head and looked at the set white face beside him and said after a moment: 'I'm sorry, Winter.'

She did not look at him and her own hurt made her desire to hurt him also. 'No, you're not! You didn't know her. To you and Conway she was only another Indian child. A "native"; what does she matter? You would both of you have made more fuss over a dog, and a great deal more over a horse. Do you mind if we do not discuss it any more?'

Alex gave a slight shrug of his shoulders and said nothing further. He did not wish to discuss it himself. He knew something of Zeb-un-Nissa and her reputation. Epileptics were often regarded in India as being possessed of devils or favoured by God, and he had seen himself the power that the child had had over wild creatures, though he had attributed it to the simple fact, unusual in a child, that she possessed infinite patience, never made any movement that was not slow and unhurried, and could sit motionless for hours at a time. But Winter's account of what the child had said last night disturbed him. It was not that he believed Zeb-un-Nissa to have had second-sight, but it seemed to him quite likely that she was repeating something, or dreaming of something, that she had heard discussed. If so, that would account for Winter's conviction that Akbar Khan had been afraid. If Akbar Khan had imagined the child to be talking of something she had overheard, she might well have been assisted to die. However, as O'Dwyer had not been prepared to interfere, there was nothing further that could be done about it. But the words that the child had said repeated themselves again and again in his brain as they had repeated themselves in Winter's last night— 'They are killing the mem-*log*!—they are killing the mem-*log*! . . .'

Perhaps it was just as well that Zeb-un-Nissa was dead, and
that there had been no one to call out during that long, burning
day that they could hear the mem-*log* screaming.

Delhi was far away, hidden behind the dust and the dancing
heat haze and the parched, blazing plains; and Mrs. Abuthnot
had not screamed as she died in the hot sunlight within the Kashmir Gate where so short a time before the officers from the cantonments by the Ridge had held that gay moonlight picnic. But
little Miss Jennings, the Chaplain's daughter, and young Miss
Clifford, who had sung 'Where are the flowers?' to the accompaniment of her mandolin and Captain Larribie's guitar, had screamed
and shrieked as the clawing, bloodstained hands snatched at them
and the reddened sabres cut and slashed. And all through that
long hot day the shrieks of women and the terrified screaming of
children, the crackle of flames and the howl of the mob, had risen
from Duryagunj—that once quiet quarter of Delhi where the
European and Eurasian clerks and pensioners and Indian Christians had lived and were now dying in terror and agony in the
blinding, merciless sunlight.

All through that long hot day frantic officers in Meerut—
where the terror had broken out and from where the mutineers
after a night of murder had ridden for Delhi—ground their
teeth and waited, or pleaded for permission to ride after them.
There were more British troops in Meerut than in almost any
other garrison in India, and not all the native Regiments had
revolted; only let them follow up the mutineers and save Delhi
before it was too late—or at least send warning! But General
Hewitt was old and fat and infirm and the magnitude of the
crisis had left him too bewildered to take any decisive action, while
Brigadier Wilson, left to take the initiative, hesitated and was
lost. 'We must think of the women and children,' said Brigadier
Wilson uneasily. 'We cannot risk a repetition of last night's
massacres. We must protect the remaining women and children.' He would not sanction any pursuit . . .

All through the long hot day the Delhi garrison waited and
hoped, and watched the Meerut road for the help that they could

not believe would fail them. And every moment that the help delayed, the mutineers of the 3rd Cavalry and those who had joined them grew bolder, and more and more of the city rabble gathered before the Palace where the tatterdemalion court of the aged King of Delhi grew hourly more confident.

'It is true!—it is true!' urged Zeenut Mahal, the scheming favourite of old Bahadur Shah. 'They say that they have killed every *feringhi* in Meerut; men, women and children also! It must be true, for see—there is no dust cloud on the Meerut road! If any remained alive, think you they would not ride with all speed for Delhi to take vengeance? They are dead! They must all be dead! Let us kill all the *feringhis* in Delhi also, and then thou wilt be King indeed!'

'It is true—it must be true!' said the scum of the city, sharpening swords and knives for the slaughter. 'They have killed every *feringhi* in Meerut. Let us do the like here!'

'It is true!' yelled the men of the 3rd Cavalry, who had fled to Delhi in dread of pursuit and the vengeance that they had imagined to be on their heels, and who now saw, with incredulity, that none pursued. 'Did we not tell you? We have slain them all! The King! The King of Delhi! Help us, oh King! *Deen! Deen! Maro! Maro!*'

Lottie had seen her father cut down by his own men, an expression of utter disbelief upon his rubicund, cherubic face, as though he could not and would not believe, even in the moment of his death, that this thing was possible. She had made no sound, because she herself did not believe what she had seen. Standing with her mother and a dozen other women and children who had taken refuge at the Main Guard within the Kashmir Gate, she had seen him ride up to the gate with his men; placid and confident, but hurrying them forward so that this preposterous situation—the details of which he could not believe to have been correctly reported—should be put an end to at once. She had heard his fussy, fatherly voice—this pleasant, kindly little man of whom she knew so little—raised in expostulation when his men had checked before the gate. And a minute later she had seen him dragged from his horse and three bayonets plunged into his body.

His Subadar-Major and his Indian orderly had fired on the murderers and been themselves cut down, and Lottie, looking down dazedly from the rose-red walls where she had picnicked and walked in the peaceful autumn days of the vanished year, had thought how red and bright the blood looked on the hot white dust.

'It cannot be happening,' thought Lottie. 'It cannot be true . . .'

'I don't see 'as 'ow we can 'old out much longer, sir,' said Conductor Buckley to Lieutenant Willoughby who commanded the Delhi Magazine. 'The perishers 'ave brought scalin' ladders——' his words were barely audible above the howling of the mob and the incessant rattle and crash of gunfire.

They had been holding the Magazine since morning, and now the sun was moving down the sky again. Was it only four o'clock? Nine of them, against a howling, yelling mob of thousands. Nine of them to man ten guns——

'Scully says the train's laid, sir!' yelled Conductor Buckley. 'Any sign from the Meerut road yet, sir?'

Young Lieutenant Willoughby ran to the river bastion and strained his eyes for a last look down the hot, empty road where the heat haze danced and shimmered under the brazen sky. 'No. They are not coming. Perhaps they are all dead. We cannot wait any longer.'

He looked up once at the blue of the sky, his eyes calm and youthful in the sweating, dust-grimed, powder-blackened mask that was his face, and then glanced at the swarming thousands who clambered in, monkey-wise, over the walls, hemming the defenders into the last narrow square of ground.

'We shall take a good many of them with us,' said Lieutenant Willoughby. 'All right, Buckley. Give him the signal to fire it.'

The ground and the buildings and the very sky seemed to rock and reel and sway to the appalling crash of sound that silenced the savage roar of the maddened city, and a vast cloud, rose-red and beautiful in the level sunlight, lifted up above the domes and minarets; above the groves and gardens of the city of the Moguls; reaching up higher and higher into the still air and spreading out like a blossoming flower on a tall white stem.

It hung there for hours, an ephemeral memorial to gallantry. But as though the sound of the explosion had been a signal the sullen hesitating sepoys within the Main Guard turned upon those who had taken refuge there, and Lottie, who had run down from the wall at the sight of Edward, saw her mother fall without a sound, a hole through her temple, and saw a sabre slash down through her husband's head, laying it open almost to the shoulder.

She had screamed then, and fought to go to him, but someone had caught her arms and dragged her struggling and shrieking to the battlements, and then friendly hands were gripping her wrists and she was being lowered down from the wall, swaying and turning against the hot stone, and screaming for Edward. The makeshift life-line of hastily knotted belts broke, and she fell and struck the hard ground and rolled into the ditch, the breath knocked out of her body, to be caught again and dragged on and up the steep escarpment, running and stumbling over the rough ground to plunge headlong into the tangled thickets of the Khudsia Bagh . . .

The crash of the explosion shivered through the hot stillness, and rocked the Flagstaff tower on the Ridge where the terrified families from the cantonments had been crowded together in helpless confusion all that long day, waiting for news and straining their eyes through the heat haze towards the city and the empty Meerut road. The women gasped and flinched to the hammer-blow of the sound, while their servants wailed aloud and the children shrieked in terror as a white column of smoke shot up from the distant city and spread into a slow, rose-red corona that hung above the mangled bodies of the thousand dead who had died in the explosion of the Magazine.

'We can't wait here any longer,' said a haggard-faced officer pacing the Ridge. 'What in hell's name are they doing in

*O

Meerut? They *cannot* all be dead! For God's sake, why don't
we do something to help those poor devils in the city? There's
still the river arsenal to draw on. We could have made some sort
of a show, instead of just leaving them to be slaughtered!'

'Don't be a fool, Mellish! We've got to think of the women
and children. As it was, we had to weaken the city garrison in
order to keep sufficient men here for their protection. We can't
try any "forlorn hopes" while we have their safety to consider.'

'Then why didn't we send them off to Karnal as soon as we
got the first news? Why the devil don't we send them now!
Every moment that we hesitate increases the danger for them
and for us, and most of all for those who are trapped in the city!
No one seems to have done a dam' thing in Meerut, and no one
is doing anything here—except young Willoughby who has
evidently had the guts to blow up the Magazine! Surely anything
is better than standing by like this and watching the few men
who might remain loyal losing all confidence in us? Look——!
What's that—there's a cart coming up the road! Is it news at
last?'

A bullock-cart creaked and jolted slowly up the road in a
cloud of dust, to halt by the Flagstaff tower where the setting
sun illuminated its contents with brutal clarity: the slashed,
stiffening, bloodstained bodies of half a dozen British officers,
thrown in as carelessly as though they had been so many bales of
straw. A challenge flung at the Ridge by the triumphant city.
A challenge that would not be taken up for many days.

The moon gathered light as the last of the daylight faded, and
those who had waited all day on the Ridge of Delhi, hoping and
fearing and waiting for the help from Meerut that never came,
prepared to leave at last. 'It will be dark in half an hour,' said
the Brigadier, his eyes still straining towards the empty Meerut
road. 'The women had better go, and they will need protection.
You had all better go while the road to Karnal is still open.'

The glare of the burning bungalows in the cantonments made
a second sunset in the sky as carriages and dog-carts and men
on foot and on horseback streamed away into the gathering

darkness to begin that long torment of flight through a hostile land during which so many were to die. The Brigadier waited until they had gone, and then with the last remaining officer on his staff he faced the sullen remnants of his command. 'Sound the Assembly,' said the Brigadier, and heard the familiar bugle-call ring out in the silence.

A single figure, a sepoy of the 74th Bengal Native Infantry, answered the summons; standing stiffly to attention, lonely and obedient in the gathering dusk. The only one to remain faithful to his salt out of all those serried ranks of men who twenty-four hours ago would have obeyed that call.

The Brigadier's shoulders sagged tiredly, and he turned at last and rode away from the Ridge, leaving the deserted cantonments to the night and the looters, while behind him, high above the darkening city, the last of the daylight and the first rays of the moon lit a fading cloud that still hung above the shattered Magazine and marked the only decisive stand that had been made in all that terrible day.

*   *   *

Winter had not spoken again during that evening ride and Alex was too occupied with his own thoughts to notice the fact. He was sorry for her, but it occurred to him that there were going to be a great many other things to be sorry for soon. He could not send Niaz to the lines any more, and his various sources of information in the city and the surrounding villages were becoming less and less easy to get in touch with. They were afraid of being seen near his bungalow, and what news they brought was inconclusive and disturbing.

He looked up at the pale segment of moon floating high above the veil of dust that blurred the horizon. A flight of cormorants making for Hazrat Bagh jheel drew a thin dark arrowhead against the opal sky, and a flock of purple pigeons circled above the jostling rooftops of the city. He wondered how Niaz and Yusaf were faring. It would be far hotter out on the plain than in the cantonments, and they would have had nothing to eat or drink since before dawn. Ramadan, when it fell in the hot weather, was no mean test of endurance, and the knife-wound in Niaz's back was not yet fully healed. 'I shall have to go myself tonight,' thought Alex. Night work was all very well for Niaz and Yusaf, who could spare the time to sleep by day, but it came hard on Alex, who could not.

He drew rein before the Residency gate and spoke for the first time in almost an hour. 'When do you leave for the hills?'

'On the twenty-second,' said Winter listlessly. Her anger had left her and she felt curiously apathetic.

'Which gives you a week in which to get there,' said Alex. 'Eight days to be precise. It should be enough. I expect I shall see you before then. Good night.'

He turned his horse and cantered away in the direction of his bungalow and Winter went on under the arch of the gateway past the stately, salaaming figure of Akbar Khan. An hour ago she would not have acknowledged that salutation. An hour ago she had hated both Alex and her husband because they would not hang him for murder. But now the apathy that had descended upon her pressed down with an almost tangible weight. She had not slept at all during the previous night and she was very tired. Nothing mattered any more. Perhaps it was true that their lives were plotted out for them and none could avoid their fate. 'What is written, is written' . . .

She slept soundly that night despite the heat and the creaking of the punkah. As soundly as Zeb-un-Nissa who lay in the Mohammedan cemetery and did not hear the yelling of the jackal-packs who slunk among the graves. As exhaustedly as Lottie who lay asleep, her thin slippers and frilly skirts torn and ripped by thorns and stained with dust and blood, in a curtained *ekka* whose kindly owner had found her and her two companions crouching in a ditch by the roadside, and had befriended them.

'I go to Lunjore, and with all speed,' said the driver of the *ekka*. 'Delhi will be no place for a man of peace for many moons, and I have a brother in Lunjore with whom I will abide until this madness is past.'

29

ALEX and Yusaf returned to the bungalow in the dark hour before dawn and by different routes, but Niaz remained invisible. He was reported to be still suffering from fever and unable to leave his bed.

Alex had hoped to sleep late but he was awakened at sunrise by Alam Din. 'Huzoor,' said Alam Din softly, 'there is a red kite caught in the thorn tree by the city road.'

'Damn!' said Alex wearily. 'Damn and blast! Oh, all right. *Acha*, Alam Din, *main jaunga*.'

He shook himself awake, and twenty minutes later he was riding through the crop-lands in the direction of Chunwar. The mile-long road that led across the open plain to the city boasted a solitary thorn tree that grew near its edge some two hundred yards from the cantonment end, and this morning there was a cheap paper kite such as children fly caught up in its scanty spiked foliage. A vivid scarlet thing, visible from some considerable distance.

Gaily coloured kites flew all day and at all seasons in the sky above the city, and a strayed one that had broken its string was frequently to be found tangled among the branches of trees on the plain. Alex did not pass the thorn tree and barely glanced at it. He took a narrow side-path that skirted a field of mustard, and checking the Eagle by a culvert where the elephant grass grew high and a wild fig tree threw a patch of shadow, he dismounted as though to tighten a girth.

There was a rustle in the grasses and a voice whose owner remained invisible spoke in a whisper that was barely audible above the creaking of a distant well-wheel and the indignant chittering of a striped squirrel:

'There is word in the bazaar that the *pultons* have risen in Meerut, and have slain all the *Angrezi-log* and ridden on Delhi, which has fallen also. It is said that they have proclaimed Bahadur Shah as Mogul and put all *feringhis* to the sword.'

'When?' asked Alex, wrestling with a strap.

'Yesterday only. The news was told at dawn by a *fakir* at the steps of the pearl masjid.'

'It is not possible,' said Alex. 'Delhi is far.'

'Do not the very birds of the air speak to the *bairagis?*' whispered the voice.

Alex said: 'Is there aught else said?'

'Nay. What need of more? The city hums like a hive.'

'Will they rise?'

'Who knows? The Maulvie's men call upon them to hold back and to wait for the Word, but it were better that none of thy people were seen in the city today. Keep them close. If even a stone were thrown there is no knowing what might follow. Thou knowest the temper of crowds. If they see blood, they run mad like jackals.'

Alex said softly: 'Go back and bring me word tonight. I will ride by the tomb of Amin-u-din at sunset.'

'I will try. But I am afraid—afraid! If it were known, they would tear me in pieces!' Alex could hear the man's teeth chatter, and he laid a handful of silver coins in the dust by the rim of the culvert and said: 'There will be fifty more tonight,' and mounting again rode on towards the open plain.

He made a çircuit of the crop-lands and returned to the cantonments by way of the rifle-range, riding for the most part at a leisurely walk that necessitated a considerable effort of will, and it was well past eight o'clock by the time he reached the Residency.

He found the Commissioner still abed, and naked save for a width of thin cotton cloth wrapped about his waist in the manner of a Burmese *lungi*. The bedroom reeked of musk and stale spirits, and the green-tinted *chiks* over the closed windows toned the light to a twilight dimness. Alex's foot struck against a cluster of little silver bells such as often adorn an Indian woman's anklet, and he found it an effort to restrain a grimace of disgust.

'Well?' demanded Mr. Barton sourly. 'What is it now? More bees?'

'I hope it may turn out to be no more than that,' said Alex curtly. 'There is a story being circulated in the city of a rising in Meerut and in Delhi. It may be entirely untrue, or there may have been some trouble there that has been grossly exaggerated by rumour. But the story is that the regiments in both places have mutinied and killed all the Europeans, and that Bahadur Shah has been acclaimed as King.'

'What rubbish!' said the Commissioner angrily. He sat upright and the movement appeared to be painful, for he groaned and put a hand to his head. He glowered at Captain Randall and said: 'Why, Meerut's crammed with British troops! Crammed with 'em!—at least two thousand. Strongest garrison in India! Poppycock! It's only another bazaar rumour.'

'Perhaps, sir,' said Alex shortly. 'The point is not so much whether it is true, as that the city believes it to be true. Such a rumour is bound to give rise to a good deal of excitement, and I should like, with your permission, to put the city out of bounds to all Europeans until the excitement has had time to die down.'

'Why?'

God give me patience! prayed Alex, setting his teeth. He said calmly and pleasantly, as though reasoning with a backward and fractious child: 'It takes very little to start a riot among people who have been systematically worked up into a state of excitement and tension as these have been. With this sort of rumour flying round the bazaars, a white face in the city might lead to stone-throwing. And as you know, sir, with a mob that is only a short step from murder. We cannot afford any unpleasant incidents at the moment. In a day or two at most we should hear if there is anything at all behind the rumours, and if there is not, the excitement will die down. May I take it that you agree to putting the city out of bounds?'

'Oh yes, I suppose so,' said the Commissioner ungraciously. 'Don't believe a word of it, but—— Well, go on, go on!—do what you like about it and leave me in peace!'

Alex did not linger. He did not return to his own office but went instead to the Commissioner's, where he wrote briefly, swiftly and to the point, using the Commissioner's official paper, and then returned to the darkened bedroom with pen and ink-well to demand the Commissioner's signature. Having seen the *chuprassi* leave with the sealed documents he asked if he might see Mrs. Barton, but Winter had gone out.

'The memsahib left but half an hour ago,' Imam Bux informed him. 'She has gone to the city.'

Alex whipped round on the speaker with a suddenness that startled him considerably. '*Where?*'

'To the city,' faltered Imam Bux. 'To the shop of Ditta Mull the silk merchant, near the Sudder Bazaar.'

'Who is with her?'

'Huzoor, the memsahib went on horseback. I do not know which syce—I will make enquiry, if the Huzoor——'

But Alex had gone.

It was after nine and the tree shadows were shortening on the white dust, while already the heat danced on the open plain so that the mile-distant city appeared to shimmer and waver in the blinding sunlight as though it were made of molten glass. There was a white foam of lather streaking the Eagle's neck and flanks, and Alex's coat was wet with sweat, but his hands and his stomach were cold with fear and rage—a rage that was entirely directed at himself.

'If I get myself involved in a riot, I may have to shoot,' thought Alex, 'and if I do that—— They won't harm her! They know her too well. They know me too, but I represent Authority, and that may set them off . . . I ought to let her take her chance. If they kill me that fool Barton will lose his head, and I have not given the order about the bridge, and—I *can't* risk everything just because of one woman! Nicholson was right —the safeguarding of women and children in some crises is such a very minor consideration that it ceases to be a consideration at all—I must not go . . .' But he went.

He reined to a canter as he neared the city gate, and fought down his fear, for a mob was a purely animal thing and like an animal could sense fear. He rode in under the gate at a walk, sitting loosely in the saddle, and called a greeting to the police havildar who saluted him as he passed.

He could feel the pulse and panic of the city swirling about him from the very dust and beating down upon him in the blinding heat. There was an ominous silence as he passed and a menacing mutter that rose at his back, and the faces that watched him were avid or insolent or uneasy. Those men whom he knew and spoke to as the Eagle shouldered his way through the crowded bazaar avoided his gaze and shifted unhappily, observing their neighbours with furtive anxiety. Normally, when he rode through the city, men cleared a path for him, but today he found that he must force the Eagle between men who made no attempt to move out of his way, and who jostled and obstructed him with deliberate insolence. His progress became slower and slower; and then a stone hurtled out of the crowd. It missed him and struck a woman, who screamed shrilly.

An indescribable sound rose from the crowd; a sound like the soft growling snarl of a gigantic cat, and Alex rose in his stirrups, and facing the quarter from whence the stone had been thrown, raised his voice and called a jest across the heads of the crowd. It was a coarse and untranslatable jest, relative to the proper treatment of prostitutes, and the crowd, taken by surprise, laughed. The tension snapped and a man called out: 'Has the Sahib heard the news from Delhi?'

'*Beshak!* I hear many lies with every morn, Kartar Singh. But I wait for the evening, and when the heat of the day is past the truth becomes known.'

'Is it then the truth?' cried another voice.

'The heat has surely turned thy brain, Sohan Lal!' said Alex with a laugh. 'Abide a little, and let it cool!'

The laugh had its effect upon the crowd. Hostility waned and doubt took its place. Perhaps the rumours that had spread like wildfire through the bazaars since dawn were false? for the Sahib, it was plain, had also heard news—yet he laughed. Would he laugh if the news were bad? The crowd drew back and let him pass, their faces sullen and unsure, and twenty yards ahead Alex caught sight of the Maulvie of one of the city mosques making his way along the street. He urged the Eagle to a quicker pace, and drawing level with the man, leaned out and touched him on the shoulder. The Maulvie turned sharply.

'*As Salaam aleikum*, Maulvie-Sahib,' said Alex pleasantly. 'Canst thou spare the time to lead me to the shop of Ditta Mull in the street of the silk merchants? I cannot call to mind the way.'

He saw the anger flash in the man's eyes, and the cunning replace it as the Maulvie looked up at him and then back at the watching crowd; and knew that he had guessed aright. This was one of Ahmed Ullah of Faizabad's men, and Gopal Nath, hidden in the culvert by the fig tree, had whispered that the Maulvie of Faizabad's men were preaching patience. It was no part of their plan to touch off premature riots, and if there was any truth at all in the rumours concerning Delhi and Meerut they must be feeling alarmed for the success of their carefully laid plans. The man who stood at Alex's stirrup knew quite well that he was familiar with every street and alley and shop in the city and was demanding protection, and he would have given much to refuse it. But it was as much in his interest as in Alex's own to prevent a premature outbreak in Lunjore, and so he smiled sourly and murmured the conventional reply to the greeting:

'*Wa aleikum Salaam*. If the Sahib will come with me I will show him.'

Furiante's impatiently tossing head, and the frightened face of the syce who was endeavouring to control both horses, were visible above the heads of a noisy jostling crowd who packed the narrow street before Ditta Mull's shop and swayed dangerously to and fro. The panic on the face of the syce did nothing to reassure Alex and once again he felt fear clutch at his throat, and forced it back. The Maulvie, walking beside him, took the Eagle's bridle and thrust his way through the crowd, who fell back and cleared a passage to the bottom of the five rickety wooden steps that led up to the shop front.

Winter was not visible, for Ditta Mull had hurriedly dropped the heavy *chiks* before the open entrance of his shop. He peered out anxiously on hearing Alex's voice and grasped feverishly at his sleeve: 'Take her away, Huzoor!' begged Ditta Mull. 'By the back way! I do not know what madness has taken hold on the city this morning. There is a tale that—but no matter. I fear that some may do her harm because she is the wife of the Commissioner Sahib. Already there have been stones flung at my shop. It is not our own people. They know her well. But there are others—*budmashes* from Suthragunj and Shahjehanpur and Bareilly who have been stirring up trouble in the city with wild tales. The memsahib is with my wife and children. She wished to leave, fearing the people might harm my shop on her account, but I would not let her. It is well that thou hast come! I will tell the memsahib.'

He hurried away through a dark doorway in the back of the shop, wringing his small fat hands and making little moaning noises, and returned a minute or two later with Winter. She was perfectly calm, and quite uninterested, thought Alex furiously—irrationally swinging from the extremes of fear to the limits of exasperation—in the dangers of the situation. She frowned a little at the sight of him, but refused to leave without a large quantity of rose-coloured sari silk that she had previously selected. She watched Ditta Mull wrap it up in a length of muslin, his hands shaking like leaves in a wind, and having accepted and paid for it, said with a touch of impatience: 'Do not show them that face, *Lala-jee*. If they see that thou art afraid, then they too may behave foolishly. But not otherwise.'

She handed the package to Alex who received it in grim silence, and went out under the lifted *chik* into the fierce glare of the sunlight. The crowd had ceased to shout and sway and had become silent, gazing curiously at the split-cane *chik* that concealed the interior of the shop and at the impassive Maulvie who stood at the foot of the steps outside it. As Winter stepped out into the sunlight a mutter rose from them and swelled ominously, but she appeared unconscious of it, and Alex saw her look up to smile at someone in a second-storey window at the far side of the narrow street, and sketch the Hindu gesture of salutation with one hand.

The crowd, instantly diverted, turned as one to see who it was whom the memsahib had greeted, and saw a small fat child hanging out over the edge of a fretted window ledge and beckoning. Winter shook her head at it and called out: 'Have a care, Bappa, or thou wilt surely fall! I cannot come today, but I will come soon.'

'Tomorrow?' shrilled the child.

'Not tomorrow. Perhaps next week.'

The brief conversation changed the mood of the crowd as Alex's jest had changed the mood of the mob in the Sudder Bazaar, but he could feel the dangerous pendulum-swing of their emotions with every nerve in his body, and knew how little it would take to sway them towards senseless savagery. Was Winter unaware of it? She seemed to be. He heard her murmur a polite and conventional greeting to the Maulvie, and then she was in the saddle and moving off down the packed street, controlling the nervous impatience of Furiante with apparent ease.

The next fifteen minutes seemed endless to Alex, riding behind her and frequently separated from her by the shifting, jostling crowds. He heard her speak to a dozen people as they edged their way through the street, her voice light and gay. He noted as they passed that more than half the shops were closed and shuttered— sure sign of panic; that despite the intense heat the narrow stifling streets and alleyways were as full of people as though it had been a fair day or a festival, and that the people talked in whispers and muttered in undertones.

The Maulvie left them abruptly at the turn into the wide stretch of the Sudder Bazaar that ended at the Rohilkhand Gate, and vanished down a side street. Three hundred yards to go . . . two hundred . . . one hundred . . . fifty. Slowly; keep to a walk . . . A man was holding forth excitedly to a dense knot of people as thick as a swarm of bees, and scraps of sentences separated themselves from the sullen murmur of the crowd. '. . . with two heads! My cousin's wife's brother saw it . . . it is a sign! What else but a sign? Their days are accomplished . . .'

Muttered curses and a man spitting loudly and contemptuously as they passed. A low-caste woman shouting at the frightened, furious syce, '*Hai, ghora wallah,* do they feed thee on bone-dust now that thou hast taken service with the sahib-*log?*'

And then they were through the gate and out on the open empty glaring road that led across the plain to the cantonments, and Furiante had broken into a canter and then into a gallop. Winter had attempted to slow him after the first hundred yards or so, but Alex had brought his whip down on the horse's quarters and they had flashed at full gallop under the shadows of the trees that lined the cantonment road. He reined in at last before the gate of his own bungalow and waited for the syce to come up with them. He had not spoken once since he entered Ditta Mull's shop, and he did not speak now. He put up a hand and wiped the sweat out of his eyes, and knew that his hand was shaking.

Winter said uncertainly: 'You're very angry, aren't you? But I did not know that there was trouble in the city. I know you told me to keep away from it. I'm sorry. But you should not have come for me. I do not think that they would have done me any harm. They were more likely to harm you.'

It was exactly what Alex himself had thought, and his anger against himself for not having had the moral courage to leave her to take her chance kept him silent.

Winter looked at him doubtfully and added: 'It was—kind of you to come. Thank you.'

'You have nothing to thank me for,' said Alex shortly. 'I probably endangered your life, and that of everyone else in the cantonment, by going there.'

The syce cantered up, dusty and sullen but still clutching the package of rose-coloured silk, and Alex observed him tight-lipped, and then turned back to Winter. He said: 'The city is out of bounds until further notice, and I should be obliged if you would curtail your rides in future, and keep only to the cantonments and the *maïdan.*'

'But——'

'That is an order,' said Alex, and turned into his own gateway.

He had ridden out at sundown that evening to the ruined tomb of Amin-u-din on the far bank of the river, but Gopal Nath had not been there. There had been no one there but the bats and the lizards and a flock of green parrots, for Gopal Nath was lying face-downwards among the high grass at the edge of the grazing-grounds with his throat cut from ear to ear, and the work that the jackals and the hyenas began that night was completed the next day by the kites and the vultures and the remorseless heat, so that twenty-four hours later no one could be quite sure who those reddened, scattered bones had once belonged to.

*　　　　　*　　　　　*

There had been a party at the Residency that night. The last of the Tuesday parties, although no one there knew that it was to be the last. And Lottie was almost thirty miles nearer Lunjore. At Meerut General Hewitt and Brigadier Wilson, with a strong force of British troops at their command, still remained in a state of helpless inaction, and on the Ridge at Delhi only the putrefying bodies of six officers, still piled one upon the other in the abandoned cart that had dragged them from the shambles of the Kashmir Gate, were the only British who remained to tell of all those who, two short days ago, had lived and laughed in the now gutted and empty cantonment.

A dispatch-rider from Suthragunj on a lathered horse arrived in Lunjore at noon on Wednesday. He had waited only long enough to deliver the sealed letter he carried to the Commissioner's head *chuprassi*, and to water his horse, before setting out on the return journey. Alex had not been told of his arrival, and the Commissioner, handed the letter on a salver by Iman Bux during luncheon, had stuffed it into his pocket, unread, and forgotten about it until the following morning. It had been nearly midday when he read it at last, and then he could not at first take in the baldly worded statement it contained. His first reaction had been incredulity. The thing was a hoax—a ridiculous practical joke! It must be, because it could not possibly be true. But it was written on official paper, and he knew that scrawled signature. The blood seemed to leave his heart and drain out of his body. His pale eyes bulged with shock and the paper dropped from his nerveless hand and slid to the floor, where the draught from the punkah sent it fluttering lazily across the drawing-room carpet like a bird with a broken wing.

It had been Winter who had picked it up and Winter who had sent for Alex. He had arrived to find the Commissioner gulping down his third glass of brandy, and under its influence returning to his first view of the situation. 'Hoax,' said Mr. Barton thickly. 'Can't be anything else!'

'I'm afraid not, sir,' said Alex, running his eye down the single sheet of paper. He looked at the quivering bulk that slumped upon the sofa, glass in hand, and said curtly: 'Where is the man who brought this? When did it arrive?'

The Commissioner swallowed the remainder of the brandy in his glass and poured himself out a fourth peg, slopping the liquid on to the carpet. 'Can't be expected to deal with everything!' he said loudly and defensively. 'How was I to know it was important? Might have been an invitation to a shoot f'r all one knew. Put it in m' pocket. Forgot it. Very natural.'

'It arrived during luncheon yesterday,' Winter said quietly. 'I think that the man left almost immediately.'

Alex said nothing. He looked at his chief with a contempt and exasperation which he made no attempt to disguise, and turned and went out of the room.

'Damned impertinence!' said Mr. Barton querulously, and finished his fourth brandy.

Less than an hour later a hurriedly convened conference of a dozen appalled men met round the Commissioner's dining-room table to discuss the emergency arising out of the incredible—the impossible news—and to decide what measures, if any, might belatedly be taken to safeguard Lunjore from the mutiny and massacre that had overtaken Meerut and Delhi. Alex had urged the supreme measure of disarming the regiments, but the suggestion had been treated as an outrage.

'If I should ever be ordered by the General to insult my men in such a manner,' declared Colonel Gardener-Smith roundly, 'he would first have to disarm me, and after me, every one of my officers!'

'Your suggestion, Captain Randall,' said Colonel Moulson, 'is not only beneath contempt, but one which it is not your place to advance.'

Alex gave a faint shrug of his shoulders. 'I am sorry, sir. Then may I suggest that we send the women and children to Naini Tal immediately? Today if possible. There may still be time.'

There was an immediate outbreak of protest. If disaffection was rife, travelling would be dangerous and difficult. The women were safer where they were. An adequate escort could not be spared. To send them to the hills now was to run too great a risk.

'To leave it until it is too late will be a greater one,' said Alex. 'The mutinies at Meerut and Delhi were premature. I am sure of it. As I have already told you, I have reason to believe that a date for a general outbreak has been set for the end of this month; and that belief is not only supported by information, but confirmed by the behaviour of the city. There is still time to send the women to safety.'

'We cannot do it,' said Colonel Gardener-Smith heavily. 'It is too late.'

'It is *not* too late!' said Alex passionately. 'At least there is a chance!'

'Perhaps. But it is a chance that we cannot take. At this stage it is surely a matter of vital importance not to show any sign of panic. You must see that.'

'I doubt it,' said Colonel Moulson with a sneer. 'It is a thing that Captain Randall has never been able to see. And I agree with you, Colonel. It is of course out of the question for any of the women to leave. Their departure at this juncture would be taken as a clear sign that we had lost our nerve, and I am sure that I speak for the majority when I say that this is far from being the case.'

'I agree. I entirely agree,' said Colonel Packer. 'To show panic may precipitate the very crisis we seek to avoid. We must place our trust in the Lord. His rod and His staff shall not fail us.'

'Possibly not, sir,' said Alex dryly. 'But will the sepoys? Are we to take it that the sight of our women and children being sent to safety will unsettle the regiments to the extent of driving them to mutiny? I had understood that you believed them to be loyal?'

'The loyalty of my Regiment,' said Colonel Gardener-Smith quietly, 'has never yet been called in question, and to send my wife and daughter away would amount to a public declaration that I had lost confidence in their loyalty. That I will not do. At this time it is doubly necessary not only to show confidence, but to avoid any action that can be construed as alarm.'

'Which means,' said Alex with shut teeth, 'that no precautionary measures whatever can be taken, for fear that any change in the present routine may be translated as panic!'

'You exaggerate, Captain Randall,' said Colonel Gardener-Smith coldly. 'Reasonable precautions will of course be taken.'

'Will you name one, sir?' demanded Alex tersely.

There was a sudden silence about the table. It was broken by Colonel Packer, who remarked pontifically that those who put their trust in the Lord needed no other armour.

'Nonsense!' snapped Colonel Gardener-Smith. 'The Lord helps those who help themselves, Packer! But at the present juncture I maintain that all that is necessary is to remain calm. There must be no appearance of alarm or any alteration of our normal practices that might be likely to call forth comment and arouse uneasiness. For which reason I myself am against sending the women and children away. What do you say, Barton?'

'Qui' ri',' said Mr. Barton. 'Mush keep calm. 'Ssential to keep calm. Where's the brandy?'

Alex came to his feet and leaned on the table, his hands gripping the edge. 'May I *beg* you to reconsider, sir? I am well aware that it will give rise to panic if we send them away. Good God, I am not entirely——'. He controlled himself with an effort and

continued more quietly: 'But I feel that it should be possible to
explain to the regiments, through the medium of the Indian
officers, that the families are only being sent away because the
services of every officer and every sepoy may be needed for
action, and not for being kept hamstrung in cantonments protecting a parcel of women.'

'I reshent that!' said the Commissioner with dignity. 'Wha'
d'yer mean, "parcel o' women"? Sweet creatures! Privilege to
protect 'em!'

Alex ignored the interruption: 'I beg of you to send them away
while there is still time. It is the lesser of the two evils, and our
paramount duty at this time is surely not their protection, but the
saving of the country. The maximum efficiency cannot be
obtained while the garrison is hampered by a horde of women
whose personal safety will be placed above military expediency . . .'

The memory of his own fatuous action of the previous day,
when he had followed his chief's wife into the city against all
reason and judgment, caught in his throat and seemed to choke
him, and he struck the table with the flat of his hand: 'Can you
not see that if they remain here they will hamper and handicap
us into virtual uselessness? How can any man make a cool-
headed decision, which he knows may involve grave risk, while
he is thinking that to take that risk may mean the murder and
mutilation of his wife and child? There are a hundred chances
that we would all cheerfully take without them, yet would hesitate to take while we have their safety to consider.'

He looked about the table at the circle of grim, drawn faces
and saw hesitation and doubt; and, for a moment only, he was
hopeful. Then Colonel Moulson spoke:

'My dear Captain Randall,' he drawled. 'You allow your
fears to run away with you. It is my opinion that the news from
Delhi will be found to be greatly exaggerated. And in any case
the Meerut Brigade will have moved by now, and Delhi has
almost certainly been recaptured. But even if that were not so,
I would like to point out that we have three Infantry Regiments
here as well as half a regiment of Military Police, and if we had

only one—my own—I would still engage to keep the city in order and protect double the number of women and children without the smallest difficulty. The rabble are notoriously chicken-hearted, and a dose of grape will be quite enough to cool their tempers should they show any signs of violence. I advocated such a course only yesterday, but I understand that it was you who preferred the more cautious method of putting the city out of bounds? A pity. Now, I should have marched my men through the streets and shot down every black bastard who raised his voice. That would have ended any nonsense quickly enough.'

'Hear! Hear!' interjected Major Mottisham.

'So you must really not expect us,' concluded Colonel Moulson, 'to make a public exhibition of ourselves by ordering a panic-stricken exodus of all the women and children, just because you yourself feel nervous!'

Alex said softly: 'I can only say, sir, that in the event of my timorous fears proving justified, I hope that you will obtain some comfort from the realization that you will have sacrificed the lives of these women, and jeopardized the safety of the Company's possessions, in order to demonstrate a confidence in the fidelity of your sepoys which you do not wholly possess.'

Colonel Moulson's face was suddenly scarlet with rage and he half-rose from his chair. 'You are impertinent, Captain Randall! Must I again remind you that you are a junior officer—and can be disciplined?'

'Because I speak the truth, sir?' Alex's precarious hold on his temper had departed and his voice was raw-edged with a rage that matched Colonel Moulson's. 'You all have your doubts! Every one of you! But not one of you will admit it. You will not even institute a few enquiries because to do so would be tanta-mount to an admission that disloyalty among your men might be possible, and so you prefer to shut your eyes rather than cast what you consider to be a slur on the good name of your regi-ments! All very laudable. But in the present crisis, you will give me leave to say that it is hardly practical!'

'In the present crisis,' said Colonel Moulson furiously, 'it is the panicmongers that we have to fear! If we could rid ourselves of them we should be a deal better off! There is no lack of confidence here, I assure you. But as you yourself feel so insecure, I can only suggest that you should apply for sick leave and set off immediately for Naini Tal!'

Alex's right hand that lay flat upon the table clenched slowly into a fist—and as slowly relaxed again. It was no use. They were courageous enough, but they did not even now realize the magnitude of this thing that was overtaking them. They had refused to take any precautions while the emergency was far away, and now that it was upon them they would take none— for fear of showing fear. They had done nothing while they could, and dared do nothing when they would.

'Qui' ri',' repeated the Commissioner with a hiccough, ' 'tirely agree. Mush keep calm!'

Alex sat down without further words, and did not speak again while the conference dragged to its inconclusive close, but when it was over he dispatched a telegram to the Governor General, in the name of the Commissioner of Lunjore, requesting plenary military powers. The nearest telegraph post had until recently been seventy-five miles away in Suthragunj, but it was not twenty by the Hazrat Bagh road, and Alex reflected grimly that Kishan Prasad's road was proving its usefulness in a way that had not been intended by those who had made it.

That night the first of the fires started, and the surgeon of the 105th N.I., Colonel Packer's regiment, had his bungalow burnt to the ground. It had been a thatched bungalow, and an arrow wrapped in blazing oil-soaked rags had been fired into the roof shortly before midnight.

Less than fifty miles to the south-west Lottie and her companions were still safe in the care of the kindly *ekka* driver and drawing hourly nearer to Lunjore. But behind them, scattered over the sun-scorched countryside that surrounded the captured city of the Moguls, the majority of the fugitives from Delhi hid and starved and died.

Men, women and children crouched all day in ditches and cane-brakes, gasping in the relentless heat. Stripping themselves of uniforms and crinolines, wading rivers, crawling through the dying grass, skulking in the jungle. Scratching shallow graves in the hot, iron-hard earth to cover the corpse of a child, and leaving the bodies of the adult dead to the vultures and the jackal-packs: robbed, stripped, insulted; hunted through the crop-lands and murdered for sport.

A few—a very few—fell into the hands of kindly people who gave them food and shelter and risked their own lives, and the lives of all their families, in order to save a hunted, helpless fellow creature. And within the walls of Delhi, in a stifling, windowless dungeon below the Palace of the aged, timorous Bahadur Shah, newly proclaimed King of all Hindustan, fifty prisoners—the last of the British and the Christians left in Delhi —had still two days to live.

30

NIAZ had reappeared in public and was once again to be seen riding with Captain Randall through the villages.

They were in the saddle for the greater part of every day, for Alex returned each night to Lunjore. He heard cases and gave judgments, sitting on horseback in the shade of a tree throughout the long, blazing days: seeing in the faces of the villagers the ominous signs of the sickness that was sweeping through India; the open insolence and hostility that must be stared down or disregarded; the quick-leaping panic that must be allayed.

The quiet countryside was alive with rumours. 'The Shah of Persia has sent an army to the help of Bahadur Shah, who is now King of all Hind, and that army is already in Delhi!' . . . 'There are but a handful of *feringhis* left in the land, and the defeated remnants of the *Angrezi* regiments have been forced back and back until they drowned in the sea!' . . .

There were stories and more stories, but no proof—until one day three men arrived in a village not ten miles from Lunjore city and brought the proof with them in the form of two flounced muslin dresses, a sword, and a long tress of silky blonde hair. The soft muslin of the flounces and the soft gold of the hair were stiffened and patched with the ugly brown stains of dried blood, and there was blood too on the blade of the sword that had once belonged to a British officer.

'We found them hiding in a ditch by the roadside,' boasted one of the men. 'Two memsahibs and a sahib, five *koss* from Delhi. There was a child also, whose crying betrayed them. The sahib was sore wounded, but when Abdullah here ran his *tulwar* through the child, he struck at him with this sword. But his arm had no strength and I took it from him and slew him with it, and the young woman also. *Arré*—how she shrieked! Like a peacock. I caught her by the hair—see, here is the lock! All the Hell-born are dead, and——'

'Not all,' said a hard clear voice behind him, and the gaping villagers drew back hastily.

Alex rode forward, Niaz at his elbow, and looked long and steadily at the three men, and no one spoke. Then he crooked his finger without turning his head and said softly: 'Kotwal-*jee*, bind me these men.'

The head-man flinched and hesitated, and suddenly there was a revolver in Alex's hand and another in Niaz's.

'Be swift, my father,' said Niaz pleasantly. 'Do not keep the Huzoor waiting—or Hell either, which languishes to receive these three.'

There was a stir and a babble among the crowd and Alex raised his voice: '*Chup!* Be still! The first who moves without an order will go quickly to his account! And if it be a woman who moves, then her man will pay in her stead. Use thy pugaree, oh Kotwal; it will serve if thou canst not find a rope. That is better! Mohamed Latif, and thou, Guar Chand, bind me these other two.'

The three men looked wildly about them, jaws dropped and

eyes starting in disbelief; but the village had known Alex for several years, and the habit of obedience, backed by the threat of firearms, was strong. If he had looked away or hesitated they would have broken and run, and guns and knives and *lathis* would have appeared as though by magic, and stones would have been thrown. But he did not look away and his eyes were cold and unpleasant. As unpleasant as Niaz's narrow-lipped grin.

One of the three men turned suddenly and ran, and Niaz fired. The man tripped and fell face downwards in the dust, twitched once and was still. 'That was too good a death for such offal,' said Niaz cheerfully, controlling his horse more by the pressure of his knees than by the reins in his left hand.

The Eagle flung up his head and backed a pace, but he had been trained to stand the sound of a shot and he gave no trouble. When the two remaining murderers dangled at a rope's end, Alex gestured at the third body on the ground: 'Hang him beside his friends, so that all may see.'

They strung up the corpse without a word and Niaz took up the sword, the stained clothing and the lock of yellow hair, and tying them swiftly into a bundle, fastened it to his saddle. Alex surveyed the shivering Kotwal and the silent villagers and said: 'If any others come saying that all the sahibs be slain, show them these three. And tell any who ask, that though every sahib now in Hind were slain, a hundred thousand more—and ten times a hundred thousand—would come from *Belait* to exact vengeance for the slaying of their women and their babes. For the blood of such helpless ones is as seed which, falling to the ground, springs up in the likeness of armed men.'

He rode on out of the village without a backward look. '*Ho!*' said Niaz, putting up a hand to wipe the sweat from his forehead, 'I did not think to leave that place alive! It needed but one among them to show his teeth and they would have been at our throats like wolves. Wast thou not afraid?'

Alex gave a short laugh and held out one hand, palm downwards, by way of answer. It was shaking uncontrollably.

'Mine also!' said Niaz. 'I counted each breath as though it

were my last. Is it true then that thy people are hunted through
Hind?'

'It is true. But the end is not yet. In the end there will be a
vengeance which will be as harsh, or harsher, than the offence:
for that is the evil that springs from such killing!'

Alex's voice was suddenly rough with anger and despair, and
Niaz said quietly: 'It is none of thy doing, brother. What is
written is written.'

'That is taught by thy Prophet, not mine!' said Alex bitterly.
'Mine would have me be my brother's keeper! Here—take the
gun.'

He sent in a brief report of the incident to the Commissioner
and was sent for to explain himself. 'You had no authority to do
such a thing!' fumed the Commissioner. 'Disgraceful! Supposing it should come to the ears of the Authorities that men had
been hanged in my district without trial? Why, I might be——
Upon my word, Randall, you take too much upon yourself! These
men should have been brought back here to stand their trial by
the processes of the law, and——'

'And been turned into heroes and martyrs!' interrupted Alex
bluntly. 'This is war, sir! What do these people know of Western
laws, which are not even their own? Those men were boasting
to the villagers of murdering women and children and a wounded
man. They had the evidence in their hands—you've seen it
yourself! Do you suppose that if I had brought them back here
it would have had a fraction of the effect on the village that seeing
immediate justice done to them will have had? They understand
justice—not law! And if I had taken those men into custody they
might have been rescued ten times over on the way here, while
if they had stood trial, half the city and possibly half the troops
would have acclaimed them as heroes who had struck a blow
against the British! We can afford no trials of that description, sir.'

'It will create a bad impression in the district,' said the Commissioner, with less certainty.

'On the contrary, it will create a very good one,' said Alex
shortly. He forced his voice to a more conciliatory tone and said:

'If you will allow me unfettered action, sir, I can maintain order in the district as long as the regiments in Lunjore remain quiet. At the moment the sepoys are quiet, but if they should revolt it would be a different matter, and I would again urge you most strongly to impress upon their commanding officers the advisability of disarming them while there is still time.'

'I shall do no such thing!' snapped the Commissioner, his pallid face becoming dangerously empurpled. 'What would happen if they did? Why—we'd be left with no defenders and no defence at all! Disarm the sepoys, and we'd be at the mercy of the scum of the city and every villager who could carry a rifle or a *lathi*!'

'It is not they whom we have to fear,' said Alex, and went out into the furnace-glare of the noonday sun. That same sun that was even now blazing down on an open courtyard in the purlieus of the palace of the King of Delhi, where stood a little cistern shaded by a peepul tree . . .

There were some fifty dazed and terrified people herded together like sheep in that hot courtyard, of whom all but six were women or children. The last of the Europeans and Christians left alive in Delhi, dragged up from the heat and stench and darkness of the dungeon in which they had spent five days, to be butchered in the harsh sunlight by men whom the sight and scent of blood had turned into beasts: men who cut and slashed and howled in frenzy until the last scream and the last moan was silenced, and who drew back then, shuddering, from the shambles and from the stench of fresh-spilled blood and brains and entrails that steamed up from the pile of the newly dead. Now at last there were no more *feringhis* in Delhi! Now at last the reluctant, trembling old King and every man, woman and child in the city was committed irretrievably to the path that had been chosen. There could be no drawing back now, for the massacre of the women and children whose mutilated bodies strewed the courtyard and whose blood soaked into the silent stones and curled and dried in the searing heat, had sealed them to their path. This was irrevocable. The die had been cast.

P

All that day while the shadows of the peepul tree and the cistern crawled across the paving-stones and the quiet dead, a shifting, peering crowd pressed ten deep about the courtyard, gaping and whispering. And towards evening half a dozen *mehtars*, men of low caste who act as sweepers and disposers of filth, heaped the stiffened, mangled bodies on to carts which dragged them to the bank of the placid Jumna, and flung them one by one into the river. Food for the crocodiles and the mud-turtles, the jackals and the scavenger birds: and a sign and a warning to a hundred villages as the bodies drifted down with the slow stream to be stranded on sandbars and burning ghats and fish traps, or caught in the eddies that washed the walls of fortified towns.

Alex walked back to his bungalow in the sweltering heat and thought about the city and the district. There was no point in thinking about the sepoys; he could do nothing there, but as long as they remained quiet there were still things he could do among the uneasy, frightened, rumour-ridden population. Things that would have to be done on his own responsibility. 'I shall have to have his authority, or they will stop me,' thought Alex; and returned to his bungalow to make plans.

'Niaz, are there any among the *pultons* who will stand by their salt?'

'None that I would gamble a single *pice* of my pay on with any certainty of return,' said Niaz flippantly. 'But the Sikhs be the least unstable. They have no love for us Mussulmans and little liking for the Hindus. They strike always for themselves.'

'And the Mussulmans?'

'We strike for the Faith,' said Niaz with a grin, 'save for such renegades as myself!'

'Give me the names of a dozen Sikhs from the *pultons*. Those who be the least disloyal,' said Alex, and returned to the Residency.

He found no difficulty in assisting the Commissioner to reach that state of intoxication where he would sign a paper without reading it—he signed many such. And the following day, backed by the authority of a dozen mounted men, he had ridden thirty miles to arrest an influential talukdar whose treasonable activities had been interesting him for some time past. The documentary evidence found in Habib Ullah Khan's house and on his person had carried conviction even to the brandy-sodden intelligence of the Commissioner of Lunjore.

'The head of the whole trouble in the city is Maulvie Amanullah of the Moti Masjid, and Abdul Majid, the talukdar's nephew. If we can get those two, the city will be left with only petty agitators, but no real leaders,' said Alex. 'But if we try to take them openly we shall have a first-class riot on our hands, and I do not think that the——' He checked abruptly and then put what he had been about to say into different words: 'I think it would be putting too much strain on the loyalty of the sepoys to ask them to fight a street action at this point. But if you will hold a Durbar, I think we can manage it. Call a conference of all the influential men in the city. The larger shopkeepers included. It's the only hope.'

It had taken an hour and the best part of a bottle of brandy to persuade the Commissioner, and it had proved harder still to persuade the Military that the risk was worth taking, but the battle had been won by Colonel Moulson's dislike of Alex, and Alex's deliberate suggestion that Colonel Moulson did not trust his Regiment.

A stately conference had been held under the sweltering shade of a vast *shamiana* erected in the coolest part of the Residency grounds. There were speeches and expressions of loyalty— genuine enough at the moment of their making, thought Alex wryly, reflecting that ten minutes' conversation with an agitator could swing the pendulum as far East as it was now West. Views were canvassed and listened to with respect, and the guests withdrew as the sun began to set. All except two of them. Maulvie Amanullah and Abdul Majid Khan, wealthy nephew of the talukdar, were delayed in conversation, and when they would have left, were detained.

There was considerable uneasiness in the city that night. The patrolling Magistrate, who had been covertly assisting the work of spreading disaffection, found himself arrested, and the following morning a proclamation was issued calling upon all inhabitants of the city to give up their arms within twenty-four hours; followed by another, imposing a curfew. It was backed by the appearance of four heavy guns that were plainly to be seen in position commanding the Rohilkhand Gate and the main road to the city.

Deprived of its leaders, the city capitulated, and the arms were collected—but not destroyed. 'For God's sake,' begged Alex, 'burn 'em. Blow 'em up! There's enough stuff there to fit out an army. Now that we've got it, don't let's take any chances of it falling into their hands again.'

'It could be in no safer place than in the care of the Military Police,' snapped Colonel Moulson.

Alex bit back the retort he had almost made, and was silent. For the moment at least the danger was averted. The villages and the city would stay quiet—for just as long as the sepoys stayed quiet. 'The thirty-first of May' . . . Ten more days. If they would only disarm them now!

There had been no reply to the message he had dispatched to Suthragunj to be telegraphed to the Governor General in Calcutta, and he did not know that it had never reached Lord Canning, but was gathering dust in a pigeon-hole while the junior official who had received it occupied himself with panic-stricken plans for evacuating his wife and family on the first ship to sail for Europe.

Calcutta was filled with panic in these days, as telegram after telegram, message after message, brought news of disaster. Delhi snatched from the hands of the British in an hour! Meerut, with one of the strongest British garrisons in India, bewildered and helpless and apparently unable to do more than protect itself from a peril that had passed from it to spread out like a forest fire over half India. A hundred pleas a day poured in upon Canning begging for troops—for British troops. 'We cannot hold out without troops. Send us help.' 'The sepoys have mutinied. Send us troops.'

He did what he could, but it was little. Help would be slow in coming. They must fend for themselves yet awhile.

*   *   *

Lottie had arrived in Lunjore at last. Lottie and Mr. Dacosta and Mrs. Holly—that same Mrs. Holly who had embarked on the steamship *Sirius* and had nursed Mrs. Abuthnot and her daughters through a bout of seasickness.

Stout, cheerful, sensible Mrs. Holly was considerably less stout and no longer cheerful. Her clothes hung in folds and her round pleasant face sagged in deep harsh lines; for she had seen her husband's head struck from his body with a single swing of a sharpened *tulwar* in the blazing charnel-house of Duryagunj, and only the sudden collapse of a burning roof-beam had saved her from a similar fate. Somehow—she could not remember how—she and Mr. Dacosta had escaped from the carnage and reached the Main Guard at the Kashmir Gate, where they had witnessed the final tragedy and escaped over the battlements. But although her stoutness and her cheerfulness had gone, her placid good sense remained. She had taken Lottie and Mr. Dacosta under her wing and it was she who had cajoled the driver of the *ekka* into taking them up, and so brought them at last to Lunjore.

Mr. Dacosta was an olive-skinned, middle-aged Eurasian, a clerk in a Government department. He had been wounded by a sword-cut and badly burned, but he had struggled on valiantly and had not complained. Mrs. Holly had bound up his wounds and taken charge of him as she had of Lottie. 'You know, ma'am,' she explained to Winter, 'it was just as well, them being sick. It give me something to do, and something else to think about than— than the things I seen that day. It was Miss Lottie 'oo said you was 'ere when that *ekka wallah* says as 'e was goin' to Lunjore. She would 'ave it that we must come 'ere, an' I don't know but what she wasn't right. We 'ad no place special to go to, you see. She said—she said as you'd invited 'er for a visit, pore young thing.'

'Mrs. Holly,' said Winter unhappily, 'do you—do you think she will remember?'

'Some day,' said Mrs. Holly. 'It'll be a pity when she does, for she's better off this way, and that's the truth.'

For Lottie had been delighted to see Winter, and she had forgotten Delhi. She wondered sometimes, a little hazily, why it was that she should suddenly have decided to come to Lunjore. Something had happened, surely? But then she had always meant to visit Winter one day, and Edward—— Why had she allowed Edward to send her on a visit just now? She had told him that she would not think of leaving him. Edward must have insisted. It was odd that she could not remember. Perhaps it was something to do with having a baby that made thinking an effort? It was easier not to think—so much easier. Thinking made her head ache, and with that ache fear would well up inside her like ice-cold water bubbling up out of an unseen spring, and her heart would begin to hammer and her breath come short. Yet there was nothing to be afraid of. Nothing. Winter was here. She was only paying a visit to Winter, and soon she would go back to her pretty bungalow in Meerut and be with Edward again. She must not think. It made her feel ill, and that was bad for the child. 'You must not think of yourself, Lottie. Think of the child . . .' 'You must rest more, Lottie. Think of the child . . .' 'You do not eat enough, Lottie. Think of the child.' Edward and Mamma and Mamma's friends had said such things so often, and they were right. She must think of the child. Edward's child——

'Edward wants a girl, you know,' she confided to Winter, 'but I want the first one to be a boy and just like Edward. He is to be christened Edward—I have quite made up my mind. But he will have to be Teddy, because we cannot have two Edwards. I am sure that Teddy will be exactly like his papa. Edward says that red hair is very catching!'

'Alex,' said Winter desperately, 'do you think she will ever remember?'

'One day,' said Alex, and added, as Mrs. Holly had done:

'She's better off as she is at the moment. When is that baby due?' He had frowned at the sight of the sudden colour that burned in Winter's cheeks and had said impatiently: 'You don't really suppose that hitching a hoop up higher and carrying round a shawl disguises a thing like that, do you?'

Winter had been taught that babies, until they were born, were an unmentionable subject in the presence of gentlemen, but the impatience in Alex's voice made her ashamed of the blush. She said with as much composure as she could muster: 'I think she expects it in about two months' time. But Mrs. Holly says one can never be sure with a first child, and that it may not be born until——'

She stopped abruptly and put her hands up to her hot cheeks. It was one thing to answer a direct question, but one did not—one *could* not—discuss such things with a man!

A corner of Alex's mouth curved in the shadow of a grin and he said: 'Don't be missish, Mrs. Barton! It's a perfectly natural function. How soon can you leave?'

'*Leave?* I can't leave now! Lottie can't go any farther. Not after what she has been through. Dr. O'Dwyer says that she must not be moved, but have complete quiet. He says that she could not support any further journeyings in this heat, and that he cannot understand why she has not had a—a——'

'A miscarriage,' finished Alex with curt impatience. 'Yes, I've heard of those too! Then you will not be leaving either?'

'How could I?'

'No,' said Alex bleakly, 'you could not. And I think in any case it is too late.'

For Alex had talked to Mr. Dacosta—Mrs. Holly avoided questions—and had heard the first true account of that last day of British rule in Delhi. The ease with which Delhi had been captured had horrified him.

'We looked all day for thee troops from Meerut,' whispered Mr. Dacosta, hoarse with weakness and fever, 'but they did not come. If only twenty British troops had appeared before thee gates that morning, those men would have run away. They were

veree fearful. Oah yess, they feared pursuit. It is all lost—all
lost. My whole family—Mamma-*jee* and Clara and the *butchas*.
Twelve we had, though five died when they were onlee small.
My Clara, she cried for them. She would not have cried if she
had known how she and thee others would die. It is not right
that I should see that and still live. I was in thee office, Mister
Randall, and when I heard that there was some *juggra* in thee
city I did not believe that it could be veree bad. I laughed at
young Pereira and said, "Nonsense, man! It is nothing," and I
stayed at my desk. That is right, is it not, Mister Randall? One
must stay by thee work and set an example when others are
fearful. We cannot run away and leave thee work. But if I had
run then, I might have saved them! No, no—that is not true.
But I could have died with them . . .'

He had died two days later, and Mrs. Holly, who had been
unable to weep for her Alfred, had wept for frail, middle-aged,
sallow-skinned Mr. Dacosta who had conceived it his duty to stay
at his work and set an example of courage.

Almost every night now there were mysterious fires in the
cantonments, and though extra guards patrolled the area they
never made any arrests. It was difficult to allay panic among the
families of the officers who lived in bungalows surrounded by
large gardens where trees and shrubs provided cover for lurking
incendiaries, and few women slept at night, while parents of
children lay awake, starting in terror at every night noise.

Only the children showed no signs of strain. They grew pallid
from the heat and the enforced inactivity in shuttered rooms
during the daytime, but the children had always been favourites
with the servants in the bungalows and the sepoys in the lines.
They loved them, trusted them, spoke their language with far
more fluency than their mother-tongue, bullied them and ordered
them about, and ran to them with their woes. The Indians—
any Indians—were their friends and allies and playmates, and
they would no more have conceived of receiving harm at their
hands than at the hands of their own parents. Less! for parents
could be stern at times and administer punishment and rebuke,

but Mali-*jee* and Ayah-*jee*, and Makhan Khan and Piari Lal and Sobra Singh, Havildar Jewrakun Tewary and Sepoy Dhoolee Sookul, the *Dhobi*, the *Darzi*, the sweetmeat-seller and old Khundoo the *Chowkidar*—never! From all these and a hundred more the children had never received anything but kindness and petting. But their mothers grew thin-faced with fear and their fathers walked with neck and shoulder muscles taut with strained alertness.

The three commanding officers still refused even to consider disarming their men, although now, when it was too late, they would have sent the women away—and dared not do so. For though Lunjore was still quiet, with the tensed, twitching quietness of a cat at a mousehole, it was not so with the districts that surrounded it. 'They are safer here,' said Colonel Gardener-Smith, whom the past ten days appeared to have aged by as many years.

The Commissioner did not appear to notice that his wife had put off her departure. He noticed little in those days, and that little through an alcoholic haze. The whole situation was beyond him. He was afraid, and his fear drove him to his familiar refuge, the bottle. Even Fatima had forsaken him. She had packed her clothes and her jewels and everything else she could manage to lay her hands on, and had slipped away one night with her three fat, half-caste children, her relations and her servants and Nilam, the blue macaw, and had not come back. Her defection had frightened the Commissioner far more than the nightly fires, the news from Delhi, the inaction of the Meerut Brigade or the endless tales of murder and massacre that trickled in daily from the outside world.

'Rats leavin' the sinkin' ship!' whispered the Commissioner hoarsely, staring into space with eyes that did not see the sly, inscrutable face of Imam Bux who had broken the news. 'That's what it is. They know. The rats know! We're sinking. She knew it, and she's gone—the lying, cheating black bitch!'

He had flung his glass furiously at the impassive butler and that afternoon he had advocated immediate flight. They **must**

P*

all of them go, and by night, in boats down the river. The
British Raj was finished. Unless they were all to die, those who
were not already dead must fly the country—reach the coast,
using the rivers and avoiding the roads—and abandon India.
They could not hold it. It was impossible to hold it! If they
stayed they would all be murdered.

'Better that than to turn tail,' snorted Colonel Moulson,
observing him with disapproval. 'I hope you don't speak in this
fashion before your servants, Con! If we can keep our heads we
shall weather the storm. Calcutta can't be idle, and strong
reinforcements are certain to be on their way.'

'How do we know that there are any Europeans left alive in
Calcutta?' whispered the Commissioner. 'If the native regiments
at Barrackpore have mutinied they could wipe out the Europeans
in Calcutta in a night! How do we know it hasn't happened
already? How do we know!'

'Y'know, Con,' said Colonel Moulson judicially, 'you're better
when you're drunk. Nothing to get worked up about. Troops as
quiet as lambs. If it's these fires that are gettin' on your nerves,
forget 'em! Work of bazaar *budmashes*. The sepoys have worked
like trojans puttin' 'em out.'

The Commissioner had retreated to the brandy bottle, and had
taken no interest in the information—relayed to him three hours
later—that the sepoys of Colonel Packer's regiment had refused
to accept their consignment of Commissariat flour, saying that it
was known to be adulterated with bone-dust for the purpose of
destroying their caste. Colonel Packer and his officers had expos-
tulated, lectured and finally pleaded, but the men had remained
obdurate. They would not touch the flour, and moreover they
insisted that it must be thrown into the river to ensure that it
was not returned to them again or handed to any of their comrades in the other regiments.

The flour had been duly taken away and thrown into the distant
river, and the sepoys, having won their point, had become
noticeably insolent and out of hand. Many of them, from all three
regiments, had that same evening openly looted the ripe fruit

from the gardens of the cantonment bungalows, and although their officers had soon succeeded in putting a stop to it, it was plain that discipline was deteriorating rapidly.

'They are a little out of hand,' admitted Colonel Gardener-Smith reluctantly, 'but that is understandable in the exceptional circumstances. We are all only human. It is nothing serious—though Packer's regiment is not behaving at all well. I begin to fear we may have a little trouble with them. Nothing of course that my own men will not be able to set to rights.'

'Old Gardener's sepoys are all to pieces,' said Colonel Packer. 'Don't like the look of it. I am thankful to say that *my* men have never given me any serious cause for anxiety. I have assured them that for the present we will discontinue the supplies of Government flour and obtain it locally, and they are quite content.'

'Wouldn't trust Packer's fellows a yard!' said Colonel Moulson. 'Or old Nannie Gardener's either, for that matter! No discipline; that's their trouble. Now *my* lot . . .'

That night Major Wilkinson, who had dined at the Residency and returned drunk to his bungalow, fired at and wounded one of a patrol who challenged him. There was an enquiry held on the following day and Major Wilkinson was acquitted of any intent to wound—on a plea of being unconscious from intoxication at the time.

'Bloody fools!' said Alex, exasperated. 'They should have cashiered him—sent him off to be court-martialled at Suthragunj —anything but this! To acquit him of wounding a sepoy at a time like this, and on a plea of drunkenness—are they mad? If it had been the other way round, they'd have given the sepoy ten years' penal servitude or hanged him! If this doesn't start something, I'm a bigger fool than Packer!'

There was a ball to celebrate the Queen's birthday on the first day of the new week. Victoria's birthday had fallen on a Sunday that year, so the ball had been held on the day following it. It had been the end, too, of the fast of Ramadan, and there was a new slim sickle moon in the sky. It hung in the green of the evening, a curved thread of silver, like the crescent of Islam embroidered on the green banners of the Faithful—like an omen in the sky.

'*La Ill-ah ha! il ill-ah ho!*' cried the muezzins from the minarets of the mosques in the city. 'There is no God but God!'

The band of the 2nd Regiment of Lunjore Irregulars stood smartly to attention, their dark faces creased with concentration, and watched the conductor's baton fall. '*God Save our Gracious Queen, Long live our Noble Queen*——' The familiar tune, the National Anthem of an alien race, blared out through the open windows across the dark parade-ground and the sepoy lines.

She was thirty-eight—that dumpy, imperious, self-confident housewife who had ascended the throne as a slim self-confident girl in the year that Sabrina Grantham had met Marcos de Ballesteros; the year that Anne Marie the second, who was Ameera, wife of Walayat Shah, had been born to Juanita in the little pink stucco palace in Lucknow City.

'*Send her victorious, happy and glorious . . .*'

Sabrina's daughter danced at the Queen's Birthday Ball in a wide-skirted ball-gown of water-green tarlatan looped up with garlands of camellias, and smiled as she danced—the same smile that was on the face of every woman who danced in that flag-and-flower decorated room, or sat against the walls listening to the sepoy band playing the 'Imogene Waltz', the 'Sultan's Polka', the Laurel; 'Angelina', 'Belle of the Village' and 'Lily of the Valley'. A smile that did not reach the eyes and hurt the heart. The smile of women who watch their men and strain their ears to listen, and who will not show that they are afraid.

Alex too had attended that ball and there was nothing in his face to show that he had spent the greater part of the afternoon arguing, urging, pleading fruitlessly and for the last time with three courageous, obdurate men for the disarming of the sepoys.

'It can be done,' urged Alex. 'There are enough of us to do it, and this ball will provide the opportunity. No one will expect anything on the night of a ball.' He had outlined a plan; rash, but possible; and the verdict had been unanimously against it.

'Until we have actual evidence of mutinous intentions,' said Colonel Gardener-Smith, 'no sepoy of mine shall be so insulted or——'

'I have yet to learn,' said Alex shortly, abandoning diplomacy and brusquely interrupting that familiar speech, 'that cure is preferable to prevention! And this Wilkinson affair may well prove to be in the nature of a last straw. I understand that the verdict was not well received in the lines?'

But they were not to be persuaded. They did, however, decide on taking one precautionary measure, for the sake of the ladies, whose nerves were beginning to suffer from the strain of constantly being on the alert. It was the custom among the European families in Lunjore to drive out in the early mornings to get what little fresh air they could before the sun rose and the heat forced them into the dimness of shuttered rooms. Word was conveyed to the families that on the morning following the ball the women and children were to drive instead to the Residency, taking with them such clothing and necessities as they would need for a stay of a few days. The Residency was sufficiently large to shelter them all without too much discomfort, and a party of Military Police were to be posted in the grounds as extra protection, while four guns under the charge of native gunners of Colonel Moulson's regiment were to be placed in between the Residency and the lines, and another two between the Residency and the city.

'The Residency is admirably situated for defence,' said Colonel Gardener-Smith. 'With that nullah and the jungle behind it, and a wall round the rest of it, nothing could be better.'

'I agree,' said Alex, 'providing one was defending it against a rabble from the city. But if the sepoys should mutiny it will turn into a trap.'

'My sepoys will not mutiny!' said Colonel Gardener-Smith obstinately. 'I will stake my life on that.'

Alex said nothing more. He was tired of vain repetitions. He had gone across to the Residency and spoken to Winter: 'I'm taking Yusaf again. I need him. What have you done with that revolver I gave you?'

'I have it.'

'Good. Keep it loaded and keep it within reach. I've brought you some more ammunition for it. And see that there is always a horse kept saddled, and——' He did not complete the sentence but looked past Winter's shoulder at the blank wall for a long minute, his brows drawn together in a frown, and then shrugged and went away without further words. What was the good of saying anything else? He had done what he could. Had that woman—Ameera?—spoken the truth? Had there been a day set, and had the Meerut rising been premature? It had been remarkably successful and its success had touched off a series of localized risings. Were those too a mistake? '*They have set the auspicious day*' . . .

'Two more days to go,' thought Alex that night, leaning against the wall and watching a quadrille danced at the Queen's Birthday Ball.

But there were no more days. Only hours.

VI

THE HIRREN MINAR

31

IT was Major Beckwith, second-in-command to Colonel Gardener-Smith, who informed his Commanding Officer half an hour before sunrise on the morning after the ball that the Regiment had not dispersed after parade, and could no longer be trusted. He had wept as he had said it, for Major Beckwith, like his Colonel, had believed with a wholehearted belief in the fidelity of his men.

'I will go back and speak to them,' said Colonel Gardener-Smith.

'It's no good, sir. They will listen to no one.'

'They will listen to me,' said Colonel Gardener-Smith stubbornly.

But they had not listened.

'We will not harm thee, or permit thee to be harmed,' said the ringleader, 'for thou art a good man. But we take no more orders from *feringhis* who have plotted to destroy our caste and to enslave us. Go quickly while there is yet time, for we know what we know, and the men of the 105th are not as us, and if they can, may slay thee.'

They had thrust him from the lines, shouting down his words, and had rushed to the bells of arms and seizing their rifles had announced their intention of marching immediately for Delhi to offer their services to the Mogul. They had opened fire on their officers, two of whom had been badly wounded, and there had been nothing for it but to leave before worse befell, and the Colonel had left.

His bungalow was empty, for his wife and daughter were already at the Residency, and it seemed intolerably dark and quiet. As quiet as the tomb. As quiet as old age. 'I am an old man,' thought Colonel Gardener-Smith. 'An old man and a fool. I have given my life to a lie. They will disband the 93rd and remove its name from the Army List. *My* 93rd!'

His mind went back to the days when he had first joined the regiment as a young ensign, and he remembered men long dead; sepoys and subadars, men who had fought with him and followed him. The names of old fights and old battles spoke their names in his brain like a roll of drums. He forgot his wife and Delia. Their faces and their names meant nothing to him, and awoke no echo in his mind to drown or disturb the memory of the men among whom and beside whom and for whom he had spent his life.

'They will disband the 93rd as they did the 19th. It will go down in the records—*Disbanded for Mutiny*. My 93rd . . .'

He left the bungalow and went to the deserted Mess, walking bareheaded in the blaze of the newly risen sun, and took down the colours and burned them in the grate, pouring lamp-oil on them and watching until there was nothing left but a heap of evil-smelling black ash. And then he shot himself.

'The bloody idiot!' said Alex furiously, hearing of it half an hour later—he had ridden out to speak to the Kotwal of a village beyond the city and had returned late—'Just when we need every man who can fire a gun! When one man is worth his weight in—— God damn these sentimentalists! Art thou ready, Yusaf? It may be that thou wilt have to wait two days. Three even. But I do not think so, for Fazal Hussain has brought word that a horseman took that road at first light. No matter, there is food and water enough for a long wait. If they come, wait until the first of them are abreast of the rocks by the two palm trees. Go now and go swiftly. *B'ism Illah*——'

Colonel Moulson had been breakfasting at the Residency, together with several officers who were engaged in assuring the ladies assembled there that there was no cause for alarm and that their presence in the Residency was merely a precautionary measure which would only be necessary for a day or two.

The Residency was noisy with women's voices and the laughter and yells of children, the rustle of poplin, muslin and barège dresses and ruffled pantalettes. Almost every woman there had danced until a late hour at the ball, and many had had no sleep before starting out for the Residency, but all were gay and in good heart, for the presence of the police guard, the sight of the guns with their attendant crews of native gunners, the high white wall of the Residency and, above all, the company of their fellows, had worked wonders on their failing spirits. They felt safer together, and in such surroundings, than they had separately in their scattered bungalows, and there was a light-hearted and picnic-like atmosphere in the crowded rooms that even the non-appearance of their host, and the news that he was indisposed, did nothing to dispel.

The information that it had been considered advisable to urge all the women and children to take refuge in the Residency, to place guns at the approaches and mount a strong guard of Military Police, had been too much for the Commissioner. The danger must indeed be great to warrant such measures, yet Fred Moulson had assured him—— Where was the brandy? Brandy and more brandy; that was the only refuge from a world that was disintegrating around him. Brandy warmed him and comforted him and cushioned him against fear.

Delia, unlike the majority of the women present, had elected to wear her widest crinoline and a dress that was more suitable for an afternoon party than an early breakfast. Her beautiful hair was not confined in a net, but tied back with a demure bow of ribbon and allowed to cascade down her back in glossy chestnut ringlets. Colonel Moulson found her enchanting, and was in process of telling her so when the sound of galloping hooves interrupted him . . .

'I might have known it!' fumed Colonel Moulson. 'Always said that fool Gardener was too soft with his men! I'll show 'em! Marching to Delhi with the treasure, are they? Where the hell's my horse! If we double three companies across the *maidan* we'll cut 'em off and cut 'em to bits!'

He galloped off into the glare of the morning, his Adjutant and a senior captain riding behind him, and his regiment received him in silence. They listened to his bellowed commands, and no man moved—their shadows lying motionless on the hot ground. Then a man laughed, loud and scornfully, and another took aim and fired.

Ten minutes later the Adjutant, his arm pouring a bright scarlet flood, slid from his wounded horse on to Alex's sunny verandah and gasped out the news.

'They shot him down—and Mottisham too—and Halliwell and Reeves and Charlie and little Jenks. They're all dead. Packer's fellows have broken too. They've killed him—saw his body. Cut to bits. And old Gardener has——'

'I know,' said Alex, knotting a strip torn from a curtain with furious haste about the man's shattered arm and shoulder. He turned his head and called out to Niaz who had ridden full-tilt round the corner of the bungalow from the direction of the stables.

'The Lunjore *Pulton* also! Ride for the river. Get the charges from the Hirren Minar. I will meet thee there. Go quickly!'

Niaz lifted a hand in salute and turned his rearing, frantic horse as Alex helped the Adjutant back into his saddle. 'If Moulson's men have broken that means the gunners will go,' said Alex. 'Get over to the Residency and tell 'em to get the women and children away over the nullah and into the jungle at once—*at once*, do you hear! Think you can do it? Good. Alam Din, run with the Sahib—be swift!'

He leapt down the verandah steps and caught at the bridle of his horse. 'Where—are you going?' gasped the Adjutant, wheeling his own wounded animal.

'Magazine.'

Niaz, already halfway to the gate, caught the word and reined in hard.

'What is it?' called Alex, spurring down the drive.

'I go with thee,' said Niaz between his teeth, and rode out level with him.

'Do as I tell you!' said Alex savagely and in English. He cut at Niaz's horse with his whip and drew ahead, the Eagle easily outdistancing the heavier horse, and yelled back over his shoulder and in Urdu: 'It is an order! This is in thy hands. Do not fail me, brother!'

The Magazine was a small, square unpretentious building of whitewashed stone that stood near the centre of the cantonment area and was surrounded by a high wall and several shade trees. There was a yelling crowd of sepoys milling round it, and Alex heard the crackle of musketry and reined back in the shadow of a clump of bamboos. Someone was holding the Magazine, then! He caught a brief glimpse of a pink boyish face, hatless, the red hair bright against the whitewashed stone above the inner parapet, and recognized young Eyton, one of the new-joined 'griffins', barely a month out from England. The other lay face downwards thirty yards from the gate and on the edge of the yelling crowd, his brains splashed in an oddly symmetrical star-shaped pattern on the hot dust.

Another face appeared beside young Eyton—a dark, bearded face that showed a gleam of white teeth; a rifle cracked and another man in the crowd fell. Alex could hear words from among the howling din: 'Join us! Do not fight for those who have betrayed us! We be thy brothers! Kill the *feringhis* and join us!' The answer was another shot fired into the thick of the mob. There were some then who had remained true to their salt. But the fight was an unequal one, for already fifty men or more had swarmed over the outer wall, and the gate was creaking under a heavy log of wood wielded by a dozen men as a battering-ram.

Alex knew that he should go. There was nothing he could do. But he did not move. He saw the boy appear briefly again on the parapet and peer down at the yelling besiegers, duck to avoid the shots, and hold up his hand as though he gave a signal—and even as he watched Alex knew what that signal meant, and he turned his horse and set him at a low wall fifty yards away, cleared it and was racing across a stretch of open ground. As he reached the far side of it he heard the roar of the explosion and felt the

shock of the blast like a blow between his shoulders. 'Well
done!' said Alex, unaware that he was shouting aloud. 'Oh,
well done!' He spurred across another piece of open ground,
leapt a compound wall and found himself among the flowers of
Captain Batterslea's garden.

Mrs. Batterslea had been one of the five women who had
considered the move to the Residency quite unnecessary and had
elected to remain in her own bungalow—'The children are far
better off here. Why, my servants adore them! I am quite sure
they would die for them.'

Mrs. Batterslea's extravagant statement had proved to be no
more than the truth. Her ayah lay huddled among the plum-
bago bushes below the verandah, in death as in life striving to
protect the small silent figure in its white frock and blue sash
that her stiffening body and outstretched arms still covered, while
in the servants' quarters behind the bungalow portly Farid, the
butler, the thin-legged *purbeah mali*, Captain Batterslea's Brahmin orderly and Bulaki, the low-caste sweeper, had died side by
side, fighting to protect the three small boys who had been reached
at last only over the bodies of four men of an alien race and
divergent faiths who had fought their own kind in defence of a
foreigner's children.

The bungalow was burning and the heat of the flames joined
the furnace-heat of the sun and shrivelled the few plants that still
brightened the flower-beds. The flower-beds had been Mrs.
Batterslea's special pride, and in them she had striven, not
always with success, to grow the flowers that reminded her of
home—larkspur and mignonette, pansies, gillyflowers and roses.
Of these only the roses now remained, wilting in the relentless
heat. The rose-bushes and Mrs. Batterslea herself, who lay
wide-eyed and open-mouthed among the withered flowers, staring
up at the brassy sky. The frilly pink-and-white wrap she had
worn had been torn away, and where her breasts had been there
was now only blood. And she had been raped before she died.
'That means the bazaar scum and the city have broken out
already,' thought Alex automatically, knowing that no sepoy

would have done such a thing, for to do so would have defiled him.

It did not need more than one look to see that she was dead, but the sight of her mutilated body checked Alex and turned him back from the road he had meant to take.

From the moment that he had heard the first news of the outbreak he had thought of only one thing and seen only one thing: the thin, tired, dauntless face of Henry Lawrence who had said: 'If it comes, I shall look to you to hold the western road for me.' And when he had learned that the 93rd had expressed their intention of marching for Delhi he had been conscious only of relief. Let them go to Delhi—let them go anywhere as long as it was not eastward into Oudh! *'Given time, I believe I may be able to hold Oudh quiet even if the rest of India rises; but it is time we need!—time most of all: and that is a thing which God and the Government may not grant me. The sands are running out, Alex . . .'*

'If I can help to give him even one more day,' had been the driving thought in Alex's brain ever since the morning that Gopal Nath had whispered the first news of the Meerut mutiny and the fall of Delhi, and it had filled his mind to the exclusion of all else during the past half-hour. But now, looking down at Mrs. Batterslea's dead, staring face and breastless, outraged body, he saw another face. Winter's. Saw it as clearly and as distinctly as though it were she and not Alice Batterslea who was lying at his feet among the trampled rose-bushes. And he turned back and rode for the Residency, hating himself; cursing aloud in a breathless, blasphemous whisper, but driven by an emotion and a fear that he could not control.

The heavy, iron-studded doors of the Residency gate had been closed that morning and the police guard ordered to keep them barred, but the door of the narrow wicket in the main gate, through which only one at a time could enter, stood ajar. There was a crowd before the gate; a swaying, yelling crowd who were being harangued by a wild-eyed figure in a white turban— Akbar Khan, the gatekeeper.

'Kill them!' screamed Akbar Khan. 'Slay all, and let not one escape! For the Faith! For the Faith! *Maro! Maro!* (Kill!)'

They heard the sound of the furious galloping hoof-beats and scattered like a whirl of dead leaves as Alex rode into them. He fired only once and saw Akbar Khan topple forward with an expression of ludicrous surprise on his face, and then he had flung himself from the saddle, the Eagle's rearing body protecting him momentarily from the crowd, and in that fractional moment he was through the narrow wicket. A bullet fired by someone within the gate smacked into the woodwork within an inch of him and he stumbled over the body of a man who lay across the threshold, and turning, threw himself against the narrow door and dropped the heavy bar into place.

He turned from it, revolver in hand, and saw the faces of the police guard, sullen and unsure as they fidgeted uneasily with their muskets, and knew that there was no security there.

'Sorry, Randall,' said a gasping voice from the shadows of the gate. 'Nearly got you. Thought it was another of those swine.'

Major Maynard, commanding the Military Police, was sitting on the ground with his back to the wall and one hand pressed to his side in a vain attempt to stem the red tide that welled out between his fingers. He held a smoking revolver in the other, a bullet from which had narrowly missed Alex, and his men watched him and did not move.

'Y'r just in time,' said Major Maynard. 'Tell 'em up at the house—run for it. 'Fraid these bastards of mine won't stand. Sorry about it.' He saw the movement of the revolver in Alex's hand and said: 'No—it wasn't them. They ain't as far gone as that. It was that gatekeeper of yours.'

Alex faced the watching men and said harshly: 'Take up the Sahib and carry him to the house. Quickly!'

'*No!*' gasped Major Maynard. 'No—wouldn't be any use. I know that—so do you. I've got—fifteen minutes perhaps—and as long as—I'm here—they'll do nothing. When I'm gone—they'll open the gate, and run fer it. Get up to the house—tell 'em t' get out. I'll hold 'em for—a few minutes——'

Alex did not wait. He had told Wardle twenty minutes ago to get the women away, and they must have gone already, but he had to be sure. He turned and ran for the distant house, across the iron-hard lawn and over the flower-beds, and reaching the verandah leapt up the steps with the noise of the mob beyond the Residency gate rising into a roar behind him.

But no one had gone. They were all there still. Perhaps a dozen men and more than twice as many women and children. A flower-garden of women in preposterous, pale-coloured, wide-hooped skirts, tight-fitted bodices and thin, inadequate, flat-heeled slippers. Women whose faces, sallow from the heat and inactivity of the hot weather, were now greenish-white with fear.

'Good God!' said Alex furiously, 'what the hell d'you think you're doing? Go on—get these women away! Wardle, I thought I told you——'

'Safer here,' gasped Captain Wardle. 'The gunners are loyal and the police'll hold . . .'

'The gunners have broken and the police will run within five minutes!—and half the riff-raff of the city is out there!' snapped Alex. 'Go on—out by the back and over the bridge. Get into the jungle! It's your only chance. *Run!*'

He saw Winter's face across the width of the room. She had one arm about Lottie and her eyes were wide and enormous but quite steady. There was a sudden and louder burst of yelling and a crash that told its own tale, and Alex ran to the window, took one look and was across the room and had flung open the door that led out of the drawing-room and to the back of the house: '*Run!*'

They ran; picking up screaming children, clasping babies, sobbing and panting, tripping over their wide skirts. Winter said: 'Take Lottie, Mrs. Holly,' and pushed them out through the door, 'you know the way.' She stood back, urging the women to speed, and then Alex had caught her wrist and was running with her, dragging her. He pulled her down the steps of the back verandah and thrusting her ahead of him said breathlessly: 'Over the bridge—quick as you can!' and then he had left her.

After the dimness of the shuttered house the sunlight was unbelievably hot and bright. The heat and the glare met her like the blaze from a blast furnace and added to the complete unreality of the moment. Far across the gardens, through the intervening trees and shadows, she could see a crowd of little figures pouring through the gate. For Major Maynard had been right. He had lived considerably less than the fifteen minutes that he had hoped for, and when they saw that he was dead his men had thrown away their muskets and unbarred the gates, letting in the maddened mob of sepoys who had now been reinforced by a rabble from the city.

'Run, damn you!' shouted Alex from the turn of the house. She saw him jerk up his arm and fire, and picking up her wide skirts she ran as he had told her to—ran after Lottie and Mrs. Holly and a dozen others who had made for the bridge over the nullah.

But they had not all run for the bridge. Many of them had checked and turned back, daunted by the glare and the empty spaces and the yelling of the mob; and deeming the shuttered house a safer refuge had run to hide instead in closets and cupboards and under the frilled valances of beds, locking themselves into darkened rooms and cowering behind the furniture. Others, confused by terror and the blinding sunlight, had lost their sense of direction and were running helplessly to and fro like panic-stricken animals, dodging behind trees and shrubs.

Winter saw Lottie and Mrs. Holly reach the bridge and cross it and run on towards the tangled thickets thirty yards beyond it. Her wide skirts swayed and swooped and the ground under her thin flat-heeled slippers felt unbelievably hot. She had almost reached the bridge when a shriek behind her made her check and turn. It was Delia, running towards her from the direction of the house.

Delia's muslin ruffles flared about her like the petals of a huge peony in the wind, and the ribbon had fallen from her hair so that her long chestnut curls streamed out behind her. Her face was a mask of terror and her mouth a screaming square. Men were running behind her, covering the ground with great bounds—two men wearing dirty turbans and scanty garments that were spattered with blood, one of whom had armed himself with a grass-cutter's sickle. His teeth looked astonishingly white in his dark face and he was gaining on Delia easily.

This is not happening, said something in Winter's brain. Her hand went to the deep pocket in her skirt and she pulled out the revolver and levelled it, but she could not fire, for Delia was directly between her and the pursuing man; and even as she hesitated, he caught her. A dark, sinewy hand clutched at Delia's curls, caught them and dragged her back. The sickle swept, and Delia's severed head, its mouth still open and its blue eyes wide with terror, remained in the man's hand, dangling by its curls, while her body fell sideways in a foam of gay muslin flounces.

Winter fired and the man tripped and fell, and Delia's head, released from his outflung hand, struck the bridge, rolled and came to a stop almost at Winter's feet. The second man had stumbled over the body of the first and fallen also, but he pulled himself to his knees. He carried a butcher's knife in his hand and there were fresh bloodstains upon it. Winter recognized him as a butcher from the cantonment bazaar, and as he scrambled to his feet she fired again and missed, and then the revolver jammed. The man ran forward, howling threats and obscenities, and Winter flung the useless weapon in his face. She heard a shot and saw him stagger and fall, and then from somewhere Alex had appeared, running towards her. He leapt the sprawled body of the man on the bridge, stooped swiftly to snatch up the fallen revolver, and said breathlessly: 'Run——'

'No!' gasped Winter, catching at the rail. 'We can't! Look——'

There were screaming women and children in the Residency garden, running across the lawns, blind with terror; dodging like hunted hares while rifles cracked and dark-faced, blood-stained, blood-crazed men pursued them, yelling and laughing.

Alex thrust the revolver into his belt, and gripping her arms tore her free and dragged her by main force across the bridge and down the path that stretched for thirty yards or so over open ground before entering the narrow arm of jungle that lay between the back of the Residency and the plain. He did not keep to the path but plunged off it right-handed, dragging her with him and thrusting his way between the high grass and thin scrub, the bamboo brakes and the *dhâk* trees; and when he stopped it was only because Winter's crinoline was hopelessly impeding their progress. From behind them they could still hear clearly a bedlam of shots and shouts and screams, but they did not appear to have been pursued. There were too many victims in the grounds of the Residency, and a too-alluring prospect of loot, for anyone to bother with chasing the few fugitives who had vanished into the jungle.

Winter was sobbing and struggling. 'Let me go! You can't leave them! You can't! There are children there—listen to them—*listen!* You coward—you *coward!*' She struck at him wildly, trying to break his hold.

Alex slapped her across the face with the flat of his palm. It was a hard blow and it jerked her back against a tree-trunk and effectually checked the torrent of words and her rising hysteria. 'I may yet be more use alive than dead,' said Alex brutally. 'Get those hoops off—quickly!' He released her wrist and stood waiting, breathing quickly and listening, his revolver in his hand.

The pain of the blow had made her head ring and Alex's curt voice did not permit of argument. She pulled up the voluminous poplin skirts and the frilled petticoat and unfastened the hooped crinoline with feverish haste, wincing and gasping at the sound of those distant appalling screams that seemed to tear thin scarlet gashes through the hot sunlit morning. She saw Alex's face flinch and stiffen but he made no move to return. He reloaded her revolver with steady hands and gave it back to her. 'Come on!'

It was easier to move without the hooped skirt, though her dress had to be lifted up to prevent it trailing on the ground. But her shoes were not made for rough walking and she knew

that they would not stand up to it for long. Something rustled
in the shadows, and two women who had been crouching among
a tangle of grass and creepers stood up, white-faced and breathing
in short gasps. Lottie and Lou Cottar. And behind them, in a
panting huddle on the ground, sat Mrs. Holly.

'*Winter!*' said Lottie on a sob. She ran to Winter and clutched
her, her eyes wide and glittering: 'I thought—I thought——
What happened? Why did they make me run? Why? *Why?*'
Her voice rose to a scream and Winter, remembering the mur-
derous rabble so short a distance behind them, spoke frantically:
'Hush, Lottie! You must be quiet! Hush, dear!'

'Why?' sobbed Lottie. '*Why!*'

Alex reached out and caught her, pressing her head against
his breast and holding it there with one hand. His eyes were
anxious and alert but his voice was neither. He spoke to Lottie
in an entirely matter-of-fact tone that somehow carried complete conviction: 'We have to go to Meerut, Lottie. You want to
see Edward, don't you? The carriage has broken down, you know,
so I am afraid we must walk. We were only running to get out
of the sun. You would not want to get sunstroke just as you are
going to Meerut, would you? This is a short cut. And you mus
not make too much noise because—because I have a bad
headache.'

Over Lottie's small head his eyes met the blaze of anger in
Winter's. 'How could you! How *could* you!' Her lips formed
the words soundlessly. He looked away again and down at Lottie.
The hysterical tension ebbed from Lottie's body and she lifted
her head and smiled her sweet, dazed smile. 'I didn't know.
I'm sorry. Why, of course I want to see Edward! Mrs. Holly did
not tell me that we were going to Meerut, and I thought—let us
hurry!'

Alex shut his eyes for a brief moment, then he released her and
said quietly: 'Are there any more of you?'

Mrs. Cottar shook her head and answered him in a whisper:
'Only the three of us. I think there are others hiding in the
nullah, and some of them ran on down the path.' Her face was

chalk-white except where a thorn had scratched it deeply, and her hair had tumbled down her back. Her smart morning dress— she too had discarded her hooped underskirt—was ripped and torn, and she was trembling violently. But her eyes and her voice were steady.

'They'll have to take their chance,' said Alex curtly. 'We can't wait.' He glanced at Lottie and said: 'She'll have to take those hoops off. And you'd better do something about your shoes, or we shan't get far. Tie 'em up with strips off your skirts—we can spare a few minutes. I don't think they'll look for us yet, they have too much to——' He did not finish the sentence but knelt swiftly to help Mrs. Cottar, who was already ripping the frills from her petticoat with quick unsteady fingers. 'You've got a pistol, I see. Can you use it?'

'Yes,' said Mrs. Cottar briefly, and sat down to tie the strips of cloth round her shoes, binding them strongly about the ankle. Alex performed a similar office for Lottie while Winter, having tied her own slippers with a ruffle torn from her petticoat, coaxed Lottie out of her crinoline and turned to Mrs. Holly who had not moved.

'Hurry, Mrs. Holly—you must take off your hoops. Let me help you——'

'It's no use, dearie,' said Mrs. Holly hoarsely. 'I can't go no further.'

'Of course you can!' began Winter, but Lou Cottar, who had heard the words, whipped round. She said in a harsh whisper: 'So he got you? I—I thought——'

'Yes, dearie,' said Mrs. Holly.

Winter dropped to her knees beside the huddled figure among the thick grass. 'What is it?—what is it? I don't understand. Get up, Mrs. Holly—please! We have to go.'

Lou Cottar said: 'It was a man in the servants' quarters. He had a musket and he fired at us as we went past. I shot him. I thought he'd missed——'

Alex pushed Winter to one side and knelt to put an arm about Mrs. Holly, lifting her a little. His hand touched a warm wetness that there was no mistaking and he saw the grey look on the plump, homely face, and recognized it.

There was a sudden renewed clamour of shots and shouting from the direction of the Residency and the screaming of someone in intolerable pain, muffled by the distance but still horribly audible in the stillness of the morning. Lottie flinched and began to breathe quickly again, and Mrs. Holly said urgently: 'Go on, sir! Make 'em go on. It ain't safe to wait. Get the ladies away. You can't do nothing for me. I know that. Go on quick.'

Alex laid her back very gently and stood up, and at the sight of his face Winter drew in her breath in a harsh gasp and caught at his sleeve. 'No, Alex! No! You can't leave her—you can't! They'll look for us, and they'll find her! And if they didn't she would—Mrs. Holly, please get up—*please*. We can carry you—we——'

'It's no good, dearie,' said Mrs. Holly. 'I'm too 'eavy—an' too bad 'urt. An' there's Miss Lottie to think of. I don't know as how I could look her ma in the face, or her Mr. Edward neither, if I was to let 'em get her. You go on, dearie. I shall be all right soon.'

Winter flung her arms about Mrs. Holly, holding her tightly; feeling, as Alex had felt, the warm tide that soaked out upon the grass. She looked up at Alex and said jerkily: 'You and Lou can take care of Lottie. I'm going to stay here.'

'That you're not!' said Mrs. Holly with sudden energy, the instincts of one who had been a children's nurse in her day rising to the surface. 'You'll do what you're told, Miss Winter!' She looked up into the young, drawn face above her and her voice softened: 'I won't 'ave it, dearie. I shall be all right. I 'aven't been 'appy since Alfred went. It'll be a pleasure to know——' The words were coming with more difficulty and she fought for breath.

Alex glanced back uneasily in the direction of the Residency. He put out a hand as though he would have pulled Winter away, and then clenched it and let it fall; knowing that she would not come for him. Mrs. Holly said urgently: 'An' there's Miss Lottie.

She knows you. She'd be that scared without you. 'Er ma was
good to you. You owe 'er something. Get along now, dearie—
hurry now.'

Winter looked back at Lottie who was staring at them with
bewilderment and a renewal of panic in her face. She looked up
at Alex with wide, imploring eyes and he shook his head in
answer to the question they asked. Her cheeks were suddenly
wet with tears and she bent and kissed Mrs. Holly, released her
and stood up.

'That's a good girl,' approved Mrs. Holly. 'Don't you fret.'
She looked at Alex and her lips moved. He bent swiftly. 'Take
me shoes,' whispered Mrs. Holly. 'She'll need 'em. Stout they
are. Not like those flimsy—I can't reach——' Alex turned
without a word and removed the stout, sensible shoes and thrust
them into his pocket. He jerked the revolver from its holster,
looked at it for a fractional moment and then laid it beside her on
the grass.

'No, sir,' whispered Mrs. Holly. 'You'll maybe need it, and
I won't.'

'You may,' said Alex in a hard voice.

'I'd rather not, sir. I might use it if they come, an'—an' I
don't 'old with it. The Commandments is plain. The Lord
didn't say kill 'em if they kills you. 'E jus' said—*don't!* I know
it's different for you, sir—an' if I could 'a killed to save Alfred,
I know as I would 'ave done. An' then you see—I might be
tempted ter use it on meself, sir, an' that wouldn't be right neither.
Take it——'

Alex picked it up again. He lifted one of the rough, worn
hands, kissed it swiftly and rose to his feet. He knew that she
had no chance; he knew that she might take hours to die; but he
had other things to think of and he had to reach the river. He
would have shot her himself and taken her death on his conscience, but he did not dare, for there was no knowing who might
hear that shot and follow it up.

He swung round on the three white-lipped women who watched
him and said savagely: 'Don't stand there! For God's sake get

on—quickly.' He thrust them ahead of him into the hot, rustling grass and the shadows of the *runi* trees, and did not look back.

* * *

Two and a half hours later they had covered less than four miles. The intolerable heat, the absence of trodden paths and the necessity of forcing their way through high grass and scrub, raging thirst and the unsuitable shoes and garments of the women had combined to slow them down to a mere matter of keeping moving.

Lottie had struggled on manfully, supported at first by Winter or Lou Cottar, while Alex went ahead, but it had soon become obvious that she could not keep up with them, and eventually Alex had carried her. Lottie, even seven months pregnant, weighed astonishingly little, but the lightest weight becomes intolerable after a time, and Alex's muscles ached and the blood drummed in his ears and he had been forced to stop and lay her down at shorter and shorter intervals.

It was Winter who said suddenly, watching his grim, exhausted face as he rested for a moment, sitting with closed eyes and his back to a tree-trunk, 'Where are we going? What is it you want to do?'

Alex opened his eyes and looked at her and his face was suddenly bleak. But for her and Lottie and Lou Cottar he could have turned back and tried to get a horse from the stables and make a detour by the plain, and he might still have reached the bridge in time. But for them he could still reach it in an hour. The bridge was ten miles by road, but barely half that through the jungle, and he had gone this way on foot often enough before, though the jungle was thick and there were no paths. But for Winter—Winter and Alice Batterslea—he would not be here at all . . . 'the safety of women in some crises is such a very minor consideration that it ceases to be a consideration at all . . .'

He said in a parched whisper: 'I know this jungle—it runs to the river—there's a ruin—use it for *shikar*—mile above the bridge. Put the stuff there—weeks ago.' He closed his eyes again.

Q

'What stuff? What stuff, Alex?' Winter knelt beside him, shaking him.

'Gunpowder,' said Alex without opening his eyes.

'*Gunpowder?* What for?'

'Blow up the bridge,' said Alex briefly.

Across his body Winter's eyes met Mrs. Cottar's. She had never liked Mrs. Cottar, but now something in the older woman that matched something in herself made a sudden bond between them. They looked at each other for a long moment and it was as if each of them had asked the other a question, and answered it.

Winter looked back at Alex. 'How much farther is it?'

'Hmm? Oh—mile. Get there soon.' He moved his shoulders uneasily and dragged himself to his feet.

Winter said with a break in her voice: 'Alex, you fool! You should have left us!'

Alex said: 'You don't know these jungles. You'd have gone round and round in circles until——' He shrugged his shoulders uneasily and winced with the pain of the movement.

'Well, we are all right now. We'll bring Lottie. Go on as quick as you can, but—but mark the way. If it's only a mile we can follow you.'

Alex did not argue. He looked at Lottie who lay asleep with her head in Lou Cottar's lap, and then at Lou Cottar and Winter. They were exhausted from heat and thirst and the slow miles they had walked. Their faces and hands were scratched by thorn scrub and sharp-edged grasses; their feet were blistered—Lou was already wearing Mrs. Holly's shoes—and their clothing was torn and soaked with sweat. But their eyes were calm and they looked back at him steadily. Two pairs of eyes, so very different; so entirely alike.

He said: 'Don't rest too long or you'll find you can't move. Keep moving, even if it's slowly. I'll mark the way. Hide if you hear anyone, and don't fire unless as a last resort. The sound of a shot carries.' He turned away, and the high grass and the thorn scrub, the choking bamboo, the *runi* trees and lantana and the hot, chequered shadows closed behind him, and he was gone.

They listened to the sounds of movement fade and die, and all at once the jungle was intolerably still. Nothing seemed to stir in that hot, breathless stillness; no twig or leaf or dry spear of grass. There seemed to be nothing alive in it except themselves.

A soft, monotonous ticking crept into the silence and Winter looked down and saw that it was Alex's watch which must have fallen from his pocket. She reached out and picked it up and the broken chain clinked as she lifted it. Surely Alex must have forgotten to wind it, for the hands pointed at ten minutes to eleven.

The watch ticked gently. Ten minutes to eleven. Only ten minutes to eleven! It had been just on seven o'clock when the first news of the mutiny of the 93rd had taken Colonel Moulson from the Residency. Less than half-past seven when Captain Wardle had ridden in on a wounded horse with his shattered arm and shoulder roughly bound with one of Alex's bungalow curtains and Alam Din running at his stirrup, bringing Alex's message warning them to leave the house and take refuge in the jungle. The warning had been disregarded, as had all Alex's warnings, for the native gunners were still at their posts and the police were loyal, but—so argued Captain Wardle and those men who had been detailed to remain in the Residency—if they should see the women and children leaving it might unsettle them and create an atmosphere of distrust and panic which must be avoided at all costs. So they had stayed; and less than a quarter of an hour later they had heard the roar of the explosion as young Eyton and the five men of the guard from the 93rd who had remained loyal had blown up the Magazine, and themselves with it.

It had not been eight o'clock when Alex had burst into the crowded Residency and told them to run—and to keep running. Surely that had been a year ago—a lifetime—an aeon ago? How many people had died in the hour that preceded that? In the quarter of an hour that had followed it? How many people were dying now? How many were hiding in the jungles like themselves, and how long would they—and those others—be able to stay alive? Ten minutes to eleven . . .

Lou Cottar spoke in a whisper. A whisper that was not on

account of the sleeping Lottie, but enforced upon her by the deathly stillness of the jungle: 'He was right. We'd better keep moving. We can follow him fairly easily if we go now, but the grass stands up again so quickly.'

Lottie rolled her head in Mrs. Cottar's lap and muttered: 'Water—please. So thirsty.'

The two women looked at each other and looked away quickly; their own throats parched.

'We shouldn't have thrown our hoops away,' said Lou Cottar getting stiffly to her feet. 'We could have made a hammock out of them. Oh, well—too late now. It will have to be my dress. It may hold.' She slipped out of it as she spoke, and they folded it and tied it with strips torn from Winter's petticoat and made a rough-and-ready hammock in which they laid Lottie. It was a precarious enough conveyance and put an intolerable strain on them, but they managed it somehow, with the aid of a makeshift harness that took the weight on their shoulders.

It was an agonizingly slow performance, but they kept moving. The sun scorched them and blistered Lou's arms and face— Winter's, more inured to the sun of late, suffered less. The dense shade held no coolness, and Lottie turned and twisted and begged for water and it became more and more difficult to persuade her to lie still.

Once a tiger bounded across their path, but they heard no other sounds in the jungle, and almost an hour later they saw something loom up out of the tangle of scrub and *sal* trees and bamboo that was not a shadow but a solid wall of creeper-covered stone, and knew that they had reached the end of that day's journey.

The ruin that Alex and Niaz had stumbled across three years ago while tracking a wounded leopard through the dense jungle had perhaps once been the hunting-lodge of some forgotten king, or all that remained of a long-vanished city. Niaz had named it the *Hirren Minar*—the Deer Tower—for they had found the antlers of a buck in the grass by the threshold. They had frequently used it as a base when on shooting-leave, but had kept its discovery a close secret, for over the last three years there had lurked at the back of Alex's mind the germ of the thought that some day a hiding-place such as this might prove more than useful.

All that remained was part of a two-storeyed building topped by a low ruined dome. Thickets of bamboo grew closely about it, and lantana and the rank jungle-grass smothered the fallen blocks of stone and pressed up between the paving. It was hot and very dark inside, and smelt strongly of the wild boar and his family who had recently been inhabiting it. There was also a distinct scent of leopard. The stairway that had led up to the top storey had fallen centuries ago, and only a gaping hole remained in one corner of the black, bat-haunted ceiling of the single cell-like lower room.

The trodden grass showed where Alex and at least one other had passed in, but the ruin was as silent as the silent jungle, the hot sunlight and the chequered shadows.

'There is no one here,' whispered Lou Cottar, and the dark stone walls about her whispered back '. . . *no one here!*'

'But there is a ladder,' said Winter. 'Look!'

Hanging from the jagged hole in the roof was a serviceable rope-ladder, and they tugged at it tentatively. It appeared to be quite fast. Winter set her foot on it and started upwards, and a minute later she had vanished through the broken aperture. Presently her head reappeared. 'Can you get Lottie up? There's water here. There's—there's everything!' Her voice broke.

Two rough-and-ready beds, a roll of matting, some tin boxes, an oil-lamp and an earthenware *chatti* containing water would not have been considered 'everything'—or even 'anything'—a few hours ago. But the world had dissolved under their feet during those hours, and the sight of these homely objects helped in some way to solidify it again.

The water in the *chatti* was warm and stale and there was not a great deal of it. There was a tin mug, recently used, standing beside it and they watched while Lottie drank, and then drank thirstily but sparingly themselves, and wetted their handkerchiefs in it to cool Lottie's hot body.

'There, there, darling,' said Winter, forcing her voice to placid reassurance. 'You'll be all right now. You must rest. We're safe now—we're safe.'

But for how long?

32

By the irony of Fate it was a bullet fired by one of the five British women who had preferred to remain in their own bungalows rather than take refuge at the Residency, that had brought down Niaz's horse. Laura Campion, standing over the body of her dying husband on the verandah of her bungalow, had fired his musket at a mob of sepoys who had pursued the wounded man from the lines. The bullet went wide, and the horse, neck stretched at a gallop, had crossed the line of fire.

Niaz struck the dry grass verge of the roadway, rolled into a ditch and lay still.

He recovered consciousness within a few minutes, and not long afterwards, shaken and badly bruised but otherwise unhurt, he was crawling down the ditch towards a culvert where the drive leading into Captain Garrowby's bungalow branched off the road. As he did so he had heard the explosion of the Magazine, and had not known if it also signalled Alex's death; but he did not turn back.

There was a tangle of oleanders growing by the gate of Captain Garrowby's bungalow, and Niaz, waiting his opportunity, left the culvert and took refuge among them. Since the night that he had been knifed leaving the lines he had had few illusions on the score of his safety if the sepoys should mutiny, and he preferred to keep out of the public eye. But he must have a horse, and there would be horses in the stables behind the bungalow.

There was a smell of smoke in the hot air and a crackling sound, and emerging from the shelter of the oleanders he saw that the bungalow was on fire. He ran across the garden, keeping to the shelter of the shrubs and trees, and saw a mob of sepoys between the back of the bungalow and the stables, cutting off his approach. Niaz did not linger. He scrambled over the compound wall and fifteen minutes later he was a quarter of a mile away, wriggling along a drain behind Mr. Joshua Cottar's stables. But Josh Cottar had taken four of his horses with him when he had left for Calcutta, and Mrs. Cottar had driven to the Residency in a carriage and pair, accompanied by a syce riding the remaining horse. The stable doors stood open and the stables were empty.

It had not proved in the least easy to steal a horse that morning, for the mutinous sepoys and the bazaar rabble had scattered through the cantonments, shouting and firing off their rifles, hunting down the British and attacking, looting and burning the bungalows. But Alex might be dead, and if so it was doubly necessary that he, Niaz, should reach the Hirren Minar and the bridge. He would have to do so even if it meant walking.

Crouched behind a prickly cactus hedge he heard a mob of men stream past, coming from the direction of the city—a mob who shouted the battle-cry of his creed: '*Deen! Deen! Fatteh Muhammed!*' An odd shiver tingled through him at the sound and he set his teeth and tried to shut his ears to the fierce cry that had been a clarion call to all men of his faith for over a thousand years.

A dried finger of the cactus overhead, withered by the sun, threw a shadow on the hot, hard ground before him. A curved shadow in the shape of the sickle moon—the emblem of that faith. Niaz stared at it, seeing it, in a sudden wave of superstition, as a sign. The sign of the once-great Empire of the Moguls, shrunk now to no more than a shadow on the ground. Men of his race and creed were fighting now to raise that Empire from the dust into which it had fallen, and if they succeeded a Mogul of the House of Timur would once again rule over the greater part of India. Once again there would be Mohammedan Viceroys and Generals and Governors.

'*Ya Allah! Ya Allah! Allah ho Akhbar! Fatteh Muhammed!*'

. . . The sounds died away, but the echoes still rang in his ears
as he ran on, keeping to the cover of trees and walls, taking short-
cuts across the compounds of burning bungalows, and making for
the road that led out of Lunjore towards Oudh.

An hour later he had dragged a portly *bunnia* from the back
of a starved-looking pony, and was riding as hard as he could
persuade the animal to gallop in the direction of the bridge of
boats.

There was seldom much traffic on the roads in the heat of the
day during the hot weather, and he passed an occasional lumbering bullock-cart, but nothing else. He had abandoned the pony
by the roadside when he took to the jungle, finding it easier to
make his way on foot, and had arrived at the ruined hide-out
barely fifteen minutes before Alex.

Something grunted and crashed away through the undergrowth as he approached it, and Niaz had entered the jungle-
choked ruin with caution and groped in the gloom for the length
of stout bamboo that he knew he would find against one wall. A
moment or two later he had operated the primitive mechanism
that released the rope-ladder, and was in the upper room collecting sundry packages with feverish haste.

He had been descending with his load when Alex arrived,
and both of them had been too exhausted for speech. They had
looked at each other for a long moment and then Alex had
climbed the ladder. He dipped a tin mug into the water that
stood in the covered earthenware *chatti* and drank it thirstily.
The water was warm and stale and there was not overmuch of it
for a good deal had evaporated since he had filled it almost three
weeks ago. There was brandy there too, and he drank some of
that, and fetching the Westley Richards rifle from its hiding-
place in the ruined dome above, loaded it. Niaz returned from
below and fetched a shot-gun from the same place, and Alex
looked up and shook his head: 'Nay, leave it. I have this——'
he touched the revolver. 'How much time have we?'

Niaz shrugged his shoulders. 'An hour—two hours—a day.
Who knows?'

He saw Alex draw a quick breath of relief and said: 'I was delayed, and therefore I came slowly'—he gave a brief account of that delay. 'But there are none on the road as yet, and there being no *risala* they must come on foot. I do not think they will come too soon. They are mad from killing and they are breaking into the bungalows to rob and burn.'

'When there are no more left to kill they will be afraid and come away quickly,' said Alex, filling his pockets with spare ammunition and reaching for powder-flask and shot.

'Assuredly,' said Niaz, following his example. 'But there is little shade on that road, and they must march. How didst thou come?'

'By the jungle,' said Alex briefly.

'On foot, then?'

Alex nodded. 'All but a few of those who were in the Residency *Koti* were slain. I came away across the nullah with three memsahibs whom I left half a *koss* from here. They follow, but slowly. I have marked the way. Let us go.'

They descended the swaying ladder and shouldering their burdens went out into the hot shadows of the forest. The river ran past less than two hundred yards from the Hirren Minar, but the banks were steep and overhung by the dense jungle so that none passed that way, and the road and the bridge of boats lay away to the right, a scant mile from the hidden ruin. No paths led there, but Alex and Niaz knew this part of the jungle well and they had their own tracks through the apparently trackless thickets and the man-high grass, the trees and the cane-brakes.

They moved with more and more caution as they neared the road, and presently the jungle thinned out a little and they heard the gurgle of the river running between the boats, and the creek and strain of the bridge.

'Wait here,' whispered Niaz. 'I will go forward and see if the road be clear.' He laid down the load he carried and wriggled away like a lizard through the thick scrub.

Alex sat down with his back to a tree-trunk and tried not to

Q*

think of a dozen things that he had seen that morning. Things
that made his stomach heave and cramp with rage, and a red
haze swim in his brain so that some primitive, unreasoning tribal
instinct had made him, for one dreadful instant, want to get his
hands round Niaz's throat at the Hirren Minar—because of the
things that men of Niaz's race had done that day. He had seen,
too, for a fractional moment, a like antagonism in Niaz's face,
and known that the drag of race and blood had pulled at him
also. It had been there for less than a breath, but he had recognized it for what it was.

'But we are not only our people—we are ourselves,' thought
Alex, '*ourselves!* No we are not—we are chained together by
environment and custom and blood . . . "*I arm their hands and
furnish the pretence . . .*" ' He found that he was unable to think
clearly and wished that he need never think again.

The undergrowth rustled and gave up Niaz who said cheerfully
and without troubling to lower his voice: 'I have locked the toll-
keeper and the police guard in the toll-house and have taken away
their muskets. Remains now those on the far side.'

Alex said: 'Had they heard aught?'

'Nay; for two slept, and that they would not have done had
the news been told.' He lifted his discarded burden and said:
'Why do we not cut the boats loose? That would suffice.'

'For a time only, for the boats would strand and they would
use them again. And I would close this road.'

They came out cautiously into the thinner belt of jungle by
the bridge-head where the grass was trampled down and the
ashes of old fires showed where travellers had stopped for the
night. The road lay long and empty under the dancing waves of
heat, and the small stone-built toll-house was silent. There was
no sound to be heard except the gurgling of the water between
the close-lashed boats.

Alex glanced at the toll-house under frowning brows and Niaz
said sweetly: 'They will not cry out. I have bound them.'

'And the others in the huts behind?'

'They sleep. And all the muskets were in the toll-house.

They will not move for some hours yet. Why should they? There was no outcry.'

They walked down the slope of the road on to the bridge, into the full blaze of the blinding noonday and the sun-dazzled water, the creaking planks hot under their feet. The heat shimmered off the wood in quivering waves that smelt of tar, and the glittering river that slid beneath them did not cool it. The banks narrowed and the river ran deep from a hundred yards above the bridge to a mile below it, for the bridge spanned it at its narrowest point, but upstream the sandbanks and the shallows widened until they were lost in the heat haze. There were row upon row of mud-turtles basking in the glare at the edge of the sand-bars on the far side of the river, but except for the turtles there seemed to be nothing else alive within a dozen miles, and the hollow sound of their footsteps on the planks of the bridge was loud in the hot silence.

A drowsy toll-keeper heard it and came reluctantly to the door of the mud hut that served as a toll-house on the Oudh bank of the river. Seeing a sahib he salaamed and hurriedly straightened his turban. Alex returned the salute and enquired as to the prospects of *shikar* in the jungles by the bridge. He had, he said, glancing down at the stain that Mrs. Holly's blood had left on the sleeve of his coat, shot a leopard that morning not a mile up the road. While he talked Niaz moved between them and the hut.

Five minutes later the two men in the hut who constituted the bridge guard, together with the horrified toll-keeper, were sitting gagged and bound in the inner room and Niaz was making fast the door. He carried the two antiquated muskets out and flung them into the water as he and Alex ran back along the causeway and on to the bridge.

They worked swiftly and methodically in the boiling sun, laying the charges, tamping and connecting fuses, never certain that the intense heat of the hot wood and the burning metal would not detonate the explosive of itself. The sweat poured off them and the dazzling glare of the river scorched their faces and hurt their eyeballs.

'Listen!' said Niaz suddenly. 'There are horses on the road!'

Alex leapt to his feet and stood for a moment listening intently; and heard the faint far-away sound that Niaz had heard. He snatched up the rifle and thrust it at Niaz. 'Four more and we have done. Hold them off for a little——'

Niaz turned and raced for the bridge-head and Alex bent to the charges again, working with feverish speed. The sound of horses' hooves was clearer now and presently he heard the crack of a rifle shot, but he did not lift his head or look round. He must have more time—only a little more time. The noise of the river was astonishingly loud under his feet, and the heat of the iron bands that reinforced the planking burnt his hands as though it were red-hot. Once again he seemed to hear Sir Henry's voice speaking from the shadows of the verandah in the Lucknow Residency—*I need time . . . time most of all*——

'Only five minutes,' prayed Alex, 'it isn't much to ask—only five minutes——!'

He heard a fusillade of shots and a bullet sang past his head like a hornet, but still he did not look round.

*   *   *

Niaz reached the toll-house and leaping the step of the shallow verandah, unbarred the door and ran to the small window that looked down the long Lunjore road, ignoring the groans of the three bound and gagged men who watched him from the floor with starting eyes.

There were perhaps twelve or fifteen riders, sepoys from Lunjore, advancing at a leisurely trot for the bridge; either men bringing the news of the rising to Oudh, or an advance party sent to secure the bridge for the main body of the mutineers who would cross later that day to swell the ranks of the malcontents in the newly annexed province.

Niaz waited until they were within range, and fired; aiming deliberately for the leading horse in order to create the maximum confusion. He saw the horse rear and fall, and the dust rose in a choking cloud as the men drew rein and came to a sudden stop.

He reloaded swiftly and fired into the dusty smother; heard a yell and the scream of a wounded horse and saw the riders scatter to either side of the road. They would not come on for a moment or two, and he fetched the muskets belonging to the police guard that he had piled against the wall out of their reach. With several muskets and Alex's rifle he should be able to save time on loading. He looked at the priming of one and noted with irritation that its owner had permitted the weapon to reach an unsoldierly state of dirt. '*Police!*' said Niaz, and spat scornfully to show his disgust.

He reloaded the rifle again and watched with interest, reserving his fire, while the skirmishers at the road's edge conferred together. Presently one of them cupped his hands about his mouth and, evidently under the impression that it was the bridge guard and the toll-keeper who were firing upon them, bellowed that they were friends and urged the guard to join them—the *feringhis* being dead and all Lunjore in the hands of its rightful owners.

The man moved incautiously out into the road and Niaz shot him and watched his riderless horse bolt down the road and gallop wildly past the toll-house. There was a crash and a splash as the frenzied animal went wide of the bridge and plunged headlong into deep water, and Niaz heard shrill feminine screams from the three small huts twenty yards behind the toll-house where the toll-keeper's family lived. A fusillade of shots spattered up the dust and chipped flakes of stone from the walls, and he saw the remaining horsemen hurriedly dismount and disappear into the jungle.

'Now they will come up under cover on either side of the road,' thought Niaz, and remembered with dread that Alex, working alone on the empty bridge, would provide an admirable target. He fired again at random into the jungle just ahead of where the men had entered it, discharging each of the muskets in turn and reloading with feverish haste.

A woman ran out across the sun-scorched ground opposite the window, and a musket-ball fired from the jungle on the far side of the road whipped past her and smacked against the corner of the toll-house, sending a shower of chips flying. She screamed and ran back again and Niaz grinned and fired in the direction from which the shot had come. Three more riderless horses galloped past with trailing reins and he heard their hooves thunder on the bridge and hoped that they had not ridden Alex into the water.

There was a back door to the toll-house and a woman beat upon it and screeched to her husband to come out and take refuge in the jungle for they were being attacked by dacoits; but the remainder of the police guard had presumably either run away or joined the sepoys. There were men now in the jungle opposite, and a bullet entered the open door and ricocheted round the small room. Niaz turned from the narrow iron-barred window in the end wall, and running to the door fired into the thick scrub on the opposite side of the road. As he did so something struck his chest and he fell sideways, the rifle jerking from his hand to slide along the floor and come to rest against the far wall.

After a moment or two he came dizzily to his knees and crawled towards the rifle, but he could not reach it. He groped instead for his revolver and dragging it painfully from its holster, raised himself a little and fired at a face that peered through the high grass at the road's edge, and saw a man lurch forward and fall on his face in the dust. And then he heard the sound of running feet, a crash of shots, and Alex had leapt the stone step of the verandah, stumbled over him and turning had fired his revolver at a man on horseback who rode shouting for the bridge.

The shouting voice stopped as though cut off with a knife and there was the sound of a fall, a clatter of hooves and a brief moment of silence. And then the crashing blast of an explosion; and another and another that joined together in a single shuddering roar of sound, and the glaring day was dark with flying splinters of wood and choked with the reek of black powder. Then the silence slammed down like an iron shutter and the river gurgled no longer, but ran quiet and unimpeded from bank to bank.

Alex spoke breathlessly into that silence: 'Quickly, before they recover—out by the back!' He had barred the door behind him and was across the room pulling at the heavy bolts that closed the back door. He drew it open a crack and said: 'There is no one there—quick!'

'I cannot,' said Niaz.

Alex whipped round, seeing for the first time that Niaz had not been merely kneeling to fire, but was wounded, and he crossed the floor in a single bound. He knelt swiftly and thrust an arm under him, lifting him: 'Hold about my neck and I can carry thee.'

'No,' said Niaz urgently. 'This is the end for me. Go—and go swiftly while there is yet time—*mera kham hōgya* (my work is finished).'

Alex looked down at the greying face against his arm and the bright swiftly spreading stain that soaked the dusty tunic, and pulling back the reddened cloth he saw that there was nothing that he or anyone could do, and desperation and a wrenching rage beyond anything he had felt that day tore at him with the savagery of a taloned paw. He heard dimly and as though through a roaring fog, the crack of rifle-fire, but he did not move.

Niaz said: 'Thou hast seen how it is with me—go now. I can still—fire a gun—it will hold them—for a little. Get to the jungle—there be the memsahibs to be—thought of——'

Lou Cottar—Lottie—Winter . . . If it had not been for them he, Alex, would have reached the river an hour or more ago. This would never have happened. How long would they live if he died? He had left Mrs. Holly to die alone and slowly. He had had to—because of those three women. And because of the bridge. But the bridge had gone. He had stopped at least one road into Oudh, and perhaps by doing so had bought, at the price of his friend's life, a little more time. Only a very little more, for there were so many other roads. Winter had courage, and so had Lou Cottar. And there was ammunition and a certain amount of food at the Hirren Minar.

Once again, and for a brief moment, he saw Winter's face quite clearly against the rough stone walls of the shadowed room; as clearly as he had seen it in Alice Batterslea's garden. But it did not mean anything to him any more. She would have to take her chance. He would not leave Niaz to die alone as he had left Mrs. Holly.

Alex drew his arm away very gently, laying Niaz back, and getting to his feet he closed and bolted the back door and dropped the shutters across the two windows, fitting the iron bars that held them into the sockets. He took up the guns one by one and loaded them methodically. There was an earthenware jar of water in the room, and he fetched a brass *lotah*, stepping over the bodies of the three bound men who lay in a terrified huddle on the floor at the far end of the room, and filling it, brought it to Niaz.

He lifted him carefully against his shoulder and Niaz's eyes narrowed in the gloom as he strove to focus him. He drank a mouthful of the water and said again and urgently: 'Go!'

'We will go together,' said Alex. 'Has it not been said that "death in the company of friends is a feast"? '

A bullet struck the heavy wood of the door and another cracked against the stone. He looked down at Niaz and smiled, and Niaz grinned back at him—the old carefree grin with which he had greeted every chance and mischance of life through the twelve eventful years that they had known each other—and he said in a clear strong voice: 'It is better this way. It is not good to have a divided heart, and there is that in me which, were it not for thee, would have me follow such men as the Maulvie of Faizabad. We have had a good life, Sikunder Dulkhan—a good life—and though thou art an unbeliever, and therefore Hell-doomed, thou hast been as my brother. Lift me up, brother—it will be a good fight——'

His voice failed, and presently he began to mutter names and odd scraps of sentences, and Alex realized that in imagination he was back at Moodkee, watching the opening of the Khalsa can-nonade, and fretting for the order to charge. Then suddenly he laughed, and raised himself in Alex's arms; pressing up as though he rose in his stirrups, and shouted aloud as he had shouted on the day of that charge—'*Shahbash bhaiyan! Dauro!—Dauro! —Da——*' A rush of blood choked him, pouring from his mouth and dyeing Alex's coat and hands, and he fell back and was still.

A musket-ball struck a leaf of the wooden shutter over the window and filled the room with flying splinters. There were shouting voices and another fusillade of shots from outside the toll-house, and the bound men on the floor writhed and groaned in terror as a second bullet smashed through the shutter and struck the wall above their heads; but Alex did not move. He stayed quite still, holding Niaz's body in his arms; his mind entirely blank. The noise outside the toll-house seemed to come from very far away and to have nothing whatever to do with him, and he was only aroused at last by a bullet fired at much closer range that smashed through the panel of the door and passed within an inch of his shoulder.

He laid Niaz down very carefully and stood up. His gaze fell on the water-jar and he picked it up and drank thirstily, and poured what remained of it over his head and neck. He did not know how many men there were outside. A dozen? Twenty? They would get him in the end, but he should be able to account for some of them before the ammunition in the toll-house ran out. He took stock of it, and discovered that unless the police guard kept their ammunition elsewhere they had been issued with only a few rounds each. But there was still the supply he had brought for the rifle.

He picked up Niaz's revolver and loaded the single chamber that had been fired. A rifle, five muskets, two revolvers. A pocketful of ammunition. He might hold them off for an hour— perhaps a little longer——

There were two string charpoys in the stifling room and he stooped, and lifting Niaz laid him on one of them. He took up the rifle and loaded it, and crossing to the window lifted the bar of the shutter and pulled it aside. There were three sepoys not a dozen yards away, and putting down the rifle he jerked the revolver from its holster and fired, killing one and wounding a second.

    *   *   *

It was nearly five o'clock when Alex fired the last round and dropped the useless weapon to the floor.

The heat of the closed stone building was appalling and his head and every muscle of his body ached abominably. The sun was sinking down towards the tree-tops and the walls of the room were hot to the touch. The three bound men who lay against the wall had ceased to move or whimper, and he wondered incuriously if they were dead from fear or thirst or one of the ricocheting bullets. He closed the shutter again and sitting down on the charpoy beside Niaz, leaned his head against the wall and waited, watching the patch of sunlight from the broken shutter creep slowly across the floor and up the wall, and thinking odd disjointed thoughts. For the moment there was silence outside, but he knew that it would not be long before it dawned upon those without that he must have come to the end of his ammunition. He had met every move with a shot so far and made it too dangerous to approach across the open, but after a time they would find that they could move without one, and draw their own conclusions.

He heard horses' hooves galloping down the Lunjore road towards the river, and heard them check some way above the toll-house. Reinforcements? He wondered how soon the mutinous regiments would arrive. They should be here by now. Unless, which seemed likely, someone had ridden back to tell them that the bridge had been destroyed and that there was no further point in their coming that way.

He wondered how Yusaf had fared, and if the blowing up of the Hazrat Bagh road had been as successful as the destruction of the bridge. It should have been—they had worked it out with considerable care. He hoped that Yusaf would not be too impatient, but wait until the guns and the wagons were well on the mined stretch of road. That should not only effectively block the road, but dispose of a considerable quantity of ammunition at the same time. Would they come that day, or would they wait until the thirty-first? A harlot's taunt had sprung the mine of the mutiny before its time, but now that it had been sprung that premature explosion, like the charges he had laid on the bridge, was setting off a succession of other explosions, and not all the pleas of the leaders could prevent the inflammable material they had prepared from catching fire from the flying sparks.

The hot room stank of sweat and urine, black powder, betel-nut and blood, and the gloom was noisy with the buzz of flies. Alex pulled down the end of Niaz's pugaree so that it covered his face, and folded the quiet hands across his chest. They were stiff already. It must be getting late. He rose and turned the charpoy so that the dead man's head was towards Mecca. There was no more water, so he could not wash as the ritual prescribed, but he rubbed his hands partially clean on his soiled handkerchief, and spoke the words of the *Du'a* over the quiet body—there being no one else who would ever speak them for Niaz.

'*May the Lord God, abundant in mercy, keep thee with the true speech; may he lead thee to the perfect path; may he grant thee knowledge of him and his prophets. May the mercy of God be fixed upon thee for ever. Ameen . . . Oh great and glorious God, we beseech thee with humility, make the earth comfortable to this thy servant's side, and raise his soul to thee, and with thee may he find mercy and forgiveness.*'

The murmured words awoke a soft echo in the shuttered stone-walled room, and when they ceased there was only the buzz of the swarms of flies once more. Alex sat down again, and presently, from very far away, borne on the hot silence and scarcely more than a vibration of sound, he heard the faint, faint boom of an explosion. It was followed a second later by another, and then a third—— 'Yusaf!' thought Alex contentedly. The Hazrat Bagh road had gone, and with it a large proportion of the contents of the Suthragunj arsenal, for the charges that he and Niaz and Yusaf had laid had not been sufficient to account for that sound at so long a range. That had been ammunition wagons blowing up. He leaned back against the wall and closed his eyes.

A voice from outside the toll-house shouted for those within to come out and give themselves up. Alex made no reply, and emboldened by the silence, footsteps clattered at last on the shallow stone verandah and rifle butts battered on the door and the window shutters. They were followed after an interval by other sounds; dragging sounds and footsteps and voices all about the small building, and quite suddenly Alex realized what it was that they were doing. They were piling wood and dry grass against the doors and windows and about the house. They were going to make a pyre of it. Well, he might as well go that way as any other. A funeral pyre for Niaz and himself. He settled himself more comfortably against the wall, and as he did so one of the men on the floor stirred and moaned.

The sound seemed to clear some numbness from his brain, and he remembered that he and Niaz were not the only occupants of the toll-house. There were three other men there, and he could not let them be burnt alive. 'Wait a minute——' said Alex, speaking aloud. 'Wait a minute——'

He dragged himself to his feet and walked unsteadily to the door, and as he did so he heard a man outside say triumphantly: 'Did I not say so? It *is* a sahib! There are sahib-*log* in there!' and realized that he had spoken in English and that they did not know who was within.

A voice immediately outside the door said loudly: 'Who is it? Who is within there?' and Alex's hand dropped from the bolt, for he knew that voice. He leant against the door because it was an effort to stand and said: 'It is I, Rao Sahib. Call off your butchers, for there are three in here who are bound hand and foot and who had no part in this. You cannot burn them alive. I will come out.'

He heard Kishan Prasad catch his breath. 'Who else is with thee?'

'None but Niaz Mohamed Khan, who is dead.'

There was a shouting and a rush of feet and he heard Kishan

Prasad say furiously: 'Stand back!—stand back, I say!' and a moment later the sound of a grumbling and reluctant retreat.

'Open then,' said Kishan Prasad.

Alex picked up the empty revolver from the floor and thrust it into the holster with a gesture that was purely mechanical, and straightening his shoulders with an effort, he drew back the bolts and opened the door.

Kishan Prasad stared at him for a long moment and then he stepped over the threshold and threw a quick look about the small room. He looked at Alex again and then turned away and stood blocking the narrow door, facing men whom Alex could not see.

'There is but one sahib here,' he said. 'The other man is dead and the three men they have bound are alive. This sahib I know, and because he once gave me my life at risk of his own, I say that he shall go free. Stand away!'

There was an ugly growl and a babble of voices: 'And what of Heera Lal who lies dead? And Dhoolee Gookul—and Suddhoo, and Jagraj—and Mohan whose leg is broken? It is a *feringhi*— kill him!—kill him!'

There was a rush of shouting men, but Kishan Prasad did not move from the narrow doorway and his voice rose clearly above the tumult: 'Stand back!' said Kishan Prasad. 'I am a Brahmin; and if you would kill this man, you will have first to kill me.'

The babble died abruptly and the men drew back, for they were Hindus, and to kill a Brahmin would be sacrilege unspeakable, dooming them to the nethermost of hells and to become outcast among their fellow-men.

'Go,' said Kishan Prasad, speaking over his shoulder to Alex. 'Move out behind me and run for the jungle. I can do no more. The debt is paid.'

Alex said tiredly and without emotion: 'Rao Sahib, if I had one bullet left in this gun, I would shoot thee now for the things that have been done this day because of men like thee.'

'That may yet come,' said Kishan Prasad. 'Go now——'

He moved out of the doorway, keeping between Alex and the group of snarling men at the far end of the verandah, and Alex backed away behind him, one hand against the wall, and reaching the end of the verandah stepped down and to one side behind the shelter of the house, and turning, ran for the jungle behind the toll-house and the huts.

He heard the uproar break out behind him, and a lone shot whistled past his head. And then he was into the high grass and had turned parallel to the road and was running and stumbling through the thickets, keeping as close to the road as he dared, in the belief that the pursuit would imagine him to be making straight for the thicker jungle instead of turning back up the Lunjore road. They would watch to see that he did not cross the road, and would not search the far side of it, so he must cross as soon as he could do so without being seen.

He wriggled into a thick patch of thorn-bamboo and lay still, listening for sounds of pursuit. There were no more shots, and though he could still hear shouting it seemed to go farther and farther away and prove that his guess had been correct, and that they had expected him to run in a straight line, and were beating the jungle behind the toll-house. The sounds did not come his way, and after a time he heard horses' hooves on the road that lay barely a dozen yards from his hiding-place. Two of the men at least were riding back to Lunjore, and the voice of one of them, high-pitched and angry, came clearly to his ears:

'What matter? He cannot cross the river and he has no food or arms. He will die slowly in the jungle. I am for Delhi; that is the place for such as——' The voices faded.

When he thought that they had gone far enough Alex crawled with infinite caution to within sight of the road and lay there for a long time, wondering if he dared cross it. He had reached a point roughly five hundred yards above the toll-house, but the road here ran straight as a spear for a mile or more, and there would be men watching from the toll-house. He must not draw them to the far side of the road. The road lay empty on either side of him but he could see men moving before the toll-house.

The sun touched the rim of the jungle and slid slowly below it, and a peacock called from the thickets behind him. Another horseman galloped towards him from the direction of the river, raising a long cloud of dust. And suddenly it was simple.

The rider drew level with him and passed him, and Alex leapt to his feet and ran for the opposite side of the road, screened by the choking cloud of dust.

33

IN Lunjore City the conches brayed and horns blared in the temples, tom-toms beat and rockets flared while men rioted through the streets shouting that all Hind was freed for ever from the 'Company Sahibs' rule—that all the *feringhis* were dead, and the great days had returned. They wore stolen finery and displayed stolen goods, and boasted of the deeds they had done and the sahib-*log* they had slaughtered; they made wild and grandiose plans for the future, and fell to quarrelling over who should be governors, generals or captains of their provinces and armies.

A mile outside the city the cantonments lay silent and deserted. Here and there a bungalow still burned and creeping figures still slunk between the silent houses, searching for any loot that might have been overlooked during the day-long orgy of murder and robbery. But as the evening shadows lengthened, the dead who lay about the cantonments filled even the scum of the city with uneasiness and superstitious fear, and they fired a few more bungalows, leaving the night breeze to carry the sparks and fan the flames, and ran away shuddering.

The sepoys whom it had been intended to march into Oudh for the retaking of the province had turned westwards towards Delhi when the news had been brought that the bridge had gone and the lines were deserted. In the silent Residency the dead lay scattered through the quiet gardens and the darkening rooms, and a quarter of a mile away, in the jungle beyond the nullah, Mrs. Holly died at last.

The jackals and the hyenas, the crows and the kites and the naked-necked vultures, would feast to the full for many days to come, for there were other dead on the plain that stretched towards Hazrat Bagh. The garrison of Suthragunj had risen at the news of the mutiny at Lunjore, and had killed their officers and seized the treasury and the arsenal, and left, as Kishan Prasad and his friends had planned, by the *kutcha* road to join with their fellow-mutineers and march in strength upon Oudh.

They had taken the guns and wagon-loads of powder and ammunition, and Yusaf had waited until those guns and wagons lay between a given mark. He had fired then, at a mark that Alex had set for him. And, as he had once told Niaz, he did not miss with a first shot, though he might be careless with a second. The charges set each other off for a quarter of a mile, and the wagon-loads of ammunition exploded with a crash and a detonation that was heard ten miles away and more. And when the smoke and the flame cleared there was no road, and what remained to be seen was not pleasant to look upon.

Yusaf waited until the shadows lengthened and the partridges began to call from among the grass and the thorn-scrub; until the last of the men from Suthragunj who were able to do so had disappeared in the direction from which they had come, and until there was no more movement from the shattered road. Then he drank deeply from his water-bottle, ate his fill of cold food, and wriggled out backwards from between the rocks.

He did not return to Lunjore, but moved off westwards, making like a homing-pigeon for the North-West Frontier. From what he knew of Nikal Seyn and Jan Larr'in and Daly Sahib, the Guides at least would be fully employed, and he had many friends among the Guides. Who knew—they might already be marching to attack Delhi? And if so, he would join them on that march.

Yusaf slung his rifle frontier-fashion across his shoulder and set off towards the red ball of the setting sun.

*　　　　*　　　　*

Winter and Lou Cottar had heard the faint, far-away crack of rifle-fire at the bridge-head, and the distant roar of the explosion. All that afternoon the firing had continued, and they had guessed what it meant and watched and listened—and waited.

For want of anything else to do they had set about turning the stone chamber into some semblance of a room. It had at least kept them occupied. Alex and Niaz had once spent two weeks in the Hirren Minar, shooting in the surrounding jungles, and they had made themselves tolerably comfortable. The room was large and square, and windowless on three sides. The fourth side consisted of three pillared arches, two of which still retained broken fragments of stone tracery, and led out on to a flat roof surrounded by a low, ruined parapet.

There were several *chiks* in one corner of the room, and though the white ants had damaged one or two of them they were in reasonably good repair, and Lou Cottar had hung them between the pillars, remarking that they would keep out the worst of the flies and mosquitoes. They had also curtained off a section of the room with sacking for Alex's use, convinced as they did so that he would not return, but denying the fear by that action.

Bamboo and dried grass had made primitive but efficient brooms, and they had swept and dusted, cleaned and tidied, in a desperate attempt to keep their hands occupied and their minds from thinking of the many things that did not bear thinking of. Of Mrs. Holly, left to die alone in the jungle. Of Delia Gardener-Smith's pretty head, with its wide eyes and open mouth, rolling along the planks of the bridge above the nullah. And of what must have happened to so many others whom they had known and left behind in the shambles of Lunjore. How many were dead? How many—or how few—were hiding and hunted like themselves, but with no refuge such as this?

It was no use thinking of these things. To think of them

was to sink into clutching quicksands of panic and horror. It was better to occupy themselves with make-believe domesticity, and they were grateful to Lottie because she needed attention and care, and because to keep from frightening her they themselves must not show fear.

Lou Cottar, standing at the edge of the open roof by the crumbling parapet, had reported that she could see a glimpse of river and would fetch water. She had taken the *chatti*—Winter had lowered it after her on a rope—and set out to find her way through the dense jungle to the river-bank that lay so near and yet took so long to reach. She had not returned for over an hour and Winter had received her with breathless relief. 'I'm sorry,' said Mrs. Cottar apologetically, 'but it's so thick out there that I lost my way coming back, even though it is so near. We must mark the way when we go again. We'll have to pull the water up. I can't carry it up that ladder.'

Winter drank thirstily while Lou Cottar filled a small rusted tin with water and arranged a spray of wild gourd and jungle berries in it for Lottie. 'I bathed,' she said, knotting up her wet hair. 'It was wonderful. The bank is very steep and there are no shallows on this side, but there is a place where the river has cut in behind a tree and made a little beach, and I held on to the roots. You had better go too, before it gets dark. It gets dark so soon once the sun is down, and——' She stopped as though she had forgotten what it was that she had meant to say.

The sun was almost at the level of the tree-tops, and they had heard no shots for some time. They looked at each other and looked away again; and said nothing because they were both thinking the same thing—that Alex must be dead.

'We are on our own now,' thought Lou Cottar. 'We shall have to get out of this by ourselves—if there is a way out. I expect we can do it. It's a pity about Lottie English—it's going to be difficult with her on our hands. I wonder if Josh will hear what happened? I wonder if—— No. I won't think about it. I won't think of it!'

'He is dead,' thought Winter. 'If he was not, he would have come back by now. The bridge went hours ago—hours. And I

called him a coward because I thought he should have stayed and
been killed at the Residency instead of doing something sensible
and dying at the bridge instead. I wish I hadn't said that. I wish
I had told him that I didn't mean it. I wish I were dead too; it
would be so much easier to be dead. But there is Lottie—and
Mrs. Cottar. And—and perhaps there are others somewhere. Or
are they all dead?'

Conway must be dead. He at least had been in no condition
to make his escape. It was odd to think that he had been her
husband, and now he was dead—and that she could feel nothing
at all. The only emotion she could feel was a dull regret that she
had made no apology to Alex. In the circumstances, a trivial
emotion. But everything else was blunted and numb. Alex had
told her once that you felt nothing but the blow when a bullet
hit you, and that the pain only came when air reached the wound.
The air had not breathed upon her brain or her heart yet, for she
could feel no pain. Only numbness.

The faint, far-away crack of a lone shot broke the brooding
stillness, and the two women turned their heads as one to listen
But there were no more shots. It was, somehow, a very final
sound. Like a period at the end of a chapter.

'I'll take some of Lottie's clothes and wash them in the river,'
said Winter abruptly, 'and my own. They'll dry in an hour.'

She removed her own torn, dusty, sweat-soaked clothes and
wrapped herself in a length of faded blue cotton cloth that they
had found rolled up in a bundle and stuffed in among a collection
of odds and ends in one of the tin boxes. It made a skimpy though
adequate sari, and she wound it about her in the fashion of the
Indian women.

'You know,' said Lou Cottar thoughtfully, 'you could almost
pass as an Indian, if you'd get a little more sunburnt. It's your
hair and eyes. It may be a help yet.'

'I should have to learn to walk without shoes,' said Winter.

'We may both have to,' said Lou Cottar grimly, and turned
away to collect a few of Lottie's underclothes for Winter to rinse
in the river.

They made a bundle of the clothes and Winter took the loaded revolver and went down the rope-ladder. The jungle that had been so silent all day was waking to life as the shadows lengthened, and there were rustlings among the dry golden grass, and birds sang and twittered and called from the thickets. A peacock fluttered up to a low bough of a tree, his gorgeous tail glinting in the low rays of the sun, and a *chinkara* fawn looked at Winter with soft, startled eyes over a tussock of grass before bounding away in the direction of the river. Making her way through the tangle of dry grass and leaves and creepers her ears were filled with the sound of her own progress, but she could hear the bird-song above it.

The river ran gold in the evening light by the time she reached it, and the far bank was already in shadow. The water slid past like silk, so smooth and still that it seemed impossible that there could be strong and treacherous currents beneath that placid surface. It chuckled softly between the exposed roots of a great tree that the wash of the stream had undermined, and lapped against a small shelving beach below the steep bank.

She clambered cautiously down the bank, and removing her makeshift sari, tucked it and the bundle of soiled clothing in a crutch among the tree roots, and let herself down into the water. It was cool and delicious beyond belief, and she lay along the shelf of the bank and let the river run over her, drawing the heat and the ache from her tired body. Her hair spread out and rippled like water-weed in the pull of the stream, and the gurgle of the current slipping through the tree roots made a soothing monotonous murmur in the silence.

She did not know how long she lay there, mindless and still, with closed eyes, but presently the slow thought drifted through her brain that it would be easy—easy and pleasant—to slide into the main stream and let the current carry her out and down into the cool darkness of the deep water. There was nothing left to live for and she was very tired . . .

The ripple through the tree roots whispered warningly against her ears, and at last she turned her head in the shallows and opened her eyes, to find that the sun had almost set and the sky and the river were no longer gold, but rose pink.

The leaves and flowers of the tree that leaned above her made a stiff, formal pattern against that vivid wash of colour, and some-thing moved in the pattern—a green parrot with a scarlet beak and long green-and-blue tail feathers . . . And all at once the Gulab Mahal was there before her. The enchanted garden of her childhood. The formal patterns of leaves and flowers and brightly coloured birds that moved against a sunset sky, and that had remained fixed in her memory as a bright promise through all the grey, intervening years. The whisper of the water was no longer a warning, but old Aziza Begum's voice, tell-ing her stories in the twilight: Zobeida's, making the old promise —'one day we will return to the Gulab Mahal, and all will be well . . .' There was something to stay alive for after all. Some-how, some day, she would reach the Rose Palace. She had pro-mised herself that for too long to relinquish it now.

A new energy seemed to flow through her with the thought, and she came to her feet and wrung out her wet hair, and reach-ing for the bundle of clothing among the roots, washed out the torn, soiled garments in the river. They made a damp, heavy bundle when she had finished but they would dry quickly. She climbed the bank again and wrapped the makeshift sari about her once more, leaving her wet hair hanging loose.

A peacock cried in the jungle, and the call echoed across the wide river and was repeated by another on the far bank. *Pea-or* . . . *Pea-or* . . . *Pea-or!* The cry seemed to underline the loneli-ness of the silent river and the dense miles of jungle, and to wail for all those who lay dead and who had been alive when that sun rose that was setting now. A savage and unbearable pain stabbed through the numbness about Winter's heart. 'The air is getting to it,' she thought, and she picked up the wet bundle and the revolver and turned from the river to make her way back to the Hirren Minar, stumbling through the tangled grass and the thickets as though she had been blind and must feel her way.

She had stayed far longer by the river than she had meant to

do, and now the sun had gone and the swift twilight was closing
in. She had marked her way carefully, but she had lost those
marks and was unsure of her direction. Fear replaced the pain
in her breast, and she stood still, trying to remember the land-
marks that she had taken note of when she had left the ruined
building. Presently she began to move again, though with more
care, but she had gone less than a dozen yards when she stopped
again at the edge of a small clearing.

Something was moving in the jungle ahead of her, as though
some large animal was walking slowly towards her through the
dry, rustling undergrowth; and remembering the tiger she froze
into stillness, her hand gripping the revolver. The noise came
nearer and nearer, and now she could see the grass and bushes on
the far side of the clearing sway to the movement of something
or someone who was moving directly towards her. *Someone*—
was the hunt so close?

Winter crouched down where she stood, seeing again in an ugly
flash of memory the dark contorted face of the man who had
pursued and murdered the screaming Delia. Her finger tightened upon the trigger of the revolver as the high grass at the far
side of the clearing rustled and parted, and Alex walked out into
the clearing.

For a moment she did not believe it. She had given him up for
dead, and the sight of him—filthy, blood-stained, dazed but alive
—was a greater shock by far than the sight of his dead body
would have been. The revolver slipped from her hand and she
stood up with a choking cry and took a swift step forward, the
bundle of clothing falling unheeded to the ground.

Alex checked, swaying, and his hand moved automatically to
the butt of his useless revolver. Through the haze before his eyes
he saw a slim Indian girl confronting him in the dusk, the blue
of her thin cotton sari and the blue-black of her long, unbound
hair melting into the shadows of the darkening jungle behind
her. Then the haze cleared—and it was Winter.

They stood staring at each other for a minute that seemed like
an hour, and then Alex stumbled forward, and as she ran to him

he dropped on his knees and she caught him, holding him to her, and felt his arms go about her in a desperate grip.

She held his head against her, rocking him as though he had been a child. His hair smelt of dust and sweat and the reek of black powder, and she pressed her fingers through it, whispering endearments that he did not hear, and listening to the terrible, grinding sobs that seemed to wrench his body to pieces. She could feel the heat of those tears soaking through the thin cloth and wetting her body, and she held him tighter, straining him against her, until they stopped at last. The racking shudders ceased, and he lifted his head and looked up into her face.

His eyes in the fading twilight held an odd, blind anger, and then his arms lifted and pulled her down on to the grass. She felt his hands on the thin cotton of the sari, wrenching it away, and he hid his grimed and smoke-blackened face between her small firm breasts. Her skin was cool from the river, and smooth and sweet, and he kissed it with an open mouth, moving his harsh cheek and his aching head against it, holding her closer. Then his hands moved again, and for a fleeting moment the fear and the horror of her wedding night returned to Winter. But this was not Conway, drunken and bestial. This was Alex—Alex——

There was neither love nor tenderness in Alex's hands or his kisses. They were deeply and desperately physical, and she knew that for the moment her cool body meant no more to him than an anodyne to pain—a temporary forgetfulness and release from intolerable strain. But it was enough that she could give him that.

Conway was dead—they were all dead. All those people who had lived and laughed in the cantonments at Lunjore and at Delhi. Mrs. Abuthnot—Colonel Abuthnot—Zeb-un-Nissa—perhaps Ameera too. The whole world was breaking into pieces and dissolving in blood and tears and terror. But here in the quiet forest there were only herself and Alex—Alex's arms and his mouth and his need of her. Alex who was alive . . .

At long last his hold slackened and he lay still. The sky darkened above them, turning from green to a violet blue that was strewn with stars. The starlight and the thin moon made odd shapes out of the trees and the thickets and the tussocks of grass, and sometimes something rustled in the jungle or an owl hooted in the darkness. Once, very far away, a barking deer called a warning that a tiger was passing, and once a nilghai, the wild blue bull of the jungles, crashed through the dense undergrowth not a dozen yards away. But Alex slept the sleep of utter mental and physical exhaustion, and Winter held him in her arms and watched the stars and was not afraid of the night noises or of anything else.

She thought once, and fleetingly, of Lottie and Lou Cottar. They would think that she had lost her way or met with some accident, and Mrs. Cottar would not dare to call her name or show a light, for fear that her failure to return might mean that there were men in the jungle hunting for fugitives. They would be frightened, but it could not be helped. Alex was asleep and she would not wake him even if she could.

His head was heavy on her breast and the weight of the arm that lay across her and pressed her down on the warm dry grass seemed to increase with every breath she drew, while her own arm beneath him had passed from numbness to prickling pain. But she did not move except to hold him closer, her cheek against his hair, and presently a breeze got up; a hot breath of wind that the river had cooled until it blew pleasantly through the jungle with a sleepy, soothing, rustling sound, dispersing the mosquitoes and night-flying insects and lulling her at last into deep and dreamless sleep.

*   *   *

The sky was paling to the first light of dawn when Winter awoke and felt Alex move and draw away from her.

After a moment or two she opened her eyes slowly and sleepily, aware, despite the rough grasses below her and the numbness of her arm, of a feeling of miraculous restfulness and physical well-being. Alex had risen and was standing beside her, his profile dark against the greying sky, and although it was as yet barely light enough to distinguish more than the outline of his face, she knew that he was frowning.

He was not looking at her, and she lay and watched him with an aching, possessive love as the light grew and deepened and his features and the forest about him ceased to be flat silhouettes and became three-dimensional, emerging from the surrounding greyness and taking on form and shape. But as the sky brightened she saw that the sleeves and breast of his torn coat were black with dried blood, and the sight brought her suddenly to her feet, clutching at his arm:

'Alex!—you're wounded!'

Alex turned his head slowly and looked at her, and her hand dropped from his arm. He said: 'No. I'm all right.'

'But—but you—you're covered in blood!'

'It isn't mine,' said Alex in a flat and entirely expressionless voice. 'It is Niaz's. He's dead.'

He looked down at the stained, discoloured coat, and began to remove it, stripping it off slowly and with difficulty as though his muscles were stiff, and letting it fall to the ground. The blood had soaked through to his shirt, and seeing it he frowned with a faint distaste and turned once more to look in the direction of the river. He said after a moment or two, and without turning his head: 'I'm sorry about last night.'

His voice did not express sorrow, or anything else—unless it was perhaps the same faint distaste that had shown in his face when he had looked down at his stained shirt—and Winter's heart contracted with the familiar ache of pain that she had felt so often when she looked at Alex. Are you, my darling? she thought. Are you really? Don't be sorry, my dear love! Anything but that!—my love, my dear love——

She wanted desperately to put her arms about him and to tell him that she loved him, and that nothing in all the terrible things that had happened or would happen mattered more than that. But she knew that she must not do it. He did not want to hear it, and he would not understand it.

She disentangled the length of blue cotton from among the

R

grasses and rewound it about her slender body. The movement brought life back to her numbed arm and wrenched a sobbing gasp of pain from her, and Alex heard the small sound and misinterpreted it. She saw him flinch, but he did not turn.

He said: 'I'm going down to the river. I shan't be very long. Stay here.'

He disappeared into the jungle, and Winter stood listening until she could not hear him any longer. She stooped then, and picked up his discarded coat. He would need it, and she could soak the stains out. She shook the dried fragments of grass from it, and as she did so something fell out of one of the pockets; a small folded square of paper. She picked it up and smoothed it out mechanically. It was her own note—the one she had written to him when she had returned from Lucknow, and which Yusaf had taken to him in camp. He had kept it. She stood looking at it for a long time and then she folded it again very carefully and replaced it.

It was growing lighter every moment and presently a bird began to twitter in the trees behind her. A hint of the terrible heat that the coming day would bring was already in the air, as though the unseen sun, still far below the rim of the horizon, had exhaled a fiery breath of warning. Winter knotted up her heavy tangled hair, and searched among the tall grass for the revolver and the bundle of linen. A jungle-cock began to cackle in the thickets, and then once again, as on the previous evening, the stillness was broken by a babble of bird-song. A flight of parrots screamed out of the trees on their way to the river, and other jungle-cocks awoke and saluted the dawn.

Alex returned at long last. He had evidently bathed in the river, for he was clean again. The dirt and grime and powder stains were no longer on his face, and his hands and arms were free of dried blood. His hair was black and smooth from the water and he had washed out his shirt and trousers and put them on again. The saturated material clung to him wetly, moulding his slim hard body, but it was already beginning to dry in the dry heat. He took the revolver and the bundle of clothing from

Winter and said: 'What have you done with Lou Cottar and Lottie? What were you doing out here last night?'

'They're all right—at least—at least I think so,' said Winter, turning to follow him. 'I went to bathe in the river, and I lost my way coming back. It was getting dark——'

Alex appeared to know his way through these jungles, for despite the absence of paths and the fact that one tree or bamboo brake or tangled thicket looked exactly like the next to Winter, he walked ahead of her unhesitatingly, until suddenly the dark entrance of the Hirren Minar was before them.

There was no sound from the ruined building, and he groped in the gloom and found that the rope-ladder had been withdrawn. He said softly: 'Lou—are you all right?' and there was a swift movement above his head as though someone had been standing there with held breath, listening, and a voice said: '*Alex!*' The rope-ladder dropped and two minutes later they were both in the upper room. Mrs. Cottar said: 'What happened to you? I thought——' She leant against the wall and burst into tears.

Alex pushed aside the *chik* that she had hung across the open archway, and went out on to the flat roof outside. The sky was bright now, and the day was already breathlessly hot. The tall bamboos that concealed the Hirren Minar, towering to the level of the ruined dome, walled in all but a small part of the roof, leaving a narrow gap through which he could look out across the jungle and catch a glimpse of the river. He sat down on the crumbling parapet and stared at that small square of brightness, and presently the sun rose and lit the tree-tops, and the temperature leapt up as though the door of a gigantic furnace had been swung wide.

There were things that he had to think about. Things that must be thought about soon. But all at once he knew that he could not do it now. He could not think about anything at all. He had not eaten for over twenty-four hours, and for months past he had considered problems that were now of no further importance. He would give himself a day in which to get what rest he could. At least he was clean again, and that in itself seemed enough of an achievement for one day. He had not expected to be clean again. He had expected to die grimed and filthy and with his face stiffened and caked with dust and blood and sweat.

The problem of the three women in the room behind him would have to wait. They could not stay there indefinitely, but they could at least stay there for a day or two; perhaps longer. He noticed incuriously that the ruined roof which was normally a foot deep in dead leaves and the debris of dying bamboos had been swept clean. A man would not have bothered. The thought of the three women pressed like a heavy weight on his shoulders, and his mind rejected it, turning tiredly away.

Winter came out on to the roof behind him, and a ray of the morning sunlight, piercing through the heavy screen of bamboos, caught her in a brilliant shaft of light. Alex turned and surveyed her with a faint surprise as though she were someone he had never seen before. She was still wearing the blue cotton sari that she had worn last night, and the scanty length of cloth moulded the slender beauty of her body with a classic perfection. Her skin glowed gold in the golden sunlight and her black hair had blue lights in it, and he thought with an entire lack of emotion that she was the most beautiful thing he had ever seen —and a stranger.

The wary, withdrawn creature whom he had met at Ware; the seasick child in the cabin of the *Sirius*; the Condesa de los Aguilares; Mrs. Conway Barton—they had all gone. The wariness and the withdrawal had gone too, and the great dark eyes were no longer unsure but quiet and untroubled. There was a serenity and a glow about her. Something that was almost happiness.

How can she look like that? thought Alex with a faint twinge of irritation. As if she were entirely content and there were no longer any problems that mattered. Had women no imagination? Had nothing of all that she had seen made her realize that her life from now on—all their lives—was only a matter of living for an hour or a day more, by luck and cunning and the grace of God?

Winter said: 'Breakfast is ready.'

The incongruity of the commonplace, matter-of-fact statement at that time and in that setting suddenly struck him, and he laughed for the first time in many days.

34

ALEX lay flat on his stomach in a thicket at the edge of a glade in the jungle. He held one end of a thin cord in his hand and he was watching the leisurely approach of a peacock and his retinue of wives. The cord operated a primitive trap some twelve feet ahead of him which had, during the past fortnight, accounted for several jungle-fowl, two green pigeons, a pea-hen and an unwary porcupine. The porcupine, as a culinary problem, had proved insoluble, and after struggling with it for an hour or more Winter had handed the charred and unsavoury remains to Alex for immediate burial.

The Hirren Minar was well stocked with salt and parched grain and a miscellaneous variety of the more durable stores, but they needed fresh food, and Alex did not dare fire a gun for he knew that the sound of a shot would carry far in the long hot silent days. They had fish-hooks and lines, however, which had proved more than useful, and he had found that it was possible to trap birds.

Cooking was a difficulty, for they were afraid of showing smoke. In that still air it would have risen straight and betrayingly above the tree-tops, and they did not know who might see it. There were probably other fugitives in the jungles, and the hunt might well be out against those who had taken refuge there. So they cooked only after dark or before dawn, and in the lower room of the ruin, blocking the door with a home-made curtain of grass and bamboo to avoid showing a gleam of light. It was a hot and choking performance, but Winter and Lou Cottar managed it without complaint.

They had been in the Hirren Minar for over two weeks now, and already it seemed as though they had lived there for months —for years even. They had settled into a routine of living, occupying themselves with petty domestic details; living a curious dream-like life in the hot, silent, shadow-barred jungle. They might have been castaways on a desert island, surrounded by a thousand miles of empty sea, but the three women appeared to be contented enough. They never spoke of Lunjore or of anything that had happened there. At least not before Alex. He did not know what they spoke of when he was not there.

Lottie's gentle, trance-like daze had survived that second escape from massacre, and though she talked continuously of Edward her clouded brain accepted the simplest lie, and the presence of Winter and Alex convinced her that all was well. Life in India was so very different from life in England—it was not in the least what she had expected it to be. But one must be prepared to make allowances for foreign customs, and when Edward's manœuvres were over they would be able to live in their own bungalow in Meerut again. She must be patient and not complain.

Lou Cottar, too, schooled herself to patience. At first it had been enough—and more than enough—to be alive and safe when so many were dead or living in dread and discomfort and danger. But as the days went by she began to take the security for granted, and ache to escape from the jungle and at least attempt to reach civilization. The British could not all be dead! That was nonsense. If only they could escape they would surely find that life elsewhere was going on much as before.

Lou had lived only for amusement, and for men, and she yearned for the society of her own kind again. For lights, noise, music, laughter—all the things that made life an entertaining affair. Josh would be in Calcutta, and she felt sure that Calcutta at least was still in British hands. She had never been particularly fond of her husband, and had regarded him with tolerance rather than affection; they had gone their own ways and had not interfered with each other. But Josh represented a way of life that suited Lou well enough. She had never taken any interest in her own sex and had little use for them, and to live cooped up in the company of two young women with whom she had nothing in common was tedious and irritating. But Lou possessed common sense and courage, and she knew that because of Lottie English they must take no chances. Lottie was no responsibility of hers, but that fact did not weigh with her. She had, surprisingly enough, begun to feel an odd fondness for the little creature: a feeling that verged on the maternal, though she would have scouted such an idea with scorn had it been presented to her by anyone else. Lottie frequently irritated her, but she knew that she could not abandon her. That none of them could.

If Alex had paid her some attention Lou might have felt more reconciled to the situation. She had always considered that Alex possessed more than his fair share of sexual attraction, and she had been interested in him both as a male and as a personality. But Alex did not see her. He did not see any of them, except as a responsibility and a collective millstone about his neck. Hampered by them, he was tied to the Hirren Minar until he could make arrangements to get them to safety—if there was any safety to be had anywhere in the country.

Outside the jungle that sheltered them and yet hemmed them in there must be so much to be done. So much that needed doing. Delhi to be retaken. Somewhere beyond the borders of Lunjore William would be doing the work of ten men: and John Nicholson too, of whom it had been said that single-handed he could cow an entire mutinous army corps into obedience. Henry Lawrence in Lucknow and John Lawrence in Peshawar. Herbert Edwardes, Alex Taylor, James Abbott; Hearsay, Grant, Campbell, Outram —a hundred others. None of them would be standing still, and they would need every pair of hands and every brain and heart they could muster to save the country from falling into anarchy. Yet he, Alex Randall, sat here idle, tied hand and foot by the necessity of protecting the lives of three women.

If he could only be rid of them! If he could only get them to safety he could reach Henry Lawrence, or the troops that must surely by now be marching to attack Delhi! And there was his own district . . . But he could do nothing yet. For the moment at least the women were safe, and he could not move them until he had more reliable news.

He had slept most of that first day at the Hirren Minar, and awakened to a ravenous hunger that had been only partially appeased by a mess of dried corn and a somewhat muddy-tasting fish that Lou Cottar—who had found the lines and fish-hooks— had caught in the course of the afternoon.

He had been unreasonably angry on discovering that Winter had cooked it over a fire that she had made in a corner of the stone chamber below, and had informed her tersely that she had shown a lamentable lack of intelligence, and that in future no fire would be lit by day. Winter had smiled warmly at him, rather in the manner of an adult humouring a cross and convalescent child, and had apologized with a lightness that had further infuriated Alex, for he took it to be an indication of the fact that she had no conception of the precariousness of their present position. He would have to take charge of them. Left to themselves they would be lost. He could not leave them to die.

He had left them to themselves the next night and all the following day, and on his return had made no mention of where he had been or what he had been doing. Winter, who knew him better than Lou Cottar did, had not even asked. Lou had asked, and had not received an answer; for Alex had gone back to the Residency.

There was a bundle of native clothing in the ruined dome of the Hirren Minar, and Lou Cottar, coming unexpectedly upon him as he set out—she had been down to the river—had taken him for a Pathan and been betrayed into a scream.

'Oh God, Alex, you frightened me!—I thought for a moment——'

Alex said: 'Does it change me so much?'

'Yes. I don't know why—it's only clothes. You look so much darker, and that hair makes a difference.'

'It's a mistake to wear false hair,' said Alex, pulling at the greasy locks that fell on to his shoulders beneath the pugaree cloth, 'but it can't be helped.'

'You should grow a moustache and beard,' said Lou, 'then no one would know you.'

'I would, except for the fact that it happens to grow too damned light; a good deal fairer than my hair. And though one can get rid of it quickly enough, it takes a hell of a time to grow again when needed. I may not be back for some time, Lou. Don't show a light if you can help it.' He had turned away and disappeared into the jungle in the direction of the Lunjore road.

The Residency had been deserted except for the kites and the crows and the scavenging pariah dogs, and a sickly-sweet stench of corruption had hung over it in a cloud almost as tangible as the clouds of bloated flies that buzzed above the dead. But there was nothing to be learned there. Not even the names of those who had died, for apart from the Commissioner and some half a dozen others, very few were still recognizable.

Alex had nerved himself to search among them for some evidence as to who they had once been, but he had been forced to abandon it. His own bungalow was empty, and like the rest of the bungalows it had been systematically looted. There had been an attempt to set it on fire, but the flames had not taken hold. The office, however, was reasonably intact, for the mob had not been interested in files and papers, and had not troubled to destroy them. Alex collected certain documents and records of importance and hid them in the roof of the deserted stables, and having made a small bundle of various objects which he considered worth removing, he filled a torn haversack with fruit and corn from the trampled garden. There had been few people in the cantonment area, and he had kept out of sight himself, crouching behind walls or in the shelter of tamarisk scrub at any sound or sign of movement.

Alex had not gone to the cantonments again, and he had not again used the roads by day. He went—when he went—by night, and returned at dawn to sleep through most of the day.

R *

On the night following his return from the Residency he had
gone to the village where his *shikari*, Kashmera, lived; walking
through the crops by the light of a narrow moon. It had been a
grave risk, for he was well known in the village, but it was a risk
that had to be taken, for he could do nothing without news. The
old *shikari* had come to the door of his hut and had known who
it was even in the faint starlight, for he, as Niaz had been, was
cat-eyed in the dark. He had turned to speak reassuringly to
someone inside the hut and had followed Alex out into the night,
and they had crouched among the shadows of a cornfield for
half an hour, whispering together.

Three days later it had been Ameer Nath and his hawks who
had met Alex at sunset at the third milestone outside the cantonments. Sometimes it would be Kashmera, sometimes Ameer
Nath, and once it was a friend of Alex's from the city, Lala
Thakur Dass, a bazaar letter-writer who lived in an alley-way
near Ditta Mull's silk shop. And so he had heard the news of the
city and the villages and the surrounding districts.

It was not yet safe to move, they told him. The countryside
was in a ferment, for there were bands of armed sepoys swagger-
ing through the villages. They had caught a sahib and a memsahib hiding in the hut of a villager, and had not only slain them,
but had slain also the man who had given them shelter, and all his
family with him, as an example to others. It was they who were
responsible for the continued panic. The villagers for the most
part asked nothing more than to be left in peace, for it mattered
little to them who governed the land provided the rains did not
fail and the crops were good, the taxes not unduly heavy and
allowances made for bad years and poor harvests. Several of the
local talukdars were taking an active part in the revolt, and the
lower elements of the city could always be relied upon to create
trouble. But others among the talukdars had remained quiet and
were watching to see which way the cat would jump, as were
many men in Lunjore.

'But if thy people do not take Delhi soon,' said Ameer Nath,
'these too will join with the others. But there is no news of that

yet, though there is talk that all the sahib-*log* are not slain, as was at first believed, and that an army marches from Ambala to retake Delhi. If that be true, and Delhi be taken, then many who now waver will stay quiet. Remain thou quiet also, and in hiding, until the worst is past. There have been many sahibs and memsahibs, and *baba-log* (children) also, who have been driven out of hiding by lack of food and water, and have been taken and slain, or sent as prisoners to those who be no friends of the Company's Raj. To move now were to run all heads into a noose, for there is no safety east or west, north or south. Oudh also has risen, and it is said that Lawrence Sahib and all the *Angrezi-log* in Lucknow will soon be slain, and that the *Jangi-lat-sahib* (Commander-in-Chief) is dead at Ambala.'

The tales that they told were all of disaster to the British. The whole of Oudh was in a ferment, and in Cawnpore General Wheeler was constructing an entrenchment for the defence of the garrison and the European population. Delhi was still in the hands of the insurgents, and there was no news from Meerut. There had been trouble in Agra, and it was rumoured that the troops had mutinied at Allahabad and massacred the British. Punctually to the given day the sepoys in Bareilly and Shah-jehanpur had mutinied, and Khan Bahadur Khan, a pensioner of the Company, had been proclaimed Viceroy of Rohilkhand. He had celebrated his accession by ordering the slaughter of all the British who had been unable to escape from Bareilly, and there had also been a brutal massacre of Europeans in Shahjehanpur.

Yes, there was news in plenty—and all of it was bad. It was obviously unwise to exchange the comparative safety of the Hirren Minar for the dangers of a cross-country flight to some district that might well prove to be in a worse state than Lunjore. There was nothing to be done but to keep the women in hiding, and Alex chafed at the inaction and occupied himself with snaring birds.

Winter alone of the four occupants of the Hirren Minar had no need to pray for patience. She was, for perhaps the first time in her life, entirely content.

The heat did not affect her to the same degree as it affected Lottie and Lou Cottar, and the jungle and the river and the ancient, hidden ruin held a strange enchantment for her. They did not belong to the everyday world. They were something lost and forgotten and right outside reality. She shut her mind to the memory of all that had happened to her in Lunjore—to the heartbreak and bitter disillusionment that had awaited her there; to the long months of degradation and misery; to the horrors of that last day and to the thought of the worse things that might even now be happening in the world beyond the forest. She would not think of the past or the future. Only of the present. And the present was Alex.

It did not worry her that Alex hardly looked at her and rarely spoke to her, or that when he did it was generally with an unmistakable undercurrent of exasperation. She felt as though she had loved him all her life and knew everything about him, and ever since the night following their flight from Lunjore she had felt so completely a part of him that she could sometimes follow the processes of his thoughts as though they had been her own. Harsh experience had taught her to expect little of life, and now it contented her that Alex was alive and within reach of her, and that she could watch him and listen to his voice, and feel his presence even when she could not see him.

The only unpleasant times were when he would go out to get news from the villages. She had never asked where he went or whom he saw, and she was always frightened, with a sick shuddering fear, that he would not return. She would stay awake, pulling the makeshift but remarkably effective punkah that he had made from bamboo and dried grass so that Lottie could sleep in more comfort, and straining her ears to listen for the sounds of his return. But even these nights had their compensations, for it meant that he would sleep for part of the day, and then she could look at him without the need for concealment.

She noticed that he talked to Lottie far more than to either Lou or herself, and also that he had a special voice for Lottie. A voice that was gay and gentle and curiously reassuring. It could always reassure Lottie, and even to hear it was an assurance of safety to Winter.

Lottie and Lou Cottar, in spite of the appalling heat, still wore the dresses they had worn when they left Lunjore. Alex had brought back needles and thread from one of his night excursions, and they had mended them neatly. He had also, somewhat unexpectedly, brought a wine-coloured cotton sari with a deep blue border, and a narrow cotton bodice such as the village women wore, for Winter.

Lottie and Lou Cottar could not be persuaded to wear such things. They had discarded their petticoats, stays and pantalettes, but they clung to what they considered a civilized garment as though it gave them some assurance that this was only a temporary interlude that would soon give place to normality. To have thought anything else would have been to lose a part of hope; to give up a plank of the raft which supported them in an uncharted sea.

'You're letting yourself go native, Winter!' snapped Lou Cottar one hot evening, in an unwonted outburst of irritation. She looked resentfully at the girl, and in the same moment thought how well the graceful folds of the cheap sari became her, and how much more effective the silky, blue-black hair was when it swung in thick plaits almost to the knee, than when it had been rolled up into the conventional heavy chignon.

Mrs. Cottar had never considered little Mrs. Barton to be particularly striking, but looking at her now she thought suddenly that she was beautiful; like something out of an Eastern fairytale—a princess from the *Thousand and One Nights*. Surprised at herself for the unexpected imagery of the thought she said irritably: 'You are the only one of us who does not look out of place in this God-forsaken hole—and who doesn't seem to mind being here!'

'I don't,' said Winter dreamily.

Lou Cottar had stared at her with an indignation that changed to sudden comprehension. She said abruptly: 'You're in love with him, aren't you?'

Not so very long ago Winter would have considered such a question an unwarrantable impertinence and in the worst possible taste, while to answer it honestly would have been unthinkable. But this was not the civilized world they had known. This was Eden. She smiled at Lou and said: 'Yes.'

'Is he in love with you?'

Winter thought of the letter that Alex carried in the inner pocket of his coat. But he might not even know that he still had it. She shook her head, and Lou said tartly: 'Then he's a fool!'

'I think he has too much on his mind to bother about anything like that,' said Winter reflectively. 'Just now he can only think of me as a nuisance. I think he has always thought of me like that. A tiresome responsibility that he would like to be rid of if he could.'

'Not only you,' said Lou with a twisted smile. 'All of us. And I can't say that I blame him. If it wasn't for us he could go. And if it wasn't for Lottie——'

She glanced towards the bed where Lottie lay asleep, and her thin features sharpened with anxiety. She said with suppressed violence: 'That damned baby! It's hanging over us all like—like the monsoon! Something that you know is coming and that can't be stopped. Not that I couldn't do with the monsoon, and I suppose that will be here before we know where we are; but if only one could stop that baby! It's knowing that she has to have it and that there's no way out that gets on my nerves. What are we going to do if we can't get her away? We must get her away! How much longer has she got?'

'About six weeks, I think,' said Winter doubtfully. 'Perhaps it's seven.'

'Six weeks! Oh God—and here we are doing nothing. *Nothing!* What in heaven's name are we going to do if she has it here? Do you know anything about babies?'

'No,' admitted Winter.

'Neither do I. Not a damned thing! I've never had any of my own and I've never been interested in women who did. They look frightful and become dead bores. We've got to get her to

some civilized place where there is a doctor. Why doesn't Alex
do something? We *must* get her away!'

Alex, lying under a canopy of leaves in the hot, dry jungle
grass and watching the shadow of a *sal* tree draw out across the
clearing, was making the same calculations and coming to the
same conclusion.

It was a conclusion that he had come to days ago, but he could
still see no safe way of translating thought into action, for the
reports he received were all the same: it was inviting death to
travel anywhere, and to remove from Lunjore would be to leave
the frying-pan for the fire. Only the Punjab—if the reports were
to be trusted—remained unaffected, but to reach it meant a long,
difficult and dangerous journey, and one which Lottie was in no
condition to undertake on foot. She would have to travel in some
sort of conveyance, and that meant going by road and not across
country. The thing was impossible as yet.

Alex remembered with a sinking of the heart certain words
from the Epistle to the Thessalonians: '. . . then sudden destruction cometh upon them, as travail upon a woman with child;
and they shall not escape.'

Six weeks . . . perhaps seven. But anything might have happened by then! Troops must be being hurried out from Home
or stopped on their way to China. Reinforcements must be
coming. And once the tide had turned it would be possible to
demand help from those who at present were watching the swing
of the pendulum and unwilling to commit themselves one way or
the other. For the moment Lottie was safer where she was.

'That damned baby!' thought Alex with an exasperation and
anxiety that equalled Lou's. 'Why on earth do women have
to——'

And then without warning a thought that had never occurred
to him before struck him with the sudden violence of an unexpected blow over the heart. It wiped the problem of Lottie from
his mind and substituted a far more frightening one, and he
forgot about the peacocks and let them mince past him unheeded

while he stared blindly across the clearing, seeing only a slim figure in a faded blue cotton sari.

'No,' thought Alex desperately—'no! It couldn't happen. It was only once——' He had not thought of Winter for days, except as one of three women who were, unavoidably and infuriatingly, his responsibility; and at the back of his mind there had lain an unjust and illogical anger because she had been the means of turning him aside from the course he had set for himself, and by doing so had been indirectly responsible for the death of Niaz. He did not want to think of her now, and with an abrupt movement he buried his head in his arms as though by that action he could blot her out of his mind and from his conscience. 'Oh God, not this!' thought Alex as he had thought once before at Hazrat Bagh when she had cried in his arms because of a wild goose. 'Not this—not now! I cannot stand it . . .'

The sudden movement caught the bright eye of a king crow who was balancing on a bough of the *sal* tree, and he cried a warning that sent the peacocks hurrying away through the jungle. But Alex lay still and did not move for a long time.

That night he took a graver risk than he had yet taken, and went into the city, riding a thin village pony that he had procured with the assistance of the apprehensive Kashmera.

'It is not safe!' urged Kashmera. 'The Huzoor is too well known in Lunjore!'

'There are few who will recognize me now,' said Alex, and it was perhaps true. His face was thinner and there were no longer any curves in it; only hollows and angles—and lines.

'Tie up the jaw as though it were wounded,' advised Kashmera. 'It is an old trick, but it serves.' He had fetched some rags from the hut, and Alex drew the blade of his knife slantwise in a shallow cut on one side of his chin, stained the cloth with it and bound it up roughly.

'That is better,' approved Kashmera. 'Perhaps after all thou wilt return. Leave the horse by the cane-field. He will not stray.'

That night was the twelfth of June, but the news that Sir Henry Barnard had fought and won a battle at Badli-ki-serai on the road to Delhi, and that once again there were British on the Ridge, and Delhi itself besieged, had not yet reached Lunjore. There was elation in the city, for the reports and rumours that had been received were all of successful risings and of Europeans and British garrisons murdered or besieged, and it lacked only ten days to the twenty-third of June—the centenary of the Battle of Plassey, which an ex-clerk of the East India Company, Robert Clive, had fought with three thousand men against an army of sixty-eight thousand, and in winning it had won half India. The rule of the 'Company Sahib', said the prophecy, would last for a hundred years from the date of that battle, and now that day was near . . .

The talk of the bazaars only served to convince Alex that he still could not move the women. He had bought food and tied it in a corner of cloth, and ridden back in the bright moonlight with angry despair in his heart.

'Is there no news, Alex?' demanded Lou Cottar the next morning, following him out into the jungle and facing him among the hot shadows of the *sal* trees. 'You must have heard something! Even if it is bad we would much rather know than be kept in the dark.'

'All the news is bad,' said Alex shortly. 'It's no good. We can't leave yet.'

Lou said: 'But we must go soon. Can't you see that if we don't, Lottie may——'

'Do you think I haven't thought of that?' interrupted Alex brusquely. 'Don't be a fool, Lou! At the moment there would appear to be nowhere to go to. She may have a bad time of it if she stays here, but she'll certainly die—and so will the rest of us!—if we are mad enough to attempt a cross-country trip just now. The jungle at least will do us no harm.'

But he had spoken too soon, for the jungle that had seemed to befriend them suddenly showed its claws.

They had gone down to the river that evening, all four of them, as they did every evening, because it was cooler there and there were always clothes and cooking-pots to be washed and fishing-lines to tend. Winter had not seen the cobra until it lashed at her, hissing, as she bent to disentangle the edge of her sari that had caught on a thorn. Her foot touched the cold coils, and the fangs bit into her left arm just above the elbow.

Alex had been less than a yard away from her and he had swung round as she cried out, and had seen the snake slither across her path, and the two small punctures on the smooth, tanned skin. The next second he had leapt at her and caught her; his fingers tight above the wound, forcing the blood down, and his mouth against it, sucking at it with all his strength.

Lou had come running and had beaten the grass with a stick, and then snatched up a petticoat that was to be washed and ripped at it frantically, tearing at it with her teeth. It tore at last and she wound a strip of it above Alex's straining hands and pulled it tight in a tourniquet.

Alex lifted his head and said hoarsely: 'Permanganate—on the ledge at the left back—quickly,' and Lou turned and ran, stumbling and tripping among the grass and thorn and creeper, while Lottie wrung her hands and wept.

Alex jerked the knife he carried from its sheath, and caught Winter to him, holding her hard against him so that she could not move; his hand a vice about her wrist. He said: 'It'll hurt. Don't move;' and cut the wound across deeply, twice.

He felt her teeth clench on the thin stuff of his shirt and her body twist to the pain, but she did not cry out and he dropped the knife into the grass. The blood poured down her arm and his in a red tide and he lifted her and carried her swiftly back to the Hirren Minar.

Lou Cottar met them a dozen yards from the entrance with the little tin of permanganate crystals clutched in her hand, and they had filled the wound with them, and had got Winter up the rope-ladder. Alex had let the arm bleed and she had looked at it with a frown of pain and said in a dazed whisper: 'It will make such a mess on the floor.'

'We can clear it up,' said Alex with white-lipped brevity. 'Lou, for God's sake get back to Lottie!'

He had bound it up eventually and given her as much opium as he dared, and later, when Lou and Lottie had returned, and he had realized that she would not die, he had gone out and been exceedingly sick behind the impenetrable thicket of bamboos.

Winter had run a high fever that first night and Alex had held her clutching hands while she twisted and turned and muttered unintelligibly, and Lou Cottar bathed her burning body with cool water. 'Is she going to die?' Lou had asked once. There had been a break in her voice, and her face had been barely more than a pale blur in the darkness beyond the line of moonlight that lay between the broken archways.

'No. She'll be all right in a few hours,' said Alex with more confidence than he felt. 'Give me that cloth and go and lie down, Lou. If you crack up too, I swear I'll go out and shoot myself!'

Lou had laughed on a sudden breath of relief and had obeyed him, and Alex had taken Winter's small fever-racked body into his arms and held it close, his cheek pressed to the burning forehead. The moonlit night had been breathlessly hot and Alex's own body was wet with sweat, but his hold seemed to soothe her, and after a while he felt her slacken and lie still in his arms, and knew that she was asleep at last and that the fever had broken.

'My love!' thought Alex, moving his mouth against the hot smooth skin and the damp waves of silky hair that were as dark as the darkness about him. 'My little love . . .'

Quite suddenly the gnawing restlessness that had lived with him hourly during the last weeks fell away from him, and he no longer cared what became of anyone else—or of India—as long as Winter was safe. He could wait patiently now. She was no longer a burden and a responsibility, but part of his heart, as she had always been. What did it matter if they had to wait here in hiding for months—or years?

'Only after this,' thought Alex, 'I must not kiss you again or touch you again, because if I do I shall only take you again—I couldn't stop myself—and it may be months, or a year, before we can get away.'

He thought of Lottie and shivered. One day the news would be better. He had no doubts on that score, for what he had once told Kishan Prasad had been true. Even if every European in all India were killed, the British would send, if necessary, every man they had, to avenge them. It would not be so much the loss of territory or prestige that would bring them, and nerve them to fight with stubbornness and fury, but the murder of the women and children. They would not forgive that, or rest until they had avenged it. One day—perhaps very soon, or if the mutiny was really widespread, perhaps later than he had thought—the British would be in control again and it would be safe to leave the jungle. They could get away then—get married. Barton was dead. It was only a question of waiting.

35

WINTER had suffered remarkably little ill-effect from the incident. The wound that Alex's knife had made had healed cleanly and given the minimum of trouble, and though the fever and loss of blood had kept her on her back and feeling absurdly weak for several days, she had soon been about again.

She saw very little of Alex after that, and suspected that he was deliberately avoiding her, but she knew that some tension in him had relaxed and that he was no longer impatient or irritable. She was aware, too, that he had developed a habit of watching her under his lashes. He would lie on the river-bank in the evening while she and Lottie and Lou washed the clothes and cooking-pots, and she would look up and find his eyes on her, and feel as always that familiar contraction of the heart.

Alex had taken to wearing nothing but a loin-cloth these days. His body was burnt as brown as his face and he could have passed anywhere for a Pathan. He had been out less for news than for food of late, and but for the relentless exhausting heat the days passed peacefully enough.

Alex, like Winter, found the heat unpleasant but bearable. But to Lou, and more especially to Lottie, it was an interminable torture. They watched the skies daily for signs of the monsoon, and longed for rain; but though the clouds would sometimes gather, and they would hear thunder rumble along the horizon and see the heat-lightning flicker, no rain fell to temper the intolerable heat, and they lived for the early mornings and the late evenings when they could lie and soak in the coolness of the river.

Alex became afraid of the river, and he drove in stakes about the narrow curve of the little beach where they bathed, in case their continued use of it might attract the attention of a mugger, and that one day one of them might be dragged down by yellow-toothed jaws into deep water. But there was too much food in the river these days for the muggers to bother with live prey. The bodies of the British came down on the current, bloated and bobbing to the undertow, and once one had stranded by the little beach: a woman whose long hair had caught in the tree roots so that her mangled corpse swung gently to and fro in the ripple as though she were swimming—or struggling.

Alex had sawn through her hair with his knife and pushed her off into the current, and the others, arriving five minutes later, had wondered why he was looking so unusually grim. He had not looked like that for some time past; he had looked relaxed and almost contented, and had taken to humming under his breath as he set fishing-lines or devised further methods of keeping the temperature of the Hirren Minar within bearable limits. But that night he had gone to the city again, and when he had returned at dawn his eyes were hot with restlessness once more; for it seemed that the tide was turning at last.

The British whom the boasters in Lunjore had declared were all dead or swept into the sea were encamped once more upon the Ridge before Delhi. The Guides had marched from Mardan and were now with the Delhi force, and Hodson Sahib, the '*Burra Lerai-wallah*' (great in battle) was also there, commanding a regiment of horse that he had raised.

They would of course be defeated—annihilated!—it was only a matter of time: but all the same there was a noticeable breath of uneasiness in the bazaars. It was disconcerting to find that the sahib-*log* were not all dead. And it was said, whispered one man to an awed group in the Sudder Bazaar, that Nikal Seyn himself was riding for Delhi! Nikal Seyn, the sound of whose horse's hooves could be heard, so men said, from Attock to the Khyber, and whom many declared to be a god, and no man. The speaker had shivered and thrown a quick backward look over his shoulder as he spoke.

'It won't be long now,' said Alex, his eyes blazing in the grey dawn light. 'We shall have to stick it out here a little longer, but the monsoon must break soon, and then it will be cooler. And when Delhi is taken we'll be able to get away. A good many of the waverers will come over to us then, and we shall be able to get help on the road.'

Another ten days; perhaps a fortnight—or a month. But what did it matter now that the end was in sight? They could afford to wait a week or two more.

'I suppose so,' said Lou, wiping the pouring perspiration from her face with the back of her hand. 'We shall have to wait. I see that. We've been very lucky—luckier than so many others. Perhaps the luck will hold.'

But it did not hold.

That same evening Lottie had strayed away to pick jungle berries, not twenty yards from the river-bank, and she had heard someone moving through the bushes and had turned, expecting Lou who had been fetching water.

But it was not Lou. It was a bearded turbanless native in torn and soiled clothing, who carried a heavy bundle upon one shoulder and bore on wrist and ankle the marks that are made by iron fetters.

She was not to know that this was one of the criminals who had been released by the mob from the city jail, or that he had subsequently murdered a Hindu merchant and his family, and escaped with the loot to the jungle. But Lottie was under no illusions as to his intentions.

He had stared at her unbelievingly, and then his lips had stretched into an evil grin. A memsahib!—a *feringhi!* His eyes glittered and he dropped the bundle he carried and drew a stained sword from its sheath. He moved towards her quite slowly, crouching a little, the dry jungle grass rustling and crackling about him, and Lottie's mouth opened in a soundless scream. She made no attempt to turn and run, but stood frozen and still like a trapped rabbit, and she did not hear Lou coming up from the river. Neither did Bishul Singh, dacoit, for he could see nothing but the petrified face of the white woman before him, and hear only the crackling of the undergrowth as he crept towards her.

Lou never moved from the Hirren Minar without a revolver, and she dropped the *chatti*, and as the man looked round, checked by the sudden sound, she pulled the revolver from the sling she had made for it, and fired. The man jerked upright and his eyes and his mouth opened in a look of incredulous astonishment, and then he swayed, coughed, crumpled at the knees and fell sideways with blood pouring from his mouth.

'No!' screamed Lottie. 'No! No! *No*——*!*'

Alex had been reinforcing a bamboo ladder that he had made to replace the rope one that Lottie found it difficult to climb, and he had heard the shot and the screams, and dropped it and ran. He had taken one look at the man on the ground and at Lou who was holding the screaming Lottie, and said: 'Where's Winter?' And then Winter had run through the bushes, white-faced and panting, and he had gripped Lou's shoulders and shaken her and said: 'Were there any others?'

'No. I don't know,' said Lou jerkily. 'He was coming for Lottie with a sword. I shot him. Lottie—Lottie!—it's all right, dear, it's all right.'

Alex said: 'Get on, get back—all of you. He may not have been alone.'

But Lottie would not go. She had struggled and screamed, and

Alex had turned and taken her from Lou and carried her back to the Hirren Minar, holding her with her face pressed hard against his shoulder to muffle her screams. He had put her on her feet for one moment at the foot of the ladder, and she had turned and fled back, and when he caught her she had fought him, writhing and twisting and clawing at him, her thin distorted body suddenly possessed of surprising strength, so that it had been all he could do to get her back into the upper room.

Alex said: 'Pull up the ladder, Winter. And close the entrance. Lou, give me the opium—and the brandy. It's all right, Lottie, dear, you're safe now.'

But Lottie had screamed and shrieked and fought as she had screamed and fought at the Kashmir Gate at Delhi when she had seen a grinning bearded man leap at Edward with a sword, and had seen her husband fall, spurting blood from that terrible wound, and had been dragged away to be lowered over the battlements and fall into the dry ditch below. 'Let me go!—let me go! They're killing him! Edward—*Edward!*' screamed Lottie. And then quite suddenly she had gone slack in Alex's arms and they saw with unutterable relief that she had fainted.

Alex laid her down on the narrow camp-bed, and letting down the rope-ladder, ordered Winter to pull it up after him and went out into the twilight jungle.

He turned the dead man over, and recognizing him realized that he was probably on the run, and he stood quite still, listening for a long time, but could hear no sounds that suggested anyone moving through the jungle. Presently he made a cautious circuit of the immediate area but found no one, and returning to the corpse he dragged it to the river-bank and pushed it off into deep water.

The bundle the man had dropped proved to be full of valuables. Silver coin, a large quantity of Indian jewellery, an assortment of bric-a-brac that could only have come from the looted bungalow of some European, and one object that told its own story: a woman's hand that had been hacked off for the sake of the rings it bore and which had presumably proved difficult to remove. Alex disposed of that gruesome and decomposed relic and carried the bundle back to the Hirren Minar. The money would come in very useful and he could only hope that Bishul Singh had not made an assignation with anyone to meet him on or near this spot. Judging from the value of the loot he thought it unlikely: it seemed more probable that the man had intended to keep it to himself.

There was an appalling smell of burnt feathers in the upper room of the Hirren Minar, and Alex climbed the ladder to find Lottie still unconscious and Lou and Winter, their faces no more than white blurs in the dusk, making desperate efforts to revive her.

'Leave her alone,' advised Alex. 'If she has remembered Delhi she is better off like that. We'd better light the lamp.'

They had used the lamp as little as possible, partly to conserve their scanty stock of oil, but mostly because it necessitated covering the open archways with solid screens that Alex had made from bamboo canes, roots and dry grass, so that the light would not show. In the daytime when the hot wind blew they poured water on those screens and it helped to cool the room, but after sunset when the wind dropped the screens made it unbearably hot, and there was no breath of wind blowing tonight.

Winter went below to prepare the evening meal and Alex handed her a revolver without comment. He was still not entirely sure that the dead dacoit had been alone, and he did not know how far the sound of that shot and Lottie's screams would have carried.

Lou lit the small oil-lamp and Alex mixed brandy, opium and water. 'It may keep her quiet for a bit when she comes round,' he said, and pushed the brandy bottle at Lou. 'You'd better have some of that yourself. You look as though you need it.' They had been as sparing with the brandy as they had been with the oil, but Lou drank, and felt grateful for the fiery liquid.

Lottie had not recovered consciousness for another hour, and when at last she had moaned and stirred they had been able to make her drink the opium brew without much difficulty. She had sat up, propped against Lou Cottar's shoulder, and had stared up at Lou's face and at Alex and Winter, and her eyes had lost the dazed sweetness that they had worn for so long.

She said at last: 'Edward is dead, isn't he? They killed him. I—I remember now. And they shot Mamma—and—and Papa. Where is Sophie?'

'Sophie is safe, darling,' said Winter. 'She is in Cawnpore.'

'They killed Edward,' whispered Lottie. 'They—they cut him with their swords, and there was a man with a knife who——'

Winter said: 'Don't think of it, darling—don't!'

'How can you stop yourself thinking of a thing like that? I should have stayed with him but they wouldn't let me. I should have stayed with him——' She turned her head against Lou Cottar's shoulder and wept, and Alex got up and went out.

He had slept in the jungle that night, in the grass before the entrance of the Hirren Minar; but he had lain awake for a long time listening to the night noises and straining his ears for any sound that might be made by men. He could hear, intermittently, a murmur of voices from the upper chamber of the ruined building behind him, but it came at longer and longer intervals and at last there was silence.

There were clouds in the sky that night, but they held no promise of rain; only of hot winds and dust, and it seemed as though they intensified the heat, pressing it down on to the gasping earth so that it could not escape, as though they were a lid on a gigantic cauldron. They were gone when Alex awoke with the first light of dawn, and the sky was clear again. Clear with the hazy clearness that promised a day of grinding heat.

Alex went down to the river and lay in the water on the narrow ledge below the bank, watching the sky turn from pale green to saffron while the birds awoke in the thickets above him and a troop of monkeys came down to drink. He lay there for a long time, until the sun leapt from below the horizon and the burning day was in full flood across the pitiless sky and the parched jungle. It was only then, when the sun flared in the tree-tops, that he realized that none of the three women had come down to the river that morning. They were usually there well before sunrise, and he would leave the small beach to them and return to the Hirren Minar. But today they had not come.

He left the water reluctantly and felt it dry on his back almost before he had reached the top of the bank. Between the tree shadows the sun was like a raw flame on his shoulders as he walked back to the Hirren Minar, and he had reached the entrance when he heard that agonized moaning, and stopped.

He stood quite still for perhaps five minutes, knowing with despair and anger and pity what it meant. Then he turned away and sat down in a patch of shadow on a fallen block of stone that fronted the low stone ledge before the Hirren Minar. This at least was not his affair. There were two women with her.

Listening to the moans he wondered why the Almighty had thought fit to inflict on womankind such a lengthy and agonizing method of populating the earth. And why, in the name of Allah the Merciful and Compassionate, had this got to happen now?

He leaned back on the warm, time-worn stone and wondered just how much difference this was going to make to all of them. The problem of this unborn child had been hanging over them all ever since the day of their escape from the Residency: marching remorselessly towards them; unavoidable and inescapable. Wars and riots and mutinies; famine, disaster and the crash of dynasties—the processes of birth stopped for none of these things. Lottie would have to bear this child even though her husband, mother, father and half her friends were dead, and India awash with blood and anarchy. Except by dying, she could not escape it.

Probably just as well to get it over, thought Alex. After all, it was a perfectly natural process. Nothing to make a fuss about. Happened half a million times a day and was a simpler matter than one would suppose. He had assisted at the arrival of Chytuc and helped a bitch who was in difficulties to produce her litter, and once he had sat up all night reading by the light of an oil-lamp a manual on midwifery, and receiving terse instructions from a doctor who had crippled himself in a fall from his horse when riding fifty miles to attend the wife of a typhoid-stricken surveyor in a lonely forest camp, who was about to give birth to her first child. It had proved a slow but comparatively simple affair. But the woman had been wide-hipped and healthy, and not in any way comparable to the childish smallness and fragility of Lottie.

'What *are* those women doing to her?' thought Alex impatiently. He could hear Winter's voice and Lou's, and Lottie's agonizing moans going on and on. The moans rose to a scream that was more fear than pain, and suddenly he could bear it no longer. He leapt the stone ledge and was up the ladder and in the comparative coolness of the upper room.

Lottie was lying on the camp-bed, fully dressed and clutching at the sides of it; her eyes wide with terror. Winter knelt beside her and Lou Cottar leant over her with a tin in her hand. They turned their heads towards him and on both their white faces was the same terror of the unknown that was on Lottie's, and Alex, seeing it, realized in that moment that not one of them had the least idea of the mechanics of birth.

The suffocating prudery of the age saw to it that the majority of young women were kept in complete ignorance of such matters, and neither Winter nor Lottie had even seen a cat having kittens, while Lou Cottar, who could certainly not be classed as either young or an innocent, had never had any children of her own and was entirely uninterested in the conversation and gossip of those who had. All three of them had only the haziest idea of what happened when a child was born, for the whole affair was shrouded in the deepest mystery and only referred to in whispers. It was, moreover, considered by many that the less a young mother knew about childbirth the less likely she would be to panic about it in advance, while once the birth had begun— well, there was nothing for it then but to endure it.

Alex could see all these things written clearly in the desperate, terrified faces of the three women, and a sudden fury of exasperation took him by the throat. He thrust Winter and Lou aside and said savagely: 'What in hell's name do you think you are doing? Come on— get her out of those clothes!' And saw again the same expression reflected on three faces. Even in this extremity they could feel it to be unspeakably shocking to remove Lottie's dress in his presence, and his exasperation mounted. He bent over Lottie and took her hands, feeling them turn and clutch frantically at his, and said: 'Listen to me, Lottie. You've got to think of your baby now and not of anything else. Forget that I'm a man—or anyone you know. Just try and do what I say. Will you do that?'

Lottie nodded, clinging to his hands, and he released them with difficulty and said shortly to Lou: 'Pull that fan and keep the flies off her. Have we got enough water in the place?'

'I—I think so,' said Lou. Her face was quite white and her assurance had suddenly forsaken her. Lou would have faced a howling mob with calm and courage, and she had not flinched in the face of danger. But Lottie's pain and fear were something that she could do nothing to relieve, and it left her feeling sickened and helpless.

'Well, make sure! And if we haven't, get it.' He turned to Winter who had removed Lottie's clothing and said: 'Get down there and heat some water. And here——' He reached for a clasp-knife from the stone ledge and handed it to her. 'Boil that in some water—let it boil for five or ten minutes and then take it off and leave it in there.'

She turned without a word and descended the ladder and Lou said: 'The smoke——'

'We shall have to chance it.' He heard Lottie's moans rise once more to a scream and went to her swiftly, taking her hands again, and Winter heard him talking as she fetched wood and dry grass and lit the fire that they had never yet lit by day. He was telling Lottie about the child. What it was doing, and what her own body was doing to help it in its struggle for release, and what she must do to help them both. It sounded, suddenly, entirely natural and reasonable, and no longer some dark and mysterious and unexplainable process fraught with terror and uncertainty. His words evidently carried the same reassurance to Lottie, for her agonized moaning ceased.

'You can't avoid a certain amount of pain, dear,' said Alex, 'but there isn't anything to be frightened of, and it will be here soon.'

'*He*,' said Lottie. 'Not "it".'

Winter heard Alex laugh, and thought again: 'He has a special voice for Lottie. Dear Alex—darling Alex!'

The long morning wore away, and the appalling heat filled every corner and crevice of the Hirren Minar as though it had been a tangible thing; a weight which could be lifted from the shoulders if only the body had possessed sufficient strength.

That day, when they had needed it so badly, the hot wind failed and the air was as still as brass. Lou and Winter took it in turns to pull the bamboo punkah and to sponge and fan Lottie, while Alex sat by her, talking to her; pulling against her as she clung to his hands, dragging at them and screaming. The sweat ran down their faces and blinded their eyes, and Winter and Lou flinched and gasped at every scream, but Alex's voice remained steady and reassuring and Lottie's eyes clung desperately to his—as desperately as her hands.

But before the morning was out he knew with a sick despair that he would not allow to show in his face that he was fighting a losing battle.

Lottie's meagre strength ebbed with the day, and Alex gave her brandy and cursed both man and nature for allowing any woman born with that narrowness of hip to conceive. He could not see how it was possible for the child to be born at all—let alone be born alive. And yet it was so nearly born. But the afternoon had gone, and Lottie's strength with it. She could do no more. He would have to do the rest himself. He looked at Lou and saw that her hands were shaking, and he turned his head and spoke over his shoulder to Winter: 'Hold her for me.'

Lottie's daughter was born just as the sun touched the level of the tree-tops; and long before the gold had left the sky Lottie was dead. She had survived the birth, and she might have lived if she had fought to do so; but she had neither the strength nor the desire to hold on to life.

She had spoken only once. Lou had washed the tiny, whimpering creature and laid it against Lottie's thin shoulder, and Lottie's sunken eyes had opened slowly and painfully and she had looked at it. A last ray from the sinking sun had pierced through the bamboo screen and touched its small head, and Lottie's bloodless lips had curled in the shadow of a smile.

'Red hair,' she whispered. 'Like Edward's. Take care of him, Lou.' And then she had died.

Lou had wept, but Winter had not cried for Lottie. Lottie was with Edward, and she had loved Edward so much. That tiny red-headed morsel of humanity, if it lived, might have comforted her, but it would never have made up to her for the loss of her Edward, or wiped out the picture of him dying cruelly before her eyes. She washed Lottie's light little body and dressed her again, and went out to the river before it became too dark to see, leaving Lou with the child.

Alex was sitting on a fallen block of stone among the jungle grass near the entrance to the Hirren Minar. He had his head in his hands, and in the dusk he had been almost invisible against the background of the bamboos that towered up behind him.

Winter stood watching him for a moment or two, and then she had gone to him and put her arms about him, and laid her cheek against his hair. He turned his head against her shoulder with a tired sigh and his arms went round her quite gently. He leant against her for a long time without moving or speaking, as though he were too tired to wish to do either, while the dusk deepened about them and the evening star shone bright in a soft green sky . . .

Alex stirred at last, moving his head so that his lips lay against the curve of her throat, and his arms tightened about her, drawing her close. And then a peacock screamed from beyond the bamboo brake—a harsh, grating cry that seemed to echo the gasping screams that had rung in their ears all that hot agonizing afternoon—and Winter felt Alex's body jerk as though he had been abruptly awakened from sleep. He pushed her away from him suddenly and violently, his hands coming up to grip her arms and wrench them away, and he stood up swiftly and said in a voice that was as hard and as rough as a steel file: 'No, I'm damned if I will! Not after today. I won't let that happen to you. I won't! do you hear! Go on—get back in there before I——' He bit the sentence off, swung round and disappeared into the dusk.

He had returned an hour later and fetched the heavy-bladed knife that was used for cutting through thick jungle, and gone out again. It had taken him the best part of the night to dig a grave that would be deep enough to protect Lottie's little body from marauding animals, but he had managed it at last.

They had buried her in the clear pearly light of the early morning, an hour before the sun rose, and Alex had said as much as he could remember of the service for the burial of the dead over her grave. He remembered a good deal of it, for India was a country where that service was used with regrettable frequency. Afterwards he had gone off to bathe in the river at a spot higher up the bank, leaving the narrow beach by the tree to Winter and Lou, and had not returned until an hour after the sun had risen.

The upper room of the Hirren Minar was clean and swept and tidy, and yesterday and all the nerve-racking torture of those long, hot, agonizing hours seemed a year away. Winter had handed him food which she had kept hot for him in a covered cooking-pot among the embers of a fire, and he had eaten it and watched Lou who was feeding the baby with water in which she had boiled a little rice. She dipped a clean rag in the liquid and gave it to the tiny creature to suck, and there was a look on her face that Alex had not thought it possible for Lou Cottar to wear. A soft, absorbed wonder. He observed it with interest and a certain astonished amusement—Mrs. Josh Cottar, of all people!

Lou said thoughtfully and with entire seriousness: 'You'll have to get me some milk. I wonder if we could keep a goat?'

Alex finished his meal and came over to look at the skinny, wrinkled little object with the fluff of reddish-gold down on its head that had cost Lottie her life, and looking at it he had a sudden warm feeling of achievement. He had not been able to save Lottie, but he had at least saved this minute scrap of new life from dying before it had lived, and all at once that seemed a thing as well worth doing as the saving of a Province. He touched the tiny waving hand, and felt it close about his finger with the instinctive and unexpected tenacity of a sea anemone.

Alex laughed and said: 'You shall have your goat, Lou, if I have to steal it! What are you going to call her?'

'Amanda,' said Lou promptly.

'Good Lord! Why? Did Lottie——'

'No,' said Lou. 'Lottie was sure it was going to be a boy. She never knew it wasn't. It's just that I think Amanda is a nice name for her. It means "Worthy of love".'

Alex stroked the downy head with a forefinger and Lou looked up at him and smiled. 'Still three women on your hands, Alex.'

'Four,' said Alex with a grin. 'You've forgotten the goat. And I can clearly see that a goat is going to be more trouble than the rest of you put together.'

It was a prophecy that was to prove lamentably correct.

Alex had slept most of that day and had gone out at sunset. He had returned at dawn dragging an exceedingly vocal goat procured for him with suspicious ease by Kashmera, whom Alex suspected of having stolen it. The goat had been loath to accompany him, and he had been compelled to carry it for most of the way.

Lou and Winter had attempted to milk it, collectively and severally, and had been reduced first to desperation and then to helpless mirth in the process. Alex had refused to help. He said that he considered that he had discharged his part in the affair by procuring the animal, and that he was damned if he was going to turn *gopi*. They must learn to deal with it themselves.

They had done so, and the baby throve. It was astonishingly tenacious of life, and survived the untutored treatment to which it was subjected, as it had survived the horrors and hazards of that pregnancy and premature birth. The goat gave far more

s

trouble. It evinced a desire to stray and could be trusted to eat
its way through any and every rope. Alex constructed a strong
door of thick bamboo poles to replace the flimsier curtain of grass
over the entrance to the Hirren Minar, and they kept the goat
in the lower chamber at night.

It had awakened them the second night by bleating plaintively
and monotonously, and when at last it had ceased they had heard
a rasping, scratching sound, and Alex, who had been sleeping
on the open roof, had looked down over the ruined parapet and
seen by the clear starlight and a waning moon the beautiful
black-barred body of a tigress who crouched before the bamboo
door, clawing at it with a taloned paw. The tigress had heard
the movement above her and had looked up, her eyes glinting
like green moons, and she had stared at him for a full minute
before leaping away into the thickets.

Alex had strengthened the door, lashing a double layer of
bamboo poles the thickness of his arm across and across it, and
the next night the tigress had been back again. He heard the
scrape of her claws, and lifting a lump of earth that he had taken
the precaution to bring up with him, he dropped it on her from
above. There was a sharp and un-tigerlike yelp and she had
bounded away into the jungle.

'Why didn't you drop something heavier?' demanded Lou,
who had been an interested spectator.

'Because I have no desire to have a wounded tiger in this bit
of the jungle,' said Alex. 'They are unpleasant things to have
around.'

'But it will only be back tomorrow night.'

'Probably. But it won't get through that door. There's that
baby of yours starting now! If it isn't one thing it's another.
Who wouldn't be a bachelor?'

Lou had laughed and hurried back to feed the wailing child,
and the next night they had been awakened at moonrise by a
leopard snarling and tearing at the bamboo door. But apart
from these disturbances the long, burning, breathless days were
peaceful enough.

The jungle dried and shrivelled and turned brown about them, and the river shrank; but still the monsoon delayed. They never spoke of Lottie, as they never spoke of all those whom they had known in Lunjore, or of anything that had happened there. Their life went on as before, except that now there was the baby to look after in place of Lottie, and Lou had lost her restlessness.

Lou had never liked children: she had not wanted any of her own, or been in the least disappointed when none had been born to her; she had looked upon it as a blessing. But somewhere, unsuspected by anyone, least of all by herself, there must have lurked an unquenchable spark of the maternal instinct; and now, unexpectedly, it had sprung alight.

Perhaps Lottie, dying, had been able to sense its presence and its potential strength, for it was not to Alex or to Winter that she had spoken. She had said: 'Look after him, Lou,' and Lou had taken the child and looked at it with a sudden awestruck and exultant sense of possession.

That sense of possession had grown stronger every day, and now she did not mind how long they stayed in the Hirren Minar. She was afraid of moving from it. They were safe here and they must not take any risks. She could even bear the intolerable heat better because the child seemed to take no harm from it, but she waited and panted and prayed for the rains. If only the rains would break!

'Alex, how much longer will it be?'

'God knows!' said Alex. 'Any day now.'

The news from the outside world, if it could be believed, was not encouraging. Sir Henry Lawrence had fought a disastrous action at Chinut and had been heavily defeated, and now he and the British in Lucknow were closely besieged in the Residency. General Wheeler and the Cawnpore garrison were reported to be at their last gasp in the torn and shattered and pitifully inadequate entrenchments that they had scratched up out of the earth, and where they had fought and died and held out under the glaring heat and the rain of shot and shell since the sixth of June. In Jhansi the Rani had urged on her people to revolt, and had offered terms to the Europeans who had taken refuge in the fort. The terms had been accepted, and they had surrendered—only to be seized, bound and slaughtered. Mutiny had broken out in Allahabad, where the sepoys had murdered their officers and massacred all Christians, and the only news that seemed to hold out hope was that the British still clung to the Ridge before Delhi, although their force was as yet more besieged than besieging.

'Wait yet awhile,' urged Kashmera, as he had urged so often before. 'Thou art safe in the jungle.'

But the jungle had finished with them, and it would not let them wait.

36

ALEX had been setting a snare at the entrance to a small clearing some fifty yards from the Hirren Minar when he smelt smoke.

He had not been feeling at all well that day. His head ached and he thought angrily that Lou or Winter had disobeyed orders and lit an early fire. Then he had realized that the hot wind that was rustling the dry grass and dead leaves was blowing towards the Hirren Minar, and not away from it. There was someone else in the jungle, and upwind of him. He left the snare and returned swiftly, pulling the grass back over the path that he had taken, and ordered the two women, who were about to leave for their evening bathe, to get back into the upper room.

'Pull up the ladder and keep a revolver handy,' said Alex peremptorily. 'And drag the slab over that hole. I'm going to have a look around. Don't move until I come back.'

He had disappeared and they had waited a long time, making no noise and listening to the interminable croon of the hot wind and the monotonous rustle and clank of the dry bamboos. Presently Winter had lifted her head and sniffed as Alex had done.

'Smoke! So that's why—— Lou, suppose it's some of the others? It might be. We can't have been the only ones to get away.'

'More likely charcoal-burners,' said Lou in a whisper. 'And if it were men hunting for us they wouldn't warn us by lighting fires.'

Alex had returned half an hour later and called up to them that they could come down. He looked strained and uneasy. The smoke had come strongly on the wind, but the wind was dying now with the dying day, and soon it would be dark enough for him to verify his fears.

Lou, carrying the baby, had made straight for the river, but Winter had stopped and looked at Alex with anxious eyes: 'What is it? What are you afraid of? Is it men?'

'I hope so,' said Alex with an uneasy movement of his shoulders. 'We could probably deal with them—or avoid them.'

He turned to gaze up at the sky to the south-west. There had been clouds in the sky all day: dirty copper-coloured clouds which he had hoped might mean rain at last. But was there something more than clouds there? He said: 'I think the jungle is on fire somewhere over there. It may burn out, but—— Oh well, we shall soon know.'

The wind died and the smell of smoke died with it, but later, as the sky darkened, a pink wavering glow that was not the sunset grew steadily brighter until it drowned out the last of the daylight and spanned the horizon from north to south.

Alex watched it from the roof of the Hirren Minar. 'It may miss us,' he thought. 'Or it may burn out before it reaches us.' But he had little hope of its doing either. So little hope that he made a bundle of those few things that seemed to him urgently necessary, and carried them down to the river-bank.

Presently the wind rose again, and now it brought with it not only the smell of smoke, but drifting ash. Soon there would be sparks, and the forest was tinder-dry from the scorching June days. He returned to find the two women standing on the open roof watching the sky, their faces clearly illumined by the distant glow. They turned together to face him, and once again, as on that day in the jungle when they had fled from Lunjore, their eyes were wide and strained but without panic, and he knew that the anxiety in Lou's was not for herself, but only for the child she held.

Looking at them Alex was conscious of a confused mixture of emotions that included gratitude, relief, tenderness, a passionate admiration, and a disgust of himself because he had once considered them as nothing more than millstones round his neck and a tiresome responsibility of which he wished he could rid himself. He found that his voice was a little difficult to control and said with unnecessary curtness: 'Can either of you swim?'

'Yes,' said Winter, who had spent a few weeks every summer at Scarborough—Lady Julia considering the sea air good for growing girls.

'A little,' said Lou Cottar. 'But—but Amanda——'

Alex said: 'We'll have to make some sort of raft. Just in case. Get me all the ropes you can, Lou, and give that child some food. Light the lamp, Winter—and get a fire lighted below. We'll have to see what we're doing.' He disappeared down the ladder and they heard him hacking down the heavy bamboo door that he had built to protect the goat.

They worked with feverish haste, tearing down the split-cane *chiks* and using them to face that triple platform of bamboo, and carrying down the box that Lou had been using as a cradle. The door made an admirable raft, and Alex found himself feeling grateful to the goat for the first time since they had acquired it. The perspiration poured off them as they worked, for the heat of the fire added itself to the remorseless heat of the June night, and the wind blew that heat across them so that soon it hurt to breathe. The air was full of smoke now, and they could hear the crackle of the flames, while the light of the fire that Winter had lit in the stone room was no longer necessary, for the world about the Hirren Minar was as bright as though it were bathed in a red sunset.

Alex said: 'Bring anything that isn't too heavy and that you think is worth bringing. I can manage this; it doesn't weigh so much. We may have half an hour or so yet, but it isn't safe to bet on it. Be as quick as you can.'

He departed with the raft, and they went back up the ladder for the last time, and collecting all the food they could carry, took a last look about the queer stone chamber in which they had lived in such discomfort and found such strange happiness, and Winter smiled at it with sudden tears in her eyes, as though she were saying goodbye to a dear friend. Then she helped Lou down the ladder with the baby, and they were out in the jungle and Lou was hurrying towards the river while Winter followed her dragging the goat.

They could not have found the way by night, familiar as it had become; but this was not night. This was daylight, and hotter than any day they had ever known. The fire was no longer a distant crackling chorus now, but a steady roar, and the sky was a brilliant rose-pink pall of smoke shot through with sparks. A bird was singing gaily among the branches of a thorn-bush as though it imagined that the dawn had broken, and the under-growth was alive with movement. Peacocks, jungle-fowl, porcu-pine, a fox, three jackals and a chital hind ran past them, making for the river, and there was a crashing among the bushes as a bull nilghai thrust its way into a clearing, saw them, and backed away snorting.

If the wind had died the fire would not have reached them for several hours, but the wind drove the sparks ahead of the wall of flame, and where they fell they started new fires, so that the roaring blaze leapt forward with seven-league boots and ate up the miles with terrifying swiftness.

Alex was waiting for them on the little shelving strip of bank where they had bathed so often. The makeshift raft floated high and light in the water, and he was lashing the tin box to the centre of it. He took the baby from Lou and laid it in the box among an assortment of bundles, and stretched a strip of wet cloth above it as an added precaution against smoke and sparks. It was less easy to get the goat on board and safely tethered, but they managed it.

'You can't swim in that, Winter,' said Lou, hurriedly divesting herself of her dress. 'I'm sorry, Alex, but this is no time for modesty.'

Alex grinned at her and waded out as far as the steeply shelving bank allowed, while Winter, following Lou's example, removed her sari and rewound it, wrapping it around her in a straight strip so that it covered her from arm-pit to knee.

Crouching in the cool water under the shelter of the high bank the heat was not so intolerable, but the river looked appallingly wide—the far bank as though it were miles away—and Lou remembered the muggers who haunted every Indian river, and shuddered. She said anxiously, looking back at the jungle: 'Don't let's go until we have to! It's still quite far away. It may miss us after all.'

Alex said: 'Not a chance, I'm afraid. Look over there. They know.'

Lou Cottar turned her head and looked. A herd of nilghai were plunging down the steep bank not twenty yards below them, and taking to the water to swim out steadily into the red-dyed river where the current took them down in a long, slanting line towards the far shore. A moment later there was a crash above them, and a wild boar, his tushes and his little pig eyes gleaming in the leaping light, slithered down the bank and without paying the smallest attention to them launched himself into deep water. And then suddenly there were animals all about them, so that the steep banks seemed alive with terrified forest creatures, and for a moment or two they forgot their own danger in the wonder of that sight.

A tawny, spotted shape leapt down the bank and crouched on the narrow ledge almost within reach of their hands, snarling with terror, its tail lashing wildly. But the leopard's green eyes passed them by, for his fear and his hate were not for them but for the fire behind him, and presently he too took to the water. From somewhere farther up the bank they heard the unmistakable snarling roar of a tiger, and a troop of frantic monkeys leapt and howled in the tree above their heads. One of the monkeys, a mother clutching a skinny big-eyed baby, sprang down upon the raft and huddled against the bleating goat, chattering and grimacing.

'Come on,' said Alex. 'If we wait any longer we shall have a cargo-load of stowaways.' He found that he had to shout to make himself heard above the roar and crash, and that he felt oddly stupid and lightheaded: he would have liked to have sat down in the water and stayed where he was. He pulled himself together with an effort and said: 'Listen, Lou. I've rigged up a sort of tow-rope and I'll go ahead with it. If you're not much of a swimmer, keep hold of the raft and keep up-stream of it. Winter——' He turned to look at her and fought down the choking fear that threatened him; the fear of the current, of the man-eating muggers of the river—'Winter, you push from behind. Give me as much help as you can, and—and don't for God's sake let go.'

He had made a rough-and-ready harness of rope, and with it across his shoulders he struck out from the bank and felt the current catch him and draw him and the raft down-stream as a shower of sparks fell hissing into the river.

He did not glance back but swam on steadily, striving with everything in him to keep from being drawn too far down the stream, for the road and the shattered remains of the bridge lay only a mile away, and there would be men there in the huddle of huts behind the mud and wattle toll-house on the Oudh bank where he and Niaz had tied up the occupants on the day they blew up the bridge. It would be dangerous to land anywhere near them, and he must not let the raft be swept too far down-stream.

The oil-smooth surface of the water was filmed with ash and charred leaves and full of frantic swimming animals, many of whom clawed at the raft and held on to it, dragging sodden shivering little bodies on to the sheltering bamboos; squirrels, rats, mice and a bedraggled mongoose. There were pig and deer; sambhur, chital, kaka, black-buck; nilghai, jackals, panthers, tigers, a scaly four-foot iguana and a solitary elephant with a

s*

broken tusk in the river that night, swimming as desperately as the three humans for the safety of the far bank.

It seemed to Alex as though they would never reach the other side. As though the river was endless. His head ached and his muscles seemed to have no strength in them, and there was a cramping pain in his stomach. The rope bit into his shoulders and caught across his throat and choked him, and he could feel the drag of the dead weight pulling to the pull of the current, for Lou could do little more than cling to it and keep afloat. And then quite suddenly there were sandbanks ahead of him as though they had lifted from the river, and the current no longer pulled at him, and he had reached the shallows.

All about him wet furry shapes were dragging themselves on to the warm white sand, licking their fur and shaking themselves and crawling or scuttling away towards the distant line of trees, and Alex freed himself from the rope harness and dragged the makeshift raft forward until it grounded.

He turned then at last, and saw that they were all there. The shivering goat, the baby lying placidly in its box, the monkey still clutching its round-eyed offspring, Lou Cottar on her knees, staring blindly ahead of her and breathing in deep gasps, and Winter lying full length in the shallows with her long hair cloaking her slim body in blackness and her chin on the edge of the raft. He walked over to her unsteadily and reached down a hand to pull her to her feet.

'I can't,' said Winter, and laughed up at him. 'I've got no clothes on!'

'I like you without your clothes on,' said Alex, and pulled her up into his arms and kissed her, holding her cool wet body close to him and tasting the water that ran into his mouth from their wet faces and their dripping hair. He held her for perhaps a minute, oblivious of Lou Cottar, and then released her gently, and putting her away from him, bent to untie the goat.

The monkey, abruptly taking fright, leapt from the raft and fled across the sand. And suddenly they were all laughing. Laughing helplessly from strain and overwhelming relief, and because they were still together and still alive. They stopped at last, and turned to look at the wall of flame that was the bank that they had left.

They had left it only just in time, for hissing burning branches were falling into the water and there was nothing but flame to the turn of the river that hid the broken bridge-head. The Hirren Minar must be somewhere in the centre of that furnace, and tomorrow there would be nothing but miles of black, smouldering desolation where yesterday there had been dense jungle.

A hot spark fell on Alex's bare arm and he winced and swung round suddenly to look at the line of trees behind them and beyond the long stretch of the sand. Lou Cottar, following his look, said with a catch in her voice: 'It can't reach as far as this!'

The flames could not leap that wide expanse of river, but the wind was carrying stray sparks across it, and the jungle everywhere was tinder-dry. But they could not remain exposed to the brilliant light at the edge of the shallows. They would have to make for the trees.

Alex bent without a word, and untying the box from which Lou had removed the baby, filled it with the various things that they had brought with them, while Winter retrieved the wet folds of her sari from about her ankles, and dragging the goat, followed them across the wide level of the sands to the shelter of the grass and the casuarina scrub that fringed it.

The long swim across the river had cooled them, but now they were hot again. Unbelievably hot. The air scorched their lungs with each breath that they drew, and the river and the wide sand-banks and the line of the jungle were lit with a bright pulsating glare as though it were a stage in the full blaze of footlights and gas-lamps. Every blade and leaf and twig of the jungle behind them stood out from its fellows, high-lighted and black-shadowed, and here and there a floating spark would alight and wink and go out, or catch at a brittle powder-dry spear of grass and show a brief spurt of flame.

A tuft of pampas-grass twenty yards from them caught alight

and flared up, and Lou caught her breath in a harsh gasp, and snatching at the end of Winter's wet sari, dragged the end of it free and drew it across the child's face. She said desperately: 'It's almost dry already! We shall have to get back to the water. Alex——'

Winter saw Alex's face stiffen queerly and knew that he was visualizing taking to the river again and going down with the current—for how far? And for how long? They might have to go for miles, hemmed in between two walls of fire and with only that makeshift bamboo raft to hold to. Then suddenly and unexpectedly he gave a dry sob of relief, and holding out his hand, palm upwards, said: 'Rain!'

It was the monsoon at last.

Unbelievingly they turned their faces up to the furnace of the sky, the hot drifting ash and the falling sparks, and felt something warm and wet splashing upon their parched skins.

'Wait here,' said Alex. 'I'm going to get the raft.' He leapt down the bank and they saw him race across the sands as the first heavy, blessed drops began to fall. He upended it and shouldered it and presently he was back again, panting and breathless. 'Get in among the trees; under the thickest stuff you can find,' he said jerkily. They forced their way into the thicker jungle with the raindrops splashing on to their shoulders and the glare from the burning trees on the far bank lighting their way, and using the raft as a roof, wedged it at an angle to carry off the rain and make a rough shelter among the trees, stowing the bundles and the baby under it as the first slow drops turned to the full drumming downpour of the monsoon.

They stood out in it, letting it pour over them as it roared out of the sky like some tidal wave such as the one that had overwhelmed lost Atlantis, drowning out the roar of the burning jungle. It was not rain as Winter had known rain. It was a solid wall of water falling on them and smothering out thought; and cool—and cool——

The glare diminished and died at last, and they were in wet darkness in the drumming, drenching rain. The thick jungle and the platform of bamboo and matting were an inadequate shelter against the torrential downpour, but they did not care. It had cooled that appalling heat and they could breathe again.

It was still raining when the dawn broke greyly over the drenched miles of blackened smoking wasteland, the pock-marked face of the river and the sodden jungle around them where the canes and the tall grass sagged under the weight of water.

Winter awoke hearing Alex stir, and opened her eyes to see him walk out into the pouring greyness. She sat up, pushing the wet hair back from her face and shoulders, and saw that Lou was still asleep wearing nothing but the cotton chemise in which she had swum the river, and with her arm about the box in which the baby slept. They had propped up the lid with sticks last night so as to provide extra shelter for the baby and the various belongings that were wedged at one end of the box, and the baby, though presumably damp in the manner of babies, appeared to be otherwise dry.

Winter rose to her knees and wringing out her wet hair, plaited it and looked ruefully at her damp sari. But there was nowhere in the jungle that was dry, for the warm rain drummed on the leaves, pouring off them in fountains and cascades and runnels, and the steady voice of the water drowned out all other sound. There would be no need to bathe in the river today, thought Winter, and then realized with a sense of shock that it was not going to be so easy to reach the river from this bank, for to gain the brink would mean exposing themselves at the edge of a wide belt of open sand a long way from the safe shelter of the trees.

Struck by this thought she turned to rummage cautiously among the few articles they had brought with them from the Hirren Minar, and found a cooking-pot which she set to catch the water that was sluicing off the roof of their temporary shelter. The noise and the movement failed to wake Lou, who slept on while Winter instituted a search in the nearby jungle for any fuel dry enough to burn. Only yesterday the whole forest could have been lit with a single match, but this morning it was no easy matter to find a handful of grass and dead leaves with which to make a fire.

Presently the baby raised a feeble wail and the sound woke Lou who sat up rubbing her eyes, and after a time came out and joined Winter. She looked up at the grey, weeping skies and round at the sodden jungle and said briskly: 'We shall have to build a hut.'

Winter looked at her and smiled, remembering Lou's previous restless desire to escape from the jungle, and contrasting it with her present and instant desire to construct a more permanent shelter so that she could remain safely in hiding during the coming months. Lou returned the smile. They could still smile in spite of all that had happened to them, and they were still smiling when Alex returned, pushing through the drenching undergrowth. But at the sight of his face their own faces were suddenly sober.

'What is it?' asked Lou sharply.

'That bloody goat!' said Alex forcefully.

Lou gave a choked cry and ran to the side of the shelter where they had tethered the goat, but there was nothing there but a chewed piece of rope, and the goat had gone. 'We must find it!' said Lou. 'We must! How am I to feed Amanda? It can't have gone far!' But the goat had gone for good.

'I can only hope that some wet and hungry tiger has made good use of it,' said Alex sourly. 'It will be a richly deserved end. Don't be silly, Lou! Give it some rice, or boil it some flour and water. No one is going to notice smoke today.'

'Will you stop calling her "*it*"!' snapped Lou in sudden and irrational fury.

Alex grinned. 'You're getting damned maternal, Lou. One day you'll persuade yourself that it—sorry, she—is your own child.'

'She is,' said Lou, and went to join Winter who was building a fire in a hollow tree that she had discovered some twenty yards from their shelter.

Alex looked after her with a half-smile that turned into a grimace of pain. He went into the shelter and found the small tin of opium pills and swallowed down a few of them with brandy. 'I cannot go sick now,' thought Alex dizzily. 'Not now——'

But no amount of brandy and opium could keep the fever at bay, and half an hour later Winter, bringing him hot food on a plate of leaves, found him lying under a tree a few yards from the shelter, his body jack-knifed with pain and his breathing harshly audible above the steady patter of the rain. His brown, sunburned skin had an oddly grey tinge to it and seemed to be stretched too tightly over his cheekbones, and there were dark patches under his closed eyes. Winter put the food down very carefully, surprised to find that her hands were steady when her heart was beating with such terrified swiftness, and laid a hand lightly on his forehead.

The harsh heat of it appalled her, and Alex opened his eyes and looked at her between narrowed lids. He seemed to have some difficulty in focusing her. His forehead creased in a scowl of pain and he said in a blurred, difficult voice: 'Be all right— only—dysentery. Tell Lou—keep that baby away—danger- ous——'

* * *

There had followed a nightmare interval of days and nights— none of them could ever have said how many, it had seemed like a month but was probably no more than three days—in which Alex's body had been torn and burned and wasted with dysentery and raging fever, and it seemed to Winter that he could not live. She had not known the meaning of dysentery, for though it was a plague common to all India, any explanation of it, or of what a severe attack entailed, was not considered a suitable subject for the delicate susceptibilities of ladies. She had stayed with him day and night, doing everything that it was possible to do for him, endlessly and tirelessly; holding his head on her lap, forcing the brandy and opium that were the only medicines they pos- sessed down his parched throat, feeding him with rice-water, listening to him rave when the fever mounted, and feeling every cramping pain as though it were a pain in her own body.

She slept only when exhaustion overtook her, and then with her hand on him so that she woke when he moved. She had never in all her short life seen an illness like this, or imagined it, and at times it seemed worse to her than the birth of Lottie's baby had been. But Alex held on to life, and it was, in the end, Lou who had betrayed them.

Lou knew something of dysentery, having experienced a mild attack of it herself and seen Josh suffer a worse one. She told Winter all that she could remember of the course of the illness and its treatment, and she had looked at Alex and said: 'I don't think it's only dysentery. I think he's got some sort of fever on top of it. Josh wasn't as bad as that. Unless—unless it's cholera——'

She had kept away for fear of carrying the infection to the baby. But the pouring rain, and the sudden breaks when the rain would stop and the sodden jungle steamed under the molten heat of the sun, had not suited the baby as the dry heat of the Hirren Minar had done. The baby wailed endlessly and heartbreakingly, and vomited up the rice-water and the thin gruel that Lou made with flour and coarse country sugar. And the supplies of even those commodities were running low.

'She will die without milk!' said Lou, wild-eyed and desperate. 'She must have proper food—she must!' She had walked up and down, clutching the wailing infant to her breast and said passionately: 'Why can't I feed her myself? Why aren't we made so that we could if we wanted to? She needs it, and I can't give her anything—*anything!*'

Winter did not hear her. She had been watching Alex's haggard, burnt-out face and dry, cracked lips, and her mind and her heart were as desperate as Lou's. She did not even notice when Lou went away, and it was only when she found that there was no fire lit—for Lou had been dealing with all the cooking—and no food prepared, that she found that Lou and the baby had gone. And even then she imagined that they could not be far away.

The rain had stopped and the jungle that had been so brown

and brittle only a few days ago was now a hot, humid greenhouse in which new grass and leaves and creepers and every variety of growing thing had sprung up overnight in lush abandon. The damp heat was less bearable than the dry heat had been, and Alex seemed to struggle for every breath he drew.

The sound of his laboured breathing tore at Winter's heart, and for the first time in the long weeks since she had run from the Lunjore Residency she turned her face away and wept: wept hopelessly and helplessly and silently; the hot tears running into the grass roots as swiftly as the raindrops that had poured down on to them the day before.

She did not know how long she lay there, face downwards on the steaming ground, and she did not hear Alex move; but his hand touched her and she lifted her head and saw that his eyes were open. There was a faint frown in them but they were entirely lucid and no longer clouded and unfocused or blind with pain. He spoke with a palpable effort and in a voice that was barely a whisper:

'What's the matter?'

Winter pushed back her hair and stared at him incredulously, the tears drying on her cheeks. He had not looked like that, or spoken sensibly, since the illness had struck him down. His frown deepened and he said: 'Why are you crying?' Winter brushed away the tears with the back of her hand and said unsteadily: 'I'm not—not now.'

She had left him and stumbled away to light the fire and boil water, because Lou was still not back. And it had been the first time for days that she had not left him expecting to find that he was dead when she returned. She had made a brew of flour and rice-water and sugar, and stirred brandy into it and taken it back to him; and his eyes were still lucid.

He drank the decoction because he was too weak to refuse it, and lay still afterwards looking ahead of him under half-lowered lids. Presently he said: 'How long?'

'I—I don't know,' said Winter with a break in her voice. 'Days. Don't talk.'

'I shall be all right now,' said Alex in the same difficult whisper, and he had closed his eyes and gone to sleep with his head in her lap.

Winter had slept too; her head thrown back against the tree-trunk behind her; and when she heard voices and someone had shaken her she had thought it was Lou.

But it was not Lou. It was a party of men armed with lathis and in charge of a man who wore a rusty sword and carried an old-fashioned musket.

'These are not sahib-*log*!' said one of the men scornfully. 'They are but the *naukar-log* of the mem.'

But one of them had peered closer and said: 'Nay, they have *Angrezi* blood in them at least. We will take them. Up, thou!' The speaker stirred Alex with his foot and Winter had said furiously and in the vernacular: 'Let be! Canst thou not see that he is sick?'

The tone and the quality of the Urdu she used gave the men pause, and they looked at her doubtfully. It occurred to them suddenly that this might after all be an Indian lady of good family. Her fingers tightened imperatively on Alex's shoulder, and he had answered the unspoken warning and remained silent. He could not have risen if he had tried. The man with the musket said uncertainly: 'Of what city art thou?'

'Of Lucknow,' said Winter without hesitation. 'Of the household of Ameera Begum, wife of Walayat Shah, who is my cousin and lives in the Gulab Mahal by the mosque of Sayid Hussain. This man is of Persia, and my—my husband.'

The men observed her owl-eyed and consulted in whispers, and Winter heard the leader say: 'What matter? The order is for all to be sent to Pari. Send these also.'

They had rifled the contents of the shelter in which Lou and the baby had lived, removing the revolvers and the shot-gun and anything else they could find, and ten minutes later they had moved off through the jungle taking Winter and Alex with them.

Alex, helped to his feet, had not been able to stand without support, let alone walk, and they had used the roof of the shelter to carry him on. It had taken them surprisingly little time to reach the road, and Winter realized that they must have been swept down by the current farther than she had supposed on the night that they crossed the river. There had been a bullock-cart waiting on the road, and a curious crowd of villagers—and Lou Cottar. Lou, white-faced and haggard and clutching the baby.

She had stared at Winter and Alex in horror and said hoarsely: 'I didn't mean—I didn't know this would happen! I thought I might find a village where I could get milk. And—and they did help me. They were kind. I didn't realize they would go back to see if there was anyone else. I only came by the sand because it was easier, and—and they followed the marks. I thought——'

Her voice choked and stopped and Winter said: 'It's all right, Lou.' And then they were thrust into the cart and jolted away down the long uneven road towards Pari.

37

IT had been dark by the time the captives reached the little walled town near the jheel; the town that Alex and Niaz had skirted on that autumn night when they had ridden from Khanwai and crossed the bridge of boats hidden under the sacks and the sugar-cane in the bullock-carts.

The cart that now carried Alex, Winter, Lou and Amanda creaked to a halt beside a gateway in a mud wall, and they were taken out and hustled across a dark courtyard and into a long, low-ceilinged room lit by a single guttering cresset. The two men who had carried Alex laid him on the floor and the door banged behind them. An iron bar clanged into place, and some-one at the far end of the room stood up in the shadows beyond the circle of light and said hoarsely and incredulously: '*Winter!*'

Winter was on her knees beside Alex, and she looked up, startled; blinking a little in the dim light that seemed dazzling after the darkness outside. A face moved into the range of the lamp and stared down at her wide-eyed: a strange, haggard face; dirty and unshaven and with a blood-stained bandage tied about its head. She looked up at it for a long moment, puzzled and uncertain, before she recognized it, and then at first she did not believe it. For it was, incredibly, Carlyon who stood there. Carlyon, whom she had last seen on the verandah of the little dâk bungalow beyond the ford on the road to Lunjore, and whom she had thought to be—if she had thought of him at all—several thousand miles away in England.

There were other voices behind him, and other faces. Eight other faces; tired, worn, dirty—and British.

Carlyon said hoarsely: 'Winter!—it is Winter, isn't it? What are you doing here? They said you'd all been killed!' His voice was as raw-edged and ragged as his clothes. And then other faces that Winter knew separated themselves from the shadows: Captain Garrowby—Dr. O'Dwyer—Mrs. Hossack——

Mrs. Hossack clutched at Lou Cottar and wept, and Captain Garrowby said: 'Mrs. Barton!—Mrs. Cottar! How did you—we thought you must all be dead! We thought that we were the only ones who had got away. Who is that with you?' He lifted the lamp and said: 'Good God!—it's Randall!'

'Only just,' said Alex in a whisper. 'Hullo, Garrowby. How did you—get out?'

There were charpoys in the room, six of them placed end to end along the walls, and Captain Garrowby and Carlyon had lifted Alex on to one of them, and he had lain there and listened to the story of another escape.

The Garrowbys and Dr. and Mrs. O'Dwyer and Mrs. Hossack and her four children had not been to the Residency, and so had escaped the massacre. Mrs. Hossack had intended to go, but had been delayed, for Dr. O'Dwyer had been at her bungalow to see her eldest child, a seven-year-old girl, who had been suffering from hot-weather fever. Captain Hossack, of Colonel

Packer's regiment, had been shot down on the parade-ground by his men, and his orderly had ridden to warn Mrs. Hossack to escape. The doctor, whose bungalow was next door, had run to fetch his wife and they had all entered the Hossacks' waiting carriage, intending to take refuge at the Residency. But the Garrowbys had stopped them. Captain Garrowby of the 93rd had been warned by his men, and he had ridden for his bungalow and bundled his wife into the trap and had turned the corner into the Residency road to see an obviously hostile crowd collecting before the gates. He had turned the trap, deciding to make for the river, and had met the Hossacks' carriage. They had all made for the bridge and had crossed it at least two hours before Alex and Niaz reached it.

They had said no word at the bridge of the panic in Lunjore, for fear of being stopped, but at Pari they had been attacked by a mob which had included mutinous sepoys from the disbanded 7th Regiment. The coachman and Captain Garrowby's syce, who had been with them, had stood off the mob for a few minutes and paid for their loyalty with their lives. But in those few minutes the party had turned and driven back furiously the way they had come, and abandoning the carriage and trap had taken to the jungle and hidden there.

One of the Hossack children had been killed and Captain Garrowby and Mrs. O'Dwyer had been wounded in the firing. Mrs. O'Dwyer had died two days later. They had wandered in the jungle, living on roots and berries, and first one and then another of the two elder Hossack children had died, and later Mrs. Garrowby too had died of heat-stroke and exhaustion. Captain Garrowby and the doctor, with Mrs. Hossack and her remaining child—a baby of six months—had been driven to ask help at a village on the outskirts of Pari, and the villagers had taken them in and treated them kindly. But three days ago they had been put into a covered cart and brought to this house—they did not know why, or how long they would remain there. They had been given food, and had not been ill-used, but the atmosphere and the attitude of their jailers was not reassuring. The

four other captives had arrived on the following day: Lord
Carlyon, the Reverend Chester Dobbie, Mr. Climpson and Miss
Keir—the sole survivors of a party of fifteen Europeans who had
hoped to escape from Oudh and had been attacked and massacred
at a village five miles way. They too had been fugitives for many
days before being captured and brought here.

Winter had paid no attention to the recital of escape and
misery, for her eyes had looked past Carlyon to Dr. O'Dwyer,
and she had gone to him and pulled him across the room to Alex,
and after that she had only watched his face and listened to what
he said. 'He'll do,' said Dr. O'Dwyer reassuringly. And then a
native woman had brought coarse food and a bowl of fresh milk,
and Lou had fed the baby and told the story of the last weeks, and
the voices and the faces and the heat of the low-ceilinged room
had mixed and melted together and Winter had fallen asleep
and had not stirred or wakened until the sun was high in the sky.

*   *   *

There was an enclosed courtyard on the far side of the room
where the prisoners had spent the night, and the door leading out
into it had been unlocked at sunrise.

The same native woman had brought food again for the captives, but she had refused to answer questions and had gone out
to the far side of the courtyard to join a crowd of gapers who
peered curiously at the *feringhis*, discussing them and speculating
about them and chewing *pan*.

'What do you suppose they mean to do with us?' asked Lou
uneasily, rocking the baby.

'Keep us as hostages, I think,' said Mr. Dobbie, who thought
no such thing but trusted that God would pardon him that
comforting lie.

'Hostages for what?' enquired Lou.

Mr. Climpson, a middle-aged magistrate who had escaped from
his burning bungalow with the assistance of a loyal servant, said:
'The local talukdar has been wavering for some time. He cannot
decide which side is going to win, and he seems to have given

orders that any Europeans found in these parts were to be taken prisoner but not harmed. I think he means well enough, but he is getting nervous. The whole of Oudh is now in revolt, and since the Chinut affair the British position looks bad. I think that is why he has had any of us known to be in the district brought here.'

'Yes, yes,' said Mr. Dobbie, nodding reassuringly at the women. 'I am sure that is right. He feels that we shall be safer here. That bar on the door may keep us in, but it also serves to keep others out.'

Carlyon, leaning against the jamb of the open door, surveyed him under drooping lids and wondered if the little man really believed that. Carlyon had heard the story of Jhansi and the public slaughter of the Europeans who had accepted the Rani's terms of surrender. That hapless garrison had been roped in three lines—children, women, and men—and bound and helpless they had been butchered in that order, so that the women had been forced to see their children die before their eyes, and the men to see both die in turn before their own end came.

He had heard too—for the news had been told to Mr. Climpson by the head-man of the village where they had laid hidden before being brought to Pari—of the massacre of the Cawnpore Garrison who had accepted the offer of surrender and safe-conduct by Dundu Pant the Nana Sahib. If Mr. Climpson's informant was to be believed, the exhausted survivors had been allowed to embark in boats that were to take them to Allahabad, but once the last man was on board the rush roofs of the boats had been set alight by the boatmen, who had then leapt out into the water as the watchers on the bank opened fire on the blazing, drifting targets. And so the last of the Cawnpore Garrison had died, with the exception of some two hundred women and children—of whom there had been close on four hundred in the entrenchments on the fifth of June—who had struggled ashore and been taken captive.

In the light of these stories Carlyon was inclined to take a very different view of their situation from those advanced by either Mr. Climpson or Mr. Dobbie. It seemed to him far more likely that they were being kept alive in order to provide a Roman holiday for the mob when a suitable occasion should arise. The type of public spectacle that the hapless garrisons of Jhansi and Cawnpore had provided.

'I should have gone home,' thought Carlyon. 'I must have been mad!'

He had meant to go. He had returned to Delhi, raging because Winter had escaped him, and had heard later, through friends of the Abuthnots, of her marriage. But he had not gone home. He still wanted her more than he had ever wanted anything in his life, and he could not bring himself to admit defeat. As long as he was in the same country there was surely some chance for him, but once he left it there was none. What did a few months, or a year, matter to him? He could afford to linger in India for a few more months, for he was convinced that a few months of marriage to this clod of a Commissioner would cure her of her romantic attachment, and then when she moved to the hills—as she was sure to do—she would find Carlyon there ready to console her.

He knew in his more sober and reasonable moments that he was behaving in an unadult and ridiculous manner. A manner which no one—least of all Lord Carlyon himself—would have thought Lord Carlyon capable of. But he had stayed. He had kept in touch with Mrs. Gardener-Smith solely in order to obtain news of Winter. Hearing that she intended to go to Simla in May, he had arranged to go there himself in April, and he had gone to Lucknow with the intention of travelling to Simla via Lunjore so that he could see this man Barton for himself. But while there he had been struck down by a severe attack of fever which had delayed him, and the tidal wave of the mutiny had swept him up into its hungry flood and brought him, after weeks of wandering and privation, to Pari—and to Winter.

Carlyon leant against the door and watched her now as she lay asleep. She must, he thought, have been very tired to sleep as deeply as that. Food had been brought hours ago and the courtyard was bright with sunlight. There was noise and talk and movement, but she had not stirred.

The three other women in their soiled bedraggled Western clothes looked haggard and shapeless and ugly with anxiety and exhaustion. But this relaxed, sleeping creature managed still to be beautiful, though it was a different beauty from that which had attracted his instant attention in the ballroom at Ware.

This was a woman, and no longer a girl. A woman thin-faced from strain and sleeping the sleep of utter exhaustion, but still as lovely a thing to look at as any man—even one as weary and desperate and as frightened as himself—could wish to see. In that hot, horrible room, surrounded by her fellow-captives in their stained and ragged clothes, she looked as colourful as a poppy growing on a rubbish-dump, and merely to look at her was a refreshment to the eye and in some way served to lessen his fear and his despairing fury. Carlyon had never known before what it meant to be afraid, but he knew now, and the fight to keep from showing it was the hardest part of living through the dragging, tormenting days. Harder than uncertainty, the intolerable heat, the torn, sweat-soaked clothing, the coarse scanty food, the memory of horrors seen and endured and the dread of worse to come.

It was an escape from that fear, and from ugliness and reality, to look at Winter lying asleep, the lovely curves of her body moulded by the thin folds of the wine-red sari whose deep blue border reflected the blue lights in her hair. The smooth curve of the bare golden arm, the line of the long golden throat and the black sweep of the lashes that lay against her thin cheek were an assurance that the world still contained other things besides hate and terror and violence.

Carlyon became aware that he himself was being watched, and looking beyond Winter he encountered Captain Randall's grey, speculative gaze.

He would not, he thought, have recognized Randall if Garrowby had not addressed him by name. The man seemed to have shrunk to no more than skin stretched over bone, and the almost black sun-tan had an odd undertone of greenish-white. Close on a week's growth of beard blurred the outline of jaw and chin, and there were dark patches like bruises under his eyes. But the eyes themselves, with their thick black lashes that were almost as long as Winter's own, were as unmistakable as Winter's had been; and meeting them, Carlyon was conscious of a sudden flare of hostility and antagonism. That familiar antagonism this man had aroused in him from the moment he had first seen him in the drawing-room of the Abuthnots' bungalow in Delhi.

He had not known then why he should have disliked him so intensely; it was enough that he did. But he knew now. The reason lay stretched between them. A woman in a wine-coloured sari.

They had escaped from violent death by the narrowest of margins; they had lived as hunted animals, and they were herded together now as captives. Their countryman everywhere were being pursued and slaughtered and defeated, and the Empire of John Company was crumbling into ruin. They had seen sights that would haunt their sleep as long as they lived—and they did not know if they might live as long as another day, or another hour. But for a moment they could forget it all and stare at each other with antipathy and cold anger; the greater issues giving place to an instinct as elementary and as animal as that which drives rival stags to fight in the spring.

Yet another bedraggled captive had come to swell the ranks of the prisoners that day, an elderly Eurasian clerk who had been found hiding in a village some five miles to the south. His tale differed little from the story of escape and flight, horror and hardship and final capture, that had been the lot of all of them. The villagers had helped him and sheltered him, but he like the others had been sent without explanation to Pari.

'It is not the country people who are cruel,' said Mr. Lapeuta in his soft sing-song voice. 'They are like us, you know—veree ordinary people. It is thee townspeople and thee sepoys who are hot against us. I think that thee talukdar of these parts, he will protect us if he can, but thee sepoys and thee Maulvies they are putting pressure on him, threatening him. He will not kill us, but I think that he wishes to be rid of us, for he is fearful of thee Maulvies, who preach against us, and he would like to wash his hands of us all. If there is better news, then doubtless he will keep us here so that he can show how he has sheltered us, and gain much reward. But if thee news is bad, then I think he will send us away. That is what thee head-man in whose village I hid told me.'

The accuracy of this forecast was proved within three days. News from Lucknow trickled into Pari, and it was news that took the heart out of the captives, put heart into the rabble, and frightened the talukdar into ridding himself, Pilate-wise, of the responsibility of the fugitive Europeans whom he was holding captive.

Sir Henry Lawrence was dead. He had died in the beleaguered Residency at Lucknow, and all over India men heard the news with a catch of the breath. Now that he had gone it would surely be only a matter of days before the Residency was captured, and its defenders massacred as the garrison of Cawnpore had been.

The talukdar wavered no longer, and hastened to rid himself of the haggard band of British before they were murdered by the mob in circumstances that might involve him in trouble in the event—which now appeared less likely—of the Hell-born ultimately defeating the insurgents and regaining power.

He sent in more and better food, permitted the services of a barber and allowed the women facilities for the washing and mending of clothes. And having impressed his excellent intentions upon them he had them hurried by night into covered carts such as *purdah* women travel in, so that they might not be seen and dragged out by the way, and sent them off under guard.

They had not known where they were going, and the unexpectedly good treatment they had received after days of surly neglect had raised the hopes of the majority of the party. It did not raise Alex's hopes, or Mr. Lapeuta's, for they had a better understanding of the native mind than their fellow-captives. That understanding enabled them to read the motives of the Talukdar of Pari with accuracy, and they had scant confidence in the future, or in the good intentions of those to whom they were being sent. Winter alone might be safe, thought Alex. Her dress and her command of the vernacular set her apart from the rest of the British captives, and this cousin in Lucknow might yet be able to save her—and perhaps Lou and the baby as well. He drew what comfort he could from that thought.

There was only one other spark of comfort to be found in the present situation, and that was that he was no longer responsible for their safety. The weight of that responsibility had been lifted from him at last, and he need no longer plan and contrive and lie awake worrying over problems connected with the feeding and protection of three women whose lives had largely depended upon him. He was as helpless now as they were—and he would have given anything to be back in the Hirren Minar, lying in the hot grass on the river-bank setting fishing-lines while the three women washed clothes and cooking-pots in the twilight, though when he had been there he had fretted and agonized against the enforced inaction and had done nothing but think and plan how to get away.

Well, he had got away. They had all got away—even Lottie. And it occurred to him to wonder if, after all, Lottie might not be the only one to be envied.

*   *   *

The four days and nights that followed their departure from Pari were a horror that equalled anything that Winter and Lou had yet endured. The carts made slow progress, for the heavy rains had turned the roads into quagmires. The torrential downpour soaked through the inadequate covering and drenched the huddled occupants, and when it ceased the sun turned the hooded carts into a steam bath in which the perspiration poured off them, soaking them afresh and less pleasantly, and the temperature rose until it became difficult to breathe.

They heard no news in those days, and did not know that on one of them the last survivors of the Cawnpore garrison had died, and with them, Sophie Abuthnot.

Little Sophie Abuthnot, as small and fair and fragile as Lottie had been, had survived both that ghastly siege in General Wheeler's pitifully inadequate entrenchments, and the horrors of the massacre in the boats at the Sati Chauri Ghat, only to meet a more terrible fate. For the guns of the British advance could be heard at Cawnpore, and Nana Dundu Pant had heard in them the bitter knell of his hopes. All the evil fury and hate of which he was capable, and which Alex had seen in his face and heard in his voice in the vault beneath the ruins at Khanwai, had been let loose on the only victims that remained in his hands—the two hundred exhausted, hopeless, helpless women and children who were herded like animals in one small building, the *Bibigarh*. He had listened to Havelock's guns and had given the order for their murder.

It had taken all day to kill them, for they had shrieked and dodged and twisted and striven to protect their children. But it had been done at last, and by nightfall the floor of the *Bibigarh* was deep in blood and littered with the bodies of the dead and dying. And when the new day dawned the butchers had dragged out the corpses and flung them into a well outside the house. Sophie had not been dead when they had thrown her down, but she had died under the weight of the dead. There had been several who were not yet dead, and one child who was unharmed and had lain all night, mad with terror, hiding under the corpses. The mob had laughed to see him run screaming round the well, and had caught him and swung his head against the stonework, and thrown him in. And half India shuddered in horror and drew back from the edge of the pit they had digged, for that massacre turned many men who would have fought the British to the bitter end to lay down their arms and return to their homes.

'There can be no blessing on such a deed,' said Ameera's husband, Walayat Shah, who had hated the British and rejoiced at the news of the risings, and had himself taken part in attack after attack upon Sir Henry Lawrence's beleaguered garrison in the Lucknow Residency. But on the day that he heard the news of the murder of the women and children in the *Bibigarh* at Cawnpore he had broken his sword in two and thrown away his musket, and come back to the Gulab Mahal and had not left it again. 'We cannot prevail,' said Walayat Shah. 'The *Jehad* is dead. Those who slew the women and the babes have slain it also. To slay in battle or in hot blood, that is well. And to kill men, if they be unbelievers, is to achieve Paradise. But to slaughter captive women who have suffered the harshness of war and sorrow, and been robbed thereby of all strength and will, is a deed to blacken the sun. I will fight no more against the *feringhis*, for God can no longer be upon our side.'

Alex had been taken from the cart in which the women travelled at dawn on the first day, and had not come back, and presently the second cart had rumbled away. One of the escort had told Winter surlily that he was to travel with the men, but she did not know if this were true or not, and when their own cart had started again without him Mrs. Hossack had given way to hysterics. 'Oh God!' screamed Mrs. Hossack, 'they've killed him! They've killed them all! They never meant to send them with us! We're alone now—we're alone!'

Winter had felt the blood drain away from her heart. Was it true? Had they always meant to separate them—putting the men to death and allowing the women to live? Would she ever see Alex again? She had tried to force her way out, and had been thrust roughly back again, and the cart had jolted forward on that long nightmare journey.

They were given little food and insufficient water, and Lou Cottar's face had aged with every crawling hour. Mrs. Hossack, cradling her small son, had wept and moaned with a hopeless and despairing monotony, and Miss Keir had suffered from bouts of sickness that added to the stench of the broiling, steaming cart. They had given the best of the food and almost all of the water to the two children, and Lou had made a paste of boiled rice and water and fed it to the baby with her fingertip.

The scarcity of food had been bearable, but the lack of water in that terrible heat had been a torment that had only been partially relieved on the second day when Janet Keir began to shriek and rave and tear frantically at the side of the cart, and Winter had flown at the escort with a flood of words that she was not even aware that she knew. Daunted by this blazing-eyed virago who could curse them so efficiently in their own tongue, the men had produced at the next stopping-place not only water but milk, though little enough of either.

There had been no sign of the other cart again, and the terrible days had crawled past without their knowing whether the men were dead or not, or where they had gone. Winter nursed Lottie's baby when Lou fell at last into a brief exhausted sleep, and longed for the Hirren Minar as a lost soul might long for Paradise. But the Hirren Minar was only a scorched and blackened pile of stone standing gaunt and exposed among a waste of charred stumps and layers of sodden ash, and Lottie was dead and her grave lost among that desolation, and if this terrible journey lasted much longer Lottie's baby would die too. Perhaps they would all die—perhaps Alex was already dead . . .

The sun was sinking again in a blaze of blood-red light that pierced through the chinks of the cart and its covering, but the darkness brought no relief. Winter's mouth was dry and her tongue swollen, her throat parched with thirst. Her head and her body ached with one vast throbbing ache that seemed to beat like a gong in her brain, and the heat was like an iron band about her neck, tightening slowly and inexorably so that soon she would not be able to breathe. The ugly scar that Alex's hunting-knife had made on her arm burnt as though it were an open wound again, and the choking stench of the cart made her famished stomach cringe with nausea.

How many days had they been in the cart? How many times had the sun gone down? She could not remember. They had had no food that day, and they had been given water only once and in the early part of the morning. Even Mrs. Hossack moaned no more, for her parched throat could produce no sound, and the children who had wailed weakly all day were silent. Miss Keir too had ceased to writhe and mutter and beg for water, and lay still at last. Was she dead? Or was she only asleep like Lou—or was Lou dead too?

Winter became dimly aware that the cart was passing through crowded streets. Lights and voices and noise pressed about it and somewhere guns were firing; guns and a ceaseless distant crackle of musketry. There was a smell of cooked food and a pungent aromatic scent of ghee and dung-fires and masala; of roasting chunna, hot dust and decaying matter, sandalwood and sewage and burning oil—the scent of an Indian bazaar.

The noises fell away and at last the cart stopped with a creaking jolt, and there were more voices. Rough voices, angry voices, shrill voices, whispering voices; and then the stout cloth that was bound over the end of the cart was unfastened, and the four dazed, semi-conscious women were dragged out to stumble and fall to the ground, their legs giving way under them.

There was a man with a drawn sword in his hand, shouting, and another man with a musket, and Winter thought numbly: 'They are going to kill us,' but it seemed a matter of supreme indifference. And then someone ran to her and lifted her, and the voices and the lights and the shouting men spun together in a circle and turned into darkness.

VII

THE GULAB MAHAL

38

WINTER awoke to find herself lying on a low bed in a strange room. It was still dark, but the greying sky beyond the window gave enough light to show the outline of the room.

She felt cleaner and cooler than she had felt for a very long time. It must have been raining again. She lifted her aching head with difficulty and saw the dark shape of an earthenware pitcher on the pale-coloured matting on the floor, and the sight of it reawoke her raging thirst. She groped for it and lifted it and drank, and drank again, as if she could never drink enough; and lay back and tried to think, and found that she could not.

She could think of nothing at all. A grey fog of utter hopelessness filled her mind, and she closed her eyes and lay still, feeling that greyness engulf her. Alex had gone—everything had gone. There was nothing to live for any more—not even Lottie.

The light brightened slowly, turning from the first pallid whisper of dawn to the clear glow that precedes the sunrise, and the silence gave place to familiar sounds; faint and few at first, but gathering in number and volume. A rustle and a twitter of birds and the hoarse cawing of a grey-headed plains crow: the chatter of a squirrel and the creak of a well-wheel: a conch blowing in a distant temple and a *muezzin* crying the call to prayer from the minaret of a mosque, *Prayer is more than sleep —than sleep!* Minas whistling and parrots talking, a ring-dove cooing softly and monotonously, and a distant murmur of voices.

The brightening light beat against her closed eyelids and the grey fog in her brain lifted and shredded away like mist drifting off the river in the early morning, and slowly and almost imperceptibly the pain in her heart lessened and peace took its place.

She felt but did not see the first dazzling rim of the sun lip the edge of the far horizon, but the glow beyond her closed eyes brightened and she opened them on the same vision that she had seen once before when she had lain in the river by the Hirren Minar and had wished for death. The rose-pink sky and the formal patterns of leaves and flowers and birds. The vision that had once before drawn her back from despair, and the dream that had glowed before her mind's eye for so many cold years . . . the moon out of reach.

But this time it was real. This was the Gulab Mahal!

She lay quite still, not stirring; barely breathing. Thinking confusedly that she was asleep—or dead. It could not be true! When at last she moved it was to stretch out a hand and touch the green parrot on the wall beside her.

Firishta—it was Firishta! The old, long-forgotten name from her childhood returned to her. So he was not a real bird after all. She had thought that they were real—the flowers and trees and birds who lived and moved against a rose-pink sky. They were not alive and they had never been alive. They were carved and moulded in painted and polished plaster. Why had she not remembered that? But it was still Firishta; and it was, incredibly, wonderfully, the Gulab Mahal!

She was safe at last. She had come home.

From somewhere in the distance there came the sound of gunfire, but she did not hear it. She rose and walked slowly about the room in a waking dream, running her hands over the dear familiar flower patterns; caressing the painted birds and beasts. She did not know that this was the room in which she had been born and in which Sabrina had died. She only knew that every foot of it was familiar and beloved. She saw the crescent-shaped shadow steal across the floor, and remembered it too, and did not fear it as Sabrina had done, for it was linked with love.

She did not know how she had come there, or know that it was the Talukdar of Pari's determination to play safe that had been responsible. The Talukdar was a cautious man, and in the unlikely event of the British returning to power he did not wish it to be said that he had sent his captives to certain death. He must cover himself, and he remembered what his men had told him of the woman who was no *Angrezi* and who claimed kinship with the wife of Walayat Shah of Lucknow. He would send them to the care of Walayat Shah, and thus his hands would be clean. Walayat Shah might spare the woman if she were indeed blood-kin to his wife, and although he would undoubtedly hand over the remainder of the party to those who would make a public spectacle of their death, the woman at least would be able to testify that he, the Talukdar, had only acted for the best.

The heavy curtain over the doorway rustled and lifted, and Winter turned at the sound and saw that it was Ameera. They clung to each other and wept and did not speak for a long time, and then Ameera had held her off at arms' length and looked at her.

'It is true then!' said Ameera. 'I thought it a dream. So thou hast come home—but in no auspicious hour. Dost thou know that I have spent the night upon my knees before my husband, begging for thy life and for the lives of those with thee? He would have turned all from the door, but Hamida was in the courtyard and she saw thee and ran to me. At first I did not believe; and then I knew that it could be no chance that brought thee here. This surely was written. For hadst thou come two days ago, or even one, I could not have saved thee. My husband was hot against thy people, and he hates them still and would rid himself of all whom the Talukdar of Pari sent hither. But because of the word that was brought from Cawnpore, he will hold his hand.'

So it was Sophie who had saved them—Sophie and all those women who had died in such fear and agony in the *Bibigarh*. And if Sophie had known that the manner of her death would play a decisive part in saving Alex Randall's life she would, being Sophie, have for her part been content to die.

For all the captives from Pari had arrived at the Gulab Mahal, though they had been brought for safety's sake by different roads. And all had been given shelter, for Walayat Shah, who had at first refused to take the responsibility of sheltering men whom he would gladly have seen dead, had listened to Ameera's pleading and remembered Cawnpore. He had had no thought of gaining from it, as the Talukdar had had. It did not occur to him that by giving them shelter he might claim immunity and reward from the army that was known to have defeated the Nana Sahib and retaken Cawnpore. He looked upon it quite simply as a penance laid upon him by God that he should risk his own life, and that of his sons and the whole household, in order to protect the lives of a weary handful of hated *feringhis*. He knew that if it should become known in the city that he was housing these people their lives, and probably his own, would not be worth a moment's purchase. Yet he took them in.

They were lodged in a secluded wing of the Rose Palace, adjoining the zenana quarters. The rooms were hot and cramped, but the one on the ground floor, allotted to Lou, Mrs. Hossack, Miss Keir and the two children, gave on to a large private garden that was separated from the rest of the gardens by a high wall, and was full of orange and loquat trees and a tangle of roses and jasmine. Six of the men shared a room immediately above it, while above that again, reached by a steep narrow stair, was an isolated square of roof, screened from the view of the zenana roofs by a wall and a pavilion that enclosed one end of it, where they had put Alex, who, as a sick man, it had been thought best to segregate from the others instead of having him share their cramped quarters—Walayat Shah having no desire to find all his unwelcome guests falling sick.

A split-cane *chik* hung over the open side of the little pavilion by day, and it was appallingly hot, but the gruelling heat of the day was compensated for by the coolness it afforded by night, and Alex lay there day after day on a narrow charpoy, listening by the hour to the firing as the siege of the Residency dragged on, and longing, as he had done in the first days at the Hirren Minar, to be gone—and for news.

Winter had been given Sabrina's room as by right, and she had begged that Lou might share it instead of being penned in the far smaller apartment on the ground floor with Mrs. Hossack and Janet Keir. Three of the most trusted servants of the household had been put in charge of the *feringhis*, who had been given native dress to wear in place of their own ragged garments, and were not permitted to go even into the secluded garden except between sunset and dawn. They were kept in complete segregation from the other inhabitants of the Gulab Mahal, and they had little fault to find with this, for they lived in daily and hourly fear of discovery and death. They knew that it was not in Walayat Shah's power to protect them should their lives be demanded by the rabble, and they felt safer behind closed doors and in each other's company, despite the heat and the cramped quarters.

The continuous rattle of musketry, punctuated by the boom of guns, came clearly to their ears all day and for a large part of every night, and was both a continual reminder to them of the peril in which they stood, and that they were not the only British in Lucknow. They could hear the crash of exploding mines as the mutineers tunnelled towards the defences of the Residency and the stubborn beleaguered garrison ran out counter-mines and blew up their galleries; and whenever there was a lull in the firing they shuddered and waited and prayed for it to begin again, fearing that silence might mean that the Residency had fallen at last.

The garrison in the Residency had numbered barely a thousand combatant British and seven hundred loyal Indian troops when the crisis had arisen, and they were hampered by the presence of well over a thousand women, children and non-combatants, as well as by lack of adequate food, by sickness and appalling problems of sanitation and the disposal of the dead. The position they held had never been intended for purposes of defence. The hurriedly constructed and inadequate fortifications were flimsy in the extreme, and the forces surrounding it numbered twelve thousand fighting men, many of them British-trained sepoys, backed by the rabble of the city. It could not have withstood a single concerted assault that had been pressed home, but the mutineers possessed no leader of real ability. The attacks were never delivered in sufficient strength, and the siege dragged on.

Alex had made one unexpected friend in the Gulab Mahal: Dasim Ali, uncle of Juanita's husband, Wali Dad, and great-uncle of Ameera who was first cousin to Winter de Ballesteros.

Dasim Ali was now an elderly gentleman whose beard was dyed scarlet with henna, and his shrewish wife, Mumtaz, was the senior lady of the pink palace. Mumtaz was as bitter against all *feringhis* as Walayat Shah, and disliked her husband's great-niece Ameera as much for her foreign blood as for her beauty. But Dasim Ali was a placid and pleasant person who harboured no bitterness towards anyone—except on occasions towards God, who had granted him no sons.

He had wandered up one evening to the roof-top where Alex lived, and had looked vaguely surprised at finding it tenanted by a sick man. He had not realized in the dusk that this was one of the *feringhis*, and would probably not have realized it even in the daylight. He had greeted Alex courteously, and when it had finally dawned upon him whom he was addressing, he had been pleased to be amused.

After that he paid frequent visits to Alex's roof-top, and they would discuss a multitude of subjects from a point of view that would not have occurred to the average Westerner, and Dasim Ali would bring Alex the news of the city and the progress of the siege, together with such scraps of news as trickled in from beyond the borders of Oudh.

Winter too made friends in the Gulab Mahal, and she was the only one who went freely to the women's quarters. Dressed in Ameera's clothes and wearing Ameera's jewels, with her blue-black hair in a heavy plait and her slim feet bare or in a pair of Ameera's flat, curl-toed slippers, she would have passed anywhere as an Indian woman of good family, or from the hills, where women's skins are fairer than they are in the hot plains. Even Dasim Ali's sour and shrewish wife ended by grudgingly accepting her presence, and had even condescended to instruct her in the art of making a certain sticky sweetmeat of which the children of the Gulab Mahal were particularly fond.

Once again, after so many years, sitting on the zenana roof in the twilight, Winter heard the old familiar stories of her childhood told to those children, as Aziza Begum had once told them to her. And as she listened she heard too the ugly sound of gunfire from the beleaguered Residency, and was disturbed by conflicting emotions.

'Mrs. Hossack says she wonders how I can endure to be friends with them, when their people are killing our people,' she confided to Alex, sitting on his roof-top one hot evening. She had carried up a strange brew made from herbs that Hamida had assured her was invaluable for those recovering from dysentery and fever, and having stood over him while he drank it under protest, had stayed talking to him in the twilight.

Mrs. Hossack's observation had evidently worried her, for after an interval of silence she returned to it: 'It is not that I forget what is happening to my own people. I could not forget it, even if I wanted to, while I can hear the firing and know that every time I hear it it may mean that someone in the Residency is dying. But—but that doesn't make any difference to the way I feel about Ameera and the others. Mrs. Hossack says it should. She hates them all. I know it is different for her. They—their people—killed her husband, and the three other children died. But . . .'

She stopped, her brows puckered in a frown, unable to explain how it was that she could feel so friendly and at ease with these women while at the same time be tortured by hope and fear and a burning anxiety for all those of her own blood who were stubbornly defending themselves in the wreck of the Residency.

Alex said dryly: 'It is considered a patriotic duty in time of war to hate every member of the nation one is fighting against, and we only remember the injunction to love our enemies and do good to those who hate us when those enemies are safely defeated!'

'But Mrs. Hossack——' began Winter.

T*

'Mrs. Hossack, poor woman,' said Alex, 'will remember the death of her husband and children, and the cause of it, until the day she dies. What she will not remember is that thousands of the race who killed them have stood by us, and died for doing it. There are not only white people in the Residency, Winter. There are Indian troops too, and Indian servants who could escape death and disease and starvation by deserting to their own people, but who are staying to help a handful of British to hold out, and who will be considered traitors to their own side and butchered without mercy if the Residency falls. There is no particular merit in fighting for your own skin when you know that it is fight or die, but there is considerable merit in being prepared to die when you know you can escape quite easily. Put at its lowest, there is a certain stubborn, pig-headed heroism in that.'

Winter turned to look out over the trees and the roof-tops to the fantastic fretted silhouette of mosques and palaces, dark now against a darkening sky, and after a moment or two she said: 'What will happen in the end?'

'That depends on what you mean by the end.'

'When all this has ended. Will we hold it for always?'

'No,' said Alex, turning over on his back and looking up at a frieze of fruit-bats who flapped silently overhead on their way to the orchards and gardens of the villas that fringed the crowded city.

'Why? Why do you say that?'

Alex considered the question for a moment and then said reflectively: 'A hundred years ago this country was a collection of quarrelling, warring, petty kingdoms, for ever at each other's throats. The Company—or Clive—put a stop to that, and we've been making a nation out of it ever since. We've done it in our own interests, because you can't mix profitable trading with continued uproar; but also because, as a nation, we cannot resist moving in and showing someone how to run his affairs when we see them being run damned badly. We regarded this country as being in a deplorable mess, and set out, fired by an entirely genuine and proselytizing zeal as much as the desire for profit, to put our neighbour's house in order and to hand on what we con-

sider to be the blessings of civilization. Which is why we have
managed to combine conquest with a pleasant glow of self-
righteousness. But once we have welded India into a more solid
whole it will become increasingly difficult to hold on to it.'

'Is that a prophecy?' enquired Winter with a smile.

'No. It's common sense. It's too large a country. Bacon once
wrote something to the effect that if a handful of people, with
the greatest courage and policy in the world, grasped too large an
extent of territory, it might hold for a time, but it would fail
suddenly. He was right.'

'What about America?' demanded Winter.

'There weren't so many Americans in America,' said Alex
lazily. 'All they'll have to do there is to exterminate the original
owners, or pen them up in smaller and smaller reservations. But
India happened to be very well stocked with Indians.'

Winter got up and went to lean on the parapet, looking down
on the garden below. The scent of dust and the sharp smell of
wood-smoke rose through the hot, still air, and there were
rockets going up into the darkening sky over the city, for it was
Bakr Id. From somewhere in the zenana quarter a woman was
singing to a *sitar*; the words quite clear in the quiet evening—
as clear as the crack of shots from the Residency. . .

> . . . *Wae nadani ki waqt-e-marg*
> *Yhi sabit hua*
> *Khwab tha jo kuch ki dekha jo*
> *Suna afsani tha.*

Winter said: '*Nani*—Ameera's grandmother—used to sing that.
"*Alas we were all ignorant and only at the time of our death was it
proved that whatever we had seen was all a dream, and whatever
we had heard was a short tale.*" It is a song that was sung long
before Plassey was fought. This is such an old country——'

'No, it isn't,' said Alex. 'It's new. As new as—as Russia, if
you like.'

Winter turned to smile at him in the dusk. 'Now you are just
arguing for the sake of argument!'

'No, I'm not. Anything that has such tremendous possibilities and horizons is new. We are old. You can predict more or less what will happen to us. But you cannot predict what will happen to her. She has lain fallow for centuries—they still use the same methods of ploughing and irrigation that they used when we were wearing skins and living in caves! They've gone to seed. But seed if it's ploughed into the ground produces something new. Think of what they could do! We've started them off again—ploughed them in, if you like. They'll hate us for it, but they wouldn't have done anything for another hundred years or so if left to themselves. We've tried to go too quickly and force our way of life on them, but in a hundred years from now—or two hundred, or three—their history may well show that Plassey wasn't an end or a defeat, but a beginning. Even this that is happening now was probably needed.'

Winter turned quickly from the parapet and came to stand at the foot of his bed. '*Needed?* Why, Alex?—why? You can't say that something as horrible and as cruel as this was needed! Mrs. Hossack and that child of hers, and that child's grandchildren, will remember some of the things that have been done. And so will Ameera's children! They'll go on hating.'

'Perhaps,' said Alex. 'Though for ourselves we are poor haters, and we have short memories. But I cannot believe that this revolt will not mean the end of the Company. I believe that the Crown will have to take over now, and if that happens it is going to mean an enormous stride forward as far as India is concerned. This may mean as much as Plassey. More!'

'And when we go?' said Winter.

'When we go Hinduism will probably come into its own again, and if they aren't careful the country will drift back into an Eastern version of the Balkans—in which case Russia may well win the game after all! But one thing at least we can be certain of, and that is that all this that is happening now will not be regarded by them as a mutiny, but as a heroic War of Liberation; and because they are a young country they will deny their own atrocities and make political capital out of the reprisals, and the truth—which is neither black nor white—will be lost. But I shall have been dead a long time before then. And so will you! Here come the rest of the castaways—unless it's old Dasim.'

There was a sound of footsteps and low voices on the narrow stair-shaft that led up to the roof, and then Carlyon was there, scowling at the sight of Winter and Alex talking together, and Mr. Dobbie and the others followed behind him, coming up to breathe the cooler air now that the light was fading.

Arthur Carlyon was a handsome man and the Mussulman garb he wore suited his tall broad-shouldered figure, and Alex lay and watched him as he stood by the parapet talking to Winter, their figures outlined sharply against the green sky in which the first stars floated palely, and disliked him with an intensity and thoroughness that he had not thought himself capable of. But Winter had lost her fear of Carlyon, and—if she had thought about it at all—had forgiven him. What he had done, or tried to do, belonged to the shadowy past and was completely unimportant. They had all passed through too much, and a yawning, unbridgeable gulf seemed to divide them from the life they had lived before the *Shaitan ka hawa*—the Devil's wind—had roared across India in the heat of May. Only the present was real, and even that possessed a dream-like unreality that was typified, thought Alex, by the two figures who stood against the darkening sky—an Eastern prince and princess; graceful, oriental, formalized; an illustration by a Persian court painter to a story from the *Arabian Nights*—Prince Ahmed and the Fairy Pari-Banou, who were, or had been, Baron Carlyon of Tetworth and Mrs. Conway Barton.

Even Lou added no touch of reality to those days. The brittle, acid, fast-living, hard-drinking Mrs. Josh Cottar of Lunjore had vanished without trace, and in her place was an anxious-eyed woman who looked ten or even twenty years older than that other Mrs. Cottar, and who appeared to think of nothing but the welfare of a tiny, placid infant with a fuzz of red hair and round, solemn blue eyes.

'Lou,' said Alex crossly one evening, 'you are getting to be a

dead bore over that baby! I have it on the best authority—
O'Dwyer's—that she isn't smiling at you. It's wind.'

'Dr. O'Dwyer doesn't know what he's talking about,' said
Lou calmly. 'Of course she's smiling at me. She knows me.'

'So she ought to. You never leave the wretched child alone
for five minutes. What is Josh going to say to this?'

'I don't know,' said Lou. And she might just as well have
said 'I don't care.' 'There, Alex—she *is* smiling.'

'Take it away,' said Alex irritably. 'It smells of sick. And so
do you, Lou!'

He was abominably bad-tempered in those days, and Winter
put it down to the natural irritability of convalescence.

He had recovered to a reasonable extent, but he did not move
from the pavilion on the roof, for the fever had an unpleasant
habit of returning at unexpected intervals and he could not seem
to get free of it. Also he preferred being left alone to being sent
down to join the other men in a room on the lower floor. He
considered that he saw quite enough of them as it was. They
were allowed to come up to his roof on most evenings, as it was
thought to be safer for them there than in the garden, and the
women would usually join them for an hour or so.

There were only three women now—four, if one counted
Lottie's daughter. Miss Keir had never recovered from that
nightmare journey in the covered cart. Her mind had given way,
and her health had already been seriously affected by the priva-
tions she had endured in the weeks before her arrival at Pari.
She had lingered on for a few days and died one hot night within
a week of their arrival at the Gulab Mahal, and Lou Cottar had
moved into Mrs. Hossack's room in her place.

Lou had said that it was because Mrs. Hossack was afraid of
being alone, but Winter confided to Alex that she thought Lou
had made the exchange because Mrs. Hossack, as the mother of
four, was a mine of information on the subject of babies and
could be relied upon to give helpful advice should any infantile
crisis threaten Amanda.

'Lou of all people!' said Alex morosely. 'I should have said that she was as unmaternally minded as a goldfish, yet here she is, reduced to a state of crooning imbecility in a mere matter of weeks! I am beginning to think that I made a great mistake in assisting that infant to get born. It will be a lesson to me to mind my own business in future.'

He turned on his elbow to look at Winter, and said disagreeably: 'I don't see you making much fuss over the creature. Are you devoid of any maternal instinct, Mrs. Barton?'

'No,' said Winter, giving the matter thought. 'But you see, it isn't my baby.'

'It isn't Lou's,' said Alex.

'Yes, it is. Lottie gave it to her.'

'And I wonder,' said Alex unpleasantly, 'what Edward English's parents are going to say to that?'

It was a thought that frequently worried Lou. Supposing that Edward's parents demanded the child?

'They can't have her!' thought Lou. 'She's mine! They *couldn't* take her——'

She lay awake at night worrying about it, when she was not worrying about the child's health. Amanda's health need not have given her so much anxiety. The tiny creature throve and gained weight and ceased to wail and whimper. It was in fact a remarkably placid baby, and as babies go a very pretty one. Lou adored it.

'Has she been christened?' asked Mrs. Hossack one day.

'*Christened?*' Lou looked up from bathing Amanda in a small metal basin. 'No, of course not. How could she be?'

'There's Mr. Dobbie,' said Mrs. Hossack. 'He could do it. She should be christened. It's safer.'

'Safer? What do you mean, *safer*?' demanded Lou impatiently.

'Supposing she should get ill, and die—you would not want her not to be saved,' said Mrs. Hossack.

Lou had glared at her, clutching the child. 'She isn't going to die! What nonsense you talk, Ida!'

But the thought of having the child christened had taken possession of her. Not because she paid any attention to Mrs.

Hossack's lugubrious view, or that she believed that an unbaptized child would be refused admittance into Heaven. It was the thought of Edward English's parents that weighed with Lou. They might have their own ideas as to names. The child was going to be christened Amanda, and also Cottar. The surname of English would be hers by law.

Fired with this idea Lou had approached Mr. Dobbie, who had instantly agreed to perform the ceremony. Lou had long ago cut up her petticoat and various other articles of underwear to make napkins and other necessities for the child, and now she made a christening robe from her pantalettes and saw nothing humorous in the action.

Amanda Cottar English was christened 'in the presence of this congregation' on Alex's roof in the late evening; Alex, Winter and Mrs. Hossack standing as godparents. The ceremony brought a considerable portion of relief to Lou. It seemed to make Amanda more her own, and the claims of the misty and far-away Englishes—Lou was not aware that Edward had been orphaned for several years—faded and became less alarming.

But its repercussions were unexpected.

39

THE fact that there was a clergyman available who was qualified to perform Holy Offices had dawned suddenly upon Lord Carlyon.

It was surprising that it had not done so before, for Mr. Dobbie had held frequent services ever since their arrival; but it had not occurred to any of them that he could also officiate at other ceremonies of the Church. It did so now, and Carlyon had managed to get Winter to himself in the garden two evenings later.

It had rained heavily that day, but now the skies were clear

and the garden smelt fresh and fragrant in the dusk. They
had all gone out to walk under the orange trees, because Alex
had suffered a relapse and had been feverish all day, and Dr.
O'Dwyer had decreed that he must have quiet.

Moonlight had filled the garden with pale shadows before the
last of the twilight had faded, and Carlyon had stood among the
orange trees and once again asked Winter to marry him. Not
at some future date when they could escape from this house and
from Lucknow—if they should ever escape—but now, at once.
Tonight or tomorrow. Dobbie could marry them . . .

'I haven't anything to offer you now. I'm just a penniless
prisoner. But when we get away it will be different. Then I
can——'

Winter put a hand on his arm, checking him. 'Don't! Please
don't!' Her voice was quick and distressed and her face in the
soft moonlight was troubled. 'If—if I loved you it wouldn't
matter if you could never give me anything but yourself. But
I don't, and I cannot marry you.'

'Why? Why not? You need someone to look after you; to
protect you. I would take care of you. I love you—I can't live
without you! What does it matter whether you love me now or
not? You would one day. I could make you. Barton is dead.
Give me the right to take care of you. Winter—Winter——'

He had caught her hand, and she drew back quickly: 'I'm
sorry. I cannot. Thank you for—for wanting to, but——'

She seemed to think the words were inadequate, and stood
before him twisting her hands together as though she were trying
to think of something less hollowly polite and baldly negative.
But the moonlight showed him that there was a sudden abstracted
look in the wide, black-lashed eyes, and he was seized with an
angry and wounding conviction that she was not thinking of him
at all, but of something or someone else.

He reached out and caught her hand again, gripping it by the
wrist in a hard grasp that she could not break, and said hoarsely:
'Is there anyone else? Is that why you won't marry me? It was
Barton before. Who is it now? Is it Randall? I've seen the way

you look at him sometimes! You were in the jungle with him for weeks, weren't you?'

His rage boiled up until it seemed that it must choke him. Some part of his brain, standing coldly aloof—some part of the bored and cynical Arthur Carlyon of the London drawing-rooms —told him that he was making a vulgar, jealous and melodramatic scene; but he could not stop himself.

'It is Randall, isn't it? What is he to you? Are you his mistress? Do you spend your nights with him on that roof? Is that why you persuaded your black relatives to let him sleep up there instead of with us?'

He saw the shadowy reflection of a succession of emotions cross the face that the strengthening moonlight threw into sharp relief against the darkness of the orange trees: disgust, anger, contempt, and finally—and surprisingly—pity. As though she could understand the cruel pain that was responsible for that torrent of insult, and could sympathize with it. She stood quite still, waiting for him to finish, her eyes grave and steady. But it was the pity in them that hurt most and which drove him to the final stupidity.

He released her wrist and caught her swiftly into his arms as he had done once before in Delhi, and kissed her with violence and savagery. Kissed her mouth and eyes and throat again and again and as though he could not stop.

She had not struggled or cried out. Perhaps she had known that it would have done little good to do either. She had stood entirely still, enduring his bruising kisses as though she had been a lay figure without life or emotions, and her very immobility had brought him to his senses as nothing else could have done. He released her at last and stood back from her, breathing in hard gasps. She had not spoken, and after a moment she had turned and walked unhurriedly away between the orange trees of the walled garden, her pale-coloured Indian dress showing like a moth among the shadows, and the Indian jewellery she wore making a soft chinking sound that died away into the dusk.

Mrs. Hossack, who was walking up and down with her small son in her arms, said: 'Mrs. Barton, I wanted to ask you if——'

But Winter had passed her without hearing her and had gone into the house and up the long narrow flight of stairs. She drew the muslin veil over her head and across her face as Ameera and the other women did on the rare occasions on which they moved outside the women's quarters, and passed along a narrow enclosed verandah and up the final flight of stairs that led to the roof where Alex lay.

The moonlight and the last touch of twilight made the open roof seem very bright after the dark passages and stairways, and the rain had cooled it so that it smelt pleasantly of washed stone.

Alex's bed had been dragged out into the open, presumably by Dr. O'Dwyer. He was lying on it with his back to her, wearing only the scanty cotton loincloth that alone made the heat of the day bearable, and his body looked painfully thin and very brown against the pale-coloured *resai* that did duty as a mattress. He heard the chink of Winter's jewellery but he did not turn, and she came to stand beside him, looking down at him and wondering if he were asleep. After a moment or two, as she did not speak, he said ungraciously: 'Well, what is it?'

The irritation in his voice gave her a sudden qualm, and for a moment her resolution faltered. Her hands gripped together tightly and she took a deep breath and forced herself to speak calmly:

'Alex, will you marry me?'

Alex did not move for an appreciable time, and then he turned slowly and looked up at her. It seemed to him that there was a tight band made of some hot metal round his forehead, and he could not think at all clearly.

'What did you say?'

'I asked you if you would marry me,' said Winter steadily. 'Why?'

She sat down on the edge of the low bed and as she did so the muslin veil slipped back and off her shoulders, and the clear moonlight showed red marks on her throat. The hand she raised to catch at the veil was bruised too about the wrist with the plain prints of the brutal grip that had held it.

Alex reached out and caught her hand, holding it with thin hot fingers, and looked at those marks; and Winter noticing them for the first time jerked it quickly away.

Alex said thickly: 'Carlyon?'

'Yes. No. I mean—it doesn't matter.'

He sat up and found that it tightened the band about his head by several notches. It should surely be impossible to feel so ill and so angry at one and the same time? Separately perhaps, but not together. He said: 'Yes, I'll marry you. And what's more, I'll do it now. Go and tell Dobbie I want to see him. And wait a minute—give me some of that opium——'

Winter never knew what he had said to Mr. Dobbie, but whatever it was it appeared to have persuaded Mr. Dobbie to accede to the unexpected request for an immediate marriage. Lou knew, for Lou had come in search of Winter and had heard a murmur of voices from the roof. She had almost reached the top of the stairs when she had heard Alex say: 'Very well, then. I'll have her without. And you can take that on your conscience! It won't be on mine.'

Lou had turned round and come down again, looking thoughtful.

*   *   *

Winter had been married at night and by moonlight, as Sabrina had been. And like Sabrina, with no preparation at all and in a wedding-dress that did not even belong to her.

She would have worn Ameera's scarlet-and-gold wedding-dress with its wonderful fringed and tasselled head-veil, but out of deference to the doubtful and anxious Mr. Dobbie she had worn instead a dress of heavy white silk, yellowed by the years and scented with the neem leaves and tobacco in which it had been kept, that had belonged to Ameera's mother, Juanita de Ballesteros.

There had been a lace mantilla too; once white and now as yellow as the silk and as fragile as the lace on the wedding-dress that had been Anne Marie's and which Sabrina had worn when she married Juanita's brother, Marcos, in the chapel of the Casa de los Pavos Reales twenty years ago. It had in fact been the self-same mantilla that her mother had worn on that night, though Winter did not know it.

The moon that looked down on that strange wedding looked down also on the ruined, looted, burned-out shell of the Casa de los Pavos Reales and the blackened, grass-grown paving-stones of the terrace where Marcos and Sabrina had stood together on that other moonlight night to watch their guest ride away. But the scent of the orange-blossom and the lemon-trees remained, and was as sweet on the hot air as it had been on that long-ago night.

The scent of orange-blossom rose too from the walled gardens of the Rose Palace, and reached the flat roof-top where Winter stood in Juanita's white dress and felt Alex's parched, fever-hot fingers push a heavy ring of beaten gold and silver on to the finger that had once worn Kishan Prasad's glowing emerald. The ring too had been one of Juanita's, a gift from her mother Anne Marie, for none of the Europeans had possessed such a thing— any trinkets they might have had having been either taken from them or parted with in exchange for food long ago.

Alex had worn Mussulman dress, borrowed for the occasion from Dasim Ali, and had only managed to keep on his feet with the assistance of opium and one of the pillars that divided his room from the roof. He had stood with his back to it, and had looked so entirely un-English in the moonlight that poor worried Mr. Dobbie had suffered yet another qualm.

But to Winter there had been nothing strange about this wedding. It was the fulfilment of the promise that the Gulab Mahal had always stood for—that old Aziza Begum had given to her and Zobeida reaffirmed so often—that once she returned to it, all would be well.

She stood in the warm white moonlight and looked down at a ring that had once been Anne Marie's as once, long ago and on just such a night, Sabrina too had done. And like Sabrina she was suddenly aware of an uplifting sense of timelessness—as if all

Time were one, and she would live for ever in the future in Alex's children and hers, as she lived in the past with Marcos and Sabrina; with Johnny and Louisa . . .

But her wedding had not ended peacefully as Sabrina's had done.

They had all been gathered there on the roof, their shadows black in the moonlight, and the fantastic skyline of the Lucknow palaces like a purple pattern at their backs: Lou Cottar and Mrs. Hossack, Captain Garrowby, Dr. O'Dwyer, Mr. Climpson, Mr. Lapeuta and Lord Carlyon. Even Ameera and Hamida had been there, standing in the darkness behind the lowered *chiks* that screened the interior of the pavilion from the roof, in deference to the fact that Ameera was in *purdah* and could not be seen by strange men.

The guests had come forward to offer congratulations and good wishes at the end of the brief ceremony, and Carlyon had confronted Winter and said in a deliberate drawl: 'Am I permitted the privilege of kissing the bride?'

Alex said: 'Not in future,' and hit him.

It had been luck more than strength or science, and rage more than luck, that had caused the blow to send Carlyon sprawling, for although Alex had recovered a good deal of his strength, the fever had once again drained an appreciable amount of it from him during the past twenty-four hours.

Carlyon had come to his feet, white with fury, and had returned the blow with a good deal more science and considerably more strength before the remainder of the wedding guests had rushed in to separate them. Alex had been unable to defend himself, for the well-meaning Mr. Dobbie had leapt at him, catching his arm, and Winter had turned and clung to the other. Carlyon's clenched fist had taken Alex under the jaw and he had fallen between them as though he had been pole-axed, hitting the back of his head on an angle of the pillar as he fell, and had not recovered consciousness for some considerable time.

'Men!' said Lou furiously. 'As if we were not in enough trouble already! Now they'll try and kill each other as soon as they get the chance! You'd think there was enough fighting going on without—— Oh God! *Men!*'

Winter spent her second wedding night, as she had spent her first, in tears and terror. But this time it was on her bridegroom's behalf and not on her own.

Alex's own recollections of the night were hazy. His head hurt abominably, his jaw ached, his body burned with fever and his parched mouth was full of blood from a cut that his teeth had made in his tongue. Somebody periodically gave him water to drink and persuaded him to spit out the blood instead of swallowing it, and someone else—or the same person—put a pleasantly cool and aromatic-smelling compress on his forehead and changed it at intervals.

The fever had lessened towards morning, and he had fallen asleep at last and had not wakened until the sun was hot on the roof. And then it had been Lou who had been standing by one of the pillars in the pavilion, peering through the slats of the *chik* and listening to the crackle of rifle-fire and the boom of guns that had been silent during the past night but had begun again with the dawn.

She had turned when she heard Alex move, and said anxiously: 'It sounds like a big attack. Listen to that! Are they *never* going to be relieved? We were told that tale about Havelock taking Cawnpore days and days ago, and Cawnpore is less than forty miles away. *Why* aren't they here?'

Alex dragged himself up and went to stand beside her. They could see the smoke from the cannonade hanging like a haze above the roofs and the tree-tops that hid the Residency, and he listened, as Lou had listened, and presently said: 'How long have we been here? Three weeks? or is it four? It feels like months. It must feel like years to them. Havelock *must* get through soon. Oh God, if only one could——'

He turned away with a groan and subsiding again on the edge of the low charpoy, closed his eyes and leant his aching head against the wall behind it. After a minute or two he opened them again and frowned at Lou:

'What are you doing here at this time of the morning, Lou? Got a sudden fit of the bore with that baby at last?'

'No,' said Lou. 'I promised your wife that if she'd go to sleep I'd see that you were all right.'

'My——?' said Alex, and stopped. 'Good God! Of course. Then I didn't dream the whole thing. I seem to remember hitting that bastard Carlyon—I'm sorry, Lou; I apologize.'

'He hit you a good deal harder,' said Lou with a grin.

'Did he?' Alex put up a hand and felt his bruised and swollen jaw tenderly. 'Hmm. He must have done. I don't seem to remember that. I thought something hit me on the back of the head.'

'It did. This pillar.'

Alex lowered himself cautiously back on to the folded *resai* and said: 'That accounts for it. I feel as though I'd been run into by a siege gun. What happened to—my wife?'

'I rather think she spent the night bathing your fevered brow,' said Lou. 'She doesn't seem to have much luck with her bridegrooms. Conway was filthy drunk.'

She saw the sudden black scowl that replaced the frown of pain on Alex's forehead, and said abruptly: 'You brought her out to him, didn't you? What possessed you to let her marry him? *You* knew what he was like.'

Alex said: 'Shut up, Lou. If you want to play at being Miss Nightingale you can give me some water. If you want to talk you can go away.'

Lou brought him food and water and prepared to depart, but with her hand on the *chik* she stopped and turned back.

'Alex——'

'What is it now?' demanded Alex ungraciously.

'Lord Carlyon . . .' Lou hesitated and bit her lip.

'What about him?'

'You won't—— Alex, we're all in the same boat! You know as well as I do that someone may give us away any day, and then— and then it will be all over with us. We've got to stay together, and that man has got a bad temper and not much control over it.

'I don't seem to have had much control over mine lately,' said Alex wryly.

'I know. But that's different. You wouldn't do anything that might jeopardize all of us just because you were in a rage. But he would. You don't know what a lot of nonsense he's been talking. About escaping from here.'

Alex turned his head and looked at her oddly, and she met the look and said with a twisted smile: 'Oh yes—I know you've thought of it too. We've all thought of it, if it comes to that! But we—the rest of us—have enough sense to see when we are well off and not do anything stupid. And we know that we don't need to escape. That we may be kept cooped up in two small rooms all day, but that it isn't to keep us prisoners. It's to keep us safe—and everyone else who lives in this house for that matter! If we really wanted to go away, they'd be thankful to be rid of us. But Lord Carlyon won't believe that, and he doesn't understand more than half a dozen words of Urdu. If he once got out of this place he'd be caught before he'd gone a hundred yards, and that might give us all away. So you see——'

Lou jerked restlessly at the edge of the *chik* and turned away to peer through it again, her back to Alex. He did not speak, and presently she said: 'He has only stayed quiet because of Winter. Because he's in love with her, and because we've told him—all of us—that it was safer for us to stay here than to take our chance outside; and safest of all for her because the Begum is her cousin. And he wouldn't leave unless he could take her with him. He asked her last night to marry him—did you know that? And then inside an hour she marries you instead and he has to watch. And then you knock him down!'

Alex still said nothing and Lou turned and faced him, her eyes desperate. 'Alex, *please!* Don't quarrel with him! Keep out of his way. Don't goad him into doing anything that may jeopardize all of us. Promise me you'll leave him alone?'

Alex said: 'Provided he leaves my wife alone.'

'Of course he will, now. But you can't expect him not to speak to her, and if you're going to hit him every time he does——'

'My dear Lou,' interrupted Alex wearily, 'at the moment I couldn't successfully hit a fly. No, of course I will not start another brawl! I must have taken leave of my senses to start one last night. But if you imagine that I am going to apologize to the man, you are wrong. Get on back to your baby, there's a good girl. My head is splitting and I can see six of you. And just at present one is more than enough.'

Lou had gone and Alex had lain on his back all through the gruelling heat of the day, and had thought as coherently as the pain in his head and desperate anxiety over the fate of the Residency garrison would permit.

Lou did not realize that there were only two things that had kept him from leaving the Gulab Mahal as soon as he was capable of walking, and that neither of them was what she had supposed. The first was the fact that a sick man was a liability and not an asset, and until he could rid himself of this damnably recurrent fever, and the weakness that went with it, it was infinitely more sensible to stay where he was. The second was Carlyon: Carlyon and Winter. Winter was safe enough—as safe as she would be anywhere at this time—with the occupants of the Gulab Mahal. But she was not safe from Carlyon.

He realized the sense of Lou's request, for they were none of them safe with Carlyon. Carlyon had an ugly and unpredictable temper and was altogether too autocratic and egotistical a person to be relied upon to exercise patience and play a waiting game. He knew little or nothing of India, and the little he knew had taught him to believe that all Indians were treacherous murderers, not one of whom was to be trusted. He refused to admit that the inmates of the Gulab Mahal were restricting his liberty and that of the other Europeans in order to save their lives. They were being kept prisoner, and would one day be handed over to provide a spectacle for the mob. Had not the fifty luckless captives in the dungeons of the King of Delhi—almost all of whom were women and children—been taken out and publicly slaughtered before a milling mass of spectators?

Carlyon had urged that they should attack the servants who

cared for their needs, overpower the adult males of the household, seize any weapons they could find in the house, and provided with arms, money and food, escape to Cawnpore where Havelock and his army were known to be encamped. He had produced other schemes, equally rash and impracticable, but he had been persuaded that any such attempts must expose the women and the two children to too great a risk, and he would not escape alone and leave Winter. And now Winter, to escape him, had married Alex Randall.

She must have been very frightened of Carlyon to have taken such a drastic step, thought Alex, staring up at the flaking plaster of the ceiling while the heat danced upon the open roof outside. What had the man done to her? Tried to rape her? Alex felt rage rise in him again at the thought and he turned over and buried his face in his arms.

Lou was right. He must keep from quarrelling with Carlyon. He had kept from doing it when they were in Delhi, and he could keep from doing it now. 'All in the same boat,' Lou had said. It was a leaky craft at best, and if two of its occupants started fighting in it they might well overturn it. As for Winter, now that she was his wife his name should be enough to protect her from any further insults from Carlyon. But he himself would have to continue to keep her at arm's length or they would be lost.

The fact that she was now his wife made no difference to that situation. It merely made it more difficult. They might be here, or on the run again, for months—perhaps a year—or more than a year. The garbled stories and rumours that Dasim Ali brought him were always more of successful risings than of defeats, and it was difficult to gain any clear picture of what was really happening in the outside world. If the whole of India was really in revolt it was going to take more than a few months of campaigning to reconquer it and restore order. Months, thought Alex, perhaps a year—perhaps longer . . . And he thought again of Lottie.

He could not forget Lottie. That appalling, agonizing day had burnt itself into his brain. Nature did not stand still for wars.

Lottie's baby had not delayed its arrival because of murder and massacre; they had merely hastened it. It had had to be born, and prematurely at that. And in the process it had killed Lottie far more painfully than any shot fired from a carbine, or any stroke from a sword.

If Alex had kept away that day, and kept out of earshot as he had meant to do, leaving her to the women, he might have felt differently about it, even though he would have returned to find her dead. Women did die in childbirth, too many of them. It was regrettable, but nothing—or very little it seemed—could be done about it.

But he had not kept away. He had stayed with Lottie instead, and he could not forget the torment she had endured before she died, or the fact that with proper medical care and attention, doctors, midwives, all the paraphernalia of modern medicine, she would probably have survived. But this was war. It was worse —civil war, rebellion, anarchy. There could be no safety any-where for any woman in the country until it was over. He could not run the risk of watching Winter die as Lottie had died, and for the first time he was grateful for the ill-health that would provide him with an excuse to keep her at arm's length.

The gunfire had continued for the greater part of the day with a fury that told of a large-scale attack upon the Residency, and an hour before noon the thunderous explosion of a mine shook the Gulab Mahal and disturbed the birds who were sheltering from the heat in the trees of the garden, sending them flapping and cawing up into the hot air.

Alex could hear the boom of the guns and the crash of the shells with shuddering clarity, and the shimmering heat of the roof-top seemed to vibrate to the sound and strike at his body with the same savage regularity as the sound itself struck through his throbbing head.

Was it just another attack on the Residency—or was it Have-lock at last? But it could not be Havelock. The city would have been in an uproar and there would have been fighting in the streets if the relieving force had arrived. This that he could hear was still fire that was being directed at and returned by the Residency.

'If only I could get away!' thought Alex. 'If only I could get news! How much longer can they hold out? How many of them are there left?' It was unbearable to lie there and listen to those sounds, knowing what they meant; knowing what it must be like inside the battered and beleaguered Residency; and to do nothing—nothing!

He had been brought a nauseous draught in the course of the afternoon by Rahim, the elderly, silent servant who looked after him. The Begum Sahiba had prepared it, said Rahim. Alex drank it to save argument, and it had relieved the pain in his head and eventually sent him to sleep. And so, for him, the day that marked the second serious assault on the Residency passed. And the flimsy defences still held.

But the hope of relief that the hard-pressed garrison had once expected hourly was receding. Havelock's army, which had crossed the border into Oudh in the last days of July and had subsequently fought and won two battles, had suffered heavy losses in the fighting, and finding their communications threatened by the Nana Sahib's forces had fallen back on Mangalwar to wait for reinforcements. Twice in early August Havelock had advanced again towards Lucknow, only to be checked; the first time by an outbreak of cholera, and later by the mutiny of the Gwalior contingent which had compelled him to secure his base and fall back on Cawnpore.

The news that the *feringhi* army was in retreat was received with wild rejoicings in Lucknow, and the position of the beleaguered garrison—and also of the handful of refugees in the Gulab Mahal—grew even more precarious. Many of the insurgents and a large proportion of the populace who had been daunted by the realization that an avenging army was almost within striking distance of the city, swung back to the wildest heights of optimism when it was learned that the enemy had not only been forced to retreat but were no longer within the borders of Oudh.

The sound of desultory firing from the direction of the Residency became an integral part of life in the Gulab Mahal: as familiar as the cawing of the grey-headed crows, the liquid cooing of the doves or the creak and squeak of the well-wheel. It was, to the fugitives, a comforting sound, for it told them that the garrison was still holding out; that the Residency had still not fallen.

There had been a third assault on the eighteenth of August. Alex had worked out the date and scratched it with a nail on the wall of the pavilion, and they had waited, all of them, with a tension that seemed to make it difficult to breathe, for the sound of musketry fire to start again after the silence that had followed the din of the assault. And hearing it had felt their nerves and muscles go slack with relief, and had breathed as though escaping from near suffocation. Three days later they had heard the thunderous crash of exploding gunpowder, and Dasim Ali had told Alex that evening that it was the work of the garrison, who had at last succeeded in blowing up Johannes House, a stronghold of the mutineers beyond the perimeter of the defence, from which a deadly cross-fire had been directed upon the Residency.

But the next day there had been another sound. The sound of gunfire from the south-east.

'By God!—they're here!' cried Alex, running to the parapet of the roof in the drumming, drenching downpour of the monsoon rains and straining to listen while the water poured off him in a warm torrent.

It could only mean one thing. Havelock was marching on Lucknow again. And presently, as the downpour ceased and a hot wind began to blow, the sound of those guns came clearly through the humid, clean-washed air.

They had heard them at intervals all that day and for much of the following one, and it occurred to Walayat Shah for the first time that perhaps God had been at his side when he had agreed to shelter those bedraggled fugitives for the sake of the dead of Cawnpore, and that perhaps because of it, he and his household would one day be saved from destruction. It was not a thought

that pleased him. Had it not been for his horror of the treachery
and the butchery of Cawnpore, he would have preferred to die
fighting the *feringhis* rather than to accept any favour from their
hands.

But they had heard Havelock's guns no more; nor any news
of what had happened to his army. And August dragged out its
slow length, and it was September. And still the dwindling,
dying, fever-racked garrison in the Lucknow Residency held out,
and still the torn rags of the Union Jack fluttered defiantly from
the flagstaff that had been shot down and replaced so often, and
at the cost of so many lives, on the topmost roof of the shattered
Residency.

40

It seemed to the fugitives in the Gulab Mahal that they had
lived in their hot, cramped quarters in the little pink stucco
palace in Lucknow for a lifetime.

Day succeeded day with an appalling, crawling monotony, and
nerves grew ragged and tempers flared. It needed very little
to touch off a furious quarrel and an exchange of blows between
the six men who passed the greater part of their time shut in
together in one small hot room where the floor space was largely
taken up by the cheap string cots on which they sat or lay for
most of the daytime, and on which they slept at night.

The lack of news from the outside world was the worst
affliction they suffered. The heat was endurable because of the
frequent downpours that roared off the roofs and gutters and
drenched the gardens, cooling the hot stone and turning the dust
to liquid mud where frogs croaked and winged ants hatched out
in drove after fluttering, crawling drove. The food was scanty,
for there was little money to spare for the feeding of a band of
Hell-doomed infidels, but it was enough, and the sanitary

arrangements, though primitive, were adequate. They were, compared with thousands of their fellow-countrymen, living in comfort and safety. But not to know what was happening to the garrison in the Residency, to Havelock's forces, to the regiments on the Ridge before Delhi, to the rest of India and the Empire of John Company, made the long days longer and frayed their nerves to breaking-point, and one night three of them, Captain Garrowby, Dr. O'Dwyer and Mr. Climpson, had climbed out of the enclosed garden, scaled the outer wall by standing on each other's shoulders, and vanished into the maw of the city.

They had told their plan to no one, for they realized that a small party stood a better chance of escape than a large one, and they considered that Lapeuta and Dobbie, both elderly and frail, were better off where they were, while Alex was not only still subject to occasional bouts of fever, but naturally could not be asked to consider abandoning his wife and leaving her in a city that might well soon be taken by assault. And they had had no intention of saddling themselves with Carlyon, who had done nothing to endear himself to any of them and whose ignorance of the language and the country, combined with his uncertain temper, would make his company a hazard to all of them.

Carlyon had stormed and raged when he had woken the next morning to find that they had gone, for he realized it might mean weeks if not months more of this enforced confinement for himself. He knew that he could not get far alone, for he could not speak one word of Urdu and had no knowledge of the city or the country surrounding it, or even in which direction to go in order to reach the British force.

Lou and Mrs. Hossack had been white with anxiety; Walayat Shah relieved, and Alex restless and either silent or curt to the point of rudeness.

But Captain Garrowby, Dr. O'Dwyer and Mr. Climpson had not gone far. They had kept together instead of taking the wiser course of separating, and they had lost their way in the maze of streets, so that dawn had found them still in the city. They had been stopped and questioned, and that afternoon they had been shot, and their bodies hung up by the heels for an encouragement to the mob.

Dasim Ali had brought Alex the news on the following evening. The men, he said, had been tortured first to make them tell where they had been hiding, for it was suspected from the state of their garments and their shoes that they must have been sheltering in the city itself and had not, as they claimed, entered it only that night. Moreover they had been captured trying to leave Lucknow and not to enter it.

They had died without divulging their hiding-place, but Walayat Shah and Dasim Ali's wife Mumtaz and others of the Gulab Mahal had been frightened and angry, and had taken immediate precautions to see that none of the remaining *feringhis* jeopardized them by escaping. That the three men had not betrayed them under torture did not mean that one of the others might prove less courageous if caught and subjected to similar treatment, and any more *feringhis* found in the city might lead to a house-to-house search. The doors were locked now at night, and the gardens patrolled, and what little liberty the fugitives had previously possessed was drastically curtailed.

To Lou and Mrs. Hossack, made selfish by fear for the safety and well-being of two small children, the loss of Dr. O'Dwyer meant more than the fact that all three men had been caught and killed, for Dr. O'Dwyer had been a tower of strength when colic or convulsions or any other infant ailments had threatened Jimmy Hossack or Amanda Cottar English, and now that he had gone their anxieties were doubled.

Neither Lou nor Mrs. Hossack would, at that time, have escaped from the Gulab Mahal if they could, and the death of the three men who had done so had only served to convince them that their greatest safety lay in staying where they were. But they hated the native dress they wore and the native food they ate; the monotony and the confinement. They quarrelled with regrettable frequency and got on each other's nerves to the point of desperation, and complained about each other to Winter.

Winter herself was far from happy in those days. She might

U

never have been married to Alex, and she was often tempted to wonder if that brief ceremony on the moonlit roof had ever taken place, or if she had only dreamt it.

She still slept and spent the greater part of each day in her own gaily painted room, and Alex still lived in the pavilion on the roof. She saw as little of him, or less, in these days as she had when they had first come to the Gulab Mahal. His manner to her was much as it had always been, and he did not appear to think that the fact that she was now his wife necessitated any change in the monotonous routine of their days.

She wondered if she had been mistaken in thinking that Alex cared for her. Had he after all only thought of her as he had thought of that auburn-haired actress whom he had taken home one night from a party at the Lunjore Residency? Would he ever have married her if she had not made him? He had never made any attempt to touch her or kiss her since the night that he had kissed her at the edge of the river, when they had fled from the fire, and she had been sure that he loved her. Had he only kissed her then from relief—because they were safe? The same relief that had made them all laugh together helplessly a moment later, despite the fact that they had been driven from the safe refuge of the Hirren Minar and were stranded in a strange jungle and within the hostile borders of Oudh?

Alex had recovered much of his former health, and the maddeningly recurrent bouts of fever left him at last, but Winter could not forget that he had been ill with fever on the night that she had asked him to marry her, or that he had been drugged with both fever and opium when he had actually done so. If he had been in full possession of his faculties, would he have consented to marry her? She began to wonder why he had ever agreed to do so, and if he had really not known what he was doing, and had subsequently regretted it.

It did not occur to her that Alex imagined that she had been frightened by Carlyon, and by some attack that Carlyon had made upon her, into taking the extreme step of asking him to marry her; for Carlyon's savage kisses had not frightened her in the least, and she had forgotten them long before the bruises they had left had faded. It had been Carlyon's disclosure that Mr. Dobbie was as qualified to perform a marriage service as a christening that had sent her straight to Alex, and it is doubtful if anyone or anything could have frightened her to the point of doing such a thing. To ask a man to marry you was shameless and unheard of, and possibly only in the case of the Queen of England, whom etiquette and protocol had compelled to propose marriage to the man of her choice instead of being in the gratifying position of hearing him propose to her.

Winter had had her own reasons for asking Alex to marry her instead of waiting in the hope that he might one day ask her himself, but she did not divulge them. Ameera and Hamida knew, and Lou guessed, but she did not ask any questions.

Winter did not even trouble to avoid Lord Carlyon. She saw very little of him, and that only in the company of the others, on the roof-top by starlight or moonlight, and in the walled garden at dusk and before sunrise. She was seen in the gardens with less and less frequency at dawn, but Alex did not think to enquire why she alone so rarely took advantage of those cooler early hours under the trees, and supposed that she slept late. Lately, on the few occasions when she had joined them, he thought that she looked tired and strained and that there were shadows under her eyes. But it was difficult to tell in the grey first light of the morning. They all looked ill and weary by that light, after the hot, restless nights.

Alex himself was silent and short-tempered these days. He knew that he was fit enough now to leave the Gulab Mahal without fear of being struck down by fever and weakness just when he needed his strength and his wits most. He knew that he should go and what he should do—as he had always known— and he was sure that Dasim Ali would help him to get safely away. But he could not bring himself to leave Winter while Carlyon was in this ugly, dangerous and unpredictable mood. He did not trust Carlyon, or the ability of any of the others to protect his wife. He told himself repeatedly that this was absurd, and that

Ameera alone, or Lou, would see to it that she came to no harm. But would the efforts of either of them—or any or all of the others—keep Carlyon's passions in check as Alex's mere presence could do, because he was Winter's husband? The opposing strains tugged and dragged at Alex's mind and his emotions, and he hated himself for not going. And could not go.

Carlyon for his part no longer regarded Alex with dislike, but with active hatred and a corroding resentment which was not only on Winter's account, but because of the greater degree of freedom and, above all, of privacy that Alex enjoyed. To Carlyon the enforced and continual company of two such men as Lapeuta and Dobbie was as near unbearable as made no matter. He had nothing whatever in common with either of them, and their views, their voices, their conversation and their mannerisms frayed his nerves until there were times when he could have shrieked aloud.

He did not know that Alex saw no more of Winter than he himself did, and imagined him to be enjoying a halcyon honeymoon while he, Carlyon, sweltered and raged and dragged himself through the long, weary, endless hours in the company of a tedious little Eurasian and a prosing parson who suffered from dyspepsia and prefaced and punctuated every platitude with a small dry cough.

And yet there was something that he did not understand about Winter and Randall. Something that did not quite square with that tormenting picture of a halcyon honeymoon. Winter did not look well, and she did not have the appearance of one who is happy. Neither, for that matter, did Randall. But then Randall had always had a trick of wiping all expression from his face when he wished, and it was difficult to know what he felt or thought. Neither he nor Winter seemed to have much to say to each other, and they might almost be thought to avoid each other's company during those evenings in the walled garden or upon Randall's roof-top. But Randall was always there: always within sight of her, or within earshot, to remind Carlyon that she belonged to someone else.

He had at times wild, insane, ridiculous ideas of killing Randall, for then she would have to turn to him. There would be no one else; Lapeuta and Dobbie would be useless in any crisis. He had been a fool, as he had been once before. He had not learnt his lesson. He had frightened her, and she had protected herself in the only way she knew, by marrying Randall. But with Randall out of the way he could prove to her that she had nothing to fear from him, and then surely she might turn to him at last?—if only because there would be no one else for her to turn to.

In his calmer moments he knew that the idea was mad, but the heat and the discomfort and the deadly days were beginning to make him a little mad, and his temperament had never been created for endurance. There had been one strangely silent day in September, when an eclipse of the sun had bathed the city in a weird, brown-tinted gloom, and hostilities had ceased while men stood silent in the streets to watch the shadow of the moon creep slowly across the blazing disk until it had blotted it out. Afterwards there had been little firing and the day had seemed curiously quiet and heavy with tension, and it was towards dusk of that day that Carlyon had seen Alex sitting on the coping of the well, and had thought how simple it would be to thrust him in. It could be done so easily—one quick movement of the arm, and the man would fall backwards down the long dank slippery shaft and drown in the black water below.

Lou, who had been watching him, had read the thought in his face as clearly as though it had been written there in block capitals, and she had seen too the moment when it occurred to him that there was a rope and a well-wheel, and five other people who would hear the fall and the splash, and would not stand by and see a man drown. Carlyon had turned abruptly away to walk restlessly up and down the narrow paths, but Lou had not forgotten that look. She had warned Alex later that same night, and he had laughed at her.

'My dear Lou!—you're letting your imagination run away with you. I agree that he would probably enjoy seeing me dead.

I'm not so sure that I wouldn't feel the same if I were in his shoes. But feeling like murdering someone and actually doing it are worlds apart. I should have been hanged ten times over long before this if I had laid violent hands on all the people whom I have felt that I wouldn't mind hitting with a meat-axe.'

Lou said: 'I'd agree if I thought that he was entirely sane. But I don't think he is any more.'

Alex had merely shrugged his shoulders and dismissed the subject, but after that he had kept away from the well.

The weather was growing cooler, and the heat was no longer a grinding torment but a discomfort that could be endured, and sometimes, after a day of drenching rain, the night air held a hint of chilliness; a promise of the cold weather to come. But although the garden was now pleasantly cool before the sun rose, Winter was rarely seen there in the early mornings, and for three evenings running she had failed to join the others on Alex's roof-top. He had asked after her, and Lou had replied shortly that she was not feeling very well but that it was nothing to worry about, while Winter herself, taxed with it on her reappearance, had said lightly that the heat and an overripe *papiya* that she had eaten had been responsible.

Alex had accepted the explanation, and might have continued to do so for some considerable time if it had not been for an unexpected storm that had blown up out of a clear sky some four nights later.

He had been sleeping out on the open roof, and the first intimation he had received of the storm was when he was awakened by what appeared to be a tub of cold water emptied over him. This was not the warm rain of the hot weather, but the colder rain of autumn, and a wind was behind the rain, driving it against him and chilling him to the bone. He was drenched almost before he was awake, and the roof appeared to be awash with water.

'This is where I catch pneumonia,' thought Alex exasperated; wrestling in the pitchy darkness to release the sodden *chiks* that hung between the pillars of the pavilion. He became aware of someone else on the roof, and of Winter's voice calling his name through the lashing of the wind and the rain and the infuriating flapping of the *chiks*.

'Alex—Alex—where are you?'

'I'm here,' shouted Alex. 'What do you think you're doing? Get on back! Where are you?'

He groped for her in the blackness and caught a wet arm, and as he did so the brief fiendish blast of the wind that had driven the storm before it died out as quickly as it had arisen, and there was only the rain falling steadily on to the roof with a soft splashing sound as though it were falling into a lake.

Alex said furiously: 'Winter, are you mad? You'll be drenched! Get on back to your room!'

He heard her laugh a little shakily and she said: 'I'm drenched already. And I won't go down unless you come with me. You can't stay up here for the rest of the night. You'll only get ill again, and we've had enough trouble with you already.'

'You sound,' said Alex, 'regrettably like a nurse I used to have when I was about six. All right, I'll come. Be careful of those stairs. If we fall down them in the dark we shall break our necks.'

The room that had once been Sabrina's seemed hot after the coldness of the wet windy roof, and there was an oil-lamp burning. The flame wavered in the draught and the painted plaster trees and birds and flowers seemed to move with the moving light as though they had been alive, and the curve of the rose-coloured ceiling was full of soft shadows so that it was difficult to tell how high it was.

Alex took the cloth that Winter handed him and rubbed himself dry with it, removing his wet loin-cloth and appropriating a length of turquoise-blue muslin—evidently a head-veil—to replace it. He sat down on the carved and painted bed and looked about the room, charmed by the gay childish grace of the formalized patterns and the clear colours which, though rubbed and worn in many places, were still jewel-bright. And then he looked at his wife.

Her hair had been unbound for the night and she was wringing the water out of it and twisting it up out of the way in a heavy shining knot at the back of her head. Her arms were lifted, and her thin cotton sari was drenched with rain and clung wetly to her body, outlining and revealing every rounded curve of a figure that was no longer the reed-slim one he had known.

Winter finished knotting up her hair and said: 'There's another *resai* over there. Will you mind sleeping on the floor?'

He did not answer her and she turned to look at him, and saw that he knew. There was a white shade about his mouth and his eyes were wide and very bright, and she stood quite still, looking at him gravely, her gaze steady and a little apprehensive.

After a long minute Alex spoke as though speaking were difficult. He said: 'Is it mine?'

'Yes.'

He held out a hand to her and she came to him as slowly as if she were walking in her sleep. Alex reached up and drew her down into his arms and said in a voice that she had not known he possessed: 'Why didn't you tell me? Oh, my love—my little love!' He laughed suddenly; a laugh that broke on a dry sob, and held her away from him so that he could look into her face.

'And to think,' said Alex, 'that I have been keeping my hands off you for weeks—for months!—because I was afraid of this!'

His hands stripped away the sodden sari and his fingers pressed through the heavy wet waves of hair, and then his mouth closed down on hers, blotting out thought.

41

THEY were allowed three days of unclouded happiness. Three days and nights of complete and unalloyed rapture and contentment, made the more sweet by being snatched out of the ugly mire of blood and fear and frenzy that fouled half India.

They had come into possession of a kingdom, and Sabrina's room was an enchanted garden a thousand miles removed from the harsh realities of the warring world outside. They had so much to talk of and to tell. So much to ask and to remember and to forget. And so much to give that needed no words for its expression.

They went up to the roof-top only after the others had gone, and lying in the crook of Alex's arm, counting the stars that shimmered and blinked and blazed in the tented velvet of the sky, Winter no longer heard the firing from the Residency or the night noises of the city, but only Alex's quiet breathing and the steady beat of his heart under her cheek.

She was entirely and completely happy with a happiness that many touch once but do not hold. At Ware she had longed for the Gulab Mahal as a child cries for the moon, and on so many nights and through so many years she had wished on a star. Now she did not need to wish for anything any more, for all that she could ever have wished for had been given to her—together with every star in the sky. She knew now that whatever happened, and however much pain or horror or parting the future might hold, she had touched every one of those stars and held the moon in her hand, and that if she died tomorrow she would die content.

They had seen little of anyone else during the three days that followed the night of the storm. Only Ameera and Hamida and Lou. Alex had not seen Ameera before, except as a veiled figure on the night of his wedding.

'But thou art the husband of my cousin now, so for a time I will forget that I am of India, and a Mussulman, and be of my mother's people, who keep no *purdah*,' said Ameera smiling at him.

Alex had looked from one face to the other and seen the similarity of the de Ballesteros blood, and had laughed and said: 'Thou art not of India only, Begum Sahiba. The West is there also.'

Ameera shook her head so that her earrings jingled. 'Nay, that is not so. There may come a time when it is possible for

U*

one person to be of both, but that time is not yet, and I do not think that my children's children will see it. Their children, perhaps. I shall be dead then, and shall not know. But those who are, as I am, of the East and of the West, must cleave only to one if they wish to avoid unhappiness. To stand with a foot in each is to be neither. I have chosen the East. It is only when the blood of one alone runs in the veins that those such as my cousin can be happy in both, for then there is no war, pulling both ways. Thy son too, when he is born, may love this land and its people as his mother does, and, I think, as thou dost also. But it will be for love alone, and not because of any tie of blood.'

Lou had come in search of Winter on that same day and had found Alex there. She had looked relieved and said: 'So you've told him, have you? I wondered how much longer you were going to be about it. Is it——' She bit the sentence off abruptly and blushed hotly for perhaps the first time in her adult life.

'No,' said Alex shortly, answering the unspoken question. 'It's mine.'

Lou drew a deep breath of relief. She said: 'I thought it might be, because you didn't come back that night, and—— But I was afraid it was Con's and that was why she wouldn't tell you.'

Winter said: 'How long have you known, Lou?'

Lou laughed. 'Probably almost as long as you have. It wasn't difficult, living as we did.'

Alex said: 'I didn't know.'

'Oh, *you*!' said Lou, and left them.

They had not seen any of the others, and did not know that their absence and driven Carlyon to the ragged fringes of jealousy and rage. While he had been able to see them—one or other of them—and to note the fact that their behaviour towards each other was almost that of strangers, he had been able to feed on the hope that Winter had perhaps only married the man as a way out of a difficult situation.

But now they had both removed from his sight, and they were somewhere together, and he could not endure it. Everything that had happened to him since his arrival in this appalling, barbaric, abomination of a country was Winter's fault. Winter's and Randall's! The discomfort and the tediousness that he had endured on the journey from Calcutta, and in Delhi. The rage of disappointment and the wound to his vanity and egotism. The sleepless nights and the gnawing, unsatisfied hunger for a woman who had escaped him. The illness and the heat and the horrors of the mutiny. The weeks of hiding in jungles and hovels, the fear that lived night and day at his elbow, and the long torture of confinement and inactivity; day after day after day of Mr. Lapeuta and Mr. Dobbie, and the all-too-brief daily sight of Winter—as lovely and disturbing and desirable as ever, and always out of reach. Of Randall, always watching.

Winter and Randall! *They* were all right. They suffered no hardships and knew nothing of the tortures he endured. Hidden away somewhere and locked in each other's arms, durance and monotony and fear meant nothing to them. He himself was the only one who really suffered, and the others were all in league against him, ranged in the opposite camp: allies of the dark-skinned, sly-faced jailers who held him prisoner . . .

And then after three days Alex and Winter had come down to the garden again, and together, and even in the soft uncertain dusk Carlyon had been able to read Winter's face.

They could all read it, and the others had looked at her and smiled, because she was young and lovely and in love. She did not touch Alex or stay very near him. She did not need to. But even the dullest and least imaginative of minds could sense and almost see the bond of love and belonging that linked them, and Carlyon had watched her, and the fury of the last three days— and of all the days that had gone before—had boiled up in him like a seething bubble of lava breaking through the thin crust of a volcano. The fumes of it rose to his brain so that he saw her through a red mist of rage as the sole author and architect of all his misfortunes.

She had been standing less than a yard away from him, her face clear in the pale moonlight, and he had leapt at her and caught her by the throat, shouting a torrent of accusations and obscenities, shaking her to and fro as his hands choked the breath from her in a strangling, agonizing, frenzied grip.

Alex had reached them first and had hit him between the eyes with all his strength, and he had released Winter and staggered back, and then come at Alex, screaming senseless, futile words.

They had overpowered him at last and dragged him, still struggling and shouting, back to the room he shared with Lapeuta and Dobbie, and Alex had carried Winter up to the painted room and held her in his arms while Ameera and Hamida had put cold compresses on her bruised and swollen throat.

Later a message from Mr. Lapeuta had been brought him by Rahim, and he had left her to the care of the women and gone up to the moonlit roof to find Mr. Lapeuta waiting for him. Mr. Lapeuta and Dasim Ali, who had both come on the same errand.

'It is not safe that that man remain longer in the Gulab Mahal,' said Dasim Ali. 'Who knows but that his shouts may have been heard by those outside the walls? He cried aloud, and in *Angrezi*, and while he remains he is a danger to us all. He must go.'

Alex's face whitened and the lines cut deeper about his mouth. Half an hour ago he would have killed Carlyon if he could, and he would not trust himself within reach of the man now. But to send him out of the Gulab Mahal meant sending him to his death as surely—and less mercifully—as though they had put a loaded pistol to his head and pulled the trigger.

The man could not be held responsible for that frenzied attack on Winter. He was mad—or very nearly so. Too mad to be trusted, and as Dasim Ali had said, a danger to every single inmate of the Gulab Mahal. But to send him to certain death in cold blood——

'We cannot do it,' said Alex at last. 'It were better to kill him here. It would be quicker. They tortured the others. He would be caught in an hour. Less!'

'If he went alone, yes,' said Mr. Lapeuta. 'But perhaps not if we go with him—Reverend Dobbie and myself. We have discussed it and we think it is possible. I, as you see, can pass veree easily as an Indian. Also I know Lucknow, and so does Reverend Dobbie. Lord Carlyon need not talk. We will tie a bandage over his eyes with much blood on it, and say that he has been injured in thee fighting, for his eyes are of a colour that is not usual in this country. We can lead him. We may be caught, as the others were, but I think we have more chance than they, for Reverend Dobbie has dark eyes and speaks thee language with great fluency. It is worth thee trying, sir. To leave him here endangers all in this house, and he can endure no longer. This has come harder on such a man than on us, sir. He is I think a brave man, but not a patient one.'

Mr. Lapeuta glanced at Dasim Ali and said: 'I had wished to see you so that you might approach this gentleman and ask his help and his permission. But he is here now, and he is in agreement with me.'

' "The raft of the benevolent gets across," ' murmured Dasim Ali, looking thoughtfully at Mr. Lapeuta. 'It may even be that thou wilt all reach safety.'

And so they had gone. Their skins had been darkened with dye and they had been given food and a little money and what clothes they would need, and had been smuggled out by a small side door in the wall. They had taken, too, the clothes that they had worn when they arrived there, tied up in a ragged bundle.

'If we are stopped, we can say that we stole them from thee dead in thee cantonments,' said Mr. Lapeuta. 'But the old gentleman has said that there is news that thee Army moves on Lucknow again, and if we can join them we do not wish to be shot by our own side.'

Alex had not seen them go, for he did not wish to see Carlyon again. He had gone back to Winter and held her and kissed her with a passionate intensity as though he were saying goodbye to her. And she had known then that he would go too.

It had rained again that night, but in the morning the skies were clear and the clean washed air brought the sound of guns. Havelock's guns.

Alex had gone up to the roof in the dawn to listen. He had drawn away very gently from Winter, and thought that he had not awakened her, but she felt that first movement and had not stopped him. When he had gone she had lain for a long time staring at the wall with unseeing eyes, and after a time she had turned on her face and wept quietly and without sound or movement.

All that day the sound of Havelock's guns shivered through the hot sunlight, coming nearer and nearer until it seemed as though they could only be a few miles from the city. And as twilight fell the four who were left of the British in the Gulab Mahal gathered on the roof-top to watch and listen.

'We shall be able to get away!' said Mrs. Hossack, her voice trembling in hysterical thankfulness and relief. 'We shall be safe at last—at *last*! When will they be here? Why don't they hurry!'

'They are fighting a battle,' said Alex. 'They will come as quickly as they can, but they won't get a walk-over. Listen! They must be at the Alam Bagh!'

He leaned on the parapet, his breath coming short and his eyes blazing, straining to listen; knowing that men he knew would be fighting out there—pressing on with everything that was in them to the relief of the battered Residency whose indomitable garrison had held out stubbornly all through that terrible, burning summer, and by doing so had occupied and held in check an army which, but for their resistance, would have been free to turn and attack the Delhi Force and create havoc throughout the North-Western Provinces.

'We shall soon be safe!' sobbed Mrs. Hossack. 'They *must* be here soon—perhaps tomorrow!'

But Winter did not speak, or Lou. Winter only watched Alex, oblivious of the guns. Absorbed in him as though he were the only person present: as though she were trying to imprint every line and angle and hollow of his face on her mind, and every tone and inflexion of his voice, so that she could keep them there sharp and distinct through the long days to come, and never forget them.

Lou was silent because now that deliverance seemed so near at hand she was suddenly frightened again. Not of possible hardships, but of the shadowy spectres of Amanda's grandparents who might claim the child. All at once she knew that she did not want to leave the Gulab Mahal, as she had not wanted to leave the Hirren Minar. She was safe here; she and Amanda. She clutched the small, solemn red-headed creature tighter in her arms and the baby set up a protesting wail.

Lou and Mrs. Hossack had taken the children away and left the moonlit roof to Alex and Winter, and Alex had forgotten, for a little while only, the thunder of the guns.

The wind shifted in the night, and in the morning the cannonade was less easy to hear, and that day it came no nearer. But on the following day the guns were no longer a mile or so outside the city, but firing from within the city limits as the Highlanders and the Sikhs and the British and Indian Cavalry and Infantry under Havelock's command fought their way through the streets.

The gates of the Gulab Mahal were barred and barricaded and every shutter closed and bolted, and none stirred outside while the city shook to the savage din of battle. And as the sun sank, the wind blowing from the direction of the Residency brought with it a new sound, faint but unmistakable. A roar of cheering.

'*They've got there!*' said Alex with a catch in his voice and a lunatic desire to cheer himself hoarse. 'Listen to that! They've got there!'

'They're safe,' said Lou, and wept.

They had got there at last. But the garrison of the Residency, though sure now of survival, had not been relieved after all. They had only been reinforced. The regiments who had fought their way through the streets had been too badly mauled, and their losses had been too great for them to be able to do more than join the exhausted defenders in the Residency and to stand siege there themselves.

The tumult in the city died down and the stench of death rose from the streets like a tangible cloud to foul the air. And once again the familiar rattle of musketry fire, punctuated more frequently now by the boom of guns, sounded from the direction of the Residency.

Alex waited for several days, gleaning what news he could from Dasim Ali, and from Rahmin who had been into the bazaars. But from what they told him there seemed to be little chance of the situation developing into more than another stale-mate, if not a retreat. The garrison was hampered by an inordinate proportion of women and children whose safety could not be jeopardized, and now that Havelock and Outram, with the relieving force, were also penned up in the Residency it seemed more likely that they would have to remain where they were until they in turn were relieved, for fight their way out with the women and children would be no easy task and would mean abandoning Lucknow and that indefensible position that had, miraculously and courageously, been defended for so long. They would have to retreat not only from Lucknow, but from Oudh, and it might be many months before another and stronger force could be marched to attack and take the city.

Alex had talked for a long time with old Dasim Ali on the last evening of September, and then he had gone down to the painted room and to Winter.

The light of the oil-lamp played upon the rose-coloured walls and the painted plaster birds and flowers as it had on the first night that he had seen that room, and once again it seemed to him that the trees swayed and the birds moved, and that the shadows made a mist under the curved ceiling so that he could not tell how high it was.

Winter was combing out the long waves of her hair, and he sat on the low Indian bed, as he had done that first night, and watched her; and did not speak.

After a moment she laid down the comb and turned towards him. The light of the lamp behind her fell upon his face but left her own in shadow, and the soft wavering flame threw an aureole about her, glinting on the long ripples of her black hair and outlining her small head.

She looked at him in silence, as she had done once before in that room; seeing in his face what it was that he had come to say. And once again he held out a hand to her, and she came to him and put her arms about him, standing between his knees with his head against her heart, as she had stood in the dusk outside the Hirren Minar on the day that Lottie had died. Now, as then, he held her quite gently, leaning against her, and presently he said: 'I can take you with me. There are troops at the Alam Bagh just outside the city. It will not be too difficult or too dangerous to get you there. You can pass as an Indian. And once you were there you would be safe. After that it would only mean reaching Cawnpore, and then by river to Allahabad and Calcutta. If Havelock is here it means the road must be open.'

Winter said: 'Would you come with me?' and knew the answer before she asked it.

She felt Alex's arms tighten about her. 'To the Alam Bagh, my darling. Perhaps to Cawnpore.'

'And after that?'

'I—you would be safe then.'

Winter put up one hand and stroked his dark hair, pressing her fingers through it; pressing his head against her so that he should not lift it and see that she was crying. She said softly and quite steadily: 'And you?'

Alex moved his head against her as though he were in pain. He said in a harsh, difficult voice: 'I must go back to Lunjore.'

He felt her flinch, and said as though she had spoken: 'I must, dear! I should never have left. There was so much that I could have done there—or tried to do. It—it is my work; my responsibility. It's my *own* district! And I ran away from it, because——'

'Because you were saddled with three women,' said Winter with a break in her voice. 'But you can't go back there now! Alex, you can't! They would only kill you. There wouldn't be anything you could do there alone—not now! You'd only be throwing your life away, and it isn't only yours—it's mine too. It's *mine!*'

Alex's arms were hard about her; he said: 'I know, my heart. But it isn't true that there is nothing that I could do there now. And—and there is more than an even chance that I shall be safe. There are several of the talukdars who I think would stand by me. Safdar Beg will lend me men; I got his revenues back for him and he was grateful for that. And Tará Chand— oh, and a dozen others. There is no one to keep order there now. But once they see someone in authority again it will quiet them and bring back order and sanity—give them the assurance that there is still a stable Government and a law that does not depend on the will or the whim of any individual who happens to be temporarily in power. That is what they need; peace and quiet and that assurance. It wasn't the villages—or even the city— that created the trouble. It was the sepoys, and they will have gone now. If I go back now I can . . . Dear heart, I must go back! Give me leave to go——'

Winter said: 'And if I will not? Would you still go?'

'I—I must. But I would go happier if I went with your leave.'

She said in a whisper, because she could not trust her voice not to break again: 'Go with it, my love,' and felt something that had been strained and taut relax in his mind more than in his body.

He leaned his weight against her as though he were very tired, and the tears that she had wished to hide from him ran down her cheeks to her throat so that they wet his face, and he felt them and tried to lift his head, but she held it closer and after a little while she said: 'When are you going?'

'Tonight. In an hour.'

She did not make any sound, but he felt the effort to control it shudder through her body, and knew what that effort had cost her. He said: 'Can you be ready by then?'

She did not answer him at once, but her hand relaxed its pressure against his head and began to stroke his hair again, quite gently, and presently she said: 'I am not going.'

He looked up then, quickly, and saw her face wet and sweet and calm above him. She smiled down at him, the soft, tremulous shadow of a smile, and laid her palm against the hard cheek that was wet with her own tears.

'Dear, I could not go. They would send me away to Calcutta. I should be at the other end of India. I shall be nearer to you here, and far safer than you will be. Ameera will take care of me, and I shall be among friends. I was born in this room, and I have thought about it and loved it all my life. Perhaps your child will be born in it too. I will wait here for you.'

Alex said: 'You don't understand, dear love. I can't let you stay. One day we shall attack this city, and take it. You don't know what that would mean, but I do. I have seen a city sacked. If you were here——'

Winter's hand moved from his cheek to his mouth, covering it so that he could not speak, and above it his eyes looked into hers steadily and for a long time. Then his lashes dropped and he kissed the warm palm that closed his mouth, and did not argue with her any more.

He had gone before midnight, slipping out by the narrow side door by which Carlyon and Lapeuta and Dobbie had left, and there had been only his wife and Dasim Ali to see him go.

Winter had stood pressed against the little iron-studded door and listened to the sound of his quick light footsteps dying out on the dusty road outside, and presently the night had swallowed up the sound, and old Dasim Ali had touched her on the arm and she had turned away.

She had cried again on the bed in the painted room when he had gone, and Ameera had comforted her. But in the morning it was the room that had comforted her most. She had woken to find it bright with the dawn, and as the sun rose and the familiar shadow crept across the floor and touched the bed on which she lay, peace and reassurance flowed back and filled her heart and her mind and her body. Nothing could hurt her while she was here. Alex would come back. She had only to wait.

42

THREE of them left. Winter, Lou and Mrs. Hossack. And the two small children; Jimmy Hossack and Lottie's daughter Amanda.

Mrs. Hossack had been horrified and indignant when she had heard the news of Alex's departure, and had expressed herself strongly on the subject to Lou Cottar.

'I cannot *understand* how Captain Randall could have brought himself to do such a thing! To desert his wife at a time like this. To escape himself and to leave her behind, alone and unprotected! Not to mention *us*. One would have thought that he would have remained to protect us all.'

'From what?' enquired Lou shortly. 'We are perfectly safe here; and if a mob should break in, one man would not be much help.'

'Well, I consider it very shocking in him,' said Mrs. Hossack, 'and I cannot conceive how he can have brought himself even to contemplate such a thing!'

'He has an odd idea that duty should come before personal inclination,' said Lou dryly. 'He also has a peculiar sense of proportion and values, and imagines that three women, who are really as safe as they can hope to be, are of less importance than the welfare of his district.'

'Personally, I should have thought that the first duty of an Englishman was to protect women,' said Mrs. Hossack indignantly.

'I'm sure you would. It is a pity that so many of them would seem to agree with you,' said Lou acidly, and had turned her back on her.

Mrs. Hossack had preserved an offended silence for at least half the day, but towards evening Jimmy Hossack had been fretful and refused his food, and had later become feverish. He had grown steadily worse and Mrs. Hossack had been frantic.

'He is going to die!' wept Mrs. Hossack hysterically, rocking herself to and fro and wringing her hands. 'I know he will die!—

with no doctor—no proper food—no medicines—this dreadful, horrible house! Oh Jimmy—*Jimmy!*'

Lou had slapped her. It had proved an efficacious remedy as far as Mrs. Hossack was concerned, and Jimmy Hossack had not died. But he had lost a great deal of weight and did not regain it, and his recovery was so slow as to be scarcely perceptible.

Jimmy's illness had frightened Lou almost as much as it had terrified his mother. What if Amanda were to get ill? —really ill? They must get away! They *must*. Alex had said that a road must be open from Cawnpore to Calcutta, and Josh would be in Calcutta. Josh would not object to her keeping Amanda. Josh had never objected to anything that Lou did. He would probably be amused at the idea, and might even one day come to look upon the child as being as much his own as she herself did. And then she, Lou, had red hair too. If only the Englishes—— Oh, to hell with the Englishes! She must get Amanda to safety. What was the Army doing? What was Havelock doing?

But Havelock, whose command had now been taken over by Sir James Outram, was still besieged in the Residency that he had hoped to relieve. And October came and went, and the air was cool now; the gardens bright with flowers and the early mornings sharp and chilly.

The news that Delhi had been recaptured by the British had reached the Gulab Mahal two days after Alex had left. Delhi had been taken, but the price had been high, for Nicholson was dead. He had been shot trying to rally his men in the attack on the city, and all that could die of him had died nine days later— to leave an imperishable legend and the echoes of those hooves that could be heard from Attock to the Khyber. 'Nikal Seyn' was dead, and the men of the frontier who had fought at Delhi— Pathans, Multanis, Afghans—had wept above his grave, and many, who had cared nothing for the Raj and had given allegiance only to him, had gone back to their own country. *There be many sahibs—but only one Nikal Seyn . . .*

The year wore slowly on, and the ceaseless, familiar sound of musketry and gunfire from around the Residency still made a background to each day, and it was not until mid-November that the roar of guns and the din of battle rattled the rickety fabric of the Gulab Mahal as another British Force fought its way towards a second relief of the Lucknow Residency, and once again the ugly tide of war surged through the narrow streets of the city.

Once again the gates of the pink palace were barred and barricaded; but fortune was with it, for it did not lie in the line of the advance, and the flood-tide of the street fighting passed it by.

For a week gunfire and the crashing detonation of buildings being blown up shook Lucknow, but no one seemed to know how the battle went. The Residency had been relieved for the second time, but had Lucknow itself been captured by the British? None from the pink palace dared go out for news, for the streets were not safe; and food ran short and there came a day when there was no milk for Amanda and Jimmy Hossack.

Havelock died in that month, and on the day after his death word had been whispered in the dusk at the barred gate of the Gulab Mahal that the *Jangi-lat-Sahib*, Sir Colin Campbell, was going to retreat from Lucknow and fall back once more upon Cawnpore, and that the evacuation would take place that very night, and in great secrecy. The women and children were to leave in carts and doolies at midnight while the city slept; stealing out under cover of darkness and making for the Alam Bagh, which was strongly held by the British.

Ameera had brought the news to Winter. 'My husband and Dasim Ali,' said Ameera, 'say that if it be thy wish, it can be arranged that thou and the two women with the children go also. There are doolies here, and men to carry them, and they will join with the other *mem-log* at a place that is known to them, and take thee to safety. But it must be decided swiftly, for already it is dark.'

Winter had smiled lovingly at her. 'I will tell the others. It may be that they will choose to go. But I will stay here—unless thou and thy husband wish me to be gone. And if that be so, then thou wilt have to send me away by force!'

'That we shall never do,' said Ameera, embracing her. 'Is this not the house in which thou wast born? Go and tell thy friends to make ready if they would go.'

They had gone.

Mrs. Hossack had tried to persuade Winter to go with them, and even Lou had urged her to leave. 'I know you are safe here now,' said Lou, 'and that you will be happier here than in Allahabad or Calcutta, or wherever they send us. But it isn't safe to stay. Can't you see that even if they are retreating this time, they will come again? Lucknow will be taken in the end—it's got to be! And when it is, the fighting will be far worse—a hundred times worse—than it has been this time, or the time before. The place may be sacked. Anything may happen! You can't risk it, Winter. You have the child to think of.'

'It is Alex's child,' said Winter. 'Alex knew that Lucknow would be taken. But he let me stay. Don't you see, Lou, that even if I wished to go I could not? Everyone in this house has risked their lives to save ours. And when they took us in they had no idea of profiting from it. We owe them a debt; a very great one. If I stay here, and I am here when the attack comes, the fact that I am in this house may save it. I could not go. Alex knew that.'

Lou had wasted no more words. She had, somewhat unexpectedly, kissed Winter. Even more unexpectedly there had been tears in her eyes. They had smiled at each other with affection and respect, their hands holding tightly for a moment, and had kissed again, saying nothing because there was so much to say—and yet so little that need be said. And then Lou had gone. Lou, Amanda, Mrs. Hossack, Jimmy.

The gate creaked shut behind them and the bars and bolts grated hurriedly back into place, and the shuffling footsteps of the doolie bearers faded and were swallowed up by the night as Alex's quick, light ones had been.

Sir Colin Campbell's army—Havelock's army—retreated from Lucknow, taking with them the women and children and all who remained of the gallant garrison who had held out so stubbornly and for so long. Leaving behind them the lonely dead and the empty shell of the Residency where a tattered Union Jack still fluttered in the dawn wind above the broken roof. And in the Gulab Mahal, the little pink stucco palace in Lucknow city, only Winter remained of the thirteen fugitives who had been taken in and given shelter on a hot night in July.

Once again the tide of war drew out of Lucknow leaving the ruin and the wreckage behind it, and there were no more sounds of the siege. Only the doves and the crows and the parrots again, and the chattering squirrels and the hum of the city from behind the high wall that shut in the Rose Palace.

There was firing still, but not from the Residency. It was farther away now, from the Alam Bagh—the 'Garden of the World'—a walled and fortified royal garden some two miles outside Lucknow, where Sir Colin Campbell had left a force under General Outram to hold at least one outpost within sight of the city.

The Maulvie of Faizabad, the best of the generals that the mutineer armies had produced, attacked the British there, and cut their communications with Cawnpore. All through the succeeding months the Alam Bagh was attacked again and again, as the Residency had been. But unlike the Residency it was not a besieged garrison holding out against insuperable odds, but a strong-post that defied capture and waited for the day when it would act as the spearhead of the final advance upon Lucknow.

There had been no word of Carlyon and the two men who had gone with him: or of Alex. But the bearers of the doolies had returned, saying that the memsahibs and their children had reached the Alam Bagh in safety, and had been sent forward with all the other *mem-log* to Cawnpore. So Lou and Mrs. Hossack at least were safe, and Winter hoped that Lou would not find that escape had robbed her of Amanda. Lou deserved Amanda.

The year drew to its close, but the mutiny still raged. Men still fought and died, and in Lucknow the mutineers dug defences and built barricades in preparation for the attack that they knew could not be long delayed. For the make-believe Mogul, Bahadur Shah's, brief, soap-bubble dream of Empire had vanished with the fall of Delhi, and Dundu Pant of Bithor was a fugitive, and many of the strongholds that the mutineers had won were once more in British hands.

But within the faded pink-washed walls of the Gulab Mahal the days passed peacefully enough, and Winter sank into the life of the Rose Palace and became part of it—as she had been part of it in the long-ago days when Juanita and Aziza Begum had been alive, and Winter herself had been a small black-haired child playing with the painted plaster birds in the room that had been Sabrina's.

The inmates of the palace frequently forgot that she was not one of them by birth, and she spoke and thought and dreamt in the vernacular as she had done as a child. She busied herself with the same household tasks, and was scolded by Mumtaz and instructed in the mysteries of drying and preserving fruits and grinding spices, of making jasmine oil or soap made from powdered gram, and preparing surma—the black ore of antimony used for beautifying the eyes. There were few idle hours in the Gulab Mahal, and there was always Ameera; and Ameera's small sons to play with, and other and older children to fly kites with on the roof and to tell stories to, and their mothers to gossip and laugh with.

Twice a day, morning and evening, Winter would go alone to the roof-top where Alex had lived, and look out across the tree-tops and the lovely battered city, towards Lunjore.

'He is not dead,' she told Ameera. 'If he were I should feel it; here, in my heart.'

But there were times when she was not so sure; when terror would suddenly overtake her and she would think of him lying dead or dying in Lunjore—tortured or wounded or sick. And when those black times came upon her she would run to her own room, and the room, as it had always been, was a talisman and a charm that could reassure her and make her believe that all would be well. She had only to lay her hand on the gay, worn curves of Firishta, and stroke his plaster feathers, to feel calm flow back to her as though his touch were indeed magic. Alex would come back.

And then in January she had heard news of him at last. Old Dasim Ali, who had friends everywhere, had heard by a roundabout route that there was a Sahib again in Lunjore who had brought back order to the district. He had been protected by a bodyguard of men provided by a Sirdar who had reason to be grateful to him, and with this backing he had taken control of Lunjore and put down the malcontents and set up courts again with native magistrates and judges and native police, and life was gradually returning to normal. The rumour gave no name, but Winter did not need one. She knew that it must be Alex, and that he had been right to go.

All through January the insurgents had kept up their attacks on the Alam Bagh, but in mid-January the Maulvie of Faizabad had been wounded and driven back. Their inability to carry the Alam Bagh by assault, and the defeats inflicted upon them, had disheartened the rebels, and they began to quarrel among themselves, and many drifted away, returning to their own towns and villages. But many more stayed and continued to attack, fighting with ferocity and valour, and towards the end of February a last and desperate assault was launched against the garrison. The Royal Begum of Oudh had accompanied the rebel army in person, together with her Prime Minister and many of the great nobles of Oudh, riding in state on gorgeously caparisoned elephants.

Winter heard the opening of the cannonade in the early morning, and it shook the walls of the pink palace and sent the startled crows and pigeons cawing and whirling above the roofs of the city. But the roar of the guns meant no more to her than the cawing of the crows, for her pains had started before dawn and the guns were only a dim and disregarded background to the ordeal of birth.

It was not an easy birth, and there had been times when Ameera and Mumtaz Begum and Hamida, and others of the women who were continuously in and out of the painted room, had looked at each other in fear and anxiety. But Winter remembered a long, hot, agonizing day in the Hirren Minar, and Alex's voice talking to Lottie—explaining, encouraging, soothing; and it was as if he spoke to her now as he had spoken then to Lottie; telling her not to be afraid. And she had not been afraid.

Through the waves of pain she could see the pink sunset sky that was the walls of her room; the dear enchanted trees and flowers that swayed in a secret breeze against that sky, and the birds and beasts that had watched her own birth and been her first playthings.

The sun had set and the moon had risen. Ameera had lit the oil-lamp, and her shadow and Hamida's and other shadows of women moved and leapt upon the walls, and the ceiling was lost in a rosy mist as it had been on the night when Alex had come down from the roof, and on the night that he had left her. And then suddenly she had thought that he was in the room, and had screamed to him by name—a scream that rang out through the open windows and across the silent garden and awoke the echo that lived within the high, encircling walls—Alex! . . . *Alex! . . . Alex!* . . . And to the sound of that echo Alex's son was born.

*　　　　*　　　　*

It was March when the long-expected attack upon Lucknow began, and day after endless day the guns had roared in the city while the streets became battlegrounds and graveyards and charnel-houses and the dead littered every yard of the contested ground.

Colin Campbell's army—Highlanders, Sikhs, Punjabis, British and Indian regiments of Cavalry and Infantry, Peel's Naval Brigade and Jung Bahadur's Gurkhas from Nepal—had stormed the defences and flung themselves on the guns, fighting forward yard by yard through the red, reeking streets; through the storm of grape and canister and round shot, and the choking smoke of burning houses; past fortified palaces and over the bodies of the grinning dead; driving the mutineers back from street to street, from building to building. . . .

Curiously enough—or perhaps justly—it was Carlyon who was largely responsible for saving the Gulab Mahal from the sack and slaughter and destruction that overtook almost every house in that shattered city. Mr. Lapeuta, Mr. Dobbie and Lord Carlyon, Lou Cottar, Mrs. Hossack and the children, had all reached safety. And they had told their stories, and told too of Captain Alex Randall's wife who had remained behind in the house and with the people who had sheltered them. And later, when the Delhi Column had joined Sir Colin Campbell's force and the army moved to the final attack upon Lucknow, Carlyon had used his considerable influence to urge that the Gulab Mahal should be granted as much protection as was possible in such circumstances. It had been promised him, and even in the frenzy of the fighting the promise had not been forgotten. With the terrible tumult of battle ebbing and surging like a furious sea through the city, rifle-butts had knocked on the barred door of the Gulab Mahal and men's voices had shouted above the clamour, demanding entrance.

Winter had gone down to them alone, wearing Juanita's white dress; not knowing who it might be. She had heard the English voices above the din and had opened the gate, tugging at the heavy bars and locks with her small hands, for the gateman had run away in terror, and had opened it at last to see the smoke-blackened blood-streaked faces that filled the once-quiet street.

They were men of the Highland Brigade and half a dozen mounted *sowars* of Hodson's Horse, and there was an officer with them. A man on horseback who laughed down at her and dismounted to take her hand: 'Do you remember me, Mrs. Alex? I met you at Delhi—William Hodson.'

'Yes,' said Winter, looking up into the white, battle-grimed, laughing face of the man whom Alex had said would always be twenty paces ahead, and thinking that no one who had ever met him would be likely to forget him: 'I remember.'

'I cannot stay,' said Hodson. 'I came only to tell you that as far as possible this house will be protected. If you see Alex before I do, tell him that the astrologer in Amritsar was right! He will know what that means! But if we get these wretches on the run I may see him before you do.'

He sprang back into the saddle, saluted her, and wheeling his horse, galloped away with his men behind him; his face as eager and his eyes as hot and bright and glittering as though he rode to meet a friend or a lover instead of the death that awaited him that day.

The Highlanders had stared at Winter open-mouthed, and had grinned at her. Friendly, amazed, half-shy smiles that had transformed them in an instant from furious, fighting animals with the red haze of killing in their faces, to kindly, ordinary men with wives and children and sweethearts of their own. Then the door had been barred again and an order signed by Sir Colin Campbell himself nailed to it; and while the fighting lasted a guard had stood at that gate and protected the Gulab Mahal from the looting and the frenzy of battle-crazed, blood-drunk troops until the worst of that delirium was past.

Food had become scarce again in the pink stucco palace while the fighting swayed to and fro through the city and none dared venture beyond the walls, and towards the end of the month, when the last resistance had been crushed and the terrible guns were silent, there was little food to be obtained in the broken burnt-out bazaars, and the shattered city starved.

Winter grew very thin in those days—as did Ameera and Hamida, and many others not only in the pink palace but in all Lucknow. But the baby throve, and her anxiety was not on her son's account. It was, as it had always been, for Alex. For the fall of Lucknow had not brought peace to Oudh.

General Sir Colin Campbell, the Commander-in-Chief, had committed one of those incomprehensible tactical errors that mar the success of so many campaigns. He had prevented General Outram from cutting off the enemy's retreat, with the result that the greater part of the opposing army had escaped. And old

Dasim Ali, hearing that news, had shaken his head lugubriously and wagged his red beard. If only part of that army crossed into Lunjore, said Dasim Ali, it would go hard with Randall Sahib— if he were there, and still alive.

April brought with it once again a warning of the molten heat to come, and the small bare rooms of the Gulab Mahal seemed airless once more, and stifling. Food was still scarce and milk was still scarcer—but news was scarcest of all, and what there was of it was far from reassuring.

The mutiny was being stamped out, and the savage reprisals that Alex had feared and predicted were accompanying that process—in the old and evil belief that only blood and savagery can repay and wipe out the stain of blood and savagery.

The British troops who had been rushed to the defence of the dying Empire of a 'Company of Merchants Trading to the East' expected no quarter and gave none. They went into battle, shouting as their battle-cry, '*Remember Cawnpore! Remember Cawnpore!*'—and they remembered Cawnpore and killed without mercy, and hung without mercy; condemning a man as often as not for the colour of his skin as from any proof of guilt.

But although it would be many months yet before peace was fully restored, it was already plain that the prophecy that the rule of the Company would end a hundred years after Plassey was to be fulfilled. India had become too great a thing to be the private possession of a trading company. It would have to be taken over by the Crown; that long step forward that Alex had spoken of.

'We have not won back Hind,' said Walayat Shah, 'but it was the Company's Raj that we had hoped to pull down, and, *Shook'r Khooda*, we have succeeded in that! For now the Company's Raj will go, and their long reign of robbery and confiscation will be ended.'

Soon it would be May again, and the breathless burning days that a year ago had seen the fuel catch fire would see it still burning fiercely, though with a dying flame, in Jhansi and Rohilkhand and Gwalior and Oudh. But there was still no news from Lunjore——

'Surely if her husband were alive he would send word?' said the women of the Gulab Mahal. 'It must be that he is dead!'

The thought was often clear on their faces and in their kind, troubled eyes, and one day it had been too clear to be borne, and Winter had answered it as though it had been spoken aloud: 'No! It is not true! He is not dead! He will come for me some day. I have only to wait . . .'

And she had snatched up her son and carried him up to Alex's roof-top although the sun had not yet set and the heat shimmered on the hot stonework, and had strained her eyes in the direction of Lunjore as though her love could reach beyond the horizon and pierce the dust-clouds and the distance and the heat haze that hid it from her sight.

The withered leaves of the trees below her rattled dryly under the fingers of a little hot wind that blew through the garden. A wind that must have blown over Lunjore. Some day—thought Winter. One day . . .

They were words that she had been saying all her life. She had said them as a child at Ware. 'Some day I shall go back to the Gulab Mahal——' And she had come back. Surely some day Alex would come back too.

The sun dipped down towards the horizon and bathed the shattered city in beauty, hiding its blackened, gaping scars, and Winter remembered what Hodson had said to her—Hodson whose star, as the astrologer in Amritsar had prophesied so many years ago, 'would arise and burn bright among much blood', and who had died in the battle for the city—'*I may see him before you do.*' Had he too spoken prophetically? Had he indeed met Alex?

Quite suddenly she could bear it no longer, and she turned and ran desperately, as she had run before, to the refuge of the painted room, sobbing and shuddering.

The reflected glow of the sunset filled it with a warm rosy light, touching the trees and the birds and the flowers into the same enchanted life that lamplight could give them, and the leaves and the petals welcomed her and the birds and the beasts nodded to her and Firishta watched her with a bright, friendly, reassuring eye.

She pushed the bed to one side and sank down on the matting with the child in her arms, leaning her head against the cool carved plaster, and pressing her cheek against the comforting curve of Firishta's round green head. Her eyes closed and gradually the helpless trembling of her body lessened as little by little the fear ebbed away from her.

The baby went to sleep in her lap and the glow faded from the room, taking the gay brightness from it and leaving it as cool and as softly colourful as an opal.

Outside the windows the birds were settling down to rest with noisy chatterings and cawings and a flutter of wings among the orange trees, and beyond the far wall of the garden the dome of the little whitewashed mosque with its iron emblem of the crescent moon cut a lilac pattern against the evening sky.

The hum of the city rose up about the Gulab Mahal, washing around it; and through it and above it Winter could hear all the familiar, friendly sounds of the house. The distant chatter of shrill feminine voices, children laughing, a baby crying, the aged gateman clearing his throat and coughing asthmatically, a clatter of cooking-pots and the creak of the well-wheel. The sounds mingled and mixed with the no less dear and familiar scents of water sprinkled on parched ground, of the spicy smell of eastern cooking and the smoke of dung-fires, the scent of orange-blossom and jasmine and marigolds, and the smell of warm dust and sun-soaked stone.

The sounds and the scents seemed to weave a web about the painted room, isolating it in safety, and Winter drew a long slow sigh and felt the last of the shuddering fear leave her.

'Some day,' she said, whispering the words against Firishta's green head. 'One day——'

There were footsteps and a murmur of voices in the passage beyond the doorway, and then someone lifted the heavy curtain that hung before it, and she opened her eyes and looked up. And it was Alex.